# THE DRAKE EPICS

# THE DRAKE EPICS

## Journey To Qara

T.M. Krieg

Copyright © 2013 by T.M. Krieg.

| Library of Congress Control Number: | | 2013918515 |
| ISBN: | Hardcover | 978-1-4931-1194-7 |
| | Softcover | 978-1-4931-1193-0 |
| | Ebook | 978-1-4931-1195-4 |

All rights reserved. No part of this book may be reproduced or transmitted in any form or by any means, electronic or mechanical, including photocopying, recording, or by any information storage and retrieval system, without permission in writing from the copyright owner.

This is a work of fiction. Names, characters, places and incidents either are the product of the author's imagination or are used fictitiously, and any resemblance to any actual persons, living or dead, events, or locales is entirely coincidental.

This book was printed in the United States of America.

Visit www.drakeEpics.com

Rev. date: 11/11/2013

**To order additional copies of this book, contact:**
Xlibris LLC
1-888-795-4274
www.Xlibris.com
Orders@Xlibris.com
134074

# CONTENTS

Prologue—Epic Poem: The Emperor's Prophecy .......................... 9
Chapter 1—Dragon of Flesh and Fire ..................................... 11
Chapter 2—Dragon of Steele.............................................. 17
Chapter 3—The Market Bizarre ........................................... 35
Chapter 4—The Temple of Marduk ........................................ 43
Chapter 5—Awakening..................................................... 63
Chapter 6—Julfa: A New Beginning........................................ 78
Chapter 7—Grandpas and Bees and Drakes, Oh My ...................... 96
Chapter 8—Ordinary Arrival............................................. 122
Chapter 9—Prolonged Lies............................................... 142
Chapter 10—Teacher's Pet............................................... 155
Chapter 11—The Novice ................................................. 182
Chapter 12—From Student to Teacher.................................... 199
Chapter 13—The Secret Unveiled ........................................ 208
Chapter 14—The Oracle of the Kur-ne.................................... 221
Chapter 15—The Forbidden City.......................................... 249
Chapter 16—Wanderers in a Strange Land ............................... 266
Chapter 17—Secrets .................................................... 298
Chapter 18—On Trial.................................................... 311
Chapter 19—Revelation.................................................. 327
Chapter 20—Happy Reunion ............................................. 349
Chapter 21—Tearful Farewell............................................ 362
Chapter 22—Of Druids and Dragons...................................... 377
Chapter 23—Blood, Fire, and Wind....................................... 392
Chapter 24—Dust Demons ............................................... 407
Chapter 25—Royal Mastery ............................................. 415
Chapter 26—Dreams Again .............................................. 432
Chapter 27—Duels and Dragon Sieges ................................... 441
Chapter 28—Howling Wind .............................................. 454
Chapter 29—The Kur-ne Again........................................... 468
Chapter 30—Of Empires and Beehives ................................... 494
Qara's Postlude ........................................................ 503

To my darling wife, Nicole, and our three lovely children, who put up with me while writing this book. May they enjoy this and share this with their children.

Specifically dedicated to my late father, Steven.

# PROLOGUE

## Epic Poem: The Emperor's Prophecy

'Twas myth and legend and lore. The three were drawn to the primordial center. Qara sought the emperor's dominion, for Marduk the brave and his sister companion. A stream of clean water, flowing through time to give rise to the fountain of redeeming potential.

Wanderers in a strange land. Their souls without blight. Mortality upon them yet honest and contrite. Their backs to the past, they plod onward boldly, in a land of great heat and cruelty and beauty.

Kings who oppress reign in eminent horror. Tyrants who destroy and seek endless harm. Ushering in death and despair under rule, the tyranny is clear, the dominance forever.

The emperor strikes at the heart of darkness and filth. His mind all ablaze with benevolent concern. Marduk gives aid to his quest's grand finale. Ending Tiamat's evil, the dragon, man, and hunter. The fallen lord surrenders to defeat and great waste. He will ne'r return to that fair land of Qara.

The three will triumph and chase away sin, they must need grow stronger as they defend and give shelter. What once was so fair and pure is laid waste, but hope shines ever brightly at their reviving grace. Their loss is but brief, their destiny is eternal order.

# Chapter 1

# Dragon of Flesh and Fire

*Evil is a myth of one's own mind.*
*It is true that evil can be inflicted upon someone, but it will never*
*control you if you don't let it!*

The mist might well have been an eternal abyss for all the boy could tell. A dingy, spongy smell hung in the air and hungrily clung to him as he blindly groped through the moist vapor. He couldn't see his hands, and he momentarily raised them to within inches of his face in a determined concentration. He swiveled them back and forth; when that failed, he waved them frantically to catch even a small glimpse of movement. After a few tries, he gave up with a grunt and began to again fumble his way through the dense moisture.

He gingerly felt along the ground with his feet as he went. But he couldn't see them either. It gave him a momentary feeling as if he were strolling through the clouds. Still, he could feel his footfalls on hard ground, which likely meant that he was in a fog instead. The earth below him felt lumpy and slanted downward. He caught himself as he stumbled and now diverted his attention to every step forward with his arms outstretched as extra precaution.

Sound was also absent from this place. As he walked along, the vapor's silence was perfectly deafening.

*Where is it?* He listened as he stepped, and hearing nothing, he stomped at the ground, but could not hear his feet strike. The boy had a sudden idea: he cupped his hands around his mouth and shouted for help. No sound reached his ears. Again, he yelled, only this time he threw his head back for added measure—nothing. Giving up all pretenses, he bellowed at the sky until his head felt like exploding and his throat grew sore. He still heard no sound, but his throat burned, as if he had swallowed a handful of nails. So he gave up, gently massaging his neck to soothe it, deciding instead to concentrate on the mist around him.

It was surprisingly whiter than anything he had ever seen before. Gentle wisps of viscous smoke formed tendrils that twisted and curled in front of his face. He was postitive they were taunting him. It was almost blinding, yet at the same time exquisitely beautiful. Small particles trapped within the vapor shone out in a myriad of brilliant colors as they rested on some invisible shelving all around him. The flavors of light were delicious.

Attempting to focus on one of the brilliant specs, a deep calming glow caught his attention, emanated from somewhere deep within the mist. The glow put him momentarily at ease—at least for a spell. He paused briefly to soak it in before the stark realization barged in on him: *he was lost!* He couldn't even remember how he got here, his memory was as foggy as the mist around him.

As if on cue, the white wisps began to turn a shade of grey, and his surroundings steadily darkened. For a few moments, the darkness was complete. Then, not unlike a giant squid changes color in the depths of its watery realm, the vapor started to flux and pulsate, turning blindingly white as lightning streaked all around him. In between the flashes, momentary hues of lighter grey pulsed to some unheard beat. For a moment it appeared almost as if an immense light were swinging to and fro behind a giant curtain.

The clouds were suffocating, converging in on him. Losing all composure, he wildly tore at the mist with his fingers, trying to rip it away. Panic replaced calm as a sudden fright welled up inside his chest. He had sudden trouble breathing, and he tugged at the collar of his shirt to give himself space to breathe. Panic turned to horror as he clutched at his throat, gasping for more air. He squeezed his eyes shut and screamed for someone to come to his aid. Again, no sound, and his sore throat protested at the repeated abuse. His faced screwed up in determination, and he jerked his eyes open to make one last frenzied attempt to rip through the darkness. The mist obligingly swallowed his hands as he struggled through it, as if mocking him in his last moments.

Just as he was about to succumb to the vapor's deathly embrace, it started to brighten ever so slightly, and the suffocating heaviness began to lift. The boy fell to his knees and gratefully gulped in the spacious air; sweat streamed down his face and splashed to the ground. He wiped at his brow with the sleeve of his shirt and lifted his head to look around. The white fog wafted into thin air and disappeared altogether as the mist drew draw back upon itself.

As he scanned the landscape that opened to his view, his eyes were immediately drawn to the center. A great concourse of people gathered, their forms boasting various shapes and sizes all jumbled together, as if they were casually mingling. The appearance resembled an immense cavern with thousands of stalagmites jutting upward out of the white vapor below.

He slowly climbed to his feet and mechanically reached out for balance from a sudden dizzy spell threatening to trip him up. After a brief moment to right himself, he strained to focus on the figures, squinting to bring his eyes into focus. They were all identically dressed, in pure white robes of the same brightness and sheen as that of their surroundings. Sometimes, they were only distinguishable from the misty background by a soft outline directly around their silhouettes, of which the boy only caught momentary glimpses, as his eyes struggled for the detail.

With a sudden flash of light, the boy was now standing by a group of the individuals who were far away just moments before. He stopped and looked around, puzzled by the sudden magnification. Upon closer inspection of the people, he noticed each wore a robe that was cut in a V around their necks. The glowing fabric fell from their shoulders and plunged to their ankles, leaving their feet exposed. Their hands were also exposed a few inches above their wrists, held closely to their bodies as if in abject worship. They all stood perfectly still, looking much like ornately carved statues.

The broader group formed a great concave circle—their attention drawn to something or someone in the center of the assembly. The heart of the circle was the size of a baseball diamond with a foggy middle.

The boy's curiosity got the better of him, and he began to paw his way through the crowd for a better glimpse. At first, he couldn't quite make anything out. He squinted as he walked and the fog revealed two lone figures, who seemed to materialize out of nowhere. They were animatedly talking, or at least flailing their arms around as if they were in a heated debate about something. As he broke through the crowd, he realized both were men. They wore flowing robes similar to that of the crowd, but were still flailing their arms. The boy decided this was likely to gesture for emphasis, as if contesting each other's silent claims. Still, he couldn't tell for sure. What were they arguing about? It almost appeared comical, if not for the foreboding feeling he felt within his heart. He quickly dismissed the feeling, after all, he had only just stumbled onto this scene.

One of the men faced him, wearing hard lines that ran down his cheeks drawn out in anger. The man's hair was jet black in stark contrast to his white robes that whipped around him, as if a strong gust of wind was furiously beating down. His features were nothing out of the ordinary. That is, except for a pair of dark, penetrating eyes set under heavy lids. Those eyes were hypnotic. They were a mixture of torment and insanity. The boy shuddered in spite of himself and momentarily looked away.

But the scene was intoxicating and the boy soon found himself drawn to the dark-haired man again, whose mouth twisted and curled as he voiced unheard words or threats. The man's mouth moved with astonishing grace, as if dancing to a delicate ballad, the boy concluded. He strained to hear what was being said, cupping one hand around his ear. He hoped he could beat the deafness, but heard nothing. Silence ruled—one thing that the mist had not surrendered when it withdrew. He glared at the man, willing himself to hear the conversation.

There was only silence.

Frustrated, the boy tried to move a little closer. But every step he took kept him in place. He never neared the man. The boy turned his attentions to the other man with his back to him and tried to maneuver around the man to perhaps catch a glimpse of his face, but whichever way he moved, the man's back remained facing him. After the third attempt, he finally gave up in disgust.

The debate now appeared to intensify. Both figures were more agitated and gestured with increased sharpness at each other. The crowd that was entrenched around the two men began to edge slowly backward to give the contenders more room to harass each other. This continued for a few moments before abruptly ending when the black-haired man suddenly raised his hands with a look of triumph oozing from his dark features. The boy resolved the man must be evil and dark, for no other reason than those suffocating eyes. The eyes of endless darkness.

Another flash of light erupted around him, and the boy was again standing where he had entered the arena. He stared back at the concourse, disappointed that he once again had to strain to see anything at all. This was all too confusing, he determined. Everything here was backward in this place, and nothing made any sense.

The circle's flank directly behind the dark-haired man suddenly broke. A wave of sharp sound erupted over the concourse, discharging in a symphonic crescendo that surged through the arena, as if a gigantic glass bowl had hit the ground and exploded in slow motion. The assembly and combatants all froze for a moment and then the crowd scattered in mayhem, all covering their ears as they ran. The boy copied the crowd, clapping both hands over his own ears at the suddenness and intensity of noise that reached him.

The black-haired man's deep voice now rose above the furor, speaking in a strange tongue. The boy unclamped a hand from his ear, as if this would help him understand the bizarre words. Another blinding light erupted at the center of the crowd, sending shock waves across the expanse, the brilliance temporarily drowning the mob from view. The light's intensity seared the boy's eyes, and he instinctively covered them with his arm for protection.

He peered out of one eye, stealing a momentary glimpse. The light was still too bright and the boy had to cup a hand over his brow while squinting to see anything at all. His eyes took a few moments to adjust to the light's brilliance. He could see something within the light . . . a dim shadow sluggishly moving within. It began to grow and crowd out the light, drowning it without remorse.

Out of the brightness hatched a ghastly black head. A long, mangled snout sprouted hundreds of dagger like teeth, encasing a long slithering tongue that repeatedly snapped in and out of its maw. Smoke curled upward from two large nostrils, set on the front of its muzzle. Two dark, penetrating eyes rose sharply from its head, crowned with a row of horns jutting from the top of its scalp.

The boy thought to himself that those eyes were eerily familiar, although he couldn't quite place them.

The head was followed by an enormous scaly body, still partially submerged within the blinding light so as not to see the whole monster in fine detail. But it was clear what the monster was.

A *dragon*.

The dragon opened its maw and threw its head backward to let out a deep-throated roar. It then glared around the arena, as if to compose itself, and halted its surveillance on the man with his back still turned to the boy.

The black-haired man was nowhere in sight, but the monster stood exactly where he had been. The crowd had now regrouped, as if in a standoff. They were now taking their places, either behind the man or behind the monstrous dragon. The figures behind the monster, cheered it on.

"I will be avenged!" the dragon presently bellowed, followed by a deafening roar. "We will rule all!"

*At least I can now understand what it's saying*, the boy realized.

The monster threw its head back again, gaping its maw wide open, issuing a gurgling, sucking sound signaling a quick intake of air. The force of it bent the crowd over toward the dragon in slow motion, followed by a moment of complete stillness. The dragon threw its head forward and belched a gust of hot air that drove the figures backward. An overwhelming flame, mixed with rancid smoke, assaulted and engulfed everything and everyone in its path.

The boy's eyes seared again. A hot stream of tears splashed down his cheeks as the first volley of hot air reached him, even from his distance. He frantically knuckled at his eyes to temper the burning, roughly rubbing them until he felt that his sockets were going to implode.

He chanced another look, peering around his knuckles, which were still raised, and immediately forgot all about the heat. He cringed in fear as a rolling blanket of flame tumbled toward him. His arms dropped to his side as he stood helplessly frozen, watching the advancing inferno draw nearer and nearer. As the frothing, burning mass reached him, he instinctively raised his arms in defense and let out a silent scream.

# CHAPTER 2

## Dragon of Steele

*Dreams are the stuff of legend—perhaps they also foreshadow what is to come?*

E than shot out of his sleeping bag, gulping in air as fast as he could. A cold sweat streamed steadily down his face, forming great drops that silently dripped onto his bedding. He was sopping wet, from head to toe, and his whole body ached as he trembled uncontrollably.

He threw his hands around his chest, cradling himself for a few moments to temper the shivering and thought to himself, *It was only a dream!* He felt a little better, so he repeated the phrase again—this time he subdued his shivering body altogether.

His dreams were happening with more frequency, almost every night, *since . . .* He shrugged off the thought. These dreams left him in a worn-out stupor when he awoke, and he still couldn't figure out who the two men were. There was also the looming question in his mind about the black haired man—had he changed into the dragon?

Ethan shivered again. *Dragons aren't real!* he reassured himself and took a slow, deliberate breath to calm his nerves.

He glared out of his bedroom window, a rough hole cut into the brown rock wall, and watched the sun lazily rising from the east over the distant yellowish Blue Mountains. The morning was still, yet the heat of the coming day already emanated off the floor directly in front of him where the sunlight steadily crept farther into his sleeping quarters. He momentarily wondered if the beads of sweat and his damp bedding were a result of his nightmare or from the muggy morning heat—it had been getting steadily hotter as the summer months neared.

At least the mugginess from last night still hung in the morning air before the overpowering dry heat of the day overpowered any moisture. *It's gonna be another hot day*, he thought rather dismally. *And I bet we'll have to ration water, again*, he spat in disgust. Ethan's mouth dried up at the thought of the excavation crews clattering around the water well for what was already a brown muddy liquid to begin with. The notion left a bitter taste in his mouth, and he grimaced at the thought of the unsavory taste. *This isn't home!* he sighed as his body wrung itself together. Bad taste or not, he already felt incredibly thirsty.

A little mirror hung from a peg on the wall directly in front of him. It was much too low, but it was the only peg in the room he could find when the family had moved in. So Ethan had put the mirror there. He paused and studied his face for a moment. A reflection of a skinny brown-haired boy with a deep tan and a tall imagination stared back at him. He generally got along with everyone around him, except for a small few. His mind presently drifted to a few of the digger's sons, who had spared him little sympathy since his arrival.

*Treat him as if he were your own*, his father's words sounded in his head.

*If he only knew . . .* The boy grimaced.

He wasn't quite sure why, perhaps because he was smaller and different from them. He certainly felt like a stranger here. It might also have to do with the fact that they couldn't pick on his older brother, Kristian, or on his little sister, Lola. But it didn't really matter why. In the end, it was him at the butt end of their jokes that they spewed at him in their *stupid* language. He only thought this because he had not mastered the language at all, unlike his brother. Anyways, actions spoke volumes more than words could, and Ethan resented the poor treatment from the other boys.

Still, he wasn't about to tell his parents or bring this up with Kristian. He was lucky Lola hadn't seen any of it, or she would have told Mom and Dad for sure. *Definitely not Mom!* he concluded. She was the enforcer and tended to be overly protective of her children, like a mother hen. If she knew about his abuse, she would set off a search-and-destroy mission for the boys, and Ethan would suffer the consequences.

He momentarily winced at the thought of the boys taking revenge on him.

So he made up excuses, and his ploy had worked so far. He simply fibbed that he had stumbled and fell or got hit with a shovel while he was digging or some other lame reason to explain away the bruises he came home with. *Could be worse,* he thought. He turned his head slightly to study a small bruise on his cheek and suddenly yearned for his grandfather, unsuccessfully choking back a rush of sudden tears that sprang to his eyes as they slid unhindered down his cheeks. He made a stern face at the mirror and brushed the moisture from his cheeks with his sleeve while swallowing hard for emphasis. He turned away from the mirror and punched his sack pillow to focus on something else, letting his anger take shape against the crew boys instead.

*Big jerks!* he hissed to himself. *Just wait until I get them back!* he plotted as he mentally made his way through the list of his usual payback plots.

Finding his favorite version, Ethan lay back down flat on his back, musing with a giant smile beaming across his ragged lips about an imaginary outbreak of desert bees repeatedly stinging the bullies in his mind. He could picture in great detail their terrified eyes bulging with fear, the beads of sweat on their faces, and the bellowing cries for Mommy or whatever word they used in Arabic as they ran helplessly from the army of gigantic bees. *Now that's a present I wouldn't want to miss!*

His smile widened as he remembered today was the day!

*Today is my birthday!* he thought excitedly.

He let his mind wander about, imagining all the presents he had asked for: *Maybe I'll get another airsoft gun or at least a decent iPhone. I wouldn't mind having a few honey sticks . . .*

Ethan's imagination went too far on the last present as he stumbled across memories of his grandfather's home-brew honey sticks. He didn't like thinking about it. His grandpa and he had been very close. *But now he was gone!* He suddenly lost all desire to celebrate, not since *Grandpa's accident.* Well, he had always been there to celebrate with Ethan, but not this year. Grandpa always had some fishing gear for the boy—and of course, his prized honey sticks. Ethan's mouth began to water, and he drooled slightly in spite of himself.

He quickly wiped the spittle away and looked sheepishly around the room, as if someone were watching him. Ethan tried again to change the subject in his mind. *Be strong, Ethan!* he quietly mouthed. *At least I'll be fourteen today. That's got to be enough, and Dad will finally let me help run the excavations and boss the bullies around!* He gloated. *Or even run errands to the market with Kristian!* He beamed at this option. *Besides,* he added, more to convince himself that he was ready, *Mom and Dad are always telling me that I think and talk more like an adult anyways. So let me act like one!* He fumed.

Ethan was dragged from his reverie as the drowsy morning silence came to a shrill end with the howling of dogs.

"Dumb dogs!" he mumbled to himself.

He covered his ears and squeezed his eyes shut, trying to drown out the barking in the hope of reviving his daydream about becoming a foreman at the dig site, but it was too late. The dream wasn't coming back.

Admitting defeat with a grunt, he briefly considered the dogs in his mind. Vizsla were awesome, and could run for miles in the heat, but most of all, *they are so much fun!* he thought. Sometimes they would get out of their enclosure and would leap around the site in a frenzied rush of enthusiasm, jumping on or running into anyone they could find, while their tails wagged their entire hind quarters in a perpetual battering motion that could knock the strongest man to the ground.

It had become sort of a game with Ethan and his brother to see who could stay standing the longest as the dogs jumped on them. *King of the mountain!* he mused at the name Kristian had given the game.

It suddenly occurred to him what the vizslas' owner was going to do with all of the commotion they were causing in the early-morning hours. *Yell and slap them, no doubt,* he thought in disgust, and his smile evaporated. *Mom won't like that!* he contemplated as he knew his mother was an animal rights activist of sorts. She had a streak of sympathy for animals and couldn't stand the mistreatment of any animal and especially of dogs.

As if on cue, he heard a gruff, groggy voice shouting hoarse commands at the dogs, which were promptly ignored, as the vizslas continued their serenade to the sluggishly rising sun. He heard the man shout once more, followed by a dull thud. One of the dogs yelped, and then silence followed.

*Oh, there's gonna be trouble!* Ethan thought as he made a mental note to inform his mother, if she hadn't already heard what had happened. *Busted!* he continued. It wouldn't be a pretty sight when she confronted the owner and Ethan involuntarily winced at the thought and then grinned mischievously.

Ethan cleared his mind of waking thoughts and pushed himself up into a crouched squat, quickly making his sleeping bag up as best he could. He swung himself around to find his shirt and jeans slung over a crudely built chair propped against the far wall of the room.

The room was simple, bare of any other decor, unless you considered his father's tools strewn about as an artistic expression. Otherwise, it was only furnished with a table and two chairs at the far corner. He had just enough space to stand and walk seven or eight paces from one end of the room to the other. His sleeping bag was laid out in the middle of the floor on a makeshift cot. His little sister's cot lay beside Ethan's, with her inside it and still very much asleep.

A brief smirk touched his lips as he surveyed the little sleeping demon. *She almost looks like a real little girl,* he thought. It often amazed him how such a peaceful little face could be filled with such fury when she didn't get her way. *Whatever Lola wants, Lola gets!* Ethan grimaced. She also had an uncanny way of getting him into heaps of trouble. *Although,* he recalled, *most of the time, it really is my fault.* Ethan held back a soft chuckle. *Na, it is all her fault!* he concluded.

Pushing himself up, Ethan crept across the room to his clothes and quickly dressed, careful not to wake his sister. He pulled on his worn-out sandals with one strap missing on one foot and a large hole in the bottom heel of the other. It hadn't taken long to wear them out. In fact, he'd done it in record time. He beamed with pride. But he needed to have Mom order another pair of sandals, he noted to himself. *That is if Amazon delivers this far out!* he doubted they did.

Quietly walking on the balls of his feet, Ethan reached the door and pulled on the latch as he slipped into the hallway. He mechanically grabbed at the lip of a rough ceramic jar on the floor and hauled it into his arms to go fetch water and quench his growing thirst.

Ethan paused and quickly glanced back at the doorway. *Lola will still be asleep if I hurry back from the well,* he thought to himself. He was never supposed to leave her unattended at any time! On the other hand, he wanted to get this task done quickly. *It's a dumb rule to begin with,* he grumbled. *Besides, Mom and Dad won't know the difference and Lola is technically still in her bed,* he rationalized. If nothing more, this gave him an excuse to go off on his own without being seen in the early-morning hours.

He quietly closed the door behind him.

The hallway ran about twelve feet in either direction, abruptly ending to his left about seven feet away with Mom and Dad's room. To the right, the hallway ended with the front door to the little clay house. Ethan looked directly across the hallway to where Kristian was staying. His older brother absolutely had to "have his own room," he mocked in a whiny tone. He paused at a faint snore coming from the room and silently grinned to himself. His brother was a known sleep talker. *Wish we were in the same room*, he thought about teasing his brother in his sleep. A symbol on Kristian's door caught Ethan's eye. The symbol of a beehive carved deep into the wooden center that his brother had etched into it. The beehive symbolized the family crest.

At the sight of the crest, Ethan's mind suddenly reopened to thoughts of his grandfather. Grandpa had made a living as a game and wildlife biologist, but he also moonlighted as a beekeeper, which was tradition and his real passion. *I wish I could have travelled around the world with him,* he mused. *Finding new kinds of animals like the Burmese cat and Sand Lions!* Ethan thought as he reflected on some of the old man's stories.

The lion is what had brought Grandpa *to this awful place*, Ethan spat. Kurdistan was dry and dirty compared to the rainy climate of Seattle that he was so used to. Grandpa had come here to help setup Dad's excavation site. The deal was that the old man could use this as his base camp to search for the lions as well as keep an eye on the dig for Dad. It seemed to be the perfect setup: Dad had someone to check in on the foreman running the local dig, searching for evidence of *primordial Neo-Sumerian temple ruins* and Grandpa got to search for the lions.

*But it wasn't perfect.* Ethan grunted. *No one cared about keeping Grandpa safe!* he thought. The boy remembered Grandpa's weekly emails; he looked forward to those emails. The last one stuck in his mind and he could recite it almost verbatim: "Ethan, today was marvelous. I had camped a few miles outside of the dig site, next to the foothills . . . it was a long day. I had just finished my evening meal, when there it was! My first sighting of a sand lion. He just stood there looking at me and I at him for an hour, before I lost sight of him in the darkness. They are NOT extinct! I wish you could have been here with me. What a discovery! Also, as you asked in your last email, I'm into the second week of domesticating the local, desert honeybee. The first batch of honey is awful—must have to do with the bitter sage flowers in the area. I plan to add some more temperate flowers around the hives when I get back from the village tomorrow. Anyways, just checking in with you on my progress. I love you boy. Take care of your mother and your family. All the best, Grandpa."

Ethan had immediately typed his response and sent it. He was almost as excited as the old man. He anxiously awaited the next email, but it never came. The news of Grandpa's disappearance came one week later, when the old man had not showed up for his routine inspection of the dig site. Dad left immediately to search for Grandpa, and an investigation began with a series of search teams led by local inhabitants. After only a month, the Kurdistan government labeled Grandpa as missing, claiming that he had either been taken by wild animals or by one of the many political factions at war within the country. But no ransom note ever came . . . no hostage video tape, and the official search was discontinued.

Of course, Dad continued the search on his own with his dig site workers and sent emails every day to the family. But after three months without a single clue, he had to reluctantly give up the search as well, fearing the worst had happened. Dad promised he had turned over every rock and climbed every mountain in the area, but there was only so much he could do. When he got back home, the family held a small funeral for the old man. Ethan didn't like to think about it, though.

He knew his father had tried his best, but Ethan still believed that Grandpa was out there somewhere, and he longed to explore the desert to find him. *It's the stupid dig's fault!* He accused as he gulped down another volley of tears. Just after Dad had called off his private searches, the locals uncovered a few clay pots, some ancient staff with an ornamental ivory pomegranate atop possibly serving as a sign of some priestly office and an insignificant clay tablet with the writing all smudged off. However, two inscriptions were preserved, and what looked like *QDŠ* and *WAP*, apparently symbolizing the words for "holy, separation, or withdrawal." His father's voice sounded again in the boy's mind. Dad had excitedly concluded that this was more than enough proof. "These are temple inscriptions. So naturally, there has to be a temple close by." Ethan parroted his father.

And so, Grandpa was all but forgotten and Ethan's father had dragged the whole family out here three weeks ago after his team got the grant money, apparently from some old wealthy eccentric who hid himself away in his remote mansion in the mountains of Scotland, somewhere.

*I'd rather be there!* he stewed moodily. At least the weather would have been more to his liking. *Why couldn't Dad have stuck to his previous job at Xbox? Maybe Grandpa would have never come out here in the first place!* Ethan reprimanded.

Mom said it was a midlife crisis and that the family would support Dad in whatever venture he took. Ethan rolled his eyes before returning to his thoughts. Unfortunately, Dad had opted to finish his degree in ancient languages and archeology, which in turn led him to join a group searching for primordial temples in the Middle East. He often talked about *computational archeology*, whatever that meant. Dad had said it was something about *the combination of old-school archeology and big data in the cloud that cataloged items and predicted dig finds* or some gibberish like that.

Ethan grimaced.

The boy thought of the 3D computerized map his father had excitedly shown the children as he recounted stories of lost Kurdistan temples housing ancient mysteries that were yet to be discovered and how he could find them through a bunch of math. Ethan hadn't taken much interest, it wasn't all that fascinating. In fact, it was altogether boring, especially the math part, which was Ethan's least favorite subject. Besides, it seemed to him that this was a very dangerous place to be dragging the family to, citing Grandpa as the prime example, let alone what the daily news claimed over the radio. It was irresponsible to force the entire family to leave their home and all for a dream his dad had, he silently scolded.

His mood worsened at the present course of his thoughts. *No electronics, no cell phones, not even fishing in this barren wasteland!* Ethan continued. *And why couldn't Dad use that 3D map and complex math to find Grandpa?* he wondered. It wouldn't be so bad, if he could at least explore and track down Grandpa. But Mom and Dad scolded him more than once for attempting to slip away from camp, pointing out Grandpa's loss as the reason for not wandering off. Ethan still couldn't bring himself to accept the facts and continued to slip away on short scouting missions any chance he got. He sighed as he remembered his parent's stern caution, "The desert is an unforgiving place! It is strictly forbidden for you to wander or explore, Ethan!"

"But Kristian gets to!" Ethan recalled his answer to his parents. This led to more punishment, but he didn't care. *It isn't fair!* his older brother got all the privileges, *because he's sixteen!* he thought in an exaggerated tone. *While I'm stuck either digging in a giant and pointless sandbox . . . Or watching Lola all the time!* he growled throwing his head back in the direction of their bedroom. It all seemed to count against him, and he blamed his parents for not giving him more freedom. What made matters worse, were the two huge guards who constantly patrolled the perimeter of the compound. This made it all the harder for Ethan to slip away. Sometimes he wasn't sure if they were keeping intruders out or keeping him *in*. He thought in contempt. Besides, the guards never answered him when he tried to ask them questions. They simply grunted and continued their vigil. Sometimes, Ethan pretended they weren't human at all, but were creatures in disguise that delighted in torturing their young captive.

His mood momentarily brightened as he again thought that his parents might allow him to go with Kristian on marketplace errands now that he was old enough. *Aah, probably not!* he sulked. "I'll probably still have to watch Lola the whole time! That or stay back in the digging pits and get beat up again!" he murmured this a little louder than he anticipated, looking around, as if he half-expected to see someone right behind him. "Would be just my luck," he hissed a little more quietly.

Ethan spat again. Any number of months of this place was more than he could stand. He hoped that Dad would hurry up and discover the dang temple and be done with it! The project was scheduled to run for nine long months. Mom had finally agreed to homeschool the children at his father's request, but she wasn't happy about it. Ethan dreamed of returning to his old school again come January. *Now I want to go back to school?* he thought in dismay. *Wow, this is bad, really bad!* he jabbed at himself.

Glancing back at the beekeeper insignia in the door, he thought once more of Grandpa, then turned and walked at a quick pace toward the front door, straining hard not to think too much.

The doorway opened into a ragged courtyard, riddled with holes and debris from bomb shells that had pounded the village years ago. This was now a makeshift dig site but the scars were everywhere to be seen. Ethan even thought he could hear the faint crackling of rifles in the distance every now and then. But no one believed him when he had mentioned this once, so he gave it up as his own imagination. Still, the area was not completely safe; hence, the armed guards to patrol the dig.

Ethan canvassed the small mountains of sand cast up by the dig, interspersed with a ragged city of tents, used by the local diggers whom Dad had recruited. One of the guards stood watch by the foreman's tent, since the foreman opted to live in a tent rather than in one of the old clay houses. Dad had insisted the family stay in a clay house to get the full effect of the experience. But Ethan was sure a tent would have given him more freedom.

Shaking his head, the boy decided he couldn't dwell on any of that right now. His focus turned to his next move. The well was halfway in between the village and the active dig site, about a half mile's distance. He needed to quickly cross open ground in order to reach it. The diggers and Dad called it the DMZ, which stood for *demilitarized zone*. He wasn't sure if this was to scare the younger kids, as the two guards had already cornered that market. But it certainly made him much more cautious, whenever he had to cross.

It was still early enough that the digging hadn't started yet. "I'll be OK. I'll keep out of sight . . . It's just to be careful anyways, and I'll stay downwind of the guards," he muttered under his breath, as if to convince some unseen critic.

Confident of his plan, he looked one way and then the other, wary of the guards. With no one in sight, he brusquely walked toward the well, hugging the walls of the shattered village as he went. Fortunately, no one seemed to be awake yet as he passed the village huts. A few lizards scurried down and across his path, and Ethan soon forgot about stealth altogether as he started to lightly jog past the one-story clay huts. Most of them were completely empty anyways, torn to pieces from previous bombardment—specters of a once-peaceful village now lying in almost entire ruin.

He finally neared the edge of the village and warily surveyed the area again, as if trying to avoid oncoming traffic before crossing a busy street. The well wasn't too far. He could almost imagine it looming in front of him in his mind's eye.

After making sure he was alone, he tensed for the sprint. He jolted forward and charged one or two paces.

"Ethan, where are you going?" a shrill voice demanded directly behind him.

Ethan tried to stop himself midstride, but caught one leg on the back of his other calf, and toppled over sideways, pitching his head directly into the sand. He slowly pushed himself up from the ground, spitting the gritty substance out of his mouth. He looked quite comical with a line down the center of his face, half covered in sand.

"Lola, you scared me . . . ," he sputtered, still trying to extract the sand from his tongue.

Lola tried to hold her giggling in, but he could hear her under her breath nonetheless.

This infuriated him all the more. "You're supposed to be asleep! Go back to the hut, right now! I need to get water!" He summarily dusted himself off and got to his feet in as dignified manner as he could muster.

Lola looked at him for a moment and puffed up her cheeks, folding her arms while shaking her head. She looked like a stubborn billy goat, cocking its head back, as if ready to charge an unwary trespasser. "No, we're supposed to stay together . . . remember?" she said stoically.

Ethan cringed out of annoyance and partly out of anxiety. He didn't want to hear yet another scolding from her about how Mom and Dad would be angry if they split up, and he most certainly wanted to avoid punishment from his parents. "OK, OK, just don't say it." He spat, fully expecting the next line to be "I'm telling!"

He finished thrashing the last bit of sand out of his hair and motioned for her to follow.

She took up her normal position next to him as they walked, and wore a triumphant look on her face, like a proud peacock. Her look infuriated Ethan, and he momentarily thought about chucking *her* head first into the sand, then reconsidered and dropped his hands to his side with a grunt of restraint.

They both walked the distance to the well in silence. Ethan dutifully scouted around them at every step, surveying the barren, sandy hills beyond them. A few desert plants sprouted up here and there, but the rest of the landscape was barren and devoid of any movement, except for occasional short gusts of wind that flung sand high into the air. In the distance, he could make out the faint outlines of another old Muslim city at the base of the surrounding ragged mountains.

He momentarily forgot about his scouting duty as he lapsed into yet another daydream. His mind envisioned him making his way through the crags of the hills. He pictured the excitement in the air, the smells, animal sightings, and breezes that navigated the ragged landscape.

*I wonder if Grandpa ever ventured onto the cliffs?* he asked himself. *No, no!* He quickly caught his thought and looked sheepishly down at his sister, as if she had been monitoring his thoughts. He swallowed hard and buried his feelings deep in his subconscious. He was a bit embarrassed about how weak he was whenever he thought about Grandpa. He silently scolded himself at this, *Get a grip, Ethan!*

The well loomed directly ahead of them, and he blinked in disbelief. He surveyed the area and realized with excitement that they had beaten the morning crowd. That meant more water for them, and hopefully, not as muddy and thick, as it usually was. Ethan sighed with relief and flashed a smile at his younger sister.

She wasn't paying attention.

The well was a crude structure made out of clay brick with an old and sand-beaten wood terrace erected over it. It was amazing the crumbling edifice was still standing. A terrace rested on top of two square beams that were rooted into the foundation of the brick well. A long frayed rope hung sulking from the beam, swaying to the sudden desert gusts that blew past. Tied to the end of the rope was a riddled wooden bucket used for collecting the water from the darkness below. Ethan knew he had to haul the bucket up quickly before all of its contents drained entirely, leaking through the rough cracks that showed visibly in the old container. Next to the well lay a tarp heap with a machine underneath. Short gusts of wind lifted the tarp at the corners to reveal a water pump. The pump was supposed to be installed in the next week. This meant Ethan wouldn't have to worry about muddy water anymore. In fact, the water would be directed through long hoses all the way back to their hut!

He sighed in relief.

Ethan reached the well first, grabbed the rope, knocked the bucket over the edge with his foot, and slowly lowered it hand over hand into the darkness below. He quickly grew bored of the task and absentmindedly examined the city's buildings again, letting his mind wander.

"Ethan, I'm thirsty!" Lola suddenly blurted out, startling her brother.

He lost his grip on the rope in his surprise, and it singed his palms as he tried to grab the rope again. The bucket dropped to the bottom, and he heard a faint splash as it hit the water.

"Lola!" Ethan yelled, blowing on his red palms and rubbing them against his chest. "You scared me again!" He shot her a furious look of contempt.

Lola shrugged apologetically. "I just wanted . . ."

"No, Lola! Just let me get the bucket back up, and then you can have your drink!" he said irritably. He grabbed the rope gingerly with his sore hands, then gave in, and began to indignantly pull on it to hoist the bucket back to the surface.

It soon reached the top, and Ethan poured the contents into the jug he had set on the edge of the well. When he was done, he motioned for his sister to drink out of the bucket before all of the water had leaked out.

Cupping her hands, she drank until she wasn't thirsty any longer, and then Ethan quenched his thirst. The water was much cleaner today. Actually, much cleaner than on any previous day. He gloated and silently committed to make it to the well earlier, at least until the pump was installed. Besides, if Mom or Dad found out the children had drunk directly from the bucket without filtering the water, they would be in a lot of trouble. *You'll get worms!* he heard his brother's voice in his mind.

His rejoicing was short-lived though. As if on cue, he saw Kristian trotting toward them in the distance. "Great," he bawled in contempt. "Kristian is going to give us both the riot act now." He sighed. "Don't tell him that we drank from the well."

Lola gave her brother a question look.

The boy sighed and reached for the jug. "Never mind Lola, c'mon, let's go . . ." He got the sentence halfway out when the earth under his feet abruptly jolted, and a large dust cloud sprayed upward directly in front of them. He instinctively fell backward, bowling Lola over in the process. He heard her shriek as she fell.

He brushed the hair out of his eyes and looked over at his sister. "You all right?" he whispered.

She shot him a perplexed look and nodded. "Why are you whispering?" she whispered back.

The Drake Epics - Journey to Qara

Ethan's face flustered bright red. "Lola!" he said in an exasperated tone while shaking his head furiously. Hadn't she heard the explosion? He inched his way back to the well and carefully peered above the brick wall. A gaping hole had appeared some thirty yards from the well over toward the city. Dust was settling around the hole, and it occurred to him that a shell must have been misfired from somewhere within the city. At this stray thought, he felt a sudden urge to throw up. *In the city?* He feared as panic coursed through his veins. That could mean real trouble.

He studied the immediate countryside then looked again at the city. "Nothing," he said with relief. His parents had told horror stories of what happened in that old city.

Kristian reached the well in a squatted run. "What was that?" his brother bellowed.

Ethan shook his head. "I think it came from the city." He pointed to the buildings in the distance.

"What? No. We need to leave now! You shouldn't be out here!" the older boy reprimanded, socking Ethan in the arm.

"Kristian!" Ethan squawked, gingerly rubbing his arm. He momentarily forgot all about the shell that had exploded, instead he scanned the area for some blunt piece of wood to go after his brother with. It didn't take long for him to abandon his musing as something moved out of the corner of his eye. He swung his head around to get a better look and instantly froze. His blood ran cold.

A large metal tank had just peaked a nearby dune and was approaching the well, roughly a hundred yards away. He elbowed his brother in the ribs as he stared transfixed at the metal beast.

Kristian, ready to punch his brother again, saw Ethan's ashen face and turned to look in the same direction. All of the color drained from his face too. "Crap, get down!" he barked.

Ethan grabbed Lola by the waist and yanked her down. She responded by howling his name before he could clap a hand over her mouth and whisper in her ear that they were in big trouble and to be completely still. That quieted her down, Ethan thought, as he turned back to inspect the tank. Although he half-expected her to punch or kick him any moment.

The tank was a rusty brown with sandy splotches painted haphazardly all around its exterior. A picture of a black dragon was emblazoned on its side armament with a plume of fire erupting from its maw. Ethan shuddered, remembering the dream from last night. A menacing cannon jutted from its front, and the hull bristled with machine guns, although Ethan couldn't see anyone manning them at present. The tank rolled ever closer, and he could now distinctly hear the squeaking of its wheels as it came within fifty yards of the children before abruptly halting.

"What is it doing here?" Kristian asked himself out loud.

Ethan shook his head.

"We've got to get back now!" Kristian ordered.

Before the children could retreat, a metallic click, followed by a scratchy whining sounded as the turret turned slowly until it was facing the city. Ethan heard another metallic series of heavier clicks, and then a deafening explosion roared as the tank's turret erupted, firing a projectile at the tall buildings in the distant city. Ethan instinctively slapped his hands over his ears and screwed his face into a small ball. He dropped to his knees as the blast rang through his head. A small cloud of white dust exploded in one of the distant buildings as the projectile found its target.

Lola sobbed, but before Ethan could turn to check on her, another blast rang out, this time a little less loud as he was still covering his ears. He opened an eye and squinted at Lola through the haze to make sure she was OK. She and Kristian were both in the same position, right next to him.

They needed to get out of there, and fast, he thought. Lola had now opened her eyes and was looking around in perfect bewilderment. Ethan motioned for her to crawl toward him.

She shook her head wildly. Her eyes were wide with fear and desperation.

Incensed, he twisted his face up in anger. "Now, Lola!" he said in a hoarse whisper. "We don't have time for your sobbing!" He extended a warning hand in her direction.

She shook her head again.

Preservation took over his senses; and he launched himself at her, grabbed her hand, and dragged her into a standing position. He broke into a dead run, with his hand locked tightly around his little sister's wrist so that he would not lose her in their flight.

He glanced over his shoulder and dug his heels into the sand, almost tumbling them both over in the process. He realized that Kristian was not following them. He silently grumbled.

"Kristian!" he yelled. No answer. "Kristian!" he roared. Again, no answer. Ethan almost cursed and turned to bolt back toward the well.

They reached the clay wall, and both crouched behind it for protection, huffing to catch their breath.

Lola fumed as they gulped down air. She rubbed at her raw wrist and glared up at her older brother. "I can run on my own!" she flatly stated, still rubbing her wrist. "That hurt, Eth . . ."

Ethan raised a finger to his lips. "Hush, Lola!" he gasped.

He realized that his brother was leaning against the well in a weird way. So, he shook him. "Kristian!" he said. No response. "Kristian, wake up!" he pleaded. Still no response. Ethan rolled his brother over and onto the sand, putting his ear on the older boy's chest. He was breathing. "Kristian!" He shook him once more. His brother didn't budge.

A myriad of solutions flashed through his mind before he landed on one. He reached up, careful to not expose his head, and pulled the water jug off the ledge that he'd left behind. It thudded into the sand; some of the water sloshed out of it and onto the ground. As soon as the water touched the earth, it immediately disappeared from view, leaving only a dark brown color in the otherwise-light sandy ground. It was too heavy for him to carry with all of the water in it, so he quickly tipped it over and begrudgingly emptied half of its contents onto Kristian before righting it in the sand.

Kristian sputtered and coughed. He looked up at his younger brother and yelled. "What are you doing? Leave it!" he commanded and hoisted himself into a crouched position.

Ethan tried unsuccessfully to hide a smile at his sopping wet brother. *That felt really good!* he thought impishly.

"We've got to get out of here! You coming?" Kristian bawled.

Ethan shrugged, "You already said that," then nodded. He wondered what Kristian would say if he'd known that his younger brother had to come back for him, but that was par for the course with Kristian. He wrapped his fingers tightly around the lid of the jar, and with the other hand wrapped back around Lola's wrist, he readied for another sprint away from the well. She tried to pull away, but his grip was still too tight.

Moments before the three could get under way, the ground lurched beneath them for a third time; and they all lost their balance, falling back into the sand. Shots buzzed and whinnied overhead, sometimes hitting the sand right behind them, stirring up tiny clouds of dust in rapid succession. Ethan desperately got to his knees and popped his head back up to peak over the wall. The tank was almost on top of them now, but the shots were coming from somewhere else. He suddenly realized that someone was firing on the tank at close range.

They all dropped back down below the well's wall and squeezed their eyes tight.

Ethan's mind raced and he fell into a momentary dazed shock. *They were in the middle of a real battle!*

Sound exploded all around him, and his mind came back to the present. He could see Kristian slowly crawling toward them, yelling for them to stay down.

He turned to look at his sister, who was in shock, and let his eyes wander beyond her. A dozen men were scrambling toward the tank and them! In a split moment, Ethan realized that they were directly in the line of fire. Another clap of thunder erupted all around as machine guns opened fire on the tank, pelting the ground around them. He could vaguely hear the bullets ping the tank as they ricocheted off the metallic armor. Ethan rolled forward and grabbed Lola with both hands. He rolled back against the wall of the well, and they huddled as shots continued to whistle overhead.

The earth beneath them rumbled again, this time more forceful than from any of the previous times. Sand showered down upon them, and Ethan held Lola closer. She gasped as he squeezed her too tightly.

Kristian had shimmied up to them, terror evident on his face. He added his embrace as they three huddled in anxious misery.

They could hear the men shouting commands in between bursts of gunfire.

Ethan glanced up to see a man drop to one knee with a long tube on his shoulder and saw fire erupt from it as a missile whizzed over their heads and beyond the well. A loud explosion erupted out of sight, followed by a moment of silence. Then the gunfire started up again.

A deafening roar rang through the air—he assumed from the tank—and Ethan tried desperately to drown out the sound in his ears as they throbbed with the loud claps of thunder. A cloud of sand shot into the air where some of the shouting men had been standing momentarily before drowning them from Ethan's view. It didn't appear to have had any effect though as the men emerged from the dust cloud, scrambling into position for another volley at the tank. Short bursts of gunfire continued to whistle overhead and pelt the sand around the children.

Ethan decided to abandon all defense or reason and make a final run for it. He pulled himself back into a crouch, hoisting Lola up by the wrist, ready for another sprint. He caught his older brother's eye. Kristian looked to be doing the same thing and slowly counted down from three, holding out his fingers for emphasis.

Just as the count reached one, they sprinted. But, again they were all knocked to the ground. Ethan felt a dull object pound into his skull as he hit the soft sand. His head exploded and reeled as he saw stars and darkness overcame him.

"Ethan! Ethan!" his sister was now screaming his name.

He jerked open his eyes. Lola was frantically shaking him. "Ethan, Ethan!" She had a tone of desperation in her voice. He wrenched himself from the dream.

He spun around just in time to see the wall of the well give way and tumble inward. The sand around him immediately followed. Kristian was right beside Lola and both of them frantically clawed at the ground to keep from sliding farther into the hole. Ethan rolled to one side and away from the growing void while thrusting both of his hands toward them.

Kristian missed his grasp and bellowed as he fell in. Lola caught hold, but it was too late, and her weight pulled Ethan in. They both followed Kristian into the pit and toppled into the blackness below.

It seemed an eternity as they fell. He could see the light above him grow smaller as he fell into the blackness. For a moment, he could hear the splash of water, probably from the clumps of clay and sand, before his body pounded into something hard, stopping his fall.

Ethan let out a soft groan and lifted his head to scan for his brother and sister. A shower of sand drown his view, but he saw Lola's unconscious form first. She lay a few feet from him. Kristian was just beyond her, groaning and holding his head, then he went limp and lay still. Ethan reached out for them. "Lola . . . Kristian . . . ," he attempted as acute pain pounded in his head.

Everything around him became hazy. He struggled to stay awake and aware, but he started to lose consciousness too. The pain was overwhelming. He just wanted to sleep; he wanted the pain to go away.

Just as he was about to succumb, something strange happened. A beam of light appeared out of the hazy blackness in front of him. It lingered for a second then expanded and grew slightly. Was it possible?

Before he could make sense of it, something reached out of the light and grabbed both Kristian and Lola, slumped together. Ethan tried to wipe the grogginess from his mind to identify what it was. A pair of hands started to pull his siblings, already half-buried in sand, and into the light. "No, leave them alone!" he shrieked.

The boy tried to roll toward them, but the pounding in his head thrust him back to the ground. He yelped and grabbed his skull, trying to subdue the pain as it seared through his head and then through his body.

The hands paused momentarily and then continued to pull the other children into the light. Both disappeared entirely from Ethan's view.

Ethan tried to scream after them and groaned as the pounding in his head reached a feverish pitch. He winced at the pain again and continued to hold his head in a desperate attempt to stop the throbbing.

The hands now grabbed at the neck of his shirt and started to pull on him. He lurched his head sideways to get a better view, wilting at the pain. He couldn't see anything through the pain, but he didn't care what happened to him anymore. He simply wanted the pain to stop.

The sounds of the shouting men and the gunfire seemed miles away now and all he could see was solid white. Time slowed, and for an instant, time seemed to stand still.

His eyes regained some of their focus through his blurry vision. He looked up, and he saw someone, a face looking back down at him. He squinted harder in disbelief. It was a warm, familiar face, someone he didn't expect.

"Grandpa?" he mumbled in disbelief. The boy faintly heard his own voice call out the old man's name.

*It can't be!* he thought. *Am I dead?* he wondered.

Ethan began to ramble, "Grandpa, you're missing . . . How are you here? Where did you go? No one knows where you went or even if you were dead or not. How are you here . . . ? Why did you go?"

He couldn't hold out any longer to get the answers to his questions. His words slurred, the haze darkened into blackness, all sound dimmed, and Ethan passed out of consciousness.

# Chapter 3

## The Market Bizarre

*Every experience has a purpose ... life is a set of building blocks.*

Kristian's senses came to him for a brief moment, although too painful to open his eyes. But, enough of a moment to hear Ethan moan one word *Grandpa!* He thought he heard Grandpa's voice too and wondered what trickery this was, but the blackness was overwhelming. He thought briefly about the trouble they were all in, but he needed to sleep first. Just for a minute. That would fix the pain. Then he would get them all back to safety, then everything would be fine.

The blackness swelled and swirled all around him as waves of pain broke upon him and then left just as suddenly as they had come. It was almost soothing as he numbed to the sensation. It was an odd feeling. He sluggishly slipped in and out of a dream as his subconscious coaxed him into memories of his last visit to the local market. The swelling playfully picked and prodded at his mind as if it were a rough breeze, replacing his thoughts of pain as his senses deadened to reality. He imagined the people at the market; they moved like a great wave. He'd been there before. It was just the day before. His mind presently gave in entirely to the dream, and his current reality vanished.

— — —

A large crowd swirled and writhed like a gigantic snake wrapping itself around the trunk of a tree. The mass filled in around little wooden shanties thrown up to house goods to be sold. The fresh odor of roasted nuts, baking breads, dates, honey, incense, and other smells reached his nostrils as they combined into an irresistible tangle of sweet aroma. A low buzz echoed throughout the surrounding shanties as merchants and customers bartered and haggled over wares of every kind.

Kristian stopped to take in the fragrance as he gulped in the hot, arid desert air. It was the only place in the village he truly felt free from his duties and expectations placed on him. "Kristian, please look after your brother and sister. Kristian, please keep your hands off your brother . . . Kristian, please clean up your mess . . . Kristian, stop talking back!" He grimaced at the stack of chores and tasks waiting for him back at their makeshift hovel they called home. At least it wasn't permanent, but that didn't mean he had to like it. He was sick of having to constantly babysit his younger siblings, and if he heard Ethan complain one more time about looking after Lola! Kristian shook his head in frustration. Still he was happy to be back here at the marketplace even if he was on yet another errand.

He scanned the small shacks around him, trying to momentarily forget about his current chore. One merchant was busy haggling with another man, trying to sell the would-be buyer a case of dried dates. Kristian had picked up the local language surprisingly fast, but wasn't always sure he understood everything, not yet at least. Therefore, he had to strain as he listened to understand, specifically noting each word. *If they would only speak a little slower!* he protested. Yet this was another wonderful reason he loved to hang out at the market: to learn the language.

The merchant was now speaking at a dizzying pace and wheezed as he spun a web of tales about the redeeming qualities of the dried fruit. "They soften the skin and ease the bowls . . ." Kristian hoped he had heard that last part incorrectly, but lost interest in the discussion nonetheless.

He eyed another merchant selling what appeared to be roasted nuts, their flavor reaching his nostrils on a slight breeze. He tilted his head to one side, much like a begging puppy, and closed his eyes to welcome the scent. He was rudely interrupted by the shrill voice of the agitated and rather-large merchant.

Kristian thought for a moment that the voice didn't quite fit the man. Upon closer inspection, he decided that the man likely overindulged himself on his own merchandise. He scolded the merchant in his mind, imagining the man stuffing every nut into his big cheeks while chewing as fast as he could.

From the sound and looks of it, the customer was winning the debate, much to the displeasure of the pudgy man. The merchant's voice echoed over the din of the shacks, "But, but, but these are like no other kind of roasted heaven—they linger on the tongue and their flavor lasts . . ."

Kristian grinned to himself before turning his head in the direction of another shanty, this one housing a slender woman with an elongated nose that stuck out from her hooded burke. She was busily stalking her shelves, apparently late for the midmorning crowd.

He could immediately tell she was in a hurry as she clumsily dropped two loaves of fresh bread on the ground. She paused and looked around with an embarrassed expression plainly visible on her face. She retrieved the loaves from the dirt and dusted them off with a ragged brown apron tied around her waist. Another quick look around, and she placed the loaves gently on the shelf, as if they were expensive jewels. She turned to look over her shoulder one last time, this time catching Kristian's eye.

He quickly turned his head, acting as though he had seen none of what had just happened.

*Enough!* Kristian thought to himself with a twinge of regret. On this occasion, he had a task he needed to quickly complete. His musings would have to wait until another day, no time to wander and wonder at the mysteries locked within the merchants' collections of wares.

He adjusted his back sack and then quickly set off down the main market street and toward his destination. He dodged and bounded through the crowd as he ran.

A sudden breeze blew in from above, kicking up small dust devils around him—it was the sensation he was waiting for. He weaved his way through the oncoming masses to avoid collisions from unsuspecting pedestrians. He picked up speed, dodging the dust devils and people, now imagining himself in the center of a great battle, avoiding blows from oncoming assailants.

He presently, and rather adeptly, sidestepped an approaching man in a long robe. He imagined the opponent was lunging at him for a direct attack. Kristian circumnavigated the frontal assault, spinning around as he passed by the man, pretending to lunge from behind with his hands, striking a squatted pose with his arms outstretched. With a brief nod of satisfaction, he whirled around and set off again down the street, ignoring the odd looks that passers-by shot his way.

He soon arrived at a cross street that led off the market road. He ducked into it and away from his pretended assault. The path was free of clutter or anyone else for that matter and Kristian set off at a light jog. After a brief stretch, he came to an abrupt halt. He took a deep breath, silently recounting the directions his father had given him, then entered a small wooden door to his right. It was set two feet into a red-brown clay wall, worn with time. A small sign written in Arabic sat on the door, the brown paint worn with time. The sides of the wall were flaking off and left a pile of clay dirt at the base of the building.

Once inside, he scanned around the room. A sudden surge of excitement welled up within him.

"Now, Kristian . . . ," his dad had said. "This is important! I need to see this artifact. Don't goof off, and please try to hold your tongue." His father had given him a stern look, and Kristian obediently nodded.

"You'll bring it right back?" Again, Kristian obediently nodded. A brief hug from Dad, and he was sent off to the task.

"Dad, don't touch me, I'm almost a man!" he contested.

His father shot him a bewildered look and then nodded.

Kristian could see a hint of sadness, but it was time to let him grow up, he justified. Besides, he was too old for hugs!

Mom would not be happy if she knew, he thought briefly. Dad was always sending him off on little excursions for artifacts the villagers had dug up. She didn't like the fact that Kristian was doing this alone. He winced at the affront to his manhood and puffed his chest out in protest. He was old enough, he thought to himself. Besides, he wasn't in any real danger. If she could only see how he handled himself in the marketplace, she wouldn't complain so much. Besides, if he were back home, he would be driving by himself anyways. So he really didn't understand why she had to be the mother hen all of the time. *Seriously!* he thought. *I'm old enough to do whatever I want.*

His mind back to the present, Kristian surveyed the room in more detail. There was nothing out of the ordinary about the small hut. It was an adequate size with a mid-sized wooden table, a few chairs, and an old wooden bar opposite the door. Rough ceramic jars lay scattered haphazardly across the floor. Directly above the bar hung a huge head of a lion, its mouth open in a horrific silent roar. Kind of cool, he thought. But probably fake. He remembered his grandpa talking about the ancient lions being extinct for hundreds of years.

However, what now caught his attention were the walls, completely lined with shelves. Shelves that shot straight from the ground and stretched all the way to the ceiling. On those shelves lay hundreds of curious objects. Artifacts from previous digs, perhaps? He assumed the storekeeper had been part of many finds in the past. After all, the surrounding deserts were the mecca of digs, just from the looks of the many small sandy mountains cast up all over the countryside.

Kristian slowly turned in a full circle, trying to identify anything of interest to him. There were vases of all shapes and sizes, many of which had faded drawings painted on them—boring. He yawned.

There were shards of pottery, stacks of faded material, miniature statues, some in pieces while others remained partly intact. Kristian noticed a small table by one of the shelves. He casually strolled over and picked up one of the statues, examining it more closely. As he turned it over in his hands, he realized that the figurine had been meticulously pieced back together. He rubbed his fingers over the minute cracks in the porcelain and suddenly thought about how fragile the statue might be. He placed it very gingerly back on the table and backed away, pretending he had never noticed the table in the first place.

Kristian skimmed through the surrounding shelving again. His eyes landed on a necklace, attached to a circular flat amulet, the size of a silver dollar in diameter. What caught his attention was how white the amulet was. It seemed to glow, if he squinted hard enough. This brought the necklace into better focus, and he now noticed it had some design in it, but he couldn't make it out from where he stood.

He glanced around to make sure he wasn't being watched and brusquely walked to the raised bar. He propped his hands up on it and peered over the side. Upon finding no one present, he turned to walk to the shelf where the amulet lay.

"Yes?" a croaky voice spoke.

Kristian jumped at the question. His heart beat twice as normal at the scare, and possibly a little at being caught, even though he hadn't actually touched the necklace yet. He spun around, almost falling over in the process, to see an old, darkly tanned, and wrinkled old man, not much shorter than he was. The elderly man was standing behind the bar, apparently appearing out of nowhere. "Where did you . . . ?" he blurted out but couldn't quite finish the sentence.

"Come from?" the man finished it for him.

Kristian half-nodded, not knowing what to say.

"I was here all along," the man stated matter-of-factly.

Kristian cast a nervous glance toward the statue table, expecting to be reprimanded for touching.

"I assume you have come for the artifact?" the man queried, seemingly not bothered by the boy's previous curiosity.

Again, Kristian nodded, this time with relief in having escaped any rebuke.

The man's voice had a rough British accent. This puzzled the boy deeply. He didn't look to be British at all. But perhaps he had been trained in England; he presently thought and shrugged it aside.

"I have it here . . . ," the man continued. "But I think you have seen something else of interest, have you not?"

Kristian's mouth dried up, and he dumbly nodded again. For some reason, this was so unnerving. He didn't know why. It just was. He usually wandered the dig sites, picking up objects and inspecting them without the least bit of guilt. But here?

It must be that he was in unfamiliar surroundings, he decided. That and Dad wasn't present to ward off any stern reprisal as he did at the dig site.

The man waddled from behind the bar and toward the shelves where the amulet rested. He looked quite at odds with the store, and Kristian noticed he limped more heavily on his left leg. Must be an old wound, the boy critiqued.

"Name?"

Surprised, Kristian croaked out his name, sounding a bit hoarse, he thought to himself.

"Again?" the man looked over his shoulder at the boy with a sympathetic grin.

Kristian coughed uncomfortably into his hand before uttering his name, still standing in the same spot, horrified at his own discomfort.

"Good to meet you, Kristian!" came the reply in a pleasant tone. Having reached the shelf, the man retrieved the amulet. He rubbed it with the edge of his shirt, spat on the amulet, and rubbed it on his shirt again. After a thorough inspection, he beamed a smile at the nervous boy and limped toward Kristian.

Kristian, having to look at the man to avoid being rude, could now see that he was of slight build, wore a long-sleeved robe that reached mid-leg,

The Drake Epics - Journey to Qara

and wore old dusty sandals. He looked to be in his fifties, no, seventies? Kristian couldn't tell, but he noticed that he had a brown leather sack in his other hand. He hadn't noticed that before.

"Here you are," the man stated as he reached the boy and held out the sack to him. "It is what your father requested," he repeated at the perplexed look on the boy's face.

Kristian nodded in discomfort. This time he ventured a quick "Thank you", regaining some of his usual composure.

"And this . . . is for you." The man presented the boy with the necklace Kristian had been admiring moments before.

"I . . . I can't afford . . ." Kristian ventured, but his eyes glowed with longing.

"Nonsense!" the man barked. "Course you can. Consider it as payment for running the errand."

Kristian's eyes brightened. He didn't know why he was drawn to the necklace. It was fabulous. He reached out a hand and accepted the reward, not taking his eyes off the prize that he now had in his grasp, rubbing his thumbs against the surprisingly chilled surface. A raised etching of a dragon graced its surface. He let his fingers explore the embossed inscription. The amulet was otherwise smooth to the touch.

He briefly studied the design. The dragon sprawled across the middle section of the amulet with its legs, wings and tail extending to the edges of the circular white surface. Three smaller dragons silently roared all around the larger version, and three people stood at the bottom, around a tree that sprouted upward and formed the platform upon which the other dragons stood. The white surface was encased in silver and a protruding rounded point extended two inches from the bottom of the circular amulet with ridges carved into the edges. It had the appearance of a key, but Kristian couldn't quite tell.

"Wow!" he said to himself, not meaning to say so out loud. Kristian immediately blushed at his outburst. Yet he forced himself to peel his eyes from the amulet and look up.

The man wore a satisfied smile on his face, obviously pleased with himself for giving such a welcomed gift.

"I can't . . . ," Kristian attempted in an unconvincing tone. He secretly hoped the man would counter. "I mean . . . I can't accept this!" he decided, firmly holding the necklace out to the man. He looked away, as if his hands were going to be slapped. He didn't want to give it back, but it was the right thing to do.

"Rubbish!" the squat man shot back. He pushed Kristian's hand back at the boy.

Kristian paused for a second, debating whether he should counter again, then decided otherwise, not wishing to push his luck and held the treasure to his chest in relief.

"I'll let your father know I gave it to you, shall I?" the old man asked with a wry smile then nodded with satisfaction, seeing the boy's delight. "No . . . he won't mind a whit," he said confidently.

This greatly eased Kristian's nerves as his thoughts filled with wonder and excitement. Wait until he showed this off to Ethan and Lola. He could hear them ranting now. "That's not fair, why don't I get one! I want one!" He smiled delightedly in spite of himself.

The man gave him an awkward look, as if he were reading his mind. Then his expression changed, and he put his hand on Kristian's back. He turned the boy back toward the door and walked with him to the exit, pushing Kristian as he went. "Off with you now. Your father will be wanting to see that artifact." He paused and gave Kristian a second glance, and Kristian couldn't help but momentarily wonder if he weren't playing a small part in a larger story that he wasn't being told about in the least. "Hurry back, no goofing off, now!" the old man warned.

Kristian was now more assured the old man knew his father well. Only his father would say something like that, he thought.

The short man gave him one last shove out the door and into the side street. He was stronger than Kristian envisioned for such a small man.

He caught himself and whirled around. "Thank you! I didn't catch your name though," he croaked.

"el'Kamin, sir. Muschle el'Kamin," the old man said in a formal tone as the door closed shut. Kristian gazed back down at the necklace and smiled again.

"This is so cool!" he exclaimed and then packed both the items he was given into his back sack and set off at a merry trot for home.

# Chapter 4

## The Temple of Marduk

*"Light conquers evil, even as Marduk conquered the chaos-monster, Tiamat."*

Ethan awoke with a start—his thoughts were cloudy and his head was swimming. The memory of his fall leapt back to mind, and he quickly sat up to look around. He instantly regretted the action as his head ached in protest. He winced, rubbing at his temples a few times to help the throbbing. *Was it all real?* he asked himself. *Or did I eat too much again and dreamed it?* which he admitted more times than not, was the primary culprit for an aching stomach and a throbbing head.

The room was bathed in blacks and greys. He scanned around him, squinting to get a better view, but could only make out the faint outline of furniture. Not enough to immediately recognize his surroundings anyway. Still, it felt like his room, even in the darkness.

He suddenly remembered Kristian and Lola and scanned the floor around him. He soon found the familiar form of his sister, lying on the ground beside him, but could see little else. He sighed, putting both of his hands behind his head, and lay back down. He must be in his room.

*It was only a dream!* he thought to himself. *Another dream!* he amended.

His mind strained to recall the battle with ammunition flying all around him, the immense blasts in the air, the collapse of the well, the children falling into the hole, his brother and sister lying unconscious beside him, and last of all, the image of Grandpa. His eyes momentarily misted over, and he felt a single hot tear roll down his cheek.

*It was just another dream!* he reemphasized mournfully. He didn't bother to wipe the tear away, instead letting it dry on his cheek.

But it would have been amazing, had it all been real, he wistfully countered, now imagining what would come next. Still, it was an unfair dream. He suddenly became irritated at the frequent visions in his head. He wished he had more control of them; he would happily suppress them, if he could. He was also sure he could recall more arguments on demand. Although now that he thought about it, this dream had been very real, too real. His mind jumped to the dreams of the dragon, and he convinced himself that those dreams appeared just as real as well, although they were somehow different.

He realized that he'd been overly preoccupied with his dreams and questions. His head was still throbbing, and he felt in no mood to continue picking apart every little detail or to investigate anything further at all. *Stupid dreams are what give me the headaches!* he concluded as the dull thumping in his head continued.

Ethan closed his eyes, trying to block out the pain. All he needed was some rest for the headache to wear off—that and no more dreams. He threw up a mental barrier as he repeated multiple times, "Don't dream . . . don't dream . . . don't dream." He fell back into a deep sleep, this time without any dreams at all.

– – –

A lone light shone through the darkness. It was small at first, but as Ethan peered upward, the light steadily grew in intensity. One ray became two, and two rays became four. Soon, he began to develop awareness and realized he was waking from his sleep. The morning's light shone on his face, and he kept his eyes shut as he slowly sat up. His body ached at any movement, and his headache was still in full swing. He grimaced and tenderly reached up to feel his head. He had a bandage wrapped around the upper part of his scalp. *That's strange*, he briefly reflected as he let his fingers work over the bandage.

He wasn't fully awake yet, and his thoughts lingered on his dreams. At least he hadn't dreamed for the remainder of the night, he announced ruefully to himself. Well, he didn't remember dreaming anyway. But why did he feel so sore? Why did he still have this infernal headache *and where did this bandage come from?* He grumbled.

He swept his legs out of his bag and over the side of the cot. Instead, his toe stubbed on hard earth. "Ouch!" he exclaimed, refraining from bad language as he rubbed his foot. He half-opened one eye to judge what had happened. He wasn't on his cot! He wasn't even in his sleeping bag. Instead, he was covered with a blanket, spread out on the ground. His mind didn't quite grasp what was happening. His head still hurt too much to think clearly, but he shook it anyway to clear his thoughts. He instantly regretted doing so and grimaced for a few moments as he waited for the painful pricks in his head to subside. He opened the other eye, trying to quickly survey his surroundings. The light was a little bright, and he had to squint and blink a few times in order to push the sleep from his eyes.

After a few moments, a new world came into view, and Ethan decided he was still dreaming. He knuckled his eyes before chancing another look. His sight now fully adjusted, his body went limp and his mouth fell open. He was not in his room at all! In fact, he had no idea just where he was. His mind struggled for an answer, clamoring for a memory from the previous day that would help his situation make any sense. All he could remember was his, well, annoying dream. The images of the dream raced through his head. He quickly studied them thinking momentarily that perhaps he might be in a dream within a dream. This all fed his ravenous headache, and Ethan fought the sudden urge to lie back down and wait for the dream to run its course. Instead, he pushed himself up from the bedroll and paused to wince at the sharp pain in his head. He shrugged it off and gingerly got to his feet, as his muscles protested at the strain. Once standing, he scanned the room, turning in a full circle for the greatest effect.

Massive columns thrust from the ground to ten—no, fifteen-foot ceilings. He raised his hand in front of him to measure, as if he were an expert. The columns were too many to count and seemed to extend in every direction with no rhyme or reason for their layout. The bases of the pillars were solidly round, thinning slightly as they rose and then fanned out a few feet from the ceiling. They gave the appearance of gigantic plants growing up from the ground, as Ethan could distinctly see the leaves deeply etched into their sides and completely encompassing the pillars at the top.

As he approached one of the pillars, he could now see that it had ornate carvings of figures and symbols, along with the leaves, totally covering the surface. The bases had what appeared to be waves of water etched more slightly into the stone, such that the pillars appeared to be aquatic plants teaming with life growing out of water. The floor echoed this theme and was smooth and glassy, as if it were a quiet pool that mirrored the massive columns' reflections.

It suddenly occurred to him that the light that had flooded the area had to come from somewhere, and Ethan looked in vain for its source. It was everywhere, but he couldn't tell where it originated from. It certainly wasn't from the sun, as it seemed to flicker and had a yellowish tint to it. He assumed it was from some kind of firelight. He started forward, intent on finding the source, but got side tracked as he studied the pillars more closely. He moved from one pillar to the next, feeling the smooth and cold stone as he went.

He halted and forced himself to look beyond the tangle of giant columns to try and get his bearings. A doorway was set into an ornately decorated wall, some fifty yards from where he stood. He hadn't noticed this before. What was more, no columns surrounded the doorway. The pillars all formed a kind of path in adjoining rows that gave the appearance of a hallway, of sorts.

Ethan squinted to see within the doorway, zeroing in on what appeared to be a black obelisk-like structure in the distance. It was a little too far away to identify completely, but the sight was nonetheless impressive.

His mind was now reeling, catching up to the reality that presented itself to the boy. Where was he? It didn't make any sense; he had never been here before. *This* must *be a dream*, he thought. At least, that is the only thing that made any sense at all right now and his mind clung to the theme in order to keep him sane. This led to more thoughts and questions: What caused this particular dream? It was certainly a new dream. Would it end like his other dreams? After all, the other dreams always had. That

The Drake Epics - Journey to Qara

must be it, he thought, trying to placate a sudden burst of fear that welled within him. He was again lost, and this dream would empty into the same arena, followed by the crowd, the two men, and the dragon, the fire, the searing heat. Ethan gulped as a fresh wave of anxiety broke over him.

He quickly turned around in an attempt to forget this last thought and cocked his head to one side as he realized that his blanket, where he'd awoke, was accompanied by two other blankets, spread out next to his—both empty. But he could tell they had both been slept in by the way they were thrown back, folding over themselves. He continued to canvass the area around the blankets and noticed rows of solid stone benches, for all he could tell. They were of seating height, and about two feet wide by four feet long each. They were all jet-black and appeared to have reeds etched into them so that they almost looked like benches made of willows instead of stone. Three of them cropped out in front of him, and another three balanced them out just beyond the blankets. That must have been the furniture shadows Ethan saw last night, his memories returning. How could he have confused this with his room? he wondered.

Still, this provided absolutely no answers, and he was quickly becoming agitated about the unfamiliarity of his surroundings. He also felt a little hungry, and he was quite alone, which sent a rush of chills down his spine. He stewed on his thoughts and memories from the previous day, now more real to him, as the pain of his headache was all but forgotten. The last dream was of Kristian and Lola—trapped, in danger, they all fell, but he couldn't remember. They all fell in with the sand, and that put him here! His thoughts picked up tempo. That meant they should both be here in his dream. He needed to find them both. Suddenly another thought occurred to the boy—Grandpa!

*But that can't be true!* he scolded himself. Yet he couldn't ignore the fact that he desperately yearned for it to be true.

He whirled on the spot, aches shooting through his entire body and throbbing head, almost drowning out any further thoughts of the others. He didn't care and forced the pain into the back of his mind. Was he here? Had Grandpa really pulled them to safety?

Ethan started to jog in the direction of his assumed hallway, still ignoring the pain in his head and now from his sore joints and limbs. He was intent on finding his siblings and finding Grandpa. He hoped this dream would be different from all the others. This dream would find him something much more valuable—his Grandpa. It sounded completely crazy to him, but Ethan clung to the thought nonetheless.

After his brief jog, he neared the lit doorway and now thought he heard voices talking in a hushed tone. He paused to listen more closely.

One voice he recognized immediately as Lola. The second was Kristian. The third voice was more raspy than the others and much deeper than his older brother's. It sounded like Grandpa! He dared not hope for it, but it was unmistakable, it had to be! Ethan charged through the door, his entire body was screaming at him with every step. He crossed the threshold and screeched to a halt in disbelief.

There stood Kristian and Lola, animatedly talking and pointing around the room with an old man in a dusty brown robe with a well-kept beard and long grey hair pulled neatly into a ponytail. It was Grandpa!

"That's right, Lola, we are in a temple . . . ," Grandpa was saying.

They all turned their heads at the sound of Ethan's approach. Grandpa lovingly smiled and immediately crossed the floor to Ethan, submerging the boy in his arms with a big hug.

Ethan stood there, frozen, sobbing in spite of himself not knowing what to do, desperately wishing this was really happening.

Both Kristian and Lola held back soft chuckles.

Grandpa comforted, "It's all right, I'm here, I'm really here." The old man soothed.

"Ethan, look, it's Grandpa and we're in a temple!" Lola now chimed in, excitedly jumping up and down. She had an uncanny way of stating the painfully obvious. She was, after all, only eleven years old and took after Dad. Dad had a knack for stating the obvious too. Well, that and talking through movies. Ethan ranted.

The joyful boy regained some amount of his composure and reached his arms as far around the old man to hug him back.

They both stood there for a minute; and then Grandpa pulled back, lowered himself to one knee, and held Ethan at arm's length. "Now, let's take a look at you!" he exclaimed. "You have grown two, no, three inches!" He measured. "You are all so big now."

Ethan stood there for a second, still not believing what was happening to him. Then a flood of questions engulfed his mind and poured directly out of his mouth. "Where have you been? How are you still alive? Where is this place? We thought you had died! I mean, that a lion got you, or you slipped off a cliff, or . . ."

Grandpa was shaking his head, a patient smile imprinted on his lips. "I see that you still like to ask lots of questions." He chuckled. "But I think Lola has you beat in that department." He now openly laughed, along with Kristian.

Lola didn't think it was very funny and folded her arms in protest.

The Drake Epics - Journey to Qara

"I've been explaining much of my story to Kristian and Lola. I'll explain to you as well. But now that Ethan is awake, I believe that you are all hungry?" The old man looked at the children for confirmation.

Ethan's stomach rumbled in agreement, and he vigorously nodded. Kristian and Lola were doing the same.

Grandpa stood and pulled out two wind-up flashlights and handed one to the boys, then wound up the other flashlight for himself. "You'll be needing this," he said as he motioned for the children to follow him. Kristian cranked on the flashlight.

They walked out of the room and turned immediately right. Ethan observed another door opening that he hadn't noticed there before either.

Lola had skipped ahead, grabbing Grandpa's hand as they walked, and jabbered about some nonsense.

Ethan quickly became annoyed because he couldn't get a question in edgewise, not with her constant torrent of comments anyway. So he dropped back to talk with Kristian, who was content to stay out of the way.

"Grandpa has been down here ever since he disappeared. I mean, this is it! The reason we haven't heard from him in so long. It's some kind of subterranean necropolis that Dad is always talking about," Kristian announced, rather proud of himself for being able to recite such large words.

"Subcroplis terranean?" Ethan asked.

"No, subterranean necropolis, Dingus. It means it's an underground city!" Kristian continued without waiting for Ethan to digest what the older boy had said. "Grandpa said he found this place by following the sand lions!"

"Sand lions? What sand lions, I don't see any . . ."

"Ethan, shut up and listen, OK!" Kristian was starting to get annoyed again. "Grandpa found this place by following lions he discovered. Remember his last email?" He looked at his younger brother and then proceeded without caring if Ethan was following or not. "Well, the lion let him get close to it, and kind of accepted him as an equal, whatever that means." The older boy paused to think about it. "Anyways, Grandpa studied it for days and slept outside with the lion and all that." Kristian scratched at his head and then looked at his hand as if he was looking for a bug before continuing. "So, one morning when Grandpa was watching the lion, the big cat was acting strange. You know, walking in circles and figure 8s and all that. Grandpa says it wanted him to follow him and then set off toward the hills. Grandpa quickly packed up some of his gear and left the rest behind so he didn't lose it. Then, he followed the lion, eventually ending up on some high cliff, you know the cliffs that we can see from the dig site?" He

49

looked at Ethan for confirmation from the other boy, who was desperately trying to keep up with the story. "Anyways, there was a lion's den on the ledge, only it wasn't a lion's den, it was a cave." Kristian paused for emphasis.

"But . . ." Ethan attempted, only to be reduced to silence by his older brother's glowering stare.

"Sooo, Grandpa camped out," Kristian continued in a slightly annoyed tone. "But the lion didn't come back out. So he decided to get closer and look around inside the cave. At first he didn't find anything, only a bunch of brush, but the lion was gone." Kristian gestured by throwing his arms out. "He thought he must have missed the lion somehow, ya know, when he was sleeping or cooking or something, so he decided to look around to see if he could find anything useful that he could learn more about the lion. So he walked farther into the cave and found a bunch of tunnels that led farther into the cliff."

"But wait, didn't the lion come back?" Ethan asked.

"Are you going to listen or not?" Kristian demanded. "Just forget it, let Grandpa tell you." The older boy spat.

"No, no, I'll listen," Ethan amended apologetically.

Kristian gave him a reprising look and then continued, "OK, so this is one of the many caves in this region, right? But Grandpa hadn't seen any with tunnels in them! So he decided to go back, you know, after the lion." Kristian was back on a roll again. "He went back out to the camp to get his gear, like these flashlights and other stuff, when he noticed that the lion came out and was studying him, as if it wanted Grandpa to follow him. But then the lion went back into the cave. So he followed it."

Ethan didn't dare ask another question for fear of being cut off from the explanation. But even he knew following any wild animal into their den was extremely dangerous.

"But when he got to the cave, the lion was gone again." Kristian paused to look at his brother to see if this was registering with the other boy. He pointed the flashlight at Ethan's face.

"Really?" Ethan said, throwing up a hand to shield him from the bright light. "I'm listening!" and motioned for his older brother to shine the flashlight somewhere else.

Kristian paused and added, "It disappeared," before pointing the flashlight back at the ground.

Ethan nodded his head more to himself than to Kristian in understanding.

"So he searched the cave," Kristian was back in the story. "and discovered a bunch of tunnels and decided to investigate each one. But he didn't know which one the lion had gone into. But Grandpa is clever and he looked around each entrance, looking for lion tracks. He found them in the sand in one of the tunnels, so he decided to follow that one, carefully of course. Ya never know if the lion was lying in wait and would turn on him." Kristian paused as they reached a bend in the tunnel they were now walking around.

Grandpa and Lola were still in the lead, and both boys picked up their pace a little.

"So," Kristian continued, "the tunnel went downhill, and Grandpa followed the lion's tracks. Every now and then, he could hear heavy breathing and grunts coming from the lion in front of him. So he had to be extra careful cause he didn't want to get too close. A couple of times, he thought he should just leave it alone and go back to camp and study the den from a safer distance, but he didn't and followed the lion deeper into the tunnel."

"Wow, remember the ape caves at Mount St. Helens?" Ethan was completely caught up in Kristian's story. "That was only one mile, but remember how we had to squeeze through the tunnels at the end and Dad almost got stuck?" Ethan grinned at the silly position Dad had gotten himself into, but he couldn't help himself in making the comparison.

"Yeah, yeah, focus, Dingus. It was like that but a lot longer, I guess." The older boy wore an exasperated look. "Anyways, Grandpa said it took him almost a day of hiking to get down, but that's not even the best part." Kristian again had Ethan's full attention and the younger boy stumbled a few times as he listened intently.

"Boys, keep close, you're falling behind," Grandpa called back to them.

They both left off talking for a moment and concentrated on catching up to Grandpa and Lola.

Once they were close enough, Kristian started up again. "Where was I?"

"You said the hike wasn't even the best part," Ethan offered.

"Oh yeah, well, Grandpa noticed that he wasn't in a natural cave anymore, the walls started to look like a corridor more than a cave." Kristian paused to look at Ethan, who hadn't quite grasped what his brother was trying to tell him. "You know, the tunnel was actually man-made. The walls were all straight, and that's what led to this place," he stated flatly.

Ethan still wasn't following.

"Anyways," Kristian forged on, again not waiting for Ethan to catch up, "the tunnel was man-made, which was weird why the lion would use it, especially because it went so deep into the mountain. Grandpa said he never heard of any animal, let alone a lion, go so far into the dark, kinda strange, eghh?" He didn't wait for Ethan to answer. "That must be why they've been so hard to find up until now. They weren't really extinct, just gone into hiding." Kristian paused as Lola gave a sudden random yell about how much she missed Grandpa and hugged the old man.

Both boys shrugged before continuing on with the story.

"So Grandpa finally reached the bottom, because it levelled off, but there was a big stone door. So here's the strange part, the lion's tracks stopped at the door, but the lion wasn't there!"

"What?" Ethan asked. "That's not possible, is it? Where did it go? I mean, there had to be another way out!"

"Ethan, yes, it is possible. Don't be an idiot and don't interrupt me again, I'm warning you," Kristian said grumpily and looked as if he were ready to punch Ethan in the arm. He shook his head and paused to figure out where he was in the story. "So the door was ajar . . . or whatever Grandpa said. But what's interesting is that the space between the door and the wall was too small for a lion or even Grandpa to get into . . ."

"I was deeply puzzled," Grandpa chimed in to both boys' surprise. They had been so engrossed in the story, neither of them realized that Grandpa had slowed to talk with them. "Where did the lion go? I had absolutely no idea. I searched the area, doubled back for a few hundred yards to see if I had missed another tunnel. Yet the lion's tracks were unmistakable. The only way out was to trek back out of the cave or to go forward, which meant I had to dislodge the door enough for me to get in."

At least Lola wasn't jabbering anymore, Ethan thought a bit too eagerly.

"What did you do, Grandpa?" she presently asked.

"Well, I had to know! So I did the only thing I could think of. I put my shoulder against the stone and pushed. At first, nothing happened, so I put my pack down, dug my feet in, and pushed harder. Finally, the stone budged, and I was able to roll it enough for me to get in. What I found was . . . well, this chamber!" Grandpa pointed around him as they all entered a large room. "Well, the other end of this chamber anyways, and you should see the mess that the lions have done on that side." The old man grinned a little nervously as he pointed into the darkness.

The children looked around in awe as they entered a room filled with hundreds of jars that multiplied until the darkness swallowed them. Each jar stood perhaps three feet tall and two feet in diameter. They had no markings on them that Ethan could see in the faint light, but looked to be a kilned ceramic bathed in light brown. They were all lined in even rows as far as Ethan could tell. It was an eerie sight as Grandpa and the group's lights crisscrossed the shiny forms. They looked like an army of small dwarfs standing in rank file.

Grandpa promptly walked over to the wall nearest them, reached inside of his pocket, and retrieved a lighter. He flicked the end to spark the flame and held it against a slight protrusion on the wall. A sudden fire roared throughout the room, filling in the dark recesses with light as it spread through the walls. Ethan could now see that the protrusion was a firebox that ran along the expanse of the walls. That must have been the source of light in the other room as well, he thought, as the light had the same flickering effect that he had seen before.

"The walls down here are all laced with an endless supply of oils, like the one we came from," Grandpa confirmed, shaking his head in reverence. "That's how I refill my lighter." He gestured with the lighter, before putting it back in his pocket. "They run all along the temple main rooms and corridors. It really is quite ingenious," he explained.

The room didn't appear to be as large as the main corridor, but still impressive in the eerie firelight.

"What is all of this?" Ethan asked. "They're jars, Dingus!" Kristian sighed with disdain at his younger brother's foolish questions before addressing the old man, "Grandpa, is this what you've been living on for all this time?"

Grandpa gave a quick nod. "Good catch, Kristian. Yes. Each jar is filled with honey and wafers. They're all sealed, and they've been around for thousands of years." The old man scratched at his beard. "I think. Don't ask me how the people preserved them for so long, but it has a good taste to it, at least good enough to keep this old man alive." Grandpa chuckled and turned to the children, pointing toward a small mountain of jars stacked by the wall, all with their lids missing.

He made his way to a nearby jar and popped its lid. "I opened this one a few days ago, it still is mostly full. I'll need to pop another wafer jar though, just ran out."

Grandpa glanced around, looking for something. "You'll be needing something to eat out of," he said slowly as he turned in place.

"Ah, that will work," he said as he suddenly strode to a mess of lids strewn about the floor. He picked one up and glanced back at the children, delighted with his find. "Can't say it will be comfortable, but probably best to use some of the lids I've removed from previous jars as dishes. Ethan, will you grab a few for you, Kristian, and Lola?" he asked.

Ethan nodded and set off on the task.

"I haven't needed them as I've been using my camping utensils," the old man said smugly.

Grandpa quickly made his way to another jar, retrieving a pocketknife from his pocket. "Kristian, can you give me a hand?" he asked while nodding his head in the boy's direction.

Kristian trotted over to where Grandpa had rolled out a jar.

"Hold it just there, yes, that's right." He smiled and winked at the boy, and then he slipped the blade of his knife under the lid and started to peel at an even rate around its lip. After restowing his knife, he placed one hand on the edge of the lip and the other hand to steady himself, with Kristian still holding the body of the jar still.

Grandpa pulled, and the lid made a swooshing sound, followed by a pop as the lid came off cleanly. "It's as easy as that," Grandpa said and smiled. "Thank you, Kristian."

Kristian nodded in satisfaction.

The family sat and ravenously ate until they were full. The honey was remarkably sweet and tasted as if Grandpa had made it yesterday. The wafers were plain and didn't have any taste, if not a little bitter, Ethan thought. But when dipped in the honey, they tasted good enough, especially on an empty stomach!

"Nothing like good, treated honey." Grandpa licked his lips after a mouthful. "I must say that living off of this has been a delight. I would even venture that whoever made this treasure trove were more expert than I!" Grandpa said in between mouthfuls.

"I still don't get one thing, Grandpa." Ethan's mind was onto another thought entirely.

The old man raised an eyebrow at the question. "Oh? What is that, son?"

"Why were you down here so long? I mean, you disappeared. We were all worried. I . . . was worried. Why didn't you come out? We had a funeral for you!" He gulped down the sudden urge to tear up.

Grandpa finished chewing and swallowed. "I would have, my dear boy. I would have. I wrote about you all in my journals, intending that someone would eventually find me. Alive . . . or dead . . . ," he trailed off for a moment before clearing his throat. "In any event, I became trapped soon after I entered this place. As you can imagine, I was deeply impressed at what I had 'discovered. What your father is now searching for as I understand it."

It was now Ethan's turn to raise a questioning eyebrow. Grandpa had disappeared before Dad had discovered the staff and tablets.

Grandpa saw his expression. "Kristian already filled me in," he explained. "I missed you all so much," he added tenderly as he looked at each of them in turn.

Ethan thought he heard a slight quiver in the old man's voice, but only for a moment.

"After I dislodged the door, I explored," Grandpa began. "I wanted to track down where the lion had gone. As I mentioned before, they did a right good number on the jars on the other side of this room. Broken jars and the like, but of course all of the honey from those jars was licked entirely clean. I wondered why they didn't go after the whole lot?" He paused while scratching at his beard again to remove some dribbled honey remnants. "Come to think of it, that is a very interesting question."

"What is?" Lola asked.

"Oh, nothing but an old man's musings." Grandpa smiled down at the young girl. "Anyways, there are a set of alcoves and tunnels that lead away from this room on the other side, and that is where I headed. After exploring for some time, I realized that I was hungry and tired. I had found the oil wells on the wall and lit the rooms as I explored each one. But I still hadn't found the lion, oddly enough."

The children all sat up, leaning toward the old man in interest at what he would say next.

"They aren't still down here, are they?" Lola asked in a frightened tone.

"Yes, but you are quite safe, my dear." The old man chuckled before proceeding. "I bedded down for the night and fell asleep. Late in the night, I heard a distant rumble from the way I had come. I decided to investigate when I was rested and went back to sleep. The next morning, I awoke and made my way back. To my disappointment, I found that the tunnel I had come through lay buried beneath the mountain, blocking my only known way out and . . . as you can tell, I never did find another way out." Grandpa scratched at his beard again in a concentrated frown. "I attempted to find a way out, and trust me, I have searched every nook and cranny, but I've . . ." He paused with a studious look. "I've never found *my* way out," he finally said.

Kristian and Ethan looked at each other. "What is that supposed to mean?" Ethan mouthed at his brother, who shrugged his shoulders.

Grandpa coughed and continued, "Imagine my surprise"—he smiled a bit nervously—"when I found you yesterday. No, I would call it a complete . . . and pleasant surprise." He smiled at the children. "I would not have imagined this in a thousand years." He shook his head and chuckled.

"How did you find us?" Kristian asked as he stuffed a wafer drowned in honey into his mouth.

"Ah, now that is something." The old man recalled. "I was exploring a series of tunnels off the main temple room when I heard another rumbling. I hear them every now and then and assumed I was in for another cave-in. Still, it was close enough to where I was, and I took a chance, backtracked to a fork in the tunnel, and headed in the direction the sound was coming from." He paused to eat a mouthful.

The children all waited for him to finish and swallow.

"It was a foolhardy thing for me to do, but then again, it was foolhardy for me to come down here in the first place." Grandpa grimaced. "In any event, the rumbling got much louder, and before I knew it, the whole tunnel was shaking. The shaking knocked me to the ground, and I thought for a moment that it was all over. In any case, that's when the collapse happened, and you three appeared. I almost didn't believe what I was seeing and thought to myself that I had finally gone mad." Grandpa chuckled in a weird high voice then corrected himself and cleared his throat, looking at the children apologetically.

"Lucky I found you when I did. If I hadn't pulled you out when I had, you would have been buried alive. As soon as I had hauled the last one of you into the tunnel, the hole filled in, and my first way of escape I've found was gone . . ."

Lola had a horrified look on her face and started to whimper as her eyes watered up.

"Oh, there, there, I'm sorry, Lola, I didn't mean to scare you," Grandpa apologized, reaching out to half-embrace the girl.

She sobbed for a few seconds and laid her head down on his lap.

He lovingly stroked her hair as he continued, "It took me three hours to get you all back down to the main chamber. Had to carry you both across my shoulders"—he nodded at the boys—"and you in my arms." He smiled down at Lola.

She smiled back up, looking a bit more comforted.

"And that's how you came to be with me," he finished.

They all ate in silence for a few more minutes, soaking in the story, before Ethan interrupted their eating, "Grandpa?"

"Hmm?"

"Did you ever find the lions?" he asked with interest.

"Ah, now that's a question. A fine question. Yes, I did find them."

Lola bolted upright and looked around in fright. Grandpa soothed her back into his lap. "Although," he chuckled, "this is the part I show just how insane I have become."

Kristian and Ethan exchanged interested glances, not knowing how to respond to the old man's last revelation.

The Drake Epics - Journey to Qara

"Well, you may see it, if we don't find a way out of here. I think we need to venture out beyond where I found you. Anyways, if we are stuck here for longer, we will meet up with the Lions."

"Meet up with them?" both boys asked in unison, ignoring Grandpa's last comment altogether. Lola shot up from Grandpa's lap again and looked like she was going to wet herself.

"Yes, we'll need to go for water." Grandpa looked at the children's questioning faces. "Haven't told you about the underground lake yet, have I? Ah well, you'll see it soon enough. You see, the lions are there as well, and they have to be getting out somehow, but darned if I couldn't find a way out. No matter how much I've studied them, I haven't found a way past them. It's all in my journals . . . ," he trailed off again before clearing his throat. "Let's finish up here, and we'll be off."

The family finished, resealed the honey and wafer jars, and set off back through the tunnel.

"What about the fire, Grandpa? Don't we have to put it out?" Ethan asked.

"Don't worry about it," Grandpa said as they left the chamber. "They will burn out in a few hours, and then the oil will replenish itself and be ready for the next lighting. The oil systems are quite ingenious really. Brilliant they were, whoever it was that built this place."

True to his promise, the light was still burning when they arrived back at the main chamber.

"I want to show you something," Grandpa suddenly announced. "You might find it interesting, it tells a story of three children, just like you."

Without another word, Grandpa ushered them back into the room with the black obelisk, which Ethan hadn't been able to study in any detail until now. So he stopped, just for a moment or two, to take in the sight, while the others continued around the structure.

Like the pillars, this obelisk also had intricate carvings etched into its surface and looked as if it were made of reeds, identical to the stone boxes he saw that morning. Only this box was hollow, stood seven feet high, and was entirely black. Ethan felt its smooth surface, also cool to the touch. The reed carvings were lifelike, and Ethan let his fingers wander across the etchings. He'd never seen anything like it. Not in all of Dad's books.

His eyes poured over every detail so that he could remember everything when they got out and returned to their parents. Dad would want to know, he thought. As his eyes reached the top of the box, he noticed for the first time that a relief mural was etched into the obelisk. He took a step back to get a better look. It appeared to be a man holding a

57

three-pronged fire bolt in each hand at the right, striking at a creature on the left that Ethan realized he knew all too well.

He gasped in spite of himself and squeezed his eyes tight to make sure he wasn't dreaming. He opened them again, one at a time, hoping that his mind was inventing the picture. It was no trick. The relief was a carving of the dragon from his dreams. A cold chill ran down his spine. "How?" he mumbled out loud.

"Ethan?" Grandpa interrupted, as the old man called back to the boy.

"Coming," he yelled back. Ethan gave the relief another confused appraisal and nervously trotted off after the others. But the carving was now etched in his mind as well. He couldn't grasp what it all meant, but he had no time to ponder it right now. He walked around the corner of the obelisk and sidled up to his brother, who shot him a stern look for falling behind.

They were all studying what looked to be an altar of some kind built directly into a wall.

Grandpa smiled at Ethan and winked. "Thought we'd lost you."

Ethan smiled back, ignoring his brother, and turned to examine the altar.

It was set against the rear wall of the chamber, sandwiched between two great pillars that rose to the ceiling. They appeared much like the others in the adjoining chamber, except these were devoid of any carving. The pillars ended at the ceiling in a flare of ovals, all encroaching on one another in a never-ending tangle of lines.

At the center of the altar was a square box opening, measuring about seven feet high and wide and roughly the same depth.

In a bas-relief above the altar's opening, a king and queen stood facing off, each with the head of a lion. The king was carrying a bow in his left hand and a tree branch in the other, the queen a palm branch in her right hand and a flame in the other. Their right hands were raised toward an orb just out of their arm's reach, resting on an ornate pillar carved in between them. Above that, three children sat, enthroned in a lunar boat within a circle of the sun. A four-winged dragon moving before them on the left and an unusual eleven-pointed star following on the right.

Ethan winced at the sight of the dragon. Except for the monster, the mural looked like one of the many drawings Ethan had seen in his father's textbooks.

Kristian's faced twisted in concentration, and he suddenly moved toward the altar as he studied another picture.

Ethan glanced back at Grandpa, who was preoccupied answering a torrent of new questions that Lola was spewing out at him.

The Drake Epics - Journey to Qara

"Kristian?" Ethan prompted, "What is it?"

Kristian didn't respond. Instead, he reached into his shirt and drew out the amulet he had flaunted in front of his siblings on the previous day. He held it out, measuring it against something.

Ethan admitted he had been extremely jealous of Kristian's find.

First of all, his brother got it at the market, the market he was never allowed to go to. Second, his older brother went on about it and wouldn't stop talking about it. Lastly, Dad had spent some time studying the amulet and talking with Kristian. They had both stayed up late into the night as Dad perused his books to find similar amulets and necklaces to identify the age.

Ethan admitted he felt a twinge of jealousy.

Apparently, they hadn't found any examples of amulets like what Kristian had, which intrigued Dad all the more. That point had made Ethan even more jealous of Kristian's find and all the attention he was receiving.

Kristian presently removed the necklace from around his neck and reached the amulet out and against a wall directly to the right of the altar. It was a bit tall for him, so he had to stand on his toes.

Ethan sauntered up behind his brother for a closer look and now realized what he hadn't seen before. To his surprise, in the wall, there was an identical carving of the amulet embossed into the altar. Kristian placed the amulet within the cavity, which fit exactly so as to look completely part of the relief. That is, all except it was an ivory white in contrast to the brown sandstone. Upon closer inspection, a mural framed where the amulet was inserted, depicting two figures approaching the insert in the attitude of worshipping what appeared to be the amulet. Much like Kristian had just done. Again, Ethan's eyes fell on the all-too-familiar enlarged bas-relief of a dragon.

Kristian shook his head, perhaps not quite grasping the utter coincidence of his discovery, the amulet, these pictorial instructions, and the amulet's subsequent use. Kristian took a step back to admire his handiwork and shot Ethan a wry smile.

"That's . . . interesting . . ." Ethan offered, but was still a bit unnerving to the younger boy.

"Yeah," Kristian joined, "but there's more, there's a hole in the bottom . . . right there." He pointed directly below where he had inserted the amulet, again standing on his toes. There was indeed a hole. "I wonder . . . ," he continued as he shimmied the amulet back out of its resting place.

"OK, now if I . . ." Kristian followed by inserting the key side of the amulet directly into the hole. It fit halfway in, right up to the amulet itself.

"Now what?" he asked, more to himself than to anyone else.

"Turn it?" Ethan ventured.

Kristian gave a shrug and reached back up. He applied pressure on the amulet to turn, and a grating sound of rock on rock sounded as the insert widened enough for the entire amulet to fit. He stared back at his younger brother with a surprised look and then at Grandpa and Lola, who stood farther back. Both had halted their conversation at the grating noise and were keenly interested in what would happen next.

"Do it, push it the rest of the way in," Ethan encouraged.

"Don't know what will happen," Kristian responded. He furrowed his brow in a moment of indecision.

"Just push it in!" Ethan said again.

"Stop!" Kristian said, "You're annoying me again . . ."

This was always the cue for Ethan to back off. *Kristian is always annoyed*, he presently thought to himself.

"OK, one . . . two . . . three . . ." Kristian applied pressure to the key and pushed the amulet the rest of the way into the hole. Then he stepped back and waited.

Nothing happened.

"Can you push it in any farther?" Ethan let his excitement get the better of him.

"Ethan, stop!" Kristian shot the younger boy a withering look then reached up to push on the amulet again. Upon finding he couldn't drive it any farther, he now tried to retrieve it back out of the hole.

"No use!" he finally said with a grunt after a few moments of tugging and pulling on the amulet. "It's stuck. That's just great, I lost my necklace!" he said in a cross tone.

His face momentarily darkened in concentration, and Ethan held back on suggesting options. Kristian immediately brightened, and he retrieved his pocketknife from out of his pant pocket.

"You're going to break it," Ethan cautioned, knowing exactly what his older brother was about to attempt.

Kristian had used that dumb pocketknife wherever he went, since they'd come out here. He took every opportunity to use the dang thing, Ethan thought to himself as he rolled his eyes.

"Dingus, you're in my blood circle, move back and stop talking!" Kristian commanded through gritted teeth as he tried to use the blade as a lever to eject his necklace. The boys had learned in their Boy Scout troop not to come within arm's length while another boy had their pocketknife open. This was called the blood circle. That was the idea, but they often ignored the rule, unless they were annoyed at someone.

When Kristian failed to dislodge his precious treasure, he tried to chip away at the sandstone around the amulet without any luck.

Suddenly a large boom erupted in the chamber, followed by a slow, deep grating sound.

It surprised both boys, and they jumped at the suddenness of the sound, Kristian almost stabbing himself in the arm in the process.

The slow grinding exposed a hidden doorway in the altar, which opened into blackness. The grinding was followed by another bang, louder than the first. The doorway released a shock wave of sand and rancid air that drove everyone to the ground.

Lola shrieked, and Grandpa groaned as they both hit the floor. Both boys somehow kept their balance as they dumbly stared into the darkness, sheer ecstasy visible on Kristian's face.

Much to Kristian's delight, the key ejected from its place and fell to the ground in front of the boys.

"What just happened?" Ethan asked.

Kristian shook his head as he moved to retrieve his precious necklace. "Don't know, but it might just be our way out!" he said excitedly as he bent over and picked up the amulet. The older boy studied the piece for any blemishes, then polished it with the sleeve of his shirt, and quickly returned the amulet to its usual place around his neck.

The boys both retreated to Grandpa and Lola and helped them to their feet.

"Where did you get that?" Grandpa asked as he dusted himself off.

"This? A wise man gave it to me on one of my errands for Dad," Kristian announced. "Muschle el'Kamin was his name, I think," he offered.

Grandpa wore an odd expression on his face that Ethan hadn't seen from his aged mentor before. It was a mixture of anxious . . . anger? The old man stared thoughtfully at the dark entrance. "Muschle el'Kamin, you say?" he asked.

Kristian nodded his head.

Ethan turned to look at the doorway too. He was stunned to see a swirling vapor around the opening. The mist magically hung in the air as it moved in a hypnotic dance.

"Well, that explains it, and we aren't going to wait around to find out right now," the old man declared. "You *are* all tired . . . Yes, you are!" Grandpa said in a half-shrill voice as he saw the complaining looks of the children. He coughed into his hand to clear his throat before continuing. "I see how you all have been limping around after that nasty fall. We need to leave this be and get some rest. There will be more time to explore this tomorrow."

It all sounded like a weak excuse to Ethan, and he couldn't fathom how Grandpa could pass up an opportunity like this one, let alone sleep while it awaited them! Especially with this amazing mystery that lay beyond. He'd never seen anything like it.

He stole a sidewise glance at Kristian, who had a look of wonder still painted on his face.

*Why couldn't we explore it now?* Ethan wondered. Maybe they just needed to wait until the old man had fallen asleep and then come back. *It wouldn't hurt to explore just a little, would it?* Ethan contrived in his thoughts.

Grandpa sensed this and presently eyed the children down as they launched another volley of protesting looks. "Not another word, off with you all!" he commanded.

He stepped forward, so that he was directly in between the children and the dark doorway. He extended his arms and escorted the children forward.

They begrudgingly turned and walked back from where they had come.

Ethan looked longingly over his grandpas' arm, his eyes still glued to the doorway and the swirling mist around it. He suddenly caught the toe of one of his sandals on the other and tripped, just catching himself before falling face-first onto the sandy floor.

"Your eyes in front of you, now," Grandpa said firmly, but with a hint of laughter in his voice.

Ethan took another longing look, as if it were his last, then obediently turned his head and walked out of the chamber with the others.

# Chapter 5

## Awakening

*Are dreams still alive upon waking from them.*

Lola couldn't sleep. No, she didn't want to sleep. The others had tossed and turned for what seemed like hours before they all drifted off. She was particularly keen on Grandpa, who took the longest of all. He was busy pouring through his journals and often paused to ponder with a faraway look in his eyes and, of course, scratching at his beard, which he always did when in deep though. Lola didn't have to be a grown-up to recognize that.

The fires, acting as Grandpa's reading light, eventually burned out in the hall. All up until that point, she snuck quick glances at Grandpa, who simply sat there, immersed in his thoughts. He kept looking away and back over his shoulder toward the room with the altar, as if he were expecting someone.

She almost gave up that he wasn't going to sleep at all. But, when it grew completely dark, she heard him rustle into his covers. It took a few minutes for her eyes to adjust to the darkness, but in the distance, Lola could clearly see that the firelight had not gone out in the altar room, casting a long stream of light into the corridor. She couldn't quite figure out why everyone was so nervous about the opening, especially Grandpa. He could protect them if there had been anything to be worried about, she thought confidently. But she also wanted to explore a little on her own.

Usually, Lola was content to follow her brothers around and have them take the lead. She would kick and scream if she didn't get her way, of course, and when that didn't work, she would ask her mother over and over again for permission before Mom finally gave in. She had this down to a pure science, and Ethan was always complaining about how unfair it was. She didn't always get her way, but most of the time she did. A sudden mischievous grin spread across her lips. Of course, it was much, much easier with Dad. All she had to do was ask, and he usually agreed, much to both of her brother's continued resentment.

Lola came back to the present and waited a few minutes until Grandpa stopped tossing. His breathing slowed, and she could hear a faint snore from where he lay. She slowly peeled back her covers and rose into a crouched position, making her way around the others, all now in a profound sleep.

She was very proud of herself for staying awake. *I'm a big girl!* she thought smugly. Of course she could stay up!

Strangely, she didn't feel the least bit worried about exploring the mysterious doorway on her own, as long as she didn't go in. Grandpa had specifically asked the children not to do so. So she wouldn't.

But it wouldn't hurt to explore around it. Besides, she thought she had seen the strangest of things when they were leaving the room, a little white bunny hopping around in the shadow. She could have imagined the little furry creature. But at least for a brief moment in the doorway, she saw the bunny before it retreated into the darkness when the others weren't watching. She wasn't sure why they hadn't noticed the hare out in plain sight, but she had seen it—she was sure of it!

Keeping her eyes rooted on the altar room, she quietly rose from her crouched position and started to tiptoe through the sleeping little group. Enough light shone from the distant door that she felt she could safely

The Drake Epics - Journey to Qara

walk towards it and rescue the bunny from sheer boredom, or worse, being eaten by lions! Lola shuddered at the thought. But the little creature was in luck. After all, she was a red belt in Tae Kwon Do, only one year away from a first-degree black belt. She was strong enough to rescue the bunny, she confidently assured herself.

She stopped once, petrified, as a ravenous growl sounded behind her. She whirled around and let out a deep sigh. It was only her Grandpa, who had plunged into a tide of deep snoring. It sounded as though a giant bear was attacking the small party. Lola shook her head and set out on her task, merrily skipping down the pathway now that she was far enough away from Grandpa and the others. She thought of how the bunny would snuggle her when she rescued it. She'd had always wanted a pet rabbit.

Just for good measure, she paused once or twice and practiced one of her defensive moves to make sure she was warmed up. This might come in handy, you know, in case she had to defend the little animal from something *bigger*. She decided not to think about it too much though. No reason to worry herself over nothing.

Her thoughts were interrupted by a quick movement that darted just out of eyesight. She came to an abrupt stop and scanned the shadows; she still couldn't see perfectly in the gloom, so she had to squint extra hard. To her delight, a little form, set against the light, hopped around and bolted for the chamber. She was three quarters of the way to the door already and now set off after the creature in a half run.

"Wait!" she called after it, risking Grandpa or the boys waking up. But she didn't want to lose the bunny now that she was so close. Besides, she could now see the little white figure reach the room. It cast a much larger shadow, and if Lola had studied the shadow more closely, she would have realized that it was not the shadow of a bunny at all! Instead it was a silhouette of something much larger and much more sinister. But she didn't notice. Her full attention was on the little mammal as it hopped around a few times and then disappeared into the room.

Lola was in a full sprint now. She punched at the air as she went. Again, just for practice. "Wait!" she called a little louder, but not wanting to wake the others, even though she wouldn't have woken them now even if she had screamed it.

As she reached the room, she looked around to find the little animal. It was hopping just near the big black tower. She couldn't pronounce the big word that Grandpa had used, *Obsik . . . obisk.* "Whatever," she said out loud and shrugged, trotting after the alluring little bunny.

"Stop, come back!" she exclaimed as the bunny continued to hop away from her. "I'm here to save you!" she explained.

The bunny continued to obliviously hop away.

Lola followed.

Soon the little rabbit was catapulting around the altar. But, it stopped and considered the girl who was so cautiously approaching it. The little creature's nose darted around, sniffing at the air to catch Lola's scent.

Lola halted, not wanting to scare the little ball of fur, and the two studied each other for a few moments. "That's it, come to me." She gently waved the bunny to come closer. "I'll save you," she cooed and again started to carefully approach the little creature with her arms outstretched.

The bunny then did something extraordinary. It talked. "You can save me, but you have to really want to," it said.

Lola was ecstatic, putting both hands over her mouth in surprise. "You can talk! Oh, why don't you come to me then and we can talk some more?" She almost sang with excitement.

"No, you must come to me," it said. "I need you to follow me in there." The bunny tilted it's head in the direction of the doorway.

"Oh, but I can't," she stated in a conflicted tone. "Grandpa told me not to go in there."

"Oh, but you must," the creature retorted. "You simply must come," it now pleaded. "It is the only way you can save your brothers . . . your Grandpa . . . ," it added. "And your parents!"

Lola screwed up her face into a questioning look. "My parents?" she asked, tipping her head in confusion.

"Yes, your parents. They would want you to do this and follow me. Think of how much they miss you! You must do this to save everyone. You will know the right way," the bunny continued.

"But Grandpa told me not to. If I do, I may get hurt and I told him I would do what he said."

"We're not talking about what Grandpa said!" the bunny said in a rather-angry tone. "You must do this. You will not get hurt, but be able to lead your family to safety," it pleaded more softly.

"Naughty bunny, come to me and I will take care of you," Lola entreated.

"No, I need to go in there." The furry mammal turned and readied to bolt into the darkened doorway.

"No! Wait!" the little girl begged.

The bunny paused for a moment and changed its tactic ever so slightly. "Follow me and save me in there," it repeated, and then Lola thought she saw it smile. "I need to save my brothers and sisters."

"Really? There are other bunnies?" Lola could not hold back her excitement. *More bunnies to cuddle with,* she thought gleefully.

*The Drake Epics - Journey to Qara*

"Yes, yes," the bunny soothed. It had her hooked now and continued to weave its tale. "They . . . they are waiting for you to save them . . . just like you will save everyone else," the bunny encouraged and began to hop around impishly. "They all love to play and cuddle, just like I do!" it continued.

Lola guiltily looked back over her shoulder. Grandpa would not be happy about this. But she would be right back! After all, she could save all the bunnies and find the *right* way home. *All those little bunnies need me!* she thought.

"Follow me. Follow me. Follow me," the little creature chanted. It presently changed course and hopped into the darkness. It reappeared for a moment. "Follow me." Then it disappeared again.

Lola took a deep breath, shook her head and plunged into the blackness.

– – –

Ethan awoke to his grandpa shaking him.

"Ethan. Ethan. Do you know where your sister is?"

He rubbed his eyes and sat up, not understanding what Grandpa was saying. "Lola? She's probably still sleeping. Is it morning already? What?"

"She's gone, blockhead!" Kristian chided.

A shiver went down Ethan's spine. "What do you mean gone? Where did she go?"

"Do you think we'd be asking you if we knew?" Kristian snapped back.

"Stop, the both of you. We need to spread out and find her. Let me light the room." Grandpa moved back toward the wall, his flashlight throwing beams of off-white light as he made his way. Suddenly the room was again ablaze.

Ethan blinked at the glaring brightness cascading around the giant hall as the fire wells lit. The room wouldn't be fully light for a few moments as it raced along, just like he saw in the chamber with the honey jars.

"Where do you want us to look, Grandpa?" Kristian asked.

"I've already tried calling her, she's not in here. That leaves either the altar room or the honey room. Don't know how she'd make her way that far in the darkness . . . Where else could she have gone?" he asked himself as he trailed off, again scratching at his beard.

"No need to look farther, you've opened the portal. She is within," came the answer in a gruff voice. They all whirled around to see a giant sand lion emerge from the shadows of one of the pillars.

Grandpa cautiously raised a hand to still the boys in an attempt to prevent them from making any sudden moves. He pulled them both behind him with a smooth sweeping motion of his arms, keeping them outstretched as a shield.

"He won't hurt you," he soothed. "Just remain very still, your scents are different from mine, he's just curious," he calmly reassured them.

"Oh, but it is much more than that, my old friend," the lion spoke.

Grandpa's knees faltered for a moment. "Did you? . . . Did you just talk?" the old man said in an unusually high tone, then he seemed to right himself. He looked sheepishly at the two boys and mumbled to himself, "You old fool, of course the lion didn't talk!" Grandpa looked back at the cat.

The sand lion stoically stood there in all of his magnificence, at least long enough for Ethan to study the feline. With the exception of any mane, this looked like any other lion he had seen on TV or from his childhood visits to the Woodland Park Zoo in Seattle. The lion was, however, much, much larger and more intimidating than the boy would have ever imagined. On all fours, the lion's head was easily the height of Kristian, if it squared off with the older boy face-to-face. His body was muscular and roughly the girth of Ethan, his older brother, and Grandpa all thrown together. But it was the lion's paws that shocked the boy, roughly the size of a catcher's mitt, with long black claws folded neatly into tufts of fur that masked their true size. In short, Ethan was in awe. At this moment, he wasn't quite sure whether to admire the beast or throw up.

After a few moments of letting himself be studied, the lion nodded his massive head. "In fact, it is by my own endeavors that I have brought you to this very temple. It is I who first entreated you at your camp. Again, it is I who led you into this place of worship, knowing that you would bring us the chosen ones." The lion continued, "Even before then, we have been watching you. We have been anticipating your arrival. For millennia, we have been in waiting, in isolation, hidden away from the world."

Ethan couldn't fathom what the beast was trying to say. All he knew is that the lion was talking with real words and he suddenly felt even more ill than he did before. Perhaps he was going mad, just like Grandpa! He stole a quick glimpse at his older brother, who looked just as perplexed as Ethan felt. But he didn't have enough time to think further on the subject.

"Come now, you must follow me. We have little time."

The lion moved slowly, with the grace of a giant skillful hunter, making his way around the small group in a half circle, taking great strides with his massive paws.

The Drake Epics - Journey to Qara

Ethan couldn't help but notice the rippling muscles and the arched front shoulders as the magnificent lion paraded around them.

Grandpa pivoted in place as the cat passed, careful to keep the boys directly behind him in a feeble show of protection. The old man might have even puffed out his chest a little, Ethan thought.

"Come, there is no reason to fear me," the lion pacified. "I will not harm you, I assure you. I will explain everything."

Ethan shot a questioning look at Kristian, who wore the same expression.

The lion stopped and looked intently at the small group. They were all still planted to the same spot.

"Follow me. Don't follow me. 'Tis there you will find your sister . . . your granddaughter." The lion raised a paw in the direction of the room with the altar. "'Tis there through which you must enter and go back, back to the world as it once was—to rescue humanity, to save it from terror and save us all from what might become."

"Now I have gone mad," Grandpa grumbled to himself. "I'm still hearing that dang cat talk!"

Before either boy could respond, Grandpa was ushering them backward and away from the lion. "It's all right, he's just curious," he explained. "Let's give him some room. Back to the altar room. Just need to give him some space." Grandpa tossed his head toward the room with the obelisk they had visited last night, keeping his arms outstretched. "Then we'll go look for Lola," he added.

"But . . . ," the boys both chimed in. "We heard him too, Grandpa!"

Grandpa wasn't listening, completely intent on protecting them. "Now, that's enough! Back with you both!" he sternly scolded, then changed to a softer but still firm tone. "Move toward the altar room, boys."

They obeyed without another word.

Grandpa continued to usher them on, keeping a watchful eye on the large sand lion for the slightest sign of aggression from the beast.

As the group shuffled along, Ethan thought he glimpsed movement between the pillars. He looked harder and saw another movement, a flash of light fur. He squinted harder to bring it into sight. But the harder he looked, the more evasive the forms were. He knew something was there, but he couldn't focus in on what it was even with the hall now fully lit. He jabbed Kristian in the ribs with his elbow and nodded in the direction of the movements.

Kristian, who would have usually punched his brother in return, nodded distractedly, confirming that he saw something as well.

69

The small group slowly made their way for what seemed hours. It was a long walk. Finally, they neared the altar room. The lion had not made any attempt to follow them, which gave the group more confidence.

Grandpa was still closely monitoring their retreat to ensure they were all safe. Once he was satisfied the boys were out of any immediate danger, he coaxed them through the doorway. "Go on, all the way into the room, now. Back by the altar." He paused. "But not too close to that opening you made," he added with a tone of caution in his voice. He turned for a moment to stare them down and seal their acceptance of his command.

Both boys nodded and quickly maneuvered around the black obelisk until they were close enough to the altar. After a quick scan of the area to make sure they were alone, the boys turned their attentions back to the old man, who had just followed them into the chamber.

Grandpa was oblivious to all else as he slowly walked backwards towards the boys. His eyes were rooted squarely on the doorway through which they had come. That is, until the same gruff voice sounded directly behind them.

They all whirled again to see the same lion emerging from the dark entryway in the altar, and both boys scuffled back to Grandpa for protection.

Ethan almost lost his balance as he moved so fast, but Grandpa steadied the boy with his hand. Ethan looked up thankfully at the older man and saw raw determination in his face.

"Boys!" Grandpa said. "Stay close, and remain still." All the while he kept his eyes glued to the lion. "It's just not possible," the old man murmured. "How did you get in here?" he asked the lion, but more for himself. Every now and then, he glanced back over his shoulder to ensure nothing else was flanking them.

"You have been hearing my voice, old friend," the great cat assured. "It is my voice you have heard now for some time since you first came here. You are not going mad," the lion added.

Both boys cast quizzical looks at their aging patriarch, who slowly shook his head.

"Ask our young saviors that you have brought with you," the lion appealed, letting his gaze fall on the two boys.

Ethan shivered as he met the beast's eyes. But he nodded at Grandpa to affirm the lion's last statement. "It's true, Grandpa, we can hear him."

Grandpa didn't seem to grasp the confirmation, and for the first time in Ethan's experience, his aging hero appeared to be unsure of what to do next. His face was an ashen white, drained of all color.

"Do not be alarmed, my friends. This is the beginning and where your journey takes flight. We are the guardians of the sanctuary, the keepers of this place." The lion cast his eyes around the room.

"We?" Ethan blurted out, which was rewarded by stern looks from both his brother and from Grandpa.

The lion waved his paw in the direction of the obelisk.

The boys turned their heads and saw what must have caught Ethan's eye as they were walking the corridor. Lions were slowly filing into the room through the open doorway.

"Grandpa!" Ethan exclaimed.

The old man couldn't take his eyes off the lead lion, shaking his head in disbelief.

Ethan tugged at Grandpa's sleeve.

Grandpa turned his head and, at the sight, quickly closed his arms tighter around the boys by instinct.

"Too tight . . . Grandpa, you are hugging us too tight!" Kristian gurgled.

Grandpa nodded apolitically and relaxed his grip a little on the boys.

The lions halted in a uniform line in front of the small group. It defied all logic. *A talking lion? More lions standing in formation? Is this all a circus act of some kind?* Ethan thought. What was worse, the line of lions now blocked the only retreat the little family group had.

"These are they of whom I speak," the lead lion announced to the little group. "They have been trained from birth to usher the rightful heirs to their journey's start. *Your* journey's start." The lion looked at the boys. "Through the primordial waters you must pass. A journey back to face the monster, the great chaos monster himself, Tiamat!" The lion looked directly at Ethan, as if to draw this information directly out of his soul. "You, young savior know of what I speak."

Ethan winced, expecting the lion's engaging stare to tear the dreams out of his mind.

Both Grandpa and Kristian turned to look at the boy.

"The mural of Marduk, the great dragon slayer, and of Tiamat, the dragon of chaos," the lion continued.

Ethan paused then nodded, as if ashamed. "Yes, I've dreamed about it," he admitted in a shaky voice.

A look of shock registered on Kristian's face. "What?" he exclaimed. "Why are you even listening to this?" he scolded his younger brother. "This is weird, we must all be dreaming or going completely insane!" he evaded.

On cue, the lion turned his focus on Kristian. "You are but a youth, but you are greater than you yet know, my most treasured friend of all."

Kristian looked around, half expecting someone to emerge from behind him. Who was the lion addressing? Upon finding no one but the lions behind him, he looked back, pointing to himself questioningly. "Are you talking to me?" he asked in a perplexed tone.

The talking lion smiled a toothy grin, which unnerved the boys at the sight of his enormous fangs.

Grandpa again pulled the boys in closer and squeezed them harder.

"Grand . . . Grandpa," they squawked in unison. "We can't breathe," they pleaded.

The old man relaxed his grip again.

"Your sister," the lion continued. "Well, she has been tempted by the cunning one, but she is brave. She has not failed you. She has started you on your journey's path, and she will bring peace and hope to you all before the end."

The lion now looked upon Grandpa. "Old friend," he said in a warm tone, "you have studied us day and night. We have freely shown you what man has not seen in a thousand years. You now know that we are different from other beasts that you have studied," he lectured. "Just how different, you will soon see as you journey through space and time to fulfill the prophecies. But you must be warned, this journey will not be easy. You know of what you have seen written on the walls, you have seen the shrines, and it is there that you must enter." The lion now lifted a paw toward the altar.

The boys looked at each other and then at Grandpa.

"What is the lion talking about, Grandpa?" Kristian asked.

The old man ignored the older boy.

"But as you enter, the children will forget all that was before until their return. You alone will remember what once was, what once will be." His counsel now given, the lion looked upon the children. "You may yet remember through dreams and fleeting thought. It may not be easy, but what *is* may yet come again to your consciousness. You have only to look in the right place. Watch for the signs. There are those who will help you unfold the mystery of your magic!"

Ethan wasn't too thrilled about all of the rhyming. He couldn't quite grasp what the lion was trying to explain to them, which frustrated him even more. He glanced over at Kristian and could immediately tell that his older brother was beyond annoyed.

The lion turned his attention back to Grandpa. "There, they must carry out a mission in innocence and self-discovery in order to save us all." The lion made a sweeping motion with his paw at the boys. "Only then will they

*The Drake Epics - Journey to Qara*

return triumphant! Only then will we be safe. He must be cast out! He must be put in his place! Exiled and smitten, must he be!" the rhymes continued. "Now go, you must fulfill what you have the agency to fulfill. I have always seen great goodness in you, great kings." The lion dipped its giant head in a sort of bow.

The boys looked at each other, bewildered and confused. Was this a dream or a nightmare? Whatever it was, it was boring and exciting at the same time. Ethan could certainly do away with all the noble speeches though.

"My kings, you are royal, you are eternal," the lion finished. He turned and walked back around them and toward the other lions, keeping to a slow canter so as not to alarm Grandpa and the boys any further than he already had. Then, the lions all retreated back through the doorway, and the boys and Grandpa were left to themselves.

The color returned to Grandpa's face, and he tugged furiously at his beard, deep in thought, presumably thinking about what the lion had just finished saying.

Kristian shook his head. "It's a trap," he said through gritted teeth. "No," he self-corrected. "This is a dream, and it is a crazy dream! I mean, lions can't talk! This place isn't even real!" he said more lightly, pulling away from the old man.

"So what if it's a dream, I still have no idea what that lion said," Ethan reported, joining in the chorus. "What are we supposed to do?"

Kristian punched Ethan in the arm.

"Owww . . . Kristian!" he bawled. "Stop hitting me!" he hissed.

"Go ahead. Hit me back!" Kristian barked. "This is a dream, and that means I can do anything I want." A mischievous grin spread across his face, and he danced around, ready to parry any attack his younger brother might throw at him.

Ethan pulled away from Grandpa too, raised up a shoulder, and prepared to charge and tackle his brother.

"Stop it, the both of you. This is no time to fight," Grandpa scolded as he continued to pull at his beard.

"But . . ." Ethan placated.

"No. Please stop," the old man said finally, making a sweeping motion with his hands.

Ethan folded his arms in protest, disgusted. He shot a withering look at Kristian, who had calmed back down, but wore a content smile nonetheless.

"Still," Grandpa added as he studied the dark doorway. "This appears to be the only way out." He looked back at where the row of lions had been, blocking the only other way out, and if we're to believe all of this, then Lola is in there somewhere." He nodded his head back at the doorway.

They all paused and looked into the blackness.

Grandpa shrugged and urged the boys forward.

Ethan was the first through and waved his hand in front of him, as if to clear cobwebs as wisps of smoke floated by his face.

"Stop horsing around. Get in there," Kristian whispered in Ethan's ear.

"You first," Ethan protested.

Kristian sighed and shoved Ethan through the doorway.

Ethan threw his hands up and momentarily winced, expecting something terrible to happen. When nothing did, he grumbled about his brother and waited for his eyes to adjust as he looked deeper into the tunnel. After a few moments, he could see that it was narrow and appeared to lead off in a straight line. He briefly looked back through the slight mist, the others' features winked in and out of view, giving them an eerie appearance.

Kristian was next in and Grandpa brought up the rear, attempting to survey the area as well.

As they made their way through the corridor, the walls began to slowly slope outward into a great hall. An eerie greenish light hung in the air, and the hall took on the shape of the chamber with pillars, but all bathed in a deep green that matched the lighting.

Ethan could hear sloshing ahead of them and soon realized that they were approaching a body of water that had appeared in front of them. Upon closer inspection, the water spread throughout the entire chamber, and directly in front of them, there was a dock with a boat tied to a lone dock pole.

Ethan didn't know how the boat played into the story, but he wasn't about to get into it. No way. He looked back at Grandpa.

"Well, looks like this is the way forward," the old man announced. "The lions haven't followed us." He turned his head to look behind them then added, "At least not as far as I can tell." He turned back to the boys. "I'm convinced that this is further down the lake that I've seen with the lions. This may be our way out. I just hope Lola is here somewhere," his voice trailed off.

"This is all insane. Completely insane," Kristian blurted out, still believing that he was in a bad dream.

Ethan couldn't see Grandpa's face entirely, but he knew from the old man's tone that he would have to get into the boat. The boy was not happy about it, he hated boats ever since he was little. But he now found himself boarding with the others in single file. Ethan found a place at the front while his brother stood mid-boat.

"Now what?" Kristian asked in a tone of contempt. "There's no paddles in this bucket. What? Do we have to paddle with our hands?"

Grandpa shrugged and unloosed the tie from the dock.

The boat lurched forward on its own. Kristian lost his balance and fell to his knees, making a desperate grab for the boat sides to steady himself. The boat listed to one side, and Ethan had to quickly shift his weight to the other side to balance them and avoid tipping over.

It was much lighter the farther they floated along, but the water's green tint gave everything a peculiar appearance that made Ethan feel like he simply didn't want to look anymore for fear of the unknown darkness all around them. Before he could look away, however, something again caught his eye. Movement between the pillars! He squinted through the dim light and to his surprise saw what appeared to be huge groups of figures. He dismissed it as trees or something else, but they were all moving. He strained harder and realized they were lions, all crowded in between the pillars in an orderly manner, filling the watery hall.

"What the carp!" Kristian said as he and Grandpa had now noticed it too.

"It appears I was wrong. They have followed us in. Just sit calmly . . ." Grandpa trailed off.

A low rumble began as the lions started to growl, or was it singing? None of the small party could really tell. But it did not help ease their fears.

Grandpa took out his flashlight and shone it in the direction of the figures. The lions were all watching them intently, thousands of bright eyes glittered as he swept the light across the expanse.

Kristian took out the flashlight grandpa had given him and did the same. But after a while, the lions' forms grew more transparent until no longer visible. The pillars remained, but seemed to slowly grow into the forms of giant aquatic plants reaching high into a black sky.

Ethan gasped in spite of himself as he realized they were no longer underground. "Maybe that's what the lion meant. This is the way out!" he excitedly exclaimed.

"Man, wait until Dad hears about this!" Kristian added.

"Yeah," Ethan blurted. "We found the lost Kurdistan temple he was looking for. We did it!"

"Yeah, yeah, but," Kristian said with a giant smile. He looked back at Grandpa. "Wait until Mom and Dad see that we found Grandpa!"

"Look!" Grandpa interrupted the boys' excited comments as he raised his finger to point directly in front of them.

The boys turned to follow where the old man was pointing.

Ethan had to squint at first, but then saw a mound of earth rising from the water. Someone stood on the mound. Ethan squinted harder; it was Lola! A dim white light shone round about her, as if it held her in place.

"Lola!" he blurted out.

"Ethan!" she replied. "Did you see the bunnies?" her voice echoed all around them.

"Bunnies? No! Forget about bunnies. I'm going to . . . ," Kristian said before Grandpa placed a calming hand on his shoulder. Kristian fell silent.

"The bunnies that brought me here," she continued.

Lola's silhouette came into clear view as a great orb of fire rose steadily into the sky, just beyond the mound. The sun looked cleaner, somehow, casting rays of light across the glimmering surface of the water and earth.

The mound itself appeared to be barren of any vegetation, it was just a mound of dirt, Ethan thought to himself. It also only rose a few feet from the surface of the water and could have been no larger than twenty or thirty feet in diameter.

The boat continued its journey toward the mound, and the lions as well as the great plant-like pillars had all but entirely vanished.

As they reached the mound, the boat slid partially into the earthy sand before coming to a complete stop. They all looked at one another in silence for a few seconds as if not knowing what to do next.

Grandpa coughed, breaking the silence. "Well, we should probably get out," he paused, "and see what comes next, I think." He finished the last part a bit hesitantly.

Lola came flying down the mound and to the boat as the boys and Grandpa disembarked.

They slowly made their way to the center of the mound as Lola jumped up and down, jabbering about her adventure to Grandpa.

The sand was soft under Ethan's feet, it was pure and beautiful. He reached down and took a handful, bringing it up to study it more closely. He let the tiny crystals slip between his fingers and watched it as the sand poured back onto the ground.

Lola finally lapsed into silence and no one talked for a while.

Ethan didn't really feel like breaking the silence. It was somehow serene. He couldn't really describe it, it felt as if it were a new beginning. But of what? He wasn't sure.

In the distance, a great thunder erupted and the family could see huge spouts of lava launching into the air. Mountains rose from the water's depth and grew in size, but never reached their little mound upon which they all stood.

*Beginning of the world?* Ethan couldn't help but wonder that someone had designed and created all of this. The feeling was palpable.

The sun was now fully risen above the water, standing alone in a vast blue sky, casting light all around them. The water lightened from a deep black to a deep blue, and the mound sparkled in a million colors. The sun continued to grow in brightness, and everything took on lighter hues: the water now turning a bright blue, the mound now entirely white. Still, the sun grew brighter. The hues of blue continued to lighten, getting brighter and brighter.

Ethan could see trees growing on the distant volcanic shores, before the sun grew too bright to see them in the distance. He stared in awe around him as if everything lacked any color at all. His attention was drawn back to his family. All color had evaporated from their clothes, faces, and even their hair! It was bizarre, as if everything had been turned entirely white.

Still, the sun continued to brighten, and it now appeared that everything was on fire. The white flames flickered all around him.

Ethan raised a hand to stare at it, watching the flames lick at his palm but yet not burn him. The sensation was surreal.

This all happened in mere seconds until everything around the boy almost entirely disappeared from view, wiped completely clean as if they were all on a giant whiteboard.

Ethan's mind soon started to follow the emptiness of his sight, and he found that he couldn't quite remember what had just happened to him or where he was. In fact, he couldn't quite recall who he was. Ethan realized that he was forgetting and desperately clung to his memories most precious to him. His name was Ethan; he had a family—Dad, Mom, Kristian, Lola, and Grand . . . he couldn't hold on to it. He didn't want to forget, he didn't want to forget about them.

The last thought in Ethan's mind was of his family. Complete whiteness replaced all form of his memories, slowly vanishing, taking shape as illusive dreams only, faintly serenading to him from the distance of another place and time.

The last words he heard were his own, recanting what the lion had said, "You may yet remember through dreams . . . and what is may return yet again to your consciousness—you have only to look in the right place . . ."

# Chapter 6

# Julfa: A New Beginning

*Another time and place, where the past is forgotten, but returns in dreams and phantom memories.*

Ethan pulled on his sandals and tunic. He might or might not have slept before rising. He was too groggy to know the difference. For a moment, he couldn't remember exactly where he was, because his mind was still awash.

This had been happening to him for *how long?* he realized that he didn't know. His entire history was a fog and it was hard for his mind to grab hold of any memory that made sense, other than the fact that

The Drake Epics - Journey to Qara

he seemed to be here now. Well, he simply couldn't remember anything beyond the last few months and even then, he felt as if his memories were somehow tampered with; maybe not even real at all.

It wouldn't have bothered him so much if his brother and sister didn't struggle with the same gaps in their memories. Grandpa was the only one who seemed to remember anything, but when the children pestered the old man about it, he told them not to worry about the past and instead focus on the future and exercise a little faith.

From time to time, the children's aged patriarch would fill in the gaps for them, but they could never quite get enough out of him to satisfy their curiosity about where they came from. None of them could remember from before. Yet there were illusive visions of another time and place where they belonged.

*Here?* Ethan looked around the room. This place was not home. That much he did know.

The rising sun was still hidden behind the jagged graphite-grey window cut out of the wall. He could already see that the sky had brightened to a crisp morning blue, even with the quickly approaching heat of the day.

His throat suddenly felt parched at the thought of caravan merchants bartering for the last few buckets of water. Still, water continued to freely flow into the Julfa village basin, and there was no immediate sign of the anticipated drought. But that could change in a day or two, as manifest by the quickly evaporating pockets of water in the surrounding desert crags. Yet the village townsmen were experts at water conservation and irrigation, and they had pulled the village through more than one dry spell as far as he knew or what Grandpa had told him.

Julfa was a small oasis basin that butted up against the Rub' al Nejd desert to the north. Beyond the desert lay the great Caucasus Mountains, and but few were brave enough to venture into those jagged canopies. In fact, Ethan had only heard tales of the rugged mountains that caravan storytellers wove fantastic stories about, and he loved sitting around the fire and listening to those mystical stories. From the precious little views of the mountains from Julfa, they simply appeared to be bluish extensions of the sky, rising no higher than his thumb, and only visible on the clearest of days.

The village was steeped at the bottom of the extensive Karabakh Uplands, also known as the plateau of Nejd to the west and that led directly into the great Scythian plains. The uplands slowly sloped downward from Scythia toward Julfa at its easternmost boundary before plummeting a great distance to the village itself. The plateau spread out as far as the eye could see and was dominated by mostly nomadic Bedouins, who were a frequent nuisance to traveling caravans; hence, why armored guards usually accompanied them while en route to their various trading destinations.

From Julfa to the east, the landscape opened to the wide Kura-Araks Lowland leading to the Abseron Sea.

This position made Julfa the perfect resting place for travelers traversing the rugged desert. This was always as it had been in Julfa's history. The village's humble beginnings started as a trading post established by nomadic tribes migrating primarily from Arabia. The people had given up their drifting to settle in Julfa's oasis. They carved out buildings and grandiose temples and tombs out of solid sandstone and cast up a wall around the village's irrigated farmlands, although Julfa was almost entirely naturally defended by the surrounding sandstone cliffs. Julfa continued to thrive over the centuries, due to its prime location, which formed the crossroads that bridged the Abseron Sea and the Scythian plains.

Caravan traders came through the small oasis to rest from their arduous journey to Scythia and water their camels, or as a staging point, before venturing through the fierce desert carrying goods to be shipped to faraway countries across the Abseron Sea. Either way, caravans converged on Julfa, making it an ideal location for trade, which made the village prosperous for the villagers and traveling merchants alike. It also didn't hurt that merchants could easily trade here without stiff penalties from other neighboring nations, bringing spices, incense, silks, gold, animals, iron, medicines, fabrics, perfumes, as well as rare gems and other caravan favorites.

Julfa also had a sea of its own, although not nearly as adventurous or mystical as the Abseron Sea, from the many rather embellished stories Ethan had overheard the traveling merchants speak of. Well, not really a sea, it was more of a smallish lake that skirted the basin to the south. But all the locals thought of it as the village sea and named it so. The sea was ringed in by a hard basalt that contained the water, like a giant dish. In fact, this same basalt was hewn from the nearby cliffs to build the village waterways used to irrigate the land through an extensive system of small dams, canals, and reservoirs.

The seawater was a mysterious deep blue hue, usually with only the reflections of passing clouds to blur its near-perfect complexion. Along with its gorgeous color, the lake was perhaps best known for a rare characteristic shared with no other body of water Ethan had ever heard tale of: extreme salinity. Due to the surrounding bowl-like coastline, the rock blocked the outflow of any water, causing the lake to bloat up with mineral-rich water from the seasonal underground oasis wells. With no river to release its waters, it maintained its size mainly through evaporation, leaving the lake saturated with unusual amounts of minerals and natural sodas.

The lake was so rich with minerals that its waters were extremely buoyant, causing swimmers to float uncontrollably. Ethan and Kristian along with other children from the village had spent many afternoons swimming in the sea, but the salt caked to them afterwards and they had to roll around in the sand after drying off in order to get rid of the unpleasant feeling of cracking skin.

The mineral saturation also allowed the locals to wash their clothes without the need of any soap. At the thought of washing clothes, Ethan's thoughts turned to his daily tasks. He had *bee* duty today, which meant prepping the beehives, retrieving honey, and cleaning the resulting mess, all without getting stung in the process.

It also meant he had to steer clear of the village bullies, at least if Kristian weren't working with him, he mumbled. The bullies steered clear of Ethan's much-larger brother. Ethan silently rehearsed his usual methodical plan he used to avoid the two bullies every morning. This morning was no exception.

Someday he would get back at them, he murmured. Suddenly a familiar picture entered his mind of stinging bees attacking the boys. *Strange!* he thought, hadn't that already occurred to him before? Perhaps in a dream, he surrendered, as he couldn't recall.

*Enough!* he charged his mind with a stern rebuke, glancing again around the small room. Lola was sleeping in her bedroll, next to his. *Why do I have to share everything?* he thought bitterly. That would soon change when he turned sixteen. He let out a wishful sigh for that day to come soon. Then it dawned on him, today was his fourteenth birthday! It seemed strangely familiar; a sensation of désavoue flowed over him as he questioned if he had lived this day once before; but he paid that no mind, he could hardly contain himself in his excitement. He'd been talking about it nonstop to his family for the past month, making Kristian a bit irritable, he chuckled.

In just two years, Ethan would get to bunk with Kristian and the other boys instead of with his pesky little sister! It seemed so close, yet so far away. He was sick of being called a child, he wanted to grow up and be treated with respect. All of the other tales he'd heard told were of young men reaching manhood at a much earlier age, fourteen or even twelve in some Bedouin tribes! "Yeah, respect!" He puffed up his chest with as manly of a smile he could muster. "That's only fair!" he bellowed a little louder.

Lola stirred in her bedroll at Ethan's outburst. He instinctively slapped a hand over his mouth to keep himself quiet. Upon finding he had not awakened his sleeping sister, he nimbly walked on the balls of his feet to the door opening, drew back the thick grey blanket that served as their door, and ducked under it and into the hallway.

He paused and stared up and down the corridor before his eyes rested on Grandfather's room directly across from his with a symbol of a beehive stitched into the door covering. Grandpa was a humble man who served the grand Sheikh's family as the village beekeeper, which was respected almost as if it were a religion. Yet again this all seemed familiar. The stitching triggered something inside of Ethan's memories. He realized that the beehive was the same from one of his many dreams. The one on the door, his family crest?

Ethan closed his eyes. Suddenly, a thousand memories flashed through his mind in a tumultuous blur, Ethan's father and mother, Father's searches for something hidden, and his mother's gentle hugs in another, another place? In fairer pastures?

The boy opened his eyes and stared blankly at the blanket in front of him. His mind was now reeling. The same questions surged within his head, battering against each other in a frenzy. Had he done all of this before? Beyond entering Julfa, his past was hazy at best, he vaguely remembered that he didn't belong here, not really. He came from somewhere? Somewhere else, another . . . ? He couldn't quite grasp it.

*Why can't I remember anything?* the frustration mounted within him as he strained to unlock his mind, reaching, stretching, but all for nothing, only fleeting glimpses of images in his dreams! They taunted him in dark shadow, always dancing just beyond his clutch. *Are they real?* He wasn't sure. Ethan succumbed to defeat and tried to squash his musings. But they continued their onslaught, unwavering, and undeterred. He squeezed his eyes shut and mentally cast them from his mind. He walled each of the thoughts out, stretching his arms wide and quietly yawning as he escaped the final thought's grip on him.

He walked sleepily toward the sunlit entrance. Emerging into the courtyard, he blinked and mechanically veered right toward the earthen Temple of Abundance for breakfast.

The courtyard was not much to boast of, even by his own standards. It was oval in shape and totaled around two stone throws in diameter with door holes carved into the walls all around. Ragged blankets served for door coverings, giving the courtyard a flamboyant appearance. A packed

The Drake Epics - Journey to Qara

brick floor spread out before him. Yet this was different from that of the other buildings within Julfa, all made of hard clay, and a mixture of small huts with reeds for roofing. No, this was the temple compound, and his family was fortunate to live here! Or so Grandpa always reminded them of. They were guests here and needed to treat others with the full respect they deserved. Ethan sighed at the thought.

He caught a glimpse of the village through an open doorway, a crisscross of walls, huts, and buildings that all contributed to the village proper. Brief open spaces appeared on the outskirts in which caravans could respite for some time as they rested against their imminent journeys.

Ethan momentarily glanced back toward his family's small living quarters backed directly into the gigantic cliff that towered above it, signifying the start of the Nejd plateau. He craned his neck to look up the face of the imposing rock face. He marveled at its size, as always; the view never failed to impress and this place always seemed so foreign to him.

"One day, I will climb you!" Ethan proclaimed. The feat had been attempted only once before, but had happened so long ago, no one remembered by whom or even when exactly. "That's bound to get me noticed by the village elders and allow me to become a man! I will climb even above the Temple of the Lions to the very top, where no one has climbed before!" he mused.

Who knows, but perhaps he'd find a secret tunnel that would lessen the time to reach the plateau above. Caravans had to either drive around the cliff for a day or more to the east, or up through a tight and precarious switchback of roads many lengths from the village to get to the plateau— taking half a day alone.

Ethan's neck hurt from the strain of looking up, so he focused on getting some food.

As he strolled past the courtyard center, a lone Qarabag tree stood erect, a true rarity in this climate. "Ugly tree," he said. Yet, the tree was considered a shrine of the seasons for some, the blessing of peace to others, although he himself wasn't convinced any of that was true. "It can't even produce fruit!" he thought in contempt. For some reason, the tree had never produced any fruit since Ethan and his family had arrived in Julfa. Not that that was an omen or anything, he quickly amended, but some of the local village bullies liked to tell him it was his fault. Some villagers, the ones who called it the shrine of seasons, even claimed it was a sign of severe droughts to come. For the droughts part, the cyclic flooding seasons, when water sprung from the depths of the aquifers, had come and gone with regularity, although he had to admit with a little less water every year.

Yet others, those who named it the shrine of peace, maintained the lack of fruit meant certain war for the village itself. There were always rumors of wars, as one nation fought against another over the rights to use the Julfa trade routes. Fortunately, none of the wars had ever made it to the village. But still, the rumor of war was always a point of discussion brought by the caravans. *It's all just nonsense,* Ethan thought. *People talk and nothing ever happens anyway,* He rationalized as he waved a hand in dismissal.

Next to the tree stood a magnificent limestone chamber. It looked like an imposing mushroom with a giant dome that sat on a horizontal wall, much like some of the algae Ethan had seen growing near the aquifer, but only when there was an abundance of water.

The dome had no other walls and was completely open. Its ceiling swung together, forming a set of half giant ovals as they rose to a pinnacle at its center with pronounced carved imprints that swirled in a smooth, wavy procession of stone woven together.

Besides the different look to the building, it was renowned for its acoustic clarity. In fact, it was called the el-Qezha or echo chamber. A man could stand within it and clap his hands or talk slightly louder than usual, and the sound of his clap and voice would be carried almost to the top of the cliff with amazing lucidity. Likewise, if one stood on the other side of the wall, the sound carried all the way to the village walls, far beyond any other sound could carry.

As extensions to this magnificent structure, there were three points from which one could communicate. Similar but smaller structures stood on top of the village walls at the east and west gates, and one was built directly into the cliff itself, hundreds of feet up at the Temple of the Lions. This allowed for emergency communication to happen in case of invasion, but mostly used for sandstorms and windstorm watches. It was only ever to be used in case of extreme emergency, and two guards always manned the building on either side. Guards also manned the cliff point and the two points on the village walls.

Ethan had seen this used before, only once, when the village got hit by an unusually severe sandstorm and the guards at the temple had sounded the warning bell (a gift to the grand Sheikh from some foreign dignitary). The village was generally safe from such storms, owing to the natural protection of the cliff face and usual direction of the breeze. Most storms were usually limited to the Nejd desert anyway. But once in a great while, the storms made it to the village proper.

Ethan pulled himself from his reverie and briefly considered two guards who gave him brief nods before he sauntered on. The boy's stomach was now in full protest against his hunger, and the daydreaming

The Drake Epics - Journey to Qara

made him all the more hungry. As he neared the midway point to the temple's entrance, he noted the south end of the courtyard that boasted a slightly larger hole, acting as the courtyard gate. This was outfitted with a wooden door to bar entrance to unwelcome visitors. Although it would probably collapse if anyone really wanted to get into the immediate grounds all that badly.

One of the village Sheikh's guards sat on the ground next to the gate, his head sagging, as if he were embracing an alluring dream.

*My dreams would cure him of any sleep—at least my headaches would keep him awake.* Ethan sniggered to himself.

The guard suddenly jerked forward as if he heard the boy and nodded at Ethan in embarrassment as the boy passed by. He mumbled something incoherent while hauling himself to his feet, using a roughly hewn spear made of sage wood and a bony tip—obviously not the most advanced weapon in the village, the boy silently mocked. But with the Sheikh and his sons out on a hunting excursion, most of the courtyard guards had accompanied them, leaving a few of the *less-able* guardsmen behind at their posts.

Julfa was governed by the royal family of the grand Sheikh, although a strong sense of democracy prevailed when the Sheikh sat in counsel with the village elders. There were no slaves to speak of in Julfa, and all members generally shared in work duties. Although some used their influence or wealth to convince others to do their work for them. *Like the two sorry excuses who seem to always get out of everything!* Ethan spat as he thought about two boys, in particular, who always got their way through bribery, *except for when they pound on me.* The boy unconsciously rubbed the back of his head from a previous incident with the boys.

Two women presently approached the guard who swung the wooden gate open to allow them passage, again muttering something under his breath.

"Why does he even mumble anything at all?" Ethan wondered.

The women took no notice of the sloppy guard, engrossed in a conversation of their own. They each carried tall baskets on their heads, likely full of clothing to be washed in the aquifer.

The boy chuckled silently about the guard and turned in time to duck into the entrance to the Temple of Abundance. He quickly bowed three times, as was required by all who entered, and walked through the carved-out doorway.

The room was large and bare, except for a wolf's head set on a large boulder at the far end of the temple galley. The room could easily seat one hundred hungry villagers and merchants who frequented the courtyard looking to sell their wares as statue shrines to villagers or possibly to the Sheikh and the village elders, if they got lucky.

On the left side of the hall stood seven large windows roughly cut into the rough wall, escorting the morning sunlight into the corridors. As the light entered the hall, it was immediately confronted by four giant sandstone pillars that supported the ceiling, and that now cast deep, long shadows to the far right, where villagers sat with their legs crossed, eating their morning meal.

Two guards sat on the floor to the right, midway down the hall, and behind the shadows of one of the pillars. They were eating and talking in hushed tones, too low for Ethan to eavesdrop on their discussion. Although this aroused his curiosity and he made a mental note to get a little closer to the pair, if he could. Kristian would certainly be game, the boy thought adventurously.

Two or three merchants were scattered across the hall, either counting their money or devouring their breakfast before leaving Julfa with the morning caravans.

"And what are you doing here?" a stern voice sounded by the boy.

Ethan almost jumped as he recognized the cook's voice, who was busily preparing the morning meal, but had paused to glare at the boy. "Nothing." He said with a smile. "Just getting my breakfast."

"As if!" the cook spat. "I've got my eye on you!" he said, as he wagged a chopping knife at the boy before turning back to his work.

Ethan didn't much care for the cook either. He and Kristian had played one too many practical jokes on the thick man. Fortunate for them, they'd never been caught, although the cook suspected them and watched them like hawks whenever the boys were in the cook's presence.

The youth kept his eyes on the cook as he made his way to a stone table of sorts that acted as a staging area for the morning meal. He picked up two pieces of dried bread and poured three or four dollops of honey into a ceramic bowl before starting off for a spot away from the cook, which meant on the opposite side of the room. "I've got my eye on you!" he mocked under his breath as he walked along. He found a seat away from the others, forgetting entirely about the two guards, and started to munch on the hard bread, pausing occasionally to dip it into his honey bowl.

He looked up just in time to see Kristian enter the room, closely followed by his little sister, Lola. He waved at them both, as if by instinct, and went back to eating. Both Kristian and Lola waved back as they walked to the food stone to retrieve their food before heading over to sit with their brother.

The cook rolled his eyes in disgust and eyed the older boy and young girl with the same scrutiny he had awarded Ethan. However, the plump man quickly gave up with them as well and went back to his work.

Kristian was a full head taller than Ethan, with light brown hair and a fair complexion. His cheeks were a bit rounder than Ethan's and sprinkled with freckles, which drove most of the village girls nuts about him.

Not that Ethan really cared. Girls were not nearly as important as Drakes, he thought.

Kristian sold himself to the girls even more so by his quick wit, which served him well in almost every situation. The only time that wit got his older brother into trouble was at school and his soldiering apprenticeship, as he often got himself into a heaping mess for saying the wrong things at the wrong time! Ethan mused.

The village school Kristian got to attend, although better than most as it taught all of the basics, was aimed at limited training. After all, Kristian was already sixteen; whereas, many started school much younger. However, the oler boy had skills and was initiated into an official apprenticeship. Grandpa had accepted Kristian's aspirations to become a soldier, although he still had time to help out with the daily beekeeping duties Grandpa levied at the two boys. Ethan wanted to do the same as his brother, but he knew full well that Grandpa would most likely hold him back to apprentice with him in beekeeping as both boys had focused so much time there.

The younger boy was Torn. He didn't feel it was fair, but still, he enjoyed the art of keeping bees and respected Grandpa for his skill. Other boys in the village proper received only meager schooling and quickly aligned themselves as apprentices to their families or to other trades. The family was very fortunate to have more. But Ethan often wondered about the beyond. There was always excitement in the air for the boy who chose to align to a caravan trader. It was sometimes enough to simply hear the legends that the caravan storytellers would weave. However, these apprenticeships were very rare, unless the boy's father or family were traders who crossed the barren landscapes in search of fabled riches in far-off lands. Still, he felt an odd connection with the nomadic traders, as if he too didn't quite belong here, as if he were searching for his true home.

Lola, on the other hand, may not ever go to school. Although, some of the women did get to attend—if they are lucky. She, of course thought this was an outrage. She was a full two or three heads shorter than Ethan with yet lighter hair than Kristian that fell around her shoulders. Her face was more slender than Ethan's, but she had the same darker complexion that

Ethan had and was very pretty. Not to mention she was a tough little girl. Most of her village friends were boys, and the village girls didn't know how to treat her in the least due to her rugged, boyish demeanor.

Ethan looked up just in time to greet his sister as she came up to him. "Where's Kristian?" he asked in between mouthfuls.

"A couple girls caught him and he's talking with them." She jerked her head in her older brother's direction.

Ethan looked around his little sister and saw a few girls clamoring around Kristian in animated discussion. *About who knows what?* Ethan smirked. *I bet he's trying to get away as fast as he can.* But he knew better. Kristian loved the attention. He caught a glimpse of Kristian's little creature perched on his older brother's shoulder. "I see Kristian has his drake with him," he mentioned a little more jealously than he had planned.

"Yeah, he doesn't go anywhere without his pet lizard," Lola rejoined as she sat cross legged and proceeded to eat. She wasn't overly happy that the boys got one and that she did not.

The boy continued to study the winged lizard. It pointed its snout around, looking to and fro, enthusiastically taking in the sights, smells, and sounds. Ethan had to admit it was very cool. Although he desperately, desperately wanted to bind to a drake of his own.

Kristian's drake was obviously a male, as females were generally larger. Its slender body had a deep red tint and was not much longer than Ethan's forearm from the end of its snout to the tip of its tail, although it would grow to triple that size in maturity. It had the body, head, and legs of a lizard, almost identical to any small iguana in every detail, but without the iguana's skin flaps under the chin and with two leathery wings extending from its side—mid-torso—presently folded neatly against its body. Well, that and it was a lot more sanitary than a dirty ordinary lizard, Ethan thought. No, these animals were every bit as clean as a pampered cat or dog, of which there weren't any in the village and only rarely seen coming and going with the caravans.

"Give it up, Ethan," Lola said as she stuffed her mouth full of bread and honey. "You're not sixteen yet and besides, the only reason that Kristian got his drake is cause of his solider apprenticeship . . ."

"And all great warriors have a red fire drake," Ethan finished for her. Although he had his doubts about how authentic that all really was. "Thanks for reminding me," he sulked as he tore into another piece of bread.

The drake's brilliant orange eyes momentarily studied Ethan as it noticed the boy's interest. Its inner eyelids snapped open and shut. However, as soon as it recognized him, the drake continued to canvass the rest of the temple hall in excitement.

The Drake Epics - Journey to Qara

"Do you think that drake will ever be able to fly?" he said out loud. From what Ethan had seen of the small drake over the last month, since his brother's binding, the little creature could fly in quick bursts for short distances, which looked more like the little drake could jump and glide more than fly.

Lola shook her head. "I dunno!" she said with a mouth full of bread. "Grandpa says it's too early to tell how far . . ." she paused to swallow. "Besides, it's not like drakes can fly like bees. Grandpa . . ."

"I know, I know!" Ethan said in an annoyed tone. "Grandpa says so." He grumbled as he recalled Grandpa's statement, "Most drakes can only ever fly over short distances, but a precious few can remain in flight that rivals any bird *or bee* around here." The emphasis on the *bee* had shocked all three children, as Grandpa never, *never* talked lightly of the bee.

Ethan continued to think about Grandpa's detailed explanation—few animals were as resilient and as industrious as that of a bee or its hive. *Only drakes can match the hive!* Grandpa had said with finality. Although the old man would never give in to a drake beating out a beehive, as drakes were more solitary creatures, sticking to their holder they had bound to most of the time, unlike the teamwork found in swarms. Besides, no one really knew where drakes originally came from. All anyone knew is that they made great companions, posing as pets that could only understand basic verbal commands, but much, much more intelligent than a common dog.

"Yeah, but wouldn't it be cool if Kristian's drake could spit fire!" Lola suddenly exclaimed, interrupting Ethan's train of thought.

He nodded and took a big swig of water, keeping his eyes rooted on his older brother's prized companion. If a drake holder was lucky, really lucky, some very few drakes had elemental powers, unusual earthen powers that were rumored to be transferable to their holders.

"Or if he could talk to it," Ethan added, talking directly into his cup. Some drakes of folklore wielded telepathy, although it was extremely rare to tell the quality of a drake before it bound. He'd bet an entire beehive on that! Still, Ethan had never witnessed an elemental drake in Julfa, let alone a telepathic one, although a few of the village elite boasted of such feats.

"I don't think that will happen though," the boy said with finality as he put his cup down. "Besides, it's one in a million chances getting a drake that could do that." He sighed whimsically. "Unless you have a really special drake, like if you're a noble or you pay a king's ransom to get one," he sulked.

Still, Kristian was one of the lucky ones. Not only did he *get* a drake in the first place, but his drake was amazingly clever. Not really telepathic and the family hadn't seen any elemental qualities, but the little creature seemed to be intuitive to the older boy's commands, although somewhat haltingly. Somehow no sign of this quality was realized by the breeders, and it was simply a miracle that Kristian had been chosen by this drake at all. Kristian had quietly revealed this discovery to Ethan and Grandpa. He had demonstrated this by rolling up his face into a comical contortion in sheer concentration. He looked like a wrinkled fig or date, and his face went purple with intensity.

"Well, at least you get to have a drake," Lola barked.

But, Ethan was still lost in his thoughts and didn't hear his little sister's comment. He smiled and had to look down quickly and cover his mouth for fear of bursting out in complete laughter.

"What's so funny?" Lola now asked, wiping at her mouth with her sleeve and looking upset. She did not like to be picked on!

"Nothing," the boy responded, regaining his stern composure.

Lola shot him a glowering look. "I want to know, now!" she demanded. "Are you laughing at me?"

"What? No!" he shot back, before returning to his own thoughts about his older brother. But he still had a wry smile on his face. Kristian had next synchronized a number of commands in his mind for the drake to follow as he shouted verbal commands. The small drake obeyed, although rather lethargically, and it protested at every command. Ethan had thought to argue the point that the drake was not telepathic at all, but he kept this to himself as he didn't want to squash his brother's dreams. This and, admittedly, the commands were beyond what he'd seen other boys accomplish with their drakes in so short of time.

Grandpa had strictly forbidden Kristian to mention any word about telepathy to anyone else. *However*, he had said with excitement evident in his voice, *this too could be due to the drake's youth or Kristian's inexperience and might develop into real talent with maturity and more study.* With Grandpa, it was always about more study.

Ethan sighed in exasperation and looked away from his brother, who was still engrossed in discussion with the girls.

This drew a deeper frown from his sister. "You always do that!" Lola stewed. "You're always laughing to yourself, or daydreaming. Grandpa says to . . ."

"To mind your own manners!" Ethan snapped back.

Lola's nostrils flared in anger. "Fine! Don't tell me. But you still have to wait two more years before you get your drake! I don't even get one!" she sulked.

"I'm sorry, Lola. It had nothing to do with you. I . . . I was thinking about something else" Ethan tried to placate his sister.

She frowned at the boy, then accepted the apology and went back to eating her breakfast. She was always fickled that way and could change her mood at will.

*Wish I could do that.* It was now Ethan's turn to silently sulk. Still, it wasn't fair! Ethan had to admit it. Drake binding was a yearly ritual for *boys only*, that is, once they reached the age of sixteen or more commonly known as the age of accountable service. That age seemed to be the magical age and was critically important for village boys. It marked the beginning of manhood and initiated the call to service in Julfa.

*That's why Kristian is so happy!* Ethan grumbled to himself as he jealously glanced over again at his older brother. Kristian had turned sixteen the month of the monsoons, just two months before the binding ritual. *And,* Ethan thought, at the same time he had begun his formal studies, *and* that which now included limited studies for drakes because of his binding.

The older boy now approached them and it was obvious that one of the girls was still animatedly talking his ear off.

Ethan shook his head and went back to eating.

". . . and I'll see you at school tomorrow, won't I?" the girl was saying.

The older boy was half ignoring her as he walked. "Uhh. Yeah. I guess so," he said in a bored tone. "Can I actually eat with my brother and sister now?" he jabbed.

The girl hardly noticed his frustrated tone, and gleefully nodded. "Tomorrow then!" as she trotted off to huddle with a group of girls.

*No doubt to talk about Kristian and how cute he is!* Ethan sighed. *Girls are fickled, just like Lola,* the boy thought.

"Day dreaming again?" Kristian asked.

Lola grinned. "He always daydreams," she said with a smirk.

Ethan frowned and ignored them both as he ate silently.

The older boy gingerly sat so as not to unsettle his drake by too much.

*As if that matters,* Ethan mused silently. Drakes had marvelous balance. The younger boy again intently watched the small drake, who was currently preening itself under its left wing while it balanced against Kristian's sudden movements with the other wing.

Ethan was reminded of the age limit. *Why do I have to be sixteen in order to bind?* he fumed. It was a dumb rule made up by conspiring men, he concluded. *It is too great of strain on younger boys . . . it could be dangerous!* he had once overheard another village magistrate telling his grandfather. *Besides, the drakes would most likely reject the bindings to younger counterparts because of their underdeveloped minds.* The man had claimed. The boy thought it was all a complete sham. It just meant that the adults could keep a tighter leash on the village boys, he silently protested. He almost spat on the ground at the mere thought. He'd heard of younger *nobles* binding. *Why would any other boy be so different?* he thought miserably.

He presently let his eyes rest on Lola, and recalled that she too had been listening in on Grandpa's conversation with the magistrate. He remembered her tugging on the old man's robe. *Why don't girls get drakes? I want a drake too!* she had demanded. *I'm just as good as any boy; I'm even better!* the memory of her shrill voice pierced Ethan's mind. Grandpa had nervously laughed and patted Lola on the head, which infuriated her and she had stormed off to her room.

Ethan looked at his older brother again, who was in process of sliding his other prized possession into his shirt, a white amulet of a dragon. Kristian didn't even know where he got if from, but he never left the hut without it. Ethan shook his head and returned his yearning gaze to Kristian's drake, trying to forget about being under age.

The older boy noticed his younger brother's interest. "You're staring again, Dingus. Seriously?" he inserted. "I mean, I wish there had been two eggs from the mother Drake that we could've shared, but you're still too young to bind anyways and they would have ignored you, which would have made you even more miserable."

Ethan winced at the sour reminder. Drakes lay one egg once per year—two if the breeder were lucky. It always happened directly following the month of monsoons. The eggs incubated for one month before hatching. The binding happened upon hatching of the drake, and for some reason, the drakes all hatched at the very same moment. Julfa's ritual was hosted within the breeding grounds, adjacent to another Qarabag tree—the only other one in the village, esteemed for its perceived qualities to enhance acceptance of a drake to its rightful holder.

If the drake didn't accept and bind to a holder within two days, it would remain wild and usually lived out its days in the breeding grounds to find a mate, although in some legends, drakes had bound later in their lives to thwart some evil mischief.

"Well maybe I could bind to a wild drake that didn't bind to anyone . . . or, or, I could get one from a caravan!" Ethan puffed up his chest in protest. But, he knew his comment was just as big of a stretch as a wild drake was wild.

"Yeah, well I doubt it," Kristian said in between mouthfuls.

Ethan admitted that he had never heard of a real case where the drake hadn't bound to a holder and instead elected to be wild, so he had cracked this up as a local myth anyways. However, due to the relatively small population of drakes, only a small handful of lucky villagers ever received the binding anyway. The drakes simply had too many selections to make. So many of the common villagers only got to passively watch from the parade stands. However, every now and then, it wasn't unheard of for some merchants to hoard a drake egg and sell it on the black market. Such eggs usually fetched a large sum of coin and was why drake eggs were tightly regulated with large fines, and sometimes even banishment, if a villager were caught in the act.

*Although that's undoubtedly what royalty does all the time*, Ethan silently complained to himself. *In any event*, he settled, *too late to hope for a binding before my age of service*. He thought gloomily. His mind raced to the tale of the drake bandits who ventured into the Nejd and prided themselves on magi-drakes in rebellion against the village and other kingdom's laws, although Julfa really didn't fall into any kingdom other than itself per se. His mind wandered into another daydream of Ethan rebelling against Julfa's Sheikh and elders and joining himself to the bandit ranks.

The boy pulled out of his reverie to overhear Kristian and Lola talking about the cook's feeble attempt to make the honey as good as Grandpa did. His lips gave way to part snarl and part smile as he continued to munch.

"Dingus," Kristian interrupted with his mouth stuffed full of dried bread. "Why didn't you wake us anyways?" the question came with a spray of crumbs.

The younger boy grimaced, raising one arm to wipe off the unwanted particles from his face.

"Yeah, I didn't hear you get up," Lola piped in with a sour look that melted into a happy grin. Lola *had* been awaken by Ethan earlier; she had simply preferred to lie in her bedroll a little longer.

"Hmm? I don't know," Ethan replied absentmindedly. All of this talk and thinking about drakes had made him grumpy. But his mood suddenly brightened. "Hey, Kristian, did you name your drake yet?" Ethan sat still, waiting on the answer. He wanted to find out what his older brother had decided after the barrage of names they had discussed last night over dinner. He had a slew of helpful names, but with most of them getting turned down as soon as they left his lips. He'd almost given up hope. Besides, Kristian had already delayed by a full month to name his drake, unlike other boys who named their drakes on the spot. Well, maybe not on the spot, but pretty close to on the spot.

"Nope . . . not yet," his brother replied, again in between mouthfuls. "Although," another pause between chewing, "I do kinda like *Dragonfly* or *Redhot*," Kristian said in a mocking tone. But this was more out of jest to tease his little brother, knowing full well that Ethan didn't like either of those names.

As Kristian predicted, Ethan wrinkled up his nose at the mention of the names. Ethan was sure that *Firebolt* and *Firedemon* were both much more fitting names for a fiery red drake. But he picked up on his brother's tone, knowing that Kristian had a great love for sarcasm.

The older boy continued eating as if the discussion weren't taking place at all. He picked up a slice of bread, broke off an end, dipped it in honey, and handed it to his drake, who promptly grabbed the piece of bread with its dexterous paws, turning it a few times before beginning to feed.

Lola plunged into the discussion. "What about *Deseret?*" she exclaimed in triumph as she slurped down a half glass of water and wiped her face with her sleeve. She stopped halfway and timidly looked about to make sure Grandpa was nowhere in sight. Not seeing the old man, she promptly dug into her meal again.

Ethan grinned in spite of himself. Grandpa was always scolding her about such inappropriate behaviors. *Lola, that is not ladylike!* Grandpa would say, or *Lola, that is not how I have taught you to behave!* But everyone knew that she desperately wanted to be a boy. After all, boys got to play in the dirt, play fight, and most of all, boys got drakes, like Kristian!

She appeared to have already forgotten about her comment by the time Kristian answered her question.

"Nah, I'll just keep mulling over a few names today and name him tomorrow." As if he were reflecting on them all right now. "Although," he added, "I do kinda like the name *BeeSting*, come to think of it."

Ethan beamed a broad grin—that was a name he had proposed, well, at least one of them anyway.

"Oh well, hey," added Kristian, "aren't you supposed to be on bee duty today, Ethan?"

"Just waiting for Grandpa." This time, it was Ethan who spat crumbs as he answered. He followed by taking another large bite out of his bread. He could never seem to get enough honey and had run out long before he was finished with the dry biscuit. This was unfortunate, as it left his mouth parched, as if he'd just eaten a mouthful of sand.

"Better hurry, I saw him getting ready to leave as we walked in," Kristian exclaimed.

Ethan wolfed down the rest of his breakfast and licked his bowl clean. With a nod of his head, he jumped up from his seat and started to dash away. He stopped and bawled at Kristian. "Can you take my bowl back for me?"

"Yeah, yeah," Kristian spat. "Don't be such a Dingus . . . Oh, and try not to get stung by those ground bees this time," Kristian jeered in his usual mocking tone. "Better take an extra tunic for padding—make that two . . ." he added to rub it in some more. Kristian always had more to say, sometimes funny, sometimes not so funny.

As usual, Ethan ignored his brother's taunts. Instead, he let out a low whine, rubbing a sore arm he'd been stung on. He felt a sudden pang of self-pity. *They didn't mention my birthday, not even once, no presents, nothing! They couldn't have all forgotten about it.*

He reached the entrance; whirled around, bowing three times; and charged out of the doorway. He rubbed his arm again as he ran. "Today is going to be one of those *long* days," he muttered.

"I wonder if Grandpa is going to finally teach me how to extract bees without smoke? It's the least he can do to celebrate my birthday, as it seems that everyone else has forgotten all about it!" He spit as he raced across the courtyard.

## Chapter 7

# Grandpas and Bees and Drakes, Oh My

*Is it the situation that makes the man? Or is it the man who makes the situation?*

Ethan skidded into view as he rounded the corner, left, into the family hallway. He almost ran headlong into Grandpa, who was carrying an armful of gear.

Grandpa, who was obviously caught off guard by the boy now hurtling himself at him, let out a forged guffaw at Ethan's sudden appearance and lightly stepped back against the wall to avoid being mowed down. He shot Ethan a dismayed look while shaking his head, which meant—Ethan knew all too well—Grandpa had another lecture on the tip of his tongue. As if sensing Ethan's thoughts, the old man shook his head again and said, "Grab the other equipment just there," pointing at a clump outside of his room. "And . . . ," Grandpa added, "don't forget your veil this time," in a sterner voice.

Ethan winced and nodded obediently, moving toward his room at a much slower and deliberate pace. He rubbed at his *sore* arm again, which was now probably much more tender due to his incessant rubbing rather than from the initial bee sting. He swung one arm down and sullenly grabbed a bee veil as he went.

Grandpa was still watching the boy. "Ethan, please explain to me the importance of the beekeepers veil," he asked in a teacherly tone.

The boy jumped at the sudden intrusion and turned to give his Grandpa a look of self-pity.

"Come now, what is its purpose?" the old man persisted.

The young student scratched at his head to remember the lines he needed to rehearse. Although, he had no idea why memorization was so important, especially about bees! "Umm, the veil . . . , next to the smoker, is easily the most important tool in a beekeeper's arsenal."

He shot Grandpa another pleading look, to which the old man only folded his arms waiting for more detail.

"Defensive bees," Ethan continued, "like those found in the Nejd, are attracted to breath—breath from any animal or person—and . . . a sting on the face could lead to much more pain and swelling."

The boy paused and strained to remember the rest of his line. ". . . Whereas, a sting on a bare hand or arm can usually be removed by a fingernail scrape to reduce the amount of venom injected." He finished with pride, as he realized he had been very lucky the last time around. The bees had only stung him on the arm and back, but he couldn't reach that spot to scratch at the itching sensation.

The old man gave the boy a quick nod and turned towards the cart.

Ethan took the opportunity and quickly ducked into his room and returned carrying odds and ends he would need. He quickly dropped to one knee to pick up the remaining items Grandpa had left on the floor before continuing out into the courtyard.

Luckily, the bees that Grandpa and the boys handled had small doses of venom, but any venom in mass quantities could be serious in nature, even lethal in some rare cases.

Ethan shuddered at the stories Grandpa had told the children of swarms of belligerent bees massing around people until their last breath. He half-rose his hand, still full of tools, to rub his arm again, but thought better of it and continued to pick up Grandpa's other instruments. The tools included: another veil with holes in it; a light tan hood; a pair of white long-armed gloves that were almost worn-out from too much use; and a smoke flask, probably meant for him, he thought miserably.

As if on cue, the old teacher asked him the next question nodding at the smoke flask, as the boy strolled into the courtyard, "Tell me about that device," he asked.

"The smoke flask?" the boy looked at the old teacher as if to ask what he was pointing at. The smoker device was made of a hard ceramic that was coated and kilned multiple times to reduce the possibility of shattering under extreme heat. It was designed to generate smoke from various woods, used as the smoky fuel. The wood was also generally applied with a special waxy coat so as to increase the smoker burn time and increase the smoke output.

Grandpa nodded in answer to Ethan's question.

"The smoke flask really is a unique device . . . The, the, the smouldering ash is the novice beekeeper's first line of defense." Ethan paused but couldn't scratch at his head because of all the gear he was carrying, so he stood still, looking comical while he recited his lines. "Smoke usually calms the bees by . . . tricking them into feeding on their honey reserves in preparation to abandon their hives . . ." He couldn't remember the rest!

"Due to fire," Grandpa helpfully finished the sentence for him.

Embarrassed, the boy continued, ". . . This, in turn, makes the bees more sluggish and less likely to sting someone when opening a hive. For this purpose, most beekeepers use a smoker device," Ethan finished. He really didn't like rote memorization and was annoyed he had to learn any lines at all! It was easier for Kristian, *senior smarty pants*, the boy mocked.

*Anyways*, he thought, *the smoke flask is a pain to carry around!* The notable exception to smoking out bees, of course, was Grandpa. Ethan, himself, would most certainly need to use the smoker again, he admitted. Although on his last excursion, the smoker didn't work as effectively as he would have liked.

Ethan reached the cart and set the contents down next to the old man in order to help him assemble a hive box. He looked down at the box frames, each with a sheet of wax as the foundation, made in part from the honey residue that Grandpa mixed with other ingredients not known to Ethan—well, he never paid enough attention to their composition anyway.

The eager student knew the next question already and plunged into reciting his lines before he was asked to do so, "The beehives or boxes are made of a special focaccia tree . . ."

Grandpa insisted on collecting wood fragments on their frequent bee explorations outside of the village. In fact, they were preparing to do just that today.

The boy continued trying not to breathe and get through his recitation as quickly as humanly possible, "The bottom box, or brood chamber, is reserved for the queen and most of the bees. The upper boxes, or supers, contain the pure honey." He paused and inhaled before proceeding. "The bees produce wax and build honeycomb using these wax sheets as the starting point, after which they raise a brood, depending upon the size of the colony, or deposit honey and pollen in the cells of the comb."

Ethan took in a deep breath as he thought about his numerous lessons the old man had taught him about the hives. Grandpa had constructed these frames such that they could be freely manipulated. The honey supers, with frames full of honey, could be taken to more easily harvest their honey crop. This was Grandpa's prized invention. Most other beekeepers made use of the more traditional *skeps*, which were baskets made of sage straw and mud. Skeps were usually made with a single entrance at the bottom where the bees entered and exited.

Usually, there was no internal structure except what the bees had to build themselves. Also, aside from the fact that it was impossible to inspect the interior of the skeps for diseases and pests, the removal of honey often necessitated the destruction of the entire hive, and the beekeepers often either drove the bees out of the skep or killed them and subsequently squeezed the entire skep in a vice of sorts in order to expel the honey. Grandpa despised these methods as they usually ended in the destruction of the bees themselves, which he considered an affront to nature.

Ethan paused for any corrections from the old man. When none came, he began to nimbly assemble the boxes, one by one. He had done this hundreds of times with Grandpa always thoroughly inspecting his work for the slightest miss.

"What do you think?" asked Grandpa as Ethan dropped the last box frame into place.

The boy looked up at the wise man with a quizzical glance. He hadn't expected this question!

"Anything missing?" Grandpa pointed at the hive that Ethan had just completed. He might as well have been asking the boy if this was a good surface to eat honey on.

"I built it like I've always done," replied Ethan, who could not imagine he had missed the slightest part of the hive in its assembly.

Grandpa gave him a reprising look, as if that were the absolute last response he should have given.

Ethan turned and looked over the hive again, frowning in concentration, before finally shrugging. "It's perfect," he concluded. He really didn't want to tear it down again, which Grandpa mercilessly made him do every time he built a hive incorrectly.

"Shall I trust you on that?"

Ethan paused as if he didn't know how to answer. Grandpa had never given him that much latitude before. "OhhhK, yes," he replied with a nod, not knowing what would come next.

Grandpa grinned in approval and announced, "Because you will be seeking the queen today . . . *and* . . . you will be using your own box."

Ethan was dumbfounded. He turned to reexamine the box. He spun around and met Grandpa's gaze with a big grin before launching himself at the elderly man, wrapping his arms around him as tight as he could.

"That will do, that will do," Grandpa said as he patted Ethan on the back, but Ethan really knew that Grandpa loved hugs from his three grandchildren.

The boy released the old man and put his hands on his head in excitement. Today really was going to be a special day!

"You will not protest to leaving now then?"

"Let's go," said Ethan with as big of grin as he could muster.

"Then load the cart with the rest of the tools, and we'll be off." Grandpa started for the gate as Ethan hurriedly gathered the tools and threw them haphazardly into the cart. He half-danced around the cart's side to the front, hoisted the two handles, used to pull it, and started forward.

—  —  —

The trek out of the village was exhilarating! They battled the caravan crowds leaving the village. The great wagons cast up clouds of dust as they slowly rolled along. Restless horses whinnied and camels snorted as they carried their loads. Armed guards accompanied the wagons, walking from cart to cart making sure they were secure.

Ethan could smell the excitement lingering in the air as they passed through the courtyard, through Julfa's farm land, and out of the eastern village gates. Unlike the village, the countryside outside of Julfa was deathly barren for the most part, with limited sages posted in groupings, as if sprinkled around by some great squall.

To the east was the road to the Abseron Sea, where the majority of the caravans now turned onto. Ethan wondered whimsically of what it might be like to venture to the bustling sea town that he had never had the chance to visit, except through caravan story tellers' stories. He was brought out of his momentary trance as he and Grandpa left the entourage of wagons and banked north and toward the desert. The Rub' al Nejd desert was a vast wasteland of red sand dunes, also known as the Nejd desert for short, or empty quarter, because of its extreme conditions and harsh climate. Only the hardiest travelers sought to venture too deep into its clutches and risk its temperament. Even then, travelers never, *never* went on their own.

Still, Grandpa and the boys had journeyed into the Nejd on a few occasions, but only for a halfday here or a halfday there, at most, and only during the daylight. Grandpa, on the other hand, had traveled extensively in the barren wasteland for days and weeks at a time, scouting out new bee species and colonies. He was quite accustomed to the climate and easily evaded predators that made the badlands so dangerous.

Ethan quit the history tour in his mind as their distance from the caravans grew. He chanced another look over his shoulder to catch a glimpse of the retreating wagons. The caravans used the main road to Abseron that only skirted the Nejd, but generally avoided the badlands at all costs. He decided there was nothing more to discover and turned his attentions in front of him and Grandpa. He recognized the typical gravel plains surrounded by huge red sand dunes that marked the start of the desert.

Suddenly, a lone dark form appeared over the rise of one of the dunes and started to descend into the gravel plain directly in front of them. Ethan squinted in an attempt to see through the bright glare as wisps of heat bobbed in front of him, caused by the burning sun. The figure was too hard to recognize, as if it were swimming in waves of heat that emanated off the gravel. As they drew closer, Ethan could gradually make the shape out as a black horse with a lone rider, shrouded in black flowing robes.

A rather-hot dry breeze picked up, but Ethan instead felt a chill run down his spine. Strangely, the rider was coming directly from the Nejd to meet the road. This went against everything he had been taught. *Never, never travel the Nejd alone!* he reflected and strained to look beyond the rider for pursuers; none came. As the rider advanced, Ethan could see a long ponytail drooping over the figure's shoulder.

Grandpa gave a curt nod, and the stranger slightly dipped his head in response before his eyes rested upon Ethan. The boy was transfixed by the man's cold gaze, and he almost dropped the cart as he stumbled on a stone. He recognized this man from somewhere, although he knew that he'd never met him before.

The stranger's eyes bore into Ethan, as if picking away at his soul. Time ground to a halt for the moment, and Ethan began to uncontrollably shiver as the man made his way into the boy's conscience. The boy forced himself to break the spellbound stare and wrenched his gaze away to avoid the silent interrogation. As he did so, a sudden warmth refilled his veins, as if all his blood had been sucked dry by the encounter and now resumed, pumping life back into his body.

The man turned his attention back to Julfa and continued on his journey, his horse not once breaking stride.

Ethan tried to suppress the unpleasant experience and quickly forgot all about it as they proceeded to wherever they were going, focusing instead on the horizon in front of them.

Grandpa was never really talkative on these excursions, and Ethan was all too happy for the silence. It allowed him to daydream about capturing the biggest and finest colony of bees the village had ever seen. He imagined himself proudly parading through the village, while everyone dropped their tools and ignored their work to rush over to look at his *mighty* beehive and glimpse the hero of the day—*Ethan*. In fact, for the whole trip, he entirely forgot about Kristian's drake and even about his own birthday, although he just now remembered.

*This is by far the best birthday, ever!* he thought cheerily. *Even though everyone has forgotten about it.* But he was too proud to mention this to Grandpa. He had already planned how he would harvest *his* honey and possibly sell it at the local village market, or even make himself honey cakes, which Grandpa would make for the children on special occasions. Ethan licked his lips in anticipation as he imagined the honey baked right into the biscuits.

As if on cue, Grandpa abruptly stopped, his silvery hair rustling, and his robe billowing in a faint breeze.

The boy stopped midstride at the unexpected halt, swallowing a tangy piece of dust in the process as he opened his mouth to speak. He set down the cart, coughed, and tried to spit out the dust before wiping his mouth on the sleeve of his shirt. As he surveyed the landscape, his attention was drawn to the rocky formation upon which they now stood. Around them spread out a series of jagged outcroppings that descended into a brief valley before immediately rising again, some two hundred paces directly in front of them. The ridge ran lengthwise to Ethan's left for a few hundred paces before the elevation gradually climbed to meet the plateau that circled back around the valley to where they stood. The small valley contained a series of short sand dunes that stretched throughout the interior, with flowering sages sprinkled about on the fringes, braced directly against the rocky bluffs. Ethan squinted to see the other side, which looked to be similar to their position.

"This is the place," Grandpa exclaimed.

"How can you tell?" Ethan asked, half-expecting the answer.

"It has the smell of honey *and* bees," came the expected reply.

Ethan smiled in spite of himself. He grabbed a flask of water, popped the cap, and took a quick swig before offering it to Grandpa.

Grandpa shrugged it away. "There," he directed, "I believe we need to set up there." He pointed to his right at a corner in the valley wedged between the bottom of two cliffs that marked the valley's start. A long shadow was already cast across the area, which meant some relief from the blistering sun.

Ethan watched Grandpa as he slowly turned, inhaling the scent of honey and bees that Ethan still could not smell, even though he tried to imitate his mentor and suck in the hot air through his own nostrils. He almost sneezed when he breathed in too much air.

"*And* I will need to go there." The old man now pointed at the top of the other end of the valley.

"What's over there that—"

"Yes, I think," Grandpa answered himself, putting his hand into his robe's pocket and drawing out a piece of wood, "that will do nicely."

"For more hives?" said Ethan, now realizing what Grandpa was talking about. "More wood for more hives?"

"Yes," said Grandpa in a distracted tone. "I see a number of tree stumps that will be perfect for the next set of hives I'm working on."

Ethan cupped his hand over his brow and squinted hard to see the trees, but saw nothing and shrugged. "But what about hunting for the queen?" he objected as it dawned on him that he might have to do it alone.

"Oh, you can manage quite well on your own, Ethan," Grandpa answered as he reached around and patted the boy on the back. "We will set up day camp first," he continued, "then we'll both be off to our own duties. We'll need to meet back at the camp two handwidths before sundown so that we make it back to the village in time, *and* you must stay in sight of the camp at all times," Grandpa said resolutely. "Understood?" he added to lock in the agreement.

The hesitant student nodded. He knew full well what Grandpa meant about sundown. The nighttime was no place for anyone outside of the village. Although the landscape looked entirely deserted in the heat of the day, it would be crawling with creatures at night. The last thing anyone wanted to do is to get caught out at night with hungry wolf packs, or worse, sand worms and the fabled lions.

Grandpa motioned for the two of them to pull the cart to the day camp previously selected on the valley floor. Together, they then set up a makeshift canopy to rest under, unloaded the hive from the cart, and dismantled it so that the brood chamber and super stayed intact. Ethan then tied a rope to one corner of the boxes and attached a board to the bottom so that he could pull it along easier through the sand while watching for bees—this made it much more efficient to capture the queen and draw out her colony.

It was near noon before all of the camp preparations were complete—that left half the day for exploration before meeting back at camp.

Grandpa took the unloaded cart and set off in the direction of the focaccia trees, and Ethan began somberly looking about for bees, keeping close to the flowering sage bushes as that was the best place to find the buzzing insects during the day.

This valley was the perfect place for bees, Ethan quickly realized. *And at the right season.* He wasn't sure why Grandpa hadn't set up a hive or two out here before, except for marauding honey thieves, of course. Bees could always be found around flowering plants, and most of the village's honey either came directly from flowering sages or from the precious crop that was farmed directly within the village walls and fed by crude irrigation ditches, dug solely for that purpose.

Ethan jumped as he heard the first buzz. He looked wildly about, finally targeting the source, and observed the bee as it landed on an adjacent sage bush. He moved closer and watched as the bee raided the flowers on a sage for its precious pollen. He stalked the bee at a safe distance from bush to bush, careful not to distract it—not that it mattered as bees are generally very intent on their crop collection. The bee suddenly changed direction and flew into the dunes instead of to another bush.

Surprised at the his prey's sudden departure, Ethan threw caution to the wind and bounded after the small escapee, but lost it over the first dune.

He kicked at the sand and turned to head back to the bushes to find another bee, but paused at another buzzing sound, this buzz had a lower pitch. He was getting much better at telling the difference between types of bees by their buzzing sounds. It was something Grandpa made him practice over and over again, and that most beekeepers would have never thought to practice at all anyway. This particular buzz sounded like a larger insect; not just any bee, but a queen bee! He turned just in time to glimpse her fly past him and into the dunes, not seven paces away.

"That's perfect!"

Ethan hunted the bee with his eyes. His original plan had been to follow bees to their colony, dig into the hive and feed them smoke—again, so as not to harm any of the bees as Grandpa always strictly ordered—and retrieve the queen. He never intended on finding a queen in midflight—that was unheard-of!

The boy found himself sprinting after the queen with the hive boxes banging around behind him as he traversed the dunes. He rounded one sand mound, then the second, and on the third, followed the queen into a small sand alcove nestled between two steep mounds of sand not two paces wide.

He stopped and bent over on his hands on his knees, winded from his quick sprint. He glanced around to check his beehive. Once convinced the supers were all in order, he turned his attention to the alcove in front of him.

At the end of the small recess, it emptied into what appeared to be a small sand hole, just large enough for Ethan to squeeze into, if he were to crawl in on his arms and legs. He paused to catch a glimpse of her and saw the queen dart out of the hole, followed by another bee, then both disappeared back into its shady recess.

He had found it! *Finally*, he cheered, *Ground bees usually produce the richest honey too. However . . .* , he counseled himself, he had to be careful this time. If he alarmed the colony, they might swarm and he would lose the queen in the mêlée for sure, and he was also in no hurry to get stung again. However, given that she was flying, she might be starting a new colony, and he would have to be completely focused in order to get her into the box. He quickly pulled his veil over his face and shoulders, attaching it to his shoulder clips, drew the gloves from his back sack, and synched them tight onto his arms.

He then crouched low, peering into the hole a second time. It was hard to see past the first few feet, and he had to unhinge his veil to get a better look. He retrieved the brood frame, forgetting entirely about his smoker in his excitement, and slowly crawled into the hole while inching the frame along the ground directly in front of him. He could still hear the bees buzzing a few paces into the small cave—so far so good.

He mentally rehearsed what Grandpa had taught him. If he could sweep the queen into the frame, slap the thin lid shut, then quickly retreat out of the hole and place her into the semihive, the remaining bees would follow her scent into the hive.

Ethan was aroused out of his self-induced trance when a bee flew directly into his face. He had forgotten to reclip his veil!

He threw his body to the side and into the wall, wildly flapping at the bee, while trying to reattach the mask. The bee was also busy, now far beyond cranky and trying to sting him on the nose. In his hysteria to rid his face of the bee, Ethan disregarded the great cracking that was sounding along the length of the tunnel followed by a low rumble; suddenly, sand and rocks collapsed in on top of him, pinning him flat to the ground.

After a few moments, the last wave of dust settled in a fine mist on top of Ethan's back, his hands now splayed out in front of him, and both his legs and arms pinned such that he couldn't grip the walls to push himself backward and out of the small tunnel. He was hopelessly trapped.

Ethan shifted his weight, trying to free his hands enough to pick through the debris, and all at once there was a horrible sensation that he was being force-fed gritty dirt as the sand flowed unhindered over his face and into his mouth and nostrils. He gasped for air, any air, but got more sand in return. He began coughing violently, uncontrollably, releasing what precious little air was left in his lungs. Every part of his face was now bulging, his head almost ready to burst.

He was suffocating, his mind screamed, which gave him renewed determination; and in a last ditch attempt to free himself of his unlikely grave, he wildly kicked, pounded, and wiggled to dislodge the would-be death trap.

Just when he was ready to consign himself to a tortured demise, the ground rumbled all around him again and suddenly gave way to emptiness beneath. He fell for some distance before abruptly thudding onto hard ground, knocking the little wind left out of him and ejecting some sand as well. Chunks of hard sand, falling with him, hammered him on the back. He rolled onto his side, coughing the sand out of his lungs and taking in great gulps of air—*musty, damp air.*

Peering upward, Ethan wiped sand and tears from his eyes. He could see the sun peering through the hole that he had just dropped through, about a half of a stone's throw above him. The cave-in must have knocked the canopy free in the tumble, he thought.

Except for the sunlight bathing the area in a shower of light immediately around him, all beyond the light was blackness, with glimpses of faint shadows forming a few paces off as his eyes grew accustomed to the darkness. With his concentration now more focused on his predicament, Ethan thought he heard a slow dripping directly in front of him and a distant roar of what had to be *a river of water?* Grandpa had once mentioned that rivers of water sometimes formed after the monsoons, and they could last for an entire month underground.

His musing was interrupted midstream as he spotted the brood frame, now totally demolished on the cave floor in front of him. *Grandpa is going to kill me.* Ethan sighed with resignation. He then remembered it was his box, which demoralized him even more so. He pushed himself into a half-standing position and reached out for the broken mess. It wasn't a complete loss, but he and Grandpa's excursion was now over. "That is, if I ever get out of this place," he muttered softly to himself.

The boy looked back up at the hole in the ceiling above him. There was no way he could jump to it, he thought. He searched around for a rock, a stick, some debris, anything that he might use to climb back out. But there was none. He appeared to be in the middle of an immense cavern with no way out, at least from what he could make out of his immediate surroundings anyway. Staring back into the cave, he slowly rotated his body to get a better sense of where he was or to find some way to get out. The shadows were now more lucid, and he could make out faint outlines of the walls all around him, but still saw nothing he could use to hoist himself back out of the hole that his fall had created. His mind raced to come up with a solution, but he couldn't think of anything offhand.

New tears started to well up in his eyes as he brusquely brushed them away with the sleeve of his arm in an attempt to be strong. But it was no use, he would have to find another way out, and night would come soon. At this notion, his sadness quickly turned to a sharp fright, digging into his mind that compelled his body to tingle and shudder all over.

He was *all* alone, and it was very unlikely that Grandpa would find him in time, no matter how hard the old man looked. The valley was simply too large, unless Grandpa could follow the boy's footsteps, which now Ethan desperately hoped would not wash out with the wind.

"Grandpa, heelloooo, Grandpa!" Ethan shouted as loud as he could, in hopes that he would be heard. But after a few moments of continued yelling, he realized this was a pointless exercise until Grandpa had returned to camp. Ethan resigned himself to the wait.

*Well, in the meantime,* he thought. *It wouldn't hurt to have a look around.* The explorer in him kicked into a high gear, and he temporarily forgot about his situation, instead focusing on the mystery that surrounded him. *Besides, I could always use the light as a map to retrace my steps.* If he carefully chose his steps.

He half-stumbled forward to the wall that appeared to be closest to him, but out of the direct light. His arms were outstretched to catch himself as he walked through the shadows, in case he tripped; fell over; or walked headlong into the wall. It took him a few paces to reach the wall of the cave, and he began to grope his way around the chamber in the direction of the rushing sound. Surprisingly, the wall was smooth and clammy to the touch, not at all what he expected. But he realized that he honestly didn't really know what to expect in this foreign place.

Suddenly, he walked into a soft trickle of water that splattered on his forehead. Ethan jumped backwards almost toppling over in the process. He threw his hands out to catch his balance, then wiped at the dampness with his fingers and licked them. The water was cold and tasted salty on his skin. Ethan had the sudden urge for a long drink of fresh water and he imagined the taste as he licked his lips.

The light cascaded down behind him causing a dark barrier in front of him that he couldn't see past. Ethan cautiously swung his right foot forward, using his toes to feel the ground directly in front of him, as if dipping a foot into a pool of water to measure the temperature. Feeling nothing but hard ground, he continued to carefully inch his way forward. After a few such attempts, he gave up on the water idea and continued along the wall at his usual pace.

The cave was deceptively smaller than he first pictured, the darkness masking its true size, probably twelve paces from one end to the other. As he reached the far end, the wall abruptly ended in a small fissure that appeared as though the edge of the cave were cleaved into two pieces. Ethan twisted his body and head to look into the fissure. To his sheer delight, he saw a faint light in the distance and immediately felt a weak, misty breeze float gently past him as he peered in, followed by the now-obvious sound of rushing water he'd heard before.

The opening was amply wide for him to walk through, and again, the corners were smooth, as if the small corridor had been totally submerged by rushing water many times before. His heart raced; he had perhaps found a way out of this dungeon, and without another thought, he slipped into the opening, using the walls as his guide as he slowly made his way forward.

He walked through the damp tunnel for what seemed an eternity. The light grew ever brighter, and he now noticed that the fissure began to slightly widen and slope uphill. He instinctively hugged the wall on his left, more for comfort and support than anything else as he continued onward. After some distance farther, the fissure disappeared all at once, and Ethan now found himself in a much larger cavern than the first one, and this one, quite a bit lighter.

The scene before him was spectacular. A few paces in front of where he stood, a torrent of water surged past him before emptying into a solid pool that stretched out to the side opposite where he stood, some unknown distance into the darkness. Ethan ran to the water and falling on his knees he used his hands to gulp down the cool water. It was

The Drake Epics - Journey to Qara

refreshing—the best water he had ever tasted! After he had his fill, he turned his head to follow the water upstream and found another dark cavity out of which the frothing water entered the cavern.

*So Grandpa was right*, Ethan thought, although he wasn't surprised. Grandpa knew a lot of things. He couldn't see much beyond the small lake, as it was immersed in complete blackness. But the source of the light was immediately to his left, and he could see the rays spilling over a rocky shelf, no more than a stone's throw high. He quickly looked for a way up and, surprisingly, easily scaled the smooth surface by navigating a series of smooth rocks that jutted out of the wall every few inches, as if they were made for that very purpose.

Ethan reached the landing and began to hoist himself up. A small sand hole another twelve paces in front of him flooded the entire landing in light. He scanned the ground in front of him before hauling himself the rest of the way up—the landing was roughly the same size as his bedroom back at the village. As he canvassed the rest of the its rocky floor, his interest about the light vanished altogether. Light was not the only thing this bluff had to offer.

To the right of Ethan, and set a number of paces in, lay a crude nest made of sage twigs and brush, lodging two eggs nestled gently within its embrace—not just any eggs, drake eggs! He swallowed hard and lost his grip in the excitement. His hand lurched out instinctively and felt for another handhold to keep him in place.

He would know drake eggs anywhere. He and Kristian snuck into the breeding grounds many times to catch a glimpse of the drakes and their eggs, just off the courtyard main entrance. The breeding grounds were never a bore, full of wonder and hopeful dreams that young boys craved. All the drake holders would drop off their drakes in the grounds, following the monsoon month when a small number of eggs were laid.

These eggs were roughly the size of his fist and they gleamed in the sunlight, although a bit more dirty than the ones in Julfa's hatching grounds. At that moment, one of the eggs began to shift back and forth, as if the egg realized that Ethan was there.

"Yes, yes, yes, this is totally happening!" he elatedly half-whispered. He momentarily composed himself enough to haul the rest of his body onto the landing, such that he lay directly on his stomach, letting his legs dangle off the side of the ledge. His breathing came in quick gasps in anticipation of what he had just found and he quickly forgot about the bees, the cave-in, and the river of water or even about escaping the cave.

"Wait until Kristian finds out," he crowed. "This is going to be the coolest thing ever. I went out to find bees and totally come back with a *drake!*" Ethan toothed a triumphant grin.

The egg was now rocking harder, and jagged lines abruptly raced across its otherwise-smooth surface. The small fissures formed a web all across the egg now, making it appear as though it had weathered a thousand years. Suddenly, a small hole emerged where a number of the fractures all converged.

Ethan held his breath and waited expectantly for what would come next. A little white-scaled paw, no larger than his index finger, pushed its way through the hole with three long fingers in the front and one opposing finger on the back.

"White?" Ethan exhaled in despair. He had never once heard of nor had he seen a white drake before; not in any of the stories Grandpa told; not at any of the bindings he had witnessed. His mind began to play tricks on him, posing questions if this were a drake at all—possibly a bird that he was not familiar with or perhaps the membrane had given the paw an unnatural iridescent color. All he knew for sure is that his heart began to sink along with all of his dreams.

Small cavities continued to pepper the shell, and the egg rattled in intense bursts as if it would shatter into a thousand shards at any moment. It promptly rolled over on its side, as the paw drew itself back into the casing. Suddenly, the top of the egg split into three pieces; and what appeared to be a small head plunged through the inner membrane, stretching the slimy mucus until it finally tore and receded back into the egg.

The small white head peered around, brandishing two gleaming blue eyes that blinked in the light. As the rest of the eggshell gave way, the creature started to bite and chew on the egg.

It was a drake, a *white* drake! Ethan lay there, stock-still, as the little drake finished its hatching process. After the head, came the drake's paws and willowy arms with a thin membrane posing as wings, followed by its bony miniature legs and at last its round little body.

As Ethan had witnessed so many times before, the little drake quickly extracted itself from the egg. The little creature crowed softly and began to devour its egg shell, until completely gone, then licked away the sticky membrane that was still clinging to its body. It was an identical miniature of Kristian's drake in every detail, but only one-thirds the size of the other red drake, and its scales gleamed a bright white in the light cascading into the cave.

Ethan regained his senses and realized this might be the chance he had dreamed about. He slowly inched his way forward, careful not to frighten the little creature but to get close enough for the Drake to notice him, as he'd seen other boys do at the ritual bindings, and hopefully accept him as a holder.

*It's so small,* he mused. A thousand thoughts engulfed his mind all at once, and he suddenly remembered the councilman's declaration that boys under sixteen simply could not bind to drakes and that the drake probably wouldn't choose him anyway. Ethan quickly thrust the thought from his mind as unwelcome and devoted his energy to focus on his tiny companion.

The drake gulped down the last piece of egg stuck to the end of its tail, paused, and turned to peer up at Ethan with interest. Its head cocked to one side, and a clear membrane closed over its pale blue eyes as it blinked while considering the cautiously advancing boy.

Ethan immediately froze so as not to alarm the little animal. He beamed a warm smile at the Drake. *This,* he thought, *this is it!* Both boy and drake regarded each other for a moment. Ethan thought about Kristian, who had recounted to Ethan the feeling that went through his mind when his drake had bound to him. *It was as if I suddenly had another presence, a presence inside of me. I know it sounds weird, but it was as if I had been missing something all my life, and now I had found it.* Ethan didn't know if the same would happen to him as it had for Kristian, but the underaged boy desperately hoped this drake would accept him too.

The drake tilted its head in the other direction before unceremoniously turning away from Ethan and stumbling in the direction of the other egg in the nest.

The boy felt a sudden pang of despair slam into him, giving him the sensation of utter loss. He thought he saw stars, as if someone had delivered a blow to his head. This hurt much worse than his now-forgotten bee stings or even from when he had fallen into the grotto.

*It's not going to happen, it's not going to happen . . .* A cavernous pain began to well up inside of him as tears again formed in his eyes. *Please, please, please, let it happen!* he suddenly pleaded.

Ethan recalled the countless other boys back in the hatching grounds as they lined up, single file, for the drakes to inspect them. The examination either ended with a squawk of acceptance from the drake, always a squawk, or the silence of rejection. He envisaged the boys' faces who weren't selected—the look of disappointment, tears, and dejection in their eyes after missing out on the bindings. Most of the time, they at least had a parent with them to console and calm them down, but Ethan knew that would never be enough for the boys to fill the emptiness; and it certainly wouldn't be enough for him either as he watched this little ghostly creature.

The little white drake reached the other egg and gingerly sniffed at the shell. It squawked at the other egg and nuzzled the shell a few times, slowly pacing around it and repeating the process. After some time, the small drake came about to face Ethan again, who was now sagging his head, concentrating on his own grief.

Suddenly, the boy felt a gentle tingling in his chest that quickly grew into a deep warmth that spread outward into his arms, legs, and lastly throughout his entire body. The sensation filled his mind with a peace he had never known before. He felt no sorrow, and the tears on his cheeks seemed foreign to him. Why had he been so sad and felt so alone? He slowly lifted his head to find the little white drake before him again, now opposite the boy, snout to nose.

The drake squawked at the boy.

*Did it*, Ethan started to ask himself, *did it happen?*

*Yes.* The confirmation came into his mind, not so much in word, but as a feeling of approval.

Ethan knew the drake had impressed this thought upon him. Somehow he knew. How did he know? The boy raised a brow in wonder, but everything seemed so crystal clear now, and a perfect calm enveloped him. More surprisingly, he somehow knew intimate details about the drake, details that were impossible for him to know about in the few short moments of their meeting, things like the drake's gender: male.

*Obviously*, the drake thought.

Personality: strong-willed and fiercely protective, excitable, sense of humor that would likely lead to mischief and a tendency to get others into mischief.

*Naturally*, came the reply.

*Oh, I don't need any help there*, Ethan interrupted his thoughts, or were they really his own thoughts in the first place? He was having a hard time telling the difference at this point. He continued on: a soft spot for his sister. *Hold on, what sister?*

*The egg that hasn't hatched yet*, came the response, again touching his mind in the form of a feeling.

Ethan now considered the egg, still unhatched, lying safely within the nest; but he felt a little alarmed she was still dormant. All the eggs in the village hatched together, why not this one?

*What is going on?* Ethan again interrupted himself. He was still having a hard time adjusting to these new thoughts that were suddenly crowding his mind. They felt jumbled, mingling with a new alter ego within him, as if he suddenly had several personalities and was going mad. *Yes! Mad,* like the beggars that sat outside of the courtyard gate, merrily talking to themselves all day long.

Ethan met the white drake's gaze, and they both studied each other for a little while longer. He had a gush of questions that flooded his mind. How did he know so much about the drake? Was this drake telepathic or even a magical drake? If so, how could a boy of his age have possibly bound to it?

*Err, him!* he found himself automatically correcting the stray thought.

The tangle of questions continued. Could the drake really hear him? Was he going mad? Where was the drakes' mother or father? What should he do with the other egg?

*Bring the egg with us of course,* came the reply, always as a feeling, but now ringing rather obvious in Ethan's mind. *That's what your back sack is for,* and *we'll have loads of time to talk about all of these questions—that is, after I get my name,* the thought announced very matter-of-factly.

*Name? What name?* Ethan countered as he squinted at the little drake. *Oh,* your *name!* Ethan now realized. *Your name, of course, of course.*

The little drake beamed up at him with an approving look. *But it would probably help you to think better if you were sitting up. Don't want you to hurt yourself by thinking too much.*

*Cheeky,* thought Ethan as the little drake remained fixated on the boy. He pushed himself into a seated position, and his little white companion promptly leapt into his lap, waiting expectantly for a worthy title.

*Hmmm.* Ethan looked at the ceiling, as if entirely absorbed in some detail etched in the gloom. He stroked the little drake's body as he thought about the name, as if that were the most natural thing in the world for him to do. A flood of names rushed by. *The problem is* he thought, most of them were the same names he had proposed to Kristian just the day before. *RedHot, er, WhiteHot? FireDemon, no, wait, PaleDemon? BeeSting?*

The drake began impatiently beating his tail against Ethan's thigh.

*Sure, you could do better?* Ethan complained.

*Not my job,* came the tart reply to which Ethan shook his head and grinned. This little drake had attitude.

The names really weren't all that good. Come to think of it, what had he been thinking when he proposed them to Kristian anyway. *Well, it's taken Kristian a month—err, Kristian is my brother and . . .* He found himself making excuses for his older brother.

*I know who he is,* came the quick reply. *I know, it's taken him a month to come up with a name, and still nothing—poor drake,* pronounced the feeling in mock pity. The little companion astonished Ethan with how much he knew about Kristian already, but Ethan was getting more used to his modestly crowded mind every moment that now passed.

*Well, it has taken him a month.* Ethan shot back under his breath, as if mumbling in response to his grandfather after being asked to do a chore. There was no response. Then it dawned on him, the perfect name.

*Seon.* He beamed in triumph. *Seon is your name! You are my little white bee!*

There was a long pause, then the drake looked up in agreement and nimbly leapt to Ethan's shoulder, which didn't seem to surprise him at all, as if that were the next logical thing Seon would do.

The little drake looked at the boy with wide eyes. *It's a good name, but why do you call me your little white bee?*

Ethan half-smiled as his mind strolled down memory lane. Yet, he wondered why the little drake didn't know this from the boy's memories. After a pause, he shrugged and proceeded with the story. *Well . . . Beekeeping is a long and honored tradition for our family. My Grandpa has kept bees for . . . well, for all of his life.* Ethan paused. *Grandpa's father before him kept bees, and his father before him. So, it has kind of been taught to us since before I can remember.* He paused to consider this, before continuing. *Well, there is a tale of the little white bee that Grandpa tells us. The little bee was a beekeeper's constant companion and lived in a wood box or hive— handmade by the beekeeper, like the one that got crushed when I fell into this place.* Ethan made a crushing motion with his fist into his palm.

*Grandpa is always saying that if a beekeeper regards his or her bees enough to house them properly, and in a worthy location, the bees would honor the beekeeper and make more honey.* "You have to treat all life with reverence, Ethan. It's not enough to simply love or fear all creatures . . . you have to take part in the nurturing and protection of all life!" the boy tried to imitate his grandfather's voice aloud, then smirked at his sudden outburst.

*Anyways, the little bee respected and loved the beekeeper because of his home. One day, the beekeeper was attacked by a family of bears who knew that the man kept bees and honey. It was the honey they were after.* He looked down at the drake curled up in his lap. *Well, the bee came up with an idea to spread pollen over the bear's eyes to blind them and without sight lead them away. He quickly gathered his brothers together and they blanketed the bears with the blinding potion. The little bee then convinced the bears that the scent of his pollen led to a treasure trove of honey. The bears groped along, following the scent of his pollen trail across a great body of water, not knowing where they went. Once on the other side, the bee returned to the beekeeper with great haste.*

*When the bears' sight returned, they were too afraid to cross the great waters and so, the beekeeper was safe.* He emphasized his last word.

*The beekeeper built a magnificent hive, even bigger and more magnificent than the last, to thank the little white bee and called him his champion because he was both fearless and used brilliant strategy in the face of danger. At least that is how the story goes. Oh, and the little bee's name was Seon.* Ethan added.

A brief silence followed as the little drake thought about the story. *It is a great name, and I accept it gladly!* he exclaimed as he jumped to his shoulder and nuzzled against Ethan's cheek.

*Well, we still need to find a way out of that hole,* Ethan interrupted their conversation to avoid blushing, now pointing beyond the nest. He instinctively rolled forward onto his knees and reached for the nest, his fingers tenderly closing around the egg and placing it safely in his back sack.

Seon intently supervised to make sure the egg was handled with appropriate care.

Once both were satisfied the egg was safe and after gently folding the flap over the egg, Ethan rose to his feet and made his way toward the light. He knelt beside the wall and fumbled around the hole, scratching at the sand with his fingers to try and dig it away, which now seemed to be made out of hard sand that had been packed in tight.

*It looks as though the hole is just my size—want me to check it out?* Seon asked.

Ethan nodded, grateful for his newfound companion's small size.

Seon alit off the boy's shoulder with ease, although he couldn't quite fly yet. Ethan knew this from watching Kristian's drake.

*I will with time,* the little drake thought rather crossly then apologized for being grumpy. He pulled his wings in, held tight to his body, sniffed at the hole, then plowed into the sand, which cast the entire cave into momentary darkness. The hole appeared to be just the drake's size after all.

After a few more moments, the light returned, and Ethan continued to dig without much luck before Seon returned. He blew on his fingers and rubbed them against his sides, as the sand dug into his skin.

*It's not sand all the way through—it's solid rock in the middle,* the drake reported. Seon registered some worry in his tone, but held something back.

*And?* Ethan asked. *What are you not telling me, Seon?* Frustration about being stuck in the cave rushed over him. Come to think of it, his stomach was now rumbling from hunger as well.

*It's getting dark.* came the reply.

The famine in Ethan's gut now turned into cold fear, and he all but forgot his appetite. All of his previous anxiety came rushing back on him. He had pushed this all aside since his discovery and subsequent initiation with Seon.

*We need to get you out of there and quickly.* The little drake said as he re-emerged from the hole.

"But there *is* *no* way out!" Ethan growled out loud. He abruptly thought about Grandpa, who was likely sick with worry at this point. With the frustration mounting within him, Ethan bellowed and slammed both of his fists into the wall.

*Umm, Ethan?* his companion intervened.

Ethan jerked open his eyes to tell Seon to be quiet so he could think. Instead, he saw sparks erupting from the rock and from his own fists. He tottered back on the heels of his feet, inspecting his hands in disbelief.

Seon, who was back on the boy's shoulder, looked up at Ethan with the same surprise, then cocked his head with exhilaration.

*Did you feel that? What a rush!* The little drake declared. *I could fill the surge of power in you, Ethan! I mean, I feel like there is a way out of here! It feels a little dangerous, but* you *are the way out!*

*All . . . all I felt was frustration and anger,* Ethan protested, shaking his head at what had just happened.

Seon wasn't paying attention, and his thoughts now came more haltingly. *We will have to . . . we both, we'll focus . . . very hard . . . but . . .* Another pause. *Yes, I feel it now.*

The little drake had Ethan's full attention. He seemed somehow different, a little whiter than Ethan had noticed before. However, Ethan innately gathered where Seon was going with this, and it hit him like a ton of bricks. For the first time since their brief meeting, he also felt it, no, *he knew* that he could use *magic! Kesem,* as the locals called it.

The boy focused inward on this feeling, not knowing why at first, trying to reach something within him that he could use to perhaps pound through the wall in front of him. *I'm ready!* Ethan announced after a few moments, sensing the natural point of his power. He stepped closer to the sandy wall and knelt, bracing his hands on either side of the hole. He hoped that this would work.

Seon paused to admire his determined companion. Ethan was picking up on their connection as quickly as he was.

Without another thought, both boy and Drake sensed what they had to do, although neither of them had the faintest idea of how to control the power now welling up within them.

Ethan counted down, then wildly exerted all of his strength. He threw back his head, eyes closed tight, and roared. He felt Seon doing the same. His mind swirled, and he could see stars, as if someone had just hit him over the head—the sensation continued to intensify as he felt pure energy gather in his chest.

Suddenly, a small pop sounded in Ethan's ears, and he opened his eyes. A blinding flash of blue light erupted between his hands to form a small sphere. Ethan concentrated on the sphere as it started to grow in size.

Seon added to the boy's own power, and the sphere's progress gained momentum. It now passed through the sand and rock, as if the wall in front of them were an apparition. Once the sphere reached the ground, white sparks began to crackle and sputter from its edges.

The sensation pricked at Ethan's brain, as if pins were being poked into every point in his head. Ethan involuntarily screamed with rage, his hands still fastened to the wall. The circle imploded, sucking in the rock as it shrunk and crushing it into smaller fragments. Then with a sudden draft of electrical current, the sphere ripped open the wall, leaving a jagged opening that revealed the desert valley just beyond and drove the condensed fragments of rock outward.

Ethan let out a laugh of satisfaction then slumped. He felt all of his energy draining at an alarming rate as the pain in his head continued to intensify. He had never experienced the total sense of power, and now the total loss of control or willpower in his life. He felt himself drifting into darkness—the shadows were overpowering. He struggled to stay awake, but it was too powerful and rushed over him in waves.

He felt as if he were going to wink out of existence, and at the moment, it didn't seem to matter if he did or didn't. A faint thought tickled at the back of his mind as it scratched at his consciousness. It was desperately trying to reach him, calling his name in a shrill tone full of worry and regret. Ethan realized it must be Seon and tried to reach out, but he lacked the willpower to do so. *Not again!* he said as he toppled to one side as his head hit the ground, then he fell into the blackness.

- - -

Darkened shadows swirled around Ethan, twisting and twirling in a dizzying tangle. He struggled to make out his surroundings, but found that he had lost control of his limbs. Suddenly, the darkness faded ever so slightly, and a sandy expanse opened up before him. The landscape, the sky, all shades around him were in black-and-white tones. He tried to rub his eyes or blink; but he was helpless, except that he was now

## Grandpas and Bees and Drakes, Oh My

involuntarily moving, eyes fixed on something directly in front of him. He fought against it, but even through his most strenuous exertions, his limbs ignored his command. Abandoning all attempts to take back control, he now focused on where he was going, trudging through the sand, although it seemed as if he were immensely tiny in this world of giant sand dunes.

*Am I dreaming?* the thought abruptly occurred to him.

The sand dunes gave way to a rock outcropping with enormous sages, and his cadence picked up speed. He could vaguely make out a figure in front of him, searching for something or someone. It was a man. As he neared the man, he realized it was a giant of a man, pacing back and forth with an immense handcart loaded down with equally large gear piled under a sheet of some kind. The man suddenly stopped pacing and turned to look directly at him.

Ethan's blood ran chill. The man was Grandpa! He felt a sudden impulse to call out to him. "It's me, Grandpa! I'm so happy I found you. I fell into a hole and worried I would never see you again, then I climbed to a ridge, I found Seon and punched through a wall, and here you are. Help me, Grandpa, help me. I don't know what is going on." Grandpa just stared at him in astonishment. No, his face reflected veneration and respect. This perplexed Ethan even more so.

Before he had a chance to act, he was again turning, turning away from Grandpa. Unwillingly, he began retracing his tracks back the way he had come. "No, don't leave him!" he bellowed. "grandpa, it's me. help me!" Ethan poured his soul into forcing himself to stop and turn back around. This seemed to do the trick, as he did stop, but his sight looked from side to side then back in front of him. Again, he started forward, pausing momentarily to look back at Grandpa, who was intently following behind him in a daze.

The boy snarled out of exasperation. Would nothing stop him! And why wasn't Grandpa answering him? But then, something remarkable occurred to him. The tracks he was following, supposedly *his* tracks he was following, didn't look at all like his footprints. They were smaller, like the size of a tiny rodent. He abruptly stopped again and instantly felt another consciousness interrupt him. The feeling was clear, it felt hurt and made Ethan suffer shame for accusing the footprints to be that of a rodent. But the awareness was gone as fast as it had come, and Ethan continued to follow those tracks around one sand dune after another; always turning back to see if Grandpa was following.

As he rounded another dune, Ethan realized he was quickly closing on a cliff wall, and that now appeared to feature a jagged hole that lay gaping at its base. An enormous explosion must have caused this scene, puncturing the cliff's face and scattering rock debris that now lay strewn all about the area. As he drew closer, he could see a figure lying on the ground directly within the wall with its back toward him. No, not a figure—a boy, a boy that looked just like him! For a moment, he felt intense and almost overwhelming sorrow and misery before the blackness shrouded around him again as he lost consciousness.

- - -

Ethan awoke. His head was pulsing with a throbbing headache. He was lying flat on his back and could make out a blurry light through his haze. He tried to concentrate and focus his eyes to clear the fogginess from his field of vision. After a few moments, he could faintly make out a light flickering off what appeared to be a smooth dark ceiling. Another wave of pain slammed into his head, and he lifted his hand to rub his forehead with a groan.

An abrupt thought interrupted his pain, *Ethan, are you, are you all right?* Seon appeared by his side, rubbing his snout tenderly against Ethan's cheek.

Ethan feigned a quick smile. *Seon, yes, I'm fine,* he thought back, welcoming the comforting peace of his little companion.

Seon cooed, which sounded a little like a cat purring, and curled up beside him, as if he knew that is what Ethan wanted most.

The boy turned his head toward the source of the light and discovered a small fire burning a few paces away from him. Beyond the fire, he could see the cart, which looked as though it was blocking a hole in a wall, and beyond the cart, darkness. He realized that he was *still* inside of the cave, it *was night* and he no longer had his back sack and the precious egg it contained, *and . . .*

*Calm down, or you are going to split your head completely open,* Seon interjected, emanating as much calm Ethan's way that the little drake could muster. *The back sack is over there, and my sister is perfectly safe.*

Ethan took the hint and subdued his fears, toning down his thoughts so as not to alarm himself, or the Drake, any further. He tilted his head to see the back sack, sitting a few paces off and secure as Seon had claimed.

He continued his train of thought. The cart was here, a fire was going, which meant Grandpa was *here!*

He swung his head around to catch a glimpse of the old man and instantly regretted the sudden movement as a wave of pain showered him in thousands of prickly stabs, followed by a dull throbbing sensation just behind his eyes.

Grandpas and Bees and Drakes, Oh My

*I told you to calm down, Ethan! He's over there.* Seon aimed him in the direction of the cart.

"Grandpa, are you there?" Ethan mouthed in a weak voice, much weaker than he had intended. "Grandpa?" he repeated.

"I'm here, my boy," came the reply as a silhouette appeared from behind the cart. As Grandpa reached the fire, Ethan could see the old man's face clearly, with a soft expression of love and concern apparent in the wrinkles around his eyes and mouth. Grandpa bypassed the fire and moved to the boy's side. He gingerly stepped over Seon, which the little drake appreciated, and bent over to tenderly rub his grandson's forehead.

"Grandpa?"

"Yes?"

"Are we safe, I mean, safe from the night animals?"

Seon raised his head in sudden interest.

Grandpa peered at the little drake and Ethan could see the curiosity in his face, then the look was gone and the old man casually reached for a flask of water resting near Ethan and looked lovingly at the boy. "Here, drink this. The water will help."

The boy sipped the lukewarm liquid. As it trickled down his throat, he realized just how thirsty he was. He tried to gulp it down more swiftly, but sputtered instead.

"Don't drink so fast, my son, there is plenty of water in this cave."

*He's right, you know,* Seon taunted.

Ethan ignored him and raised his hand to signal that he was through drinking for the moment.

Grandpa capped the water skin, then took up a seat next to the boy, glancing up at the cave opening every few moments.

"Grandpa?"

"Yes, Ethan?" he sounded as if he were contemplating some great mystery, but his voice was no less full of love.

"I'm . . . I'm sorry." Ethan felt a great guilt well up inside of him.

"For what?"

"For falling through the hole, for not getting out in time, for trapping us here at night . . ."

"Ethan," Grandpa interrupted, his voice full of warmth and reassurance, "there is no need to be sorry for what happened to you. You cannot control everything around you. It is the way you react to your circumstances that defines you." He paused for a moment, considering something else before continuing. "In fact, I believe that you've grown to be a man on this day—your birthday, I believe?" he said with a wry smile.

"You remembered!" the boy said gratefully with a hoarse whisper.

"You have experienced something special. Something I have never seen in my lifetime, Ethan."

The boy listened intently, so as not to interrupt.

"In fact, something that pales next to any present that I or anyone else could give to you. You have bound to a drake—not just with any drake, but with a white drake." The old man paused again. "A white emperor drake."

The boy wasn't sure he grasped the importance of what Grandpa was saying, although emperor drake sounded very cool.

"That is something to be proud of, my son. This drake," Grandpa paused to peer down at Seon again. "This drake would not have bound to just anyone. Do you see? This is why you must not sorrow, you are very special." Grandpa lovingly rubbed his grandson's head. "You and your brother and your sister—you are all special, and I love you all very, very much." Grandpa paused again as if he were going to add more, but thought better of it and turned back to the fire.

*Oh, I like him, I can see why you love him so much.*

Ethan blushed, but he knew the drake was right.

"I love you too, Grandpa."

"Now get some rest, I will stand watch. In the morning, we will be off, when you feel up to it, that is."

Ethan nodded. *Goodnight, Seon,* he thought sleepily.

*Good night, Ethan,* Seon answered. *By the way, you aren't going mad.* he added, *But next time you feel the urge to call me a rodent, you better think twice.* The little drake croaked, sounding very much like a little chuckle.

Ethan smiled, closed his eyes, and drifted off into a deep sleep.

# Chapter 8

## Ordinary Arrival

*A tranquil conscience invites freedom from anguish, sorrow, guilt, shame, and self-condemnation.*
—Richard G. Scott

Morning arrived earlier than Ethan had wanted it to. He still felt sore from the events of the previous day as he sat up and grimaced at the sharp twinge of pain that shot through his skull. He cradled his head to steady the pain. The action did little to stay the throbbing, but he felt a little better anyway. The boy considered the marvels of yesterday as he gently massaged his temples to avert another surge of dull throbbing building inside his brain.

Seon was sleeping peacefully, coiled around himself on the ground.

Ethan absentmindedly stroked at the little creature with the back of his fingers. He could feel the drake's presence and sensed his companion was dreaming of something happy, although he couldn't tell just what about at the moment.

The fire still crackled and burned, illuminating the landing. Just beyond, a soft purple light cast its pale tendrils across the cave's entrance as dawn quickly approached.

Grandpa was already quietly preparing breakfast and turned at the sudden rustle of Ethan's movement. He beamed a broad smile in the boy's direction. "Feeling a little better, I take it?" the old man crowed, then turned back to the fire. "You gave me quite a scare last night, Ethan!" he exclaimed over his shoulder.

The boy began to nod, but quickly thought better of it, not wanting to provoke his headache any more than he already had. Besides, he didn't feel like answering beyond his usual morning grunt. He gently stood and skillfully picked his way toward the old man, careful not to wake Seon. He was expert at this every morning with Lola and took great pride in his self-proclaimed stealth. He found a smooth spot on the log that posed as a sitting bench adjacent the fire and gingerly sat down. He placed an arm around the old man in a half hug.

Grandpa flashed him a welcoming smile and offered the boy a cup of hot water that had been sitting halfway in the fire. "Drink this, it will help the throbbing in your head."

Ethan removed his arm and accepted the cup. He blew on the water and sipped with his lips. His face wrinkled at the bitter drink's taste. He swirled the sour concoction around his tongue before forcing himself to swallow. The liquid oozed down his throat.

"Sage tea," Grandpa answered Ethan's sour look. "It's a bit more tart than you're used to, but I drink this all the time on my journeys."

Ethan raised an eyebrow, momentarily setting aside his revulsion of the herbal tea. "Tell me more about your adventures, Grandpa." He looked up with the best longing expression he could come up with.

The old man chuckled kindly, only as a grandfather can. His laughter always filled Ethan with such warmth. "You've heard most of them anyways, drink up," he dismissed. "It really will help clear your head." Grandpa paused and looked whimsically in the direction of the hole that Ethan had made the day earlier. "We have a long day ahead of us," he said in a soft tone.

The comment almost escaped Ethan's attention, but he was quick to jump on it. "Long day?" he asked in a confused tone. After all, they were only a half day away from the village, and it wouldn't take them long to clean up camp and set off.

Grandpa chuckled again, more to avoid answering the question rather than anything else. "I gathered a little more wood than I had intended."

Ethan figured this was as good of explanation as any. So he set aside the thought and drained the unpleasant contents of the cup that was now cool enough to take bigger swigs from. True to Grandpa's promise, the tea did ease the pounding in his head, almost instantaneously.

"Grandpa?" the boy ventured with a newfound resolve. "What do you know of drakes?" Then he paused. "I mean, really know about them?" he stressed.

Grandpa turned himself around and studied Seon, sleeping peacefully where Ethan had left him, before looking back to Ethan. "Drakes are special, Ethan. They are great companions and good friends," he began. "Although, as you've seen with Kristian's little pet, most drakes can't really think and simply obey the rote commands they are given. Still there is an amazing quality about them indeed." The old man paused, choosing his words more carefully now. "You have a special drake, Ethan, as I said last night. I'm not sure how special yet and I aim to find out." He again turned to look at Seon.

"But I sense you already know that, don't you?" Grandpa studied Ethan's face for acknowledgment before prodding the boy further, "And that you can talk with it—"

"Him! It's a him," Ethan blurted out before he could catch himself. He blushed at interrupting the older man.

Grandpa hesitated, still regarding the boy, but wore a smile that spread across his face. "Him it is!" he corrected. "You can talk with him." The old man picked up a stick and casually poked at the fire. "And that hole in the cave is new to this valley." He nodded at the crevice.

Ethan knew that Grandpa had already made the connection. But he himself couldn't completely recall how he had created that hole before passing out. He briefly considered if he should tell Grandpa the whole truth. The old man was always expert at drawing information out of him anyway, in fact, whenever he and Kristian got themselves into trouble from their frequent brotherly escapades. But this time was different. At least the boy felt differently. He felt, well, it felt extremely personal, as if by sharing this he would defile his experience. Besides, he rationalized, his relationship with Seon should not be broadcast, but kept to himself for the time being.

"It's no natural hole," Grandpa continued at the boy's blank stare. "It was made with magic," the old man announced, "Your magic." He was really pushing the boy now. The wise man studied the young boy for any response, as if he could sense Ethan's most intimate thoughts and was trying to surgically draw the truth out of him. "Your combined magic, perhaps?"

Ethan stared blankly at his hands and kept quiet. But his mind was abuzz, and he yearned for Seon to be awake so that he had someone to consult with. This last round of questioning, in particular, worried Ethan how his grandpa could have deduced all this without a single word to the wiser. He'd heard Grandpa lecture on drakes before, whenever the boys came rushing in from the drake breeding grounds or when Kristian received his first drake. However, he didn't realize the extent of the old man's knowledge until just now. Besides, how could he know so much of what had happened?

"Ethan." The old man nudged as he rested a hand on the boy's shoulder and lifted Ethan's chin with the other to meet his gaze. "You must keep this knowledge to yourself," Grandpa lectured. "Until I tell you it is safe, you are not to share this information with anyone, and you must keep your drake out of sight." He smiled at the boy, his eyes reflected a mixture worry and love.

The questions boiled over in Ethan's mind, and he felt he couldn't hold them back. But he also couldn't ask anyone else. *Why is it not safe?* he thought. *I want to know more about Seon, my white emperor drake! Besides, how does Grandpa know about the magic Seon and I used? How does he know we can event talk?*

*All good questions, Ethan.* Seon yawned. *I think he's just trying to tell us to be careful until we know it's safe. I wouldn't overthink this, it's your grandpa."*

Ethan felt better at his companion's reassurance. But only a little. *And where were you just now? I could have used your counsel!* he jeered.

*Me? I am sleeping!* the little drake concluded, and his thoughts went dark again as the little drake fell back asleep.

"You must trust me for now, Ethan," Grandpa was saying.

Ethan couldn't tell if he had just missed part of the conversation and listened more intently.

"I know it is hard to understand, but there are dangerous forces at work here that you will learn of in time." The old man sighed and released Ethan and sorrowfully stared at the fire. "I don't have all of the answers, and I'm not qualified enough on elemental or telepathic drakes, to give you enough of the answers that you will need."

Ethan marveled at this revelation. "Grandpa doesn't know the answers?" he accidentally said aloud in disbelief, before slapping a hand over his mouth in instant regret.

Grandpa chuckled, taking the edge off the rather-serious conversation. "I'm sure you'll get over it. Now, eat this." He handed Ethan a piece of dry bread with honey spread and motioned for him to eat. The boy promptly began to hungrily devour the meal.

"You must trust me," Grandpa said again in a lighter tone. "I will tell you when you're ready, but now we need to get back to your brother and sister."

Ethan knew all too well this meant the discussion was now at an end. But the unanswered questions still burned in his mind.

—  —  —

Ethan roused Seon, who was not happy about the lack of sleep. The boy and his grandpa quickly packed up the remaining gear, put out the fire, and started back. The sun had peaked over the distant mountains and spread a warm light on the sandy countryside in front of them. The sand dunes cast their shadows in a swirl of shades of brown, painting the whole scene in a rather surreal picture.

But the trip back to the village was even less eventful than the trip to the valley on the previous day, and Grandpa was more quiet than usual. Ethan hardly noticed, using the time to recount his and Grandpa's morning discussion to Seon. Seon perched nimbly on his shoulder as Ethan pulled the cart.

*He seems to be very wise,* Seon realized. *I feel like we should listen to him,* the drake counseled.

*I guess so.* Ethan shrugged. *But,* he added, *I will have to tell Kristian too, we never keep secrets.* Now feeling a little guilty that he should have told Grandpa more. *Lola is a different story though,* he said in an attempt to deflect the guilt. *She can't keep any secrets, and her mouth is always running.* He sniggered.

The rest of the journey was a blur. Ethan and Seon continued their conversations, each learning more about the other with every passing moment, although it felt rather like they were old friends to begin with and they were simply getting reacquainted rather than launching a new, blossoming friendship.

They reached the village by midmorning and stopped a few hundred paces outside of the main gate.

Grandpa turned to Ethan. "The drake, err, Seon," he corrected, "needs to be kept out of sight, even from Kristian!"

"But . . ." Ethan's thoughts of confining his little friend somewhere so small didn't appeal to him nor to his companion much. He knew that Seon shared these feelings of disdain. Besides, he couldn't keep this secret from his older brother.

"I know," Grandpa said with a look of pity. "But we can't risk him being seen by anyone beyond this point. Even by Kristian." The old man stared them both down with a stern reprisal.

Both Ethan and Seon sheepishly nodded their heads. Ethan opened the flap to his back sack, and Seon reluctantly crawled down inside his miniature prison as Ethan closed the bag, careful to give Seon enough room to get fresh air and take in some of the sights.

"Comfortable?" Ethan asked awkwardly.

*As comfortable as I can get,* came the annoyed answer, and Ethan again felt very strongly that Seon was not at all happy about riding in a stinky leather pouch.

Grandpa nodded in satisfaction, and they started again toward their village home.

"It really doesn't make sense to call our home a village," Ethan contemplated as he held back just out of earshot of the old man. "It looks more like a great city with some of it in that gigantic half cave rising above the ground. Do you see it?" he said under his breath.

*It is amazing. I did not believe you until seeing it for myself!* the drake marveled.

"See how most of the homes are built directly into the cave?" he continued with the wave of his head. The cliff exposed thousands of small holes that represented windows and doors and outlines of buildings that stacked on top of one another.

"It totals twenty levels in all. That and the network of ladders." He pointed out. The ladders climbed and weaved their way up its face, twisting upward by the homes all extending from the wall's surface.

Seon sandwiched his head in between the bag and the flap to get a better look and cooed at the sight.

They soon approached a set of towering wooden doors, which had just opened to admit visitors in the early morning. "They are always closed in the evening to keep animals and intruders out." the boy clarified.

Ethan lapsed into momentarily silence as they passed through.

Two guards, who were armed to the teeth with giant spears and swords strapped at their thighs, stood at attention on either side of the door. They monitored admittance, although not many visitors came and

## Ordinary Arrival

went from within the village proper today. The guards both nodded to Ethan and Grandpa as they entered the massive walls on either side of them, rising twelve lengths or so into the air and encircling the village's irrigated farmlands.

*Amazing!* Seon cooed again.

The grand Sheikh's courtyard came into view surprisingly fast as Ethan continued his tour of Julfa for Seon. The courtyard was set at the base of the cliff and in the center of the village that sprawled out in both directions, giving it a half-moon appearance if you were to stand directly on top of the cliff and look down. Its door stood lazily open with the same guard standing at attention and at the same time trying to wave away a fly that was busily buzzing about his face. He paused and nodded to both of them before returning to his task of frantically waving at the little pest.

"I need you to unpack the cart, remove Seon to your bedroom, or at least keep him out of sight while I go to visit with Limnah."

"Limnah?" Ethan asked. "Why do you need to see him, Grandpa?" The old man did not visit the wise village elder very often. *Why visit him now?* But he thought better of asking more questions aloud, owing to the serious expression on his grandfather's face. "I will. I will," he grumbled, acknowledging what he had been told.

Grandpa nodded with a satisfied look and then continued, "After you've finished unloading, you will need to attend to your daily duties and make your rounds to the rest of the hives, and don't forget to take your gear along with you," he lectured. "Kristian will still be in school, but he will join you back in the courtyard to help bottle the honey as soon as school lets out at noon."

Ethan swallowed hard on his jealously of Kristian. *Kristian is sixteen,* he feigned in a whiney tone. *That means he gets to go off to classes for half the day and I'm stuck with all of the hard work!* he quietly explained to Seon. Since Kristian had started his formal education, Ethan did have more chores heaped on top of him, and although he wouldn't admit it, this meant less time to goof off.

*Sounds like you want to be in school too. Isn't that why you always pepper him with all of your questions when school lets out? You know that it really does bother him when you do that,* Seon explained.

*Hey, those were private thoughts,* Ethan balked. *See what you do, when I go digging around in your private thoughts, hmmph,* he thought sourly.

*Well, I just hatched yesterday. Go ahead, my life is an open book.*

Ethan wasn't amused.

Grandpa pulled Ethan out of his reverie. "After your chores, it would be best if you stay in the courtyard. I need to be able to find you quickly."

Ethan unenthusiastically nodded and set off with the cart to unload the gear. Upon arriving at their home, he was halfway through the door when Seon interrupted his task.

*The egg needs to be safe, probably better stash her in your room for safety,* the little drake suggested.

*Now?* the boy asked with a hint of annoyance in his voice. *You just want to get out of there, don't you?* Ethan nodded at his backsack. *Besides, how do you really know she's a her, I mean how do you know that the egg is your sister anyways?* He stopped midstride and peered down at his bag as if in deep thought.

*I just know, Can we move her now?*

Ethan nodded with a sudden realization that he had forgotten to tell his grandfather all about the second unhatched egg. He whirled around, but Grandpa had already left the courtyard. He sighed and walked to his room.

Once inside, he let Seon out to stretch and carefully placed the egg on his desk. He wrapped it in a blanket and piled some gear around it to hide it from view. Once satisfied, he then packed his bee gear into his back sack, working out a good position for Seon in one of the pouches before preparing to collect the drake and set off on his daily duties.

Seon cast a nervous glance in the direction of the other egg.

*She'll be fine, Seon. I promise.* Ethan ventured. *Besides, no one ever comes in here, except for Lola and she never goes to the desk.*

The little Drake looked up at the boy and then nodded and jumped into the backsack.

Harvesting honey was more enjoyable with Seon around, and time passed much more quickly than performing his chores alone. It reminded Ethan of days past when he had worked together with Kristian. *Before he started his precious schooling,* he thought in a rude tone. *We had a riot,* he told Seon, *although, more times than not, we'd find some way to get into trouble.* The boy maniacally smirked.

But with Seon, it was different and not at all in a bad way. They passed the time talking about everything they could think of, and it was great to have a second pair of eyes, although he got a little sick of Seon for being a nag about what he was doing wrong.

*You forgot to clip in your veil. Check if the smoker is still going. Remember to use your gloves at this hive,* and every other hive they stopped at.

*You're starting to sound like my brother!* he commented once. Ethan even let Seon out a few times to chase bees or taste the honey directly from the honeycombs. This helped remove his guilt about not offering the little drake breakfast that morning.

Before either of them knew it, they had loaded the last frame into the wagon and were now heading back to the courtyard towards what the boys had named *the bee pit* to make the final preparations of their day's harvest. As they crossed the threshold to the courtyard, Kristian came bounding toward them, his drake was clinging wildly to his tunic with his wings fully spread, in an attempt not to be swept off the jubilant older boy's shoulder.

*Easy, Seon,* Ethan soothed in a low voice as the little drake excitedly tensed at the sight of Kristian's companion. *Remember what Grandpa said.*

*Bah!* spat Seon in Ethan's mind, but kept still as Ethan had requested.

Kristian almost toppled Ethan over as he embraced him in a tight bear hug, barely missing squishing poor Seon in the fracas, to which Seon was not all that happy about.

"Grandpa told me all about it as I was leaving school" Kristian gasped as he released his younger brother.

"Why was Grandpa at your school?" the younger boy asked, before remembering the old man was visiting Limnah. This was followed by a wave of relief that washed over him. *Grandpa told Kristian about you, Seon, great!"* Ethan thought with relief.

*Ethan, wait a moment . . .*

"I know, isn't it great?" Ethan overrode Seon's warnings in his sheer excitement. He lowered his hand to his back sack, ready to pull the flap open and give Kristian a peek at the little drake.

"Great? Not great, you Dingus!" The word *Dingus* was Kristian's favorite taunt. "You almost kicked it, and for what? A queen bee?" The older boy shook his head in disapproval. "I'm just happy that you're alive, you've gotta be more careful when you're hunting for bees," Kristian scolded.

"Queen bee?" Ethan realized with a great pit in his stomach that his brother didn't know anything about Seon or of his incident with magic. He quickly removed his hand from the pouch and awkwardly placed it on his hip to recover from his question. "Yeah, well, it was my fault" Ethan sighed in despair, now trying to get off the subject, entirely.

Kristian's drake, who now looked to have caught his balance, stared intently at Ethan's pouch and appeared on the verge of pouncing on the back sack at any moment, threatening to uncover Seon's hiding place.

*His drake can talk!* Seon eagerly announced. *At least with me, although he's not advanced enough to talk with your brother, and your brother doesn't know how to connect with him either,* Seon's thoughts were erratic and jumbled as he elatedly rushed on. *Oh, I've told him to be patient upon our meeting. Oh, you need to make an excuse to let us talk, and don't worry, he couldn't tell your brother about me, even if he wanted to*, he added, sensing Ethan's rising alarm.

This last message put the boy a little more at ease, although he knew that he had to find a way to tell Kristian about Seon anyway. He simply had to wait for the right place and time to do it. The boys had never kept secrets from each other before, and he wasn't about to intentionally start doing so now.

"Well, c'mon, little brother, let's get our work done, and we can talk about what happened. I had to take care of Lola all night, and we were both super worried . . . she kept crawling into my bedroll." He slapped Ethan on the back in that older-brother's-sign-of-affection way.

Ethan winced; he never really appreciated those slaps very much in the first place.

As they started off, a dark form suddenly crossed their path, and Ethan felt a chill cold spread through his body. He quickly averted his eyes and hugged close to a nearby wall. It was the same man they had passed by yesterday, outside the village gate. Ethan had all but forgotten about their first meeting, but his blood now ran cold at the memory.

Kristian stopped and glanced back at Ethan with mock concern. "Wassup?" he asked. "C'mon Dingus!"

Ethan timidly motioned for Kristian to come back.

"Ethan, just come, what's the matter with you?" The older boy placed both hands on his hips in protest. However, when Ethan didn't budge, Kristian shrugged and walked back to him, walking with an annoyed gait.

"Kristian . . . who's that?" Ethan croaked then coughed into his hand and repeated the question in his usual voice. He pointed at the tall figure who was just entering one of the minor temples. Ethan couldn't recall offhand the name for the temple as it wasn't frequented by many in the village. *Temple . . . of the . . .* , he probed in his mind.

*Temple of the Dragon*, Seon spouted.

"Right!" Ethan said in a congratulatory tone.

Kristian gave him a peculiar look at the sudden outburst and looked in the direction of the temple.

"Oh . . . yeah, that's bad news," the older boy stated flatly. "He's auditing drake holders. But best if you and Lola keep your distance. I don't trust him, none of us do."

The older boy now turned to look at Ethan. "A bunch of us had to interview with him last night," he said with disgust. "In fact, he lined us all up as if we were prisoners, and we had to answer a few questions about where we got our drakes. He was checking off our names on some official drake list." Kristian paused to ponder why the man would do such a thing. "He's looking for something, something unusual, I guess . . . ," he concluded. "C'mon, Ethan, let's go, you don't need to worry about him anyways."

A quick jolt shot through Ethan at the mention of a drake audit. He paused. "I . . . I need to drop off my stuff first." He hedged. "But what if I drop your drake back at my room since I have to get my gloves anyways . . ." He momentarily hesitated, "And then I'll be in and we can talk?" The idea was a little shaky, Ethan reflected. But this way, both drakes would have a chance to talk.

Seon happily approved of Ethan's sudden stroke of genius.

Kristian smiled wryly at his younger brother. "You'll get your drake soon enough, little brother," he chirped, amused at Ethan's impulsive interest in his drake. "But OK, sounds all right. He could use a nap, anyways."

Ethan felt a sudden twinge of guilt for not telling Kristian about Seon, but quickly suppressed the feeling as he had no time to think about it. Not right now, at least.

Kristian squeezed his face together again in concentration and spoke a single command, "To Ethan!"

The younger but wiser boy knew his brother was trying to communicate with his drake and wondered why it came so easily to him when it was so hard for, well, for his *more experienced* older brother. He mused.

Kristian's drake cocked its head, looking first at Kristian then at the younger boy. Ethan could feel that Seon was linking with the red drake already. The little animal launched himself and landed precisely on Ethan's shoulder, using his wings as balance.

"Wow—I must be getting really good at that!" Kristian said in triumph. "Hurry up though," he chided. "I know you'll want to play with BeeSting, but we have work to do!" he taunted still maintaining his smile.

"You named him?" Ethan squawked with a half-nervous laugh. He now felt even more guilt, if that were possible. The moment was a bit awkward as Ethan thought of the previous day when he had offered up *BeeSting* as a name for Seon.

*Well, that's fortunate!* Seon cut in.

Ethan swore he could feel the little white drake giggle to himself.

"I'll be right back, quick, I promise," Ethan exclaimed as he trotted off in the direction of their room. As soon as the blanket dropped behind him, he opened his back sack and let both drakes down on his bedroll to socialize. "Seon, keep out of trouble and out of sight!" he stressed. "If anyone were to find you?" He stopped to contemplate various tortures.

*We'll be fine!* the white drake countered. Again, Ethan sensed a faint chuckle.

"Well, just the same, if anyone . . . and I mean anyone comes in, hide! They won't care if BeeSting is in here, but they'll care if they see you."

Seon shot him a bewildered look. *You were going back with Kristian, right?* he coaxed, then he turned to BeeSting, engrossing himself in some conversation that Ethan could only make out a few bits and pieces about.

Ethan hastily retrieved a pair of dirty cloth gloves that had been treated with wax and left the room, returning to the bee pit where Kristian was already hard at work, scraping the honeycombs free of honey and into a set of large ceramic jars.

"Well, I haven't seen you work like this in a while!" Some of Ethan's humor had returned to him.

"Ha-ha, very funny!" Kristian remarked in a sarcastic answer. "Hurry, let's get this done with so we can talk!"

That was exactly what Ethan didn't want to hear. He sluggishly made his way across the room to join his brother. If only he could draw this out, perhaps he could avoid the conversation altogether. He took his time and studied his surroundings as if they were new to him.

One wall was lined with every piece of beekeeper gear imaginable and many of Grandpa's inventions, including the items that ended up not being such great ideas. Ethan noticed one of Grandpa's early beehives that had seriously backfired on the old man. Grandpa had told the story of his worst honey harvest, resulting in more bee stings than he could count.

The other wall was lined with a set of washing tubs, used to harvest the honey, and a long row of large honey pots, prepped and ready to be served, if needed. This is where Ethan joined his brother.

"Hurry up, Ethan. Stop moping around," Kristian said with a mischievous grin, "and remember, that drake is mine." He placed additional emphasis on *mine*, as he quickly eyeballed his younger brother.

"Yeah, I know," Ethan replied, not looking up as he lazily closed the gap to the tub on Kristian's right and began studiously scraping out honey.

After Kristian waited a while, he glanced up at his younger brother. "So?" He waited expectantly.

"So what?" Ethan fiddled with his honey scraper, keeping his head down to avoid direct eye contact.

"What's the scoop? I mean, you got stuck in a cave, right? How in the world did ya do that anyways? And how did you get out again?"

Ethan shrugged. "Just lucky I guess." He tried to avoid the conversation altogether.

"Ah, come off it, Ethan." He paused to consider something. "Oh, OK, if I say I'm sorry about the comment about BeeSting, will you tell me then?" he said apologetically.

Ethan sighed, knowing full well that Kristian wouldn't shut up until he gave him something to chew on. He began at the beginning, telling Kristian about the valley, how he followed a flying queen bee, the collapse and Ethan's fall into the cavern, and finally tracking the source of light to the exit. He purposefully left out the part about finding the eggs and Seon, although he felt the guilt rise in his chest about that part and convinced himself that he would make amends later. When he had finished, Ethan glanced sidewise at Kristian to see if he had bought it.

The older boy stood as still as a statue for a few moments. "That's it?" he finally balked. "Grandpa wouldn't go to see Limnah 'cause of a cave-in!" Kristian said this very nonchalantly, as if they were talking about how bees produced honey. "Well?" Kristian intently stared Ethan down, waiting for a reasonable answer.

Ethan's mind raced through a thousand stories that he could tell his brother. He felt an intense longing for Seon's company before finally landing on an idea he thought would work. By this time, Kristian was impatiently taping his foot on the ground.

*I'm here!* Seon announced. *Sorry, busy with BeeSting. Besides, you should do this on your own. But remember that Grandpa told you not to even tell Kristian,* the little drake's thought warned.

"Well . . . ," Ethan started, still feeling concern about not telling Kristian everything, "I kinda . . . fell off a ledge again and passed out until Grandpa found me right before night time . . . and . . ." He added when Kristian still didn't look convinced, "We kinda found an underground spring of water!" Ethan closed, not wanting to add another string of half-truths.

Kristian shot him a quizzical look as he dissected the story. Then the older boy finally nodded, taking the bait. "Dingus," he muttered before telling his own story. "Not much went on here. Although Lola had a tantrum because she couldn't boss BeeSting around." He mused with a slight smile. He scraped the last hive super clean and into a bee jar.

"Kristian?" Ethan queried.

"Hmm?" the older boy grunted.

"You ever heard of a drake that has laid two eggs and one of them didn't hatch?"

Kristian was a bit stunned by the question. "I don't believe I have," he said, furrowing his brow, as if he were a resident drake expert. "All drakes are supposed to hatch at the same time, you know that!" he added as an afterthought. "Hey, why do you ask anyways?"

"Oh . . . uh, no reason." Ethan awkwardly coughed and continued his task trying again to avoid his brother's gaze. However, his guilt grew more the longer he kept his secret and he started to debate with himself if he should tell his brother or not.

*You know what Grandpa said,* Seon interjected.

*So? Grandpa tells us not to do a lot of stuff,* the boy rationalized. The last thing he wanted to do is to lie to his best friend, *We never keep secrets and this one is killing me. Can't you feel it too?* he pleaded. Ethan subconsciously sped up his scraping, as he knew Seon was right. At this point, he would do anything to escape from his brother and from his own sense of swelling guilt.

Kristian had finished his scraping portion and was now cleaning up his area.

"Can you clean up the rest, Kristian? . . . Don't feel so good." Ethan grabbed at his head, acting out a sudden migraine.

*Too dramatic,* he heard the little drake bark in his head, *Don't hunch over so much!*

*You can't even see what I'm doing!* he thought, as he quickly righted himself and momentarily thought about how close his connection with Seon was. *Annoyingly close.* He grumbled to his little companion.

*Well, I know what you were thinking!* The little drake replied.

His brother looked up at him with an air of concern visible on his face. After a brief moment, he nodded and waved his younger brother out, much to Ethan's surprise. Kristian never, never let him get away with anything!

Ethan hastily peeled off his wax gloves and hung them on a nearby hook, careful to continue playing his part. He then exited the bee pit, only too glad to get away from his brother. As soon as he was out the door, he felt slightly better, but looked sorrowfully back at the bee pit. At least he didn't have to worry about lying to Kristian anymore, although he briefly considered he was going to have to tell a lot of lies in the following days. He realized that he now felt sick and very alone after all. That is, except for Seon, he quickly amended.

He turned to walk back to his room, wondering how he would ever feel right about himself again, when an abrupt large shadow crossed his path.

"And where do you think you're off to?" the question came from a familiar and rather-unwelcome voice, a voice Ethan frequently tried to avoid altogether.

He peered up, hoping he was mistaken. Unfortunately, the two eyes that stared back at him were filled with the same loathing and contempt that Ethan had seen too many times before. They belonged to Hem, Ethan's arch nemesis, sitting astride his prized desert stallion.

Hem was a plump boy with sandy brown hair and a rather-round face. *Probably from stuffing way too many crackers and honey down his throat,* Ethan chided to himself. The older boy wore a muffled tan robe, dusty from riding, and that draped around his rotund body.

*The next grand Sheikh,* Ethan thought with disgust.

Hem was the Sheikh's eldest boy and roughly the same age as Kristian, although Kristian had him by sheer strength. Something Hem resented, but was helpless to do anything about. Astride his shoulder sat an equally pudgy brown-and-black-speckled drake measuring a little larger than BeeSting. The squat little reptile shot Ethan the same sour look that Hem was giving him.

*Do you need us to come to your aid?* Seon's thoughts felt highly agitated.

Ethan craned his head to see around Hem's horse, surveying the courtyard behind him for help. He saw the rest of the hunting party entourage returning through the gates as they led their horses off to the stables. The figures appeared tired and worse yet; Hem's younger brother, Yeb, had just ridden up, positioning his mount next to his older brother's horse. *Well, I don't think I'm going to get any help.* Ethan realized.

*BeeSting and I will be right there, Ethan!* Seon's thought came again to the boy.

*No, it's too dangerous, you heard what Grandpa said.* It was now Ethan's turn to scold the drake. *Stay where you are and I'll find a way out of this mess,* the boy soothed, but he could still feel Seon's apprehension. *Besides, Hem has got to be tired,* he guessed.

*How do you figure?* Seon balked.

*Well, the grand Sheikh and his whole house has been on the hunt with a guest for the last few days.* The Sheikh had been entertaining some foreign dignitary, *probably trying to steal him blind* Ethan thought with amusement. The grand Sheikh was a very good horse trader and had bargained himself into the lap of luxury on more than one occasion. It suddenly occurred to him that the black-caped auditor may have come with the dignitary. If so, he wasn't so sure the Sheikh would prevail on this occasion. He quickly dismissed the thought as he had seen the lone horseman arrive, and he was certain no one had accompanied him.

*Ethan, get back on track! Are you going to be all right?* Seon interrupted in a worried tone.

*The Drake Epics - Journey to Qara*

The helpless boy's attention abruptly returned to his present situation as Hem maneuvered his horse around Ethan, such that the boy had to step forward and towards Yeb in order to avoid being trampled. But by so doing, he lost his only way of escape back into the bee pit. *Not now, Seon!* he barked as he tried to think his way out of the situation. There was no response.

"Oh. My mistake," Hem hollered as a malicious grin spread across his face.

Sandwiched between the boys and with no retreat available to him, Ethan let his temper flare. "Bug off," he retorted as he whirled around in an attempt to round the horse and retreat into the bee pit. Suddenly, he was anxious to be back in his brother's company, even with all of the guilt he had felt about his fibs.

Hem's eyes narrowed. "Show some respect, *Atzer*," which was dirty slang for foreigner. "Or I'll have to remind you whom you owe your allegiances to!" The stocky boy urged his horse forward and blocked Ethan's path, almost toppling the boy in the process. "I didn't say you could go! Stick around, maybe ask some more of your dumb questions," Hem sneered.

*I'm in for another beating.* Ethan hung his head in resignation. At the same time he realized that Seon had withdrawn his thoughts from Ethan after being yelled at by the boy.

"Ya!" Yeb now joined in, "He doesn't know authority when he sees it." He bantered to his brother, before turning his comments on Ethan. "You realize that you're in *our* village, right, Atzer?" Yeb was an extremely thin boy, a little taller than his older brother, but with darker hair and a lighter complexion. He was a little older than Ethan, by three or four months. Yeb spat at their would-be victim.

Ethan anticipated the incoming missile and sidestepped just in time to avoid it.

The other boy's spit landed on the horse's leg that Hem was astride, and the spittle slowly oozed down onto its hoof.

"Ah, ya big qaba," bellowed Hem at his younger brother for being an oaf, as he whipped his long lead line in Yeb's direction.

The action was pointless as the other boy was obviously out of reach, but Yeb gave his older brother a sheepish look nonetheless and hung his head in a moment of shame.

Hem turned his anger back on Ethan and continued his jeers, which were getting more insulting by the moment. "You're not welcome here, atzer. Never were and never will be. If it weren't for your precious

Grandpa's honey, we would have left you for the vultures long ago or sold you to a caravan."

"Caravan is good!" Yeb interrupted but fell silent as Hem shot him an angry glare.

"Anyways," Hem scoffed, "you are a good-for-nothing nuisance. Still, as a punching bag, you are pretty good practice even if I have to wash my hands when I'm done with you. I mean, who knows what filthy place you hatched from, Atzer. You know, strike that, you and your whole stinking family don't even deserve to lick the dust off my boots." The older boy pulled his boot from the stirrup and mockingly wagged it in front of Ethan. "Want to give it a try?" he provoked with a sneer, noting Ethan's face contort in anger.

Both of the boys laughed down at Ethan from their mounts. Even their horses brayed, as if they were in on the same joke.

Ethan's mind snapped, *"You'll pay for that, Hem! The both of you will pay!"* he bellowed and charged the boy and his mount, taking a wild swing at Hem's leg in an attempt to protect his family's honor. He was a little too slow for Hem as the older boy landed a kick to Ethan's skull, knocking the boy on his back a few paces from where he had lunged from. Pain shot through his head as a warm fluid filled his eyes. Both Hem and Yeb roared even louder in laughter.

*Ethan?* screamed Seon's voice in his mind. *Ethan!*

The boy slowly regained his senses. *Stay there, Seon!* Ethan sluggishly commanded. *Can BeeSting do something to ask Kristian for help?* he amended.

A pause followed, then Seon prompted, *All he could do was make Kristian feel in danger. But I don't know if it will work—he's not very good at it.*

*Thanks, Seon! I'm sure that's enough. I'll be there soon.* Ethan forced himself to focus through the throbbing pain in his head.

*It better be, or no one, not even you can stop me from ripping these two bullies apart*, Seon threatened.

Ethan didn't argue the case.

Kristian abruptly came bounding out of the bee pit and looked around wildly from Hem to Yeb, sizing up the situation. He noted Ethan lying on the ground, clutching at his head. "You alright, Ethan?" he barked.

Ethan nodded.

Pure rage replaced reason as Kristian guessed at what had happened to his younger brother. Without another thought, he barreled toward Hem, who in the other boy's shock and dismay, was too slow to yank on his reigns and get out of the way.

The stronger boy grabbed Hem by the leg and yanked him off his mount in one fluid motion, setting Hem's horse off into a full buck as it galloped away toward the stables. Hem groaned as he hit the ground at the sudden attack.

Ethan now tried to wipe the blood from his eyes and make his way to his older brother, but felt too dizzy to stand.

Kristian started to pound on Hem, throwing punches at his head as fast as he could manage. "Teach you to pick on my younger brother . . . ," he ranted. "How do you like this?" He punched the flailing boy's face. "Or maybe this . . ." he continued the assault.

Yeb, too frightened to do anything but watch in terror, reigned his horse around and fled at full gallop to go for help.

Ethan slowly staggered to his feet and made his way to Kristian, straining to pull him off the other boy. "It's not worth it, Kristian. Let him go . . . You'll get into trouble . . . ," he pleaded.

His brother shrugged him off and continued to throw punches. He abruptly wound up to take a knockout swing at the now-flailing Hem. The pudgy boy's arms were wrapped around his head, and his body was curled up as he tried to avoid the blows being showered down upon him.

Suddenly, an arm appeared from behind and, grabbing hold of Kristian's tunic, hauled him up to his full height and off the other boy. A large man with dark, tan skin, his arms muscular and lean, held the thrashing Kristian at bay.

Ethan immediately recognized Heramon, and he knew they were in good hands.

His older brother still wildly punched at the air, trying to reach Hem.

One of the gate guards approached to give assistance, but Heramon waved him off, and the guard walked grumpily back to his post.

Hem peered up as the pounding ceased, realizing that he was out of harm's way. He sobbed and pushed himself up, wiping at the corner of his mouth that was bleeding. He pointed a judgmental finger in Kristian's direction, "He . . . attacked me and I did nothing!" the boy blubbered.

"Liar!" Kristian howled and continued to wildly swing at the air.

Hem's nose was now bleeding, and bruises lined his right check and forehead, where Kristian's fist had connected multiple times. He again wiped at his face with his thick hands and looked down at the blood in outrage. "I'm gonna—"

"Do what? Kick Ethan in the head again?" Heramon growled. "Is that how you treat Julfa's citizens, you openly taunt them and then beat them?" The man let this sink in before continuing, "I'm sure your father, the grand

Sheikh, will be only too happy about that bit of information." He reproved in a calm, cold voice.

Hem's face sagged, partly from being caught and partly out of fear of what his father would do to him if he found out. He brusquely turned and hobbled after his horse and Yeb, glancing over his shoulder every few steps to make sure he wasn't being followed.

Kristian made a final lunge for Hem as the other boy hastened his retreat, but Heramon held Kristian fast and shook his head.

"Give it up, Kristian, he's not worth it, and you'll probably get licked for losing your temper anyways." Heramon now tried to talk a little sense into the wildly thrashing boy.

"He . . . he . . . deserved it." Kristian gasped, trying to catch his breath. His face was still flustered as he gulped in air. He eventually slackened and hung limply in Heramon's grasp, glaring up at the stronger and much wiser man.

Heramon nodded, satisfied that Kristian was subdued. He released the impulsive boy as soon as he was convinced Hem was well out of reach. "He did, but still no reason to lose your temper," the man scolded.

"You would have done the same to that little rodent." Kristian snarled.

"Aye, that I may have, but never if it meant that I lost my control," Heramon countered. "If you are to be a wise warrior, you would do well to learn this, boy," he lectured.

Kristian shot him a pained look, but fell silent.

Ethan thought back to the first time he had met Heramon. He had wandered into the village half dead and collapsed. No one knew who he was, nor where he'd come from, but Grandpa took pity on him, being himself a stranger or at least one not born to Julfa. The family had taken Heramon in and nursed him back to health. This is likely why the three children had taken to him right away, and Lola had a special place in her heart for him in particular. She talked about him whenever the opportunity arose. He was just like them, wanderers in a strange land, not really sure how they fit in.

Heramon didn't talk much. But when he did, he did so only out of necessity, and he *never* spoke of his life before Julfa. However, he had quickly proven his worth to the Sheikh, leading the village to victory not once but twice against a band of roving raiders who had breached the village's weaker parts of the walls. All of the battlements had since then been repaired and fortified making them stronger. Heramon was skilled with a sword, and a skilled tactician. The village general had readily accepted him, and he now even taught part of Kristian's soldiering curriculum.

"Can you walk?" Heramon turned his attention to Ethan.

Ethan nodded his head, trying to wipe off the remaining blood, while covering his wound to stop the bleeding.

"Very well, your grandpa sent me. He said for you to proceed to Limnah's study in the Temple of the Lion straight away . . . and to bring your back sack . . ." He paused, now glancing back at Kristian, who was still glowering after Hem.

"And what you found in the desert," he said more softly. "But first, we need to bandage your head. Wait here." Heramon ducked into the bee pit.

An awkward silence followed as Ethan continued to clean off the blood as best he could. Kristian seethed with anger and still kept looking between Ethan and where Hem had now disappeared into the stables. He was unusually quiet.

After a few moments, Heramon returned with a wet rag in one hand and a makeshift bandage in the other. He quickly dabbed at Ethan's wound.

Ethan tried to be brave.

After Heramon was satisfied with his cleaning job, he wrapped the bandage around the boy's head and tied it in a knot. "Too tight?" he asked.

Ethan shook his head. "No, it's fine."

Heramon put his hands on his hips and nodded for Ethan to depart. "Off with you then."

Ethan nodded, discarding his sudden thoughts of revenge, and lightly jogged to his room, hoping his older brother wouldn't follow.

Kristian tried to follow, but not before Heramon caught him by the shoulder. "We will talk about this . . . incident in the morning."

Kristian looked over his shoulder in the direction that Hem had fled. Then he turned to look up at Heramon and nodded.

"Then off with you too," Heramon added.

Kristian ran to catch up with his younger brother.

# Chapter 9

# Prolonged Lies

*Lies and fibs eat away at the soul. So don't lie!*

As the two boys neared Ethan's room, Ethan wildly tried to grasp at ideas, reaching to come up with a plausible detour for his brother. Kristian had caught up with him and both boys had walked from the incident without a single word. He didn't know what was worse, the dull pain he felt from Hem's blow or the awkward silence that fed his own guilt.

He couldn't hold this ruse any longer. He felt he would go crazy trying to remember all the half-truths and lies he had to tell. With just a few steps from the door, he stomped out of desperation and raised his voice, "Kristian, thanks for protecting me." He shot a quick glance back toward the older boy. His older brother didn't look amused, and Ethan could clearly see that Kristian was now beyond agitated. The one thing he didn't want to do was to annoy the older boy. Ethan gulped, in spite of himself.

"What are you playing at, Ethan?" Kristian exploded. He thrust his arm against the wall in front of the younger boy before Ethan could throw open the rug that posed as his room's entrance.

"Excuse me?" Ethan asked in total surprise. He didn't think far enough ahead to worry about his older brother's reaction, but at least it stalled them for the moment. Long enough for Seon to hide.

"Don't give me that, Ethan. You didn't tell me you found anything in the desert, and why are you acting so funny all of the sudden?" Kristian narrowed his eyes, as if trying to discern what Ethan was thinking.

"It's nothing." Ethan feigned with an innocent shrug. "Really!" He plodded on in order to avoid Kristian's gaze now glowering at him.

"Don't make me beat it out of you, Ethan, don't you hold back on me!"

Ethan immediately recognized his brother's tone as the point of no return.

"Give it up, c'mon, what is it? There's a reason you're going to see Limnah, and I'll bet my fiery red drake it isn't because of a cave of water!"

Ethan's mind raced, but he felt too much guilt from the lies he had already told. That, and once Kristian latched onto something, it would take an army of men to pry him away from it, unless it was Heramon of course.

Giving into defeat, he shrugged. "I'll tell you when I get back."

"I promise!" he said again after Kristian gave him an incredulous look.

This seemed to placate his brother with only one response from Kristian, "Dingus!" and they entered the room.

Ethan's eyes darted around, and at first he couldn't see BeeSting anywhere. His eyes fell on his bedroll, then to Lola's bedroll, and he suddenly realized he hadn't seen Lola since his return.

"Kristian, where's Lola?" he said conversationally, hoping to stall any further fury from his older brother. "I haven't seen her since I got back," he surmised.

"Nah, she's being looked after by Abenish, been there all day. Guess I should go pick her up after I get BeeSting." Abenish was the wife of the Sheikh's butler. She was barren of any children and looked after Lola as a surrogate mother.

At the sound of his voice, Kristian's red drake suddenly appeared and launched himself from the desk and glided nimbly to the older boy's shoulder.

Ethan anxiously looked back over at the desk where BeeSting had taken off from, hoping that the egg was still safe and that Seon was out of sight.

*It is quite safe,* came the reply from a familiar thought. *Although, you didn't have to stomp outside of the room, you could have thought it to me . . . hello.* Ethan felt a sudden blush of embarrassment coming on. He'd forgotten about the telepathy, even though they were using it at the bee pit. He quickly considered practicing distances to see how far apart he could be from Seon and still talk with him. Perhaps he'd try walking all the way to the village gate or to the Temple of the Lion to try and reach him. It had at least worked from the bee pit to his room.

"Come and get me when ya get back," Kristian announced, "*if* you get back. You have a lot of explaining to do!" He sounded like he was back to his normal self and had that brotherly taunting grin on his face again. "Besides, your acting is *horrible!*" Kristian snickered. He opened the door flap and ducked out of sight.

Ethan quickly snatched up his back sack and emptied its contents onto the ground by the desk.

*Seon, we need to go visit Limnah—err, the village priest, err, wise man, whatever he is.* He stopped to contemplate that thought. *He and Grandpa are asking for us,* he said absentmindedly as he held open the flap to the pouch that Seon had ridden in during the trek back into the village.

Seon looked at the pouch in disgust. *I'll go if you promise to never get into trouble again when I'm not around,* the little drake bartered.

Ethan shrugged and agreed, as if he could help that anyway.

Seon nodded and then reluctantly hopped into the sack, not happy that he had to return to his leathery prison.

Ethan locked the flap firmly in place, again allowing Seon an adequate view, then crossed the room to the door and started for the wise man's quarters.

He made his way up the long flights of ladders. *I could have used the tunnel stairs* that were carved into the cliff, he conceded to his little companion; *but this is so much better to be out here, especially with the view that I can only see from the cliff.* As if in response to this, Ethan met a pleasant breeze that the cliff seemed to issue. The sun was just setting, sitting halfway between the horizon and the sky, as if it were a giant glob of honey being dabbed into a bowl and now falling out of sight.

The boy and his drake paused and looked down at the spectacle.

The valley sprawled out before them in a delicate contrast of golden browns and dark greens across Julfa's farmlands, and the giant sand dunes and rock outcroppings outside of the village walls sprinkled with

The Drake Epics - Journey to Qara

a smattering of green sages and the blue mirror of the Julfa Sea. In the distance, he could faintly make out the Caucasus mountain range with a slight blue and orange hue, due to the setting sun.

After a few moments, Ethan returned to his climbing. He finally reached the top landing of the cliff, reserved for the Temple of the Lion, and the priest's quarters at the far left of the landing. Ethan set off toward a door opening a few hundred paces away, supposing that for where Limnah would be. For a brief moment, he was happy to be out in the open as another light breeze rustled his clothes. As he reached the priest's doorway, he halted in anticipation of the unknown that crept into his mind. Coincidentally, he could hear hushed voices inside, and his curiosity got the better of him, as in so many times past.

*Let's take a look,* Seon enthusiastically urged.

The boy needed little encouragement. He hugged the wall outside of the door and edged himself cautiously toward the entrance, crouching low to peer inside.

There wasn't much light because of the setting sun, and Limnah hadn't lit his chandeliers yet. But Ethan could see a rough outline of statues made of clay and stone and bookshelves that disappeared into the blackness, laden with sheaves and sheaves of scrolls. He also glimpsed a number of ceramic pots, with rolls protruding from their necks, and a few sitting rugs set here and there throughout the room. A great rug extended from the door and followed the shelves back into the darkness.

A man suddenly strode over to a chandelier and lit the candles, using a light stick with a waxy candle attached to the end that was used to reach ceiling lamps. This cast better light within the chamber, and Ethan now saw that the room ended a little beyond where the darkness had begun. A large bedroll was stationed at the far end of the room.

*That's Limnah,* he explained as he squinted to see the wise man, who wore a plain robe, as usual, with long white hair that fell around his shoulders, but was neatly combed. He also identified two figures standing by the right row of shelves who were still quietly discussing something. Limnah added his commentary as he lit the chamber lights.

*He looks wise,* Seon thought offhand. *Who is the other man by your grandfather?*

The boy recognized him immediately. *That's Ezera, one of Limnah's priests.* Ezera was a self-pronounced reclusive in the village, who avoided the other villagers, and they him. *He keeps to himself mostly.* In fact, Ezerea rarely ventured far from the temple grounds. Ethan never believed the ridiculous stories told about him, but was nonetheless surprised to see Grandpa talking with him.

Ezera, quite the opposite of Limnah, wore an exquisite robe with embroidered drakes, wolves, sand worms, and other animals. His hair also fell around his shoulders, but was jet-black as well as neatly combed. He had a hooked nose, taut lips drawn over his face, sunken cheeks, and dark brown eyes, giving him the appearance of a hairless wolf, except for his mane of hair.

Ethan strained to hear just what they were conversing about.

"I've never seen its equal, Limnah, and he's only fourteen years old. I worry about him being pushed too hard," his grandpa was saying. His voice sounded a bit out of sorts, as if in desperation to prove a point.

The old priest listened intently and looked off into space for a moment, as if lost in his own thoughts. His gaze was interrupted as Ezera commented in answer to Grandpa.

"Yes, but surely the boy . . ."

"Ethan is his name!" his grandpa corrected.

"Yes, well . . . Ethan, is it?" Ezera corrected disdainfully. "Strange name for a boy, as is Kristian and Lola . . ." He sidetracked before coughing into his hand. "Yes, well, Ethan must be the boy of prophecy, he will need proper . . ." Ezera suddenly hesitated, turning his head in Ethan's direction, as if noticing sudden movement at the door.

There was a moment of awkward silence, and Ethan held his breath.

Seon couldn't help himself and asked Ethan what a prophecy was, a concept quite foreign to him for some reason.

"Not now, Seon!" Ethan hissed under his breath.

"Ethan, you may come in," Limnah's warm voice rang out. "You mustn't lurk in doorways, my boy, come in, come in!"

Ethan stood slowly and moved completely into the doorway. He shyly looked at Grandpa, who wore a forced smile on his face, waving for the boy to enter.

He bowed three times as was customary before entering any priest's lodging and trotted over to Grandpa.

The old man embraced him in a half hug and asked him if his daily duties went without trouble before noticing the bandage.

"It's nothing, just bumped my head," Ethan prompted.

Grandpa nodded and patted the boy on the back.

"Good, good. Ethan, you know Limnah," Grandpa introduced them. "And this is Ezera. He is a priest here at the Temple of the Lion," he said, motioning to the other man.

"He doesn't leave the premises much, but you will get to know him quite well when you start your training," Limnah inserted.

The Drake Epics - Journey to Qara

Ezera took a forced, rigid bow. A small shiver tingled down Ethan's spine, but he quickly righted himself before his body started to show it.

"Wait . . . ," Ethan spouted. "Training? What training?"

Grandpa shot him a look that quickly quieted him.

*This is very interesting, you mean you will get to study just like Kristian?* Seon injected. *Perhaps you are receiving this great honor because of the prophecy?* the little drake mocked. *Oh, wait a moment, I'm not sure what a prophecy is because you wouldn't tell me!*

Ethan squirmed a little and gave a brief answer. *It's something that tells about what will happen in the future. I have no idea why I would be part of any prophecy,* he reasoned.

Limnah cleared his throat. "Now, I would like a moment with Ethan," at which point Ezera excused himself and left the way that Ethan had come in. "Ethan, would you like for your grandfather to stay?"

Ethan looked up at his grandpa's face and briskly nodded.

"Very well. If you would be so kind?" Limnah motioned for the both of them to sit on the rug at their feet. After they had all found their spots, Limnah continued without missing a beat, "I want you to tell me what happened on your beekeeping excursion yesterday."

Ethan shot his grandpa a questioning look, a sudden wave of fear washing over him.

The kind patriarch nodded to him with a smile of encouragement, and Ethan felt a little better inside, but still wasn't sure of what to say.

*Can we trust Limnah?* he asked Seon.

*He looks to be trustworthy. His heart is beating normally, he's not sweating, so he's not nervous or anything.*

*You can tell all that just from looking at him?*

*Of course!* Seon answered. *I'm a drake!* He lapsed into silence, as if this explained all things.

Ethan pressed onward, *Well, Grandpa told me to keep this all quiet, and now he wants me to talk about it openly even if it is Limnah?* Ethan was now thinking more to himself than with Seon. *Besides, I haven't even told Grandpa much of anything yet. How am I supposed to tell the whole story to an old man I hardly even know?* He certainly would not tell the wise man more than what he had told Grandpa, even if he'd seen him talk with Grandpa on many occasions before.

*If you're all that concerned about it, then don't tell him.*

*Seon, now is not the time to be cheeky,* Ethan rebuked his companion.

*You're right, I can see that he's holding something back from us now. I'm not sure about what though,* the drake pondered. *Choose your words wisely. I*

147

*now don't feel good about this, try to avoid talking about our bridge and how you blasted that hole in the wall,* Seon counseled.

Ethan nodded. *Try to think of a story for the hole. I mean, Grandpa recognized a lot of things that were true without even talking to me. I bet he's told Limnah this already. We need a way to explain ourselves out of this.*

Seon didn't answer, but Ethan knew his companion was thinking about the plan.

The boy began with the story he'd told Grandpa, careful to leave out the parts as Seon directed. He also left out the part about the unhatched egg.

"That is an interesting tale, Ethan," Limnah remarked after Ethan had finished. "Is there anything else you want to tell me?" Ethan hesitated, not quite sure what to say next.

*What do I do, what do I do?* he frantically asked Seon, to which his little friend only responded that he wasn't sure either. Ethan quickly brainstormed some ideas before one emerged. *Yes, this will get 'em off my back. Besides, he already knows about you. He just doesn't need to know any more about you.* He resolved, and Seon knew where this was headed.

"Do you want to see Seon?" Ethan suggested in an excited tone, successfully changing the subject and deflecting any more questions. He could see the old priest's eyes light up as Ethan lifted the flap on the pouch. He quickly looked at his grandfather, who gave an approving nod, as Ethan inserted his hand into the pouch and slowly drew out the white drake.

Seon played his part well, looking around and sniffing in Limnah's direction as if he were a rote animal. After a few moments of this behavior, he promptly climbed on Ethan's arm and perched himself on the boy's shoulder, still sniffing at the air.

*Brilliant!* Ethan congratulated the little drake.

Seon beamed.

They all sat in silence for a time. All eyes were on Seon, as if to study his every move and behavior.

Ethan grew uncomfortable and moved on to the next step in his plan, "I can even tell him to do tricks."

Limnah now looked very interested and stirred where he sat.

Ethan screwed his face up, imitating Kristian as best he could, forcing his face to turn a shade of bright red. It was all he could do from bursting out in laughter. He pointed with his finger to one of the bookshelves that stood in the hall and uttered a command, "Go there!"

Seon, playing the part perfectly, crawled down Ethan's side and leapt to the ground. He took a few steps, hesitated, taking a step back toward the boy, before whirling around and running to the bookshelf.

Ethan then turned his finger back to his shoulder, uttering, "To me!"

Seon dallied a few moments, so Ethan repeated the command. The little drake paused a moment more, then sprinted back to the boy, leaping to his arm, and crawled onto his shoulder.

All the while, Ethan kept his face creased, his features now turning a shade of purple with his finger frozen in the pointing position. He finally exhaled, as he'd been holding his breath the whole time, and looked merrily at the priest.

Ethan could hear hearty laughter in his mind as the two enjoyed their little game they were playing with the priest. It wasn't fair what they were doing, but they both felt anxious about Ethan's underage binding in the first place and now felt much more jovial and relaxed after their little charade. The boy exerted all his strength not to laugh, and it took all of his resolve to keep a straight face. If he were lucky, Limnah would take one look at him in disgust and dismiss him on the spot.

Instead, the wise man peered intently into Ethan's eyes with a broad smile etched on his face.

The boy realized he was being studied and suddenly felt as though the priest were looking directly into his soul, or worse yet, perhaps the priest had uncovered their little plot. The boy, unaccustomed to such attention, couldn't take it any longer and looked away, not wanting to meet Limnah's gaze again. The laughter went perfectly silent in his mind. He looked up at his grandpa, who was also studying him. Yet, Grandpa wore concern on his face.

Limnah calmly asked the question again, "Is there anything else you want to tell me?" To which Ethan again hesitated, feeling doubly uncomfortable before shaking his head in the negative.

*Is there anything you wish to tell us?* Seon mocked in a calculated attempt to lighten Ethan's worry.

Ethan again refrained from giggling. *Stop it!* he thought. *You're going to make me laugh and then we're both in trouble.*

"Very well," Limnah concluded. "I shall see you every morning for the next month here in my quarters—that is, if you are all right with this?" He looked at Ethan's father figure, who gave a nod with strained excitement showing in his face.

The boy registered total shock at this turn of events. *Maybe we should have told the truth instead of messing around with him?* he probed.

Yet something told him deep down that would have been much worse for them both.

Seon confirmed this feeling, now taking on a more serious tone. *It's safer this way. At least until he has earned our trust.*

*Yes, but what if we need to earn his trust, maybe he knows something that we don't. I mean, how does he know so much? Is he testing us for something else?* the boy silently deliberated with the little drake.

Seon seemed to simply shrug.

The boy looked back up and realized that Limnah was intently studying both of them, and Ethan blushed as if he'd just been caught in the act of what he was so worried about to begin with.

"Tomorrow then, at sunrise," Limnah said as he seemed to realize that the two had finished their silent dialogue. "Ah, and we mustn't let this out—the four of us know and no one else." He was now addressing Ethan and referring to Ezera as the fourth party. "It is very important that this stay between us, there are terrible forces . . ." Limnah appeared to suddenly change his tactic. "Understood?"

Ethan nodded. But he knew he would break this rule as he had already resolved to tell Kristian the truth, not just what he'd shared here or even with Grandpa, but the whole truth.

*There it is again. Don't tell anyone, but we can tell each other,* Seon balked.

The boy didn't argue.

With that, Limnah stood up and clasped hands above the wrists with Grandpa as a sign of agreement.

As they left the temple grounds, the sun had dropped behind the mountain ridge. A faint hue of purple light escaped the horizon, casting its rays as far into the sky as it could muster, before the night defeated it and drove it back into the ground.

The three—boy, Drake, and grandparent—walked together in silence, choosing to take the tunnels instead of the ladders, for Grandpa's sake, as the tunnels were all lighted and much easier to traverse.

Grandpa wore a disappointed look on his face, which made Ethan feel even worse, as if he'd now betrayed his confidence too.

He wanted to ask if he'd performed poorly, but was having a hard time bringing himself to the point. "Grandpa?" he finally asked, his voice more brittle than he had wanted it to sound.

"Hmm?" came the absent reply.

"Are . . . are you . . . disappointed in me?" Ethan barely got the question out and felt even worse as the question hung in the air for a few moments.

Grandpa's face immediately softened, and he looked down at his grandson. "How could I ever be disappointed in you, Ethan? With any of you children?" He considered his next words, as always. "I just expected more out of this meeting with Limnah. I thought there was more—ah, an old man's dreams . . ." He spat.

Pain and anguish welled up within Ethan's head, as if the pressure of a great thunderstorm approached. This mental pain was much worse than his experiences of the previous day. *I let him down, Seon. I let him down and I betrayed my brother.* He mourned. *I have to make this all better,* the boy resolved. "I didn't mean to . . ." Ethan choked down a sob.

"Oh, Ethan, I'm sorry." Grandpa stopped, dropped to one knee, and embraced his grandson, who was now openly weeping.

Seon added his comfort to the boy, sorrowing with him.

Grandpa pushed Ethan to arm's length and gently wiped at the boy's cheeks with a thumb to dry his tears, looking into his eyes. "You must not feel guilt, Ethan," he consoled, now looking at the boy's bandage with more interest. "I won't ask where you got that bump, but it must have hurt a little."

Ethan nodded.

"Well, let me tell you this. Guilt is to the soul what pain is to the body." He let this sink in for a moment. "You mustn't allow guilt to weigh you down at such a young age. That is the realm for old men like me." He chuckled.

Ethan smiled in gratitude as he sniffed and chocked back any further tears. Now was the chance to tell Grandpa. *Now.* He really could talk with Seon; he really had used magic—it was amazing!

Even Seon agreed he should tell the wise patriarch.

Yet something deep within Ethan's mind wouldn't allow him to reveal their secret. That something held him back, and he felt Seon's turmoil similar to his own. The regret knotted up like a big welt inside of his stomach. He felt like exploding and yearned to disappear from existence entirely.

Suddenly, his mood brightened as he remembered about the egg. This was a chance to redeem himself before his loving grandparent. He felt no remorse in this.

*Go ahead, tell him,* Seon urged the boy.

"Grandpa, I have something I forgot to tell you." The story of both eggs washed out of him in a torrent of words, as if he were trying to rid himself of the secrets that had consumed him in so much guilt over the last day.

Grandpa shook his head in disbelief. "Thank you for telling me of this, Ethan . . . we need to get back to your room quickly." Grandpa ended the hug as they stood together, and both picked up their pace.

After an eternity of fast walking, they arrived at his room's entrance. From inside, they could here Lola talking and singing to herself, and they both smiled before opening the flap that posed as the room's door. The blanket dropped back into place, and Ethan stood frozen, utterly beside himself at the picture that presented itself to them.

Lola had not been talking to herself at all. She'd been talking to a drake, a little blue drake stretched out with her on Lola's bedroll.

The merry girl craned her neck around to greet them, a welcoming smile spanned her face. Strangely, she seemed a little more mature, somehow, a little more in control of herself than before, although Ethan couldn't quite put his finger on it. Grandpa was also in total shock, but quickly regained his senses and beamed a smile back at Lola.

"Hi, sweetie, where did you find your pet?" Grandpa tried to sound casual, but Ethan heard the strain in his voice.

"She came to me. She hatched from over there, and now she speaks to me. She's my friend." Lola pointed her finger at the desk, and Ethan leapt toward it, uncovering what used to be an egg but now only a few shell scraps remained. He clenched his fists, his knuckles turning a pale white under the pressure. He turned back toward his sister in muted anger.

Seon, who had fallen quite asleep while riding in Ethan's pouch, suddenly awoke in a heightened alarm he sensed from Ethan. *What's wrong, Ethan, are you—?* He suddenly paused, and Ethan could feel him talking to the larger blue drake before he responded to the boy. *She hatched, she hatched, she's OK!* he bellowed in Ethan's mind. *And she has bound to your sister—what a match! Let me out! Let me out!* It drowned out any uneasiness for Ethan, at least for the moment.

"Lola, you do have a new friend—I do too." He quickly unstrapped the pouch that Seon had been sleeping in and deposited him on the bedroll as the little drake started to immediately tumble and play with his surprisingly larger sister.

Grandpa was calm, as always, and seemed to soak in the sight and the occasion, a look of complete happiness spread across his face. The old man walked to the far side of the room, by Lola's bedroll, and plopped himself down to get a closer look at Lola's drake and to talk with her. "Lola, do you have a name for her yet?" he asked.

"Blue Deseret," came the reply, "for bees and water, because she's blue, my favorite color."

At this, Grandpa smiled and cleared his throat. "Lola, Ethan, we need to keep this development even more quiet. It will be hard, but I don't want anyone to know about this." He paused for a moment. "It is not the custom for a drake to bind to a girl—it has never happened before, at least that I'm aware of and at this young age and . . . ," Grandpa was talking more to himself now.

"The point is that, Lola, you must keep Deseret a secret. Understand?"

Lola nodded, although neither Grandpa nor Ethan really believed she could keep it a secret for very long.

Grandpa spent the next long while explaining and repeating this to Ethan, more for Lola's sake, until he was completely sure they both understood and that the warning was clearly imprinted on their memories.

They had just wrapped up when, to everyone's surprise, Kristian stumbled into the room.

"Doesn't anyone ask before they enter?" Ethan moaned.

Kristian didn't seem to notice the comment. All of the color had drained from his face as he stood rooted to the spot, frozen, jaw open, with a look of dazed bewilderment. "I . . . I . . . I," he kept mumbling, never getting the rest of the sentence out.

"I was going to tell you, Kristian, really," Ethan said more out of pleading than as a statement. He knew deep down that this would not turn out well between the boys. It was clear that Ethan had betrayed his brother's trust. He could have at the very least told the older boy about Seon and the egg instead of him having to find out this way, he scolded himself.

"Come, Kristian, sit and let us all talk." He motioned for Kristian to take a place next to the old man. The older boy sluggishly made his way over to Grandpa and sat in a trancelike state.

Ethan realized this might all be too much for his brother to handle and felt a sudden pang of sympathy for him. Still, it was better for all of them to know about this rather than to continue keeping secrets from each other. Ethan had to admit. Besides, this meant that he wouldn't have to keep Kristian in the dark on anything now. He thought excitedly.

Grandpa and Ethan spent the remainder of the evening explaining the course of events to Kristian. Lola added her commentary every now and then too, not that it really helped any. But she too had come up to speed through Deseret, who had apparently absorbed the story through the thin shell of her egg as well as from Seon.

Kristian came out of his daze and listened intently. As the story wore on, he seemed to rather resent the whole thing as he looked up at Ethan a number of times with pained contempt in his eyes.

153

The younger boy noticed this and felt awful for not trusting Kristian in the first place. Yet he held out some hope in reserve that Kristian would get over this quickly, even if his brother had a tendency to hold grudges for a long time. Ethan resolved to tell Kristian everything, the first chance he could. He would even tell him what the others did not know. He again concluded.

"I told Ethan to keep this completely quiet. So, please do not blame him." Grandpa declared and then repeated his warning to all of the children one last time, "You must not tell anyone of this! It is for all of our good."

They all nodded their heads in agreement.

"Well, time for bed then," Grandpa announced. "Tomorrow will be a new day, and we can all start out fresh . . . together!" he counseled, noticing the tension building between the two boys.

Kristian now scowled at his younger brother. He rose, keeping his eyes fixed on the other boy, and left the room without another word.

"He'll come around," Grandpa consoled as he saw the pain on Ethan' face. "Good night." The old man kissed Ethan and Lola on their foreheads, excused himself, and disappeared through their doorway.

Ethan lay awake most of the night, struggling with the reality that Kristian might be mad at him for a long time to come. He tried to think of ways he could mend their friendship, but nothing really came to mind. In all of this, he was left to himself. Seon and Deseret remained locked in conversation late into the night, and Ethan didn't want to interrupt that.

Suddenly, a random thought occurred to him, he would be going to school; at least he thought it was a *kind* of a school. He'd forgotten about it altogether in all of the excitement. He brightened a little at this thought and finally turned in to get some sleep.

# Chapter 10

## Teacher's Pet

*Learning opens our minds to the eternities. What's more compelling than infinity?*

The next morning didn't come soon enough. Ethan was already dressed, sitting impatiently next to his bedroll, glancing at his little companion every few moments to see if the drake was awake yet. But, Seon peacefully slept next to him, completely unaware of the boy's musings. In fact, the boy had woken a few times during the night, only to find that both drakes were still animatedly chattering in his mind. Even so, he now would have gladly woken his little comatose friend without another thought, if he felt that the drake had gotten any sleep at all. But, instead, he studied both drakes and watched their little bodies move to their steadied breathing as they slept. They were unsurprisingly similar, even if Seon was two-thirds Deseret's size.

Lola lay sprawled out on her stomach with one arm wrapped around her little drake and the other twisted around on her back, appearing quite comical. Deseret's snout lay nestled in the little girl's bed of hair. Seon lay one or two paces away, curled up in the same position that he always slept in, with part of Ethan's blanket rolled around him.

The blanket's rolls brought to memory the powerful magic back at the desert valley, tugging at his thoughts as Ethan wondered if Limnah would allow him to learn and practice the art. He had so many questions about the magic and was both excited and at the same time a little scared to use it again. The boy studied his hands, wondering how he had known how to use the raw energy in the first place. *Will I be able to stand it, the next time I use it?* he mused as he turned his hands over. The notion made him shiver and he quickly deflected his attention to his dreams in order to avoid that memory. He gratefully realized he hadn't dreamt for the last few nights. But they still taunted him, picking at his mind as if they had somehow foreshadowed Seon's discovery, and he now desperately hoped they would not return to foreshadow other more sinister things to come. He brushed the thought of the black dragon from his dreams aside too and decided he needed air and would start for the temple early.

Ethan finally woke Seon, who was not happy of being waken, let alone having to ride in that wretched pouch again.

*You will do well to make a new back sack that suits me better!* the little drake barked as Ethan let out a soft chuckle.

Seon sluggishly entered his leathery prison again and both boy and drake walked the tunnels to the Temple of the Lion.

He was too excited to even think of eating, even though Seon sleepily reprimanded him for not taking care of himself and something about forcing his little companion to eat leftover scraps. But he didn't pay this much heed as he quickly made his way through the temple grounds to Limnah's chambers. As he reached the door and bowed, Limnah immediately met him much to his surprise.

"Good morning, Ethan." The priest smiled. "And I don't recall your drake's name?"

Startled by the forgetfulness of the question, Ethan fumbled over his answer, "Oh, uh . . . Seon," he finished, wondering if Limnah were as great of a wise man as the boy had built him up to be over the events of the previous evening.

"Good morning, Seon," Limnah said with equal enthusiasm and a quick bow to Seon's little muzzle poking out of Ethan's sack.

*Would be even better if you let me out of this dungeon*, Seon criticized, apparently now fully awake.

"Let us begin! Do come in," Limnah said invitingly. "And you are now allowed to have Seon accompany you on your shoulder, but only while in my quarters of course . . . ," he advised.

Ethan felt Seon's eagerness, but hesitated looking around the room, still a little unsure of this course of action.

"It is quite safe, I can assure you," the old priest insisted. "No one, except for Ezera, is allowed to approach the temple precinct or my chambers."

The boy thought this quite peculiar, as no one had ever stopped him from entering the grounds. Why would it be any harder for someone else to do the same?

*Just, let me out. Let me out!* the drake bawled.

Ethan let the thought vanish and conceded, letting Seon out of the bag.

The little drake stretched in triumph at his release, reaching out his miniature tiny paws while curling his back not unlike a cat does, such that his front was low to the ground and his rear curved higher up. At the same time, he yawned, opening his maw as wide as he could and extending his pink tongue. Once satisfied, he quickly took his perch on the boy's shoulder for some morning preening he had been denied, due to their rush to the temple.

The boy smiled in spite of himself, happy to see his companion once again content.

The room was as it had been last night, with a notable exception of a short table now placed over the rug where they had all sat before.

Limnah led them to the table and motioned for them to sit on the ground beside it.

"I wish to know your abilities," Limnah announced. "The both of you," he amended.

Ethan impulsively reached up to stroke Seon's head. *He's doing it again*, he thought with worry as he wondered why the priest had addressed them both.

*Obviously, he didn't buy our little show*, Seon observed.

*Yeah, well, I thought that it was a great performance*, Ethan complimented them both.

*It was rather good.*

Limnah continued his sermon as if he openly understood the ongoing dialogue in their minds, "I believe that we got off to a slow start last night. Although I must say that the face you made and Seon's simple movements were quite amusing."

Ethan dropped his jaw in near panic, losing all composure. "But . . . but," he stammered. How was it possible that the old man knew of their secret? *This isn't happening. I mean, it's not possible, unless . . .*

*Unless he could read our minds!* Seon finished the sentence. The stark revelation hit them both like a sack of bricks, and Ethan never finished his comment to the old man, preferring to let the discussion take its own course.

Limnah casually watched their reactions, as if this were the most obvious observation in the world. "I believe it is a matter of trust, no?" the wise man resumed, "And perhaps a sense of mischief that runs in your blood?" this he said with a wry smile, and Ethan had the distinct impression that the priest was now toying with them both. He strolled to one of the many bookshelves and perused the contents with a finger, moving from scroll to scroll. "Writing is one of the great gifts given to us by the gods," he stated as he continued his search. "There are but few who can read and write, and this should be considered to be a treasure beyond all others . . . ," the old priest instructed. "Ah, here it is!" Limnah found the scroll he was looking for and slid it off the shelf as he walked back to the desk.

"Have you studied runes?" he directed the question primarily to Ethan.

The boy, not knowing what runes were, shook his head.

"I mean, can you read?"

Ethan bobbed his head slightly, still reeling from Limnah's surprising insight into the boy and his drake's most intimate thoughts. "I've always been able to read," he stammered, regaining some of his composure, "since before I can remember. Grandpa always has us read with him over our evening meals, and I have to study the scrolls on beekeeping," he continued with more courage. "But I'm not great at it," he added.

Limnah nodded, as if in perfect understanding. "I believe you will be able to read this then." He handed a scroll to Ethan, who hesitated to take it. "Please proceed." Limnah pressed the scroll into the boy's hands and turned to leave. "It will also be good practice for you and your drake to learn to read together. So leave him ample room to see the scroll." Limnah observed over his shoulder before disappearing through the doorway into the temple compound.

Ethan missed the comment entirely as he unlatched the scroll and carefully read the title before slowly reading the text:

## ~ Drake Holders and the Less-Common White Emperor Drakes ~

*I, Nejdm'el'sharim, the great researcher and scribe, write by my very own hand that emperor drakes are very rare and the signal of royalty. Only a few from the annals of history are known to me at the time of this writing. It is not known where they come from, and no other knowledge is available on how they are bred. Even I have never seen one of these majestic drakes. Those who have been recorded in lore and legend have manifested a few impressive traits that seem to be common among the legends:*

1. *They are telepathic and exhibit enhanced communication with their holder and can communicate over vast spaces between them and their holders, most of the time, immediately upon the binding.*
2. *They are known to grant their holder with magical gifts that can be exercised at a very early point in their training. The potency of this magic is difficult to measure, and has differed greatly in all known legends, but is developed and controlled only through careful study.*
3. *Emperors are amazing flyers, capable of flying at high altitudes, and are reported to be one of the fastest flying drakes, even outpacing the fastest birds of prey. Although this trait in legend develops later than in other drakes species and requires direct training and practice.*

*In all other traits, they match elemental drakes, although they do not have the specific abilities of each elemental, instead imbuing the holder with general magical powers that range far beyond the elementals potential in their varied combinations and potency.*

The scroll was slightly more advanced than what Ethan was used to reading. He stopped a number of times to reread words and sentences to retain their meaning and read the scroll seven more times to make sure he got the true message.

Seon started to pick up on the runes at an amazing rate, which greatly astonished Ethan. By his fifth time reading it through, Seon was reading at Ethan's level without having to examine the boy's thoughts for comprehension.

*The scroll isn't wrong*, Ethan remarked. *That does sound like you.*

*And it explains why Limnah knew what we were up to yesterday*, Seon added.

Ethan felt a momentary twinge of guilt at their poor behavior in front of Limnah, then remembered his grandpa's warning and discarded the feeling.

Seon agreed, *We didn't give a good impression at all, did we?* Then he added, *I think we should trust him, Ethan. Just a little more . . . ,* Seon said at the look on Ethan's face. *I am curious what other things he has to teach us.*

The boy gave the drake a quizzical look at the sudden change in alliances. *Do you really think that wise?* he asked as he felt the drake's excitement well up within him.

The drake gave him a sarcastic look. *Of course I do, I wouldn't have thought it if I didn't mean it!* came the response.

*Yeah, well . . .* The boy smirked while nodding his head in agreement. *I guess we can trust him just a little more.* He still felt he needed more time to understand the old man than what Seon wanted. But he felt the encouraging warmth emanating from his little friend.

As if on cue, Limnah appeared in the doorway and strolled toward the unlikely pair. He stopped briefly, examining both students, and peered down at the scroll. "I assume you are finished with your readings then?" he inquired.

Ethan nodded.

Seon yawned and sniffed at the old man.

Limnah retrieved the scroll and rolled it together with a leather strap. He then placed the resulting tube on a nearby bookshelf and went to one of the ceramic vases strewn throughout the room, this one with scrolls extending out of its glossy neck. The priest pulled out a dirtier, more worn scroll before returning to the students. "I wish for you to both read this tonight," he instructed. "Don't worry, it is a copy, otherwise all originals must stay within my quarters. Of course, you are welcome to read any of the scrolls in my chambers . . . all you need do is ask."

Ethan and Seon both felt a rush of excitement. *Finally!* they thought in unison.

"That will conclude your studies for the day. Please think upon your readings and come prepared for tomorrow's lesson, at dawn," Limnah declared. "I do hope that I have gained some amount of your trust?"

Ethan bowed, and Limnah dismissed them with a wave of his hand. His mind was rooted on what they had read as he left the priest's chambers, *There must be scrolls in there about everything? We need to read as much as possible!* He settled.

Seon agreed, *Absolutely everything we can get our clutches on.*

- - -

The next few weeks were uneventful. The homework scroll that Limnah had given them was entitled "Everything You Need to Know about Drakes." It was boring reading and almost put Ethan to sleep that night. But he had pushed through and read it completely.

Seon, on the other hand, had devoured the scroll, studying its contents and drawing conclusions about his family tree and classifications. The little drake spent long nights debating his readings in greater detail with his sister. They felt a closer connection beyond their memories, which had not clarified their lineage before.

Ethan, himself, began to think more on his own ancestry, and he had made a note to inquire of Grandpa on this matter more, when he got a chance.

The lessons continued to focus purely on reading, much to both Ethan and Seon's dismay. Not all disappointing as they ravenously read anything placed before them as well as by their own selection of topics, of spells such as control, levitation, defensive shielding, attacks and even a bit on scrying. But, they had hoped that Limnah would have instructed them on how to use Kesem, but the old man had not mentioned this practice, not even once! The routine was always the same: Ethan and Seon would enter for their lesson, and Limnah would direct them to the table, unroll a scroll in front of them, and ask both to read. This was followed by early dismissal, once they completed reading the scrolls at the desk.

On the upside, however, both were showing marked improvement in their reading abilities, and Seon continued to keep perfect pace with Ethan. The little white book worm even read to Ethan a few times, which the boy felt was something he could get very used to. Although, he fell asleep one night during a particularly dull reading and got a stern reprimand from his little instructor.

Ethan enjoyed learning more about drakes, but he was becoming more impatient with his assignments. He wanted to practice the Kesem he was learning more about, or perhaps even teach Seon to fly, but there was no space in which the two could practice, much to their continued disappointment. Although he did try speaking to Seon from the village gate to test long-distance communication; it worked just as they'd read on the first day. The boy also took a page out of Seon's own play book and spent his evenings talking with Lola about her little drake, whom she was keeping strictly in their room and out of sight from prying eyes.

She had mentioned to Abenish that she had a drake a few times, but just got patted on the head whenever she brought it up, which sent her into tantrums. Fortunately, she hadn't tried to smuggle the little blue drake out of her room to prove her point—at least not yet.

Grandpa was also busy at this season of the year, and the family only saw him at their evening meals. He usually asked Ethan how his lessons were going, but they didn't get into many details over dinner. When Ethan had tried to discuss topics after school, although very loving and attentive when he had the time, Grandpa usually had other pressing tasks he needed to attend to and so couldn't spend much time with the boy. He wasn't quite sure if his patriarch was trying to avoid him. *Or was he?*

He also hadn't seen much of Kristian, who was now hanging out more with his soldiering buddies rather than spend time with his younger brother. At least, he always seemed to have at least one of them tagging along whenever Ethan saw him, even in the bee pit while cleaning out the honeycombs. The older boy scowled at Ethan whenever they made eye contact, which wounded his brother at the harsh resentment and Kristian's complete lack of attention. Still, this also meant that Ethan was free from Kristian's ritual of brotherly teasing.

And so, Ethan spent most of his time with Seon, the only friend available to him; and he immersed himself in discussions with the little drake, memorizing spells, focusing together on their core energy, meditating together and talking about . . . well just about everything. The most interesting topic is what would come next, and they had hatched more than a few plans of how to find solitary places where they could practice Kesem on their own.

A few of the days, Ethan had off from instruction, so he left Seon behind to socialize with Deseret as he went about his daily chores. Besides, this gave him an opportunity to talk with the drake over greater distances, even when Ethan was far away in the farmlands cleaning out hives.

— - —

Upon one such day, Ethan found himself returning from the fields, his cart full of honey remnants he was taking to the bee pit for harvesting. He rounded a shack and was approaching the courtyard when the tall black figure appeared at the gate, not fifty paces away, talking with a guard. Ethan looked around quickly and ducked into a nearby alley, barely getting the cart to fit in the close quarters. He winced at the unpleasant sound as the cart scraped against the sides of the walls, so he decided not to go farther in and risk it getting more stuck than the cart already was. The boy dropped to the ground and shimmied himself under the back of the cart so as to peer around the wall and watch the auditor.

"Seon?" he announced in a quiet voice, preferring to talk aloud instead of in his mind. He often felt his thoughts more jumbled when he couldn't speak out loud to his little friend. "Seon, are you there?"

*What is it? Are you all right? I can feel your heart racing*, the little drake answered from the confines of their room.

"He's here!" the boy hissed. Ethan had luckily avoided all contact with the mysterious stranger up until now, but he knew it was only a matter of time before he'd have to face the man. Still the whole experience didn't quite feel right. He knew the sensation he had felt when the stranger had passed him, as if death itself had form, a very cold form. But what was worse, this stranger had the uncanny ability to read minds. Ethan could have sworn that is exactly what he had done on his birthday as they passed one another, and this is what Ethan feared most of all.

*Wait there, I'm coming!* Seon reacted, knowing full well what Ethan meant. The boy had explained the encounter with the auditor to Seon, who had also shivered as a result, feeling Ethan's experience by proxy.

*No. Stay there! I'm in no immediate danger,* Ethan shot back, reverting back to his thoughts for emphasis. *I'm watching him now at the courtyard gate, just need to wait for him to leave before I can go in,* he explained. *I . . . I just need you to be here in my mind . . . just in case.* The boy involuntarily shuddered before righting himself and continuing his surveillance.

Seon didn't respond, but Ethan could feel the little drake's disappointment, and that meant brooding.

*What do you think he is really up to anyways?* Ethan pushed on, more to calm his own nerves rather than engage in conversation. *I mean, why is he here in Julfa of all places? Why now? What or who does he expect to find, and why the interest only in drakes and their companions?* Ethan explored. He'd heard more of the auditor's continued inquisitions around the village, as if the auditor were taking a census of some kind. *It just isn't right!* He thought. *At least Limnah hasn't exposed us.* This thought reminded Ethan that he was gaining more confidence in the old priest.

The village had never had a drake census before, that was mostly managed by the Sheikh. More times than not, the Sheikh used this to his own personal advantage to limit village participation and barter with caravan merchants to turn a profit. *Unless!* Ethan had a sudden epiphany. *Unless, the Sheikh is the one who brought him here!* he plowed onward. *Wow, maybe that's it! The Sheikh wants him here!*

*I think you are now jumping to conclusions,* came the lackluster reply.

*Seon, now is not the time to mope around,* Ethan scolded before continuing. *But why would he want him here? What's different now?* he investigated. These questions often puzzled the boy as he tried to think them through to their natural conclusions. Ethan lay there in a daze, looking at the dirt beneath him in deep concentration on the topic.

*You have enough hobbies, without adding this one to your already-long list, don't you think?* Seon nudged. *Just don't get distracted and get yourself into trouble with him.*

Ethan shrugged as he ran his hands through the dirt. *Don't you feel the least bit worried about this?* he prodded.

*Well . . . yes, but with all of our chores and studying, there isn't time. Besides, he is an unknown, and that doesn't sit well with me,* the drake commented as he preened at a wing.

*Ha!* Ethan said with contempt. *You're just as worried as I am!* The boy smirked.

Seon continued to preen.

*I felt you tremble when I told you that story. We need to find out what he's up to,* he said, determined to reveal the stranger's true intentions.

*Perhaps so, but we have other things to stew about right now, like keeping you safe and what about tomorrow?* Seon reminded in a serious tone.

*Yeah, well, I am quite safe, and as for tomorrow, I . . .* Ethan fell silent to think up a comeback for the drake, but instead he froze as a sudden chill ran down his spine. A black form was approaching. Ethan instinctively pulled himself backward and under the cart to stay out of sight.

*He's coming!* Seon announced. *I can feel your fear, Ethan!*

The boy didn't hear him. A long dark shadow emerged in front of him, followed directly by a black robe with its skirt dragging through the dirt. Ethan couldn't see any higher, but he knew it was the auditor.

The man abruptly stopped, and Ethan felt his eyes on him, scanning the would-be abandoned cart.

He secretly hoped that the auditor wouldn't see him hiding underneath, and he said a brief prayer in his mind, concentrating on the words. *Please! There's nothing here. There's nothing here. Please!* He felt something icy tickle at his mind as he continued to recite the lines. It latched on and started to probe in an attempt to peel back the words and look deeper within, but Ethan was scared witless and continued to recite the same lines over and over again as his only refuge. After a moment more, both the feeling and the stranger were gone.

*Ethan?* Seon was back with him. *All you all right?*

Silence.

*Ethan, snap out of it!*

*I'm here! I'm here.* The boy exhaled. *That was close. I'll be right there, I just need to be alone right now,* Ethan announced. He hauled himself to his feet and pushed against the cart to dislodge it from the walls. After a moment of pushing, he drove it into the street and peered in the direction the auditor had gone, then looked at his hands that were visibly shaking;

The Drake Epics - Journey to Qara

he concentrated to hold them still. After a few moments more, he briskly walked toward the courtyard looking over his shoulder every few steps. Once through the gate, he dropped off the cart at the bee pit, leaving it for his brother to clean and he headed for his room at a fast clip.

The sun had set by the time he arrived. The incident had drained him much more than he had realized. As he entered, Seon was in an unpleasant mood.

The drake peered up from his preening. *I'll just let you be alone, shall I?* he fumed. *After all, you do need your space, don't you?*

Ethan had no strength for a retort, but he knew that he'd be in for a stern reprimand in the morning. *Tomorrow morning!* he said in a moment of clarity. Ethan had forgotten all about tomorrow, the last day of instruction. *I'll come up with something.* He strained. *Just need to get some rest.* He rationalized as he yawned and pulled the covers over his head, still fully clothed.

Seon, who had now concluded his evening cleaning ritual, smirked back at the boy. *I'll bet*, was the drake's only thought, then he picked at the blanket with his claws, turning himself in a circle a few times before finally settling in beside the boy.

*I will*, Ethan said sleepily. *Don't you worry your little head about it*, the boy ended as he drifted off to sleep.

The next morning came all too quickly. Ethan lay wide awake in his bedroll thinking about what he'd learned over the past month, compiling all of the facts as if preparing for a last-moment quiz. Today might be his last day of instruction for who knows how long, or at least until he was sixteen years old, which seemed like an eternity away just now. He needed to pick up as much as he could, and he decided to talk to Limnah about continuing on with him for a while longer. He'd practiced a few lines he would use on the priest, ignoring the sarcastic chuckles coming from Seon, whose attitude had much improved from a good night's sleep but who was still acting a little scornful.

*Funny*, Ethan said sarcastically at a particular chuckle from his companion. Then he surrendered, *Oh, you're probably right!* in a sad tone.

*Well, get ready and we'll think of something on the way up*, Seon noted in a more measured tone, realizing he had hurt the boy's feelings.

But no better ideas came to either of them as they walked the inner hall to the temple. It wasn't for the lack of trying. They both tried to think of any way to convince the old priest, and before either realized it, they were standing in the temple grounds just outside of the priest's row.

Ethan sighed, set down his sack with Seon inside, and took up a seat by the entrance to Limnah's chambers. He waited patiently for his last day to start, practicing the various lines he'd thought up.

*Sir . . . hello, sir . . . Excuse me, sir . . .*

*Oh, do get on with it,* Seon said in exasperation.

Ethan shot the bag a foul look. *I've been wondering . . . that is to say, Seon and I have been wondering if . . . we could continue our lessons with you. He says you are very wise, and . . .*

*I didn't say to tell him everything,* Seon interrupted.

*Well, you're not helping me much right now, other than correcting me on what I say for this or how I'm not saying that!* Ethan spat. *OK . . . sir, I've been thinking about our lessons, Seon and I. No. I would very much like to continue on with you and learn more about how I can serve in the community. If so, I will promise to follow your every instruction!*

*Much better!* Seon complimented. *Really good. I don't see how he could say no to that.*

Ethan beamed a giant smile.

"Ethan, come in." To his alarm, Ezera, not Limnah, appeared in the doorway and invited him into the old priest's chambers.

The boy quickly stumbled to his feet, bowed three times, and collected his back sack.

"I will provide your instruction for today," the priest exclaimed over his shoulder as he escorted Ethan toward their usual study table. "And Limnah asked that you report back here tomorrow morning, again at dawn," he said in an airy tone.

Ethan silently celebrated with Seon, punching at the air behind the younger priest's back, a flood of relief washing over him that he had yet another day to convince Limnah to keep up his training. He stopped to look at a scroll spread across his reading table, anticipating Ezera's next instruction. He moved to sit at the table and begin his daily ritual.

"Oh, we won't be reading today," Ezera explained as he motioned to another small rug. "Come."

Ethan quickly obeyed, his interest peaked for the moment. He took his seat as Ezera had instructed.

The young priest sat directly in front of the boy. "It is time to test your abilities with Kesem, or magic as it is sometimes called in the common tongue. But, here we will refer to it only as Kesem," he amended.

Ethan's heart leapt within him.

*Finally! We have a chance to try this out!* Seon exclaimed.

They had read enough with Limnah that both boy and drake felt they could accomplish anything they might be tasked with. Still, deep down,

Ethan feared he might not be able to control the Kesem, and the memory from the cave formed a sudden lump at the base of his throat.

"Now, I want you to start with a calming technique before we begin." Ezera continued, "Fold your arms and legs, close your eyes, and concentrate on a pure white field. Good, now breathe deeply." Ethan followed every instruction.

"Now, listen carefully before you begin . . . You will focus on a blank white field with a white sky and exert yourself, push the white to be whiter, think of peace, then . . ."

Ethan pushed on, blocking out Ezera's words more out of annoyance of his whiney voice. The priest's words grew fainter and fainter. Ethan could feel a sensation of calm wash over him, not unlike the feeling that he experienced when he first bound to Seon. It was amazing, he could feel peace and calm flowing through his veins—all of his worries were worlds away.

*Ethan!* Seon called in the background, the thoughts barely audible. *Ethan, you need to wait and listen to Ezera!* the drake complained then wavered, *You are glowing Ethan, a white aura is shining about you,* the drake declared in wonder.

The boy redirected his attention in an attempt to respond to Seon. He concentrated, exerting his strength to draw the drake into the scene before him.

But the white field had evaporated and Seon's thoughts were now entirely missing. Ethan began to panic as he heard nothing but perfect silence. It started buzzing in his ears. He was now standing in a thick grey vapor, almost tangible, and fear welled up within him as he realized that he was back in his dream again, but this time he wasn't sleeping, not really sleeping.

The mist drew back upon itself and opened to the same concourse of people, the same two men in deep discussion. Then the dream changed. For the first time, he heard and understood what the two men were saying. This time he sensed the voice was directed at him, "One of you must fight to live, and yet die to live."

From there, the same events unravelled as in his previous dreams, yet he perceived but fragments, only bits and pieces this time. The dream came at the boy in quick bursts followed by deliberate moments that lingered in slow motion. The words were his only focus.

The same voice was speaking again, shouting the challenge at the would-be dragon, "We need agency to learn and to be tested! That is our purpose, not to be slaves to you and your kind."

"We will do no such thing!" uttered the man with the black hair in a reassuring, yet still-icy tone. "Don't you see? We will control you by force and remove the heavy burden of freedom from your minds. Rejoice— for none shall be lost!" His voice was confident as he raised both hands in victory. "We will all reap the reward!" The crowd behind him erupted into a deafening cheer. The dark-haired man continued, "Therefore, this place no longer has room for you. Return to your own land or become my slave. It does not matter. Simply, you will have no more power and you will bother us no more!"

"No, it is you who have cast yourself out! Not only from our home, but now you have created this bleak land. It is you who shall bother us no more," the calm voice rejoined.

The dream closed with the same blinding light. The dragon emerged, and a torrent of fire encompassed everything in sight, including Ethan.

Ethan awoke, lying flat on his back with a cold sweat pouring down his face. His clothes were wet, and he was shivering uncontrollably.

A concerned Ezera knelt over him, dabbing at the boy's forehead with a cloth rag.

"Dragons aren't real! Dragons aren't real!" Ethan realized he was chanting to himself.

A familiar presence burst into his thoughts, *Ethan . . . Ethan, what happened? Why are you going on about dragons?* The little drake lovingly nuzzled at the boy's cheek.

Ethan could feel his drake's distress.

*I sensed great fear in you, a great evil that you alone were facing, but it felt elusive. I couldn't enter your thoughts. It . . . it kept me out!* Seon sounded on the verge of tears, as if thoughts could sound like tears, and as if drakes could cry.

"I'm fine, Seon. I'm fine," Ethan muttered out loud. He was still groggy, but didn't want to over worry his little companion about his current condition. He would tell Seon about the dream later, in every detail.

"Dragons? Dragons?" Ezera bleated. The priest sounded distraught, and Ethan couldn't tell what was more alarming to the young rector, the mention of dragons or his assigned stewardship gone wrong. "Are you . . . are you able to stand?" Ezera croaked, his voice sounded a little raw with a hint of regret.

Ethan forced himself to look up at the priest and clearly saw the discomfort in his face. He nodded as vigorously as he could manage. "Yeah, I'm fine. Just a bad . . . bad dream . . . is all," the answer sounded a bit shallow to him as soon as he said it.

Ezera regarded the boy with the same concerned expression.

"I must have wielded wrong," the boy hedged. "I guess I lost track of the white field," he acknowledged, straining to think up a suitable alibi.

The priest stared at Ethan for a moment longer then shook himself out of his trance to close their session. "We will . . . we'll," he paused to clear his throat, "conclude the lessons for today. Limnah will lead them in the future." He then hastily added, "Don't try this again!"

*I am going to try it again!* Ethan thought rebelliously to Seon. The drake didn't respond, but Ethan thought he felt his companion's hesitation. He allowed Ezera to pull him to his feet. He still felt a tad dizzy, but tried his best to mask it, which seemed to convince the priest. Once he felt part of his balance return, Ethan nodded thankfully to his benefactor; and without another word or even looking back, he picked up his sack and stumbled toward the chamber's entrance.

Seon kept his wings outstretched to keep balance as Ethan strained to stay on his feet.

"The drake," Ezera said, his voice still shaken. "The drake must go in your pouch," he reiterated to Ethan's annoyance.

The boy turned and looked at Ezera and nodded. From this distance, the man looked deathly pale. He quickly motioned for Seon to take his hiding place, then nodded to the priest again and ducked out of the doorway.

The boy gingerly walked along the ledge and reflected on the vision, although he admittedly had no clue of what it meant. His companion rummaged through the boy's memory of the dream, but Ethan was too groggy to force himself to explain.

*This is the dragon you've been dreaming about?* he asked.

Nodding in answer to Seon, Ethan knew that the drake found the rest of the story rather dull, but dragons were a drake's kin. At least he intuitively figured this out through his combined consciousness with his little white companion. Still, this meant that Ethan would have to figure out the rest of the dream for himself. The boy strained to concentrate on putting one foot in front of the other.

The two rounded the corner and into the tunnel when Ethan almost stumbled into Kristian, who grunted in contempt at the sight of his younger brother.

"What are you doing up here?" A sour look spread across the older boy's face. "You're not allowed up here yet."

"I can be here too!" Ethan retorted. "There's no law that I can't be up here!" This last comment rang a bit whiney in his own ears. But he didn't care. His head was swimming, and he just wanted to be back in his room and in his own bedroll, sleeping the Kesem off!

Kristian shook his head and looked as if he were ready to smack his brother. But Ethan held his ground.

"Kristian, what's wrong with you?" Ethan tempted the older boy as a measure of his strength returned. "Why are you avoiding me?" he mustered all of his remaining strength to stare his brother down.

Kristian gave another grunt, slightly softening to the question. "We both dreamed about our drakes. Do you remember?" His head jerked from side to side, upset at his brother's forgetfulness. "No secrets, that was the deal! Together, we would use our drakes to make the world a better place for Grandpa and Lola . . . but you kept yours a secret!" He looked around as he remembered he wasn't supposed to talk about it. "Hold on!" he sighed. "Let me grab my scroll I left in class, then we can talk about it."

Ethan nervously shuffled his feet as he watched his brother disappear into a side room before quickly reappearing.

The two boys walked in an awkward silence back to Ethan's room, neither one wanting to break the silence. They arrived without being noticed, which was refreshing for Ethan as he hadn't seen Kristian without one of his little buddies for days now.

They let their drakes down onto Ethan's bedroll to play and were immediately joined by Deseret, leaping from behind the desk to playfully pounce on the other two. She was now bigger than BeeSting and used the size to her advantage; whereas, Seon was still only two-thirds of the fiery red drake.

"All right, you wanna hear it?" Kristian now demanded in a rather-loud voice. He belted out the rest of his triage without waiting for Ethan. "You're a Dingus!" he flatly stated and slapped the back of his brother's head.

All three drakes paused to watch the two boys.

"Ha! That's it? That's all you're going to say?" Ethan mocked while rubbing the back of his head.

"Just getting started," Kristian growled. "When were secrets part of our pact?" He continued without waiting for an answer. "I mean, you're a *Dingus*!" He looked like he was readying to smack is brother again, but instead folded his arms in protest.

"Finished?"

"Not even close, shut up and listen!" the older boy continued. "I'm the one who turned sixteen! I paid the time, but *you* . . . you and Lola get to skip on by. You're too young . . ."

"Is that what all your ignoring me was about? That's stupid!"

"I didn't say I was finished!" Kristian barked. "And wipe that Dingus smirk off your face! I'm the one who bound the drake! I'm the one who started school! I'm the oldest, and it's my right to get there first! You always had to trump me." Kristian shook his head. "When are you gonna learn, you're just a little kid!" He momentarily savored this last outburst before closing. "How am I supposed to trust you when you flat out lie to me, then go tell'n' Grandpa and who knows who else?"

All three drakes looked at Kristian in anticipation for what was coming next. When nothing did, they went back to a game of wrestling.

Ethan hung his head low, a fresh wave of guilt and exhaustion overwhelming him. "I . . . I didn't mean to, I mean . . ."

Kristian shook his head in disgust and made to pick up BeeSting and leave.

"Wait, Kristian," Ethan croaked in an unusually tired voice. "I have to tell you something." He paused to reserve some strength. "Something that I haven't told Grandpa or Limnah . . . or anyone," Ethan pleaded.

Kristian gave him a stern look, then conceded, taking a seat on Lola's bedroll.

Ethan started at the beginning and told Kristian everything he could think of. He paused to consider the parts about the telepathy and Kesem, but decided to let him in on it in the end. He also recounted his sessions with Limnah, his readings, and lastly his lesson with Ezera.

Kristian sat in silence the entire time with his eyebrows slightly raised. "Whoa, what the—?" Kristian finally spouted. "That's quite a story, you really can do magic? I mean Kesem?" Kristian asked in a surprisingly excited tone.

Ethan nodded, feeling another wave of exhaustion hit him.

"And you can talk with Seon . . . just like that?" Kristian snapped his fingers with a mixture of amazement and disgust registering on his face.

Ethan slowly nodded, half-expecting to get punched again.

Kristian rolled back on his arms and let out a long whistle as all of the drakes turned to look at him again.

"Show me some!" Kristian suddenly demanded.

"What? Now?" Ethan was stunned at Kristian's order. He also felt Seon whirl around, looking intently at the exhausted boy. "I told you what happened both times I tried to use it," he weakly protested.

"Ya didn't get hurt the second time, just had a dream, right?" Kristian debated. "How scary can that be?"

Ethan remembered that he had left out the contents of his dream for some reason, only saying that he had a nightmare. He now guessed it couldn't hurt again and slowly nodded his head. "OK, I'll try what Ezera taught me."

*Ethan, no! You might really hurt yourself this time. You are too tired!* Seon shot him a glowering look that momentarily reminded Ethan of his older brother.

*I'll be fine, just stick with me this time and keep a lookout for me, OK?* Ethan waited. *Ohh-kay?*" he goaded.

Seon gave a curt nod. *Do as you must, just don't come running to me when it all goes wrong,* he said in a wounded tone.

Ethan knew he'd have to repair hurt feelings with Seon later, but he owed at least this much to his brother. *After all of the lies, Seon? I need you to understand that I need to do this.*

The little drake softened. *Ok, but if you so much as wince, I'm pulling you out of this,* he warned.

The younger boy relaxed his mind, careful to retrace all of the instructions Ezera had given him. His body felt immediately peaceful, all of his worries and exhaustion stowed away somewhere that didn't matter now. He could feel Seon's mind pinging him in the distance, but this time it was different. This time, he felt the drake's calming power all around him. He waited in the trance for a few moments, then realized he didn't know his way out. He'd missed that part of the lesson due to his dream. Panic started to crowd out his thoughts, and the white surroundings began to swirl with darker colors.

*Calm down, calm down,* he heard Seon's faint encouragement. The little drake was much more clear in his mind this time and the boy wondered what was different.

Ethan forced himself to think of white again, and the swirls disappeared. It occurred to him that if he wished to be awake that his senses would all return to him. He didn't know how he knew this, but he felt that this was the right action.

Seon felt it too and urged Ethan to follow this line of thought to the end.

The boy exerted his strength to return from the spell, and in slow amounts, he felt as if the white began to vanish around him and that he was coming back into full consciousness. He opened his eyes to see his room and Kristian sitting in front of him, his face inches from Ethan's, wearing a gigantic grin.

"That was the coolest thing I've ever seen. You were totally white, you lit up the entire room," the older boy croaked. "I had to drop the drapes over the window, in case someone saw it!" he exclaimed.

The Drake Epics - Journey to Qara

Ethan smiled, now even more drained and tired than before. He knew he'd taken a chance and that he was lucky.

*Very lucky!* Seon whispered in his mind.

Even though Ethan was exhausted, he claimed newfound strength as the two boys continued to talk and banter into the early-morning, just like old times. Ethan hoped that this would go on forever and finally turned into bed completely happy that night. Happier than he had felt in a very long time.

The next morning was difficult. Ethan did not want to wake up, but his little companion was nudging at his cheek.

*Ethan. You need to get up!*

The boy groaned about the drake's cold, wet snout and rolled over. *Not Now Seon, I'm sleeping.*

*No, Ethan! This is the last day and you need to get up, or we'll miss Limnah.*

*Oh, right,* he thought, but not any happier about how quickly morning had come. He arose with a yawn, sluggishly dressed, stumbled to the temple hall to grab a quick mouthful, and they were both standing at Limnah's door a few moments before dawn.

Limnah was not in his room.

Ethan waited for a while as he continued to recite his lines from the previous day. *Where is he?* he thought. He could recite the lines for only so long.

*Let's go in,* Seon announced on a whim. The little drake had escaped the pouch and was perched on the boy's shoulder.

*What, and get into more trouble?* the boy bleated.

*Stop worrying so much. It will be fun. Besides, we can look up a scroll to read. After all, Limnah has given us his permission,* the little drake prodded.

The sun started to crest over the distant mountains, which would provide more than enough light to read. So, they decided to go into Limnah's chamber with or without the priest.

The hesitant boy admitted that he wanted to have a closer look at the scrolls as well. He thought about a topic, something about controlling other's thoughts perhaps?

*That sounds intriguing,* Seon admitted. *Maybe we can use that on Limnah!* he mischievously considered.

*Maybe,* Ethan replied absent mindedly, as he started with the first shelf he came across, this one full of scrolls of all shapes and sizes, bottles with strange colored liquids, and some quills for writing.

Each scroll had the title written lengthwise on the outer surface to make it easier to identify the subject. "A Hunter's Best Friend, Regional

173

Desert Creatures . . . ," he read aloud as he worked his way through the scrolls. "Trapping Techniques: How to Control Animals."

*Grandpa could use that for Lola*, Ethan chuckled to himself.

Upon losing interest, he and Seon moved on to the next set of shelves. They soon discovered that each shelf was related to a specific subject, but still they couldn't find anything relating to the controlling thoughts.

The boy sighed in resignation and glanced up, toward the door.

The sun was higher, and its light cascaded deeper into the empty chamber, throwing the room into a different view altogether. In fact, the light uncovered objects that would have otherwise remained hidden from the two explorer's inquisitive eyes.

Still no Limnah, so Ethan continued rifling through scrolls. He moved toward the next shelf when something reflected in the corner of his eye. He slowly turned, trying to locate the glimmer again. He didn't have to search for long. The reflection was coming from something hanging on a wall directly beside the old priest's bedroll. Ethan slowly inched his way up to it while his mind tried to register what it might be.

It looked like a sand-blown frame with a white light set within it, like a window. Yet it wasn't a window at all. As he drew closer, he could see a shadowy reflection approaching the frame and a duplicate of the room behind him. The middle looked like a pool of water as impossible as that seemed to be.

He wasn't sure why he'd not noticed this before all the times he'd been in Limnah's chamber. But it was out of the way and no wonder, as most of that time had been spent with his nose buried in reading scrolls. He stopped a few paces from the frame to study it and tapped its metallic surface, leaving a slight smudge from his finger on its surface. It felt a little cold to the touch. He took a step back and studied his reflection then made a silly face, the surface reflected this.

*It's a mirror!* Seon announced and struck as intimidating of a pose as he could muster.

Ethan chortled in spite of himself.

Seon glared at the boy then broke into laughter, sounding like a chorus of grunts and whinnies.

The two spent a few moments enjoying their reflections when Ethan noticed a neatly wrapped scroll leaning against the wall. Seon now noticed it too.

The boy grabbed the tattered parchment, lowered himself to his knees, and slowly unrolled it on the old man's bedroll using both palms to spread it out fully and study the surface in more detail. *Strange*, he thought. A pile of sand lay heaped up in the middle of the scroll. *How did that get there?*

Seon shrugged. *Look at the runes all around the edges,* he stated. *But I can't read any of them.*

The boy squinted at the runes, himself, but without success. *It's old,* he surmised. *Very old.* He peered harder at a single rune trying to study every detail, but to his surprise the rune vanished from sight. "Whoa!" he shot Seon an inquisitive look, but the drake had apparently not noticed. *Did you see that?*

*See what?* Seon asked.

*That rune.* The boy pointed to an empty spot on the parchment. *It disappeared.*

The drake shook his head.

*Let's try again with . . . ,* Ethan thought for a moment then pointed at another rune, *that one!*

Seon nodded, and they both studied it for a few moments before it too vanished. Ethan felt a sudden jolt. *Whoa, that's not right,* he clamored, but stopped midway through what he planned to say next.

The runes all suddenly started to swirl around the outer edges of the parchment. The sand sifted towards the same edges, leaving an otherwise-placid interior, then spun up into tiny sand dervishes, framing up the parchment all seemingly of its own accord. A faint light danced in the scroll's interior with a hypnotic rhythm that drew the boy in closer, as if he were compelled and had no control of his body's movement.

"What do ya make of it, Seon?" Ethan asked out loud.

*I can sense power!* came the awestruck answer as Seon also stared spellbound into the scroll.

They were now a nose length from touching the swirling surface. Suddenly, an arid breeze escaped the parchment, spraying sand over the two.

Ethan snapped his eyes shut in reaction to the sudden movement. But when nothing seemed to have happened, he peered through one eye.

*We're floating . . . no . . . we're flying!* Seon exclaimed, as he spread his wings and lit off of Ethan's shoulder.

The boy grinned. *This is amazing!* he shouted.

It felt as if they were moving with incredible speed in a vast blue expanse with a hazy white mist rushing at them from below. Ethan stretched his hands out in front of him to brace for the impact as they dove into the vapor and were absorbed in a white swirling haze. The blue expanse disappeared altogether. White streaks hurtled past them and started to fade, a new brownish landscape opening up below.

Ethan craned his neck, captivated by the scene around him. He thought he could make out a barren sandy wasteland, walled in by giant looming mountains as barren and rocky as the sandy expanse.

They were still plummeting earthward; and sage, rock outcroppings, and trees sprouted across the surface as if they were growing in fast-forward.

*We're going to crash!* Seon screamed in Ethan's mind.

The ground loomed in front of them and, without warning, lurched upward and swallowed the pair in one swift bite. For a time, the boy and his drake fell headlong through the earth before opening up into what appeared to be a dark cavern below the sandy fields.

They slowed to a brief halt, hovering over the cave floor.

Ethan and Seon at once recognized the cavern from a month ago as Seon's hatching site. They didn't have much time to relive the memory before they sped off through a maze of caverns—so many that Ethan quickly lost track. After a series of dizzying twists and turns, they again started to slow as a pool of water opened up before them, briefly hovering over its black lurid surface, but only for a moment. Before either could react, they plunged into its depths, picking up momentum as they sped through the watery darkness.

Again without warning, they burst from the water's surface and into another much smaller cave. They lingered over the water's surface as the ripples they created moments before grew more calm.

When all was still, Ethan floated across the pool and touched down on a rocky shore.

Seon glided back to his perch on Ethan's shoulder.

They both stared at what was presented to them. Directly in front of where Ethan stood was a small pillar, atop of which rested a round sphere made of some unknown metal. A glowing metal.

Both Ethan and Seon tried to concentrate on the object, but it evaded their understanding.

*Ethan . . . Ethan . . . Ethan*, the orb called out to him. *The way is clear. Find the orb to reveal the path.*

Suddenly with a great gust of wind, the scroll erased the scene from their view, leaving windblown ripples behind, which slowed, until the leather was quite still again with a heap of ordinary sand piled up at the center.

"What was that?" Ethan asked aloud, more to himself rather than to his companion.

*It's the map to the great temple!* Seon answered in awe. *It's waiting for us, all we need to do is find it and revive it.* Ethan could feel Seon tremble with excitement.

*I don't understand. How do you know what it is? What was that round orb? How did it know my name?* Ethan thought in confusion.

"Ah, and what exactly is it that you have just seen?" a voice interrupted them.

Ethan immediately recognized the old priest's voice. He slowly turned around with a blank look. "I . . . I shouldn't be in here without your permission. Forgive me." Ethan groveled, trying to give himself time to think his way out of the situation. *Seon, help me come up with a story, quick,* the boy clamored.

Limnah raised an eyebrow as he waited patiently for the answer. "Ethan, what did you see?" he repeated, his tone the same calm as always.

*We trust him about what we just saw?* Seon suggested. *But we don't have to tell him the location.*

Ethan almost laughed out loud at the latter comment and leaked an impish smile onto his lips, which he quickly corrected as he prepared to act out his plot. He sighed, as if trying to remember the experience, then recounted his journey, but kept the details vague. When he got to the part about the object, he mentioned that he saw a cave like any other, but didn't go into any details beyond that.

"Is there more you want to tell me?" Limnah finally asked after Ethan was through with his recital.

"No," he lied. He was annoyed Limnah always fell into this line of questioning. It always made him feel so uneasy. It was not a pleasant feeling, he decided.

"Very well, perhaps you will trust me enough over time?"

Ethan took this to mean that Limnah knew he was lying, which made him feel all the more guilt and some amount of anger. But still not enough to tell the priest the whole story. He felt a sudden pang that Limnah would never accept his request for schooling.

*I told you to tell him,* Seon scolded.

"And now, I think we shall start with our lesson," Limnah concluded before Ethan could right himself or respond to Seon.

The boy nodded in defeat, deciding to take his chances and hope for another practice session, like Ezera's lesson from the previous day. Even though he didn't deserve it after his dishonesty, not really, he thought. He sheepishly started toward the old man, then remembered that the scroll was left open and turned to roll it back up. However, the leathery parchment was not there. Ethan quickly scanned the area and found it rolled together where he had found it. Confused, he turned himself toward Limnah and walked to him in a slight daze.

To Ethan's chagrin, the lesson was not another practice but instead consisted of more reading, this time, a scroll on controlling thoughts.

*Well, at least we get to read the scroll we were looking for in the first place*, he consoled the drake. But he wondered if Limnah knew this is what they had been looking for to begin with. The old priest seemed to know an awful lot about what he and Seon thought. He knew too much, Ethan considered.

As both boy and drake dove into the scroll, the topic turned out not to be about controlling other's thoughts at all. At least not directly. Instead it read about why it was important to master oneself before attempting certain magic, or Kesem. Kesem drained energy from the practitioner if used incorrectly. Furthermore, Kesem took study, pondering, and practice.

The last section, however, seemed a bit out of place and caused a stir for the two. It covered a self-mastery blocking technique. In fact the only one in the scroll that prevented others from entering their thoughts, or even more strangely, recognizing their conscience or even their presence, making them almost invisible to detection.

*Can drakes and drake holders really detect each other's presence and thoughts?* Ethan asked in disbelief.

*Well, BeeSting and Deseret both detected me, and I them . . . and you've caught bits and pieces of their thoughts when we've been talking*, Seon reflected. *And there's always the auditor's probing thoughts . . .*

Ethan shivered in spite of himself, but Seon's thoughts rang true.

Suddenly, both boy and drake came to the same conclusion, *What if that's how Limnah knows?* they thought in unison.

Ethan stole a quick glance at the priest, who was sitting at the other end of the room with his back to them, but noticeably immersed in another scroll. The idea had merit, and they both began to greedily read on, covering the section two times to get as much out of it as they could. It really wasn't a magic Kesem, the scroll read, so words didn't have to be used.

*I have no idea by what the scroll means about no need for words, but let's practice!* Seon hungrily asserted.

The boy nodded, and they mentally practiced on each other with varying results. Ethan got through to Seon on the first try, but was hindered on further attempts; whereas, Seon broke through Ethan's barrier every time, much to the boy's continued humiliation.

*I'm sure you will get better with practice,* Seon consoled Ethan unconvincingly after they had finished. This did nothing to bolster the boy's hopes.

Ethan shrugged off the disappointment and now concentrated on his next task. He decided to chance his request with Limnah about continuing their lessons. He forced himself to focus on the mind-blocking technique before walking over to where the old man was sitting.

"Master Limnah?" he timidly asked as the priest paused and looked up at him. "Seon and I were wondering if we will continue on with you?" he ended the last few words as his voice faltered.

Limnah raised an eyebrow. "We?" he queried.

Ethan immediately realized his blunder in implying he and Seon were linked. He was furious at his slip. He had to come up with a counter argument, and fast.

"I . . . I mean . . . I would like to know." He shot back, mentally flogging himself that his reply was even more revealing.

The old priest studied the two for a few moments before answering, "I feel you will do well in the advanced courses, yes. I'm sure you already know the other classmates, Hem, Yeb, and a few other students?" he now asked in a rather-paternal tone.

A sudden knot twisted in Ethan's stomach. "Hem and Yeb?" he said. "Why not just with you?" he quickly repealed, suddenly trying to get out of his need to school with the two bullies.

"Oh, you will meet with me a few times per week as well. However, it is good to meet with others of your own age, it enhances and increases your learning retention."

Ethan still wasn't convinced, but let Limnah continue.

"The classes will consume every day of the week, except for the day of the Great Spirit. Breakfast and lunch will be provided. It will also—"

"But what about Grandpa and my chores?" Ethan interrupted, unintentionally overriding the old man. How would Grandpa fare without the two boys, he thought. It was tough enough to have Kristian absent half the time. Ethan knew this all too well as he had to pick up most of Kristian's daily chores, he thought with disdain.

Limnah feigned a quick smile at the interruption. "Your Grandpa will be just fine. I will consult with him on this today, and he will receive additional help in your absence."

"But . . ."

The old man raised a hand, warding off further unnecessary questions. "You are young to start schooling indeed. We have never made an exception of this sort. But you will do well I think, yes," he concluded.

Ethan's mind buzzed with bittersweet excitement, as if a great hive of bees took up residence inside his skull. He was not sure what to make out of this latest opportunity. How was he supposed to start school? This was much more than he'd hoped for. How would he deal with it? How would he deal with the bullies? He had always tried to avoid them. Now he would be sitting in the same room with them almost every day!

*Something is very strange about this, Ethan,* Seon chimed in. *This is definitely out of the ordinary.*

Ethan didn't respond, but he knew it too.

*We need to be even more careful than before . . . ,* the little drake advised.

"Arrive at dawn as you have done this last week," Limnah was now giving Ethan instructions. "Oh, and you must either keep Seon concealed, or you may leave him here while you study. Your assignment for tonight is to practice with Seon on the mind block you learned today."

Ethan and Seon again marveled how the old man knew so much about them. Yet somehow, Limnah had gained a measure of their trust. They were both beginning to like the old man more with every passing day.

Limnah concluded, "You are to use this technique while at school with the other students. All other magical practice sessions or other drake-related training will take place in my quarters as directed by either myself or Ezera. Any questions?"

Ethan shook his head, not wanting to push his case further at the moment.

"You are excused."

Ethan momentarily paused, then nodded in subjection, and dismissed himself. He quickly pushed down the thought of school with his childhood bullies and thought about his experience with the frame on the wall and the strange scroll, his heart now pounding at the prospect of both adventures.

*We need to retrieve that ball, the map,* Seon said. *Besides, the adventure is too great to pass by. I feel that it's important.*

*Important? How do you figure that?* Ethan asked.

Seon sent Ethan an image of the little drake peering into the ball, and they both felt a sudden boost of energy, as if the memory itself had power.

Ethan shook his head, avoiding the sudden excitement welling up in his chest, then thought better of it. *It's too dangerous,* Ethan replied to Seon. Their roles seemed reveresed at the moment. He tried to rationalize that the power he was feeling was from his own adrenaline rush and not from the actual memory. Either way, it didn't feel right.

The Drake Epics - Journey to Qara

Seon blathered on, as if he hadn't noticed the thought at all, *We'll have to plan it at day, and make plenty of time. We'll also need to come up with an excuse to skip out of school for a full day.*

Ethan privately mulled over the idea in his head and felt another jolt of excitement surge through his body. *We have to find Kristian, he's great at coming up with unbeatable plans. He'll know what to do!* He finally gave in.

This adventure would be the supreme undertaking, the king of all adventures, surpassing anything they had ever tried before, let alone dreamed of—leaving the village unattended to explore some dangerous cave. The more he thought about it, the more the idea became perfectly reasonable. That is, as long as Kristian was along for the ride.

# Chapter 11

## The Novice

*Perfection is attained over a lifetime—it's the striving that counts.*

Kristian wasn't in any of the smaller temple classrooms. "School must have let out early," Ethan remarked with disgust. Regardless of this small setback, the excitement built with every passing moment. He did not let this deter him and kept up his vigil to search for his older brother.

The boy and his drake talked about their plans for the adventure as they searched.

It was early afternoon before he finally caught up to Kristian and BeeSting in the bee pit, thanks to Seon's keen senses that lead them there. The older boy was just finishing up his chores, and by the way he was throwing around the cleaning tools, Ethan could see that his temperamental brother was in another one of his foul moods.

*This will cheer him up!* he thought optimistically to his companion. His enthusiasm got the better of him. "Hey, you hungry, Kristian?"

*Watch out!* Seon bawled.

Ethan instinctively ducked as a pan crashed into the wall directly where his head had been only moments before.

Apparently, Kristian hadn't noticed his younger brother come in, and had reacted by flinging what was in his hands in his younger brother's direction. "Don't do that, Ethan!" he bellowed, placing both hands on the edge of the metal sync and shaking his head to deal with the sudden rush of adrenaline at the surprise.

The younger boy stayed in his crouched position with a mixed look of relief and shock.

After a few moments, Kristian regained his usual composure. "Dingus! Yeah, guess I'm kind of hungry." The larger boy motioned to a sack laying in the corner that Ethan assumed contained a midday meal.

The boys sat and broke bread and dipped them in honey.

Seon had found a way out of the satchel and promptly perched on Ethan's shoulder, as the boy absently offered the hungry drake a small morsel. Seon took the bread in his clutches and began to devour it.

BeeSting seemed to also be ravenous, consuming his piece of bread in one gulp and then expectantly waited for his next, which Kristian promptly handed to him.

Ethan didn't waste any time as he launched into the story in between mouthfuls. "Kristian, I'm telling you, it felt so real!" He explained about the wind scroll before taking another giant bite out of his bread.

"I just can't see it," the older boy lectured. "Are you sure you didn't see this in a dream or something?" he scrutinized.

"Nope." The other boy shook his head. "Limnah even encouraged us to think about this more. If he believes, then we believe." He nodded his head at Seon, who peered up momentarily from his meal. Ethan studied his older brother and recognized the familiar facial expressions that his more experienced brother made when materializing a plan or strategy in his mind.

Finally, Kristian nodded, and poured through a laundry list of items they would need. "But that's just off the top of my head. I'll need to think about this more and make sure we're covered."

Both boys fell silent as they chewed.

"That and I need to find a way out of school." The older boy mused.

"Well, I certainly won't worry too much about missing any classes with Hem and Yeb." Ethan spat, still not happy that he would have to meet with them every day.

At the mention of this, Kristian's thoughtful expression turned into an indignant frown. "What do you mean about classes with Hem and Yeb?" he said in a low and deliberate tone.

"Umm . . . that's not the point," Ethan balked, perplexed by his brother's tone. "I mean . . . it's no different than what I've been doing with Limnah, and . . . besides, you know what Hem did to me"—now trying to skirt the issue and focus the discussion back on the bullies—"they pick on me, and I gotta spend full days with their taunts!" he concluded, his words all coming out in a jumble.

Kristian's face darkened all the more at the comment about full day training. There was an awkward silence between the two. Ethan glanced sidewise at Seon and fidgeted with his hands, while Kristian tore at an unusually large chunk of bread with his teeth.

"Well . . . uhh . . . what do ya think about the adventure?" Ethan said in a timid voice. "You in?" The words were almost coming out in a hoarse whisper as he tried to deflect any further discussion about schooling.

"Don't get off subject now, Dingus," yelled the older boy.

Ethan realized that his older brother had latched onto school, and there was no thwarting him now. If he were lucky, this one would blow over quickly. If he were unlucky, he had days, possibly weeks of hardship ahead of him, or worse yet, the silent treatment. Somewhere in the back of his mind, he realized that sharing too much information sometimes does more harm than good. He sensed the fight coming on, but felt helpless to stop it.

*Better to let this one ride itself out and not make it worse,* Seon counseled as the drake chewed on his piece of bread.

*What should I do?* Ethan braced for the worst.

Seon remained silent, pretending not to acknowledge the conversation any further. *Probably because you're feeling it too?* Ethan sulked as he realized he'd have to deal with Kristian all on his own.

"I'm not getting this special training! It's unheard-of! I mean, I've gotta train with the others"—Kristian now fumbled in the air with his hands to grope for the words—"my age, and you can't even call that training!" His voice now sounded shrill, his face red, and Ethan even thought he saw his brother's veins show at his temples, as if this whole thing were a giant parody being played out on him all at once. "It's not fair!"

Kristian would have figured this all out on his own anyway, Ethan thought with remorse. But he was especially frustrated by his poor timing, *Why can't I keep my big mouth shut?* He fumed. How could he not have known this would infuriate his brother, *Just dumb luck!* he thought in frustration; and instead of letting this blow over, which would have been the smart thing to do, he instead reached a boiling point at the prospect that he might not get his adventure after all. This in turn led to his own irritation and bitterness that Kristian always had to have his own way! "Look, I didn't ask for any of this, Kristian! Besides, you always get to do everything that I don't. You always get more than me, you always take my stuff, you are always better than me at everything . . . Why can't you be happy for me just this once?" Ethan paused, trying to catch his breath to his list of grievances. But he instantly regretted the outburst. He'd gone too far.

"Dingus. You're such a baby, Ethan!" Kristian shot back. "I'm gonna pound you into the dirt!" Ethan winced and braced for a licking. But instead, what came was much, much worse. "Just . . . go sob to Grandpa like you always do! I don't care about your school or your adventure or about you anyways!" the older boy hollered, throwing his arm out apathetically.

Tears welled up in Ethan's eyes. "Fine, I'll do it all on my own." He spat. "I don't need you, Kristian! I never have! You only care about yourself and no one else, unless it benefits you!" he tried to jab the words at his older brother to make his own wounds feel better, but the insults fell rather ineptly from his lips.

"That's just ripe, little brother!" Kristian retaliated. "Fine!" he yelled even louder and again dismissed the younger boy with a contemptuous wave of his hand.

Ethan stood up, calling to Seon, who made his farewell to BeeSting before promptly leaping to the boy's shoulder. Ethan angrily stomped out of the bee pit. He'd have to come back later and finish his chores when Kristian had gone.

*We always have to fight. Things were going so well. Then, he has to blow up and we get all mad. He's always grumpy and he always thinks only about himself.* Ethan spouted, furious at his brother for not supporting him more, and a little about his own reaction about dumb school. Instead of hatching a plan together that could have been quite possibly the biggest adventure ever, not to mention life-saving for he knew not why. He clenched his fists in a silent protest.

*Ethan, are you all right?* Seon nudged.

The boy half-nodded in answer, unclenching his hands as the little drake nuzzled close to his neck and cooed. This always seemed to calm him down. He set off on a brisk walk around the complex once or twice until Kristian left the bee pit. Once the older boy had gone, Ethan quickly ducked in to finish up his chores in silence, after which both he and Seon practiced their blocking technique the requisite seven times before retiring to bed for the night.

The next morning, Ethan reported at dawn to the Temple of the Lion as Limnah had instructed. A breeze rushed through the temple entrance, feeling a little cooler than usual, and he paused to enjoy the rare treat. He took a deep breath and detected the faint smell of incense, probably coming from one of the temple shrines in the courtyard.

He presently considered the entrance to the temple, with two imposing lions carved out of solid sandstone, opposing each other with their mouths agape in a silent challenge.

Memories of the previous night flooded his mind, and he couldn't help but feel betrayed by his older brother. Were they so different from the lions? He shrugged off the thought and entered the classroom at the far end of the temple courtyard.

The room was dark and empty, except for seven short tables, each with an adjoining rug underneath them for sitting. The tables were all arranged in a half circle in the center of the room, facing the wall opposite the entrance.

Ethan let his eyes adjust and realized that the walls themselves were lined with shelves containing everything imaginable—scrolls, bottles, quills, and an assortment of other items—much like Limnah's chamber, but not as exotic.

*Where is everyone?* Seon asked from his usual hiding place in Ethan's back sack. He tried to squirm his little snout through the bag's flap for a better look.

The boy shrugged. "We'll wait until they get here, I guess," he answered as he sat at one of the tables and patiently waited.

*Remember, you need to send me thoughts when others are around, don't speak them out loud*, the little drake reprimanded.

Ethan nodded in embarrassment as he remembered how he unwittingly revealed some of his secrets to Limnah last week by speaking out loud when he shouldn't have.

*Better?* he thought in jest.

Seon ignored the comment.

The two companions decided to practice their mind-blocking technique again and tried to hold it in preparation for the day's events.

They didn't have to wait long, Hem and Yeb entered the room, bragging to each other about their recent hunting excursion and their heroic feats of valor. They both halted midstep when they noticed Ethan. This was quickly followed by utter revulsion.

Hem curled his lip in loathing and quickly closed the gap between him and Ethan, pounding one fist into his other hand. "You little," he began.

Ethan could still see the bruises on his right cheek that Kristian had given him and choked down a spiteful smirk.

"Egh, um," someone cleared their throat from somewhere in the room.

The boys jerked their heads upward, looking for the source, homing in on the shadows in the back of the room.

"Take your seats, boys." Ezera now emerged from the darkness as he stared down the two brothers standing but a few paces from Ethan.

Hem thought wildly, trying to find an excuse for his outburst. "He's in my place!" he protested unconvincingly.

"Hmm." the priest grunted. "Ethan, you may sit here." Ezera motioned at a seat at the end of the half circle. The boy stood, retrieving his back sack with Seon still inside, and took up the seat as directed.

Hem glared at him as he moved. The bully slowly sat, keeping his eyes fixed on Ethan all the while.

Ezera walked slowly around the room, lighting the oil chandeliers with a light stick, such that light shone directly around the little circle of tables where the students would sit for the balance of the day.

Two more boys soon entered the room, followed by two girls. Ethan instantly recognized them all, but realized Seon might not. *The first boy's name is Kreshk*, Ethan explained to his companion. *He is the village general's eldest son, and he turned sixteen the same week as Kristian.* Kreshk had the same muscular build of Kristian, had rusty brown hair that curled at the ends, and his eyes were a deep hazel. He paraded an orange drake perched on his left shoulder, roughly the size of Seon.

The next boy to enter was Khalin. *That's Limnah's great-nephew*, Ethan announced. He was more slender than Kreshk with a narrower face, darker eyes, and dark brown hair, sporting a red drake perched on his right shoulder, identical to BeeSting.

*Cynthia*—the first girl to enter—*is the general's daughter.* She had light brown hair that fell around her back. She looked like her older brother, although much, much more beautiful and slender. Ethan blushed. By her walk, the boy recognized her usual haughty temperament as he could attest to from past brushes with the older girl. *It's only a matter of time before she asks me about Kristian,* he chided as she had a penchant for his older brother.

The last girl's name was Sherah. *And she is the grand Sheikh's daughter, sister to Hem and Yeb,* Ethan concluded. She had soft glowing brown hair, a cheery disposition, and didn't much care for either of her brothers. *She's stood up for me with her brothers before.* Sometimes this had saved him from a severe beating. *But not always!* Ethan grimaced.

*Interesting,* Seon thought.

Ethan looked questioningly at his sack. *What is?*

*I can feel all of the drakes, but they cannot sense my presence. It's working!*

The boy grinned, *Well, you're better at this than me—the mighty Seon,* he mocked.

*Funny.* The little drake chided. *No, I can feel their power. They are all elemental.*

Ethan remembered about village royalty getting special attention. Usually, he would have been furious about this, but found that his feelings had softened somewhat with his binding to a much more powerful Seon.

*You know it!* Seon bragged, causing Ethan to grin widely.

The girls didn't have any drakes, as per the village custom that drakes were man's domain.

*Deseret and Lola would disagree!* Seon announced rather proudly.

Ethan imagined his little sister and wondered what would happen as soon as everyone found out about her drake. He quickly repressed the thought as he didn't want to follow that course too far down the line.

The four students took their seats, exchanging questioning glances between each other about the new student.

*Not like I can't see or hear them!* Ethan fumed. He knew they were whispering about him.

*Easy now,* Seon soothed.

"Sir, why is *he* here anyways?" Hem regained his usual arrogant composure, pointing his pudgy finger in Ethan's direction.

"Ethan is now a student in our class," Ezera continued, ignoring the soft gasps of shock from the students. "You will do well to welcome him into our midst and treat him with every respect that you show to one another."

The new student looked nervously around the room and suddenly wondered what he had gotten himself into.

"Very well then," Ezera continued. "We will pick up from where we left off in yesterday's lesson. Sherah, because you are sitting next to Ethan, please help him through the lesson materials."

She nodded and smiled at Ethan again as he blushed a bright red at the extra attention.

"Kreshk, please pass out the scrolls on . . ." the priest continued.

"Hi, Ethan," Sherah leaned over and said in a soft whisper. She wore a kind smile on her face, which immediately put Ethan into a nervous twitch. "Just let me know if you have any questions. The lessons go by pretty fast, so it can be hard to keep up, but you'll catch on soon enough," she remarked confidently.

Ethan nodded in gratitude. "Thank . . . thank you," he whispered back while blushing a deeper purple at his lethargic response to the girl.

The lessons sped by even faster than Sherah had said, and Ethan found it impossible to keep up with Ezera's tempo. He realized this was going to be much harder work than he had anticipated. Even Seon found it difficult to keep pace.

The day was split into seven lessons: three before lunch with the remainder following.

The first class focused on history and village lore and included reading, reciting, and some singing. Ethan almost fell asleep as he read through a brutally boring scroll on village genealogy. At first, he had been excited, but upon finding no mention of Grandpa or the children in the record, he felt even more out of place than before. But he did find some interesting anecdotes about some of the villager escapades that he'd not known about before.

The second class was even less interesting. The theme was language and rune study, similar to the studies Limnah had advised Ethan on. The session was broken into two halves, the first lesson included memorizing words, names, and their runes. Ethan regretted that Seon could not sit on his shoulder and participate, as did Seon. After all, the little drake was much better than he at this. The boy stole quick glances at the others and their drakes, careful to not get caught, and noticed they all read over the boys' shoulders too; however, only Hem's drake looked remotely interested as Kreshk's companion kept swiveling its neck around to look at anything else that caught its attention and Khalin's busily preened himself.

The second lesson included rune writing, which Ethan never remembered having attempted before. At first, his fingers felt like giant toes trying to etch something onto a stone surface with a piece of brittle wood. Twice, he dabbed too much ink onto the scroll and came close to breaking the tip right off his quill, not to mention the scribbles on his paper, which were not legible in the least. However, once he got over this hurdle, it came to him with remarkable ease. He had a vague feeling that

# The Novice

he had once before mastered this, but the thought was fleeting, like that of his dreams.

Lunch didn't come quickly enough for Ethan. The students made their way to another hall through a door cut into the back wall of their study room. The hall was one-quarter the size of the Temple of Abundance. Two long tables stretched out in front of the students with an assortment of foods already laid out in preparation for their arrival.

The meal was deliciously prepared. *Look at all of this meat and vegetables, and . . . well, I have no idea what that is.* He pointed at a round blob of glue on a plate that wobbled as the others bumped into the table.

"That is a delicacy from the Abseron Sea!" Sherah explained, noticing where Ethan was pointing to.

The boy grinned impishly. He had never witnessed its like and devoured the sight in hunger. His stomach joined in and began to noisily rumble, louder than he thought possible, as Ethan held his sides hoping none of the other students had heard.

Sherah giggled.

Ethan blushed and quickly gathered food onto his plate and found a seat. As soon as he was comfortable, the boy began to sneak small quantities of food to Seon, careful not to be caught. But no one seemed to notice.

Seon gratefully tore at the meat that Ethan slipped him, exchanging a quick *Thank-you* with the boy before gorging himself on the small feast. This, especially considering the dry bread and honey Ethan had been feeding to the poor little drake for the last month. It occurred to him that meats might be more to Seon's liking.

*Yes, they are, Ethan. This is much tastier than that wretched bread. Although the honey is sweet enough . . .*, the little drake conveyed.

Lunch passed without major incident. Hem, Yeb, and Kreshk all sat together at the opposite table, much to Ethan's relief. Hem looked up to glare at Ethan every now and then, while whispering something to the other boys. Ethan tried to ignore them.

Khalin and the girls sat with Ethan, as they discussed the goings-on in the village. Ethan purposefully paid little attention to the conversation as he ate, just happy to have such a feast for the first time in his life.

"Isn't that right, Ethan?" Sherah was now asking.

"Um, sorry, I didn't' hear what you said," he sheepishly answered, now feeling a little guilty for not listening.

"You used to work with your grandpa to harvest honey, right?"

"Oh yeah, still do. We work the hives at interval days." He dove into another helping of meat and stuffed his mouth full so that he didn't have to talk any further.

"Did Kristian help you?" Cynthia jumped in.

Sherah and Khalin rolled their eyes, as they knew full well what she was up to, trying to pry the tiniest bit of information out of Ethan about his older brother.

"What did I say?" she asked the two. They both shrugged.

Ethan nodded, his mouth still full, and she looked disappointed when he didn't offer up anything else.

"So . . . how did you get into this class, Ethan?" Khalin was now asking, stuffing his own face with a large helping of meat. He continued talking with a mouth full of food. "After all, aren't you only fourteen years old and a bit behind the rest of us and . . . ?"

Ethan noticed that Sherah shot Khalin a withering look, which cut the other boy short. This did little to ease Ethan's concerns, and he now felt even more self-conscious. He shrugged at the older boy in answer for fear of divulging too much information.

Khalin presently handed a piece of meat to his red drake, who quickly set to work devouring it as fast as it could. He pressed on, "Well, whatever the reason, you're definitely in for an interesting ride, especially 'cause you don't have a drake yet . . . But that's OK," he amended as he met Sherah's stern gaze. "Yeb . . . over there." He motioned toward Hem and Sherah's younger brother, sitting silently at the adjacent table, completely engrossed in the two other boys' conversation.

"Well, he doesn't have one yet either," Khalin concluded, taking another bite.

Ethan looked up, and it suddenly occurred to him that Yeb worshiped the other boys. He remembered many times where both boys had commanded Yeb to do things, horrible things, to himself, yet he still did them. Ethan now suddenly understood that all Yeb wanted was attention and acceptance, and he felt sympathy, almost compassion for the boy.

He was brought out of his brief reverie as Cynthia humphed. "He doesn't deserve a drake anyways!" she said irritably into her cup before gulping down the remainder of its contents. Sherah glowered at the other girl, but held her tongue.

Ethan decided to change the subject to his interrogator's red drake in a sudden stroke of genius. "What can your drake do, Khalin?" he asked, trying to glean any information about the other boy's drake that he could pass on to Kristian.

"Ah, you've come to the right place!" Khalin beamed.

Now it was the girls' turn to roll their eyes, and Ethan would soon find out why.

Khalin embarked on a sermon on fire drakes.

Ethan was especially interested to find out that Khalin's drake was an elemental *fire* drake and that the older boy could exercise a small amount of Kesem to cast fireballs!

"Currently the size of a small stone," he was saying. "Hey, wanna see it?" Khalin exclaimed, more as a statement rather than as a question.

Both Cynthia and Sherah gasped and shook their heads while waving their hands wildly behind the boy in disapproval. Apparently, Khalin practiced this a little more than either cared for.

Ethan avoided any encouragement, hiding himself in another helping of food.

Khalin's face briefly clouded over with a faraway look as he said the word *yangin*. A tiny flame lit up in his hands. He opened his eyes and threw it against the rock wall before it snubbed out, leaving a little black mark.

"It's supposed to get bigger over time, with more study," the boy said proudly. "I may even have the ability to exercise fire in different ways, eventually."

Ethan was unquestionably impressed. He hadn't realized this before, and his mind raced through options for how to impart this knowledge to his older brother, momentarily forgetting they weren't on speaking terms right now.

"Also, fire drakes don't communicate very well," Khalin mentioned. "You have to really focus hard to talk to them. It's even harder for them to talk to us. Not like sand drakes, like Hem's." He waved a surreptitious hand in Hem's direction. "Sand drakes are the best at telepathy, but it takes a long time for the holder to break through to them before that can happen, which Hem hasn't mastered yet." Khalin chuckled.

Ethan presently wondered why Seon was so much easier to communicate with.

*Don't get overconfident . . . ,* Seon cautioned, still busily shredding a piece of meat. *I'm simply more advanced than they are.*

*Who's the one who is over confident now?* the boy pressed without a response.

—  —  —

After lunch, the boys all returned to the same classroom. Ethan was disappointed to learn that the girls separated into other lessons for the remainder of the day. Sherah had mentioned this to him during lunch. The girls studied topics under another priest, which included proper etiquette, the arts, music, and medicinal studies. This would all apparently help them when they wed to other royalty.

Ethan winced at the thought. He found the idea of girls so young getting married. In fact, it was revolting to him, but he didn't know exactly why. He looked longingly after Sherah, as he knew he would have little help.

"That's ok. I'll help you out." Khalin said, as he slapped the younger boy on the back.

Ethan winced and was reminded of his older brother.

"This lesson is split into two sections; one on astrology and mathematics and the other, of course, is all about the sciences."

*What's astrology?* The little drake asked Ethan.

*I'm not quite sure, but I think it's about the stars. Beside, you're about to find out.* The boy thought back.

It was, in fact, about the stars and Ethan felt completely overwhelmed with the topic, although he was much relieved when he was paired up with Khalin instead of with one of the other boys. The group was now an odd number and that meant that one of the boys always had to pair up with Ezera if another partner was not available. Each group received a scroll of the planets and stars, and they had to use geometry to chart planetary courses.

Khalin mentioned they had to also use math for building construction blueprints, land boundary maps, and other uses. Lastly, Ethan not only had to learn geometric algorithms but also had to memorize stars, constellations, and names used for navigation.

The second lesson concentrated on sciences, such as seasonal climate and the study of the four elements: earth, wind, water, and fire. Most of this included reading out of some boring text that Ethan couldn't remember half of, even after reading it through twice.

Ezera was adamant that this study was crucial for all students. "These sciences are studied at all of the temples at all of the large sanctuaries," he said.

*I wonder where the other sanctuaries are?* Ethan exclaimed to his drake. *Somewhere on a cliff looking over the Abseron Sea?* He let his mind wander about temples in far-away lands where other boys like him were learning about the gods, the cosmos, and how mankind lived in harmony with their teachings. But, before he knew it, the lesson was over, and Ezera was announcing the next session.

*The Novice*

"It is now time to turn to magical technique and control," Ezera said flatly. "Put down your scrolls, stand for a moment and stretch." He exclaimed.

Ethan was only too happy to stretch out his sore limbs. *I've never had to sit for this long before,* he complained to his companion.

*Well, it could be worse.* The little drake fumed. *You could be stuck in a stinking leathery pouch!*

The boy felt a sudden pang of sympathy for his companion and wished he could sneak him out somehow. But his thoughts didn't linger on the little drake for long.

"This is my favorite lesson!" Khalin said to the boy. "Ezera teaches us strategy, drake telepathy, theory, and self-mastery. Best of all, the lesson on theory includes practice drills from what we read," he said with a yawn. "Ah, don't let my yawn fool ya though. It's pretty tough . . . that is for those of us with drakes. Sorry Ethan, I guess you just get to watch," he concluded in a pitying tone.

True to Khalin's revelation, the lesson's topic was on the principles of magical control. Ezera covered sounding out commands to their drakes before he opened up to questions by the boys about their magical progress.

It was here that Ethan learned Hem could already move rocks and sand in small degrees through his drake named Colbert. Kreshk's orange drake, Storm, was an elemental wind drake that gave Kreshk control of mini wind gusts.

Both Ethan and Yeb sat quietly. Yeb, in particular, wore a look of misery mixed with boredom on his face for the length of the class. Ethan half-listened while he devoured as much of the scroll as time permitted, immersing himself in each section. He took a number of mental notes to practice with Seon that evening, when they retired to their room.

The last lesson of the day quickly became Ethan and Seon's favorite—the exercise of magical abilities and enchanting skills. For this lesson, they were both excused to meet with Limnah, while the other boys remained in the classroom with Ezera to practice together. Before leaving, Ezera told Ethan that the class changed every other day to sparring and the study of weaponry, which the boy already guessed would be his least favorite class of all.

"You can let Seon out of his little cage now." Limnah observed with a smile as Ethan entered his chambers.

*Finally!* Seon discharged with relief as Ethan opened the latch to his back sack. The little drake quickly clambered up to the boy's shoulder, taking up his typical perch and started to preen.

"How were the lessons on your first day?" the old wise man queried.

*"Fine,"* responded Ethan in a fatigued tone, still trying to take it all in.

"Over time, you will get used to the routine . . . and you will develop your skills to match what is required of you."

*How does he do that?* Ethan asked.

*Cues!* Seon paused before diving back in.

*Cues? What are cues?*

*You know, when you stand in front of him like you did and act tired, he's going to pick up on that and know that you are tired.* The little drake replied and sent a mental image of Ethan looking pathetically tired.

*I don't look* that *bad!* the boy grumbled before their little exchange was interrupted.

"Today, we shall practice the calming Kesem that Ezera had you perform previously. As I'm sure you've started to learn in magical theory, exercising Kesem is a delicate process that can drain you, if not done correctly."

Ethan nodded in answer and Seon finished his preening.

"This makes Kesem hard to calibrate—it is different for every holder. Usually, this magic is specific to the drake that a holder is bound to. But you have already learned this from your readings, I imagine."

Ethan silently nodded again.

"For example, Hem's brown sand drake is a ground elemental. Meaning that Hem can control elements in the ground directly around him by exercising mastery over it." Limnah paused and looked into Ethan's eyes as though to silently quiz him on what he'd just said before continuing.

"Often, it is easier to express a feeling in a small way that develops and grows over time and with practice. The easiest way to develop the feeling is to attach a word to its meaning." Limnah brought his hands together in one motion for emphasis.

"This must be done verbally, although accomplished holders can sometimes, and only very rarely, perform this completely within their own minds." The old priest again paused, thinking of an example before giving up. "As in days of old. These words are captured in the lesson materials and perfected over many generations to correctly capture the essence of the feelings in order to perform the action correctly . . . nel'Alchezim'klat, as it is called, or more well known as the tongue of the drake in the common language."

Ethan concentrated hard on the old priest's lecture. He didn't necessarily have need for the words when using his Kesem, but he was very interested in the feelings they imbued. Feelings he would need to master control over.

# The Novice

"I understand from Ezera that you did not recite any word for the calming Kesem yesterday. Can you share with me how you were able to perform this?" Limnah suddenly asked.

Ethan felt a quick pang of sobriety.

*And so it begins!* Seon sighed.

*I hoped Ezera wouldn't notice!* Ethan knew he'd made the blunder yesterday, but thought that he could evade notice. He silently scolded himself as he was constantly revealing too much information about the combined powers he shared with Seon.

*Still, Limnah doesn't miss a beat, does he?* Seon claimed.

*What do you mean?* the boy asked as he strained to think up a good excuse for Limnah. Although he was extra careful to think the question through, instead of saying it out loud.

*Meaning, no matter what we do, he somehow knows what we're up to,* Seon clarified.

Seon was right, and Ethan knew he had to redouble his efforts to be more cautious around Limnah and Ezera from now on. Suddenly, an idea bubbled up that gave a perfect way out of this latest mess. Ethan was fast becoming an expert at diverting attention.

"But it didn't work . . . ," he weakly protested to Limnah's question. "I . . . I muttered another word under my breath that I learned in one of the scrolls you gave me." He hung his head in mock shame.

The wise man raised an eyebrow, but was silent.

After a few moments of uncomfortable awkwardness, Ethan coughed into his hand. "Can we try it again, if you tell me the word?" He hoped his ruse would placate Limnah.

*Brilliant performance,* Seon chirped.

The old man stared intently at Ethan, as if he were deliberating. He finally nodded, as if satisfied. "Sessiz," he stated. "The word is *Sessiz*. But—" Limnah raised his voice in warning. "You have to say the word aloud, then memorize the feeling that is attached to it . . . This last part is important." The high priest paused, as if considering something else, then continued, "The word will invoke a feeling within you in order to employ the technique."

Limnah slowed his words for emphasis. "As your training progresses, the feeling will grow, hence evoking a stronger reaction and a stronger outcome, but it must be attached to the feeling. This is why it requires the novice user to concentrate harder, sometimes sapping all energy . . ."

The old priest paused to study the boy and his drake. "You really must understand this. If you learn this now, this will become easier for you later on. If you continually hide behind your mask and ignore the motions, you will not learn this important lesson!"

*The Drake Epics - Journey to Qara*

*He's onto us,* Seon announced.

*What? How?* Ethan looked at his little companion then back at the old priest.

*I think that we better start listening to him more. Perhaps, we shouldn't be practicing without words,* the little drake continued.

*That's nonsense!* Ethan countered. *Of course we don't have to . . .*

"If you two are finished, are you ready to try again?" Limnah asked, looking at the boy and then at his drake.

Ethan blushed bright red. *Seon! Stop talking to me when* he *can see us. He can tell! Somehow, and I have no idea how, but he can tell.* The boy fumed with disdain.

Seon fell silent.

The boy sat himself down in defeat.

Limnah repeated the instructions that Ezera had given them previously. This time, Ethan waited until the instructions were complete before executing the command.

"Before you begin," Limnah cautioned, "the last part of the technique is the most important of all, for that is how you end the Kesem's spell to return to your normal state." The priest raised his voice in warning again, "You must think of the outcome at the time you perform the action, and in this case, the outcome is a relaxed peaceful state, followed by your safe return to consciousness."

Ethan knew full well what this meant, and Seon's comments came to mind that perhaps he should listen more to the old priest. But he had performed this technique already with Ezera and then with Kristian, why did he need to change up his routine now?

*Yes, but remember how exhausted you were afterward? You could barely stand, let alone walk out of the temple!* Seon countered.

*Stop!* Ethan barked. *Limnah is watching! Besides, it was my dream that did that,* he stated flatly.

Seon again fell silent.

"This is important!" the old priest snapped his fingers to get Ethan's attention.

The boy blushed a deeper purple.

"As the holder may be lost to the Kesem. If"—Limnah raised a finger—"this isn't performed at the time you recite the word. Very few holders can execute an outcome while they are in the midst of the spell. I have yet to see someone successfully do this without depleting their energy entirely, sometimes ending in death." The priest added the last word for emphasis to prove his point.

*That is why you passed out at the cave!* Seon said in amazement. *We both felt the power, but didn't know how to control it. And that is why you were so exhausted with Ezera. It was* not *because of the dream!* Seon declared in triumph.

Ethan gave in and nodded in answer to both Limnah and Seon. He now wondered how close he had come to death in the cave followed by the thought that he performed this successfully with Kristian the other night without any drain. He suddenly wanted to ask Limnah more about this, but thought better of it. *Perhaps when I trust him more,* he thought to himself.

*Perhaps,* Seon repeated, but Ethan knew the little drake was mocking him.

The boy followed Limnah's instructions to the letter and clearly said the word *Sessiz,* careful to think of the outcome at the time he said the word. He immediately felt the peaceful sensation he'd experienced before. But strangely, the feeling was nowhere near the strength or intensity he'd previously felt.

*I know. I feel it too,* Seon joined in. *I admit that maybe I was wrong.*

Ethan grinned at his companion's honesty. Perhaps if he'd ignored the feeling attached to the word and used his own instead? Yet he felt too peaceful to feel confused. He knew this required more study and thought; there were so many unanswered questions. Questions he wanted answers to, but questions he couldn't ask Limnah about, not yet. Ethan let go and enjoyed the moment of pure serenity.

---

That night, Ethan was entirely exhausted. All of his mental and physical strength were spent. The lessons had drained him in a way he had never experienced before, yet a sense of excitement stirred in his belly for what would come the next day. He slogged into the Temple of Abundance, where Grandpa called the family together for dinner, as he did every night.

Ethan usually enjoyed the dinners because the family could come together and talk about the day's events. However, tonight was torture, and Ethan yearned for his bedroll and a peaceful sleep. Moreover, Kristian still wouldn't talk to him and shot him dirty looks, while Ethan recalled to the family all that he learned that day. Ethan was too exhausted to put effort into a reconciliation with his older brother tonight anyway. *Maybe tomorrow,* he thought to himself. *Maybe tomorrow.*

# Chapter 12

# From Student to Teacher

*Talents are meant to be shared, even if it fosters fear or misunderstanding. Our talents are ours to develop and ours to teach. Use them or lose them!*

The next few weeks came and went in a flurry of lessons. Ethan only had fleeting discussions about the adventure with Seon, which was all but forgotten by the duo in the blur of catch-up homework. He was getting more used to Ezera's swift pace and was able to at least keep up with the session's blazing tempo, but the homework was murder as the two spent every spare moment studying.

The boy and his drake still did not give Limnah or Ezera their complete confidence and would purposefully fumble through the techniques to ensure their performance remained subpar. The trouble was, however, that Ethan still outperformed expectations in both the classroom and in his practice sessions. Both priests seemed to have an endless amount of patience for the young boy. This carried across to the other students, who were also impressed with how quickly their new classmate had picked up the subjects in all of his classes; and at last, some of them began to treat him as an equal. Well, all except for Hem and Yeb. Even Kreshk seemed to welcome the younger boy, much to Ethan's delight.

The mind-block technique was also becoming more natural. Seon was now only getting into Ethan's mind half the time; however, he still could not get into Seon's mind at all. Ethan didn't take this personally, as this appeared to be paying off for them in class, as Kreshk's, Khalin's and Hem's drakes didn't seem to have taken notice of the hiding emperor drake.

As predicted, the one session Ethan absolutely loathed was the off-day sparring lessons. He was much too young, and usually got paired up with Ezera, due to the odd number of boys in the class. It was at these times, he wished that Kristian could be in school with them. The part he disliked most was when Ezera would trade sparring partners. Ethan had gotten doubled up with Hem almost every time now, and the bully had taken every opportunity to leave his mark on Ethan with heavy-handed welts all across Ethan's back, chest, and legs. Whenever Ezera noticed this abuse, he reprimanded Hem, but the older boy feigned innocence and would make up excuses that Ethan wasn't blocking properly.

To make matters worse, Ethan was still not on talking terms with his brother. The older boy had barely said a word to him and seemed to be engrossed in his own activities with his school buddies. Ethan figured that this was out of spite for his own schooling. He rarely saw his older brother alone for long enough to make peace. He tried once or twice, but gave up after the last attempt when Kristian had conspicuously ignored him. Kristian's apparent absence of support left a gaping hole for the boy, and although his nightmares were all but gone, the only reprieve he felt was his constant vigil with Seon. Well, that and his growing friendships with Khalin and the girls. He also treasured his brief nightly discussions with Grandpa about his progress.

Grandpa gave wise council that Ethan appreciated, but the boy still felt awkward in keeping things from his father figure.

Teaching had become another pastime for Ethan. He had taken this up with Lola, training her on some of the more basic techniques he had studied with Limnah. If he had stopped to think about it more, he wouldn't have believed it himself.

At least this act kept her content and stopped her incessant whining about keeping Deseret a secret. Time after time, he reminded Lola that she was to keep this top secret and often wondered if it had sunk in all the way. He feared that eventually she would talk out of her pride, during a rash temper or simply out of just being a kid. It was a race to see which won out. Ethan cringed whenever she opened her mouth at dinner, but fortunately, she hadn't said anything too harmful—at least, not yet.

Ethan actually found that his little sister wasn't such a demonic pest after all; and for the first time he could remember, he enjoyed her company as a capable student, instead of as a raving lunatic posing as his little sister.

Of course, it helped that Lola was a quick learner. She could now perform all of the basic techniques and seemed to be doing well with the blocking technique, although he had to admit that he really didn't have any way to assess how she compared to his other co-students. At least she could block him now, and Deseret could block Seon. That was good enough for him. In fact, Deseret kept perfect pace with Lola, and together, they had easily broken the telepathy barrier. What's more, Deseret seemed to be every bit as intelligent as Seon. This was surprising, considering that most drakes were as intelligent as the average two-year-old child, that much, Ethan had learned from his studies.

The two children also weren't yet sure if Deseret was an elemental yet, although Ethan spent some of his free time in between school classes pouring through scrolls seeking for some material on blue drakes. But he couldn't find any story of a blue drake, and he began to worry that he never would. However, this fact did give him pause for thought and added to the mystery, making him wonder about Seon's now-larger sister all the more.

The tall auditor had also been absent, much to Ethan's relief, although before the tall man had left, he felt the auditor's eyes boring into him a few times on the way to class. Upon some discreet inquiry of his classmates, he had discovered that the foreign dignitary had indeed brought the auditor along, and he bet Seon all the money in the world that the grand Sheikh was behind it all. It felt odd, especially considering that Julfa fell under no dominion or kingdom and was considered a free state.

Still, Ethan didn't dwell on the stranger. He had felt the man's chilling power twice before and the boy was not keen on repeating the experience. Besides, as long as he kept his nose clean, he wouldn't call any unwanted attention to himself. Why would the auditor bother with someone so insignificant as Ethan? As long as Seon's secret was kept safe, he had nothing to worry about.

All of these thoughts flooded Ethan's mind as he walked toward the Temple of Abundance to join his family for their evening meal after another fast-paced day with Ezera. He reached the door and rubbed his back, wincing in pain from the new welts that Hem had left him the day before, added to countless older welts he'd received at the bully's hand. This infuriated the boy, as Hem had complete permission to beat him up; and he knew this is exactly what Hem wanted, a free pass to wail on Ethan! Gritting his teeth, he let the pain pass, bowed three times and entered the temple.

The family ate quickly, as usual. Grandpa tried to encourage a conversation between the two boys; but they remained stubbornly quiet, committed to their ongoing silent treatment and only offering grunts when a response was required.

Lola, as usual, wanted to talk about every detail of her day. So Grandpa turned his attention to her for the remainder of the meal.

However, Ethan thought he saw Kristian steal a few awkward glances at his younger brother when he thought the other boy wasn't looking. Ethan dismissed this as coincidence and tried to avoid any eye contact.

*I think that he wants to talk*, Seon suddenly announced.

"What? Who?" Ethan asked out loud.

The family all looked up from their meal at the interruption.

"Sorry, never mind," Ethan sheepishly amended, and the family went back to eating.

*Who wants to talk?* Ethan repeated to Seon, who was still buried within his back sack. He quickly slipped the little drake a piece of honey bread.

*Kristian does!* came the reply before the drake fell silent and devoured his meal.

Ethan looked up with interest and caught his brother in the act, but the older boy instantly looked away and began diligently eating when caught. *You're right!* he exclaimed.

*Course I'm right!* the little drake thought in between mouthfuls. *I think you should also hoard more meat for me, by the way*, Seon bartered.

Ethan let a smile creep across his face and finished his last mouthful of food.

Kristian's bowl was already empty.

Grandpa closed the meal and excused the family.

Ethan and Lola quickly cleaned up and returned to their room for another one of their private lessons.

"Lola, you have to concentrate," Ethan said, almost losing his temper.

Lola was playing with Deseret again. They both liked to constantly goof off and shared the same tendency to lose focus very quickly.

Ethan sighed and rubbed his temples with his fingers. Understanding now dawned on him of how his own instruction might appear to his teachers, and he felt a sudden jolt of sympathy for the two priests. "Can you pleeeaaasse pay attention long enough to do this?" he repeated, making a dramatic gesture with his hands.

Lola peered up at him, a bright smile beaming on her face. "Yes!" she said. "I just wanted to play with Deseret. See what she can do?" Deseret stood on her hind legs and performed a perfect pirouette, at least as perfect as a drake might do.

"Yeah, that's really great, Lola. Now can you concentrate?" he said in an exasperated tone.

He heard a soft chuckle from Seon, who was ruefully spectating from the side lines. The little drake had perched himself on the desk watching all the action with enthusiasm, in between mouthfuls of food Ethan had brought back from dinner for the drake.

"Would you like to come over here and teach the lesson yourself?' Ethan chided his little companion.

*No, no, you are doing a superb job of . . . what is it you're doing again?* Seon playfully bantered.

Ethan ignored the little white drake.

Lola nodded her head and looked up at Ethan with her undivided attention.

Deseret imitated the girl.

"OK," Ethan said as affably as he could. "Let us start with the calming Kesem to get yourself ready . . ."

Lola closed her eyes, relaxed her breathing, and uttered the word *Sessiz*. She began to immediately glow in a soft white light.

"Good, good." Ethan could feel the calming effect extend throughout the room, something he found very interesting the first time Lola had performed this technique, and wondered if the same thing transpired when he performed the commands as he practiced them. Still, he had to admit to himself that Lola might be better at this particular spell than he, but Seon disagreed on this point.

In any event, he'd noticed that he could squeeze more focus out of his little sister after she performed the calming Kesem—well, at least a few precious moments of her uninterrupted attention as opposed to her usual attention span of a gnat.

The light began to fade and Lola sluggishly opened her eyes, ready to try the technique they had been reviewing tonight.

This Kesem was more advanced than prior lessons, as it required levitation. He'd only just perfected this technique himself with a small clay bowl he had placed in the far corner of their room. Ethan had partly performed the technique with Limnah a number of times to keep up his ruse, but had not yet seen the same Kesem even attempted by any of the other students. He wasn't quite sure what would happen with Lola, but felt it was safe enough to try, at least with how well she was able to perform the other more basic techniques he'd already taught her.

Lola concentrated and said the word *kemand*. Nothing happened.

"OK, it's OK." Ethan raised an encouraging hand. "You have to find your concentration and hold on to it. Focus . . . ," Ethan prodded. He felt a tinge of regret that he'd pushed her too far, but didn't let this show.

She nodded her head, now with a determined look of concentration etched into her face.

*Ethan! Kristian is coming!* Seon suddenly interrupted with alarm.

Surprise, followed by rushed anxiety tore through Ethan's mind. "Lola," he started, realizing too late that he shouldn't be disturbing her at this point in the spell.

A blue light suddenly emitted from her hands. Ethan took a step back in surprised delight, temporarily forgetting about Seon's warning.

*Ethan? I can't hold him back,* Seon urgently repeated. *And BeeSting isn't advanced enough to tell him to stop!*

*Then tell BeeSting to create a distraction . . . I don't know—bite him! Just tell him to do something until Lola can finish!* he barked. He had to end this now, and in the safest way possible for Lola. He grabbed his head in disbelief, trying to think of a way to get out of this gracefully.

*Tell him to bite Kristian,* Ethan clamored.

*Not enough time . . . ,* came the reply.

Ethan felt trapped between overseeing the safety of his little sister and stopping Kristian from entering the room. He couldn't raise his voice for fear that Lola would lose control of the Kesem. No time, he made his decision as he whirled around, and lunged for the doorway—but it was already too late.

Kristian had drawn aside the blanket and now gawked at his little sister and then at Ethan in total disillusion.

Ethan halted midstride, realizing he could do no more and turned back to Lola, momentarily ignoring Kristian completely.

The blue light was fading, and something was taking its place—a liquid, a clear liquid.

*Water?* both Ethan and Seon thought in unison.

The realization slapped Ethan in the face as he stood in a slight daze. Lola's drake was a water drake!

*A blue water drake . . . of course!* Seon interrupted.

Ethan smacked his forehead. Although, come to think of it, he'd never read of a water drake either. Still, it made perfect sense. He had studied the elements and had seen earth, wind, and fire drakes, then why not water? Then why not blue drakes? Ethan reveled in his new discovery.

The water was now forming into a small spiraling rope that swiftly and abruptly thrust itself toward the clay vessel, shattering the bowl in turn. But instead of dissolving there, it lassoed a shard and pulled it back toward Lola. The liquid seemingly evaporated as the shard reached her hand, slicing her palm in the process, as her fingers closed in upon it moments too late. Tears formed in her eyes as she let out a gasp of pain and dropped the broken piece of clay.

Ethan sprinted back to his sister in three wild steps and held her hand to look at the wound. He sighed in relief as he saw that the cut was very small, no worse than if she had cut herself on the edge of a scroll.

"Don' touch it, don't touch it!" she yelled, now in full panic as she saw the blood.

Ethan clumsily uttered a quick healing spell, cursing himself for not practicing his rather-boring healing techniques more often. Once finished, he changed tactic and embraced his little sister, much to her surprise and to his own. This seemed to pacify her completely. He brought her around at arm's length and beamed a smile at her. "You did great, Lola!" he exclaimed. Next, the boy reached behind him and quickly fumbled for a scrap of cloth from off his desk.

Lola toothed a slight smile as he wrapped her hand for extra measure.

When he finished, Ethan stood back to size up his work. She was a tough little girl, growing up with two older boys who were as rowdy as any boys should be. "And wow! Deseret is a water drake!" he interrupted his own thoughts.

Lola half-absently nodded, studying the bandage wrapped around her little hand. After she was satisfied, she turned to look in Kristian's direction.

Ethan realized he needed to face his older brother and slowly turned around.

Kristian stood motionless, still dazed at what he'd just witnessed. He had not moved from the spot where he had entered, his hand still holding the door drape open with his mouth agape.

# From Student to Teacher

"Ethan, what are you doing?" Kristian finally croaked. "There's no way you can do that. It's not possible. How did she do that?" He wagged his finger at their little sister.

"It is possible, she just did it. You just saw it!" Ethan retorted, his temper now flared in response to the last few weeks that Kristian had completely ignored him.

"No, I didn't'!" The older boy shook his head in denial.

"Yes, ya did!" Ethan clenched his fists, now pale white under the strain of his grip.

"No, I . . . didn't!" Kristian was back to shrieking at this point.

"Whatever!" Ethan bellowed as he flung a hand in his brother's direction.

Neither one cared presently if they got caught or not.

"OK . . . I did. But what are you, thick in the head? Do you ever think, Dingus?"

"I don't care . . . I don't care one bit of what you think, Kristian!" Ethan snapped. "And, stop calling me that!"

Both boys stared each other down for a few moments.

"You think you're so high and mighty, can't even take time to talk to me because I get to do something you don't. *You* get off it, Kristian, you're not the best at everything!" Ethan continued to bellow at his older brother. The words came all too easily, having had enough time to rehearse them over and over in his mind over the last few weeks.

"Please stop fighting," Lola now pleaded.

Both boys looked at their little sister.

"You could have really hurt her," Kristian said in an uncommonly gentle voice, his tone full of sudden anguish.

Kristian's sudden submission took the wind out of Ethan's reply that he was fixing to lob back at his brother. He'd never heard Kristian talk like this before.

"You could have . . . ," the other boy stumbled over his own words. "I am . . . I'm sorry for the last few weeks." His head drooped. "That's why I was coming to see you." He kicked at the ground with his head hung low.

Nothing could have prepared Ethan for this, and after exchanging a few quick glances at each other, he and Lola crossed the room to their older brother and embraced him together.

"Ethan, can you . . . can you teach me too?" Kristian pleaded in a hushed voice.

Ethan pulled away from his older brother and grinned from ear to ear. "Yeah, you bet!" he exclaimed.

Kristian grinned back at him as he stroked his little sister's hair.

Ethan found it refreshing after the long weeks of frowning and scowls. He was happy and content to see Kristian back to his old self. Well, not quite himself, but it was a welcomed change and Ethan hoped it would last. The younger boy remembered how much he had missed his older brother, regardless of all the other friendships he'd made over the last few weeks. No one could really fill the hole that Kristian had left, except for Kristian himself.

All of Ethan's worries seemed to vanish, and he basked in the moment.

# Chapter 13

## The Secret Unveiled

*Secrets are one of two flavors. Those to be cherished and those to keep hidden.*

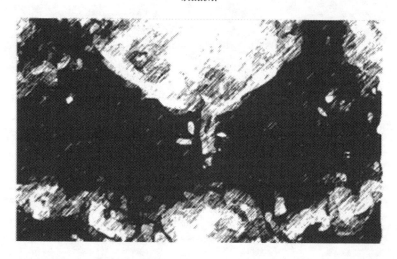

The next few months were filled with happiness for the family. They had their squabbles, but nothing serious in nature.

The hot, dusty summer months were almost at an end. Soon, the temperature would start to drop into a milder zone that allowed them to spend more time outdoors.

Ethan, Seon, Kristian, and BeeSting were back to their old mischief and regularly colluded together in how they might retrieve the ball. The plans hadn't gotten very far at first, but it seemed as though everything would work out in the end. Ethan felt a sense of security, now that he had his brother's full support. Although he felt that Seon was a tad jealous of the connection the two boys shared. Still, the little drake shared Ethan's enthusiasm for Kristian. After all, their minds were linked, and they held many of the same likes and dislikes in common.

Kristian showed improvement and could now speak to BeeSting without squinting; and BeeSting could link to Kristian in broken strands, which was progress nonetheless. However, he still had a harder time than Lola with his Kesem. Apparently, it was much harder to perform the actions for a fire drake, true to Khalin's word. It certainly took more energy and practice than Ethan had expected. Kristian could only partially perform the most basic of techniques, although he was able to perform the calming Kesem once or twice.

Ethan tried to encourage his brother as best he could, and Kristian mostly left their sessions feeling upbeat about his own progress. However, the younger boy kept these sessions separate from Lola's, so as not to give Kristian a contrasting allusion. Ethan had simply explained that Lola had been at it longer than Kristian had, which seemed to satisfy his brother's penchant for the time being.

Yet the most puzzling and bizarre part of all was that Kristian could perform his fire techniques better than Ethan and Seon could. It made sense as BeeSting was a fire drake, and the older boy seemed to be advancing with this at a much faster rate with each passing day. He could now conjure a fireball the size of a small rock, exceeding even Khalin's prior demonstration. Ethan had Kristian attempt this technique out of desperation one night when his older brother was feeling particularly dejected. Luckily, Ethan had him aim at the open window, remembering Khalin's fire singe left on the wall at the temple. They were fortunate that Kristian had a good aim and that no one witnessed the flame that hurtled through the small opening that posed as a window.

Ethan's daily progress also seemed to accelerate at an amazing rate. He attributed this mostly to his cause as a teacher, which forced him to study the spells in more detail in order to help Kristian and Lola develop their own Kesem. Sometimes he wondered if he wasn't learning more than his siblings. The young pupil frequently interrupted his readings in class to ask Limnah and Ezera questions about his Kesem. The boy's intense interest seemed to please the old priest and that perhaps, he was truly getting through to Ethan. Of course, this not only helped Ethan to become increasingly proficient with every passing day but also allowed him to be a much wiser teacher, as Limnah's proxy for his siblings. At least, he liked to think of himself in that way.

His own power was also developing and increasing, or at least he had more control over it. The techniques came more easily, and he felt he had to use less energy with every spell, as if the energy were simply an extension of his soul, much like another leg or an arm. What's more, he continued to innately recite the spells in his mind and only used the words as a shield to mask his true abilities from the priests. This seemed to infuriate Ezera, when he was instructing the boy, as Ethan had to continually ask for the words or at times used the wrong words altogether.

Ezera insisted that the boy study harder to memorize these words as it was for his own good. But Ethan saw no value in it. Besides, he had enough that needed memorization, mathematics and astrology, for example, with which he constantly struggled.

Limnah, on the other hand, wasn't as keen to pester Ethan on his apparent lack of discipline. They had an unspoken understanding, he and Ethan. The boy guessed that the priest already knew that Ethan had no need of words, although Limnah never brought this point up.

What's more, Lola had also caught up to Ethan, much to his own chagrin. Although at first, the fear from the retrieval technique slowed her down a little. After a few painfully slow attempts to boost her confidence, she quickly forgot her fright and plunged into the new studies. Ethan would barely learn a new technique in class and would find he was teaching that same technique to Lola the very same evening with wild success. Of course, her techniques were completely inclusive of water only, but she and Deseret were every bit the match for Ethan and Seon. Although he hated to admit it.

The most exhilarating moment was to discover how the technique differed in her Kesem from that of his own. Ethan's Kesem seemed to be more transparent and, in most cases, much more powerful, although he had yet to exert himself as fully as in the cave for fear that he might misuse the Kesem and fall into another self-induced coma.

He longed to spar with his little sister, but didn't dare do so as he couldn't measure how the force of their Kesem would react when colliding.

Kreshk and Hem were also supposedly now just beginning sparring with their drakes, and Ethan longed to participate. He had yet to witness their abilities, due to his physical separation from them during the sparring session, when he was meeting with Limnah. But he heard enough about it from Khalin, who was more than happy to relay all of the gory details.

Ethan also hoped the time would soon come when Seon wouldn't have to hide in his leather back sack anymore, and they could both spar with the other boys, or at the very least, make them cringe a little.

Seon, more than Ethan, hoped for this to come sooner rather than later, and they both looked forward to the end of the year and hoped that Limnah would allow this to happen.

However, as the year drew close to its end, approaching the ritual of the new beginning, they had still not heard anything further about sparring from their wise instructor. Still, Ethan couldn't believe how fast the last year had passed. He paused to peer down at the elaborate alabaster water clock in the Temple of Abundance as he prepared to eat. The local priests kept it here next to the red granite shrine of Armasian of plenty.

*The clock really is an ingenious solution that your people have created,* Seon contemplated.

Ethan nodded as he patted his back sack and let his thoughts roam free for the moment.

Within the clock's bowl, lines divided the varying lengths of night into twelve equal portions, which allowed the priests to perform their duties in a punctual fashion. Also painted on its interior was a circle of the year that divided into three seasons of four months each. Farther down, the scale of dots below the appropriate month measured those nights as the water sank and passed through a seated ape and golden tube. The open heavens of Julfa were carved on the exterior; above the ape was carved the North Pole and its constellations that Ethan knew all too well from his studies. He let his fingers run along one constellation, in particular, with two turtles facing off each other signifying the New Year as he thought about how the time had passed.

*We've all grown so much this year,* Seon commented in a ponderous tone, while basking in Ethan's peaceful conscience. The two of them often practiced these moments of meditation wherever they found themselves. It rewarded them with increased perspective.

All three children and their drakes had grown much in the last year, and Ethan felt as if they could accomplish any task that was put before them. *Hmmm, yes. I am stronger than I've ever been before,* he mused. He still had his dreams on occasion, which was a cause for concern. But he and Seon learned how to talk them through, staying awake late into the nights discussing what the dreams meant and how Ethan should interpret them. What Ethan found most useful from these discussions was that somehow he felt they were premonitions for what was to come, although he often didn't know how or when.

A merchant broke the pair's momentary reveries as he bounded into the temple and raised a glass to toast the crowd. They all saluted him in response with a jubilant chorus of voices.

Julfa was abuzz with the preparation for the New Year celebration. But this year was more special than most, signifying a new decade and even a new century. This special year would be ushered in with a substitute Sheikh selected to reign for a day while the real Sheikh remained in private, signifying death from battle with a pantheon of evil spirits. The ensuing day at sunrise, the great Sheikh would rise at the Temple of the Lion, overcome the acting Sheikh in a final mock battle, and be crowned for another year. This would be followed by the grand Sheikh and his entourage touring throughout the village countryside to participate in various crafts to confirm he was at one with the people. The entire event lasted a total of one month.

At the center of this procession was the honeybee. The king could eat only honey from a virgin honeycomb during the month while he traveled and served the people. This he did to take a census and demonstrate his own humility and supplication to the will of the people and so to reap the loyalty of his subjects. And so, that meant that Grandpa had to rigorously prepare for the event every year.

*This is my most favorite time of year, Seon,* Ethan readily admitted with a smile, as he piled food onto his plate. Today, as in all days leading up to this event, had been filled with games, celebrations, and worship. The caravans had continuously poured into the village over the last week in preparation for the events, adding to the preparation ceremonies with throngs of strange and wonderful traders all celebrating with a common purpose. It was spectacular!

*Mine too,* the little drake cooed.

Rebirth had become something of an obsession with Ethan. His studies helped him assuage the continued forebodings that he didn't belong here, as if he were a stranger roaming in an unknown land. He felt that he had a mission to accomplish before he and his siblings could return to their true home. Perhaps the orb was the key to unlocking the mystery? His dreams even portrayed this feeling; sometimes they lingered in his waking thoughts and in daydreams, or perhaps it was intuition that urged him to think on the matter. Still, none of that could be definite or real—they were just fleeting pursuits, he convinced himself.

*Speaking of rebirth, we'd better get a move on. We've got a lot of work to do, and if your Grandpa finds out, you will have to be reborn after what he'll do to you,* the little drake chided.

Ethan nodded and stuffed the food into his mouth.

Grandpa, as he did every year, had set out on his annual excursion to find the virgin beehives that the Sheikh would eat the combs from. His travels customarily took upward of a week's time, coinciding with the start of the village celebration, taking him to some remote location in the Nejd to retrieve the hives. As always, he usually traveled alone, but had promised he would take the boys next year, after they had passed his homemade beekeeping tests.

The timing couldn't have been more ideal as the boys' training had come to a close for the next month to commemorate the New Year. This was precisely what the boys had awaited to make good on their adventure to the tunnels. Kristian and Ethan were left in charge of Lola, and for the first two and a half days, all three children spent every waking moment practicing their techniques and strengthening their Kesem. Oftentimes, they paused only to horde food from the Temple of Abundance and smuggle it back into their room to conserve time for more practice.

Ethan pulled away from his thoughts, remembering his task. The boy quickly opened his pack's secondary compartment so that Seon would stay concealed and started to cram food into it.

*Careful!* Seon urged.

Ethan looked up just in time to see the cook coming his way. He quickly threw the flap over his pack and picked up a piece of bread, as if he were munching. "Thanks!" he mumbled to his companion.

The cook cast him a wary look and waved the boy away from the table. Ethan curtly bowed his head and moved toward the temple's entrance. "I hope we got enough food," he moaned. He hadn't had time to gather more last night. When Lola fell asleep, the boys crossed to their grandpa's room to plot out their little escapade to the tunnels, and they had lost track of time. Ethan glanced at the water clock as he passed it and wished they had such a device at home.

*All of our careful practice has prepared us for this. We can't mess it up now!* he thought to Seon. Ethan had carefully mapped out the route he and Grandpa had taken to the desert valley and then into the caves. He did this entirely from memory with some of Seon's help. It was only a half-day journey anyway.

*Some of my help? I know the journey by heart,* Seon crowed. Seon had convinced the boys he remembered the route perfectly.

*Yes, if we were as perfect as you are,* Ethan chided as he again patted the sack.

Kristian had charted out the change of the guards in the outer village gates to allow them to sneak through the township unnoticed. It was to be at day, while the preparation festivities were in high gear. They'd planned to sneak out alongside one of the caravans leaving the city. So the festival would cover their movement to the caravan, and the caravan would cover them until they were far enough outside the village to separate and head for the tunnels.

They could leave nothing to chance.

This was of course harder than either of them expected, owing to the festivities. Most caravans were just arriving to participate in the market bizarre, and not many were leaving. But Kristian had finally rooted out a caravan planning to depart for the Abseron Sea. Otherwise, the two boys might be noticed and they'd be done for if caught leaving the village without an accompanying adult.

They had also planned to leave Lola with Abenish for a few days to give them enough time to retrieve the ball and return without being missed. The ruse was that they had heavy chores to do in Grandpa's absence and they would be gone late into the evenings. Besides, Abenish was unfamiliar with bees and hadn't realized that this was the off season for honey collection in the first place. Their plan was brilliant!

One thing Ethan obsessed about, however, was that the sinister stranger who had returned from wherever it was he had gone, now seemed to have taken an ardent interest in the young boy. Ethan saw the tall man much more frequently, and once or twice, the man had asked Grandpa about the boy. Grandpa wasn't overly worried as he trusted that the children had kept their secret safe, but the children had noticed Grandpa was a bit more edgy than usual. This prompted a curfew from the patriarch and continued reminders for secrecy. He left nothing to chance. Of course, the boys ignored this, but it still worried Ethan immensely.

Lola was under strict orders to keep Deseret hidden from view back in their room until the boys' return. She would smuggle food to her companion every morning and evening. Neither Deseret nor Lola were thrilled about this arrangement, but Ethan had promised to train her on a technique he had been holding back on. Of course, they both had to also promise her whatever she wanted if she did this. The little girl graciously accepted and was already compiling her own list of chores and tasks her two older brothers would take over from her.

Tomorrow at dawn was when their adventure was to start. All Ethan needed more was a small almanac of spells for some of the techniques they might need and some he hadn't yet learned. These included such spells as the sharding spell he wanted to perfect. Ezera had offered this to him to borrow for the month, but only if he memorized the words of enchantment for every spell in the scroll. Ethan had reluctantly agreed to

*The Drake Epics - Journey to Qara*

this charge, even though he knew he would find absolutely no use for the names, if only to please the priest during practice.

*I guess this will be in the name of the adventure!* he justified to Seon, who openly sniggered about the whole thing. Still, Ethan knew that finding the ball was much, much more than an adventure. He dared not reveal this part to anyone, other than to Seon and Kristian.

Reaching the door to the temple, he bowed thrice and ducked out, making his way to the Temple of the Lion and to Ezera. The priest had told Ethan to come later in the day, so as to avoid the mobs of crowds at the temple.

The immediate Sheikh's compound was still full of people, some still in open celebration, dancing to flutes and other instruments. Many were still wearing their celebration masks to mimic evil spirits and others as heroes playacting as they vanquished the masked demons with wooden swords. But many were either leaving or now entering the Temple of Abundance to eat an evening supper.

Seon was mesmerized by the entire scene. *We should stay a little longer and play!* he half-begged and pleaded as he watched from Ethan's sack.

"And what good what that do you?" Ethan laughed. "All you could do is watch and yearn anyways." He didn't much worry about speaking out loud. Given the size of the crowd, no one was really paying any attention to him anyway.

*Just a thought . . . really,* Seon concluded, sounding rather depressed.

"Well, you'll have enough time to play out in the open soon enough," Ethan prodded. "Tomorrow will be more fun than you've had in a very long time . . ."

This seemed to placate the little drake, and Ethan could feel Seon's spirit lift considerably at the thought of an open range to fly across and play with BeeSting.

"Besides, think of all the fun we had earlier today!" the boy reminisced. They had left the Sheikh's compound to play at the market bazaar. It really was no different than usual, but there were considerably more caravans and the atmosphere was electric. People of all shapes and sizes sold the usual objects—only, they were all seasonally dressed in fantastical costumes, the theatrical spectacle of the New Year festival observably augmented the overall market experience; with merchants breathing fire and others eating swords or even lying on swords, snake charming, and acrobats performing amazing feats. Ethan admitted to himself that he could spend all of his time in the market, alone, that is if they didn't have something more important to attend to.

*Well, that is something. But I still want more,* Seon whined.

"And you will, Seon. We'll be back in a few days, and the real fun will start at the New Year celebrations." Ethan could sense the drake's excitement.

*Yes, I've felt your love for these events. I can't wait to experience them for myself!* Seon enthusiastically squawked.

The corridors leading up the cliff had considerably fewer people in them. The sun was two thirds of the way to setting, and Ethan assumed the villagers and guests were returning to their homes and caravans to continue their celebrations in family groups.

Sooner than expected, the temple loomed in front of them. Ethan quickly jogged through the temple courtyard toward Limnah's chamber.

Ezera was seated, reading a scroll. Limnah was apparently elsewhere still making the preparations for the Sheikh's big performance.

The boy bowed three times and announced himself to the young priest.

Ezera looked around. "Ah, Ethan, come for the almanac?" he said as he stood and took the scroll from the table at which he'd been sitting.

Ethan nodded gratefully as Ezera approached him. At least the two were on better terms of late. After the long months of training, Ethan had grown accustomed to Ezera's quirky mannerisms and had even grown a measure of fondness for the priest.

Ezera held out the scroll to Ethan as the boy tried to grab at it. Ezera quickly pulled it out of his reach. "And you remember what you are to do with it?" the priest asked.

"Memorize the words of enchantment," Ethan said sourly. "Yes, I remember, Ezera."

"Good. Then it is yours for the next month. I expect you will do much better upon your return," the priest stated as he handed the scroll to the boy.

Ethan nodded, as he wrapped his fingers around the almanac. He bowed once to the priest and again at the door. Then he turned, running along the temple courtyard to get back to Kristian and Lola, waiting in his room. He rounded the lion statues and got a few dozen paces into the corridor darkness that led to the inner stairs.

Suddenly, a shadow of a figure appeared from behind a statue. It was Hem, and he looked to be in an unusually sour mood. Yeb stood next to him in his usual stance with his arms folded. It looked as if they had both been lying in wait to belay or ambush their prey.

"Why do'ya alwaysss tottle away to sssee those priestsss?" Hem asked harshly with a sinister smirk. "Does the honey boy need sssomeone to help translate the lessonsss for him?" At this, he turned to Yeb, and they both heartily laughed. Hem's words were slurred together, and Ethan realized the two boys had been drinking a little too much of the imported wines brought in with the caravans.

Grandpa had never cared for the drink and was adamant that he and the children were never to partake of it, due to evil and conspiring men, or something to that effect. In fact, this was of religious importance to him, and the children had never questioned the patriarch's commands. But Kristian certainly enjoyed joking about doing so, much to Grandpa's annoyance.

Ethan shook his head. He had no time for dealing with this right now. "Come on, guys, we should be celebrating," Ethan bartered, trying to find a way to talk himself out of a beating.

*I don't think it's working!*" Seon exclaimed.

Ethan looked at the boys and agreed with the little drake. He changed tactic and tried to take advantage of the situation, assuming both boys would be a bit sluggish. He charged forward to push his way through the two bullies quickly enough to get by and then run for it.

The plan almost worked, but at the last moment, Hem grabbed Ethan's tunic and threw him backward and onto the ground. The older boy was surprisingly agile while under the influence.

"Where do'ya think . . . yoooou're going?" he spat. "I need ssssomeone to practice on."

Yeb's grin faded from his lips, and he looked hesitantly at his brother at this remark. He tugged worriedly on Hem's sleeve.

The older boy threw off his brother and continued his tirade. "You been missssing all the fun withhh our Kesem sssessions . . . thought you'd like a little tassste of what'ssss to come . . . You won't ever get a drake anyways!" He laughed again, swiping his arm in front of him to emphasize that Ethan lacked the intelligence.

Ethan suspected what might happen next but halfheartedly sputtered his retort anyway, "Hem, bug off. You're not supposed to use that on other students, if Limnah caught . . ."

"Limnah thisss and Limnah that . . . *and* who'ssss gonna tell? You? I don't sssee any witnessezesss!" He looked around, almost falling over before turning to Yeb. "Do you?"

Yeb hesitated for a moment. He appeared not be as intoxicated as the older boy and seemed a bit embarrassed by his brother's behavior.

"Do ya?" Hem repeated in an imposing tone.

Yeb slowly shook his head.

Hem turned to look back at Ethan again, who was checking his sack to make sure Seon was OK.

"Get up, I wanna do thisss right!" Hem fumbled with his tunic and smoothed it down with his palms as if being presented in the grand Sheikh's court. A grin twisted across his lips, making a full maniacal smile. "Trussst me, you haven't ssseen anything yet." He smirked.

Ethan's blood began to boil. Hem had picked on him for the last time! He wasn't going to stand for this again. He knew the rules for not using his Kesem, but he had enough sense to only use it as a defense, at least enough sense for the time being—as long as Hem didn't push him too far. He slowly stood, determined to end this bullying once and for all.

*Ethan, I want to take this boy out. I'm sick of this pompous windbag!* Seon added to the chorus. *It's time to show him who's boss around here!*

Hem stood erect and lethargically incanted with a single word, "el'Khaxular!"

The would-be victim could see a rock fragment rip out of the side of the sandstone cliff, roughly the size of his fist. The stone hovered for a moment before hurtling toward Ethan's stomach. Hem was smiling with glee at the success of the spell.

Ethan dug into his Kesem and thought of the feeling to protect himself that he'd practiced with Limnah many times before. He raised his hand, evoking a transparent shield. He swiped the rock away with ease as it fell harmlessly to the ground. He was now the one smiling back at Hem.

Hem and Yeb faltered and took a step back in horror. "How did . . . how did ya do that?" Hem stammered. He shook his head, anger replacing shock. "One isss not nearly enough!"

Yeb stood fearfully behind his brother, still tugging on his robe.

Hem shrugged his brother off again. This time, he said, "el'Khaxiler" And three stones of the same size as the former materialized from the wall and hurled toward Ethan.

Reaching deep within himself for the feeling, Ethan again formed the shield, and waved the stones aside.

A look of mad insanity stretched across Hem's face. He looked ready to charge Ethan at full tilt.

Ethan didn't care. He was enjoying seeing fear in Hem's eyes as he thought of all the times he had been pummeled. There was never any mercy from the other boy. Besides, Hem and Yeb might not remember this in the morning; and on the off chance they did, then it was a drunken dream of madness.

Hem screamed another word, "Qenber." The earth started to vibrate, escalating into a rumble that shook the ground directly around Ethan.

*Watch out!* Seon screeched.

The Drake Epics - Journey to Qara

Ethan looked down in disbelief as six pillars grew out of the rock. The sandstone closed in around his waist. Ethan struggled and gasped for breath at the tightness of the spell. His thoughts were immediately on Seon's welfare.

*I'm fine*, his companion soothed. Seon had cast a small protective shield around the bag to keep from being smashed.

Again, Hem had a maniacal grin on his face. "I'd like to sssee you get out of thisss one, that should at leassst squeeze some senssse into ya!" He laughed out loud.

Yeb stood looking conflicted as he glanced back and forth, trying to decide if he should run for help.

Before Yeb could choose, the fury inside Ethan erupted.

*Let's finish this!* Seon raged.

"So many times I've been the victim, so many times I've come home bloody because of *you*." Ethan gasped for more breath. "It is *not* going to end like that again! Not here! Not now! It's over, Hem. You rule me no more!" Ethan dug deeper into himself and found the fury. He had learned two techniques he invoked simultaneously, surprising even himself.

He started to levitate up and beyond the reach of the pillars, shattering them in the process; and at the same time, he threw an invisible shock wave at Hem that easily picked the larger boy up and threw him backward.

For a split moment, Ethan could see Hem's mad expression turn into terror as he was flung backward. He hit the wall and slid down its surface, slumping to the ground. Ethan felt his liberation, and it felt exhilarating.

"What did you do?" Yeb screamed in disbelief, entirely forgetting to go for help at all. Overcoming his fear of what he had just witnessed, he ran to his brother's side. "Hem, you all right?"

Hem moaned and raised a hand to his head, having hit it hard against the wall. With his brother's help, the larger bully started to climb to his feet, still clutching at his head.

Yeb kept hold of his brother, a look of concern still etched on his face.

Ethan could tell that the small amount of sympathy Yeb might have had for him was all but gone now. He slowly descended back onto the ledge, just behind the bars of rock, their broken fragments still jutting out of the ground as if they were confused on what to do next. He touched down; and now both Yeb and Hem, who had regained their senses, stood, staring at Ethan in amazement and terror.

In a moment of clarity, Ethan realized that Seon had escaped his confinement in the leather back sack, and sat, perched on his shoulder. He glowed a bright white, lighting the entire landing around them.

219

*I could not offer you my help in that leathery prison.* Seon reacted to Ethan's outright concern. *It must be this way, Ethan!*

The boy shook his head in horror. *No. We're in big trouble, Seon.*

Seon nodded, but seemed to not be overly worried, the bloodlust still coursing through the little drake's veins.

The boy and his drake both stood magnificently in that dark corridor, knowing that this would become a real problem for them both very shortly.

Just then, Ethan realized that one of the priests from the Temple of the Lion stood in the shadow, having just reached the top landing. What's more, the boy realized that the priest had seen Seon, and his fears came to the forefront that he had been discovered. Ethan had a stark realization that both he and Seon might have put his family in jeopardy. Would they be safe in Julfa? Another thought barged into his mind—the auditor! He felt the memory of the dark figure's icy touch.

A vengeful smile now spread across Hem's ragged lips as he too saw the priest. "I've got you now, *Atzer*," he spat, again referring to Ethan as a dirty foreigner. "You're not sssupposed to have that!" He pointed at the white emperor drake.

# Chapter 14

## The Oracle of the Kur-ne

*We often seek for what we don't or can't have. Perhaps, we should focus on what we already have and dream of that instead?*

Ethan shoved his way past the two boys, who weren't about to impede him in his hasty retreat. The two boys and even the priest's expressions were ashen, but Hem's vengeful smile remained imprinted in Ethan's mind—a wretched sneer.

"You can't escape, *Atzer*! My father and the council will find you! No!" his rant reached a feverish pitch, "The auditor will have you!"

Ethan momentarily glanced over his shoulder as he ran. A look of evil joy crept across Hem's face, his hatred evident for Ethan. The older boy seemed to lose his drunken facade now altogether.

"You're an outcast, Atzer, never to see the Qarabak tree again. They'll ban your family from the village! You are *lost*. you'll . . . be . . . sorry . . . !" Hem's laughter rose into a satirical scream with every syllable ringing in Ethan's ears.

He ignored the next stream of insults as he catapulted down the stairwell at a full run. He knew he had to reach Kristian and Lola quickly. The fastest passage led to the bottom of the village cliff and a back way into the courtyard. If he were lucky, he wouldn't be noticed by anyone else. He scrambled down the steep, winding stairwell and caught himself from tripping a few times, his hands now scraped and bleeding from grazing the walls, as they plunged behind him with the speed of his sprint.

Seon was still perched on his shoulder, wings extended to remain in balance.

As moments passed, the boy didn't care if anyone saw them now. Besides, it was only a matter of time before everyone in the village found out anyway. He needed to get somewhere safe, somewhere away from the Sheikh, the council, and the auditor.

*Seon,* Ethan gasped in between breaths, *send word to BeeSting and Deseret. We need to pack . . . quickly!* He knew full well that his little revelation would have a ripple effect throughout the village and would bring his brother and sister under scrutiny. That scrutiny would undoubtedly expose Lola. He didn't want to take time to consider what would happen to her, if the council found out she had bound to a drake, or for that matter, what the auditor would do.

*Tell BeeSting to talk slowly so that Kristian gets the message clearly!* he added as he lumbered down another set of stairs, bypassing the bottom three entirely and onto a ledge as he lunged forward. *Tell them that we are discovered!*

Seon nodded and set to work on reaching out to the other drakes.

It took too long to reach the bottom, which seemed like an eternity to the boy. Ethan had to pause to catch his breath, hunching over and grabbing his knees. After a brief pause, he sprinted again, entering the back door into the courtyard, hoping and praying that he wouldn't be noticed.

He glanced up at the sky to gauge the sun. He figured they had just enough light left, which gave them enough time to make their way to the cave entrance. He hoped that the cave hadn't taken up residents with its new opening, but cast the idea aside as something he'd have to deal with when they arrived.

As he made the last turn, someone suddenly loomed in front of him. Before he could sidestep or slow his canter, Ethan plowed into Heramon at full gallop. The much stronger man caught him with a grimace, his hands wrapping firmly around the young boy's arms, half-attempting to catch his own balance, then smiled when he saw it was Ethan.

Seon squawked and launched himself upward at the impact before gliding back to his perch on Ethan's shoulder.

"Whoa . . . Ethan, what's the rush?" Heramon suddenly paused as his eyes wandered to Ethan's shoulder. His face instantly turned pale at the sight of the white emperor drake. "Ethan! You are not supposed to have Seon out in the open, you might be seen, and that would be bad . . . very bad. Get him back in your back sack, now!" he firmly commanded.

*He knows!* Seon said in disbelief. *But how?*

*I don't know, but we don't have time, we need to get out of here!* Ethan shrieked back in his mind, now trying to struggle free from Heramon's brawny hands, but to no avail.

"I need . . . to . . . get past. Heramon . . . let me go . . . I need to get past . . ." He wheezed, trying to catch enough breath to speak.

Heramon's expression now turned to fear for the young boy. "Ethan, what happened? You must tell me!" he asked frantically, shaking the boy in the process for emphasis. "Do others know about Seon?"

Ethan paused then nodded in shame, still trying to catch his breath, but not struggling as much against Heramon now. "Hem knows . . . saw me use my Kesem . . . only protecting myself . . . going to his father and the council . . . I'm in trouble." He spat out while taking huge gulps of air. "Heramon, I'm in big trouble.'

Heramon whirled around, Ethan still firmly in his grip, much to Ethan's surprise at his superhuman strength. "We need to get out, now. Get to your room and get your stuff . . . Get Seon out of sight . . . Meet me in the courtyard proper quickly as you can!" Heramon gave him a little shove in the direction of Ethan's room.

The boy stumbled a few paces, stopped and turned while shaking his head. "Heramon, I need to get Kristian and Lola out too." His eyes were pleading for understanding.

*Tell him about Lola, Ethan. We need to trust him, he might be our only hope,* said Seon.

Ethan nodded in agreement. If Heramon already knew about Seon, then he had to be in the confidences of Grandpa or Limnah, and that was enough for Ethan.

"No, it's too dangerous. Now hurry . . . ," Heramon said, turning to leave.

"Wait . . . you don't understand . . ." Ethan paused then committed to the next few words. "Lola has bound too!" The words tumbled out of his mouth as a great relief washed over him that someone other than Grandpa and the three children now knew about their secret.

Heramon stopped midstride and turned his head slowly; and for a moment, terror and disbelief were plainly evident on his face before he regained his usual stoic composure, his facial expression again clouding over. "I will have two horses ready just outside of the courtyard, we will double up and ride. We'll have to pack lighter than I'd like to, if all four of us are to set out . . . I don't want to attract attention," he concluded, much to Ethan's relief.

He thought a little further, then added, "There is a side exit from the city that we will follow. Be there as quickly as you can with both Kristian and Lola. You have to hurry though. If I am right, Hem and Yeb will not be allowed to use the el-Qezha echo chamber to call down to the temple grounds. However, once you are discovered by the elders, they will waste no time in sounding the alarm from here and all guards in the city will be on the watch out for you, including at the gate!" With that, he turned and quickly strode away.

Ethan muddled over what had just happened, and he was glad to have the extra help. They now might have a chance. He turned and bolted for his room. As he reached the family hut, he dove into the doorway, ripping aside the blanket.

Lola was frantically packing.

He feigned a small smile. "Lola, are you OK?"

She paused and looked up at him with a horrified look on her face. "Will we be OK, Ethan? I miss Grandpa . . . I want Grandpa." Tears started to form in her eyes.

Ethan quickly stepped to her side and embraced her, but she pushed him away—an unusual calm and maturity coming over her.

"Yes . . . we'll be fine . . . we need to hurry and pack . . . just the stuff we need," Kristian said. She quickly brushed the tears away on the sleeve of her tunic and continued packing.

Ethan shook his head in disbelief. *This little girl is growing up fast*, he thought.

*Too fast!* Seon added. *She didn't have enough time as a child, and that time has now passed.*

*Don't be such a drag, Seon . . . you're usually the optimistic one . . .*

Seon shrugged and lit off Ethan's shoulder to make his way over to Deseret, currently clawing at Lola's bedroll.

The boy grabbed another back sack and threw as much as he could into it, stuffing it full of clothing and bee gear for the trek. A sudden thought came into his mind. "Lola . . . where is Kristian? Is he packing?"

Lola nodded her head. "He's packing right now and getting some honey pouches and dried bread."

Ethan nodded with satisfaction. Between his and Kristian's food haul, they had at least a few days of food for the four of them, including Heramon. His stomach rumbled in protest at the mere thought that he wouldn't get the full-course meals at school anymore.

As if on cue, Kristian appeared at the door. "Ready?" he asked as he drew aside the blanket, now noticing Ethan. "Ethan, what happened? Are you OK? We got the message from Seon to get ready, but that was it."

"I don't have time to go into details right now, but they know about Seon, and it's a matter of time before they find out about Lola."

Kristian nodded his head. "That much I figured. I'll get more from you later . . . but I'm not sure where we'll go. I asked Asara, ya know, one of my bunk buddies. Anyways, I asked if we could hull up in his father's cellar on the outskirts of the village until this whole thing blows over or at least until Grandpa comes back and fixes it . . ."

Ethan shook his head. "No, Kristian, we need to leave the village!"

"We don't have time for the ball right now, Ethan. I know you wanted to go, but this is kinda serious and it changes things. Besides, we had planned for a few days only. We can't survive out there for longer than that!" Kristian said in as low a tone as possible so as not to over worry Lola.

"Heramon is getting a few horses ready to leave . . . We'll exit by the side entrance to the village, then make our way to the cave . . ."

Kristian's face now flashed with indecision. "Heramon?" he said. "Does he know? Can we trust him?"

Ethan quickly nodded his head. "I don't know how, but he knows about Seon . . . He didn't know about Deseret." Ethan reflected aloud.

"And you told him?" A look of frustration now replaced indecision. "Dingus, you can't go telling everyone you feel you can trust about her drake. This is really, really bad!"

"That's what Heramon said . . . Look, he's our only way out right now, and"—a sudden glimmer of hope now crept into Ethan's mind—"we . . . can use the time to look for the ball!" he exclaimed with excitement. "That part of the plan is still in motion!"

## The Oracle of the Kur-ne

"Dingus, not now! I told you, we have bigger problems! We're in real trouble, right?" Kristian sternly reprimanded.

The younger boy's dream shimmered for a few more moments then expired; Ethan knew that Kristian was right. He nodded in subjection. "We need to hurry and meet Heramon right outside of the courtyard." He remembered aloud. "And I hope that word hasn't gotten out about Seon yet," he added, now in full remorse for his impromptu decision to face off with Hem. "But he was drunk, and it will take him time to get down here from the temple. That and they probably won't believe him at first—there is that," Ethan amended. "But, they'll believe the priest, when he's asked . . ."

"Yeah, yeah, concentrate, Dingus . . . wait a moment. What priest?" the older boy belted out before shaking his head. "Never mind. I think we need to go out separately. We don't want to attract any attention. Lola and Ethan, you two go first. Act as if we're gathering honey. I'll follow, will get some honey sacks, and I'll ditch into the bee pit to get one of Grandpa's mobile beehives to take along with us."

Both Ethan and Lola nodded.

They all quickly finished packing. Ethan and Lola stowed their drakes in their back sacks, crammed to the brim with clothing, bedrolls, and other necessities, which happened to include an extra warrior doll in Lola's case. Then the both of them set off to meet Heramon.

They strolled up the hallway and into the courtyard, blinking in the waning sunlight and glancing around to make sure that they wouldn't be detained. When no one approached, the crowds still engrossed in the courtyard festivities, both children walked as casually as they could toward the courtyard gate.

Two new guards now stood at attention on either side of the large wooden door.

Ethan hoped they could blend in with the crowd to avoid detection.

But a guard singled out the two children as they walked past.

"That's a lot of stuff, you got there." The guard pointed at Lola's back sack.

A sudden jolt of fear struck Ethan. He forced himself to smile at the guard. "We've got some honey harvesting to do, and she wanted to come along and watch from a distance . . . So she gets to pack some of the equipment," he stammered, thinking inwardly that it wasn't going to fly.

"A little late to be gathering honey, isn't it? It will be sundown soon."

Ethan froze, not knowing what to say, so he shrugged in response, "Not for night ground bees." he fibbed.

"Night time bees? Hmm." the guard nodded and bent closer to Ethan.

226

The boy remained perfectly still. He'd never been so scared in all of his life, his muscles went rigid, and cold sweat dripped from his brow.

"Hey," the guard said in a low tone, "bring us back some of the honey. It'll be our little secret, you and me." The guard smiled back and nudged Ethan with his forearm.

"Oh . . . yeah," Ethan said with relief. "I can do that."

The guard straightened back up and gave Ethan a wink as the two children moved off.

The boy chuckled to himself that the guards would never get the honey.

They only had to walk a short distance, keeping close to the crowd, before they dodged into an alleyway and met up with Heramon, who was waiting beside two large mares, their manes were a jet-black and their bodies were rippling with muscles. The mare closest to Ethan was bobbing her head up and down, eyes big, and stomping her front hoof on the ground at the approach of the children. Heramon was dressed in his full hunting garb, a sword latched to his right side, a smaller dagger the size of Ethan's arm on his left, and a bow and quiver on his back.

Ethan had only seen him dressed like this once before when he accompanied the grand Sheikh on a hunting excursion. But even then, the boy had never seen the swords.

"You two get out all right? Where's Kristian?" the man asked.

"Kristian is getting some beehive equipment for the journey. We used that as our excuse to the guards."

"Good thinking!" Heramon nodded in understanding and reached out his arms for the children's back sacks.

"Umm, Seon and Deseret are in these," Ethan offered in order to caution the guardsman from carelessly throwing the sacks around.

Heramon nodded. "I will place them cautiously . . . Let me know if they're too uncomfortable." He grinned at the children and winked.

Ethan barely caught his meaning and eyed the larger man. *How much do you figure he knows?* he asked Seon.

*Enough to know that you can communicate with me, and I with you . . . He must be helping Limnah. Your grandpa doesn't know this much . . .*, Seon trailed off.

Heramon strapped the back sacks into place—Lola's on the lead horse and Ethan's on the other. Kristian now came around the corner, an older beehive strapped around one of his shoulders and his back sack on the other. Heramon, finished strapping the younger children's sacks, then walked over to Kristian to relieve him of the heavier beehive, which he promptly attached to the lead horse.

"Heramon?" Ethan now asked. "I know where we have to go!"

Heramon raised an eyebrow, and a slight grin drew across his face. "You do, do you?"

Ethan nodded, glancing at Kristian and Lola, then took a deep breath before sucking up the courage to tell him. "I saw . . . I saw it . . . when I first discovered Seon. It's the cave I found, which is big enough for all of us to camp in." He decided at the last moment not to mention the scroll in Limnah's quarters. "With plenty of water and a ways into the Nejd so that we won't be bothered by anyone from the village," he amended to seal the deal, glancing back at his siblings.

Kristian nodded in approval.

*Good call!* Seon said. *We need to convince him it's the safest place . . .*

Ethan grinned. *I know full well why you want to go there.*

*What . . . me?* Seon asked, but Ethan could see the image of Seon grinning about the treasure.

Heramon synched up the beehive tight and now turned to face Ethan. "Good, good . . . I had another campsite in mind, but the cave will be much safer. I went out there after you discovered the place. As long as the lions and wolves haven't taken up residence, we should be good . . ." He winked at Ethan again.

The last comment did little to ease the boy's concerns.

"They could only use the top part of the cave . . . ," Ethan blurted out as his memory came back to him. "Beyond that, it's a stone throw's drop to the water landing that I had to climb straight up in order to get out."

"Yes, that's about what I remember too!" Heramon now said, but Ethan could sense that he was jesting with the boy.

Ethan gave the coordinates to Heramon as best he could remember them. Heramon nodded. "Yes, I know. Thank you, Ethan." He looked at the younger boy. "It's going to be all right. We'll get you there safely." Then he looked up at the sky. "We need to hurry though . . . We've taken too much time already and don't have much sunlight left. It's about a halfday by foot, so I'm hoping to get there before sundown by horse . . . Come this way." Heramon grabbed both of the horses' harnesses and led them to the side entrance, careful to remain in the alleys so as to avoid the concourses of people returning to their homes and caravans.

Once through the maze of clay homes, they followed the courtyard wall around in silence until it ended at the cliff face. The red cliff jutted straight up into the sky and stood in stark contrast to the greener farmlands that sprawled out in front of the little company of travelers.

The children continually looked over their shoulders and into the farmlands in case they were noticed, but there was no one in sight here.

# The Drake Epics - Journey to Qara

The path ran along for a time before reaching the outer wall, with a small door set into its side, just large enough to pull one horse at a time through without a rider. The door was old and weathered and appeared as if it were about to fall off its hinges by the looks of the decaying wood.

Heramon pulled a lone key from a pocket and inserted it into the now-noticeable keyhole set into the door. A distinct clicking sound followed, and Heramon swung the door inward into darkness.

"This leads into a brief chamber we must enter in order to get out," Heramon offered at the children's questioning looks. He grabbed one of the horses by the reigns and led the animal uncomfortably into the dark room. He had to press the horse's head down with the palm of his hand in order to move her forward, and she only just squeezed through. Kristian followed Heramon to secure the horse, while Ethan remained inside the gate. The second horse wasn't so lucky and had to be relieved of the beehive and back sacks before she could fit through the gap.

Heramon lit a small torch and handed it to Lola to hold aloft, followed by closing the gate behind them and locking it shut. He motioned to the boys to quickly load the horse then led them a few dozen paces to another much sturdier and slightly larger door and drew the keychain from his pocket to open the gate. Once outside the village wall, Heramon took Lola as the lead, and Kristian and Ethan followed behind him on the other. They set off at a slow trot.

The sun sat a few finger lengths above the horizon, casting a yellowish red haze across the barren landscape, casting long shadows that made the travel more treacherous. So, they kept to the more solid areas, where their horses had firmer footing, avoiding the sand dunes, unless they loomed directly in front of their path.

Ethan spent the journey filling Kristian in on all of the details of his encounter with Hem.

The older boy especially liked the part about the scuffle with Hem and turned around briefly to beam a big smile at Ethan for handling the situation so well. He was also intrigued by Ethan's skill in handling his Kesem.

Ethan noticed that Heramon was straining to overhear the boy's conversation as he kept the lead horse in stride with the boys, only slightly ahead of them.

The boys slowed their horse, and Heramon finally gave up and set off with an increased cadence, motioning for the boys to do the same. Once satisfied he was out of range, the boys turned their attention to the treasure that had been sitting alone for the last month since Ethan had discovered its existence. They came up with a rudimentary plan to retrieve it, more to keep their minds off what was really happening to them and what would happen to Grandpa upon his return to Julfa. If only they could reach him, both thought and decided to ask Heramon if he was aware of their grandpa's whereabouts so that he could possibly leave for a day to retrieve the patriarch.

True to Ethan's word and Heramon's estimated timing, the little party reached the valley just before sundown. The large sphere sat on the horizon, casting a blood-red glow across the dunes, giving the sand an orange-red hue. Ethan directed them toward the cave's entrance, careful to stay on the outskirts of the valley, remembering his previous experience when venturing into the dunes and the resulting collapse. They reached the cave and dismounted. Ethan heard the familiar faint sound of roaring water as they neared the entrance.

To be safe, the boys held the tethers to the horses, while Heramon investigated the entrance of the cave. By the time he returned, the sun was barely peeking over the horizon and a hush had fallen over the valley as deep blue shadows crawled their way across the basin.

"It looks as if a pack of wolves spent a few nights here, but they couldn't have made their way into the cave proper." He patted Ethan on the back. "We're safe, but we'll need to get the horses inside and onto the ledge. It will be a little tight, but I'd rather have them inside during the night and out of harm's way." This again did little to boost the children's spirits about what might be lurking just outside that night, but they didn't push it further.

The cave's mouth was roughly the size of the village side door, although a bit wider. The boys got the horses into the cave, unsaddled them, and unloaded their gear, while Heramon scraped around for firewood. He dragged a few hefty sage bushes to the entrance that looked like he had ripped straight out of the ground.

"To close up the cave entrance and double as firewood," he answered at the children's questioning expressions. He claimed the horse blankets and pinned them to the inside of the hole, with the bushes directly outside.

They all nodded in appreciation, hoping this would prove an effective barrier against what might be lurking outside of the cave that night.

Heramon pulled together some of the firewood and lit a small fire toward the entrance to avoid extreme proximity to the horses, but far enough away so that the blankets and bushes concealing their lair didn't take fire. The group silently ate a hasty dinner of honey and dried bread that Kristian had brought along with him before rolling out their bedrolls. Lola was careful to sleep in between Kristian and Ethan for safety, and all three drakes curled up around her. The sound of the rushing water lulled them into a sound sleep as the exhaustion of the day's events overtook them.

*The Drake Epics - Journey to Qara*

Heramon took the first watch and stayed awake half the night, keeping the fire lit, before waking Kristian in the early-morning to take his place. The night passed without incident.

At dawn the sun's rays peered through gaps in the blankets and sage, casting lines of light into the cave before disappearing into the blackness just beyond.

Ethan sat up in his bedroll, rubbing his eyes and swinging his feet out and onto the stony floor, cool to the touch. He stretched his arms wide and rubbed his back with a yawn. He looked over at Kristian sitting by the fire, poking at it absentmindedly with a stick. BeeSting, as always, was dangerously close to the burning flames, curled up by its warmth.

Ethan quickly pulled on his sandals and tiptoed around the sleepers on the ground about him. The horses whinnied softly and stomped their hooves a few times at the sudden movement, but looked no worse for the wear.

Kristian peered up from his reverie and greeted Ethan with a nod before looking back into the flames.

The younger boy took a seat next to him, picking up a second stick to poke at the fire too.

"I had BeeSting up this morning and flying around the cave," Kristian started in a soft voice. He glanced over his shoulder at the sleeping Heramon for extra measure they weren't overheard.

Ethan glanced up at Kristian in surprise. "He can fly now?" BeeSting could only fly extremely short distances before the boy's falling out, and since then, the topic had never come up that the fiery drake had developed the ability to fly for longer periods of time.

Kristian nodded. "Yeah, he's right good at it now, I suppose . . . ," he responded. "Anyways, he can see pretty good in the dark as I'm sure all drakes can. He surveyed the area . . ." Kristian moved his arm in the direction of the dark cave. "From what I could gather, there's a pretty large pool of water just below us, and the water is coming in somewhere from the other side . . . Also, there's an opening on the other side of the cave. He didn't' go in too far, but said that it leads to other caverns . . ." He paused with a big grin spreading across his face.

"That's it . . . ," Ethan exclaimed louder than he expected. He quickly glanced around, fearful he'd woken the others before leaning in toward his brother. "That's it . . . ," he quietly said with relief. "That's what we're looking for, it's the beginning of our adventure!" Excitement began to well within him. "Seon has an excellent memory and said that he could find his way through the maze to the ball, although he can't really fly all that well yet," he added, furrowing his brow.

"So . . . tell me what's so all important about this ball again? I mean, you saw it in this parchment scroll . . . how do you know it's special?"

"I don't know," Ethan confessed. "I guess I felt power when I saw it . . . so did Seon . . . It's kinda hard to explain," he concluded.

"Well, we'll need to convince Heramon or come up with some excuse to get him out hunting for us so we can go and get it." Kristian waved his head in the direction of Heramon. "Or . . . we could trust him . . ."

Both boys fell silent as Heramon stirred in his bedroll.

Ethan took up poking at the fire again.

Heramon sat up in a half yawn. The larger man stepped carefully through the sleeping drakes and sat next to Ethan. "Morning," he offered.

Both boys nodded and replied in earnest.

Heramon picked up a stick and mimicked the boys poking at the fire. Red-hot embers crackled and floated toward the cave ceiling. He studied BeeSting for a moment. "Drakes are wonderful creatures." He ventured then changed course. "It's best we talk before Lola wakes . . . I need to know what happened last night," he urged. "I also would like to know how she bound to an elemental water drake. Blue drakes are very rare. I've never encountered one in my travels. But then again, I've never encountered a white emperor drake either."

Both boys looked at each other in bewilderment. Heramon had always been a good friend to the children, but he had never embellished much about his past, even with the children's constant harassments. He now seemed to know an awful lot about drakes, but they trusted him almost as much as they trusted their grandpa.

Ethan cleared his throat, buying some time to think about how to respond. "Didn't Grandpa tell you about Lola and the egg?"

"Nope." Heramon sluggishly shook his head and continued to poke at the fire.

A burning desire rose in Ethan to know why Heramon didn't know this detail when he knew so many other things. "I don't understand. How did you know that Deseret is a water drake and why didn't Grandpa tell you about her?"

Heramon looked up from the fire, surprise registering on his face at the query, before jabbing his stick at the flames. "Fourteen-year-olds binding to emperor drakes is a risky enough business . . . Eleven-year-old girls binding at all, well, that is unheard-of, let alone to an elemental drake . . . I suppose your grandpa feared for your welfare, at least I hope that he swore you all to complete secrecy?"

The Drake Epics - Journey to Qara

Both boys nodded their heads, convinced of Heramon's sound arguments. At least, Heramon seemed to be saying all the right things.

He continued, "I suspect he didn't want to share this bit of information with anyone . . . not even me." He sighed. "With regard to my knowledge of drakes, let us just say that I have dealt with drakes in far-off lands."

The boys looked at Heramon in eager anticipation. But their excitement was short lived.

"In any event, I need to understand what happened last night," he said with finality.

Ethan cleared his throat again and started at the beginning, careful to stick to the storyline he felt Heramon needed to know. He spoke about his first encounter with the eggs, how Seon hatched, how he'd hidden the other egg, how Lola had discovered Deseret in his room, and lastly about his encounter with Hem and Yeb. He was careful, although sorely tempted, not to discuss the experience in Limnah's quarters or of the ball in the cave.

"Well, you can't go back right now, that's for sure." Heramon sighed. "I'm sure there's a flurry of activity going on in the village council right about now. They've never had to really discipline anyone for hording drakes before, at least from what I've been told . . . But they can't be very happy about it either, and they still don't know about Lola, which might push them over the edge. And then there is this business with the auditor . . ." He paused as if considering this in particular.

Ethan felt a cold chill run down his spine.

"Still, the start of the New Year rites are fast approaching and they will be quite engaged in . . . other matters." He stirred in his seat before changing course. "We'll need to get a message to your grandfather, of course. He should be back tomorrow. Once he arrives, he can discuss with Master Limnah and work out the details. Until then, we're on our own."

Both boys sat silently, staring at the glowing embers, deep in thought about ways to get Heramon out of the cave while leaving them behind.

Suddenly, Ethan had it. He only needed Heramon out of the cave for a day at most. "I suppose that you will go into the village to find out what the mood is, and"—he now tried to lay his trap—"leave a message for Grandpa on how to find us?"

Heramon looked up at Ethan again. "Yes, I suppose that is a good course of action . . ." Heramon scratched at his unshaven face, considering the boy's proposition. "I could leave the note during the festivities, but that would leave you three here unattended," he quickly amended.

233

*The Oracle of the Kur-ne*

"We can scout for queen bees . . . and be careful to stick to the sages," Ethan quickly added, remembering his last experience with a queen bee in this valley. "We'll be fine as long as you're here by nightfall to watch over us." He inserted this last flattering compliment.

Heramon gave Ethan a quizzical look. "What are you boys up to?" he asked.

Kristian swallowed hard and sucked up his courage. "We're in trouble, Heramon, we need Grandpa here to help us figure this out."

The older man studied the boys even harder then slowly nodded. "Sounds all right, but you have to promise to stick close to the cave and get inside at the first sign of danger . . . and protect your little sister?" He looked over at her sleeping form.

Both Kristian and Ethan nodded in agreement.

"Very well, I will leave one of the horses behind and will be back before nightfall. I'll leave right after breakfast."

The boys struggled not to show their excitement, but Ethan sensed that Heramon knew they were up to something, even if the man didn't know just what it was.

Heramon and Ethan set to work clearing the cave's entrance and saddling Heramon's horse, while Kristian prepared a quick meal. Lola woke and beamed cheerful smiles, excited to be camping out for the first time in her life. She added an extra air of cheerfulness to the otherwise-drab morning.

They ate to her animated comments about yesterday's journey, about how well she had slept and her explanation about Deseret's good sleep. Both boys squirmed at her mention of Deseret, and Kristian shot her a dirty look.

Heramon didn't know she could communicate with her drake. However, Heramon didn't think to ask follow-up questions, although he looked up at her from time to time with interest.

After their meal, the boys escorted Heramon's horse out of the cave.

Kristian closed it up again, with only enough room for the children to fit in and out of.

"At the first sign of danger, get back in the cave, and block it off . . . understand?" Heramon said as he mounted his horse.

The children nodded again as this was the fifth time Heramon had reminded them of this.

He paused, noting each nod, then nodded to himself in acceptance. "I will be back before sundown." Then he wagged a finger at Kristian as if he'd forgotten. He reached down and handed his dagger to the oldest boy and nodded at him in unspoken understanding he was to protect his siblings.

234

The Drake Epics - Journey to Qara

Kristian gratefully accepted the dagger and pointed to his sling attached to his hip for some reason that Ethan didn't really understand. But he smirked to himself anyway. He, Lola, and Kristian could take care of themselves no matter what came their way.

*It's the thought that counts, don't disregard it 'cause you don't like to spar,* Seon commented.

Ethan promptly ignored his companion and huffed with distaste.

Heramon reigned his horse around and set off at a gallop up the side of the valley.

The children watched until he crested the valley's ridge and was out of sight. Once they were sure he had gone, they hurried back into the cave.

Kristian quickly took charge of the group. "We don't have a lot of time . . . I hope that we can get the treasure in time." Ethan and Kristian began making preparations.

"Treasure?" Lola piped in. "What treasure? Where is it?"

The boys paused and looked around at their sister in alarm.

Kristian sighed loudly. "And what do we do with her?"

"Can't we just leave her here with the other horse and Deseret? She'll be safe." Ethan knew as soon as he had said it that they would have to take her along.

"What? Don't be stupid, Ethan. She needs to come with us."

*Not to worry, Ethan, Deseret and I will keep a steady eye on her . . . remember that her talents might come in useful when we have to submerge,* Seon now spoke up.

*Nope, no good, she can't come in the water with us, we'll need to come up with a plan.*

*You worry too much, let's go,* retorted Seon.

Ethan nodded, realizing there was no substitute for taking her with them. *Perhaps we can leave her at the water's edge.*

"We'll need torches. Even if our drakes can see in the dark, we can't," Kristian announced. "Ethan, grab my back sack."

The younger brother retrieved the sack and handed it to Kristian, who dug around inside it for a few moments before pulling out a canister of beeswax.

"What's that for?" Ethan asked.

"The torches . . . Dingus, find two sticks . . . 'bout the size of my arm." Kristian pointed at his inside elbow and measured it to his hand. "Like that."

Ethan stood rooted to the spot, curiosity getting the better of him.

"Now?" the older boy commanded as he looked around and found Ethan hadn't started off yet.

235

Ethan nodded then turned toward the entry, frequently looking over his shoulder to see what Kristian was up to.

Next, Kristian took out the knife that Heramon had presented to him and scraped off slivers of the wax, dropping the shavings into a small pan. After the pan was half full, he placed it over the fire, which still radiated heat from the burning red coals.

Finally, Ethan returned with two large sticks for the boys to carry. Kristian grabbed one of Ethan's burlap tunics lying on the ground next to him. "Mind if I use this?" He lifted the tunic toward Ethan, who shrugged that it was OK.

Kristian grabbed both ends and ripped, shredding the shirt into smaller fragments, then wrapped it around the sticks. He then lifted the pan from the fire, the wax reduced to a bubbling brew, and gently poured it over the burlap. Next he took each stick and held them over the fire until they ignited, the burlap burning slower than Ethan would have expected burlap to burn, but he prayed that the light would last long enough to find the treasure.

"Where did you learn that from?" he asked in amazement.

The older boy looked up with a furtive smile. "You aren't the only one who learned important things in school," he said. "We need some firewood," he suddenly announced, and the boys looked for wood that could be easily packed into their back sacks, throwing out random clothing to provide enough room. Once they were satisfied that they had enough, they launched their quest into the cave.

Ethan was the first to scale down the wall and into the main grotto. He clung to the wall with both torches in his hands, slipping once or twice and almost dropping them. When he reached the bottom, the rushing water pounded his ears much louder than what he remembered.

Kristian was now yelling something at Ethan, but he couldn't hear, so Kristian pointed to Lola and motioned for her to start her climb down the smooth surface.

Ethan quickly propped the burning sticks against the wall, only releasing them when he was sure they wouldn't fall over and go out. This seemed to give him more light anyway, and he guided Lola's descent once her feet reached his hands without incident.

The older boy was next and reached the bottom easily, now picking up his torch and motioning for Ethan to do the same.

The children's drakes perched unrestfully on their shoulders. They each could sense the exhilaration building in their holder's minds as Ethan recounted the adventure he and Seon had seen again.

Kristian sent BeeSting to scout ahead. The drake could relay advance warnings back to Seon, who interpreted for Ethan, much to Kristian's disappointment as that meant that Ethan understood BeeSting better than he did.

They slowly made their way through to the crag that BeeSting had discovered that morning. Halting for a brief moment, they edged onward and exited the cavern where they had encamped on the previous night. The rocky corridor's walls were smooth, like the last one Ethan had groped along to reach the main cavern. But in this one, he had barely enough room to walk and had to haunch over as he made his way forward. He could now see much more detail than on his prior visit as the firelight flickered off the smooth rocky surface. The rock was a rich black that shimmered in the firelight as the light danced about them, flicking wildly, urging them on to the treasure that lay in wait for them.

The glittering canal continued onward, seemingly without end. It started to widen slightly, at least enough for Kristian and Ethan to straighten out of their forced crouch into a full-standing walk.

BeeSting still flew ahead and reported back from time to time that they were nearing an opening into another cavern.

The small group held their breath for what awaited them on the other side as Ethan relayed this to the others. They walked for what seemed an eternity to Ethan before they finally emerged into the next cavern.

He looked around for the great lake, but his heart sank as he remembered that they had many more such crags they must pass through before reaching their destination.

This cavern was much smaller than the main cavern they had just come from. The torchlight flickered against the rocky walls and ceiling, and they found themselves in a half-oval chamber around seven paces wide and deep, with the ceiling perhaps thirty hands tall. At the far end, two small fissures, the size of the one they had just emerged from, opened up into more blackness. Seon directed them through the fissure on the right, and they set off through it at a faster pace, now that they were standing perfectly erect.

This continued on for an eternity, passing through each cavern in the same way. The total darkness that bathed the passageways in black seemed to also mask the time from the intrepid adventurers. Regardless, the boys' excitement grew with each passing cavern. This was unlike any exploration they had been able to conduct before. The boys occasionally waved their torches in different directions to catch brief glimpses of their surroundings, watching the darkness flee from the assault of the chasing flames.

Even with the excitement from the boys, the small group walked in an unnatural silence in awe of the darkness that cloaked every corner. Even

Lola was silent, usually talking and jabbering about anything that came to her mind, Ethan thought.

As they marched on, the roar of the campsite river soon dissolved in their ears until they could hear nothing but their own footfalls, an occasional bead of water dripping onto rock that echoed throughout the chambers, or a small lizard or amphibian scattering away from them as the light revealed its hiding place.

Ethan also realized that each cavern looked the same as the others, perhaps because of the lack of light rendering any details quite invisible, except upon immediate inspection. The only unique sensation the children felt was the gradual descent as they marched deeper into the bowels of the earth.

They soon discovered that without Seon's keen eye and memory, they would be hopelessly lost in the labyrinth sprawling out before them in a jumbled tangle of twisting passageways. Ethan was quickly disoriented after passing through so many caverns that he lost count and questioned if they weren't lost.

*Certainly not!* Seon snarled when Ethan thought to ask, *We are exactly where we're supposed to be!*

True to form, a few moments later, they emerged into a spacious cavern, identical to the one Ethan had seen in the scroll. Immense stalactites hung motionless from the ceiling, their sluggish forms hiding behind jagged points.

Lola quickly sidled up to Ethan, hugging his side at the ominous sight as she looked upward.

A vast body of water unrolled before the little group as they peered around. Ethan tried to scan beyond the water, but the cavern swelled around them into darkness just beyond the reach of their torches, leaving an eerie glow that flickered and bounced on the water's placid surface that would have remained motionless otherwise. Ethan couldn't identify the source of the lake, but could hear a distant rumble.

*This is it!* claimed Seon victoriously. *We now need to enter the pool . . . here . . . yes, and swim under there.* He sent Ethan a clear image from their encounter they had envisioned.

Ethan paused, not fully comprehending what they needed to do next. "Seon says we're here . . . I recognize it too," he alerted the others. "We need to go in . . . there." He pointed to the area that he and Seon remembered during their fantasy flight. Even as he spoke, he now wondered how they were going to succeed and how they would handle Lola as she couldn't swim.

The Drake Epics - Journey to Qara

Lola looked up at him and then at Kristian with a horrified expression plainly visible in the faint torchlight. "Swim? In the dark water? Without light?"

Ethan admitted to himself, he hadn't thought this through far enough to figure a way into the other cave. What's more, he hadn't counted on Lola, which complicated matters. He rattled his brain, trying to come up with an answer. "Kristian?"

"Don' look at me, Dingus . . . you're the one with the image in your head . . ."

Ethan shook his head, stumped at this new challenge. "This is the only way in . . . the scroll led us, Seon and me, through the water . . . I don't remember for how far . . . I just assumed we'd need to swim for it . . ." He sat down, holding his head in his hands as if this approach would provide him with the answer.

Kristian strolled along the side of the lake, scouting for alternatives. The torchlight bobbed as he walked off, and the outline of his body slowly disappeared until the fire looked like it was moving of its own accord. The light grew smaller and smaller until it was the size of a small marble, and Ethan had to squint to see it before it stopped and started bobbing back toward them. Kristian returned, shaking his head. "It goes on forever, I couldn't see the end of the lake . . . even from where I stood!"

"I'm gonna have to swim for it!" Ethan finally proposed. "I saw it in my dream, it's gotta be it . . . I'll go in and retrieve it then swim right back," he resolved, proposing the group split up.

"No, we agreed that we would stay together!" Kristian retorted, shaking his head again.

"I don't see another way in . . . ," Ethan countered.

"We may have to try this again, perhaps we let Heramon in on this . . . We've been gone for ever and it will probably take us even more time to get back . . . ," Kristian's voice drifted off as he calculated the time it was going to take to reach their campsite.

"What about Deseret?" Lola asked.

"What? Not now, Lola," Ethan responded, his head buried in his hands again, trying to think of another way.

She gave Ethan a soft kick in the ribs.

"Owwww, Lola . . . what did you do that for?" he said, rubbing his side.

"Deseret says she's born to swim and can tell us how far to go," she replied.

Kristian was now looking at Ethan. "That makes sense to me."

*She's right, Ethan! Besides, you're a lousy swimmer*, Seon added.

Ethan turned and grimaced at the drake.

*What? Don't look at me like that. You've shared your thoughts about your little swimming escapades with Kristian after rainfall . . . he had to save your life two or three times as I remember it . . .*

*I thought you really wanted this treasure?* Ethan jabbed back.

*Don't get snippy with me, Ethan . . . Deseret is probably a great swimmer . . . probably . . . I mean she is a water drake after all . . .* Seon tried to get the point across confidently.

Ethan nodded in surrender to the idea.

Lola's eyes beamed with pride and then glazed over as she talked to Deseret. The little blue drake looked at Lola, then half-nodded in understanding before launching from her shoulders toward the water, before diving in, with surprising speed. The action happened so quickly that the small group blinked in amazement.

They waited for a time without any sign of Deseret. Lola began to worry as her attempts to reach the little drake failed.

Seon informed Ethan that he also couldn't reach her, apparent worry in the tone of his message.

Kristian paced back and forth in front of the water, looking as if he were ready to dive in after Deseret at any moment.

Suddenly, a blue dart shot out of the water and landed on the beach. Deseret, much like a wet dog does, shook the water off her head, body, legs, and tail.

Lola quickly knelt by her side before turning to Ethan. "Deseret says that it's a long time under the water, and no one of us can make it."

Ethan drew his face up in frustration. What was the scroll to have meant? Everything had been correct until now, so it had to be real! Why this when they were so close? It didn't make any sense to him.

*Seon, there has to be another way in . . . Do you remember anything that we might have overlooked?*

*I don't remember anything else. We saw the water, traveled through it before coming out into a cave . . . We have to go through the water,* the drake said in an exasperated tone.

*Is it meant for you or Deseret to retrieve it?* Ethan prodded.

*No, Ethan, I feel that it is for you and you alone to retrieve . . . I'm not sure I understand either . . . Let me talk with Deseret.*

Ethan nodded at the plea.

Lola was now talking again, but Ethan had missed it, "Lola, can you repeat that again?"

"I said that it's too far to swim."

"No, no, the next part," Ethan urged her on.

"Oh . . . um . . . there was a tunnel into the rock. Deseret swam through it for a long time then came into a cave, like the caves we walked through . . ."

"Did she see it?" Ethan blurted out, not letting his little sister finish.

Lola gave him a stern look, as if she were an adult scolding a child. "I wasn't finished!" she said indignantly then beamed a broad smile. "Deseret saw a ball on a rock and another tunnel behind it."

Ethan didn't remember any tunnel in the vision, but shrugged it off. At least it was real. He looked up at Kristian, who had the same excited look on his face.

"OK, OK, so how do we get to it?" Kristian said, scratching his head. "I don't see any end to that lake." He threw his hand out in the direction of the water.

Ethan shook his head as well.

*Ethan . . . ,* Seon called out. *Deseret says there's a stone lever in the wall by the ball. She didn't touch it because she wanted to get back . . . It might be a way in!*

*Can she go back?*

*She says she's fine underwater, but she's frightened . . . She sensed she wasn't alone while she was swimming . . . Shadows following her or something like that . . .*

Ethan paused. *Does Lola know?*

*No, too hard to explain . . . but I don't see what that's got to do with . . . ,* the drake answered before pausing. *Ethan, I'm ashamed of you!* he finished.

Ethan's face now flushed bright red. He'd thought to send the little drake back down and take the chance, but that would be harder if his sister caught on about another presence. The thought had raced through his mind so fast that he'd reacted to it too quickly before weighing the consequences.

*Sorry . . . sorry, Seon. She only sensed it—it doesn't mean there's any real harm.*

Seon gave him a severe look before accepting the apology. *Don't underestimate our premonitions. But there is a way through. I think I can go with her,* he said, and Ethan could sense the anxiety in his thoughts.

*But . . . I thought it was too long for you to hold your breath?*

*Oh, I've been practicing . . . Well, since Deseret went for her first swim . . . thought I might have to go in after her and all.* Seon sent Ethan an image with the little drake puffing out his cheeks with his face bright red.

The boy had to refrain from laughing out loud at the comical image.

*I think I can hold my breath for long enough. Also, we've tried the protective barrier in our practice sessions,* Seon continued, *and I think I can duplicate it for long enough . . . for the two of us . . . underwater.*

*But those sessions were my practice lessons, you haven't tried them, have you?* Now dawning on Ethan what Seon was about to attempt.

*Well, no . . . but I figure that it's like the blocking technique that we both practiced. I have the ability to do it as well . . . so . . . this should be the same! Besides, it worked with Hem,* he suggested.

Ethan nodded, worry swamping his mind. *I want to see you do it before you go in with Deseret.*

Seon agreed.

"Well?" Kristian now asked, frustration mounting in his voice.

Ethan knew Kristian wasn't very good at communicating with BeeSting, and he often got irritated when either Ethan or Lola's eyes glazed over and they started talking with their drakes.

Lola looked up at Ethan as well.

"There's a lever in the cave," he stated slowly. "Seon and Deseret are going in again and will try to pull it to see what happens."

Kristian's face clouded over in concentration. "Can Seon make it?"

Ethan nodded.

"No . . . Deseret is afraid. I can feel it!" Lola blurted out.

"That's why Seon is going with her. He's going to cast a protective shell around them both." He looked at Lola, who still appeared fearful. "He'll protect her . . . promise!" he added.

Lola slowly nodded her head.

*Practice now before you go under.* Ethan turned to Seon, who nodded and jumped to the ground.

Seon stood motionless for a moment, then Ethan felt the drake draw on his powers, and a small oval shield popped into existence and formed around him.

Kristian and Lola stepped back, wonder evident on their faces.

The shield emitted a half-transparent-white barrier immediately around the drake and sputtered sparks here and there, but it was still too small for two drakes.

Confusion flashed through Ethan's mind as it appeared that Seon's power seemed to be weaker than his own, something he would have to ask Limnah about, that is if he ever got out of this mess. He quickly cast the thought aside.

As if Seon sensed his thoughts, he now walked over to Deseret; and the barrier grew, reaching out to encircle both drakes. Apparently, the sparks didn't harm his sister drake at all.

*I can hold it for long enough . . . we're ready*, Seon informed Ethan.

Ethan nodded. "They're ready . . . going in . . ."

Just as the two drakes reached the water's edge, Seon added, *By the way, it seems that the water blocks our telepathy . . . I'll contact you once we get to the other side. I'm assuming that Deseret can't communicate at the same ranges that I can.*

Ethan nodded. *Be safe!*

He suddenly realized he didn't know what would happen to him if Seon were injured, or worse. He'd heard horror stories from some of the villagers about instant insanity, but had never paid much attention to the stories—not until now. He silently scolded himself for not looking this up when he had had the chance back at school and resolved to study harder if he got the chance again.

Both drakes dove in.

It seemed an eternity to Ethan. He soon lost count of time. None of the children spoke in anticipation.

Abruptly, he felt Seon's presence in his mind again and realized he'd been holding his breath. He inhaled sharply, feeling dizzy as if he were mere moments from passing out.

*Ethan, we made it . . . close call . . . The shadows attacked us, but I was able to keep the barrier up . . . We're pulling the lever now."*

"They made it!" he said aloud, choosing not to share the part about the shadow creatures. Relief flooded Lola's face, which, as Ethan now thought about it, looked a little pale. He hoped that the lever would work and the drakes didn't have to swim back again. It just had to work!

"They're pulling on the lever now . . ."

Ethan was interrupted by a sharp, grinding sound that vibrated through the cavern. The children backed away from the water's edge, hugging the wall behind them. Their torches were starting to burn low, but they could make out a faint opening growing in the wall directly above the water in front of them. A stone slab was also now extending outward from just below the opening. It invitingly reached out over the water before crashing with a loud bang on the rocky beach in front of them, forming what they now realized was a small bridge to the breached hole.

*Ethan . . . Do you see an opening?* Seon asked.

*Yes.*

*Come quickly, the treasure awaits!* Seon flamboyantly called.

"Seon is telling us to enter," Ethan explained as he started for the bridge. He wasn't going to miss being the middle man. It made him feel odd.

Kristian and Lola overcame their initial shock and followed Ethan into the new gap. The corridor was no different from the others they had passed through, although this one was not as smooth. They walked for a few moments before reaching an abrupt ledge, which opened into a small cavern.

Ethan's heart beat faster as he looked out and saw both drakes perched around a stone pillar set in the middle of a rocky outcrop. The rest of the chamber was buried in water. The pillar was identical to what he'd seen in the scroll. On top of the pillar rested the ball. He turned to look at Kristian, who had an expression of shocked amazement mixed with wariness painted on his face as he had noticed the ball as well.

The little group quickly joined the drakes, jumping half of Kristian's body length to a rocky path below the ledge.

Deseret leapt onto Lola's shoulder when she approached to get a better look and nuzzled the little girl at the same time.

Upon closer inspection, the ball was of a curious workmanship roughly the size of Ethan's fist. It was made of a metal that none of the children had ever seen before, but had a bronze tint to it like some of the special cutlery they had seen in the hall of abundance before, and it seemed to shine of its own accord. Ethan inspected the treasure, and Seon quickly leapt to his shoulder to do the same.

*It's the Kur-ne!* Seon said abruptly.

*The what?* Ethan inquired.

*The Kur-ne . . . I somehow know its name . . . it told me.*

Ethan didn't grasp how Seon knew these things, but he'd been impressed by other events when the little drake innately knew about new objects and surroundings.

*So what does it do?*

*Not sure, but don't you feel the power?"*

Ethan nodded, half to himself. He had sensed an energy, an intensity as soon as he entered the chamber.

Kristian and Lola also now stood around the pillar, hypnotized by the glowing orb in front of them. "Well . . . go ahead, Dingus. Pick it up . . . and then we need to get back. That . . ." he nodded at the orb, "and this place gives me the creeps," Kristian said in a hurried tone as he looked warily over his shoulder at the unnaturally calm water.

Ethan hesitated then slowly reached out to retrieve the glowing orb.

*Ethan*, the ball called out his name!

The boy quickly withdrew his hand in surprise and looked around. No one else seemed to have noticed, and Kristian was motioning at his younger brother to hurry.

*Go ahead, Ethan. The orb wants to connect with you. It's all right*, Seon encouraged.

The boy cautiously reached his hand back out and let it hover over the ball for a few moments. His fingers grazed the metallic orb, and it felt immediately cool to his touch as he caressed it, surprising, as the air in the chamber had a warm and muggy texture to it. He paused again, then his hand closed around the ball, and he lifted it off the pillar. He studied its glowing surface for a few moments. All time seemed to halt as he turned it over in his hands and studied it.

Suddenly, a large bang erupted from directly behind the little group. The ground broke free in a quick series of tremors, and they struggled to stay on their feet.

"The tunnel!" Lola shrieked.

The boys followed her gaze just in time to see the walls around the gap slam shut.

"No!" bellowed Kristian, reaching his hand toward the opening as if to stop it from closing by sheer will.

The two walls met, followed by an immense quake that threw everyone to the ground. Ethan braced before striking the stone ground beneath him. Searing pain shot through his hand that held fast to the ball as he collided with the clammy surface.

He jerked his head up, realizing that the impact from his fall had driven the ball from his grasp. His eyes tore across the ground for any sign of the orb. The light sputtered and flickered all around him, and he realized that the torches were bouncing on the ground and rolling toward the water.

"Ethan, the ball!" Kristian warned.

Ethan spun his head around and quickly located the metallic orb, which to his horror was rolling along the descending slope and toward the water. He scrambled to a crawling position, wincing at the pain in his hand, and lunged for the ball, gripping it moments before it was lost in the black swirling pool. His instant relief was replaced by a great lump that formed at the back of his throat as the bouncing light now revealed the water rising about them. He quickly deposited the ball into his pocket and patted it for safety before looking up at his brother.

Kristian struggled to a half-standing position and snatched up one torch. The other had now gone out. He grabbed Lola with his other hand and hauled her to her feet.

"Go!" Ethan hollered as he scrambled behind them. They ran for the tunnel behind the pillar, barely visible in the faint light.

As they made the gap, Ethan wrenched his head around to get his bearings. The dying torch provided brief glimpses of the room, no larger than a closet with no noticeable exits except for the way they had just come. However, a few moments of searching revealed on the far wall, what looked to be shelving was actually a stone ladder extending upward beyond the ceiling.

Kristian was the first one up the rails, throwing the torch down to his brother as he began to ascend. The older boy was soon out of the torchlight's reach.

Ethan heard fists against stone, followed by a few loud grunts. Ethan guessed Kristian was trying to punch the ceiling open.

"It's no use, the way is blocked!" Kristian roared out in frustration. A few grunts later, the older boy gave up. "It's no . . . use . . . won't budge!"

Kristian quickly climbed back down the ladder and seized the torch from his younger brother, desperately searching for another way out. He made it to the opposite wall and felt along the surface.

Lola shrieked again and pointed at the door.

Both boys spun around and immediately saw the reason as the water flowed unhindered through the doorway. Soon, it was at their ankles and rising fast. Ethan thought he felt something cold in the water.

*Ethan! They're here!* Seon announced in his mind. *If we do not find a way out, something terrible is going to happen. Much worse than drowning,* the drake warned.

"Come on!" Ethan exclaimed. "Is this what is supposed to happen?" He pulled the orb out of his pocket and yelled at it. "Work, dang it! Work! Aren't you supposed to show me the way?" he roared.

*Well, yelling at it won't help you!* Seon reprimanded.

Suddenly a halting thought formed in the boy's mind. It twisted and swirled in his conscience as it gave him silent instructions. "I'll do it!" he blurted out.

"Do what?" Kristian yelled over his shoulder, still feeling his way around the closet for another way out.

"Get back!" Ethan commanded his brother. The water was now at their knees, and Ethan could feel the water's icy touch strike him to the core. He wasn't about to let the water demons get anywhere near them. The boy hesitated for a moment more, depositing the orb back into his pocket. Then he quickly grabbed his injured wrist and cast a simple healing spell to mend the sprain, but couldn't spare enough time to restore it completely.

"What are you doing?" Kristian yelled.

Ethan ignored his brother and quickly cast a shield across the doorway. It crackled into view and held steady. He then turned and reached out for the ladder as he started to climb, overriding the throbbing in his right hand.

"I already tried that, Ethan, you can't get it open!" Kristian bawled, pulling his eyes away from the shield his younger brother had just cast. "Besides, the water is still coming through."

"Trust me!" Ethan shouted back down the ladder as he continued to climb, reaching the top, terrified of what would happen next. He knew what he had to do.

*Are you sure you want to go through with this, Ethan?* Seon asked, now perched on his back, as the boy hunched over to brace himself.

Ethan gave a quick nod then fixed his legs against either side of the wall and placed both hands on the surface directly above him. *I hope that my learning has taught me to control this—at least I can think of the outcome when I try it this time,* he feebly answered, trying to console himself.

*I will add my strength to yours, Ethan.*

He was happy for the support and concentrated, digging deep into his core feeling around for the energy. His breathing slowed, and he forced himself to be calm, locating the dormant fire within him just as he had on that first day in the cave. It was easy to stoke the flame, and the power began to stir within his chest as he focused his attention on the ceiling—forcing it upward, unblocking their exit, then for a safe return from the spell. The intensity of the power increased.

Suddenly, something pounded against the shield, momentarily distracting the boy from his errand.

"Ethan! You'd better hurry up!" Kristian shouted from below.

Another attack on his shield, this one with double the intensity of the last strike.

*Ignore it!* Seon soothed. *Just focus and block it all out."*

The boy shut his eyes tight and concentrated on the action. As in Seon's hatching cave, a small blue orb burst into existence and grew, the familiar annoying needles pricked all around Ethan's head. Suddenly, another familiar presence fortified his own, and he realized that Seon had joined him. Ethan counted backward from three, two, one, and drove the rock up and out in his mind.

A blinding flash emanated all around him. He could see it through his eyelids. The brightness grew, followed by a shattering bang, followed by complete darkness. Ethan heard someone yell from below, but couldn't tell if it was Lola or Kristian.

The rock at his hands was now gone, replaced by a shower of sand flowing down upon him. He thrust his head downward and felt a little panicked, remembering when the sand caved in on him before. *Seon, hang on.*

*I'm here, and it will take more than this to dislodge me from you*, the little drake courageously replied.

Ethan waited for the torrent to jettison him to the ground below or drown him. It did neither. Instead, the pouring sand subsided. He slowly opened his eyes, blinking and wiping small particles from his lashes, looking up into blackness above him. He'd really done it!

*It worked!* Seon congratulated the boy. *Do you feel all right?* the drake quickly added out of concern.

The boy nodded and gave a great toothy grin to his little companion before turning his attentions to his siblings.

"Kristian, Lola, are you all right?" he bellowed back down the shaft.

Kristian responded in a flurry of words, "Yeah . . . what's going on? You OK? We saw a bright light and an explosion . . . There's no way out, and the water is already at my waist. I'd say we have to swim for it, but there's something out there that keeps crashing into your shield. It's not good."

"Send Lola up, I found a way out!" the younger boy yelled back.

"What? How?" Kristian shouted in an unbelieving tone.

"No time, send her up with the torch, then you follow!"

Ethan climbed the rest of the way up and into the darkness, above.

# Chapter 15

## The Forbidden City

*Challenges crop up all around us. We can withdraw from them, or we can stand and fight, even if we're not entirely sure what we're fighting against.*

Lola whimpered as the little party squeezed their way through a narrow tunnel, similar to all the others they'd passed through before. She clung tightly to Ethan, and he could feel Deseret's tail whipping at his arm as they trotted onward, almost afraid to look back. The water and whatever was in it, never caught them.

His hand still hurt from the fall, and he cradled it gingerly, careful not to rub it against anything as he walked. Again, he wished he'd studied the healing art a little more closely over the last year. At least it was just a sprain, but it stung nonetheless.

The torchlight was on its last leg, but held on for much longer than they could have expected. Kristian had run out of the burlap strips to add to the flame. So the children all had to squint to make out the path directly in front of them. None of them dared call attention to the fading light, for fear that bad luck would put the meager fire out completely.

The passage now seemed to be slowly climbing, and it weaved back and forth in sharp directions as they continued onward. A number of times, they had to stop and tediously make their way through large stones and rubble that had apparently broken free from the ceiling at some point in the past. The rocky ground beneath their feet gradually gave way to sand, and hope rose within Ethan that an exit might be nearby.

The path eventually straightened out but still gradually sloped upward, and Ethan could now see a pale light wandering along the tunnel that gave form to the outlines of the walls and the ground beyond the reach of their torch. The brightness intensified the farther they walked until they could see the pasty white sand without the need of their torchlight. In fact, he realized the torch had gone out altogether; although, Kristian still held the stick out in front of him as if it were a beacon.

They seemed to all notice the swelling glow and walked on at a healthier pace in anticipation of what lie ahead.

Suddenly, the path bent upward and climbed at a steeper grade in front of them, and the pale white light cascaded down upon the family.

Ethan had to blink a few times as his eyes adjusted.

"The end of the tunnel! It's gotta be!" Kristian broke into a dead run, followed closely by Lola and then Ethan, who held his hand against his chest as he jogged behind.

The older boy was the first to reach the end and suddenly stopped, flailing his arms as if bracing against a fall.

Lola slowed not knowing what to do and Ethan finally caught up to his brother and pulled the older boy back to safety.

As Ethan peered around is brother, he could see that the tunnel opened onto an enormous cliff above a vast graveyard of fallen pillars; most of which was bathed in shadow. The graveyard formed a sunken valley set deep within the earth's belly. Colossal cliff faces rose from below and towered above them.

*This puts Julfa's cliff to shame!* Seon said with awe.

An icy breeze blew past him from below as the boy shivered at the unexpected coolness of the night. He craned his head to look up the cliff face, much larger than the one he'd known at Julfa, and suddenly realized that the pale light they were seeing from the tunnel was a full moon set against the bright starry heavens. The moon was much lighter than he had ever seen before, almost as light as the noonday sun and just as big, Taking up a big portion of the sky. It appeared that Ethan could reach his hand out and touch the glowing planet. Wisps of thin clouds high in the atmosphere lazily accentuated the dark blue sky above them and were almost drown out, as they passed over the moon.

"That's our way down," Kristian announced. A small jagged pathway wound its way down the steep cliff, with enough space for only one person to shimmy down. The path was barely discernible as it broke every few paces, which made it treacherous, even with ample lighting. There was no path leading upward.

The children cautiously made their way to the valley floor, careful to hug the side of the precipice as they went.

Ethan gingerly guided himself with one hand, keeping a tight grip on Lola with the other. He didn't spend time to take in the scenery, due to their steep and treacherous descent.

The pathway abruptly ended in a sheer drop, the last twelve paces to the valley floor. Kristian leapt first, hitting soft sand and rolling into a crouched position. He turned and motioned for Lola to jump next. She shook her head violently before Ethan and Deseret convinced her that Kristian would catch her and that she would be fine. She finally agreed, closed her eyes, and leapt. Kristian caught her.

Ethan jumped next, and landed more roughly than Kristian, momentarily knocking the breath out of his lungs.

*All right?* Seon prodded, as he glided lightly down to his perch on Ethan's shoulder.

The boy nodded and pushed himself up slowly, sucking in air. Relief washed over him as he glanced back at the cliff face in the moonlight. He couldn't even make out the pathway they had just traversed, and he was suddenly grateful that they had even made it down.

*Clearly, there is no going back!* he thought gloomily. *At least not that way.*

*Ah, but we have the Kur-ne,* the little drake cooed.

The sunken basin around the children was eerily beautiful, casting long shadows all around them in the moonlight. It was shrouded in more sand and walls, half-standing under the otherwise-open sky. The silence was deafening.

Suddenly, a sharp howl broke the momentary dreamland appeal, and the children nervously threw their heads around in apprehension.

Lola jumped at the sound and clung to Kristian, wearing a look of abject horror on her face.

All three drakes launched into the air. Seon was in flight only for a moment before he was back on Ethan's shoulder.

*You know where the sound came from, don't you?* Seon asked.

"It is a nightmare," Ethan mumbled. "It is night time!" His mind was in motion at the thought of the unpleasant creatures attached to those howls claiming the night as their own, especially in the open desert.

"We've gotta find some shelter and get a fire started!" Kristian half-whispered, trying not to attract unwanted attention.

The howls suddenly broke into a chorus coming from all different directions.

"Now!" the older boy demanded, raising his voice, as both of the other children stood there in a frozen trance.

Ethan regained his senses and quickly closed the gap to his brother, who started to scan the plaza for a protected shelter or room of some kind to safely camp in.

The little group walked from wall to wall, peering into dark doorways that were set into the free-standing structures about them, occasionally stepping over more rocky debris that lay strewn all about.

The first few darkened doors drained into larger courtyards that weren't defensible, and they quickly passed on to others. After a few attempts, they finally found a small alcove with its walls and ceiling still intact, and with just enough space for them to defend themselves, if there was need.

Kristian hauled them inside and hastily began emptying the firewood onto the ground that they had brought along with them.

Ethan was now even more grateful for the forward thinking of his older brother as it occurred to him that he hadn't seen one scrap of wood in the area outside—not that he had been looking for it.

*I hope the wood has dried out enough to catch fire,* Seon interrupted.

*Ever the optimist,* Ethan taunted.

Kristian hastily dug a rough fire pit in the sand with his hands, and the children found ragged shards of stone to line the trench properly—likely pieces of debris that had fallen from the walls and ceiling. He piled some of the wood in the pit, making a tepee, and stacked the rest in a corner before whispering, "Yangin." An immediate flame formed in his hands, and he lit the wood, which thankfully started to immediately burn and crackle. "We'll keep the fire low to conserve our wood throughout the night," he stated as Ethan and Lola huddled around the flames for some warmth.

They broke into Kristian's back sack and ate a hasty meal of dried bread and honey. The one thing Ethan regretted is that they had not brought the beehive with them, but that wouldn't have ended well anyway, he reflected.

After the meal, Kristian ushered Ethan and Lola to bed. "I'll take the first watch then wake Ethan halfway through the night. We need to watch for what . . ."—he shot a furtive glance toward Lola before continuing in a lower voice—"what might be out there. Now get some rest. We'll need to get our bearings tomorrow in order to get back."

The two younger siblings nodded and curled up together in the sand as best they could, using what little clothing they had in their back sacks as pillows and blankets. Lola laid her head on her brother's chest and immediately fell asleep, although her body jerked whenever a howl ripped through the evening air.

The last thing Ethan remembered was the small fire crackling directly in front of him as small embers floated gently toward the door opening. Kristian was sitting cross-legged beyond that, intently looking out the doorway.

Ethan closed his eyes, and a fitful sleep embraced him.

—  —  —

Sand blew all about Ethan in a feverish pitch. He was perfectly alone, lost in a barren wasteland. The surroundings were bathed in almost total darkness, and he couldn't see but a few feet in front of him with raised hands shielding his eyes from the biting dust that impaled his face with tiny jagged strikes. The wind gusts continued for a while then abruptly stopped, and a dim light peeked through the settling mist.

As the sand sifted earthward, a vast sandy wasteland came into view, devoid of any noticeable life, stretching without an end in sight in all directions. He slowly turned himself around, looking for any distinguishing marks that might give him some bearing as to where he was. But the only feature that stuck out in his mind was the rolling hills of more sand.

The boy started to aimlessly wander, not knowing where his feet would lead him. He glanced back over his shoulder once or twice to find that his footprints were being wiped clean by short gusts of wind. Ignoring a growing sense of urgency forming in the back of his mind, he continued onward, taking one step at a time. Moments turned into an eternity of aimless roaming. Ethan's urgency turned to despair, and he finally chose to give himself up to ruin, dropping to his knees as the heat beat down upon him from a blood-red sky. The sand singed his palms and he felt the hot arid air through his clothing, as the shiny pebbles reflected the sweltering heat upward. He didn't care.

He remembered Seon and tried to reach out to his drake. No answer, no presence—nothing but emptiness. He was perfectly alone.

A memory presented itself to his mind—one of Grandpa's teachings about the Great Spirit. He had never paid much attention to this before. Frankly, his family had been enough for him, and yet he always had a nagging feeling there was something more. Besides, he was too independent most of the time to rely on anyone else, let alone someone or something he couldn't see or even fathom.

"If you call on him, you will be answered!" came his grandpa's words into his mind. He tried to drown out the thought and mentally shook himself free. But the feeling kept tugging at him with growing strength each time he thought about it.

He finally resolved to try. It couldn't hurt any more than this, he realized.

Ethan lay face flat in the sand and squeezed his eyes shut, forcing himself to think as piously as he had ever done and to beg and plead for mercy. He lifted his head off the ground to peer around for a sign, some sign of rescue—nothing happened. He decided he wasn't being fervent enough and tried again, squeezing his eyes tighter this time and clenching his teeth in concentration. He ignored the dull headache now forming at his temples at the strain of his prayer. Again, he jerked opened his eyes—nothing.

Perhaps nothing would happen?

Yet he felt he shouldn't give up just yet; after all, he had ignored this aspect of his spirituality for so long, it occurred to him that it might take some effort for him to get back on track. The boy slowly arose, turning himself around once again to get another view of the landscape. Half the way there, he caught sight of something he did not expect—a grove of pure white trees loomed in the distance. At least that is what it appeared to be. He raised a hand over his brow as a shield from the red sun to perhaps get a better look. It still appeared to be a grove of trees. Relieved, he thought to thank his good fortune and set off at a half trot.

After a time between full-out sprinting and lazy jogging, he noticed that the trees seemed to remain the same distance, no matter how hard he tried to reach them. "Why is this not working!" he cried in agony. But then he stopped and prayed again. Another thought suddenly occurred to him that he needed to dig deeper within himself, much like he did with his Kesem, in order to get to the grove. He wouldn't be able to approach it by only walking or running in its direction; instead, he had to focus and exercise a little faith. He closed his eyes and concentrated on the trees, praying this would work. Yet another thought popped into his mind: Was this what he desired most? Would he give anything to reach the trees? *Well, yes*, he thought. *It is as good as anything to wish for right now*, as he considered the situation he was in.

Ethan opened his eyes, and to his astonishment, the grove appeared to be much closer! He continued thinking of the trees, and as he walked, the grove drew ever closer. Finally, an enormous gnarled trunk rose sharply in front of him towering over the boy. A few bright white leaves floated down to him on a gentle breeze. The entire tree was much whiter than the sand all around him, and yet, these trees seemed to emit light from within and not from the sun.

He cast his eyes to the rest of the grove and counted twenty or more trees in all, skirted by knee-high grass, which Ethan had only read about in scrolls Ezera had lectured him on in class, about the Abseron seaside beaches and grassy plains.

The boy reached his hands out and caught one of the tender leaves. It was soft and velvety to the touch. He absently let his finger move up and down the leaf's spine as he passed through the trees, moving farther into the belly of the orchard. Soon, he came upon the center of the grove, where lay a small pool of water, its surface dazzling from within and reflecting a few lazily moving clouds above.

As Ethan approached the small pond, he attempted to look into its depths. He could see nothing but a reflection, a reflection of fruit hanging in a nearby branch. He realized that he was quite hungry, glancing up at the tree and instinctively reached out in his eagerness to pick one of the fruit from the tree's lowest branch.

His finger grazed the fruit's skin and a sudden bolt of energy ricocheted through him, throwing him backward and into the grass.

Recoiling from the unexpected shock and resulting pain, he shook his head. "Why can't I get a hold of it?" he wondered aloud.

—   —   —

"Ethan . . . Ethan . . . Ethan . . ." the boy abruptly woke from his dream.

Kristian was standing over the boy, his face contorted with concern. Ethan was wet from sweat and shivered as a cool breeze entered the small doorway and stole some of the warmth from the room. He squinted and rubbed his eyes, glancing around him. The fire was still going, but most of the firewood was now gone.

"You all right?" Kristian asked, anxiety evident in his voice.

Ethan shook the sleep from his eyes and nodded. "Yeah, why shouldn't I be?"

"You started to scream in your sleep . . . I was worried something might be wrong." Kristian looked up at the doorway. "And . . . that you might warn something about us . . . you know, that we're here," he whispered, as if careful not to invite any misfortune upon them. He looked back at Ethan.

"No, I'm fine . . . just a bad dream . . ."

Kristian nodded. "You should take over watch now anyways. I figure we have just a little while till sunrise. The howling died down 'bout an hour ago . . . Luckily, it never got closer, so I hope we're safe for the time being."

Ethan stretched and slowly pulled himself up. He rubbed the back of his head with both hands and stumbled over to where Kristian had been sitting before.

Kristian lay down where Ethan had been, careful not to disturb Lola, and closed his eyes.

*Are you OK?* another concerned thought entreated.

*Yes, but . . .* , he paused to consider if he should go on or not.

Seon glided to his side. *I sensed pain and frustration from you, it woke me. It was different from the dreams you had before.*

Ethan didn't really want to discuss it right now, but questions pressed in upon him about the scene, the grove, and the fruit that he wanted—*no*—needed answers to.

*This was a weird dream*, he finally conceded. He shared his conscience with Seon then recounted the dream to the little drake, who sat silently by his side.

When he was finished, he drew out the metallic orb and toyed with it in his hands, the surface still smooth and cool to his touch.

*We need to get to Limnah, but I don't know how we will get back. We need to find out the meaning to your dreams. I feel they are significant for us*, the drake said ponderously.

*It's . . . It's just not fair*, Ethan exploded. *Why does this all have to be so difficult? Why can't it be easy, like for Kristian and BeeSting?* Ethan was on a roll. *Seon . . . I want for you and me to play. I mean, we shouldn't have to care who knows about us . . . We should be able to use our magic to do whatever we want to do, like find out what this Kur-ne does, for example.*

He raised the ball in his hand and touched it to his nose, peering more closely at the black fog rolling within the sphere that he had just noticed. After a few moments, he tossed it from hand to hand before continuing.

*These dreams just weigh me down . . . I . . . I just want them to stop.* He cried in frustration.

*Be careful of what you ask for, Ethan. Men's dreams signify things they see by day, albeit in strange and wonderful combinations. You may not want the dreams, but they will help you . . . they will help us, if you try harder to understand them . . .*

*Whatever . . . I guess I'll talk to Limnah when we get back . . . ,* he said more to placate the drake than to admit it to himself. *If we get back!* he thought with a healthy dose of skepticism.

Seon decided to let Ethan stew on this and work it all out in his own mind. The small drake curled up next to the boy and fell asleep.

Ethan continued to play with the ball and occasionally study it. He wondered what the Kur-ne's purpose was and suddenly had a stroke of genius play through his mind. *That's it!* he contrived. *I'll return at some point to Julfa, right?* Then when he did, he would look into the scroll again. *It worked the first time, why won't it work again?* It would tell him what to do with the kur-ne and finally he could get free of this whole mess! His mind raced through all the ways he could distract Limnah in order to accomplish this, and renewed enthusiasm flowed through his veins once more.

A sudden movement in the shadows brought Ethan out of his reverie. He glanced up and stared hard at the spot. Was it a shadow? Did a cloud pass over the moon? He couldn't tell.

For added security, he quickly dropped the ball into his pocket and surveyed where he thought he'd seen the movement. For a time he saw nothing more, convinced his mind had played a trick on him. The more the boy concentrated, the more he believed he was imagining things, at one point, even hearing soft footfalls in the sand, but that couldn't be real. Whoever heard someone walk in the sand? Unless they were really, really heavy.

He decided to return to what he had been doing before. Just as he leaned back, another movement caught his eye. Ethan quickly rolled into a kneeling position, poised for action, a quick jolt of nerves tingling throughout his body. Seon was now awake, having felt Ethan's sudden surge of adrenaline.

*What is it? What's going on, Ethan?*

## The Forbidden City

*Thought I saw something a few times . . . I don't think we're alone . . . Better wake BeeSting and get him in the air to scout as you can't fly well enough yet.*

Seon shot him a glowering look, but nodded and alerted BeeSting.

Kristian was now up and scrambled to Ethan's side as BeeSting zinged out of the doorway in a red blur, circling higher to get a better view of the surrounding scenery. The morning light was now breaking upon the clutter of rocks and pillars just outside of their hiding place.

"See something?" Kristian whispered to Ethan.

Ethan nodded, trying to concentrate on the area. "Twice, and I heard footsteps . . . I know it sounds weird—"

Suddenly both Kristian and Seon interrupted him at once, "Wolves!"

It was an odd sensation, Ethan had to admit, hearing this at the same time by ear as well as in his head. He quickly shook off the irony and threw a magical shield against the door, almost instinctively.

"Where?" he asked both of them.

Seon responded first, *Circling the area. They know we're here . . . at least BeeSting thinks they do . . .*

Seon's thought was interrupted as a wolf emerged from a nearby boulder, baring its teeth in a low growl.

*It knows we know!* Seon said in a startled tone.

Without further warning, the wolf charged headlong into the shield. The creature gave a quick yelp and fell backward.

The surprise and speed of the attack threw Ethan off, and the shield dissolved. Kristian fell backward from the attack as well.

The wolf was on its feet again, now cautiously advancing on the tiny group, and Ethan thought he saw more pairs of eyes approaching from behind it.

Lola was now awake and in full hysteria at the back of the room, which did little to help Ethan's concentration.

Suddenly, a flash of fire streamed past Ethan from somewhere behind, targeting the wolf. The fireball caught the giant canine on the paw, and it yelped in pain, running in circles in the sand trying to put the fire out. The wolf retreated, but three or four now stalked the children, cautiously approaching on their position.

Ethan recovered from his shock and threw another shield barrier at the doorway. He didn't know how well it would hold against multiple intruders, nor if they possibly knew of the blockade's existence. Perhaps it would hold, perhaps he'd just been lucky the first time. Either way, he wasn't about to find out. He thrust his hands out in three successive rapid

258

motions, adding more layers as a precaution. Then he invoked the same technique he had used on Hem—this time with more power.

Three wolves were simultaneously picked up and cast backward against a rock wall across the way. All of them fell to the sand and retreated, whimpering their complaints. One of the wolves turned and barked angrily at the three children before following the others into the shadows.

"There's too many of them, Ethan . . . ," Kristian interrupted as more wolves advanced on them. "But wow, I'd hate to be Hem if that's what you used on him."

Ethan turned to see Kristian throwing a wishful smile at his younger brother, but only momentarily.

The older boy's face turned pale. "Look! There's . . . two more . . . another two there . . . Whoa, three more over there . . . ," he continued, counting in silence.

Dawn was fast approaching, and the surrounding courtyard was growing lighter. "The only hope we have is to hold the wolves at bay until the sun hits them." Ethan declared. *Wolves hate the sun,* he explained to Seon.

"And you know this how?" Kristian asked.

"Lots of reading." the younger boy shrugged.

"Well, we might not have that long," Kristian warned.

A continuous stream of wolves poured into the street. The sheer numbers of them made Ethan think of a procession of ants in search of food. They seemed to be emerging from every nook and cranny.

"I don't know how long my Kesem with last." Ethan groaned. He silently scolded himself for never trying to max himself out previously, just as a proof for how far he could go on.

*You didn't know this was going to happen, Ethan,* Seon thought. *Keep your thoughts focused on them, not about what you might not be able to do.* He counseled.

"It's gotta be long enough for us to hold them back and wait on the sun. You're gonna have to push yourself, little brother," Kristian coaxed.

Another wolf charged and bounced off the shield barrier. This time Ethan was ready, and the shield held strong.

Lola crawled forward and crouched low, next to Kristian. She was just behind the wall so that she could see part of the action. Her face was a mixture of absolute fright and seething anger at the sight of the snarling wolves, baring their fangs at the children.

"Stay back, Lola!" Ethan shouted as another wolf pounded into the shield, bouncing off the crackling blue surface in a yelping retreat.

Lola raised herself up and hollered "Knahast Sans!" and abruptly launched a spear of water toward another charging wolf, which landed in its hind quarters. A loud yelp erupted from the animal as she snapped its hind leg in two, and it limped out of sight while holding its leg off the ground.

"They're testing our defenses!" Kristian said in a tone of disbelief. "They're testing us! How is that possible?" he bawled.

*He's right, Ethan . . . ,* Seon inserted. *BeeSting is reporting to us that the wolves are regrouping just out of sight. It appears they are communicating somehow and launching waves against us to break us down . . . They also have patrols circling our encampment, looking for another way in, but have mostly given up and are concentrating their attacks at the door.*

As if on cue, Ethan jerked his head upward at the sound of scratching on the rock ceiling. The wolves kept coming one by one, testing the barrier.

*So how do we stop them?* Ethan countered. *I don't know of anything powerful enough to drive them all off. All I can think of is holding them long enough for the sun to rise, but it doesn't look like that will work . . . they look really hungry, and they just keep coming.*

*Wait . . .*

*Seon?* Ethan asked at the sudden interruption. The drake didn't answer.

*Seon?* The boy looked at the drake.

*Ethan, something is coming . . . something else, not wolves . . . BeeSting can't identify what they are, but they're big. Really big!*

The news came as a heavy blow to Ethan. A knot twisted in his stomach, and he suddenly felt drained and feeble. He glanced sideways at Kristian and saw in his eyes that he'd just received the same message from BeeSting. Ethan's mind was now whirling. What else could be out there? Whatever they were, were they working with the wolves?

*How many . . . are there?* he managed to think through the haze of fear building in his mind.

Three wolves abruptly rammed the barrier together. Ethan hadn't prepared himself for the charge as he'd been preoccupied with the news. The force of the impact threw him backward, and he wrapped his hands around his torso, gasping for breath, as if someone had just punched him in the gut. Stars twinkled in his periphery vision, and he felt lightheaded.

The next few moments were blurry for the boy, but he could vaguely hear Kristian and Lola scream together. Fire and water erupted from both sides of Ethan, and he heard yelping from more of the brutes.

*E-than . . . E-than . . .* Seon was trying to reach him, but the pain had knocked him into slow motion.

*Ethan, Ethan, are you OK?*

The boy regained his breath and rolled over and onto his stomach, hoisting himself back up to invoke another shell. More wolves were charging the doorway.

Kristian and Lola were busy with another set of the dogs and didn't see the charge.

He didn't know if he could get the shield up in time.

Suddenly, a furry blur lunged across the doorway from just outside of the children's line of sight. It slammed into the charging wolves. A mess of paws and bodies flung in every direction, and the dogs let out high-pitched yelps of agony as they ran for cover.

Ethan shook his head in perfect surprise. He looked at Kristian who wore the same expression and then at Lola, who had shrunk back behind the wall with renewed fear.

"What was that?" he mouthed.

Kristian shrugged. He had no idea. "I think we're really in trouble." He balked.

The boys broke eye contact, now witnessing the same spectacle happening all over the courtyard to the pack of wolves.

From a distance, Ethan now identified the hulking masses just as Seon announced it.

"Desert lions!"

The boy's heart sank. Desert lions, or sand lions as they were called in Julfa, were known for their ferocity when guarding a territory. The little group didn't stand a chance against one of these gigantic predators, let alone this many of them! He'd never heard of them grouping up like this. *It's impossible!* he thought. A second thought then occurred to him: Ethan realized that he couldn't shield his family from such an attack—he had never faced something this big!

True to form, the lions were decimating the wolves at every turn. Limp bodies lay strewn across the courtyard, and Ethan almost had to cover his own ears to block out the continuous yelping from the wounded animals being tossed about. He hoped this was not a territorial display and that the lions wouldn't turn on the children after the wolves had been driven off. The pit in his stomach tried to leap up his throat, and he swallowed hard to keep from vomiting.

He was interrupted in his thoughts by Seon again, *Ethan, get a hold of yourself!* Seon unsympathetically scolded, *There is a way out . . . While the lions and wolves are busy, we can slip out and away from the mayhem.*

The boy took the ray of hope in this last bit of the message. But he had not time to bask in it.

*BeeSting has found a path for us to follow, but we'll have to be quick about it . . .*

Ethan tore his eyes from the grueling scene in front of him and nodded at Kristian, assuming he had the same message. The boys locked eyes for only a moment.

"Lola, get your stuff together—fast! We need to get out, now!" Kristian demanded, hastily gathering and cramming his belongings into his back sack.

Ethan did the same.

The morning was now light enough for them to easily make their way through the rubble.

Kristian peered around the edge of the doorway. Finding the way clear, he motioned to Ethan and Lola and led them out of the small room and around a large boulder.

The children paused for a moment, while Kristian took his bearings.

Ethan could now clearly distinguish between the lions tan fur versus the wolves' darker pelts, all of which were still in midskirmish with loud growls, snarls and barking echoing throughout the courtyard.

Kristian nodded and directed them from boulder to boulder until they entered a roughly hewn doorway that emptied into a larger courtyard beyond the battle fray. Once on the other side, the children threw themselves up against the wall to catch their breath.

The younger boy relaxed a little as the sounds were muffled behind the large stone walls. But he still didn't feel completely safe, not until they had some distance between them and the battle. They needed to find a way out. He feverishly scouted around, canvassing the courtyard. To his astonishment, he found that they had ventured into a great demolished, sunken city of some sort. He hadn't noticed this on the previous night, assuming the shadows all fell from the rubble. All around them, great cliff walls rose above them. He estimated that the cliffs were over three or four times the size of the cliff at Julfa, and he wondered how this could be possible.

Apparently, Kristian had now noticed the same thing and stood gaping with his head tilted backward. He looked like he had just been bucked off a horse and was suffering from whiplash. "What the . . . ," Kristian blurted out.

Ethan shook off the revelation. "Let's go!" he said hurriedly. Grabbing his little sister's arm, he bolted for the other end of the courtyard, where he could make out another small dark entrance. At least he hoped it was an exit.

Kristian followed in close pursuit as BeeSting swooped in from above and joined him again.

The children reached the center and halted to catch their breath.

After a few gulps of air, Ethan was ready to run again, but something was different. The battle sounds were gone. He looked over his shoulder at Kristian, who wore a look of terror as they both turned to look behind them.

At first, they saw nothing, but they heard it and it made their blood run chill. They could hear something lumbering towards them. Something massive.

Fear overcame Ethan, and he ran full tilt at the opening opposite him with a renewed sense of preservation. He barely noticed that Lola was kicking and screaming that he was hurting her as he dragged her along in an attempt to escape. They made it three-quarters of the way to the dark entrance when an enormous form crashed down in front of them. He dug in his heels and skidded to a halt.

Kristian had done the same, just a few paces behind them.

All three children huddled with their backs towards each other and anxiously looked around.

Another form appeared to their left then to their right.

Ethan craned his head to look over his shoulder to see an army of lions approaching them from behind. The thunder of their giant paws made the earth tremble, as pebbles danced in front to them in a dizzying rhythm.

They were surrounded!

In his shock, Ethan released Lola, who promptly sat down, whimpering and rubbing the arm that he had been gripping during their flight. Deseret licked at the young girl's arm, pausing only to indignantly glare up at Ethan for his mistreatment of her companion.

The two boys slowly orbited their little sister in defensive poses, examining the lions that had now formed a great circle around them.

The lions started to slowly close ranks on the small group.

"Kristian, we gotta do something . . . ," Ethan snarled over his shoulder. He knew his shield would not hold against such powerful creatures. Then it dawned on him, perhaps fear would do the trick where brute protection could not! "Form a ring of fire around us," he barked. "We need it high, really high . . . I know you've only done this small scale, so you'll need to reach extra deep this time!"

# The Forbidden City

Kristian looked uncertainly over at his younger brother then finally nodded and closed his eyes tight. He screwed his face up in a menacing growl then uttered the word *Uzuk*. A flame circle burst into view around the children, but the flame was barely a few hands tall.

Ethan looked around nervously as the lions continued to advance on the little group. He tried to keep his voice calm and composed so as not to alarm his brother any further. "Good! Kristian, now keep your eyes closed. Find the energy deep within you . . . got it?"

The older boy paused then nodded again.

"OK, now stoke the flame, let it grow, believe that it is an inferno . . . build on it . . . then invoke the fire again when you're ready."

Kristian fell silently still for what felt like centuries to Ethan as the lions drew ever closer.

*I do not think they mean to harm us*, Seon announced.

"Now is *not* the time, Seon!" Ethan said under his breath. Still, he paused to study one of the advancing lions. He could see its solid black eyes, and they somehow seemed different from any animals' eyes that he'd seen before. The eyes did not appear to be wild at all—in fact, there was unfathomable intelligence behind them; it all didn't quite fit. They appeared as if they could think!

"Uzuk!" Kristian finally shouted, letting his energy go all at once.

Ethan could feel it in the air, and his hair stood on end. Sudden flames cast up around them sprouting into the heavens. Lola backed closer into the circle, horrified by the sudden explosion and covered her face at the extreme heat.

Ethan knew that the flames would cook them. He could already feel the scorching effects as sweat streamed steadily down his face. He stole a quick look through the towering flames and saw the lions halt their advance with trepidation as they swung their heads around not knowing what to do next. The boy smiled to himself at the success. He quickly formed a defensive shield in his mind, finding the lucid energy within himself and invoked the barrier around the children. The cooling results were immediate. Ethan couldn't feel the heat any longer, and the perimeter around them was as comfortable as it could be.

He looked sidewise at Kristian, who now had his eyes wide open, a look of astonishment spread across his face at the size of the fire.

Ethan gave him a pat on the back. "Wow!" he commended.

Kristian grinned with pride. Even BeeSting seemed delighted by the show.

The younger boy turned his attention back to the lions. He hoped that this display of strength would scare them away, with a little coaxing, that

The Drake Epics - Journey to Qara

is. He readied himself to launch one of the lions high into the air to scare the rest off. He worried about the amount of energy it might take to do so, given their large size, but quickly shrugged it off as something he just had to do.

*Is it really necessary?* Seon was asking.

"What is with you, Seon?" Ethan growled. "Can't you see that we are trying to deal with this?"

*Do what you will. But you aren't seeing the bigger picture here,* the little drake said in a reproachful tone.

Ethan growled again. "Not seeing the bigger picture, eh?" Using his Kesem, he formed a small hole in the fire, enough for him to see through it and prove to Seon that the predators meant them harm. He was surprised that it worked the first time that he tried, as breaking through another holder's Kesem was something he hadn't attempted before.

However, nothing could have prepared him for the next turn of events. Ethan expected to target a large monster of a lion, but instead, he saw a squat little man haltingly walk up to them. At least it looked like a little man. It was much too hard to tell through the waves of heat that emanated from the inferno. All he could see from the short man's stance was that he was extremely uncomfortable as he wiped at his brow with the sleeve of his arm, but maintained a safe distance from the blaze. The lions had all regrouped behind him and a host of other squat men?

The little man opened his mouth, and a little raspy voice called out, barely discernible above the roaring flames, "Great Sheikhs, we are come to escort you from the Forbidden City."

# Chapter 16

# Wanderers in a Strange Land

*We are all wanderers ever seeking our true home. We may find that our current homes are only way stations, and we have simply forgotten our true origins.*

The two boys gaped at one other, completely perplexed. Kristian peered out of the hole and scratched at his head while trying to make sense out of the squat little man. A similar crowd of stocky-looking folk trailed behind him with odd expressions on their faces. They appeared a bit anxious and looked at the flames with veneration.

The Drake Epics - Journey to Qara

If Ethan had studied them a little closer, he might have noticed that the men bore an interesting likeness to the lions, but in miniature.

Lola missed the announcement, giggling uncontrollably in her own little world now, as she shot small water missiles at the fire and poked holes in the raging flames. "See that, Deseret?" she exclaimed. "Watch this one." And she let another one loose.

"Well, Lola has lost it." Ethan announced as he rubbed at the back of his head.

"Where did the lions go?" Kristian asked and stood aside to let Ethan have another look.

Ethan shrugged as he peered through the hole a second time. The same question loomed in his mind.

*Perhaps the little men are the lions?* Seon chided. *And they aren't so threatening as you may have thought. Perhaps, you should look at the bigger picture*, he urged.

Ethan cast him an irritated grin. "Just say I told you so," he mumbled, but he knew that his little companion was right and that he should have listened to him in the first place.

The squat man continued to stand just outside of the reach of the flames, mopping at his brow every now and then and waiting for some sign from the children.

"Well, we need to answer him, don't we?" Ethan asked.

"Guess you better make sure there aren't any lions left . . . and then ask him?" Kristian recommended.

"Me? You're the oldest! Fearless leader, you ask?"

"Nope! You're going to do it."

Ethan shook his head in frustration. "No way!" He folded his arms.

"My brother, Ethan, wants to know where the lions went!" Kristian yelled.

The squat man's face immediately brightened at the response as he dabbed at his brow with the cloth.

Ethan jabbed Kristian in the ribs with his elbow as hard as he could, outrage flustering his cheeks. "I did *not* ask, it was *you!*" he bellowed.

Kristian grinned and punched Ethan in the arm.

"Don't hit me!" Ethan bawled.

"If you had done what you were told, Dingus, wouldn't have happened."

"What is *that* supposed to mean?" Ethan thought about casting a spell to wrap his brother in a knot, but reconsidered when Seon sternly cautioned him against such antics. *I was just thinking it!* he retorted.

"Excuse me, Great Sheikhs . . . egh, um." The man's raspy voice called out again. "All will be explained in due time. You are quite safe to proceed with us. We await your decision." He bowed and now appeared as though the heat of the flames had gotten the better of him as he bowed again and took a few steps backward. He tripped and toppled over, quickly jumping up looking utterly embarrassed, but appearing relieved to be farther away from the inferno as he tugged at his shirt, wet with perspiration.

"Well?" Ethan asked, trying not to burst out laughing at the sight. He felt in a much better mood all of the sudden.

"We don't . . . we don't have a . . . better choice . . . do we?" Kristian said, barely containing his own laughter. He put a hand to his mouth and coughed, regaining his composure. "They can wait out there all day. We can stay in here . . . as long as the Kesem lasts." Kristian winked at his younger brother.

Lola was all the while erupting into full laughter every few moments, launching boulder-sized water torpedoes that momentarily poked huge gaps in the fire.

"At least Lola's happy," Ethan admitted.

She glanced up and smiled, not grasping the tone of sarcasm in his voice, then launched another torpedo at the flames. "Deseret, that was a good one!"

*Hmm, not sure if I trust the gnome, but they may be of use to us. We need to find our way back to the caves, right? Besides, I can't find our way back, unless we can go back through the caves. Perhaps they know of another way through?* Seon suggested.

It made sense. They might as well try, Ethan agreed.

"All right, we know we can't go back the way we came. We know that wolves and lions prowl . . . well, wherever it is that we are. These . . . little people seem to have sway over the lions, and they seem to be kinda scared of what we did with our Kesem, so . . ." He paused to take a breath. "We'll drop the fire ring . . . and be prepared to pull it back up if there's any funny business," he proposed. "All we need to do is to drop it."

"Drop what?" Kristian asked.

"The fire!"

"Oh yeah. Hold on." Kristian contorted his face in concentration to snuff out the fire. "Etmak," he recited. Nothing happened. He peeked through one eye and grunted, trying again. "etmak!" he commanded. This time he opened both eyes, but the fire still burned just as hot. "etmak, etmak, etmak!" he yelled in quick succession with no different outcome.

"OK, I can't do it!" he whined, throwing out his hands in frustration.

The Drake Epics - Journey to Qara

"OK . . . well . . . fire can't survive without air so . . . we put it out with . . . water!" Ethan concluded

*It should work,* Seon chimed in. *Have Lola cast a wall of water around the fire . . . she should be able to pull it off, given her already-advanced level . . . ,* Seon trailed off, not sounding completely sure.

The boy slowly nodded, wondering if this was going to be the first time that Seon was wrong, but it couldn't hurt. "Lola"—he said, turning to his little sister—"can you invoke a ring of water right on top of the fire?"

Lola looked up at Ethan with a questioning look on her face.

He pointed at the fire. She looked at it, Ethan's question dawning on her. "Yes!" She nodded in excitement, a broad grin spreading across her face at the thought of displacing the blaze.

"Might help if you concentrate," Ethan suggested supportively.

Lola invoked the calming technique, and the same bright light filled the little shielded area. Then in an instant, she immediately uttered the word *su Uzuk.* A mischievous grin spread across her face. An immediate pool of water materialized over the flames, dousing them for a few moments before the flames shot back up again in a great cloud of steam and smoke, but this time half their height.

"Again?" Ethan pressed.

Lola tried again, all the while smiling. This time the flames went out completely. She looked up mockingly at Kristian, who shrugged, as if he didn't care.

"Not that great," he mumbled to himself, scowling at the ground.

They could now clearly see the squat little man and his relatives. The lions were nowhere in sight.

Lola took notice of them for the first time. "Little gnomes!" she announced in awe at her new discovery as she pointed in the squat figures' direction. "I found them first, they chased the lions away." She giggled.

"Lola, be quiet!" Ethan scolded.

Lola gave him a sour look, but fell silent nonetheless and whispered something to Deseret.

They all looked the same, Ethan thought. Their little hosts were a cross between small plump men and the small sand gnomes that the pottery makers would create to scare the children away from their projects back at the village. Their skin was a deep brown tan and wrinkled, and their ears were pointed at the top. They wore robes a shade lighter than their skin, most with hoods, some of which were drawn over their heads, some of which were not. From what Ethan could see at a quick glance, they all had a mane of white hair that flowed down and around their shoulders.

The lead gnome didn't have his hood on, but looked very pleased with himself for successfully talking the children out of their fiery blockade. He approached the children cautiously in a slight bow, but with a grace that contradicted the shape of his plump little body. He came to within a few paces from the children and just outside of the crackling shield around them. He bowed deeper, almost touching the ground, and remained in this position for a few moments before twisting his head sideways to peer back up at the children.

Kristian caught the drift and bowed himself while elbowing Ethan to do the same.

Ethan grunted at the blow, rubbing his side and grimacing at his brother.

*I think he means for you to drop the shield and bow, Ethan,* Seon claimed.

*Yeah, I kinda got the point on that one.* The boy dropped the shell, and bowed.

Lola stood rigid, with the same awe painted clearly on her face, looking as if she were ready to burst into a torrent of questions.

The little man smiled, apparently satisfied and pulled himself out of the bow. At full height, he was roughly the same size as Lola, although much, much larger around the midsection, as opposed to the much slimmer girl.

"I am Muschle," the little man prompted placing a hand on his chest.

Lola's face changed from one of awe to one of determination, and before either Kristian or Ethan could stop her, she exclaimed, "You're funny looking. Why are you so short and fat?"

"Lola . . . ," Kristian growled under his breath. She paid no heed to her eldest brother.

Muschle gave her a quizzical look then smiled, letting the comment drop completely. He quickly glanced at the drakes on the children's shoulders, and a look of reverence flashed in his eyes.

Ethan watched him intently, studying his mannerisms. *Why is he so interested in you?*

Seon shrugged.

Muschle's gaze passed over Ethan, and he hastily averted his eyes, realizing that the boy had caught him observing the children's little companions.

"Please accompany us, Great Sheikhs." The little gnome bowed again. "Our king and mistress await you," Muschle added.

"Who?" Ethan asked.

Muschle raised slightly from his bow. "Why, our king and queen, of course!" he exclaimed. "They have foreseen your arrival. You are to do great things . . ."

The Drake Epics - Journey to Qara

A gruff cough broke their attention from somewhere in the crowd.

Muschle looked back over his shoulder at the company of gnomes with an annoyed smile.

Another squat figure wagged his finger, indicating their little spokesman had gone too far.

Muschle coughed himself before turning back to the children and continuing. "Well . . . we'll have plenty of time to talk about such matters later . . . please follow." He waved his hand and started back toward the group of little gnomes, sneaking a few glances at the drakes as he turned.

"We're not going anywhere until you tell us what happened back there!" Kristian bellowed as he tossed his head in the direction the children had retreated from. "Those lions; where did they come from and where in blazes did they go?"

The little gnome halted and look back at the older boy.

Ethan thought he saw a quick flash anger show on the little man's face. But the expression was gone as fast as it had appeared. Or perhaps Ethan hadn't really seen it at all.

"Lions?" the little gnome asked. "Was that what you witnessed?"

"Don't play games with us. We know what we saw." Kristian held his ground.

"They are our companions and we theirs." Muschle glanced at the children's drakes and plead, "Surely this you must understand."

"Then, where are they?" Lola blurted out, putting her implicit trust in the little man's words. "Will we see them again?"

A chorus of deep-throated laughter broke out in the ranks of the gnomes. Muschle chuckled. "Aye, you will, soon enough you will. Come! You are quite safe. We have driven those dirty wolves from our valley. They won't be back for some time." The little gnome turned and started walking.

Ethan looked at Kristian, who simply shrugged and followed the gnome. *He gave up too easily,* the boy grimaced.

*Perhaps, but I think he knows what he is doing, Ethan. Follow his lead,* the drake encouraged.

Ethan shook his head in disgust and followed after Kristian and Lola. *Don't expect me to trust this little Muschle,* he warned.

Seon thought it wise to let this last comment ride without a response.

The group of gnomes parted as the little company passed them by. But, like Muschle, they all stared at the children's drakes in apparent veneration—something Ethan felt very disconcerting about as he wasn't quite sure what that really meant. "Haven't they ever seen a drake before?" he whispered to Kristian, having caught up to him after passing through the crowd.

"Apparently not, but they won't take their eyes off BeeSting, and it's really starting to bug me." The older boy scowled. "And him," he said as he rubbed his little companion's head.

Lola skipped ahead, past Ethan and Kristian, and was currently merrily jabbering away with Muschle at the lead of the company.

Ethan couldn't tell if the gnome was annoyed or not, but he'd rather have Lola talking their little guide's ear off rather than his own. He glanced over at Kristian, who seemed to be deep in thought with BeeSting. His eyes had the familiar glazed-over appearance.

*Seon, do you have any ideas about this?* Ethan asked

*I don't fully comprehend all that is happening here or where we are going. It is beyond my understanding. But they're bound to know how to get us out of this place. I can't say what will happen, but this path feels right for now.*

*What do you suppose he meant by great things . . . are we expected to do great things? And how did they know we were even coming?* Ethan shot back, reflecting upon the strange dialogue. *That part really doesn't feel right to me,* he countered.

*We've both felt the same. But it's probably best if we let this story unfold before us . . . and we probably shouldn't mention the Kur-ne to any of them just yet.*

Ethan patted his pant leg pocket to make sure it was still safe, having forgotten about it as the morning events unraveled. He felt the small ball under the leather material and sighed with relief. *Well, they certainly seem to be interested in you, Deseret and BeeSting,* he added, to which there was only an awkward silence.

*You actually like it!* he realized as he looked at his drake.

Seon shot the boy a strange look.

*Don't deny it, Seon.* Ethan plodded on. *The attention makes you feel important! I can feel that you feel it,* he said in surprise.

*Well, it certainly doesn't hurt to be revered every now and then,* Seon said rather piously and turned his head away from the boy in mock disdain.

Ethan guffawed and shook his head. He was about to give Seon a good ribbing about it too, but caught the tail end of what Muschle was saying.

"We are humble sand people, working sand and glass. It has been our way for a thousand years since before the creation of the desert," the little man proudly exclaimed.

The boy reprimanded himself for not paying attention to the discussion in front of him. "Sand and glass? A thousand years? Before the creation of the desert?" he recited, interrupting midconversation.

*The Drake Epics - Journey to Qara*

Lola turned and shot her brother a glowering look, which Ethan promptly ignored.

"Ah, yes," answered the little man. "You will see some of our most notable handiwork when we arrive. Thousands of years old, some of it . . . ," he paused. "And . . . you will see what I mean about the desert, which was once a lush and beautiful savannah with tall peaceful trees sprinkled around the countryside." The little man stared into the distance with a wistful expression. "If only I could go back."

"Are . . . are you . . . How old are you?" Ethan stammered.

The squat gnome turned with a wry smile. "Not the type of question you would ask of a stranger upon your first meeting, now is it?" He didn't offer anything more.

The group passed through the doorway that the children had been running towards earlier. This entrance drained into yet another larger courtyard, strewn with yet more rubble and debris.

It appeared to be an elaborate maze concocted by both man and nature, but Ethan couldn't make heads or tails how it came to be this way. Only that rocks had fallen in some cataclysmic event that he could only speculate about the destruction and havoc it must have wreaked on the inhabitants. He momentarily wondered if he could retrace his steps back to where they had come out into the valley. But, he already had another question on the tip of his tongue. "Do you know what happened here?" he asked shyly, not wanting to push his welcome too far. "I mean, this place looks awful, like something terrible happened here."

"Ah . . . now that is a sad story better told at another time. But I will say that a wise and righteous people once lived here, in this very valley. They succumbed and then fell into mischief and sought only for their own wealth and profit. Then came the oracles, warning them of impending doom and fire, unless they repented of their evil ways. They of course ignored the warnings, because of the pride in their hearts. They cast down the oracle's temples and dragged them into the streets to kill them. Others, they cast out of the city." He punched at his hand for emphasis and shook his head in grief.

"Sadly, true to the prophecies given by the oracles, a great calamity resulted, destroying most of the citizens in one fell stroke and sinking this once-glorious city into the depths of the earth, almost as deep as our fair city . . . well, at least that's how the tale goes . . ." He turned and gave Ethan another wink.

*He talks in half-truths*, Seon said in an irritated tone. *He hides behind pretense and stories as if to keep us away . . . away from the truth . . . I can't*

273

*pin him down, and this bothers me*, the little drake complained. *I don't think I like them staring at me now, after all.* He revealed.

Ethan wasn't sure if he trusted this little storyteller either as he rubbed Seon's head, behind the eyes. *We need to watch ourselves here.* He thought. *Perhaps we can turn their worship of you to our advantage.* He glanced up and noticed they were approaching one of the towering cliffs. Its shadow reached out to the company approaching it, even while the sun was almost directly in the center of the sky. *But we can talk about that later.* Ethan excused.

As they neared the bluff, he could vaguely pick out something standing at the cliff's base. He squinted harder and recognized the figure as a massive sand lion standing alongside an equally massive half-circular stone. The boy immediately froze, as did Kristian who had noticed the figure too.

The whole party halted with the boys.

"We are companions—they and us. Don't worry about him," Muschle offered. "He won't harm you." The little gnome pointed to the lion. "It's only Kant. He is one of us," he soothed.

The children looked at the gnome, still not understanding. Kristian looked ready to encircle the children in fire again.

Muschle sighed. "All you need know is that the last thing you will worry about here is desert sand lions, as I believe you call us . . . erm, them." The little man shook his head quickly as if he were caught in the act of lying. He hurriedly motioned for them to follow, obviously flustered.

*Us? The lions are these little men . . . the little men are the lions?*

*I told you, didn't I?* the drake gloated.

*Well, not in so many words*, the boy shot back. Ethan shook his head in disbelief. "Did you hear that, Kristian?" he said in a low-enough tone so as not to be overheard.

"Yeah, not sure I believe it—would be super cool though, eh?" the older boy added.

"How is that cool?" Ethan asked. "I mean . . . that means they could shred us at any moment. Besides, how is that even possible?"

"I dunno," Kristian said. "Stop being such a Dingus and follow along." The older boy reprimanded.

The lion guard bowed and growled at the traveling party.

Muschle said something out of earshot and after a few moments, motioned for the rest of the party to follow.

The massive feline lumbered over to the boulder.

Ethan could see the lion's giant leg muscles expand and contract as it walked, and he half-wondered why a gnome would ever choose to be

The Drake Epics - Journey to Qara

a gnome at all, instead of looking like that magnificent lion. At least he would never choose to be a squat little gnome, he decided. *I can't even believe that I'm discussing this with myself,* he balked.

*I don't know,* Seon answered. *You're not that crazy. But, I wouldn't discount these little gnomes. There's much more to these miniature men than meets the eye. I'm still trying to process the whole thing through. But, maybe it's just another one of his lies,* the little drake offered.

The boy shrugged. *Maybe,* he thought. *What's he doing now?* the boy asked.

*Don't know, I suppose he intends to push that round boulder aside . . .*

The lion pressed itself against the stone and let out a great roar that ripped through the early-morning still as it slowly rolled the boulder to one side, revealing a dark opening in the cliff face. The stone creaked under the weight of the friction as it came to a stop. The lion bowed its head and took up watch directly in front of the stone.

Muschle again motioned for the troupe to follow him, this time into the darkness.

"And we're ok with this?" the boy asked his older brother in a low voice.

Kristian narrowed his eyes, as if that would help him to see into the blackened tunnel ahead of them. "I don't think they are going to hurt us, Ethan. Just stay close to me if you're scared." He grabbed at Lola and pulled her closer to him, as Ethan also stepped closer to his older brother.

As they walked forward, the shadow of the tunnel cast its blanket over the little company, and Ethan noted that each of the little gnomes had taken little torches out of their robes. These weren't anything like the torches Kristian had made; instead, they were quite striking, with an ornately decorated glass handle, boasting a pair of dueling dragons clawing their way up the shafts. But the most peculiar part of all was the crystal orb fashioned at the tip of the handle, as three glass fingers wrapped smoothly around the ball, melding flawlessly into the orb itself. The orb glowed with a soft white light that remained completely steady immediately around the torch that emanated a soft glow into the handle shaft, unlike the children's crude torches that harshly flickered and wavered in comparison. The light grew brighter the farther they moved into the cave.

*Do you see that?* he asked his little companion. *Do these gnomes use Kesem?* he wondered.

*Naturally, they must.* came the reply. *How else would this be possible?* The little drake concluded.

*Well, if they have magic, then what?* the boy pondered.

275

*Then we had better be extra careful. Now concentrate on where you are going before you trip and fall,* Seon scolded.

Suddenly, a distinct grating sounded behind them, and the children spun around in surprise to see the sunlight vanish as the hole closed back up. The orbs immediately burst into full light before their surroundings could be plunged into darkness.

Ethan shielded his eyes for a few moments at the sudden change in brightness. He blinked a few times, giving his eyes time to adjust before dropping his arms again to take note of his surroundings.

This tunnel also had smooth walls like that of the cave; however, the farther they marched in, the more he realized that the tunnel had been meticulously cut into the cliff side rather than naturally formed. It produced a great half circle with a flat walkway, flagged with menacing glass shards that protruded from the walls. Amazingly, the lights from the crystal torches seemed to light up these shards, radiating more light into the tunnel directly around them as they passed. Upon closer inspection, he couldn't make out even the tiniest flaw in the walls around him or in the protruding glass shards. He wondered how many gnomes and how much time it must have taken to build this, and a new sense of reverence resonated in him at their industry and attention to detail.

"They double as a defense," Muschle announced by Ethan's side, having noticed the boy's interest in the shards.

Ethan almost jumped in surprise.

"In the event of an attack, the shards extend to here." Muschle measured with his hands to depict the shards protruding almost to the center of the tunnel. "Then they retract and strike again. It is quite effective, and the shards are nigh impossible to break," he finished proudly and motioned for them to continue. "Another one of the great accomplishments of our people. Indestructible glass!" the little gnome said over his shoulder.

The pathway led steadily downward as it twisted its way back and forth around unseen obstacles. A small gust of refreshingly cool air brushed Ethan's cheek, and his muscles immediately relaxed at the welcome breeze.

He continued to study the walls as they marched downward and couldn't help but think about what lay ahead. He really couldn't imagine what would occur next. "Hello . . . um . . . Muschle . . . where exactly are we going?" He risked another awkward question and another curt answer.

The little man twisted his head over his shoulder. "You're about to find out," he announced.

Ethan glanced up at the reply and saw a colossal door folded into a wall in front of them. On either side of the door stood two magnificent-looking lions, molded from transparent glass, their jaws agape in a silent roar. It immediately reminded him of the Temple of the Lion back in Julfa, except for these two lions were much more intricately carved and made entirely of crystal. This, and the fact that the lions weren't facing off with each other, like in the village.

*Still, these are remarkably similar to the Temple of the Lion,* Seon remarked. *I assume that there is a connection somewhere.*

*I guess.* Ethan offered, completely mesmerized by the size of these gates. As he drew closer, he realized they too were made of a darker glass that seemed to magnify and radiate the light from the group's torches back toward them, forming a perfect circle of light on the floor.

Muschle raised a hand for the company to halt as they entered the center of the lighted circle. He cupped his hands around his mouth and let out an inhuman roar, startling all of the children.

BeeSting squawked in rebuke at the sudden noise.

*Interesting,* Seon declared.

*What is?* Ethan asked. *What is so interesting?*

*Why, his roar, of course.*

*Oh, I see. OK, you've had your fun. You can stop gloating now,* Ethan reprimanded.

Seon snorted, which was his way of laughing. *Of course, this is probably the only signal to open these doors. Once we're inside, I hope this isn't the only way out,* he said in a more serious tone.

*So we may be walking into a trap?* Ethan prodded. *Well, it's too late now, because, hey—we're already trapped! There's no way we can get past the boulder back there . . .* He jabbed a thumb over his shoulder wishing that the others had listened to him before they entered the tunnel in the first place.

A single click echoed throughout the tunnel, followed by the rumble of giant invisible gears swinging the massive doors open. As the gulf widened, rays of sunlight streamed into the tunnel, bouncing off the shards on the walls. The brilliance canvassed the tunnel in a dazzling prism of liquid colors, before turning white-hot, directly where the group stood. The whiteness and heat was almost overpowering as the door and walls seemed to fade from view, as if they stood amidst the clouds in the sky.

Ethan was temporarily blinded and again raised his hands to shield his eyes. He blinked a few times and let his vision get used to the light. Once his sight was clear, he exhaled at what lay before him.

The little party moved sluggishly through the door and into a sprawling garden of greenery and sand basking in the light of day. A neat path of brick wound itself deep into the park before splintering into tens of fingers, weaving their way through a sandy world, sprinkled with a lush green oasis, as if they were large green islands in a sandy sea.

"A hidden sanctuary!" Ethan mumbled, although it seemed unnaturally calm. Surprisingly, he couldn't make out any other rock formations beyond the land in front of him, just a hazy blue expanse.

"How is that possible?" the boy asked aloud.

"I have no idea, little brother," the older boy answered.

BeeSting immediately launched from Kristian's shoulder, spreading his wings and soaring high into the sky above them.

When Ethan looked at Kristian, his brother simply shrugged with an impish grin.

Ethan squinted to measure the distance to the other side and estimated that it was perhaps a half day's journey, and about the same distance from end to end, before abruptly ending in a light blue sky on all sides. He looked upward toward the source of a light, cupping his hand over his brow to protect his eyes from even more brightness. There he saw a brilliant sun, much smaller than the one he'd known aboveground, hovering directly in the middle of the heavens, quite motionless, casting its light in all directions. The sun was crowned by more blue expanse above it, and Ethan couldn't see any flaws or clouds in the otherwise-perfect sky blanketing the sanctuary.

*This has to be the work of Kesem,* Seon thought.

*There's no other way this is possible!* All of Ethan's senses told him that he was miles under rock and stone. *I mean, how could an open garden exist in such a place?* He craned his neck and followed the blue horizon plunging down to meet the ground on either side of the doorway they had just entered. He turned and studied the blue shell, reaching out to brush his fingers against it. He almost fell over in surprise when he realized that they were in a massive bubble that felt like smooth glass to the touch. The glass seemed to absorb the sun's brilliance as Ethan couldn't see any real evidence of the light reflecting off its surface. He squinted hard to look through it, but could see nothing but the light blue haze, as if it were the sky reaching out into infinity.

"Welcome to Qara!" Muschle boasted, swinging his arms wide toward the gardens. "A thousand years it has stood and protected our people!"

*Ethan, this place is filled with a good magic . . . very strong magic . . . It must hold this land together . . . and the source of it seems to be coming from*

*The Drake Epics - Journey to Qara*

*directly in the center where that tower stands*, Seon said, his tone filled with a sense of wonder.

Ethan turned to look at the direct center of Qara, having missed this before. A magnificent city rested in the center, sparkling with equal brilliance to the sun overhead. It appeared to grow out of a massive green forest island that lay at its base. Thousands of lights shone from within, giving it added radiance to the already-bright sunlit expanse, like twinkling stars. A lone tower thrust itself upward, towards the sun, reaching out and ending in a delicate spire, like a giant finger pointing to the heavens above.

"What is that place?" he asked their small leader. "In the center there," he pointed.

Muschle smiled and excitedly urged them onward. "We march to the Qara's palace city!" he announced, waving the children to follow.

"I told you we could trust them, Dingus," Kristian announced in a soft whisper to Ethan, who ignored the foolish comment from his older brother. "BeeSting says that we're encased in glass . . . ," he continued. "This is cool. Wait till Grandpa finds out!" Kristian wore a grin as Ethan momentarily glanced back at his brother in surprise.

"You can't be serious," he said.

Kristian didn't seem to care for an answer and promptly followed the gnome's lead.

Lola was in yet another full discourse with their guide, and Ethan could hear the spew of questions pouring out of her mouth.

Muschle wasn't answering much, but Ethan could tell the little man was getting a little annoyed at the incessant questioning. But there was no stopping Lola once she got started.

As they made their way down the winding path, Ethan could now make out the first grove they were to pass around. The trees loomed in front of them, their foliage reaching out in every direction, and a sweet perfume wafted by the group, tempting the children to drop everything at a dead run for the forests.

Lola even fell silent for the first time they had entered Qara, gulping in the soft fragrance that lingered in the air.

"That is the smell of our lilac trees." Muschle conveyed. "I never get tired of the welcoming fragrance of Qara!" he boasted. "It especially smells best, when I return!"

Ethan could see the momentary relief in Muschle's eyes. But with the little man's moment of reprieve, he continued to steal glances at the children's drakes, which strengthened Ethan's hunch that something more was going on that he hadn't yet grasped.

*I know. I know. I was wrong to enjoy it and it is really starting to annoy me,* Seon barked. *It's as if they are expecting something from us, but I can't quite tell what or why,* he said with an irritated tone.

They eventually skirted the grove, while the children took in the new sensation, gulping in as much of the sweet air as they could. Walking at half pace, they gaped at the lush grove, which they had never seen before in their lives.

"I could lie down in that"—the boy pointed at the grass—"and fall asleep for years." Ethan fantasized. It reminded him of his last dream, and he suddenly wondered if there was any relation. But, his thoughts were soon forgotten, as his attention was drawn to glass sculptures that dotted the pathway in the sand. The glass was exquisite and took the shape of every known desert animal that Ethan knew of, and some that he didn't recognize at all.

"Muschle . . . um . . . what are these glass statues for?" he asked.

"Ah, these are the work of my people. We pride ourselves in our glass work. They protect us on our journey, along the path that leads to the great palace," he boasted, adding a side note. "You will find that our palace is made entirely of glass created by our great father, Sheshank!"

"Sheshank?" Ethan asked.

"Yes. He founded our land a thousand years ago, for our refuge and haven, when the desert began to overthrow our land. It is his Kesem that preserves Qara to this day. His son, Corin, is now our king." Muschle paused, considering if he should continue. He decided not to.

"He must be really old," Lola inserted. Both boys gave her a dirty look, which she ignored. "Do we get to meet him?"

"Yes," Muschle answered. "He wishes deeply to meet you all." The gnome let his eyes pass over the children and the drakes again. "However, you must be rested and washed clean before admittance into his presence," He declared. "He and the queen will most likely see you on the morrow."

The children fell silent and admired the glass statues that lined the path around them. The landscape seemed much larger, now that they were level with it.

Ethan could only just see the tip of the tower over the treetops as it glistened in the sunlight.

The group passed four more groves identical to the first. The landscape appeared devoid of any other life. However, Ethan caught glimpses of desert lions standing guard in the shadows of the trees a few times; but when he looked a second time, they always disappeared into the shadows without a trace, as if they were ghosts.

They now neared the forest of the city-palace, this one quite a bit larger than any of the previous groves. Trees sprang up all around the city, blanketing it in greenery. The structure itself was even more impressive up close than when they first saw it. Its walls towered over them, and the children had to twist their heads around to glance up, as if they were staring up the side of Julfa's cliff. The tower seemed to be much taller than their village cliff and looked like a frail string that somehow magically hung from the sun. Ethan half-wondered if a strong-enough gust of wind wouldn't tumble the tower down upon itself. On its outskirts, Ethan could make out more towers and buttresses much shorter than the lone tower directly in the center of the city, but no less beautiful.

The palace's glass walls radiated a soft white light. Intricate designs wove their way through the glass, telling wondrous stories from times past through intricate designs and pictures. Small windows melded into the glass structure, and the whole palace looked peculiarly natural to the surrounding forest. In fact, if not for its translucent color, the palace would not have been noticeable to the naked eye, effortlessly camouflaged with the surrounding trees.

The group approached a set of gigantic doors with two massive crystal pillars rooted on either side. The doors were no less impressive than those they used to enter Qara; these made of a smoky white glass and mixed with weaving colors and shades that made them look like the sandy expanses in between the groves. The doors opened on hidden hinges. This time, no announcement was needed as they effortlessly and surprisingly quietly swung inward.

The inside of the city was the same as the exterior, except for articulate sculptures and murals that lined every inch of the capital. Everything here was also made entirely of glass, or whatever this substance was. The walls, doors, street, benches, stairs, railings—literally everything, except for the gnomes and lions, themselves.

The inner courtyard was abuzz with life. Gnomes and lions intermingled in their daily rituals. A market appeared to be in full motion as creatures scurried to and fro in a whir of commotion, buying and selling clothing, sculptures, animals, food, and other items that Ethan couldn't even begin to describe. The rich fragrance of fruits heightened the children's hunger.

Ethan's stomach growled reproachfully as he realized now that he was insanely hungry. He held his side to silence his unruly bowels.

"And we will get you something to eat before you retire for the night," Muschle now added, noticing the boy's discomfort.

Ethan nodded in appreciation. As the little company made their way around the market, he realized that every gnome they encountered quickly stood back at their approach and bowed with awe as the children and their drakes passed them.

*Again! They are doing it again. What is so all important to them about us? Have none of them ever seen a drake before?* This greatly puzzled the boy as drakes were quite common in Julfa—well, common enough for the lucky ones who bound to them.

*It is now annoying Deseret, and BeeSting is ready to launch himself at these little creatures*, Seon hissed.

Once they were through the market, the group wound their way up a series of steps to a small set of doors. The rest of the gnomes took up posts at the bottom of the steps, next to two massive lions that stood at attention on either end.

Muschle rapped on the door and stood back. After another moment, he knocked harder before it opened to a small demure figure in a soft blue dress, and a white apron affixed to her front. Soft brown hair flowed around her shoulders, and she had a gentle look upon her face.

Ethan realized that she was also a gnome, and she was much softer looking than the hardy men who had accompanied them from the Forbidden City.

"Dear me . . . I . . . I wasn't expecting you so soon . . . Come in, come in!" she exclaimed in a soft singing voice. "Why did you knock?" she glared at Muschle, who simply grinned and gave her a soft kiss on the cheek. She blushed red before eagerly motioning for the children to enter. She too looked at their drakes with reverence, but her face quickly turned to one of concern. "Oh, look at you. You must all be very tired and famished," she exclaimed. "I just happen to have a hot meal of worm soup ready for you . . ."

Ethan's stomach turned inside him at the mention of the revolting soup. No matter how much Hem had always gone on about how it was the cuisine of royalty and that he and Kristian, as *atzers*, didn't deserve to eat it.

*Can't be all that bad, if everyone likes it*, Seon mocked.

Ethan turned a sour face at his companion.

"And honey and bread," she added.

"You have honey here?" Kristian blurted out in relief.

"Of course we have honey!" Muschle answered. "We couldn't live without honey! It adds much-needed flavor to our lives." He smiled with a tranquil look.

The Drake Epics - Journey to Qara

Kristian and Ethan grinned at each other. They couldn't wait to see what kind of bees the gnomes housed and how they harvested the honey. Grandpa would certainly like to know about the broods of bees that the gnomes must be keeping.

Ethan's reverie was interrupted as the little gnomish woman spoke up again.

"Enough talk of food. Muschle can draw baths for each of you when you are ready . . . then we can eat . . . My name is Mesa," she added as an afterthought and gave a quick curtsy. She eyed each child as they crossed the doorway, eyeballing their measurements. "I'm not sure if I have the right clothing sizes for the boys, but I certainly do for the girl. We prepared many sizes in anticipation of your arrival, you see."

"But . . . how did you know . . . ?" Ethan asked again, hoping for a more detailed answer than what Muschle had provided before.

"The king and queen have awaited you for some time," Muschle reminded him.

The boy nodded, having failed again at his attempt. Instead, he studied their surroundings and found that they all stood in a large entryway. Everything was made of glass, except for fresh flowers, which were arranged in a few of the vases standing on either side of the door. Two large staircases wound their way up to a short landing, sandwiching the entry, and were flanked with two doors made of a clear glass exposing a small hallway that opened just below the landing.

The children were hurried into the hall and asked to sit in wait for the hot water to be drawn.

Muschle helped Mesa with buckets of water into three separate washrooms.

The boys offered their help, but Mesa gave them reproachful looks and commented that they were to do nothing of the sort.

Once the tubs were filled, the children were directed into the adjacent washrooms as Muschle and Mesa disappeared into another set of doors that Ethan guessed led to the dining room.

Ethan stepped into the room he was given and closed the door behind him. The room was small, but was lavish with glass murals and a few sculptures. A large tub sat in the middle of the room. Four large legs sprouted from the sides of the tub's white glass and twisted their way to meet the ground in a seven-clawed paw that dug into the floor. The tub was filled to the brim with water that birthed evaporating wisps of moist steam rising from the hot liquid. A smaller bucket lay next to the tub, also with hot water that Ethan assumed was for Seon.

283

The little drake leapt down from Ethan's shoulder and peered into the bucket, sniffing at it, before jumping right in. Ethan could sense the drake's pleasure as Seon hummed, as he often did when completely content.

The boy smiled in spite of himself.

A neat bench lay to the side with a set of clean trousers as well as a tunic that looked to be about his size, and a pair of sturdy sandals made of soft cork insoles and hard outer soles made of some material he wasn't familiar with.

A body-sized towel lay draped to one side of the bench. Ethan caressed the towel, which was soft to his touch, much softer than any cloth he had felt before. However, what now caught his attention was another boy, standing at the far side of the room, peering through a glass oval. Ethan jumped back at first glance then realized that he was looking at a reflection of himself, like in the mirror in Limnah's room. His heart jumped. Could this be like Limnah's?

*No, it is only made of glass, Ethan.* The drake chuckled. *These folk seem to have refined the art of glass making from all of the sand around here. It is beautiful, and we're treated with such respect.* Seon bubbled in Ethan's mind as the little drake playfully preened at himself in the bucket of water. Ethan couldn't help but again smile at the little drake's complete comfort.

He quickly disrobed, ensuring that the Kur-ne was safe and hidden from sight, and gingerly entered the hot bath. He had to ease his way into the water as it was much, much hotter than what he liked. Finally, he rested in the warmth and felt completely at ease.

*Seon . . . what do you think of these little gnomes?* he asked.

*They are a good people . . . I can feel it . . . I felt it,* the drake quickly added.

*But you don't trust them?*

*No, I don't,* the drake answered.

*Then, why do you say they are a good people?* the boy queried. *And, what do they want with us? I've only heard bits and pieces of what Muschle has told us. There is still a lot of questions that need to be answered.* He stopped and thought about his grandpa, suddenly thinking of what Heramon must be doing. *Heramon must be out of his mind with worry by now.* He grimaced.

*I sense that Heramon is fine . . . your grandpa may be returning home even now and I am sure that he will pick up on Heramon's clues . . .*

*How do you sense these things, Seon?* Ethan now questioned. *I mean, you say that, and it seems that as soon as you say it, I feel the same way. But, you can't really guarantee it, can you?*

*Don't know . . . it's something that I . . . I feel,* the little drake concluded.

Ethan wasn't satisfied. He wanted to know more about why this happened, but decided to let it go, as it was apparent Seon did not know how to explain it in the first place. He sighed. *Well . . . I still don't trust them. Not until I know what they want from us and what they are up to. I mean, the way they look at you, Deseret and BeeSting . . .* He let the rest of the conversation drop, enjoying his bath.

The pair finished bathing.

Seon leapt out of the pale and shook himself dry, splattering water all over the room.

*Really?* Ethan said with disdain. He dried himself off with the soft towel and quickly dressed. The clothes were a little baggy, having been made for a boy of Kristian's size and not his own. Yet they were comfortable. He strapped on his belt and pulled on the new sandals, which unlike the clothing, fit perfectly.

They both exited the room to find Kristian and Lola already waiting for him. All of the children were clean, and they radiated from the restful warm water. Their drakes were just as content. All they needed now was a warm meal and a good sleep.

Just then, Mesa bustled into the room.

"Ah, you are ready then? Yes, yes, the dining hall is this way." She lowered her head and pointed down the hallway. "I have set out bowls for you with piping hot soup." She grinned and motioned for the children to move towards a doorway. "Come, come," she urged.

Ethan was the first to enter. The room opened to a long glass table with chairs lining its sides. He had only seen chairs used by the Sheikh and was puzzled why they were placed here. The room was narrower than the Temple of Abundance, and its walls were lined with pictures, each with smiling faces of older gnomes. A giant fireplace stood at the other end of the room, although Ethan wasn't quite sure why one was needed. A pair of statuesque lions stood at attention on either side.

But something was not quite right. A lone man sat at the head of the table with his head bowed.

Ethan blinked and rubbed his eyes to make sure he wasn't dreaming then stared with his mouth agape at the figure.

Heramon was seated, mid-dip of his spoon into his bowl of steaming soup. As soon as the man noticed the children, he jumped up in surprise, knocking his chair over with a loud clang in his excitement, and bolted toward them. He rounded the end of the table and swooped all three up into his arms.

Lola giggled, but Kristian and Ethan grimaced, red flushing their cheeks, embarrassed by the sudden show of affection.

Ethan glanced around at Mesa, who was acting as if she hadn't noticed, her back turned, dusting off a nearby already-spotless statue. But she turned slightly and wore a small grin across her face nonetheless.

"You're safe!" Heramon belted out, squeezing the children even harder.

Ethan felt as if his eyes were going to pop.

"You're safe!" he repeated, but this time his voice dropped in pitch and sounded sterner. He put the children down and glared at them, with most of his focus directed at Kristian, much to Ethan's relief. "Why did you go so far into the caves? The wolves stopped at the ledge. There was *no* need to wander farther in."

"Wolves?" Ethan and Kristian asked at the same time.

"Yes, I assume that's why you ran for it . . . although it really doesn't explain how you had time to make the torches . . . ," Heramon trailed off, as if he had made a new discovery that he hadn't quite thought completely through yet.

"We didn't see any wolves," Ethan answered.

Kristian gave him a hard jab with his elbow.

Ethan grimaced in pain, but refrained from yelling at him about it.

"Ahh, so you didn't get chased down the shafts. Then what were you up to?" Heramon crossed his arms, looking at the boys as he waited patiently. A moment of odd silence followed, but both boys held their ground and didn't answer.

"I followed your tracks a half a day into the caves. They disappeared at the edge of the lake . . . Why in the blazes would you wander so far?"

Mesa's eyes lit up at the mention of the lake, and Ethan noticed that she was now paying full attention to their conversation.

"I walked its edges. I even fell into the lake once after traversing a narrow path that crumbled below me—that was awful, I was . . ."

"You were attacked by the shadow demons?" Mesa answered in a hushed tone.

The small group spun around. Mesa realized that she had commented out loud and looked awkwardly from side to side, as if desperately looking for another place to clean.

"But how did you know . . . ?" Ethan started.

*Ethan, I have a bad feeling about this. She can't have known about the shadows, and you told no one. I wonder how Heramon made it through himself . . . If she knows about the demons, she may know something of the Kur-ne!* Seon announced.

The boy thrust his hand into his pant leg, wrapping his fingers tightly around the small ball with relief, but kept his hand over it, just in case. Mesa glanced at Ethan at the sudden movement, but was hopefully too preoccupied to notice exactly what he was doing in her discomfort.

*It's safe, but I agree, we need to make it safer, at least until we find out what it's for*, Ethan thought back.

*And what these confounded gnomes are up to!* Seon declared.

Just then, Muschle burst into the room, panting heavily. He paused to catch his breath then surveyed the little group standing to the side of the table.

"What are we doing? Sit, sit, we must eat," he announced. "Mesa, dear . . . the soup?"

Mesa looked relieved she had found an escape and took the opportunity to duck out of the room to fetch the soup, careful to avoid the others' questioning glances.

They all took their seats, with the three children sitting together.

Heramon pulled up his chair to move closer to the children and slid his bowl along as he went.

Muschle sat in a chair directly across from the children.

Mesa re-emerged carrying a tray with soup bowls for the company. She was careful not to look directly at any of the children or at Heramon while she passed out the bowls, and she quickly retreated out of the room once the meal was set.

Muschle rubbed his hands together. "Eat, eat!" he said as he lifted his own spoon to his lips.

Ethan glanced at Kristian and Lola, who both stared at their bowls in horror. He decided to try it and laboriously dipped his spoon into the hot liquid and raised it to his mouth. He gently blew on the spoon to cool it then slurped some into his mouth, swishing it around to catch the flavor. He realized it was amazingly good and swallowed. He noticed that both Kristian and Lola were intently watching him for any sign of distaste, and when he nodded with a smile, Kristian tried a little.

Lola paused and finally gave in to try a few spoonfuls.

"I have sought audience with His and Her Majesties. They will meet with you on the morrow . . ."

"What majesties?" Heramon choked on his soup in apparent confusion. "I'm still not sure what's going on here, Muschle," he said, setting his spoon down on the table with a loud clatter.

"Not to worry, Master Heramon, all will be explained on the morrow," Muschle said as he quickly filled his mouth with a helping of bread and honey. Ethan noted a twinge of apprehension in his voice.

Heramon shook his head with a grunt and went back to eating.

The children continued to eat in silence.

A thousand questions buzzed in Ethan's head. *Seon, we need to know what's going on. How does Mesa know about the shadows? Also, does she know about the Kur-ne?* he asked. *Also, why these gnomes seem to worship you?* Ethan quickly added, catching Muschle yet again sneaking glances at the children's drakes in between spoonfuls of his soup.

A sudden impulse came over him. *Seon, can you . . . can you probe Muschle or Mesa's minds?* He knew it was a stretch, even when the idea first popped into his mind, but he wanted to know something of these little creatures and what they had in store for them.

*Ethan, I do not believe it is right for us to probe them for information. We need to respect their privacy, even if it bodes ill for us*, the drake reprimanded.

*I don't want to know their life stories, just what they're planning for us . . . To protect us! It may save our lives*, he pleaded, hoping that the sense of compassion for their companions would overwhelm the little drake into attempting the feat. It didn't work.

Seon didn't answer, obviously frustrated with Ethan's line of thought.

*All right . . . I guess you're right. I won't try it either. But I do want to know what is happening.* Another thought popped into his mind, *Maybe . . . maybe if you, BeeSting, and Deseret take up posts to listen for any conversations?* he prompted.

*I can do that, but we won't eavesdrop*, Seon said warily.

Ethan nodded, *No eavesdropping then. But I need to talk to Heramon and Kristian . .'. We'll try to get him alone after dinner.* He knew full well that listening for conversations was exactly eavesdropping.

The party finished their meal.

Mesa once again appeared and began to timidly clean up the guests' eating dishes. She once looked up to sneak a glance at Seon, found Ethan staring at her, and quickly dropped her gaze, flushing bright red at getting caught. She rounded the table and began to gather Ethan's utensils, while keeping her head down to avoid further eye contact.

"Mesa . . . ," Ethan whispered, "Mesa, it's all right, you don't need to worry about us." He paused. "Thank you for all that you've done," he said quietly.

The little gnome looked up at the young boy with wonder in her eyes. She nodded, and a broad smile spread across her face.

"Now, you must be exhausted, and we have a big day ahead of us tomorrow," Muschle announced. "Mesa and I will show you to your rooms."

They all stood and filed out of the dining room.

Ethan glanced back over his shoulders and caught Mesa's eye as she beamed a big smile at him. He quickly smiled back.

She neatly stacked the dishes at the end of the table and scurried over to accompany them to their rooms.

They entered the familiar hallway and back out to the entry where Muschle motioned for them to climb the stairs to the large glass doors at the top of the landing. As they approached, he threw the doors open, and they filed into another long hallway with doors on either side.

"You each have your own room, except for the boys. We've prepared a room for you to bunk together in . . ."

"No!"

The group halted and looked around at Lola.

Ethan realized that his sister had been unnaturally quiet for the duration of dinner.

*She's fine . . . just a little out of sorts. Deseret is keeping a close watch over her*, Seon advised.

Ethan nodded, suddenly conscious and grateful of the great gift that perched on his shoulder.

The little drake nuzzled him at the thought. *I too care for you, Ethan.* Seon radiated.

"I want to sleep with Kristian and Ethan!" she demanded. Her voice was full of resolve, and for a moment, she sounded like an adult. Too much like an adult.

Muschle and Mesa looked at each other in bewilderment. Then they both nodded and presented a door to the children's left. "Heramon is staying in the room just across the hallway."

Heramon nodded. "Night," he said and slid into his room.

Everyone responded together, "Good night."

"I will bring another bed shortly," Muschle announced, and the children nodded before Kristian turned the doorknob and disappeared into their room.

Ethan entered next. A spacious room opened before him with the same white glass walls, flooring, and adornments that he had seen throughout the rest of the home. A large glass window let in the day's remaining sunlight, giving the room an amber look. He briefly wondered how it was possible for the bright orb to set, like the sun did. Under the window was a white dresser fashioned out of wood, an oddity in this house, as he hadn't seen a lot of wood in its interior.

On either side of the room stood two large poster beds, each with four glass spiral pillars that twisted their way toward the ceiling, ending in a sharp point. A soft white canopy attached to the tips and hung gently over the beds. Each bed had soft white pillows and down comforters that rested on the surface. Ethan had never seen such comfort and wondered if he could even sleep on them. The thought of his bedroll suddenly occurred to him. He had completely forgotten it in the washroom and absently patted his pant leg to comfort him that he still had the Kur-ne. Feeling the small round globe in his pocket, he sighed in relief and poked his head back out of the doorway to catch Muschle. The little gnome had already gone.

"Ethan, shut the door and come over here," Kristian called after him.

Ethan let the door close behind him and strode across the room to where Kristian stood.

Lola had already flung herself into the far bed, in sheer ecstasy, as she rolled around in the soft bedding.

"We need to know what is going on," Kristian quietly announced.

"I thought you trusted them?" Ethan said with a bit of irony in his tone.

Kristian ignored the comment. "We need to talk with Heramon!"

"Yeah," Ethan acknowledged. It felt good to have the brothers plotting together again.

"Just don't know what's gonna happen with the king and queen tomorrow . . . and . . . what they want with us." Kristian frowned in deep thought.

"Seon and I hatched a plan!" Ethan announced excitedly, not waiting for his older brother to respond. "The three drakes will take up posts around the house tonight. They're small enough to go unnoticed and can listen in on any conversations that might help us find out more about what's going on."

"Too bad we can't read minds," Kristian smirked.

Ethan consciously half-smiled, glancing sidewise at Seon. "I just don't know what kind of Kesem we're up against," he said, deflecting further discussion about Kristian's last comment.

The older boy nodded, while rubbing his chin. "Maybe it's safer for one of our drakes to stand watch at our room while the others check around?"

Ethan nodded.

"Anyways, we should still check with Heramon. I'll bet he knows more than we do . . ." Kristian was cut off midsentence by an abrupt knock at their door.

Both boys jerked their heads around.

Ethan paused momentarily then walked to the door and opened it a crack. Heramon stood outside. The boy swung the door open with a giant smile as Heramon stepped inside and quickly closed the door behind him, keeping his back pressed against the door.

"Kristian and Ethan," he said quietly, motioning for Kristian to join the other two.

The older boy obediently crossed the room.

Heramon waited until he was close enough before speaking in a hushed tone. "We need to meet tomorrow early," he whispered.

The boys glanced at each other, happy their plan was all falling into place.

"I will come get you," Heramon continued, "then we will proceed to the garden. I want to review what happened over the last few days." Heramon listened cautiously at the door, as if someone were trying to listen in on their conversation. "I've been here since yesterday . . ." He prompted, seeing the confused looks on the boys' faces at the mention of a garden. "And . . . I've scouted out the premises . . . Just be ready to go." He stared down the two boys, who obediently nodded. Satisfied, Heramon concluded, "Now get some rest."

He reached for the doorknob, cracked open the door, then paused. "Someone is coming," he announced. He swung the door open and was out, quietly shutting it in one fluid motion.

The timing couldn't have been better. Muschle trundled around a corner with a small bed in tow.

"Help you with that?" Heramon suggested casually, acting if he were just strolling down the hallway.

"Most appreciated," the little gnome said thankfully.

Heramon grabbed one end, and the gnome pushed his end up high with an unnatural strength that caught Heramon by surprise.

"The bed is going to the children's room," Muschle explained.

Heramon nodded and stepped to their door, lightly tapping on the glass.

Kristian opened the door with a look of staged surprise as Heramon and Muschle navigated the bed in through the small doorway.

Heramon winked at the two boys and helped the little gnome set it alongside of the canopy bed that Lola was now jumping in, still giggling uncontrollably and completely oblivious to anything else going on around her.

*The back sack?* Seon reminded Ethan.

*Oh! Yeah.* He heartily thanked the little white drake. "Eghm, um . . . Muschle? I left my back sack in the washroom . . ."

"Never fear, young sir. It is over there." The gnome motioned toward the drawers on the other side of the room. All three of the children's back sacks lay at the foot of the dresser.

Ethan thought it curious that Lola's sack was placed in their room, considering that moments before, she was to have her own room. He didn't like the gnomes being one step ahead of them and he told Seon to remind him to mention this to Kristian when next they talked about their hosts.

"Good night then," Muschle announced and motioned for the two adults to exit the room.

Heramon gave the boys another quick nod and winked.

"Good night," Kristian and Ethan said.

"Oh! Good night," Lola pitched in, realizing they had company.

The door closed behind the little gnome and the tall man that dwarfed over him.

Kristian quickly stepped to the door and placed his ear against the glass to listen as the footfalls grew quieter until the hallway was silent.

*Seon, have you let both Deseret and BeeSting in on our plan?* Ethan asked.

*Yes,* came the reply. *And Lola knows that Deseret has to do something tonight so as not to be concerned.*

Ethan frowned.

*She won't breathe a word of it,* Seon consoled, knowing full well what Ethan was feeling at that moment.

The boy sighed in relief and motioned for the three drakes to glide to the door. He cracked it open and peered up and down the hallway. Once satisfied no one was in sight, he let the three drakes out of the room and quietly closed the door behind them.

"How will they get back in?" Kristian thought out loud, suddenly dawning on him that the drakes would likely not be able to turn the doorknob on their own. He shook his head. "Never mind, I'll keep watch and will let them in when they get back," he concluded.

Ethan nodded and motioned that he would take the smaller bed as he strode over to it and seated himself.

The children wished each other good night. Lola calmed and climbed into her covers and fell asleep almost instantly.

Ethan watched his older brother for a time, who had now blown out all the candles. He could faintly make out the older boy's outline, who had taken up a sitting position in the other poster bed across the room, determined to stay awake until their drakes returned.

The glass in the room seemed to absorb all transient light and their sleeping quarters were thrust into an immediate darkness, except for the soft light that filtered in through the window and the light coming from the hallways through the glass door.

*See anything yet?* Ethan asked Seon.

*Nothing yet,* the drake replied. *BeeSting is heading down to the floor below us as he's much faster than my sister . . .*

*Or you,* Ethan added with a wry smile.

*Or me,* Seon said grumpily. *Deseret is taking the post in the hallway, and I am exploring this level, but all looks to be quiet right now. Better to get some sleep while you can. I will awake you when I get back to recount anything we have picked up,* Seon said.

*I will say one last time that it would have been easier to try to read their minds,* Ethan grumbled. Seon didn't answer, but the boy felt the little drake's frustration, so he let the topic drop again.

*Seon?* Ethan asked. The drake didn't reply, but Ethan knew he was still listening. *Did you ever think that our little adventure would take us so far . . . I mean, so far from home, that is?*

The drake paused. *Well, no. But ever since the vision in the scroll, I've known that we had an important work to do. Something we needed to discover.*

*But how did you know?* Ethan tried to calculate it out in his mind. *I mean, it seems like a bunch of random dreams, situations, and bad luck that we blundered through. How can that have any meaning?* he added.

*I don't really know, it's more of a feeling, you know that. But all of this is anything but random. Things happen for a reason. We just need to find out why they are happening to us, and how to solve them,* the little drake counseled.

*I guess that makes sense,* Ethan thought in defeat.

*Ethan, I have to concentrate now. Just saw Muschle heading into the library. I will alert you if there is any trouble,* the little drake announced.

*Be careful. I don't trust these little gnomes one bit,* Ethan resolved.

He pulled off his sandals and slipped under his covers. The bed was deceivingly firm, but soft enough for him to sleep soundly on. He maneuvered into a comfortable position, drew the covers up over his head, pulling out the Kur-ne to study it. He was quickly disappointed, only catching a glimpse of the round form in his hand and nothing more. He trained his eyes on it, as if that would help him see any better in the dark, but to no avail. A few more moments, and he decided to put it away.

Suddenly, he felt power being drained from him. Unnerved, he tried to put the ball down, but he found he couldn't move. He tried to avert his eyes, but instead he lay transfixed on the orb. A soft glow now emanated from the glass ball, and Ethan didn't quite know what would happen next.

His world swirled around him like a mist, and he realized to his horror that he was surrendering his thoughts to the orb. He cried out to Seon in desperation. *Orb . . . the orb . . . the Kur-ne . . . is glowing . . . can't control it!* He wasn't sure if the message had gotten through, but soon he didn't care if it had or hadn't worked, and soon thereafter he couldn't remember if he had even sent a message in the first place. His whole energy and focus was now on the glowing orb in front of him.

The light grew steadily brighter, and he could see thousands of lighted pinpoints glowing from within the ball. He was being sucked downward and inward. The expanse around him was growing the further he was drawn down into the small orb. He concentrated on the lights, which were now growing in size and hurtling past him with increasing momentum. The lights whirled by as he tried to count them: one, two, ten, twenty, fifty, one hundred. He lost count.

A single light was growing near, and it felt as though he were slowing down. He realized that the light was a radiant woman, whose beauty was far beyond anyone he'd ever known before. She reached out to him with something in her hand. He opened his arms to embrace her, but she would not. What was in her hand? His attention was drawn to it, but he couldn't comprehend what it was. What was in her hand? A small point of light? She took the light and balanced it on his forehead, then pushed it into his head. He winced, expecting pain, but instead he felt something new, something different.

Then she was gone, and another light approached him—a sphere, no, it was a star, like the star constellations Grandpa used to point out to him on clear nights in Julfa. He drew closer to the star, and the nearer he got, the broader the expanse became. If he had his wits about him, he would have concluded that this was all quite confusing. He hurtled through clouds that clung around the star, like in Limnah's room—once through the clouds, the ground came at him with dizzying speed, and he slammed into its surface and into the darkness.

The orb released him, and Ethan's eyes closed as he dropped off into a dead sleep and a single dream.

- - -

He was back in the grove of white trees again.

He looked up and saw the fruit once more and tried to reach it a second time. Much like the first attempt, he was thrown backward into the tall grass, clutching at his sides. His head swam in pain, and he scolded himself for not learning his lesson on the first try.

Another thought suddenly occurred to him; and he closed his eyes, wishing for the fruit above all else to quench his hunger and thirst, which now seemed to envelope his entire frame. He opened his eyes and reached for the fruit with a trembling hand. This time he grasped it, plucked it from the tree, and began to voraciously eat.

The fruit was more delicious than anything he'd ever tasted before, even more so than all the fruits and lavish meats he'd gorged himself on at the village school, and it filled him after a few bites. He suddenly felt the presence of others and yearned for his siblings to partake. He cast his eyes around him to see if they were nearby.

The landscape around the grove had mysteriously transformed, and the grove was now set on top of a lone hill with sheer cliffs that dropped off all about it, except on one side, which lead down to the barren sandy wasteland. At the bottom of the path, he now saw Kristian, Lola, Grandpa, Heramon, and two unknown figures but somehow familiar: a man and a beautiful woman-the same woman with the light. He wondered who the strangers might be, but a sense of calm flowed over him, and he simply knew they were welcome.

Ethan fleetingly wondered if they were his mother and father, and the thought encircled him in joy. He motioned for all of the group to join him, and they did so. After explaining how to obtain the fruit, they all gorged themselves on the pulpy nectar with looks of contentment plainly visible on their faces. He now cast his eyes again toward the bottom of the path and saw the villagers he'd grown up with milling in the sand below, as if they didn't know where to go next. He motioned to them, but they simply ignored him and would not come.

A rude shadow abruptly shrouded the host of villagers; and as Ethan looked up at the source, he saw an immense, familiar form appear in the distance, hovering listlessly in the air.

He blinked and tried to wave off the head of the dragon.

It glared down at him and gave a wheezy, throaty laugh. The head began to bear down upon the villagers.

Ethan shouted at them to run, but they didn't seem to listen, ignoring his pleas. He perceived Limnah, Ezera, the grand Sheikh and his sons, Ethan's friends, and a few others who all took notice of him.

They reluctantly started toward him, but only slowly, lethargically—and too late.

To the boy's horror, the head halted just beyond the villagers and was drawing in its breath, as he'd seen many times before.

All time froze as the dragon's mouth contorted and a torrent of sand blew out a massive sandstorm, clouding out everything, including the dragon. The sand consumed the villagers, but didn't upset the perimeter immediately around the grove.

The dust storm howled for what seemed an eternity. It swirled and railed against the giant tree in the grove, with a blood-red sun at its apex. The harsh light reflected off the whirling particles in the air, giving it a monstrous, reddish appearance. Then, abruptly, the storm vanished, and a curtain of sand plummeted to the ground. The dragon was no more, and the villagers were all gone.

All Ethan could see was sand all about him, and instead of the grove resting on a cliff and looking down upon the sandy wasteland, the sand was rising all about them in great shifting mountains.

He turned to look at the man and woman. "Who are you?" he asked.

"Ah, but you know who we are . . . We've waited for so long to meet you," they responded in unison.

—   —   —

Ethan stirred and awoke. He felt weak, as if all of his energy was entirely drained.

*You had another dream?* Seon's thoughts penetrated his own. *I sensed great fear in you this time!* A note of worry carried in his tone.

*I had another dream 'bout the dragon,* Ethan replied, thinking Seon was still on patrol. A sudden thought shot through him, and he quickly fumbled around for the orb, which he located in his pocket, although he wasn't quite sure how it got back into his pocket just now. *Seon . . . the Kur-ne . . . It drew power from me . . . it pulled me inside . . . it tried to overtake me . . . ,* Ethan stammered to the drake.

*The Kur-ne lived?* Seon asked with curiosity.

Ethan nodded. *It's as if it needs me in order to operate. But its power was frightening . . . I'm not sure if it's good or bad . . .* Ethan paused to consider what had happened. *I think it drew me into my dream, but I'm not sure.*

Seon contemplated this for a moment. *Ethan, when did this happen? Did it happen when I was with the others? I felt you cry out and disappear for a few moments last night, but thought it was some interference from a magical barrier the gnomes had put up . . . and you were back again in an instant . . . peacefully sleeping. So I thought nothing of it.*

Seon's thoughts rushed in upon Ethan, and the boy thought he sensed a momentary twinge of guilt from the drake.

Ethan nodded. *Yes, last night . . . I'm all right, Seon . . .* Then it occurred to him. *Did you find anything out? I didn't hear you come in.* He realized the drake was curled up by his side.

*Hmm?* Seon said, still pondering about what Ethan had just recited to him. *Oh . . . nothing happened, so we came back. Better to find out from*

*Heramon in the morning . . . We will continue to keep post and watch as long as we stay in this place.*

Ethan nodded and was suddenly happy to be in a comfortable bed, much better than sleeping in the Nejd, he admitted. *Would it be so bad to stay here forever?* he thought to himself. But the thought was short-lived as the Kur-ne and the dream quickly returned to his memory and frustration welled up inside him.

He recounted more of the dream, about the dragon, the two people, and the sand. Seon still lay curled up at his side, but the boy could tell that the drake was intently concentrating on the story that he laid out before him

*I just don't know what to make of it, Seon,* he concluded. *I mean, these dreams keep coming to me, and they're not happy. Now, this time, I think that the Kur-ne drew me into the dream . . . I don't know what it all means, but it somehow seems connected!* Ethan gave in completely to his frustrations. *I still don't know why I keep seeing the dragon, and this time, he destroyed the village or took them captive—at least I think he did . . .*

*I feel that we'll both know the answers in time . . . maybe sooner than either of us expects,* Seon counseled.

*I suppose,* Ethan thought absentmindedly as another wave of exhaustion hit him. *I need to sleep, Seon . . . Let's talk more tomorrow . . .* He closed his eyes again and almost immediately fell back into a deep, albeit dreamless sleep.

# Chapter 17

## Secrets

*Everything is not as it seems. Shadows are light, and light becomes shadows.*

Sunlight poured in through the open window at the far end of the room. It was almost blinding as all of the glass fixtures and even the floor itself radiated the light. Ethan groaned and pulled his covers over his head to avoid the glare. *It's too early for morning,* he sleepily protested. But, it was too late. He was already awake and now couldn't go back to sleep.

The boy sighed, giving in as he peeked out from underneath the blanket. He pulled the blanket back over his head and growled, then he quickly sat up, throwing the bedspread off of him, stretching his arms wide and knuckling at his eyes. *Too early!* he grumpily repeated to himself.

Seon still lay curled up beside him, as he carefully swung his feet over the little sleeping drake and grasped the edge of the bed with both hands. His toes caressed the smooth floor as he swung them back and forth a few times. It felt surprisingly warm.

Glancing up at the big posted bed, a small bulge in the covers hid Lola, who was still sleeping. Yet, Kristian's bed was empty.

A sudden lump formed in his throat. *Kristian wouldn't leave the room without waking me first,* he contemplated and scanned the remaining room for a clue. Much to his relief, his brother was sitting next to the window in a glass chair. The only reason Ethan had not seen him before was due to the glaring sun that bathed the older boy in a bright light, almost drowning him completely from view. The younger boy relaxed and chided himself for jumping to conclusions.

Seon stirred next to him at the mental convulsions of his companion.

The boy quickly subdued his own fears and recited a calming technique that put him immediately at ease.

The older boy looked up as Ethan stirred in his bed, and his face melted into a look of relief when he realized it was just his brother.

Ethan covered his mouth in a half yawn as he stumbled over to his brother. He pulled up a chair and sat.

Qara's sun, orb, or whatever it was, was already one-quarter of the way up in the sky. The courtyard below sported a few gnomes who were busily setting up their makeshift stands for the day's activities.

"The drakes didn't see anything last night," the older boy announced in disgust. "Nothing! It's like . . . like, the gnomes knew we were watching them or something." He spat out the window and leaned over to prop his elbows on the ledge to get a better view.

"Well, at least Heramon can fill us in on some of the details." Ethan suggested, "Like how he got here in the first place, if he got the message off to Grandpa, and . . ." Ethan stopped as another stream of thoughts poured into his mind. "Hey, Kristian?" He didn't wait for a response. "Heramon might know . . . I mean they brought him here . . . He's bound to know how to . . ."

"You're talking gibberish again!" Kristian rolled his eyes. "Dingus, make some sense and slow down!"

"Heramon knows the way back!" Ethan said more deliberately. "You know, back home!"

"Other than being painfully obvious, what's your point?," Kristian shot back.

"Well, yeah, that's all I was going to say."

"Dingus." Kristian muttered and slugged his brother in the arm.

Ethan slugged him back. "Owww, that hurt, kristian!"

Lola stirred in her bed.

Both boys fell into silence, and Ethan glared at his brother as he rubbed at his sore arm.

A light tap sounded at the door, and the boys jumped out of their seats. All three drakes poked their heads up in unison from their respective beds.

Kristian was the first to move and half-trotted to the door.

Another knock sounded again.

"I'm coming, I'm coming." the older boy growled. He reached the door and opened it slightly to peer out of the crack, then swung it wide as Heramon entered.

"All awake?" the man asked in a forced pleasant tone.

Kristian shook his head. "Lola is still asleep," he said.

"Wake her, and let's go."

"Uh, have you ever tried to wake up our little sister?" Kristian answered as he rolled his eyes. "Trust me, it's not a pretty sight," he declared.

Heramon frowned in thought. He suddenly looked up and crossed the room to Ethan. "Can you cast shields yet?" he asked in a hushed tone, glancing about, as if someone would sneak up on the conversation and overhear the question.

"What?" Ethan asked in surprise and confusion. How did Heramon know about shields? "Wait . . . But how . . . ?" he started.

"Never mind, can you do it?" the man demanded, still considering the room. He sounded a bit agitated.

Ethan stole a quick glance at Kristian then sheepishly nodded.

"Around more than one person?" Heramon persisted.

Ethan slowly nodded again, still puzzled about this line of questioning and where it was going.

"Good, Kristian, over here!" Heramon waved his hand for the older boy to take a seat. Then, he pulled up another glass chair alongside of Ethan and sat down. "Now," Heramon began, still in a hushed tone, "all you need to do in addition to the invocation is to think about complete silence . . . more specifically, think about muffling all sound coming from within the barrier," he counseled.

Ethan had no idea what Heramon was talking about.

"So that Lola can't hear a word we say," the man noted, seeing the perplexed look on Ethan's face.

*Or so that no one else can overhear what you say*, Seon joined in sleepily.

"Well, that makes sense, I guess." Ethan admitted, more to Seon than to Heramon.

"OK then, let us see it done." Heramon sat and waited with his arms folded.

Ethan drew from the familiar strength inside of his chest, and his eyes glazed over as he harmonized himself with his surroundings. He heard Heramon tapping his right foot, Kristian shifting in his chair, Seon and BeeSting beating their wings as they both flew to their usual perches on the boy's shoulders. Ethan instinctively reached up and stroked Seon's head in welcome. Having enough power now, he closed his eyes tighter, and the familiar translucent blue crackling shield snapped around the small group.

Heramon stared at Ethan in astonishment. "How did you do that?" he marveled.

Ethan was now even more confused, as he thought this is what the older man had asked for in the first place. "Do what?" he asked.

"Invoke without sounding out the words to the spell?" Heramon pressed.

Ethan shot an uncertain look at Seon and silently scolded himself.

*How many times must I remind you to go through the motions when others are around?* Seon added to the scolding.

"I . . . ," he thought ferociously. "I whispered it . . . been practicing without moving my lips," he lied a little guiltily. "The word is *Qalxan*," he amended, suddenly thankful that Ezera had forced him to memorize the command.

Kristian nodded in support of Ethan's story. "Ya, he always does that," he said offhand as he cleaned his fingernails. It was a convincing performance.

Heramon eyeballed both boys for a moment, skeptical of the excuse, but then moved on. "Plug your ears!" he advised. "I want to test your sound barrier!" he added at their questioning looks.

The boys clapped their hands over their ears as Heramon roared for Lola to wake up. Nothing. He yelled a second time. No response. Satisfied, Heramon took his seat again and, to Ethan's delight, immediately began to recount his journey to Julfa and of his attempt at a search-and-rescue for the children.

"As I crested the hill from the cave and rode into Julfa, I couldn't help but wonder that you were all up to something."

Kristian and Ethan shot each other worried looks.

"But I didn't have another choice. I arrived at the village and kept to the same route we took when we left Julfa . . ."

—  —  —

Heramon tethered his horse near the cliff wall on a post lodged into the ground. "It's all right. It's all right," he soothed as he patted her shoulder while she anxiously pawed at the dirt. He ducked under her head and started for the nearest alley in the village proper. Merry sounds came from the street musicians and he realized that the festivities had already gotten underway for the day. He had seen a number of caravans entering the main gates to the city, and more would come that day. After all, the ceremony was only a few days away. He had to be quick about this and leave the message conspicuous only for Grandpa, but hidden from unwanted prying eyes.

It was easy to keep to the shadows as he made his way through Julfa.

No one paid him any attention, instead focusing on other matters of entertainment.

He rounded the last hut and pulled the hood over his head as he walked to the edge of the temples' wall, not expecting he would be able to pass through the gates to the Sheikh's courtyard.

Upon finding no one in sight, he ran and leapt at the wall. He caught the edge and easily hauled himself up to peer into the premises. This was a good spot to enter, he determined and hauled himself the rest of the way up, nimbly swinging his legs over the wall and letting himself down on the other side. The inner courtyard was a little quieter, probably due to the fact that most of the villagers were en route to their morning meal. He skirted behind a few of the clay structures, avoiding the windows that would expose him, making his way toward the family's dwelling.

"You two, stand guard here and let me know the instant they return!" a voice commanded upon Heramon nearing the hut. He recognized the Sheikh's voice instantly. "You three! Scour this courtyard for any sign of them! If you don't find them here, then search the village farmlands. I already have guards searching the Temple of the Lion . . . What are you waiting for, get to it!" the Sheikh barked. "And you're sure you saw them yesterday, going for more honey?"

"Yes, my lord," another man replied.

"Incompetent fools!" he insulted. "Why do I even pay these guards?"

Heramon put his back to the edge of the wall and cautiously peered around the corner.

The Sheikh, the auditor, one of the village elders and a half-dozen men all crowded around the hut. The Sheikh did not look at all happy. "Come!" he said to the auditor, and they both disappeared into the premises.

*I need to get closer!* Heramon thought as he pulled himself back. He quickly skirted the hut around the back. As he came to the corner, he looked again and waited for the guards to look away. After a few moments, his chance came and he stealthily closed the gap between the huts, making it to the back wall of the family's home without being seen. He crouched and made his way along the wall until he was just under Ethan and Lola's window. He craned his head around so that he could see into the room.

"Are you sure?" the Sheikh was saying. "But . . . but that's impossible! How could she?" He threw his hands out in contempt.

The Sheikh looked like a magnified version of Hem. That is, except for the extravagant clothing, the turquoise-colored turban, and the heavy eyeliner he wore. Other than that, he was every bit as plump as the boy, and his fingers were littered with exotic rings of every make imaginable. He wore large, heavy earrings and had a dark brown goatee that carpeted his pudgy face.

"My Sheikh, it is painfully obvious!" the auditor's cold voice rang out. "The girl has bound to a drake. I can sense it. But that is not nearly as disheartening as the boy's binding to a white emperor drake."

"Yes, I know! This enrages me! I, the purveyor and protector of this village, of this family . . . I have been lied to! This will most certainly not go unpunished," the Sheikh said angrily. He cast a hand out in a sidewise slicing motion.

"We must launch a full inquisition!" The auditor continued standing perfectly still. "A village tribunal to publicly interrogate anyone who had dealings with the family. No one must be spared the investigation."

"Wait a moment, I don't see why . . . ," the Sheikh complained but was cut off.

"You must see it this way, my grand Sheikh. For it is the only way in which we can uncover this treacherous plot," the auditor said in a hypnotic tone. He waved his hands in a smooth motion in front of him.

"But I refuse to believe that my trusted beekeeper had any part in this! He simply could not have!" The Sheikh began to nervously pace back and forth in the small quarters. "After I took him in. After I gave him a seat in my presence."

"But he did," the auditor countered. "See here." He pointed to the wall next to the window.

Heramon immediately swung around and laid his back flat against the wall. *Too close,* he thought.

"These markings tell me that the drakes were known for quite some time. At least a year they have lived here, at the same time I came to Julfa."

After a moment more, Heramon peered back into the window. The auditor had turned back to address the Sheikh.

The large man stopped pacing. "A year?" he demanded. "A year, he kept this from me? When he returns from the Nejd, he will certainly pay!" He seethed.

"Yes, he will, Great Sheikh, and I will take them all with me." The auditor's voice soothed.

"No, but you can't. Those drakes are mine! You cannot, I will not . . ."

"Oh, but you will." The auditor raised a hand that seemed to completely pacify the Sheikh. "It is your will that I escort them from Julfa. I shall escort them from Julfa." The man's words slowed, as if he were compelling the Sheikh to obey him.

"As is your will, of course," the plump man finally acknowledge and drooped his head in disappointment.

"Good, now, you must deploy all of the guards to search the village. Leave no stone unturned. We must find them!"

"And what if they have fled Julfa? What then?" the Sheikh challenged.

"How would they have?" the auditor disputed. "They wouldn't have had any help."

"Well . . . ," the Sheikh paused, and Heramon sensed that the conversation had turned in the auditor's favor. Strange as it was, for the Grand Sheikh of Julfa was always presented as the master and never the slave. Yet he was beginning to sound like a puppet in this whole affair.

"Witless dog!" Heramon growled to himself.

"Well, what?" the auditor demanded. "I mean, what, my Sheikh?" he amended.

"My guards tell me they have not seen Heramon today."

"Ah yes, the guardsman. I wouldn't be surprised if he did help them. I've wondered about him and what part he would play in all of this," the auditor regarded. "I suggest that we tell the guards to look for him as well," he advised.

The Sheikh whistled and a guard appeared at the blanketed door. "Find me Heramon, immediately!" He barked.

"Yes, my Sheikh." The guard nodded and was gone.

"And what of the priests?" the auditor now questioned.

"Tread carefully, Auditor." The Sheikh had regained some of his usual composure. "The priests' power equals that of my own in the sight of the people. They form an important part of the elders. After all, without them, the New Year rites would be void! I cannot offend them. By so doing, I also offend the gods!" he said reproachfully. "I shouldn't even be out here! If they knew that I had broken with tradition and had exposed myself before the year-rites ritual . . ." he complained.

"Nevertheless," the auditor said in his hypnotic voice, ignoring the last part of what the Sheikh had said, "we must counsel together with them in this matter. We will find the meaning to all of this. The boy must have been in the confidences of Limnah, I am certain of it, and if so, then Limnah must have known about the drake!"

"No!" Heramon said in a low voice. In his unease, he slid down the wall.

"What was that?" the Sheikh asked.

Heramon secured himself under the window and hugged the wall as tight as he could underneath the ledge. He controlled his breathing and lowered his heartbeat as he had been trained.

The auditor closed the gap to the window in a few short steps and scanned the area outside.

Heramon held his breath and concentrated as an icy probe grazed his thoughts. He immediately blocked any entrance and concealed himself behind a thoughtless barrier, focusing on the sand in front of him. The coldness latched onto his consciousness and attempted to drive itself further in, but he held his ground. For how much longer he could do this, he did not know.

Suddenly, a lizard scurried down the wall next to him and scuttled across the sand toward the cliff.

The icy touch lingered a moment more then released him.

"It was just a common lizard." The auditor hissed and turned to walk back to the Sheikh. "At your request, my Sheikh, we must start the interrogations," he announced, and they both left the room.

With the situation avoided, Heramon exhaled. "That was far too close," he muttered. He had to warn Limnah, get back to his horse before she was noticed, get out of the village, leave markings around the gate, and make it back to the cave all before dark. He had a lot of work to do, and no time to do it in. "Sounds like my kind of work," he grimaced.

One thing was quite clear, these children were much more important than he had anticipated. They were the three of the prophecy. "And I left them alone!" he muttered. "I need to get some answers from Limnah, and when the old beekeeper returns, we need a plan. This will get very ugly, very fast. This auditor isn't who he says he is."

- - -

"Heramon?" Ethan asked as he shook the man's arm. "Are you all right?"

The soldier shrugged off the daydream and focused back on the two boys. "Yes, yes. I am fine." Heramon stood and moved toward the shield, tapping at the barrier as the sparks arced and painlessly touched his hand.

This turn of events in the village was deeply disturbing, and both boys sat on the edge of their chairs waiting for Heramon to finish his story.

When Ethan had questioned him about Limnah or Ezera further, he didn't know, except that Limnah was quite safe and said he would do what he could for the others. Ethan hoped they were protected from the Sheikh's rule, but it was certain that the auditor had an unmistakable influence over the Sheikh, from what Heramon had recounted.

"I left a message for your grandpa," he explained. "It was a rather-cryptic message at best, and I repeated this at different points both within and outside of the village. Let us hope that it was enough." He looked over his shoulder at the boys. "Your grandpa is a cunning beekeeper. I just hope that the message was neither too clumsy nor too rushed for the old man to recognize it." the guardsman looked back at the shield and touched it in wonder a second time. "I left one final message at Julfa's east gate when the guards weren't looking, in case he makes it that far." He didn't go into any detail, but Ethan could tell that he was hopeful Grandpa would steer away from the melee and rendezvous at the cave without being followed.

"Lola has been discovered as well," Heramon finally announced.

Ethan's heart sank, and he looked over at his brother. Kristian's face looked ashen and somber.

"How?" Ethan asked with his mind abuzz.

Seon shared his concern.

"I don't know, but this auditor . . . he knows things . . ." Heramon fumed before shaking his head and continuing, "He knows elemental drakes and has declared that Lola has bound to a water drake. Don't ask me how, it is beyond my understanding. He also knows that Kristian's drake is a fire drake . . . Apparently, you invoked techniques in your room?" Heramon said with a tone of reprisal in his voice as he turned to look at the two boys.

Ethan shrunk back in his chair and felt as if he were going to throw up. Kristian stared at the floor, perfectly still.

Heramon continued, "If it had only been found that Kristian's drake was really an elemental, which binding had been sanctioned by the council in the first place . . . well, you wouldn't have had any trouble. But between the appearance of the white drake, the grand Sheikh's sons description of Seon, and Lola's binding . . . well, Julfa is no longer safe for any of us."

The Drake Epics - Journey to Qara

Ethan felt an immediate pang of despair, as if the entire world had been pulled out from underneath him. He was now an outcast. No, he had plunged his family into this mess . . . they were now all of them outcasts. What would they do? Would they live here, deep within the Nejd forever? Would his family forgive him for this when he was the cause of this entire drama!

*As always, you are much too hard on yourself, my friend. I'm sure that your dreams have meaning—this is the path you must take*, Seon attempted to console Ethan. *I feel that things will turn out the way they are meant to turn out.*

Ethan felt a little better, but not much, as he moped around inside of his head about alienating his entire family from the village. He looked up hopefully at Kristian, but his brother wouldn't return his gaze, still sitting perfectly silent while he examined his hands. *I guess. But will they forgive me?* He nodded at his brother.

Seon didn't answer; he only nuzzled his head against Ethan. The boy did the same and lovingly rubbed the little drake's head.

"Anyway, after finding out all that I could about Julfa's frenzy, as well as leaving the messages for your grandpa"—Heramon swung his hand toward the two boys—"I made a hasty return to the camp, arriving just before nightfall. The horse you left behind vanished, but the hoof prints weren't deep enough in the sand for riders, so I figured you had gone farther into the caves." He paused and scratched at his short beard. "I tracked you for too long in those caves. You all had me worried sick! I feared the worst after your tracks went cold at the water's edge of the lake." He shook his head as he relived his frustration.

The boys didn't respond, but they both drooped their heads a little lower, avoiding any eye contact with the man.

"The gnomes found me at the mouth of the cave, frantic about where you must be," Heramon continued. "It was to my greatest relief when they informed you were all safe and were to arrive in Qara shortly. That and they promised to search for your grandpa and find him before the village does."

Both boys sat up and looked Heramon in the eyes. "But how did they know about us? We only just arrived, and you were already here!" Kristian exclaimed.

"This I do not know." Heramon admitted, caught off guard by the boys' sudden interested. "They must have been watching you all along."

Kristian made a solid fist and punched his leg as he glared at his younger brother.

Ethan knew the older boy was glaring about the gnomes and not at him directly. Still, he was in shock. *They've been watching us!* Ethan thought angrily. *All this time . . . with the wolves . . . with the water shadows . . . the quakes . . . they've sat idle and simply watched us?* he fumed to Seon.

*I am conflicted, Ethan. I no longer have any trust for these little gnomes, but we have no way home, and even if we did, we are discovered. What awaits us back in Julfa? And what of the Sheikh, the council, and the auditor?* the little drake questioned.

*I . . . I don't know,* Ethan resigned. *But we need to get out of here!* he finished.

"What aren't you two telling me?" Heramon asked as he squinted his eyes at the boys.

"We will tell you, Heramon. But first, how did you get here? Do you know a way out of Qara?" Ethan asked.

Heramon kept his eyes on the boy, not sure if he was willing to let this go just yet.

"We will tell you," Ethan repeated.

Heramon shook his head. "I was asked to follow the gnomes, but I was blindfolded for secrecy's sake. Still, I have other senses about me, but alas, it is unlikely I can find my way back."

Ethan and Kristian gave each other pitiful looks; Ethan had a fleeting hope that perhaps BeeSting could scout the way ahead to get a bird's-eye view. Seon was getting stronger every day with his abilities to fly. He could match BeeSting's flights, but Ethan wasn't sure what distance and how fast the little drake could fly.

*Far enough and fast enough!* Seon bragged.

Ethan half-smiled to himself.

*If we can just get back, I'm sure I can set things right!* he thought with renewed hope. *I can win the village council over to our side. I can fix this for our family!* he bravely charged himself.

*Yes, you are brave. But some things are meant to happen,* Seon answered then changed tactic. *And what about Qara? What does Heramon know about this place? We need a way out of here, past all of the gates!* the little drake urged.

"What about Qara?" Ethan asked. "Is there a way out of here?"

Heramon was still eyeing the boys. "I know even less than you do. I was blindfolded all the way to this prison." He made a sweeping motion with his arms, as if to take in the scene before him. "These little gnomes have kept and annoyingly close watch on me." He made his way back to his seat and sat down. "But this much I do know. This shield is required to

308

mask the sound around us . . . You can hear from the inside, but no one can hear from the outside," he said matter-of-factly. "I have learned that these walls have ears . . . some kind of magic, and the gnomes seem to pick up the conversations all to easily . . . ," his voice trailed off as he tugged at his goatee in thought.

Kristian slapped his leg. "They have no right!" he barked to the other's surprise.

"But . . . how . . . how did you know . . . ?"

"How do I know about Kesem, drakes . . . and shields?" Heramon thrust out a hand toward the barrier. "I have studied drakes all of my life. Although I've never encountered a drake of the royal line," he said as he studied Seon more closely.

*I'm not a piece of worthless meat!* Seon fumed.

*Easy, Seon,* Ethan consoled. *Heramon isn't looking to eat you.*

"Of the royal line?" Kristian asked.

Heramon turned to look at the oldest boy. "An elemental, like BeeSting . . ." He nodded his head in the direction of the red drake. "Or the white emperor drake, which is the drake of true emperors," Heramon said more slowly, turning to look back at Seon.

The boys both stared at Heramon, not grasping what he meant.

"I don't understand," Ethan admitted.

"Nor do you have to understand this right now." Heramon feigned a gentle smile, but Ethan heard the finality in Heramon's voice and decided not to probe any further.

"Heramon?" Ethan changed the subject. "What happened in the lake . . . ? I mean in the underground lake . . . Mesa mentioned shadow demons?"

"Yes . . . I guess you could call them that. I've never encountered such creatures before. As I fell into the lake, I saw nothing but darkness in the water. I groped around blindly, trying to reach the shore, but these creatures were even darker. They attempted to drag me to the depths . . . I managed to free myself and make the beach."

Heramon studied the boy's face. "Now, enough questions from you. It is my turn to hear of your events. What aren't you telling me?" he stated as he slapped Ethan's knee and stood again. He glanced over toward the window then turned with his arms folded, waiting for either boy to speak up.

Ethan paused at the sudden change in topic and shot Kristian an awkward glance.

Kristian shrugged and motioned for Ethan to begin.

The younger boy fumbled through the first part, but warmed to his version of the story, careful to leave out anything about the Kur-ne or the water caves and the children's knowledge of the shadow demons. He made up some story of finding a hole in the cliff that the children had climbed through to get out of the caves, followed by a collapse that filled in with water. The half-truths sounded shallow in his ears, but he hoped that Heramon would believe them.

It appeared to work for the time being. "And this is why you are so angry, Kristian? The gnomes must have seen this, but did not come to your aid?" the man prodded.

Kristian looked up in surprise, then his face hardened. "That is exactly why I do *not* trust them!" he said with finality.

Ethan coughed into his hand "May I continue?" he urged.

Heramon shot him a questioning look, then nodded.

The boy next recounted the demonstrations of Kesem they had used in front of the lions and gnomes, assuming that Heramon would most likely learn of the truth of these events from the locals anyway.

The warrior listened intently, raising his eyebrows when he heard of the children's accomplishments, although Ethan tried to play these down as much as possible.

Finally, Kristian jumped in and described to Heramon where they really were.

Heramon's face went rigid and stoic as he listened. He shook his head at the discovery that he was in a giant cave. He turned again to look out the window, as if pondering on the significance of where they were. "I thought that sun looked contrived," he stated.

"And then we met you in the dining room." Kristian closed the story.

Heramon sat silently for a few moments. Then, he nodded. "I'll leave it at that for the moment. We can pick through some of the gaps in your story at a later time. But now, it's getting late, we should not keep our hosts waiting on us. They'll wonder if anything is wrong, and it won't do to have them barge in on us, when this shield is still up." He motioned for the barrier to be dropped, paused, and held up a hand. "Better we all go down separately," he added with a nod.

Both boys nodded in answer.

Ethan was careful to clearly whisper the shield word to close the spell. "Naxos." And the sound barrier vanished.

The larger man strode across the room without another word and listened at the door. Once he was satisfied, he cracked it open to peer outside. He straightened, waved to the children, and then quietly shut the door behind him.

# Chapter 18

## On Trial

*The evils we fear most might in fact be a simple misunderstanding.*

The boys sat, looking at the door where Heramon had been moments earlier and then at each other with the knowledge every word of their conversations were likely overheard. They both had many thoughts run through their minds, but were wary of saying anything to each other, even in whispers.

Lola was now stirring, and the boys acted as if nothing had happened. She promptly sat up in her bed. "I had a great dream," she exclaimed.

The boys looked at each other, and Kristian grumbled, "That's great, Lola," as they both moved off to their respective beds to pull on the remainder of their clothing.

"No . . . really. I dreamed that we were eating the best fruit ever. It was really white, and . . ."

Ethan stopped dead in his tracks and slowly turned around to look at his little sister with amazement. "What did you say?" he interrupted.

"I said we were eating fruit with pretty trees. I ate so much that I got full . . . then I woke up," she exclaimed with a big smile on her face while rubbing her belly.

Ethan shook his head to clear his thoughts. "Lola, did you see any sand?" he paused to consider the other parts of his dream. "Or anything else? I mean, anything strange?"

Kristian looked up with a bewildered expression visible on his face as if to ask his brother why he was encouraging her.

Ethan took no notice. His full attention was on Lola, and he quickly closed the gap between them, trying to draw more information out of her.

Lola looked off into the distance, as if pondering hard about the dream, then shook her head. "Nope. Just the fruit and the trees." Then she quickly added, "You brought us there, Ethan, and there were two others." She smiled again and started to roll around in her soft bed, much like the previous night. "This is so comfy," she stated.

"Egh, um. Ethan, Lola, let's talk about this later." Kristian's patience wore thin with the interrogation.

The younger boy glared over at him, but could see his brother's stern face and remembered about others listening in on their conversations. He decided not to ask a follow-up question, but brooded over the experience. How could she have known?

On cue, Seon jumped in. *She knows part of your dream, Ethan. Deseret confirmed it to me—you both had the same dream, but hers was just part of your dream.* Seon paused. *This is an omen, Ethan, we need to find the grove! You need to get more out of the Kur-ne . . .*

*But . . . how? How could she know? This is getting too strange . . . ,* his thoughts trailed off as he glanced back at his playful little sister. He was still confused. What did she have to do with this? He knew he had to talk with her more about the dream, but didn't want to risk it, not now, not here.

A sudden thought occurred to him. *Seon, the walls might have ears, but we don't have to talk to be heard.*

*That's sheer genius!* Seon praised, catching on to what the boy was thinking.

Ethan flushed bright red. *Tell Deseret and BeeSting that Lola and Kristian both need to talk through their drakes so we can all communicate without being overheard.* He rubbed thankfully under his companion's chin with affection.

The other two children momentarily paused, and Lola stopped rolling in her bed as Deseret and BeeSting relayed Ethan's message.

Kristian looked up and swiveled his head in Ethan's direction, a giant smile spreading across his lips.

"Why?" Lola belted out.

Both boys turned on her at once. "Lola! Shhhhh!" they urged in unison, putting their fingers to their lips.

"Just do it!" Ethan added in a warning tone and pointed to Deseret.

Lola fell silent then nodded her head with a shrug.

Seon piped up again, *Lola is asking Deseret why and Kristian wants to know what's going on with the bit about the dream . . . I already explained to them both; Deseret about why we need to do this silently, and BeeSting that you both had similar dreams. I didn't go into any detail.*

Ethan nodded in gratitude for his new little middle man, and the children readied for breakfast.

For the next while, Lola talked only through Deseret to both Ethan and Kristian about anything and everything. First she wanted to talk about her soft bed, then how she slept so well, followed by many more unentertaining subjects.

Ethan finally got so sick of her silent chattering that he asked her to just talk out loud and abandon thinking through Deseret altogether. Seon relayed this message to Kristian, and he looked over at Ethan with a relieved look on his face. At least she'd have others at breakfast she could bug, instead of the two boys. Besides, that might seem odd to the gnomes, as she was always chatty . . . always.

The children finished making their beds when another knock sounded at their door.

Mesa popped her head in as she shot Ethan a healthy smile. "Breakfast is ready!" she beamed.

"Great, I'm starving!" Kristian said.

All three filed toward the door and followed Mesa silently to the dining room. That is except for Lola, who began her barrage of questions about what food had been prepared and how ravenously hungry she was.

By the time they arrived in the dining room, Heramon had almost finished his entire plate of food. He stood and welcomed the children, as if he only just met them for the morning.

An assortment of breads, honey, and fruits lay on the table; and three places had already been set for the children.

Ethan looked around for their host, who was nowhere to be seen. "Where's Muschle?" he prompted.

Mesa blinked in surprise, but smiled nonetheless. "Why, he's gone to make ready for your court appearance," she announced. "But he'll be back shortly. Now eat, eat. You don't have much time." She rushed all three to their seating places and motioned for them to dig in.

The three drakes leapt onto the table and started to feed from the dishes that were prepared for them.

*This meat is divine,* Seon pleasantly declared.

*I know, I know, much better than stinking dry bread and honey,* he mocked, still with his mind on his own questions. But he was too hungry to venture it. He wolfed down his food as fast as he could. He wanted to talk to Mesa about the shadow creatures before they left. However, his hopes died when Muschle burst into the room, just as Ethan was finishing his last bit of bread.

"Time to go, time to go. The king and queen await your arrival!" he proclaimed. His eyes darted back and forth, and he was impulsively rubbing his hands together, as if he were in an immense hurry.

Startled, the children looked up at Heramon in anticipation. He slowly nodded then rose himself. He motioned for the children to do the same, but remained oddly quiet.

Lola crammed more food into her mouth, giving her the appearance of a giant squirrel stuffing her cheeks beyond capacity.

"Seriously Lola, that is not healthy. Don't eat so much!" Kristian demanded. He was always after his siblings if they ate too much and he didn't approve.

The small company proceeded into the entry, out the door, and down the main stairway. Seven lions stood at attention near the bottom of the steep and joined the group as they veered right and away from the marketplace that they had waded through the day before in order to reach Muschle and Mesa's home.

*And why do we need guards?* Ethan asked Seon. *Do we really need protection here?*

*I'm not sure why. Perhaps they don't want to let us out of their sight?* the little drake offered.

Muschle led them onto another side street, and Ethan could now see they were heading in the direction of the lone tower, which soared above all of the other buildings. *Isn't it strange that this place hasn't been discovered? I guess it makes sense, since this is somewhere in the middle of the*

*Nejd. Well that and it's underground. I certainly have never heard of this place from Grandpa before.*

*I'm sure the Nejd is not a wasteland to trifle with. Besides, who would dare come through the cliffs into a barren place, and they would never discover the entrance to Qara. It is well hidden, guarded, and enchanted. Put that all together, and it makes sense why no one has heard of Qara,* the little drake lectured.

*Know-it-all!* Ethan scoffed.

Seon snorted, but did not answer.

As the company turned down another shallow alley, the bright reflection off the glass buildings made the street appear much wider than it probably was, as light cascaded down all around them. In fact, Ethan couldn't pick out any dark recesses anywhere in sight. The children were all speechless, all craning their necks around to take in the scenery and gape at the spectacle of the glass buildings until their heads hurt. The farther they marched in, the more elaborate the buildings became.

One of these structures caught Ethan's eye. The building was no bigger than Muschle's home, but had ornate siding that ran its length. As the boy let his eyes wander, he noticed large windows that were set into the siding, such that they appeared to slant inward ever so slightly, giving the edifice an appearance of having shiny scales. The roof was gabled with bluish ice-like glass shingles that curved up at the ends and were stacked one on top of the other, making the entire structure shine with an iridescent color. A lone door was set into its frame on the left side of the house. It was the only feature that was not transparent, made of a dark mahogany colored wood with carvings of sand trees and gnomes dancing around their perimeter.

The door is what first drew Ethan's attention as he momentarily thought he saw the figures move. *Did you see that, Seon?*

*See what?* the little drake answered.

The boy convinced himself that figures etched into doors couldn't move and dance. In fact, upon closer inspection, they were set deep within the wood. He must have imagined it. *Never mind,* he dismissed.

The group continued their onward march and turned through yet another alley with more buildings similar to the one Ethan had studied. They continued on a while, before the alleyway drained into a panoramic view of the central palace plaza. Ethan heard Lola gasp at the sight that stretched out before them. He had never seen such a thing.

The broad center of the palace grounds formed a concave bowl that slanted downward, a few hundred paces across. Seven neat pathways, meeting at the center, branched out and led in opposite directions away from the tower. Each pathway was banked with hedges on either side, and finally intersected with two cross streets that skirted the ground's full circumference. In between these paths were hedges, flowers and vegetation of all shapes, sizes, and colors that filled in the remaining earth, braced with giant fountains erupting water high into the air at interval blasts.

Seven large glass buildings matched the pathways, more exquisite than any of the buildings they had passed by before. Each structure stood directly above one of the seven paths with voluminous tunnels running through their middle that acted as entrances to the gardens. These buildings balanced out the base of the sprawling palace tower taking up almost half of the grounds. Two guards stood at attention at each entryway of the edifices.

Ethan was sure that an aerial view of the tower would reveal an appearance of a giant wheel with seven spokes. At this thought, he looked up and had to cup his hand over his brow for shade as he realized he could no longer see the top of the tower. The sun was almost directly on top of the spire.

Muschle motioned for them to proceed down the nearest path.

As they passed through one of the seven buildings, Ethan glimpsed faces pressed up against the windows watching them. They looked comical as their features flattened against the surface of the glass. *Again, why are they all staring at us?* he wondered. They were all staring down at them, giving him an eerie feeling that he didn't appreciate.

The boy quickened his pace and sought momentary refuge in the brief tunnel underneath the building. At least he was out of sight, and he was determined not to look back once he was out the other side to avoid eye contact. But the eerie feeling remained—this time he felt their eyes bore into his back. *This is not natural!* he complained to his companion. In fact, come to think of it, he felt some amount of chatter going on inside of his head, like walking through an immense crowd.

Surprised, he broke his promise and looked around, half-expecting to see a large concourse of gnomes converging on their little party. But no one was in sight. He glanced up at the building and saw more faces pressing up against the glass. This made him shutter; something was not quite right. He should not be hearing people's voices, hundreds of people's voices. He glanced at his siblings.

Lola was covering her ears, visible distress painted on her face.

Kristian wore a grimace and shook his head once or twice, as if a bee were buzzing in his ear.

*Ethan!* Seon burst into his thoughts. *Ethan . . . you need to put up your mental block! Someone is trying to gain entrance into our thoughts!*

The Drake Epics - Journey to Qara

*I know, I can hear the chatter too, but that doesn't mean they're trying to gain entrance, does it? Besides . . . we won't be able to communicate then . . .* the boy realized.

*Never mind that, I've practiced long enough with you to penetrate your thoughts in case of an emergency. I hope that the same won't be true for whomever is trying to get in. It is not the chatter I'm concerned about. Put up the block. Now! I've already told the others to do the same,* Seon charged.

Ethan sighed, but trusted Seon's intuition. Again, he drew on the familiar power inside of him and invoked the blocking technique. To his relief, the chattering stopped altogether.

He had a faint thought from Seon. *The other's defenses . . . are up.* Then nothing. Ethan felt a sense of accomplishment. He had never blocked Seon this successfully before. However, he also now felt perfectly alone, even though the white drake was perched on his shoulder.

The boy reached up and nuzzled Seon with his hand for comfort, but he still didn't like feeling so ill prepared to meet with the king and queen. What would he do without Seon's counsel? A thought suddenly occurred to him that he would now have to rely on Kristian or Heramon. *We should have come up with another way to communicate,* he thought. What's more, he wasn't sure if they could even whisper, for fear of being overheard by others in their party or by whatever magical endowments their surroundings had been coated with.

Kristian sidled up to his little brother, making sure that their guards were far enough ahead of them and far enough behind. Once satisfied, he softly whispered to his brother. "This Qara is one surprise after another. I mean it's beautiful. But, so is Julfa. I could do without all of this, if I could just be back in Julfa." The older boy smiled and continued to look around.

Ethan found that he too longed for the simple surroundings of their village. Julfa had its own beauty in the sandstone. It might not be their true home, but it seemed so much more sincere than this place.

As the little company approached the palace, a pair of massive doors loomed in front of them, inlayed into the base of the tower wall. Two massive lions, at least five hands taller than the largest lions they had seen already, stood at full attention on either side of the doors. They were dressed in fantastic golden flocks and wore dramatic golden headbands that shrouded their manes above the brow with slits that allowed room for their protruding ears.

Ethan paused to study the tower at arm's length. He gathered that the tower wasn't made of glass, as he had first thought. It was made of some kind of translucent stone, different from all of the other buildings they had seen up until now. As he studied the tower more closely, he realized that

317

On Trial

the stone wall gave off an aura. No, a crackling aura. It looked like . . . *It can't be!* Ethan exclaimed to himself. He reached out for Seon in his mind, but hit a mental wall and he remembered about the blocking. He screamed in silent frustration.

Looking around, he caught Kristian's eye. Somehow, he had to get his point across to someone! He made a small gesture with his hands and hoped Kristian got the idea. He did. Ethan was going to cast a protective shield and needed the others to huddle a little closer.

Kristian quickly reigned Lola in, who gave out a gasp before Kristian clapped a hand over her mouth and raised a finger to his lips. Heramon apparently realized what was happening and stepped in closer to Ethan on his own.

Once satisfied they were all in range, the boy drew from the power inside of him. It grew and was now ready to cast. In his excitement to get the shield up, he overlooked a new and benign presence that had penetrated into his consciousness. Before he could invoke, a soft, comforting woman's voice interrupted him, *Ethan, Kristian, Lola, Heramon, welcome! I can assure you that you are quite safe with us. Why cast your shield?*

They all felt an odd sensation of peace. Uncertain of what just happened, they all glanced at one another—the voice hadn't come from any of their companions. Yet, Ethan felt a new sense of safety with this new presence. He couldn't put his finger on just why, but he innately trusted in the voice.

*Your power is miraculous, little ones, and with such little experience and preparation. I am profoundly impressed. It took me great lengths to reach you through your mental walls. You are truly great Sheikhs,* the voice continued. *Of course, I cannot breach your drake's walls. Speak to them. Tell them to drop their protection. They have no need of it here,* the voice pleasantly requested, as if they were sitting down to bread and honey.

Ethan felt a sense of reassurance and found that he yearned for the voice to last. He threw caution to the wind and let his power drain entirely, and promptly turned his head to speak to Seon in a soft whisper, "Seon, drop your mental block . . . a voice is talking to us . . . I can't explain how she got in, but she wishes you to join the conversation."

Seon looked at Ethan, disbelief and disappointment registering in his eyes. Ethan nodded to encourage him.

Seon's consciousness joined Ethan's mind again. *Ethan, what's going on . . . ?*

*Shhh . . . Seon, listen,* Ethan interrupted, placing a finger to his lips.

The drake looked frustrated at the interruption, but conceded all the same.

For the first time, the boy presented his mind to someone other than to Seon. He almost felt a little guilty, as if he were scrying and he could sense the drake's distress at this exercise, but Seon held his thoughts to himself for the time being. *Who . . . who are you?* Ethan asked.

The question was followed by a momentary pause. *Welcome Seon!* the voice replied to the both of them. *I will bring you both up to speed. Ethan, your brother and sister have asked the same question, and I have now met BeeSting and Deseret. You are all welcome in my humble palace. We have been expecting you.*

It was immediately obvious who they were speaking with. *Your Highness, we will do as you command,* Ethan said with as much reverence as he could muster.

Seon abandoned his disdain and shared his respect and warmth with the boy in reverence for his show of maturity.

The little drake's feeling of admiration permeated through Ethan's thoughts, and he blushed, in spite of himself.

The soothing voice also conveyed this sentiment. *You are truly a mighty leader . . . a somber boy with amazing talent, who will lead your people to freedom.*

Ethan openly balked at the revelation, but somehow he knew she wasn't wrong.

*Never fear, young Ethan. I sense your concern. Your secret of the Kur-ne shall remain safe with me. We have much to discuss about the amazing orb you have obtained. It is yours and yours only to command.* The voice paused, *We will talk when you arrive.* Then it fell silent.

The boy felt his blood run chill and fought the sudden impulse to run. Should he have kept the mental shield intact? Had he failed? He quickly felt for the orb. It lay perfectly safe in his pocket. Relief and a fresh sense of wonder flooded his mind with newly forming questions for the queen. But he still felt completely exposed, the same way he always felt with Limnah, when the Wiseman had interrogated him all those times, almost as if he had been toying with the boy and his drake. Was this the same thing?

Seon was deathly silent, but Ethan felt the little drake wanted to tell the boy that he told him so. Still, the drake was also experiencing a touch of amazement mixed with anxious concern that penetrated the boy's thoughts. Whatever the outcome, Seon also felt exposed and had now nuzzled closer to the boy for comfort.

Quickly glancing around him, Ethan saw vacant, surprised looks on his siblings' faces.

Kristian jabbed Ethan lightly and nodded his head in Heramon's direction.

The warrior looked completely ashen, and he was starting to noticeably tremble.

"Now, what could make Heramon look like that?" the older boy asked in a low whisper. "What do you suppose the queen said to him?"

"How do you know it was the queen?" Ethan asked back.

Kristian shrugged. "Who else would it be?"

The boy's quiet conversation was interrupted as the two great doors swung silently open on hidden hinges, followed by a loud clang, as they locked into position against the inner walls of the tower.

The small party entered the breach and were immediately confronted with another set of smaller redwood doors directly in front of them. On either side, Ethan could see a winding hallway that wrapped around and climbed its way along the outer wall of the tower and out of sight. Translucent, fireless torches, identical to the handheld variety that Ethan had seen during the previous day's journey through Qara's tunnel entrance, now lined the hallway just above his head. They were affixed around the outer wall of the hallway and ran its length until they too disappeared behind the tower's inner walls.

The doors behind them now swung closed, again clanking as they locked into place, shutting the garden and its alluring fragrances out. Ethan realized now that the garden's aroma had soothed him, and he savored the remaining scent that lingered in the air. The torches energized, and the brilliance in the tunnel raised a few notches.

Ethan glanced at the inner doors in front of him again, and his facial expression turned to one of fascination as he studied them more closely. A beautiful mural lay etched into grains of the deep red wood.

From right to left, the mural depicted a beautiful woman with flowing robes, almost lifelike, due to the exquisite detail carved into the wood. He wouldn't have been surprised if she had sprung to life and jumped out of the door itself, and he immediately thought of the other figures he had seen carved into the door they had passed by on their way here. Next to her sat an immense dragon, whose tail raised and crossed to the other door and around both doors' edges, eventually encircling itself and the woman. The dragon looked down upon them with a look of maternal compassion.

The other door was just as captivating. A great tree perched in its center, with flowing branches. It looked uncannily familiar to Ethan, and he suddenly remembered the great tree from his dreams. Next to the tree stood a tall, elegant man, also with flowing robes and a flowing beard. Ethan passed over the man a second time, and he noticed that the man's hands and feet looked like branches and roots that sprung out in every direction. Plants and flowers blossomed around him, as if by his sheer willpower. The closer the plants were to him, the larger they were.

Ethan's appreciation of the mural was short-lived as the inner doors began to swing open as well and a brilliant light burst in open the small company. As the gap widened, Ethan lifted his arms to his eyes to shield himself from the overwhelming glare. He let his eyes adjust for a few moments before lowering his hands. To his amazement, before him lay a land even more vast than that of Qara, at least twice its size by his best calculations, as he thought back on the previous day when he stood at the entrance to the underground world.

*How can this be?* he wondered to himself. He had seen the outside of the tower, the inside couldn't be this large by any stretch of the imagination.

*Spectacular!* Seon's thoughts radiated in his mind. *This place is filled with Kesem—it flows freely and enables much to be that defies the laws of nature we are so accustomed to,* Seon stated this fact more to himself rather than to Ethan.

The skies spread out indefinitely and were a soft hue of purple and red, mixed with a deep night time blue and bright shining stars that twinkled in the heavens, as they did in Julfa. Ethan couldn't tell where the bright light emanated from, but it seemed to come from everywhere in a perpetual dusk. In front of the little group stood an immense city made entirely of dark redwood. He had a peculiar thought that the wooden city was alive, as its branches twisted into the forms of buildings and pathways.

The landscape beyond the city was unnaturally divided into even sections. One side was flowing sand such as the lands that surrounded Qara, the other was a vast garden of greens, yellows, and reds from the thriving plant life, even more intense than the gardens they had just passed through. Ethan caught himself deeply inhaling in an attempt to catch a faint whiff of the vegetation, but he got an earthen, woody odor instead. The aroma was not what he'd anticipated and had a bitter tang to it that burned slightly in his nostrils.

Leading along the center of the division lolled a narrow sea that stretched out into the distance and out of sight. It was all indeed beautiful, but it seemed constrained, forced to live, unnatural, and Ethan felt every muscle in his body begging to cry out that the scene before him was contrived. He could sense that Seon agreed with him on this point.

This all made him a bit jumpy, and he squawked in spite of himself as the wooden doors clanged fully open. He shook his head in embarrassment at his sudden outburst.

"Need me to hold your hand?" Kristian said in a low, but mocking voice.

"Funny." the younger boy said.

Muschle motioned for the small group to proceed, and they continued their march.

His adrenaline satisfied, Ethan found he was now becoming numb to all of the dramatic surprises in this land of Qara. It now almost hurt to think of the vast differences between this *inner* land, that of Qara just outside and of his own home at Julfa. Still, this added to his feeling that he was a wanderer in a strange land, and he felt a yearning for another home and time that was just beyond his thoughts and his reach.

"Beautiful, isn't it?" Lola mused aloud.

Ethan wondered what she was thinking, but didn't dare risk thinking about it too much. At least, not until he knew more of what to expect and how to better combat eavesdropping.

*Wise choice,* Seon commented.

*You know, for having us not to think or talk, we seem to be doing a lot of it,* he mocked his little companion.

There was no response.

The group moved forward in a shroud of silence, as if the awe of their surroundings clamped its hands over their mouths and imposed silent reverence. A small path led tens of paces in front of them before they entered the wooden city proper. This time, little gnomes scurried in every direction, but again paused on both sides of the path in abject veneration, as the children and their drakes made their way to the center of the city.

Again, this annoyed Kristian, Ethan and both of their drakes. But Lola reveled in it, and merrily said "Hi" to the little gnomes each time they did this.

Ethan cringed every time.

Different from Qara's glass structures, everything here was indeed made entirely of wood. Streams of flowing purple liquids lazily sloshed within the knotty recesses of the branches. Ethan strained to find the source of the branches or even the flow of the liquid, but found none.

After a few moments of marching, they approached a large courtyard, completely free of debris, except for a majestic tree directly in the center. As they drew nearer, Ethan could now make out the tree's branches and roots that reached out to the city. *This must be the source of the city's buildings and walls . . . ,* he realized with amazement.

In front of the tree stood the woman from the mural. Ethan immediately recognized the queen of Qara, although he'd never met her in person before. She was draped in beautiful white robes, flowing in some imaginary breeze, although Ethan couldn't feel any wind. The man from the mural stood by her side, dressed in flowing blue robes, and Ethan recognized him as the king from the mural. Behind them both were two thrones, formed by the giant tree.

The boy paused to take this in when an abrupt memory coursed through his mind. This man and woman, king and queen, were the couple in his dreams. The couple he had assumed were his parents. Were they his parents? Was it possible? It seemed too remote to be true. He gave Kristian a wild look, but Kristian failed to grasp the importance and the older boy mouthed back, "What?"

Ethan shook his head. He suddenly wished he had told his brother more about this dream, although he didn't realize at the time that they were relevant, let alone that they would come true.

*Ethan, I do not feel that these are your parents,* Seon cautioned. *They are strange, removed from us, yet they are from your dreams, and we must talk with them . . . Perhaps . . . she is listening, even now?* Seon settled.

The eager would-be son wasn't sure either, but he didn't feel her presence in his consciousness this time. Just to be sure, he probed his mind further, but he only felt Seon. So, without thinking any further, he reached out to the queen in his mind before Seon could stop him. *I know you . . . I have seen you!* he declared. A pause followed. Ethan could feel Seon hold his breath in anger, but also with a sense of anticipation.

*Yes, we have met in a dream . . . I too have dreamed of you, along with the king! I dreamed of your coming far before you were born.*

*Before I was born?* It suddenly dawned on him that she might have more knowledge of where he came from; of where they all came from, and the excitement rose in his chest.

*All in good time, Young Sheikh. I knew you as a child, I knew you as older than you are now, and you have come to me many times in times that are past and in times to come,* came the response.

*Ughh Riddles!* Ethan hated riddles! He tried to cover up his disdain so as not to risk offending the queen more than he probably already had.

Seon snorted and wheezed as he chuckled at the boy's feelings.

"Very funny!" he muttered to the little drake. Besides, how could she have known him before he was born or even as a child, or in the future for that matter, when he couldn't even remember any of it himself? It was all impossible.

*Improbable, yes. But not impossible,* Seon said in a sudden somber tone.

*Not you too?* Ethan feigned in a mock tone.

As the group drew nearer to the royal throne, Ethan's attention turned to the king, who was crouched over, talking to a little gnome, dressed in the most exquisite armor that he had ever seen. Its iridescent colors glimmered in the light and was completely transparent. He could see directly into it and make out the clothing beneath, as if the armor were made of some sturdy glass. The gnome held a shield, identical to the armor, but with ornate decorations that outlined some epic battle. The shield ended abruptly in two spires that gently curved back to the center. He could also make out a faint aura around the gnome, as if the armor were infused with Kesem.

Just beyond the throne stood a column of gnomes, standing· at attention, all dressed in the same manner. Although their armor and shields were not as decorated as the gnome engaged in the quiet conversation with the king.

The king suddenly looked up, as if startled at their approach. His eyes quickly passed over the party, and he beamed a broad, friendly smile at them. He looked back at the gnome and said something that Ethan couldn't hear. The gnome saluted the king and whirled around in a pronounced march back to the column. He sounded some command that Ethan couldn't understand, and the column spun on the spot, now facing the little company. Another command was shouted, and the column marched past their party and out of sight. Ethan could still hear their armor clanking in the distance. The armored gnome returned to his position a little behind the king, but still in full view of their small group.

The king stood at his full height, and as they closed the gap to the royalty, Ethan realized how very tall this pair was.

Muschle halted a few paces from the two figures and ceremonially bowed on one knee, uttering something in an unknown tongue, again which Ethan didn't understand.

The rest of the group did the same, followed by the children after Heramon motioned they should mimic the others.

The king raised his hand in satisfaction. "Welcome to our land, Great Sheikhs," he said. His voice was a gentle, deep rumble, sounding like hundreds of rustling branches and leaves when a gust of wind sways great trees in the forest. "We have been expecting you, as I'm sure my queen has already informed you."

The children and Heramon looked at one another then at the queen, who smiled in return as she bowed. Her countenance was radiant. She seemed beyond human, almost transcendent. Ethan felt intoxicated by her

The Drake Epics - Journey to Qara

presence. Her face radiated with a delicate cheekbone and soft nose. Her long flowing white hair wrapped her elegant head and shoulders.

"I'm sure you have many questions for us," the king continued. "You seek audience with us, although you do not know why." He paused to let this last comment sink in a little. "There is a great evil at rule in this world. One that only you can conquer . . ." The king looked directly at Ethan, as if delving into his mind.

Ethan quickly looked down to avoid his gaze.

The king continued, "But . . . it will take great courage and wise counsel to defeat this evil." He now looked directly at Kristian.

The older boy defiantly held his ground without diverting his eyes.

"And great support." the king continued, now looking upon Lola, who was paying more attention to a giant purple butterfly that was lounging on a nearby flower.

Heramon just stood in place, still trembling with his head bowed.

"Yet you stand here on trial before us," the king said resolutely.

The children looked at the king in shock.

Heramon noticeably held back, showing a measure of self-discipline, but his head came up and his hand went directly to his sword nevertheless.

The king didn't seem to notice, or he didn't much care.

"On . . . on trial? How are we on trial? We have done nothing wrong!" Kristian blurted out. "O Great King," he amended as an afterthought, suddenly embarrassed by his own outburst as he quickly bowed his head again.

The armored gnome brandished his spear in distaste, and Muschle looked up at Kristian in horror that he had addressed the king in this manner. Both gnomes watched the king expectantly.

The magistrate nodded his head and motioned for Muschle and the other gnome to be still.

"I'm afraid so. You are on trial before the people of Qara. But not for what you suspect. Not for what you have already done or because of some wrongdoing, but of what you might do."

Kristian looked at Ethan and rolled his eyes. He never did very well with authority, which constantly got him into trouble in his soldiering apprenticeship with Heramon.

"This people revere you . . ." the king continued. "They may even . . . worship you." He let this fall heavily, choosing his next words carefully. "They will measure you, watch your actions, hang upon your every word, and even probe your feelings—if you don't guard them carefully . . ."

"Although that does not seem to be a problem for these Sheikhs," the queen spoke her first words since the arrival of the little group. Her melodious voice was almost hypnotic, and Ethan again felt entirely relaxed. She examined the children with a look of delight, as if she had just unearthed a colossal treasure.

The king raised one of his bushy eyebrows, glancing sidewise at the queen before returning his gaze to the children. "Nevertheless, it is important that you conduct yourselves with honor and nobility while you sojourn in our humble world." He paused again for emphasis. "You are constantly on trial for all that you do. You must take care," he said pointedly.

The children all shifted uncomfortably under the strain. Ethan half-felt as if Grandpa were standing in front of them, giving another one of his stern lectures after one of the boys' incidents.

"But come," the king said in a more merry tone. "Let us not dwell on such matters. We must counsel together. You have much to learn, and we have much to teach you."

# Chapter 19

# Revelation

*When in training, do as the master commands.*

Ethan felt a dull headache coming on. He desperately wanted to insert himself into the one-sided conversation, but the king's voice trailed on and on and on, as the druid's words slowly fell out of his mouth. For the first time in the recent past, he couldn't bring himself to ask any of his rather-more-important questions. Why did the people revere them? Did it have to do with their drakes? Why were the gnomes spying on them? He screwed his face up in distaste and finally smothered the questions out of sheer frustration. But he knew he wouldn't get the chance to ask them, even if he wanted to.

Seon nuzzled closer to the boy in an attempt to pacify him. But this did little to ease Ethan's tension.

They had all been taken on a brief tour of the wooden city, hosted by the king and queen, prancing ahead of them. Much to Ethan's chagrin, all of the excitement was literally sucked out of the whole experience. The king was so very boring, Ethan felt to pull his own hair out just to be done with it . . . and the king's jokes! They were drier than the hot sands of the Nejd. It seemed to him that the king simply liked to talk for the sake of talking.

*The only thing more important to the king, other than Qara, is the sound of his own voice!* Seon had commented.

Lola was unusually fidgety, and the boys had to scold her for wandering off, or deciding she wanted to sit down every ten paces as they were walking. Even Kristian appeared ready to jump out of his own skin.

"Did you know that this piece of wood—the one right here—was the branch that the great Krumer slept on for one hundred years? Well, that was some story . . ." Ethan turned himself about, rolled his eyes, and let out an audible sigh so that only his siblings could hear. If it wasn't about this branch or Krumer, whoever that was, then it was the rather-dry history of how this building was built and by whom, why the city planning took its shape, and so on and so forth. Ethan might have missed a number of the details—well, most of the details as he let his mind freely wander.

Finally, the small group made their way into the core temple. The structure was different from the others, with inlaid wood as the branches intertwined with one another in intricate designs and pictorials. The temple was serene and calm with a simple altar at its center and two murals hanging on the opposite wall, one of which depicted some goddess. "Hecteress," the king mentioned, bowing herself to the ground in sorrow. But it was the second mural that caught Ethan's eye.

The king continued to prattle on about the importance of the temple and its future meaning that Ethan didn't completely understand or grasp anyways.

*This old stump won't stop talking!* Seon almost hissed, absorbed in his own boredom.

Ethan sensed Seon's frustration. He had not seen the drake so irritated before, except for when he rammed his own ideas down Seon's throat. *Let's wait and see what he has to say,* Ethan found himself thinking to the drake. He needed to hear this next part. The mural, it was eerily familiar to Ethan.

The Drake Epics - Journey to Qara

Seon resentfully withdrew himself in silent protest.

*Seon, I'm sorry, but look at that mural. What is it?*

The drake remained silent, but Ethan sensed the drake was coming around to what the boy had seen.

The mural was a relief of a man facing off with a dragon that blew fire from his mouth. The man was a blaze with a giant trident in his hand. He held the spear as if to throw it at the dragon.

*I feel that I've seen this mural before, Seon. But I don't remember it from any of my dreams.*

*Ask your new friend, the king,* the little drake jealously retorted.

*Come on, Seon . . .*

"Ah, I see you have an interest in this mural," the king suddenly spoke down to the boy.

Ethan almost jumped at the intrusion. But he realized that he had inadvertently made his way over to the mural and now stood directly under it, gazing up at the picture.

"It is a mural of Marduk, the great Sheikh of our freedom," the king continued. "He has freed us from the dragon once before, and may do so again." He winked down at the unassuming boy and then looked over at his brother in a slight bow.

"What is he talking about?" Ethan mouthed at Kristian, who was grinning across the room at his younger brother's apparent confusion. Ethan knew this was somehow amusing to his older brother, but had stopped trying to figure out why Kristian found anything funny a long, long time ago.

"When the battle is at its bleakest, Marduk will charge into the fray and vanquish the dragon lord," the king mused before regaining his senses. "Well, at least that is how the prophecy, err . . . legend goes," he quickly corrected himself.

*There it is again, Seon! Something about a prophecy!* Ethan thought with renewed energy.

The drake wasn't speaking to the boy and turned himself about, whipping his tail against Ethan's cheek in spite of the boy.

Ethan shot the little drake a hurt look and turned back to the mural, masking his thoughts from his companion.

The king finally raised a hand and ended his boring tour. He motioned for the group to reverently exit the temple compound.

A little gnome appeared from somewhere in the eaves waiting to be summoned. "Shahir, please escort our guests to the training room. I'm sure they grow tired of an old man's rambling." The king chuckled more to himself than for anyone else's sake.

The children didn't find his comment amusing, but were all overjoyed to be through his lecture series.

"Please excuse me, we haven't much time to train and I must talk with Muschle, so I cannot escort you further," he announced apologetically. "But the queen will follow shortly, and I hope that you have found this discussion educational," he added in a tone that sounded like Ezera when instructing his students in Julfa.

Ethan couldn't say he was disappointed. For the first time since meeting the king, he felt a twinge of excited anticipation. Even Seon perked up, although he still refrained from talking with Ethan.

Shahir bowed, almost touching his nose to the ground, then swung his hand out, motioning for the small party to follow.

Ethan looked sidewise at Kristian, who shrugged and followed the little gnome toward a doorway set into one of the trunks lying about. The boy studied the little gnome more closely. Something was out of place, but he couldn't quite put a finger on it.

*Seon, I know you are angry with me!* Ethan said apologetically. *But something is wrong. I can feel it! This gnome appears to be out of place, somehow,* he finished.

The little drake didn't respond.

Lola sidled up to Ethan, hugging tightly to his arm, interrupting his mental inquisition. The two siblings' relationship had grown over the last few months. Before their *adventures*, the slightest cross-eyed face from Lola drove him huts, but now only occasionally. She seemed different, much more mature and seemed to look at Ethan as her mentor for encouragement and protection. It must have been their lessons. He smiled to himself at the newfound realization of his love for his little sister. She wasn't a little beast after all.

The group now circled the great tree. As Ethan gazed up into its towering branches, he thought he saw a movement within the lumbering plant, but it was so fast that he couldn't focus his eyes long enough to make out what it might be. He blinked a few times, determined to catch sight of whatever it was, then gave up after a few moments as it was giving him a headache. Instead, he turned his attention to the little gnome in front of them.

Shahir was walking with a slight limp in his stride. Ethan had not noticed that before, again giving rise to his previous premonitions. The gnome wore a simple brown garb with a green belt strapped around his rather-large midsection. Shahir's face was clean shaven, unlike the other gnomes that Ethan had encountered. But he had the trademark white hair, neatly combed and tucked behind his ears and pulled together into a neat ponytail that hung to his waist. Ethan finally admitted that he must be imagining the differences. After all, he was very new to Qara and unacquainted enough to tell what might be normal or out of place here. So, he suppressed his feelings.

They were presently being led up a narrow path that wound its way around a slight hill toward a very small wooden cottage burrowed between two giant trees. As they approached, Ethan could see the trees' massive branches sprouting from the ground to form the base of the small building as they twisted their way around to form a spire at its peak. Roots separated to expose two small windows and a little door nestled into the woody tangle. The other side of the cottage dropped off steeply into the long, narrow sea of what Ethan realized was the same purplish liquid he saw streaming through the city branches.

Shahir pushed open the door, and it squeaked on its hinges. The little gnome bowed and stepped to the side with his back against the door to admit the little group into the hut.

"Can we all even fit in there?" Ethan asked Kristian. "It's barely large enough to hold you and Heramon." He balked at his older brother.

Heramon motioned for Shahir to proceed first.

The little gnome looked surprised at Heramon's favor then nodded and muttered something under his breath as he entered the building.

The group followed him through the doorway, having to bow their heads through the entry. Heramon almost had to get on his knees. But it seemed to be the right size for Lola and the little gnome.

Ethan followed directly behind Heramon, but froze as soon as he stepped across the threshold. He saw a little creature scurry above the door, but much too fast and just out of the line of sight to make out any distinguishing characteristics. He momentarily thought this might be the same creature he saw in the tree branches. But, all he knew for sure is that a tiny voice had called out to him. "Things are not as they seem. This gnome is a bad omen. Beware. Beware." Ethan paused to ask Seon if he had heard the voice. He had not.

The older boy grunted as he now walked into the back of Ethan and bumped his head on the doorway in the process. "We're walking, Dingus?" he said in a sarcastic tone as he rubbed his sore head with one hand and gave the younger boy a hard shove with the other into a spacious interior. However, Kristian himself stopped to crane his head around and take in the sight. "What the?"

Ethan barely caught his balance and glared over his shoulder at his other brother. He had forgotten entirely about what he thought he saw or heard and instead looked around with the same awe as his brother. The hut wasn't a hut at all! The boy could have sworn that the building was a small cottage, but this room was anything but small. Instead, a massive hall, easily a few hundred paces deep and wide spread out before him, and the ceiling rose twelve lengths above him. "It's huge!" Ethan thundered.

Seon had caught interest as well and seemed to have forgotten being upset at his companion. *There is a strong Kesem in these walls!* the little drake thought.

The boy was happy to have his little friend back with him and tenderly rubbed the drake's head with love.

The hall revealed tens of gnomes, sparring one with another in small groups of no more than four combatants each. Spears and swords clanged together and glinted in the pale light. The tiny weapons looked like toy daggers to Ethan.

In one group, Ethan watched a giant sand lion leaping around, avoiding blows from seven little gnomes lunging at it with drawn weapons. The boy paused and sized up the lion and then turned to measure the doorway. "There is no way that lion could have gotten through that door!" he pointed out, but intended it for Seon.

*There must be another way in?* the drake thought.

"Must be," Ethan said.

The mock battle in front of him continued. One little gnome finally managed to grab a handful of the lion's mane and nimbly hoisted himself onto the large cat's back in one fluid motion. The lion jerked itself around to dislodge the little intruder, but the rider held tight. The gnome shouted something unintelligible at the lumbering beast and made a quick series of moves that ended with a thrust of his small dagger into the base of the cat's skull, stopping just shy of drawing blood. The lion halted against the tip of the gnome's blade and bowed itself in defeat with a ragged grunt, followed by a frustrated roar. The gnome smiled and jumped nimbly to the ground, triumphantly shouting. The lion sat up on its haunches, shaking its great mane in contempt.

Kristian was over his brief sightseeing and gave Ethan another shove forward. "We need to catch up." was all he said.

The younger boy stumbled to catch his balance, glaring over his shoulder at his brother. By now, the others were many paces in front of them so that the boys had to trot in order to catch up.

Ethan continued scanning around, careful to not slow his pace and risk another shove. At first glance, the little men all looked harmless enough, but he could tell from their quick and agile maneuvers that they were anything but harmless. An intriguing thought came to mind. *Seon?* he asked. *Are they preparing for something?*

*I think they are not telling us everything!* Ethan persisted. *But what could it be? Will we get drafted into whatever this is?* A brief silence followed from Seon, but Ethan knew the drake was thinking about his statement.

*Ethan, not here, not now. Wait until we're somewhere quieter to talk about that subject!* His companion finally answered in a cautious tone.

The boy let it slide, even if he didn't feel the queen's consciousness, he agreed that they all needed to be more careful. He felt suddenly vulnerable and touched his center of strength, casting up a quick mind block to shield himself—not that it would do him any good, he reflected. The queen had already successfully broken her way into his conscience once before; she could easily do so again. So he determined to monitor his thoughts for any sign of an intrusion.

He changed his line of thought, and his mind now raced to think of a way out of their situation. He wasn't ready to be pressed into service, and he desperately hoped his latest idea was dead wrong. He quickly tugged at Kristian's sleeve.

The older boy grimaced and yanked his arm away.

Ethan repeated the action, this time with a consequence as Kristian thumped Ethan's arm

"You're annoying me again, and I'm going to . . ." Kristian stopped short of landing another blow as he noted Ethan's ashen expression.

The younger boy mouthed a silent warning to his brother, who shook his head, not understanding. Ethan pointed to his mouth again, looking around to make sure no one was watching before repeating, as he mouthed the words more slowly, silently, momentarily safe from immediate prying ears, "Something is not right!"

Kristian shook his head again. "Speak up, Dingus!"

Giving up all pretense, Ethan whispered what he'd told Seon and stood back to measure his brother's response.

"Whatever," the older boy snorted, turning back toward the others.

"Fine!" Ethan fumed in a hoarse whisper. He hated it when Kristian got into one of his surly moods.

The group stopped, and Ethan realized that Shahir was talking to a lion and another gnome suited up in a glasslike armor, like the gnome by the king's side.

*Where did they come from?* Ethan asked, reverting back to his quiet thoughts, still angry at his older brother.

*I don't know. I hadn't noticed them there before,* Seon replied. *I think that we're right about this gnome. Something is not as it appears to be.*

The lion suddenly turned its massive head toward the children and bowed, keeping one eye fixed on them. The animal grunted, turned, and strode toward a nearby sparring ring, with Shahir in close pursuit. The group followed. The ring was roped off and set against the far wall. Two gnomes jumped back and forth to avoid each other's lunges. As the group approached the ring, the gnomes paused their battle and leaned on their weapons.

Heramon turned and shot Kristian a warning look. The older boy reigned in Ethan and Lola.

Ethan's first reaction was to punch his brother as his temper flared. He took one look at his brother's expression and gave in.

"Don't use Kesem!" the older boy stated flatly, and that was all. He moved over to stand by Heramon.

Lola looked up at him with a question waiting on her lips, but she swallowed it when Kristian frowned at her while sternly shaking his head.

Ethan thought it was an odd request and didn't grasp the full meaning. His mind was still abuzz about being pressed into battle and what horrible things would transpire while trying to figure out how they were going to get out of it all.

*He's right, Ethan. I think they want to test us—I mean, test our abilities,* the drake said haltingly. *This is very odd.*

Ethan looked at his companion, who appeared to not want to say anything more. *What?* his mind was now halfway between thoughts of the war draft and this new topic escaped him.

*Oh, do pay attention, will you?* Seon said in disgust.

Both Kristian and Seon's comments finally dawned on him, and he curtly nodded and hugged Lola tighter to himself. His feelings were a jumbled mass, but the same thoughts still flooded his mind that Qara wanted them as slaves—no, that didn't make any sense, drafted soldiers. *That's it!* The thought at least occurred to him that they were pawns in some larger game that he wanted no part of. "Not our battle!" he muttered. "Not our battle." Yet he still couldn't shake the feeling that the queen would protect them at all costs, if she could. He had, after all, seen her in his dreams. Shouldn't that be enough? Enough to trust them? He wasn't sure.

"And we'll start with her!" a voice interrupted Ethan's reverie. A new gnome had appeared from nowhere, or Ethan hadn't been paying attention. Either way, the little man was pointing at Lola.

"You what?" Ethan said, shaking his head to clear his mind.

Heramon had already placed himself in between the gnomes and the children, folding his arms as a sign of dogged contempt. "Stay behind me," he muttered to the children.

"You have much to learn." The gnome pointed to them. "And we have much to teach you." He pointed both of his hands at himself. "We will start the teaching with the girl," The gnome said through gritted teeth.

Ethan glanced around, but didn't see Shahir anywhere. He had vanished. Come to think of it, where were they now anyways? He'd lost track while he was daydreaming.

"Not until we understand what is going on here," Heramon said gruffly.

The gnome looked at Heramon in surprise before a stealthy grin stole across his face. "Ah, but you are not to be tested, filthy man. Stand aside!"

Kristian had crept his way back to stand by Ethan. "OK, you were right!" he begrudgingly whispered. Instinctively, he reached for his sling and notched a small stone in its pouch. He handed his dagger to Ethan.

Ethan reluctantly accepted the blade and grimaced in concentration, trying to remember his limited and painful sparring sessions with Hem. These gnomes looked like hardened veterans with much more experience than Ethan's former pudgy combatant though. He also couldn't shrug off the feeling that this was all wrong.

*I don't like this!* Seon warned.

A list of questions flooded Ethan's mind. Since their arrival in Qara, the people revered and worshiped them. *The king said it himself!* Ethan recalled. But this? This was all wrong. Why was this happening? Where was the sense in this? Did the king and queen put these gnomes up to this? After all, Shahir led them here directly under the king's command. *Are they really testing us?* he probed Seon.

The drake shifted uneasily on his shoulder, ready to take flight at any moment.

Ethan reached up to calm his little companion, but fully admitted that he felt his own adrenaline building. He was torn of what to do next, but one thing was for sure, he would not allow the gnomes to bully any of them. He was quite through with bullies.

The lead gnome warily advanced on Heramon, followed by his giant companion.

Heramon drew his sword and took a few practice swings crossing his sword in front of him, looking very confident with himself. "I said *no!*" Heramon challenged.

The gnome momentarily paused, sizing up the guardsman, but did not answer him.

The two boys huddled together, pulling Lola behind them for safety. Kristian menacingly twirled his sling.

*Don't they know what we're capable of?* Ethan shot at Seon. Only the day before, the lions and gnomes had barely avoided the children's power in the Forbidden City.

Suddenly, BeeSting lit from off Kristian's shoulder and bore down on the advancing gnome. The drake veered right, came around, and swiped at the gnome with his talons, ripping a gash above the gnome's ear and across his forehead. The gnome shrieked, flailing his arms about him in astonishment, trying to shield his unprotected face from the drake's razor-sharp claws. BeeSting made one or two passes, ripping at the gnome's clothing as the gnome writhed in momentary panic.

Kristian laughed out loud. "Aren't you supposed to avert your eyes, like all the others?" he teased. "BeeSting will make sure you remember your place!"

The second gnome called out to the cringing creature and hurdled a shield into the ring, landing just shy of his reach. The squat man dove for the shield and brought it up above him in one fluid motion for momentary protection. BeeSting continued to assault the gnome, but the shield now successfully deflected his attacks.

Heramon gave the boy an impatient look and shook his head.

The drake retreated to his perch on Kristian's shoulder. The soldiering apprentice flashed his companion a broad smile. "Teach you to mess with us," he mumbled to himself, but loud enough for both Ethan and Lola to hear.

"Are you sure you want to press us further? Look, you need medical attention. Let us discuss this more calmly," Heramon offered.

The gnome recovered, pulling himself to his feet, still clutching the shield close to him in case of another attack. He drew his fingers over the gash above his ear and stared at the blood. "You fool!" he bawled. "How dare you let that *thing* attack me?"

Kristian's face contorted in rage. "Careful . . . ," he muttered through gritted teeth.

The gnome paid him no mind. "We're not here to train you, but I will most certainly kill you now!" the little man spewed, drawing his sword.

"I'm terribly sorry for your unfortunate introduction to BeeSting, but I assure you, he was only acting out of the children's best interest," Heramon negotiated. "Come now, let us see to that ear of yours."

The gnome spit on the ground. "You really don't get it, do you?" the gnome ranted. "Must I spell it out for you, we are here to kill you!" He fumed as he began edging around the little group.

Heramon sneered, refraining from laughing out loud. "Come now, this is no way to treat your guests." He mocked as he swung his sword a few times in front of him.

The Drake Epics - Journey to Qara

Ethan realized that the other gnome and the lion were already circling them as well.

The gnome was now in striking distance to Heramon and both leapt and thrust his sword at Heramon's neck for a kill shot, uttering something unintelligible that Heramon and the children didn't understand. But it felt like a foul spell to Ethan. The blade glowed bright green at the incantation and seemed to have a life of its own as it writhed in the little gnome's hands.

Heramon easily sidestepped the attack, but the cursed blade unnaturally curved around and forced him to duck, narrowly missing being skewered.

The lion also advanced on Heramon, with an indignant sneer at his defiance.

Heramon recovered his stance and took a halting step backward, measuring up the three advancing foes, then back at the children to make sure they were out of harm's way.

Ethan could see the gears turning in the guardsman's head to come up with a strategy. *Seon!* he thought. *Get ready to attack!* He felt the drake prepare himself. "We may have to use our Kesem after all," he muttered to his brother.

Kristian nodded in agreement.

Heramon planted both feet firmly and continued to take a few practiced swipes to and fro, twirling the sword in his hand with ease to buy some time.

*Now!* Ethan sounded. This time, all three drakes launched in unison, targeting the lion and whirling around the massive cat's head. The lion seemed oblivious to their attacks, but was momentarily distracted by the commotion.

Heramon took his chance, deflecting the first gnome's lunges, and flanked the lion from behind. With a few skilful steps, he leapt onto its back and held tight to its sparse armor plating.

The lion roared in fury, trying to dislodge Heramon, but he hung on.

The second gnome launched an attack on Heramon from the other side.

Heramon didn't see him coming.

"Heramon! Behind you!" Lola screamed.

Many things happened all at once. Kristian let a sling stone fly, aiming for the head of one of the attacking gnomes. At the same time, Heramon sunk his left hand into a tighter grip on the lion and brought his right hand up to bash the other charging gnome in the face with the hilt of his sword. Both gnomes were struck in unison, and their limp forms struck the ground unconscious.

Heramon whirled back, brought his sword upright, and pressed the tip of the blade into the base of the lion's skull, holding both palms against its edge as if to drive it into the giant animal. He yelled. "enough!"

The lion froze instantly, growling softly to itself. "Do you surrender?" Heramon demanded. No answer. "Do you yield?" he repeated, sliding his sword around and under the lion's throat. He leaned over. "Is that enough training for you?" he whispered as he nimbly dismounted, while holding the tip of his sword at the lion's throat.

By now, a group of gnomes and lions had crowded around the spectacle. Ethan didn't know what to expect next and prepared to cast a shield around them if the need arose. He glanced up to see the gnome with the shield stumble to his feet.

The gnome looked around frantically then dove into the newly formed crowd and disappeared from view.

Ethan heard abrupt clapping coming from somewhere behind. He whirled around to see the gnomes parting down the middle. The queen emerged in the resulting rift as she clapped her fair hands together. "Well done! Well done!" She studied the lion and his unconscious companion lying a few feet from him.

"You have defeated three worthy opponents. But where is the third, I wonder?" She stared down the lion, who shrunk in terror from the queen. "Find him!" she commanded a gnome standing next to her side. The gnome immediately disappeared into the crowd.

*But how did she know about the third gnome?* Ethan asked Seon. *I mean ... ah, never mind. She always knows,* he said in dismay.

The queen turned her attention back to the lion. "You are a wolf in a lion's clothing, I think," she said. "I wonder, are you sent here to spy on us? Can you possibly know of the prophecy and of the great Sheikhs?"

Ethan's mind reeled. *Again, with the prophecy? Are we the only ones who don't have a clue?* He quickly cataloged all the times he heard of it.

*Perhaps she will be the one to tell us?* Seon encouraged.

The queen muttered something, and a light shrouded both the lion and the gnome. As the light faded, the former lion now exposed a man in a hooded black robe, kneeling on the ground in abject horror. He collapsed under the weight of the armor, trapped within it, muttering, "We are discovered! We are discovered!" The gnome, slumped over on the ground, also revealed a man, still unconscious from Heramon's blow.

A sudden clamor erupted behind the group, bringing Ethan out of his daze. Two gnomes were dragging a third behind them. As they came into view, Ethan recognized the gnome who had threatened them, kicking and screaming something unintelligible.

The queen repeated the phrase with strange words, and the screaming gnome lay subdued as a man, but still awake and frozen, staring up at the queen.

"Why did you try to kill these guests?' she demanded as she elegantly waved her hand in the direction of Heramon and the children.

The man began to tremble and violently shake his head. "They will die, they won't live much longer." A maniacal laugh escaped his lips. "The prophecy will die with them!" he continued. "Especially that one!" He pointed a bony finger at Ethan. "I will tell you how he dies and fails to . . ."

"Away with them. I will not hear another word!" the queen boomed, her voice once beautiful and soothing, now deep and harsh as it reverberated across the room. The man fell deathly silent. "And find Shahir! I do not believe that he is whom he professes to be!"

A gnome appeared instantly at the queen's side, and summoning others, they quickly retrieved the men and hauled them away.

"What just happened?" Ethan bawled.

No one answered. Kristian shrugged. Lola was oblivious, now talking to a gnome standing beside her.

*Where was Heramon?* Ethan looked around in search of the man.

*Ethan, she has power . . . the queen . . .*

The boy turned to his little companion, forgetting about Heramon for the moment.

*We need an audience with her, Ethan.* The drake's tone was suddenly serious and somber. *It is time to get our answers and we need to understand all this talk about the prophecy, about your dreams, about the Kur-ne . . . ,* Seon trailed off, as if considering if he should continue.

Ethan still wasn't sure, but felt an increasing level of reassurance emanate from his companion.

Muschle suddenly appeared beside the queen. His face was drawn out and pale. He raced toward Ethan, who stepped back, not knowing what to expect from the little gnome. One thing was for sure, he had lost all trust in these gnomes not that he trusted them to begin with. Yet the queen seemed still to be a beacon of peace for him.

"You need not fear him," the queen consoled. "Those whom you just battled were neither friend nor ally. Yet they knew how to infiltrate into our most sacred grounds, uninvited, undiscovered . . . waiting until you arrived . . . waiting . . . . ," the queen trailed off in deep thought. "Amazing, really."

"What? They were not trying to train us? That gag about them killing us wasn't just a ruse to get us to fight them as part of the test?" Ethan took a breath, allowing himself enough air to continue. "Then, who were they?

Why were they here? What about the prophecy?" Ethan was sure he could blurt out more questions upon request.

"Now is not the time, Young Sheikh," she calmly replied. "Enough training for today, you must all be very hungry . . ." She looked each one of them in the eye and nodded to herself in satisfaction.

"Muschle, please escort our young Sheikhs to the dining hall . . . Take others with you to guard their safety. We must be ever vigilant!" the queen closed, as if ending a sermon. "And find Shahir!"

Another gnome and two cats sidled up next to the little group as their escort. The boys looked at each other in concern, but Lola was jubilant to have a growing audience for her questions and comments.

"Ethan, if I may have a word with you?" the queen asked graciously, now turning toward the boy.

"Oh, me?" he uttered in surprise, pointing to himself.

*I don't want us to split up. What if we . . . I mean, what if something happens?* he asked Seon in desperation. But his mind drew all blanks on coming up with a way out of this one. *And where is Heramon?*

*I don't know, but we need to talk with her. This is a perfect opportunity,* Seon insisted. *It's the right thing to do . . . She will give us the answers we need,* he counseled.

Ethan knew the little drake was right; however, he felt an odd sensation about the whole experience. It felt as if he were in a dream where things, well, things just happened. There was no rhyme or reason why, they just did. "But what of my brother and sister?" he let slip and realized he now had to commit to the rest of his statement. "Can you promise they will be safe . . . As long as you promise they will be safe?" he added.

Her smile widened in sympathy. "Muschle will watch over them, my dear Sheikh, I promise you no harm will come to them. Upon his life, he will protect them," she placated.

Ethan shot Kristian and Lola an anxious look.

The older boy urged him to go with a sweep of both hands. Clearly, he was a tad infatuated with the queen.

Ethan had only just realized this and expected to give his brother a good ribbing about it tonight when they were all back in the room.

"Go on, we'll be fine," Kristian pressed.

"And where is Heramon?" Ethan blurted, no longer willing to hold this back.

"I'm here," the man said as he appeared from behind the crowd. He coughed into his hand, as if embarrassed, then joined the little group. "Go ahead with the queen. You will be safe."

The queen smiled at the warrior. "Thank you for tracking down Shahir," she said gratefully.

He smiled and bowed. "It was my duty." With that, he shepherded the others toward the hut's door they had entered through, and Ethan turned his attention back to the queen, who was already strolling in the other direction.

She paused, turning back, and motioned for him to follow. He looked between his siblings and the queen then awkwardly stumbled to pick up his pace to catch her.

The gnomes parted as she continued toward the opposite end of the hall. Ethan glanced at the squat men as he followed behind her. They all bowed as he passed, careful to avoid his gaze.

*I know what my first question will be: Why do they keep doing that?* he fumed to Seon.

Seon looked at Ethan as if to shrug. *It's better than the alternative. We could be fighting them instead,* he offered. *Besides, perhaps this is how we know they are genuine. If they bow, then they are friend. If they do not, they are foe.*

Ethan mulled the comment over in his mind. Seon had a very good point.

As the crowd thinned, he realized two heavily guarded gnomes fell in directly behind him. A small door came into view. He hadn't noticed it there before, but thought there was much he hadn't noticed when he first entered this strange arena. As they neared the door's entrance, he was sure that the queen would have to duck in order to enter. However, the door appeared to be growing with every step they made until it was quite large enough for the queen to walk through without ducking. She didn't break stride as the door opened of its own accord and they entered the room.

The interior was dim with a few chairs and a small fireplace on the opposite wall. It was roughly the same size as the bedroom he had stayed in last night. Above the fireplace a picture hung, portraying a barren landscape with an overcast sky. A streak of lightning illuminated a lone, wilted bush that took up a prominent position directly in the center.

The queen suddenly turned toward Ethan and the rear guard. "Wait outside," she commanded and nodded at their questioning glances. The guards obediently bowed and shut the door behind them. "Ethan, please take a seat." She motioned to a chair on her left.

The boy nodded and moved slowly to the chair.

The queen also sat down in a chair next to his, but appeared to be in deep thought at the moment.

"You are on a quest, Young Sheikh," she began in a revealing tone.

"Quest?" Ethan didn't know where she was going with this, and he didn't understand what she meant. He'd been wandering the last few days and felt he had stumbled his way through a number of unplanned, haphazard events, nearly getting himself and his siblings killed in the process. In fact, if it weren't for him, they wouldn't be in this whole mess in the first place. No, she must be wrong, everything leading up to this point was a series of random blunders.

"Ah, but you are!" she answered, perceiving his confusion by the quizzical look on his face. "The path to your quest has led you here . . . to me."

Ethan still didn't fully understand, but listened intently anyhow.

"First you sought the Kur-ne . . . ," she continued.

Ethan squirmed uncomfortably in his chair, instinctively reaching out for his pocket to confirm that the small orb was still there.

Seon also shifted his feet on Ethan's shoulder, and the boy felt the drake tense up.

"You may reveal the orb . . . I will not take it from you." She nudged as if she had again read Ethan's mind. This was curious as the boy felt something leave his mind, but didn't feel her presence there, and he suddenly worried she knew how to enter his thoughts unobserved.

"But how did you . . . ?"

Seon shifted again then added in a forced tone, *Protect your mind.* Then he added, *But show her the orb. I will guard its safety.*

The queen didn't answer, peering deep into Ethan's soul.

He slowly eased his hand into his pocket and drew out the Kur-ne. At the same time, he carefully began casting up barriers around his mind, but ever so slightly so as not to cause alarm. However, he soon abandoned the attempts as he noticed that the surface of the orb was glowing, much to both his and Seon's surprise.

"Ah, it remembers me," the queen said with some emotion.

"Remembers you?" Ethan spoke, his curiosity getting the better of him.

"Yes, long ago it offered me a quest. Like your quest, this was mine alone to follow—until I had finished my task . . . ," she trailed off in thought of some past event.

"I don't understand." Ethan fumbled, bringing the queen back out of her reverie.

She smiled and nodded. "Of course, I haven't divulged this to you yet. Where shall I begin?" The queen put a finger to her lips. "Ah yes. You see, the Kur-ne appeared millennia ago. Some say that it was given to this world to preserve its goodness and love, and yet others insisted that it was an object of great power. Regardless, it has been passed down from generation to generation to the righteous, or something to that effect, until it was lost a millennia ago."

Ethan listened intently. He also felt Seon's interest peak, and they waited, as if to snatch the next few words out of the queen's mouth.

"I was the last to have seen it," she finished, and Ethan sensed a twinge of pain in her voice.

This baffled him even more so. "What do you mean you were the last to see it? You are not old . . . I mean you are so . . . Are you thousands of years old? You are so beautiful . . ." He realized he had gone too far as soon as it slipped off his tongue. His cheeks flushed scarlet red in embarrassment.

The queen bubbled in sweet laughter that enveloped him in warmth. "Thank you, my young admirer. A lady always appreciates comments on her beauty, but it is the beauty that you see within that is most important." She nodded toward the orb.

Ethan broke the queen's gaze and peered into the orb; the glowing colors were exquisite.

"Yes, I am quite old," the queen narrated, "or young. It all depends on your perspective really. Yes, my race has great longevity." She paused again.

"Your race?" Ethan asked, again looking back at the queen.

"All in good time. However, I will tell you that your drake and I are not so unlike each other . . . in many ways." Her eyes turned on Seon, and she nodded out of respect.

Seon bowed to her in response.

She presently pulled herself upright as if to refocus her attention. "Ethan, you *are* on a quest. You sought the Kur-ne." She nodded to the orb in his hands again. "After your discovery that it existed, your mere thoughts set events in motion, irreversible events, and you were soon drawn to it in ways . . . well, in ways you did not expect . . . you see . . ." She slowed her speech and precisely emphasized each word. "The Kur-ne works through small and simple means. It prepares its holders and draws them to it . . ." She paused again and looked up into Ethan's eyes. "As *you* . . . were drawn to it."

Ethan couldn't break from her gaze, he was mesmerized—frozen. He didn't know how to respond. This was eerily familiar to him. The auditor had the same effect on him, but instead of an icy touch, the queen's touch was warm and comforting.

Seon was also deathly silent, and Ethan could hear the drake's breath coming in rasps. He sensed and felt the tension in his companion's feelings.

The queen broke off the silent inquiry as she abruptly stood and strode to the fireplace.

A flood of relief washed over Ethan at his freedom from her gaze.

"But you must behave yourself," she said over her shoulder. "If you are to reap its rewards . . . if you are to be led to your quest's end," she lectured. "The quest that only you and Seon know of. The quest that only you two can finish." She placed a delicate hand on the fireplace mantle and studied the mural, as if seeing it for the first time. "Trust no one else, unless you know for sure they can be trusted, even if you have to peer into their minds for that insight and root it out of their souls."

Ethan shook his head, and he sensed an immediate distaste from Seon at the mention of mind scraping or scrying. But Ethan already had an entirely different question on his mind. "I still don't understand. How do you know that I have a quest? How do you know what I'm supposed to do?" he braved.

She was silent for a few moments before responding in a far-off voice. "You forget, I too had the Kur-ne as my treasure at one time. I too had a quest. I too had . . . similar experiences," she said whimsically.

She turned to look at Ethan and Seon again with a much more serious look on her face. "You must follow your quest . . . whatever is shown to you, that you must do. The Kur-ne seeks out those who have an important question after all." She emphasized each word again. "You must interpret what you see. You must study it out in your minds. You must come to a solution and ask yourselves if it be right, or your Great Spirit, as I believe He is called."

The young boy blushed. He had never divulged to anyone that he believed.

"The Kur-ne will show you the way, and your hearts will confirm it." The queen turned back to the fireplace, grabbed a fire stick, and poked absentmindedly at the small burning fire that unexpectedly sprang to life.

"And you must do this alone. No one else can do it for you, although they may give you guidance from time to time." She paused, stoking the fire, and looked back at Ethan again. "But it is you who must decide. The fire will burn within you . . . within your heart . . . when you feel that your path is right, it will guide you to your journey's end. When you ask something that is wrong, you will have a stupor of thought."

The boy didn't grasp what the queen was trying to tell him. None of it made any sense at all. Still, he was intrigued by what she was saying, even if it were all too much to cope with. *Seon, do you know what she's talking about?*

The little drake didn't answer, but Ethan knew Seon didn't know what she was talking about either. At least not for the time being, but he knew the little drake would figure it out sooner or later; probably sooner than he, himself, would.

The queen set the fire stick down and strolled back to her seat, sitting with her hands folded neatly in her lap, again staring intently into Ethan's eyes. "The Kur-ne comes to those who are worthy, from a higher power. It leads the worthy back home. But it is not for free, and it is never to be trifled with." She paused, hung up on something in her own mind. "The bearer must learn and grow with every experience, continue on the path of worthiness. Failure to comply means failure to receive the Kur-ne's instructions, and eventually, the bearer, if still unworthy, will lose the Kur-ne altogether." She looked guiltily at her own hands. "And such a loss it is." The trembling tone in her voice sounded vulnerable for the first time since Ethan had met her.

He wondered what must have happened to her to give her so much pain, but didn't dare ask. For the first time, he felt he could truly trust her, he could sense that Seon did as well.

"Your Highness," he started as gently as he could, "how do I know when it's time?"

She looked up at him with a puzzled look on her face. For a moment, Ethan could have sworn he saw a tear on her check, but when he looked again, it was gone.

"I mean," he stammered, trying to keep his focus, "I have seen my . . . well, I think it is . . . I've seen my quest."

The queen's face brightened, and Ethan could tell he had her complete attention.

"But," he continued, "I saw this many times in dreams before I ever knew about the Kur-ne." He paused to read her face then selected his next words carefully. "I know that I must now find . . . this place . . . and make things right. I don't know how, but I will make things right before it all goes wrong."

The queen's face turned to excited wonder at this latest revelation.

"Even if the Kur-ne consumes me . . . ," he ventured in midthought, hoping that the queen would catch on.

"Ethan, I'm amazed at your wisdom," she answered slowly. "The Kur-ne will never consume you, but you must learn to control it." Again, her eyes misted over as she remembered some event in times past. "The Kur-ne has great power, it will leave you drained, true. But it will never, can never, harm you."

The queen blinked, smiling to herself, and drew a hand through her shining hair as if pulling herself back to the present. "All that I have told you before still applies." She paused to think of what she would say next. "You have also taught me something today," she began. "The feelings within you are yours and only yours, the Kur-ne is simply a director that leads you toward your destination . . . but it is you, who must study it out, feel it, and choose to follow the path."

Again, Ethan thought he heard her voice tremble, as if choking back tears. He looked into her glistening eyes and saw something he didn't fully intend to see, as if subconsciously, he could now see directly into her soul. He felt warmth inside of his chest, but he didn't know why. It was all so confusing, yet until this moment, he had only experienced such clarity of mind once before—at his binding with Seon.

The drake snuggled closer to Ethan, feeling the same warmth. The two of them shared the experience.

In fact, Ethan felt as if he were waking up from a long sleepless night as pure intelligence flowed through him. More so, he sensed this clarity in Seon's mind as well—they both knew what they had to do next.

The queen must have also realized what was happening as she reached out to cradle Ethan's hands in hers. "Then, the prophecy is true. You will make things right, Ethan . . . you will!"

*Ask now, Ethan. Ask now!* Seon prodded.

Ethan couldn't hold his questions in any longer, feeling now was the time he could finally get the answers he'd been seeking for. "What is the prophecy? What does it mean?" he asked in a longing tone.

The queen looked intently at him before answering. "Young Sheikh . . ."

Just then, the door behind them banged open as the king burst into the room. The queen stopped abruptly, ripping her hands away from Ethan. She stood up, and in an instant, her stoic countenance resumed, impenetrable, as if a great wall had just been cast up.

*Wow, we can't catch a break!* He sighed mournfully to Seon. Ethan was not going to get his answers now, if ever, he thought miserably. He stiffened even more as he saw the outrage plainly visible on the king's face. He also realized that Kristian, Lola, and Muschle were following directly behind him, and he gave them a questioning look.

Kristian shrugged and nodded at the king while rolling his eyes.

Ethan tried not to laugh, but caught the queen's glowering stare she shot at Muschle, who also stood behind the king, using the monarch as a giant shield.

"Are you all right, Queen Arsenath?" the king belted out. "How did those fiends gain entrance into our kingdom?" he demanded into the air.

Ethan felt a sudden twinge of bitterness and anger toward the king. The queen had never been in danger! Those *fiends* had attacked him, Kristian, and Lola, not the queen! He paused to consider his feelings of outrage that boiled up inside of him, much different from the calm he had experienced sheer moments before. He concluded that he didn't like the difference.

The queen spoke, interrupting Ethan's thoughts, "I am fine, my king. All is well. However, they were cloaked."

"Hmmph," the king croaked as he scratched at his beard. "Those imposters escaped before I could get my hands on them."

Ethan glanced back at the queen and thought he saw her controlled face contort in anger. A moment later, she had recomposed herself.

The king noticed the change in her countenance and walked to her side to comfort her. "I'm sure we will catch them. I've sent my best men to round them up . . . They cast hypnoses spells on the guards, who promptly escorted them out of the tower. Once they were free of our protection spells, they teleported. One, if not more of them were magi." He spat. "As was Shahir. How he made it into our good graces, I do not know. He passed all the tests," he said in a perplexed tone, completely baffled how his Kesem had failed him.

Ethan had heard of magis before from his grandpa's tales—and warnings. He searched his memories for their description . . . *Magis use their Kesem for self-gain. They are wicked and care for no one, giving themselves over completely to the Kesem and often cut themselves repeatedly to evoke emotion enabling them to enact their gruesome magic.* He remembered this stern lesson from Grandpa once when Ethan had been caught rummaging through an old caravan that apparently had belonged to a shady group of magi. Grandpa never cared much for them and spat at the ground whenever he saw one of them.

The queen turned to the king. "Then, it begins!" she said, her voice now filled with resolve. "We are exposed and must fight to defend our world!"

The king nodded without another word.

Kristian and Lola had now moved over to Ethan. They all felt out of place as they looked around the room at the strangers around them. They didn't fully grasp what was implied by the queen, but Ethan had a pretty good idea what they had been thrown into.

"We are going to war, aren't we?" he blurted out before he could stop himself.

The king looked up at him, as if questioning his motives, then nodded. "Yes, we are, Young Sheikh. Yes, we are." The king paused for a moment then continued on, "They are come for you. We will make our stand in your defense . . . as we have foreseen . . . !" The king wandered off in some thought for a few moments, looking at some invisible point in the corner of the room. Then he turned his attention back on Ethan. "They also come for the Kesem of this land. We will double our defenses. They cannot teleport in, only out, and that will soon be remedied." He looked at his guards with a determined look on his face. "The only entrance to our domain is through the Forbidden City, and that is where we will make our stand!"

Ethan felt his world crushing in around him. *War?* He was only fourteen, Kristian only slightly older, and Lola was so much younger. They couldn't go to war! This was much worse than being pressed into service. His mind whirled around him looking for a way out, some way they could continue on their quest that he'd only just discovered. He desperately yearned for the feeling of peace and warmth he had been feeling to come back and replace the growing sense of dread he now felt. But before he could decide on a course of action, Heramon appeared in the doorway.

*Heramon will know what to do!* Ethan gambled. Although he couldn't help but regret that he had brought folly down upon this kingdom for a moment. Heramon would help them fix this. He stood and started toward the warrior, then abruptly stopped when he saw someone else standing behind their protector.

Heramon wore a giant smile on his face. He looked perfectly composed, yet he was somehow different. He wore a look of complete confidence and happiness. He stepped aside, and Ethan saw who had followed Heramon into the room.

All of Ethan's fear and uncertainty instantly evaporated.

# Chapter 20

# Happy Reunion

*You don't really know what you have until you've lost and regained it again!*

"Grandpa!" Lola shrieked as she bolted for the elderly man and thrust herself into his arms. He laughed and picked her up, hugging her close to him as she squealed in excitement.

Ethan and Kristian grinned and walked over to him, both wanting to act the part of the adult. But the younger boy could barely hold back from launching himself at the old man.

Grandpa reached out with his other hand, first grasping their hands, followed by a fierce half hug for each of the children, as he drew them into him.

"Welcome!" the king and queen both beamed at the old man.

He kindly smiled in response. "Thank you, I am in your debt!" he said before turning his attention back to the children.

There was a moment of peaceful silence; then everyone burst out into a fury of questions all at once, each wanting to know of the other's story. In the commotion and torrent of the next few moments, Ethan forgot entirely about the king and queen. He glanced up and realized that they had left the room to allow the family a proper reunion. He thought little of it and went back to the matter at hand.

"But how did you find us?" Lola was now asking.

Grandpa gave her one of his paternal looks. "The gnomes directed me here. I have known them for quite some time now. Although"—he motioned for the children to all sit down—"we have kept our distance from each other, other than for important matters," he concluded.

"You know about the gnomes?" Kristian asked in disbelief.

The older man nodded. ". . . The Nejd is a dangerous place. It is important to know one's surroundings and inhabitants of any land."

Ethan knew their father figure was spinning up for another lecture, unless he could change the subject quickly. "Grandpa?" he asked.

The old man turned to give Ethan his attention.

"Who are they? Really?" the boy asked.

Kristian and Lola looked at Ethan then back at their beloved patriarch.

Grandpa frowned for a few moments then chose his words carefully. "They were once a great civilization, but alas, times change and they have lived, or rather survived, in this sanctuary for quite some time, hundreds of years in fact." The old man scraped at his beard in thought. "Some might even call the king and queen gods, by all accounts, they have wonderful powers, and the people of Qara hold them in high regard, as do I . . . as do I."

Ethan realized that Grandpa would be lost in his own thoughts if he didn't ask a follow-up question. "They've been kind to us . . . but this land is strange. I mean, the things that have happened to us . . . ," he paused.

Grandpa studied the young boy for a moment. "Yes, I imagine so, my boy. I would never overly trust them, Ethan, and I know that you haven't. Still, they have housed you because I asked them to look after you if ever there was need. They have been watching from a distance. Did they not find you at the cave and bring you here?"

The children looked at one another, and Ethan shook his head. "No, Grandpa." The wise old man had a lot of catching up to do.

For a spell, Grandpa and the children sat and discussed their adventures. Heramon stood by the fire, almost in the exact same position as the queen had with Ethan. He too poked absentmindedly at the fire with a metal rod, pretending not to listen. But Ethan saw him strain to overhear the finer points of the conversation and heard him grunt a few times when Grandpa asked a follow-on question.

A number of times, both Ethan and Kristian had to override Lola, as she went too far with her descriptions. Kristian passed it off as the over imagination of an eleven-year-old girl. Lola was too excited to notice, which made it easier to skip her comments and continue to the end of their story.

After the children had rehearsed their experience, careful to leave out the secret parts as they went along and keep it consistent with what they had told Heramon, Grandpa sat back with a look of amazement on his face. Ethan could tell he was trying to take it all in and make sense of it. They all intently watched him in silence for a while with expectant looks on their faces.

The fire burned and crackled behind them as Heramon poked at it to stir up the flames. There was the feeling of energy in the room, but none of the children dared interrupt it, waiting on what Grandpa would say next. But he simply sat there, meditating.

"Grandpa . . . ?" Ethan finally inquired, interrupting the silence. He tried to think of the best way to ask the question. "I . . . I don't understand why they're . . ." Ethan gulped. "Why they're after me!" He looked at the others, then quickly corrected, "I mean us. Why are they after us?"

At this mention, Heramon abandoned all pretense and strode over to the little group.

Grandpa sat up and sighed. "Why?" He looked at Ethan. "No, it isn't your fault, Ethan. It is the prophecy!"

Ethan looked intently at the older man, but knew that nothing more was coming about the prophecy. He couldn't take it any longer. His patience could only go for so long. "Why is it always later with the prophecy? Limnah wouldn't tell me, you won't tell me, the queen couldn't tell me . . ." He winced.

"What prophecy?" Kristian now joined in. "I've never heard of any prophecy. What am I missing?"

Grandpa pulled at a tuft of his beard, as he always did when deep in thought. "Ethan, we need to get you out. Once we do, I will explain. But first, we need to find some way to defend this people. I fear we have brought this down upon their heads . . ." Grandpa paused again, the suspense was killing Ethan.

"Someone will need to remain behind and help them—after their gracious hospitality," Grandpa announced. His face suddenly showed a firm resolve. "Someone will need to stay back to create a diversion, a diversion for Ethan." Grandpa furrowed his brow. "Besides, the gnomes have served us well these last few days, as they have done for our family in times past."

"Wait, in times past?" Ethan asked. He still didn't fully grasp why he was the center of all of the attention, but what did Grandpa mean with his last comment? What did he mean in times past?

"Our family?" Kristian piled on. "And I still haven't heard a good answer about any prophecy!"

"Aye, our family!" Grandpa replied. "And, Kristian, you will all know of the prophecy soon enough. The gnomes helped us to Julfa when we first left the great cities." The children all sat forward, hanging on every word. He rarely talked of their life before Julfa.

"We were lost in the Nejd—I thought we could take a shortcut in our hasty retreat from the city. But I was wrong, dead wrong. I ventured into an area I did not know. If it weren't for them." Grandpa paused. "Well, it would have ended badly. They took us in and nourished us, the king and queen offered us refuge, but we needed to move on to Julfa. Once we were strong enough, they escorted us to the outskirts of the village . . . ," Grandpa trailed off. He often only shared bits and pieces with the children of their life before the village, and they knew that once he had ended the story, there was no getting more out of him.

"Why don't we remember any of this?" Kristian complained, before Ethan and Lola broke out in a chorus of chatter.

"Now, now, I know that you do not remember. Your childhood events were traumatic for you and it is understandable that you don't remember." The old man tried to sooth.

*He's holding something back!* Ethan thought in dismay. *Why is he holding back on this and the prophecy?*

*He must have his reasons to protect you,* Seon answered.

The boy shot the drake a frustrated look. *I don't need protection!* He fumed. *I need answers!*

Before Seon could respond, Heramon cleared his throat and spoke, "It is not safe for you here, sir. I propose that you make a retreat . . . for the children's sake." He added, seeing Grandpa's face darken. "I'm strong enough to stay behind and fight in battle. I am more than worthy to perform this task in your place as a distraction," he volunteered, bowing his head slightly.

Ethan had never seen Heramon address his grandpa in this way before. He knew that Heramon had taken a liking to Grandpa and that Grandpa had taken the man into their home, nursed him back to health, and all. But he now questioned if Grandpa hadn't known Heramon before, before Julfa. He shot Kristian a questioning look.

The older boy wasn't paying attention to his younger brother.

"Hmmm. I cannot argue with you, Heramon. But it is not an easy task I leave you with," the old man answered.

Heramon nodded. "It would be my greatest honor!" he replied.

Kristian suddenly cleared his throat, determined to cast in his voice.

The old man was still deep in thought and didn't notice.

*What is he up to?* Ethan thought in a worried tone. *Seon, I don't like this at all. He isn't going to . . .*

The eldest boy made a fist, raising it to his mouth, and cleared his throat again, this time loud enough for everyone to hear.

Grandpa glanced up at the interruption.

"I . . . I will also stay!" Kristian blurted out.

Ethan's face flushed bright red as he stared at his brother in disbelief.

"No . . ." Heramon and Ethan gasped together.

"Let him speak." Grandpa raised a hand, nodding his head in thought before responding, "Kristian, you are now a man. The decision is yours. I will not stand in your way . . . however, if you fall into the hands of the enemy, it could be very dangerous."

"But, Grandpa . . . !" Ethan started.

"Kristian will remain behind with Heramon." The old man concluded, overriding Ethan. He looked at their two would-be saviors. "Heramon, keep him safe from harm's way, you are his protector." He turned to look at Kristian. "Kristian, I leave you with my blessing. Seek the goodness in your heart, remember what you have been taught, and you will return to us, again."

Ethan sat in a total stupor. His mind went rigid and blank.

Seon remained completely silent, but tried to support the boy as best he could.

Ethan desperately needed some reassurance right now, feeling immense guilt over being the single cause of war, bloodshed, and now his brother was rushing into its deadly embrace. *And what if Kristian . . . ?* Ethan couldn't bear to think about it any further. His concern turned to anger *It's selfish! Of course he would do this to us!* Ethan grumbled that his

# Happy Reunion

brother would choose such a foolish path. However, he didn't have time to mull it over in his mind though.

"It is settled then!" Grandpa concluded. "Lola and Ethan will come with me. We will leave at sunrise. But first, I must seek audience with the king and queen," he added in a thoughtful tone. "Muschle is directly outside of the room. He will escort you back to his home." He motioned to Ethan and Lola. "Heramon and Kristian will remain behind with me."

"We will join you shortly," he added as he saw the indignant looks of disdain on Ethan's and Lola's faces.

They all slowly stood. Kristian made to hug his younger brother, but Ethan pushed him away. Kristian's face looked hurt, but Ethan didn't want to dwell on it at this point. He needed to think in peace, somewhere away from his brother to resolve his bitter feelings. *Why didn't he tell me he was thinking about this?* he fumed in frustration, even though there was no warning and Kristian couldn't have told Ethan beforehand anyway. *He's gonna get himself killed,* Ethan continued. *And I can't be there to protect him! We all just got back together! We were supposed to go home as a family! He is so selfish! He can't leave us!* His anger was replaced by remorse.

Seon didn't answer, letting Ethan work through his anguish. But the little drake nuzzled more closely to the boy to comfort him.

Muschle escorted Ethan and Lola back to his quarters in silence. Ethan walled everything out including Seon, trying to think out a plan, some plan that would fix this whole mess he had gotten them into.

Lola was also somber and quiet, only briefly answering some of Muschle's questions, as they marched along.

They reached Muschle's home and proceeded to the dining room, where they ate a silent meal. By this time, Muschle had registered something was wrong and had stopped asking questions or trying to make small talk. After supper, the children retired to their bedroom and sat on their beds quietly.

*Seon?* Ethan finally asked.

*Yes?*

*I've been thinking about . . . about today. We need to finish the quest. We need to tell Grandpa. It's up to us now—you and me. I realize that now . . . Kristian must find his own way, even if it means . . .* , he trailed off, choking back a sudden sob.

*We need to read the Kur-ne again,* the drake suggested.

*I know,* Ethan agreed as he reached into his pocket to caress the orb. The ball was smooth and cool to his touch, as always. He didn't feel any fear for it anymore, only respect. The queen had helped him to realize its potential. The queen, he suddenly realized. What was to become of her?

The Drake Epics - Journey to Qara

He desperately hoped that Qara, Heramon, and Kristian would be safe. But the queen was on his mind as well, and he wasn't exactly sure why.

*I think the queen is more than she has led us to believe*, Seon said after a moment's quiet.

The boy nodded his head. He wasn't quite sure of what she was, but he at least knew that she wasn't human.

"Ethan?" Lola had quietly made her way to the end of her bed so that she had a clear view of her brother.

The older boy turned to look at his sister, surprised by the interruption. He'd almost forgotten she was in the room. "Hi, Lola." He feigned a quick smile.

"What's going to happen to Heramon . . . and to Kristian?" She wore a concerned look on her face.

Ethan turned back to look at his hands. "I don't know, Lola," he said sheepishly.

She slipped out of bed and walked over to her brother. She had to jump up, taking a seat beside him on his bed. Her feet dangled off the floor, and she absently kicked them back and forth. "I'm scared . . . Deseret is scared." She almost sobbed. "But she's been teaching me to be brave."

A smile spread across Ethan's lips as he looked down at his sister. They hugged each other as Ethan patted her back. "It will be all right, Lola," he consoled. "Heramon will protect Kristian. It will all be alright. Now, off to bed," he said as he helped her back onto the ground.

She looked at him for a few moments then turned and walked back around the bed and climbed into her soft blankets. She fell asleep quickly enough.

Ethan focused his attention on the orb that he had now drawn out of his pocket. He needed to know what was next. He took a deep breath then closed his eyes to draw on his power, focusing on the orb. He felt the same drain from the previous night and opened his eyes to look into the Kur-ne.

—  —  —

The familiar bright stars, Gnolaum, as the orb called them, shone within the orb. Ethan wasn't quite sure how he knew these things—only that the orb's bond with him was similar to what he shared with Seon and the queen. Similar, yet different.

The Kur-ne immediately drew the boy into the sphere, racing through the Gnolaum, as the earth approached him with dizzying speed. He saw the sun, Shinehah, and the moon, Olea, as he hurtled past them.

He soared through the skies. It felt more exhilarating the second time, he admitted. It wasn't such a surprise this time and gave him the opportunity to scan his surroundings. A bright flash of light pulsed in front of him, and he was now gliding over the same earthy ground, falling through the sky and bursts of clouds until he reached the ground. The earth swallowed him as he fell through sand and rock, as though they did not exist, and all was dark.

The darkness evaporated as he tumbled through emptiness and into a burning light so bright that it seared his eyes to look at it. He could feel the scorching heat all around him that would just as soon envelope him in its deadly embrace, and he desperately wanted to scream out in anticipation of the pain. Then, just as suddenly as the light had appeared, it was gone and he felt the immensity of open space.

Ethan opened his eyes and saw a sandy expanse below him that he now realized was Qara. He ventured a look around and recognized Qara's sun-orb directly above him. He must have fallen through it in his descent.

As he neared the ground, he slowed and hovered for a moment before his feet touched down. All around him, he recognized the familiar scenery of Qara. The palace tower rose directly in front of him, its glass spires jutting up from its bulky foundation.

The queen and king stood by his side, along with an entourage of gnomes, lions, Heramon, and his family. The king was shaking his head, his face drawn up into a profound grimace. He was muttering in a language Ethan didn't understand; however, he somehow caught bits and pieces of the sermon. The king was not thrilled that Ethan, Lola, and Grandpa were leaving, as it risked destruction. Destruction of what, the boy could not glean. But he understood it likely meant the destruction of Qara and its people, of the beautiful landscape, and of the Kesem that held the landscape intact.

He had no time to ponder this mystery further. He was airborne again. Heramon and Kristian were waving as he left, and Ethan felt a twinge of regret and longing for the other boy, as well as a deep-seated fear that he would never see his older brother again. But, he had not time to dwell on this as he burst through the top of Qara and sifted to the surface, opening to the azure-colored sky above.

Shinehah glared garishly down upon him, scolding him for his absence, and he closed his eyes to adjust to her brightness. He squinted around him and recognized the familiar bleak landscape of the Forbidden City below. His ascent slowed, and he again hovered a few hundred paces above the ground. He twisted his body around to see behind him. The

The Drake Epics - Journey to Qara

sight made him recoil in horror. Dark, ominous clouds rolled in from all directions, threatening to block out Shinehah and her sunlight altogether.

Upon the plateau above the Forbidden City stretched a jumble of tents, people, wolves, and other animals as far as his eyes could see. Little black forms peppered the landscape, and wisps of smoke curled upward from hundreds of fires. They looked like a colony of ants moving about, so that the surface of the land perpetually moved.

Ethan studied them more closely. He could see preparations of monstrous wooden carts, of which he had no idea what they would be used for. Most of the figures, people and animals, appeared to be dressed in armor, their metallic suits glinting from the sun's rays. Then the severity of the scene suddenly hit him. *They are . . . they are warriors!* Ethan gasped.

He strained to think about what it all meant. They were preparing for war, *Not just any war.* He wildly twisted his body back again and looked in front of him. In the distance, he could clearly make out a gigantic hole in the ground that appeared bluish in the daylight as the sun didn't reach all the way into its depths. He couldn't see the bottom from his vantage point, but he already knew in his heart that the Forbidden City lay at its floor and, farther in, the land of Qara!

The boy turned back toward the encampment to study it again, perhaps to catch some detail, some weakness—anything that might give Heramon and his brother the advantage, *At least a fighting chance?* As he surveyed the moving masses, the orb opened his understanding, and he thought he saw familiar forms moving among them; but could he be sure that the figures were his people of Julfa? He determined to find out more. He had to be certain. However, the harder he concentrated on the picture, the more the panorama faded from his sight. Eventually, a deep mist settled about him; and in an instant, all forms were shrouded from his view.

The mist cleared and the landscape showed no sign of the war preparations. He was now closer to the gaping hole in the earth, even though he still couldn't see the valley floor. He briefly wondered to himself how deep the valley really was. But before he could do the little geometry he knew from Ezera's teachings, he was again interrupted, as columns of soldiers appeared out of nowhere and marched into the crater.

A stray thought struck him and he suddenly remembered his brief military lessons back at Julfa. The leader was always at the head of his armies. He studied the lead column, and at their head was a rider, the only rider, in fact, a dark rider on a dark horse. Ethan shook his head to clear his thoughts and looked again, in case his mind was playing games with him. There was no denying that the rider was the *inquisitor!* It made no sense. "Why? How?" he asked aloud to the emptiness.

357

Again, he didn't have time to study the situation as the vision dimmed. "No," he cried out, followed by, "wait . . . please wait." His attention instead turned in the opposite direction as he soared above the rolling dunes, slowly at first, then with quick bursts of speed. The air sounded like a thousand rushing rivers followed by a sonic boom, and everything whirred by him, unrecognizable at his growing velocity. Soon, the landscape became streaks of browns and yellows for a time.

Finally, he slowed enough to get some bearing, realizing that he was approaching more cliffs. He leapt over them to see mountain after mountain stretch out in front of him—some with strange white tops that rose into the sky and above the clouds. The sight lasted only a moment, and he broke into another burst of speed as the landscape again whirred unrecognizably by him.

He slowed yet again, and the mountains dropped away from him into a sea. *The Abseron Sea!* he sighed as the thought reached him. How he had longed to see its beauty and explore its shores. He rushed over the breaking waves and out into an open stretch of water. But soon he approached another beach and beyond that, a sandy wasteland. Yet this bleak expanse was somehow different than those he had seen before. In the distance, there stood a solitary grove. Not just any grove, a grove of white trees—the trees from his dreams!

A quick flash of light forced him to close his eyes. When he opened them, he was standing in the midst of the white orchard. The rest of his previous dreams flashed before his eyes in fast-forward—the grove, the sandstorm, the dragon—until he was now standing in front of the two figures he had seen before, both in dream and in person: the king and queen of Qara.

"I don't understand. How did you get here? How did you journey to this place?" he asked in an attempt to grasp the meaning.

"You've eaten of the fruit?" the queen asked.

He nodded sheepishly, although he didn't know why he did so. He had no recollection of eating any fruit. As he looked down, he realized that he held the fruit in his hand, half-eaten. Ethan blinked, looking up into her soft eyes.

The queen was somehow different from his last dream, different from his meeting with her. She had an eerie glow about her, and he thought for a brief moment that he saw the trees right through her, as if she were an apparition.

The queen spoke again, pulling Ethan out of his trance, "Now! Now you must battle the dragon. You and Seon! Only you two together can defeat the dragon . . . the great black chaos dragon, Tiamat."

# The Drake Epics - Journey to Qara

Ethan recoiled in fear. He was utterly confused and lost. The dragon of his dreams? The dragon was too great! He couldn't possibly. It wasn't real.

"There you may find the grove . . . ," the queen urged. "There, you may yet find peace for us all . . ."

- - -

A sudden clatter awoke Ethan as he jolted up in his bed. The room was perfectly dark, except for a dim glow directly surrounding the door. Ethan waited for his eyes to adjust to the darkness and saw a shadow moving on the other side of the room. Kristian had just entered.

*Ethan, are you all right?* came Seon's familiar thoughts into his mind.

*Yes,* he answered. *How long was I out?* he asked.

*Half the night . . . Did you get the answers? Do we have a direction?*

Ethan nodded his head and knew that Seon could see him in the dark. He shared his stream of conscience with his small companion to mull over then excused himself. *I need to talk to Kristian.*

Seon acknowledged and patiently withdrew any further questions.

"Kristian?" Ethan said, as he silently crept to his brother's side.

The older boy spun around in surprise, half-drawing a sword.

BeeSting also raised his head and spread his wings at the sudden interruption. The red drake nestled back down as soon as he realized it was Ethan, lifting a wing to preen before retiring for the night.

Ethan raised his hands in mock surrender.

Kristian sighed. "Don't do that, Dingus!" he grumbled before sheathing the sword. He seemed unusually tense.

Ethan could now see his face as he neared the older boy. The ambient light cascaded through the door magnifying the older boy's features, and his nose in particular. Ethan restrained a soft chuckle as he looked at his brother's appearance. "I see you have a new toy," he offered, trying to breach the awkward silence that followed.

The would-be solider nodded and grinned with pride. "The king gave it to me as a gift for staying . . . um . . . defending Qara." He paused, a bit unsure of himself, before launching into the sword's description. "It's a sickle sword. It's enchanted! Look how it glows red." He beamed. "He also gave me an armored cloak, a magical sling, and the coolest helmet I've ever seen! Also enchanted," he added out of pride. Kristian turned slowly for Ethan to show his younger brother the armor he wore, while placing the helmet over his head. "Well?" He thrust his arms out while turning in a circle as if starring in his own personal fashion show.

Ethan nodded with a big smile and quietly clapped. Then, he grabbed at his brother's cloak. Upon closer inspection, it was made of a sturdy leather that plummeted to Kristian's ankles and had a shiny brass strap affixed around his neck. Small metal disks with raised spines were sown across the entire cloak, giving it the armor-like appearance. The meta-studded cloak was impressive. It must have been fairly heavy as Ethan noted that Kristian was slightly hunched over.

Next, Kristian pointed at the helmet, made of exquisite bronze that shaped down his face and around the back of his head. It boasted a round top that lowered just above the ear, followed by a pronounced band around the entire helmet and an embossed ear with a hole through which he could hear commands through. The helmet glowed green. "It has healing qualities!" he announced.

"The best of all is the sword though!" Kristian unsheathed his sword, swinging it at the air. "It's enchanted with a fire rune!" he exclaimed, pointing to a glowing red rune etched into its hilt.

Ethan admired the gifts. They were kingly gifts for sure. He suddenly felt a twinge of envy that Kristian was staying and had to quickly suppress it before he could think more of it.

The two boys stood silently for a moment in an awkward silence; then both abandoned all pretence and launched into the day's events, letting their excitement get the better of them. They forgot all about potential eavesdropping from their benefactors.

Kristian recounted what had happened with the king. He gave details about the king's plans, about the war preparations and the queen's calming influence, of Grandpa and Heramon laying out methods of attack, and finally of the king's gifts to both Heramon and Kristian.

"Heramon?" Ethan raised an eyebrow with interest.

Kristian nodded. "Heramon received a magical bow," he said uninterestedly. "It has two runes, one for distance and the other for frost, A green cloak of near-invisibility and a horn of some kind . . . ," he trailed off.

"Ethan?" he continued. It was clear that he wanted to talk about something different.

The younger boy looked at his brother expectantly.

"I know it came as a surprise today . . . but . . ." He looked like he was grasping for an explanation.

Ethan knew where his brother was going with this and drew up the courage to recite his practiced apology about his behavior earlier that day, "Look, Kristian . . . I . . . I was angry that you were staying behind. I know that you've always wanted to be the soldier . . . I just don't want to lose my brother." He choked back a sudden sob that he didn't expect and forced himself onward. "I need you to be . . . careful. There is a strange magic about this war . . ." He stopped short, vulnerably looking up at his brother.

Kristian looked like he was about to respond, but stopped short and gazed intently at his younger brother with a surprised expression etched into his face.

Ethan couldn't tell if the older boy was touched by this last confession or not.

In one quick motion, Kristian grabbed Ethan and pulled him into a bear hug. "I love you too, little brother. Don't worry, Grandpa has taught us to believe in a higher power, and we should trust in his words," he said before releasing the other boy and pushing him to arm's length. "Don't ask me how I know about Mom or what she taught us because I don't know how, I just know that she would want us to be strong, wherever she is!" Kristian consoled.

Ethan was taken aback by Kristian's comments about their mother. The children rarely mentioned their parents if at all, and then only in the tenderest of tones they could muster. He only recalled very vague memories of her. But the memories were scratchy, as if they came in and out of focus only long enough for him to sense she was real. Sometimes the memories were painful, but sometimes they consoled him to think of her maternal love for him.

"Now get some rest," the older boy said. "We have a big day ahead of us tomorrow. We will be back in Julfa before you know it. Grandpa has it all planned out for our return," he said. "I promise we'll be OK," he assured.

Ethan desperately wanted to tell his brother about his own dreams and that things would turn out a little differently to be sure. Yet something held him back. He knew that he had to tell Grandpa though. So he simply nodded and stumbled in the semidarkness toward his bed. Ethan drew the covers over his head, wiping sudden hot tears from his eyes. Would he ever see his brother again?

# Chapter 21

## Tearful Farewell

*Saying goodbye is always hard!*

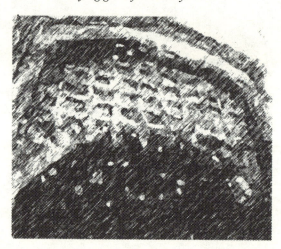

Morning came all too quickly. Ethan awoke just before dawn, feeling strangely renewed, probably because of his resolve to speak with his patriarch, or maybe it was the bed. Either way, he knew that he shouldn't be feeling this way, especially on a day like this.

Seon was already awake, grooming himself in the early-morning.

Ethan quickly reviewed the Kur-ne's latest instructions with the drake and clarified gaps in the consciousness that he had shared with his companion on the previous night.

Seon sat quietly listening to the story.

*I think that I'm not only seeing the direction, but I'm seeing bits and pieces of the future,* the boy thought excitedly.

*We must tell your grandpa. But . . .*

*But, what?* Ethan thought. *Don't hold back on me now.* He encouraged.

*I just feel that we need to be extra careful of what you seek through the Kur-ne. It is never good to see too much of the future!* the little drake warned. *Dangerous to see any of it!* he corrected. *You must control yourself, Ethan,* Seon counseled like a scolding parent.

The boy grumbled.

*Remember your dreams before this. Do you want all of those to come true? That is a heavy weight to know of, to have no control to change it and to carry that around all the time,* Seon persisted.

Ethan realized the drake was right and nodded his head in defeat. He quickly, quietly dressed and slipped out of the room to find Grandpa. He stole one last glance to see if he had awakened Lola or Kristian. Both lay perfectly still.

Seon nimbly flew across the room to take up his perch on Ethan's shoulder, and the boy quietly shut the door behind him.

He walked down the hallway. *Kristian told me last night that Grandpa is just down the hall from Heramon's room.* He passed Heramon's door and softly knocked at the next door, hoping it was the right room.

He heard Grandpa clear his throat from somewhere inside and hoarsely croak, "Come in."

Ethan slowly opened the door and peeked his head inside.

Grandpa was sitting on the bed, pulling his sandals onto his feet. He looked up and smiled as Ethan entered. "Ethan, come in, come in. Good morning to you." He beamed, but Ethan could already tell his grandpa was hiding something by the tone in his voice. "I'm afraid that as you grow older, it is much harder to dress yourself." The old man chuckled, as he struggled with one of his sandals.

Ethan took a deep breath, peered at Seon, and then quietly shut the door behind him. As he strode to where Grandpa sat and glanced about the room. It looked identical to the room that the three children were staying in, only a little smaller.

"Ah ha!" The old man said, as he successfully slid the sandal into place and looked up. He patted a spot on the bed next to him. "Sit here my son. What seems to be on your mind?"

The young boy paused, looking around the room again, not fully trusting his surroundings, before deciding on his next course of action.

"Grandpa," he announced, "I need to cast a protective barrier around us. I need to tell you something."

A moment of silence followed as Grandpa stared up at the boy, puzzled for a moment, then sighed in resignation. "You've been talking to Heramon much too much. We are quite safe. I can assure you of that." He smiled and patted the spot to sit again.

Ethan sat down reflexively, then stood back up. "Grandpa, I need to do this!" He had learned to trust the queen, he couldn't say the same of the king; and at this point, he wasn't quite sure of who was listening in on what he had to say. He gave the older man as serious of a look as he could muster, but ended with a look of pleading.

The wise old man stared intently at the boy for a few moments, his face was stoic and unmoved.

Ethan was sure a lecture was coming, but he saw a slight curl of a smile in the old man's lips.

"Do what you must." Grandpa finally nodded, acknowledging the boy's request.

Ethan reached inside himself for his energy, found it quickly, and muttered some word he made up. He cast a blue crackling shield around them, shrouding them in a protective sound vacuum.

Grandpa whistled then slowly stood to admire Ethan's handiwork. "Well done, my boy, well done. You have learned much indeed." Grandpa tilted his head to and fro with a giant smile on his lips and reached out to touch the barrier.

Ethan looked at Seon again, pleading silently with the drake to avoid the oncoming discussion, then took another deep breath and readied for the plunge.

*Go on, Ethan, we have to tell someone. Your grandpa is as good as any, if you truly trust him.* Seon nodded in the direction of the old man.

Taking another deep breath, Ethan swallowed hard. He had to know if he were talking to the *real* grandpa, and not some magi, for all he knew. Besides, this was what the queen had previously instructed him to do. He tried to block this thought from Seon, in anticipation of the drake's reproach. He hated to do this, but he had to know. He found the familiar strength within him, the power came faster now.

Seon felt something was off and reached out to Ethan asking what he was doing.

Ethan sensed the concern and quickly drove the drake's question out of his mind.

Grandpa touched the barricade again and let out a boyish "ahhh." It fizzled and sparked as he did so. He was oblivious to what Ethan was doing. Or was he? The thought lingered for a moment in Ethan's mind, then vanished.

Reaching out to pull some memory from Grandpa, Ethan selected a random memory that they both shared. It didn't matter what it was, he would let the Kesem decide. It would only be a moment. Grandpa would never notice . . .

- - -

Instantly, Ethan was standing in a strange land with towering green trees. Grandpa was by his side looking much the same, but dressed differently than he had ever seen before. To his surprise, a much younger-looking version of the boy stood just to the other side of the older man, also dressed differently.

*This can't be right.* He thought to himself. But, deep down, he knew that this was a memory they both shared. Yet, somehow, Ethan had forgotten this. *How is this possible?* He thought.

They were standing at a river's edge, holding long, *fishing poles?* Ethan remembered hearing of such things from caravan story tellers before. He'd always thought that nets would be much easier. *But, I've never fished with a pole before, have I?* The answer came to him that he had.

Confused, he pressed on. Suddenly, his younger self caught something and squawked with delight. "I caught one grandpa, I caught one!" he shrieked.

"Reel it in son. That's it don't fight it too much." The old man had set his own pole down and was guiding the young boy through the process. "That's it." He repeated, "Carefully, carefully . . . Now yank!"

The younger boy threw his pole backwards and a fish, attached to the pole's line flew out of the water and onto the beach.

Ethan had seen such things before, but by the time they reached Julfa, the caravans had dried the fish out and they were leathery and wrinkled compared to what they should look like. He momentarily marveled at how round they were and so full of life. Even their scales sparkled.

"Good job, Ethan. That is a fine catch!" the old man commended. He presently dehooked the fish and set to cleaning it out in the river.

His younger version had a look of expectation on his face, completely drawn to what Grandpa was doing.

After a few moments of staring and exchanging a barrage of questions and answers between the youth and his grandfather, the old man turned to the much younger boy. He looked over at him with gentle eyes. "Ethan," he said in a reverent, loving tone.

Ethan turned to peer into his grandpa's eyes with an elated smile etched into his face.

Grandpa wiped his hands and put the fish on a tethered line in the river. He grabbed both of the boy's shoulders to speak to him, "Ethan, one day you will be mighty, and you will do things . . . amazing things . . . beyond your wildest dreams. The dreams of an emperor!" he laughed, "I love you, son . . . your parents love you, son. Always remember that!"

The discussion ended in an embrace as Grandpa drew the younger version of Ethan into his arms.

- - -

Ethan abruptly withdrew from the memory, blinking to pull himself back into the present. He realized that his eyes were wide open, and he tried to adjust to the ambient light in the room. He felt a lone hot tear roll down his left check and wondered briefly why his emotions weren't completely in check.

He had a vague memory of that experience that lingered before starting to evaporate. He felt that this was the first time he really knew Grandpa's love for him.

The old man had turned to face Ethan and was intently studying the boy with a tender smile on his face.

*How long has it been?* Ethan prodded Seon.

*Only an instant . . . but . . . I sense that your grandpa knows you were in his mind*, the drake replied in a scolding tone. *I still feel you should stay out of other people's minds!* The drake stuck out his tongue and turned his head in the other direction in disgust.

Ethan half-ignored the comment to avoid his own conscience, but the damage had already been done. He cleared his throat and looked away from his grandpa in shame, while fidgeting with his hands.

"There is no reason to be ashamed, my son. I let you in," Grandpa stated flatly as he again took his seat next to the boy.

Ethan looked up in shock.

*You're right, Seon! He knows! But . . . how?*

*You cannot treat such actions lightly, Ethan! This is what I've been trying to tell you!* the drake scolded again.

"I can block mind attacks if I need to, but you needed to know it was me, and now you know." Grandpa reached out and patted Ethan on the arm. "Now you know," he repeated gently.

"But how . . . ?"

"How did I know of your abilities? Well, call it a grandpa's intuition. I know what you are capable of becoming . . . ," his voice trailed off into some distant vision.

Ethan's mind was swimming again. Had Grandpa known all along? His mind raced back to Limnah's quarters upon their first encounter and Grandpa's look of shock when he purposefully sabotaged the commands to Seon. He looked back at his hands in even more shame at the thought of the memory.

His mind lingered on it for a few moments then jumped to the next conclusions from their recent mental exchange. Grandpa knew precisely where Ethan had been in his thoughts. But how could he have known? Ethan looked deeper into his grandpa's eyes, looking for some hint he could latch onto; perhaps he could drag it out of the old man by sheer willpower. Yet, all he could see was an endless eternity behind those eyes. They were dark and devoid of any further information, at least for the time being.

The older man suddenly shifted on the bed, crossing one leg over the other. He placed a hand on the back of the bedpost and sighed. "There are many things that you don't know, my boy. Things you must learn. But I have a feeling that you'll catch on quickly enough. You always were a fast learner." He turned and smiled at Ethan again.

*Tell him, Ethan. Tell him everything*, Seon prodded.

Ethan mentally shrugged off the comment. He had too many other questions filling his mind.

"Grandpa . . . ," he began, but still a little unsure of himself. He reached deeper for the courage to continue and swallowed. "Grandpa, I need to know who I am . . . and . . . and what's happening to me," he finished and looked away.

Seon grunted at the snub.

The boy felt the drake momentarily withdraw from his thoughts, but he'd be back soon enough. Ethan knew he would have to make amends with his little companion later.

Grandpa nodded in understanding and sighed.

Ethan felt the patriarch's love for him, and it was a fair-enough question that he had asked. But he knew deep down by Grandpa's expression that he wasn't going to get the answer he wanted.

The old man contemplated the question before answering. "You have much to do . . . as your adventures . . . no . . . as your *quest* unfolds. The answers will come to you. It will all happen in time . . . You will learn more of yourself . . . of emperors . . . of prophecies." Grandpa looked toward the window.

A bee busily flew into the room, studying the environment, before speeding toward a vase of flowers resting on the inside window ledge. Grandpa stood in anticipation and started to stroll toward the window before remembering about the crackling barrier around the two. He again admired the shield with hands outstretched before refocusing on the bee, now actively collecting pollen from one of the biggest flowers in the vase. "Ethan . . . I wish you to be as steady and dedicated as that bee, always abounding in good works—that *your* work will bring forth fruit and sweet honey . . . that your path may be in the service of others."

*Ugghhh, rhyme!* the boy thought to Seon as he rolled his eyes. Grandpa had an annoying tendency to break into verse every now and then. But suddenly, he had another unintentional thought. Grandpa had lost all of the beehives. It had been his lifelong passion collecting and building hives, and now, it might be all gone. Ethan had been so preoccupied thinking of himself and his own challenges, he had not thought of Grandpa's feelings, or anyone else's feelings. His mind now spun an image of Kristian and Lola losing everything they held dear. He yearned for this all to end, for their safe return to Julfa. He had brought folly upon his family because of his own selfishness. If only he had kept his whit about him in front of Hem and Yeb. He hastily thrust his own issues aside in desperation to bury his mounting guilt.

Grandpa turned and smiled at the boy as if he knew the boy's thoughts.

Ethan tried to look away again, his guilt still too fresh within his own mind. But he locked eyes with the old man and noted an intense longing in his guardian's countenance. The intensity surprised him, and he couldn't bring himself to break the gaze.

"They thrive because they work together . . . ," the wise old man continued. "No matter what the challenges or struggles that lay ahead of them. No mists of darkness to block their way that they are lost in forbidden paths or lack of water or lack of pollen to hunger or thirst after. No ferocious attacks upon their very hive can deter them from their duty. They push on, they find a way, they create and rebuild."

Grandpa maintained his gaze with Ethan for a few moments longer then looked back at the bee still busily buzzing around the flowers. As man and boy watched the intrepid worker, the bee finished its task, and upon finding no more flowers to pollinate, zipped out of the window.

Ethan suddenly felt Seon back in his thoughts again. He welcomed the warmth that he now realized had been missing in the drake's mental absence.

*He's right, Ethan. Will you tell him now? Tell him the entire story!* Seon rebuked the boy for not listening to him the first time.

Finally, Ethan nodded in agreement. *Yes, Seon!* He half-grinned at his companion's impatience. *I will.* He felt Seon beam in approval.

"Grandpa? I have a story to tell you," he began slowly. "The complete story," he added, looking up at Grandpa submissively.

For the first time since his discovery of Seon, Ethan was going to tell someone else of his story from beginning to end. A nervous anxiety surged within him, but he sucked up his courage and waded through it one sentence at a time.

Grandpa took a seat again and listened intently for the duration.

Ethan started at the beginning.

Much to his relief, Grandpa didn't stop him at any point in the tale. He listened with an interested gaze, nodding his head and grunting from time to time. Ethan told him about Seon and Deseret's discovery, his recurring dreams, the air scroll, even about his Kesem's mental abilities and all details of the children's flight through the water, the Forbidden City, and the journey into Qara. Lastly, he revealed the Kur-ne, holding it out for Grandpa to study. As the old man peered into the translucent orb, Ethan told Grandpa about his discussion with the queen and of the prophecy. "That is why I want to know of the prophecy and my part in it," he concluded. "I've been searching for some meaning in all of this, and the harder I look, the harder it is to find."

Then Ethan sat there for what seemed an eternity, awaiting Grandpa's reply. A flood of relief washed over him. He felt as if a great load were suddenly removed from him, taking in a deep, renewing breath. He felt free for the first time in a long while.

Grandpa continued to quietly caress the ball in his hands, deep in his own thoughts.

Ethan barely noticed the time pass as he reveled in his newfound freedom—a gigantic smile painted across his face.

*Ethan, are you going to tell him about your dream last night?* Seon interrupted.

*Oh . . . I forgot about that. You're right, Seon, we need to warn him about it. Thank you!* He reached up and rubbed the drake below his chin. Seon purred in response.

"There's more, Grandpa . . . ," Ethan added as the old man glanced up at him. He quickly recounted the dream and the army advancing on Qara with the inquisitor at its head.

Looking at him without surprise, as if he'd already known about this, the old man spoke. "Then the pieces are placed and the events are finally set in motion," Grandpa said more to himself rather than to Ethan as he reached up to run his fingers through his thick beard.

Ethan didn't quite catch what Grandpa meant. "What events?"

Grandpa shook his head and let out a sigh. He handed the boy his orb and waited until Ethan had placed it back in his pocket, then the aged man embraced the boy, much to Ethan's surprise. It had been a while since their last embrace, but Ethan didn't mind. Grandpa released him, grabbing him by both shoulders, and looked into his eyes. "Thank you for confiding in me, son."

The old man stood. "We need to drop the shield, Lola is coming, and we must prepare to leave," he announced.

Ethan looked at his drake in surprise. *How does he know that?*

Seon shrugged. *She is coming. Deseret just told me,* he claimed.

"Ethan?" Grandpa repeated.

The boy shook his head and obeyed, reaching for his familiar power. He severed the source, thinking of its end, and the blue void immediately vanished.

Grandpa strode over to a chair beside his bed and retrieved his tunic draped over the back of it. He nodded for Ethan to stand as a quick knock sounded at the door and Lola burst into the room.

She squealed a good morning and launched herself into Grandpa's arms.

Kristian stood at the door, annoyingly shaking his head at Lola's overenthusiasm. Grandpa and Lola exchanged quick kisses on each other's cheeks before he announced it was time to go down for breakfast.

Lola jumped back down and was out of the door before anyone could tell her to wait up.

The three entered the hallway just as Heramon closed his door behind him. They briefly greeted and walked down to the eating room all together, with Lola at a full gallop ahead of them. No one was around to serve them breakfast, but the table had been set with a myriad of fruits, cakes, drinks, and of course, honey, all ready to be consumed.

Breakfast was eaten in silence, in anticipation of what was to come or what might come to pass.

Grandpa and Heramon sat at one end of the table, talking to each other in hushed tones, as adults often do.

Ethan, Kristian, and Lola sat at the other end. Ethan kept glancing up to wink at Lola, who was giggling at the little game they were playing. The drakes were sparring with one another in the corner, probably for the last time they would be together in a long while. They attempted to grab at one another's necks in playful bites in between tiny growls and snarls as

The Drake Epics - Journey to Qara

they tussled on the ground. Then, one of them would momentarily stand on their hind legs, extend their wings wide, and pounce on the others. Lola and Kristian had noticed it too and were watching the three play fight in between mouthfuls of food. Ethan half-caught himself drooling down his chin due to his interest in the drakes' mock battle.

At the end of breakfast, Grandpa stood. "We must be off," he announced. "It is time to say our goodbyes." They all stood and strode toward the door. The drakes paused and launched themselves to their respective perches on the children's shoulders.

Ethan had dreaded this moment ever since Kristian had announced his decision to stay behind. He loathed goodbyes.

Lola was the first to launch herself at Kristian. Tears were flowing freely down her cheeks, much to Kristian's and everyone's surprise. "Don't stay, Kristian, come with us. We need you!" she pleaded in between sobs. "Why can't he come with us?" she cried up to Grandpa as he approached the two.

"Now, now, we must all be brave. We will see Kristian again." He bent over to touch her gently on the cheek. "I promise."

Lola turned and threw herself into Grandpa's arms, burying her head in his side, her sobs surprisingly more pronounced than before. "But . . . I don't want him to stay," came her muffled voice.

Ethan noticed a single tear roll down his older brother's cheek before Kristian noticed it too and quickly wiped it off with the sleeve of his tunic.

"I love you, Lola, but you've got to be brave for me. That will help me more than anything else," the eldest boy said in a soft voice.

She stopped crying for an instant and turned to face Kristian. She quickly brushed the tears from her cheeks, nodding in agreement. "I love you too, Kristian." She hugged him again, this time as a much braver girl.

Everyone shuffled their feet at the awkward intimate moment. Most of them, not used to such a show of affection.

Ethan coughed to break the silence and reached out his hand to shake Kristian's.

With a wry smile, the older boy took his younger brother's hand, and pulled him into a bear hug. "Take care of Grandpa and Lola, Dingus," he said. "I'll be fine, and we will meet again in Julfa. I promise!" He pushed Ethan back to arm's length. "Promise?" he prodded.

"I Promise!" Ethan replied, trying his best to not show any emotion.

Nodding, Kristian pulled him into another briefer hug. This time, he whispered in Ethan's ear, "Keep the Kur-ne secret. Keep it safe. I have a feeling that it will guide you to help us all out of this mess we're in." He paused for a moment. "We're wanderers in a strange land, the

371

# Tearful Farewell

Kur-ne will guide us home." Kristian patted Ethan on the back and released him.

This last comment pounded Ethan. *Wanderers in a strange land? How could he have known that?* He thought, turning to his drake.

Seon shrugged.

They had been traveling through the Nejd over the last week, true, but that didn't make them wanderers. Ethan thought back to the new mysteries uncovered over the last few days and his eerie dreams, and finally agreed, perhaps just like Ethan, his brother felt like a wanderer indeed.

The rest of the farewells went quickly. Ethan and Lola hugged Heramon. Grandpa exchanged some parting comments with both Heramon and Kristian. Then they all walked to the door, ready to part company, when Muschle burst into the house.

"Wait . . . ," he gasped, trying to catch his breath. His face was red and his hair disheveled. It looked as though he'd been running for some time. "The king and queen would like to make their farewells." He gasped in between gulps of air.

"No time, Muschle, I already made our farewells last night. We need to be off." Grandpa shook his head.

Picking up on a sense of urgency in the older man's voice, Ethan assumed it was due to what he had relayed to him earlier that morning. But Grandpa seemed to be a bit nervous, unusual for the normally stoic figure he knew.

"They do not wish to have audience at the palace . . ." Muschle was hunched over, leaning on both of his knees, gulping for air. "They will meet you on the way out of Qara."

Surprised for a moment, Grandpa quickly recovered his usual soberness. "Very well," he acquiesced.

The small company exited Muschle's home and made their way down the stairway. At the bottom, two marvelously large lions stood at attention and fell into line behind them, as they walked along. The courtyard was busy as usual, but not like before. This time, the gnomes and lions were too busy to notice the small company, stocking supplies, stockpiling weapons, and organizing—for war!

Ethan shivered as he realized this. His thoughts rushed back to Kristian, and he looked in the older boy's direction. Kristian walked, looking about, proudly parading his new sword, armor, and helmet he had been awarded on the previous night. He seemed somehow different. It took Ethan a moment to zero in on the change, but he finally realized that Kristian walked with his head held a little higher. He had the appearance

The small company marched out the way they had come a few days earlier. Ethan was still amazed at the size of the palace gates they now walked through. The glass doors swung open in a throaty yawn as the hinges squeaked their way open. The familiar desert and islands of trees stretched out before them. The journey passed by more quickly than Ethan remembered from the last time, most likely due to his thoughts about Kristian and the war ahead of him. He was also silently plotting what his next steps would be when they left the city. He hadn't discussed this with Grandpa in the morning's events, but he knew he needed to set a course toward the grove of trees. He had barely recited the dream to himself before they were already approaching the great gates of Qara.

Before them stood an entourage of gnomes and lions at the gates' outskirts. As they drew nearer, Ethan recognized the same group at the gate as from last night's dream. The king and queen stood at the front of the concourse. The queen was smiling; the king looked to be in a sourer mood. When they got to within a few paces, the group all bowed in reverence before the king raised them with a wave of his hand.

"I would still counsel you to stay with us, but I know you have made up your mind. Just know that we could use your strength, and she would be quite safe here." At this, the king motioned in the direction of Lola.

Lola hmpphed in protest. Ethan saw the look of mutiny on her face and momentarily feared she might say or do something rash. She didn't, much to his relief.

"Great King, I have already decided. We will be quite safe, and you have two"—Grandpa paused to look at Kristian wearing a proud smile and then at Heramon with a nod of his head—"mighty warriors whom I am leaving behind. They will fight nobly and will bring you a great *victory!*"

The king grumbled to himself before answering, "It is your decision to make. We wish you great success. You are truly noble and worthy of the people of Qara!" The king paused. "To aid you in your journey's end, we gift you with the loyalty of two of our finest warriors—the lions that accompanied you from Muschle's quarters!"

Ethan looked at the two lions in astonishment. He had never heard of such a thing. Seon purred on his perch in a mock whistle.

Grandpa glanced at the king and queen with a poised look and nodded. "We graciously accept your offer, Great King, and thank you for your hospitality."

The king nodded in acceptance of Grandpa's flattery.

"This . . . is Koran!" the king continued, motioning for the lion on the right to approach him in introduction. "And this is Helam!" The king now motioned the same to the lion on the left. "Both are loyal and will serve you well. Take counsel with them, for they know the Nejd as well as you do, albeit in parts you have not dared wander yet."

Ethan was intrigued by this last claim. He thought that Grandpa had traveled the entire Nejd and knew it better than any living creature. The normal surge of questions built up within him, but he suppressed them for a later chat with Grandpa.

*Ethan,* the melodious thought flowed into his mind, as it had done thrice before. *Ethan and Seon, I wish also to give you a gift. A gift that none, except for the king, has knowledge of.*

Both Ethan and Seon stared intently at the queen in anticipation. Suddenly, their minds were flooded with a vision of a great dust storm. The storm beat upon the ground, and shrouded the sky. It was magnificent and terrifying at the same time. Suddenly, the dust swirled inward, and the great storm shrunk in upon itself, until it began to take form. At first, the form was vague; but as the dust settled, Ethan made out a solitary figure in shadow, a gigantic figure. Rays of light pierced through the dust, thrusting down and around the hulking form, highlighting parts of its body, until completely solid. The form of a golden brown sand dragon!

The dragon stretched its wings, tilting its head, and roared. Then, she looked down at the boy and the drake, and Ethan knew in an instant that the dragon was the queen.

*You are a dragon?* Ethan stammered in his mind. He had to cover his mouth for fear of blurting it out loud. *But . . . but how?* he asked in awe.

*I am. We can take the form of but one other creature. I chose the form of a human,* she exclaimed.

*We do not have much time. Ethan and Seon, I also gift you with dragon strength. 'Tis a rare gift that a dragon may willingly give to another, but twice in our lifetime. Once, if prudent, and once at death.* She paused again at this last statement. *I gift this to you freely of the former. It will strengthen you in time of need.*

The queen continued, *Note that this gift comes with a price . . . The giver gives it with a blessing and a curse. In your case, the blessing is for all that is good—to vanquish evil. The curse is to suffer and fall if your nature becomes evil. Do you accept this gift?*

Ethan paused to analyze the price. *Seon?* he asked.

Seon was momentarily silent before responding, *I feel that we are to have a place in this world as workers of goodness. I will accept this price, if you will accept it!* Seon radiated.

*The Drake Epics - Journey to Qara*

Ethan felt a complete peace in the drake's answer, and he made up his mind. *Great Queen, we are workers of goodness. We will accept your gift to aid us in vanquishing evil.*

The queen smiled in approval. A white flame emanated from immediately around her. It grew until it enveloped both Ethan and Seon.

Ethan suddenly felt a surge of power flow through his veins. He could sense that Seon felt the same. His eyes glazed over momentarily, and then it was over. He felt clean, as if a cleansing purity streamed through him guiding him by a clarity of conscience. He felt renewed, ready to take on any challenge against impossible odds, as if the past couldn't hold him back any longer. He had only the wish to look after the others and to the future.

*We are clean, Ethan. We will accomplish our task!* Seon spoke with power.

Ethan had not felt such confidence from his drake before, and he could feel Seon's presence deepen within himself than ever before. It was invigorating.

*Young Sheikh, remember your feelings. They will serve you well.* She paused again for a moment, as if considering something of great import. *Young Sheikh . . . ,* she started, *the fruit that you seek through your dreams. You know of what I talk. That fruit is one hundred fold what you experience now. It is the means to save your village of Julfa. It is the means to save us all. Now, time is short. My greatest wishes go with you, until we meet again.* She trailed off, then was completely silent.

Ethan had a thousand questions come immediately to mind. *Wait!* he stifled, but the vision had ended and he came to his senses. As always, he had more questions and absolutely no answers.

He looked around. The king and Grandpa were still exchanging pleasantries and, from the sound of it, had been doing so for quite some time, although Ethan wasn't quite sure how long he and Seon were in their trance.

Kristian wore a strange look on his face as he studied Ethan, but the others were oblivious to what had transpired, their attention completely on the two old men, serving volley after volley of praises at each other, as was the custom.

Ethan lifted his fist to his mouth and coughed.

Grandpa turned and nodded. "Oh, King, we must now go. May your paths be straight and sure. Until we meet again." With that, Grandpa made to move toward the gates.

Lola grabbed a hold of Kristian and hugged him as tightly as she could one last time before releasing him and trotting after Grandpa.

Ethan smiled at Kristian and turned to leave.

Kristian caught hold of his shoulder and pulled him back around. The two stood briefly studying each other, then they embraced in farewell. Kristian whispered, "Ethan, I know the queen gave you something, I saw you both glow. You will be protected by her. Protect Lola. You are the oldest, now. Follow Grandpa's instructions word for word. You'll be all right." He released Ethan. "You'll be all right, Dingus!" he tapped the younger boy on the face and grinned.

Ethan smiled and held back his tears. He shook Heramon's hand followed by a bear hug from the giant man and then followed the others out of the gate.

The two lions were waiting for him, and as soon as he crossed the threshold, they turned to walk with him. The great gates groaned as they began to close behind the departing party. Ethan turned and stood with Lola and Grandpa, looking at Kristian and Heramon, as the doors swung inward.

The light of Qara flowed into the chamber and then began to shrink until only a sliver of light was left. The doors lurched and slammed shut, and the light was snubbed out. The torches in the dark chamber immediately sprang to life, and a familiar soft blue glow emanated around the passageway.

Ethan wondered if he would ever see the beautiful Qara again. He wondered if he would ever have audience with the great king and queen. He wondered and yearned that his brother and Heramon would be safe from harm. He slowly turned with the others, and they walked away from the land of Qara and back to the world above.

# Chapter 22

## Of Druids and Dragons

*Bravery is not about the lack of fear, it is in knowing one's fear and facing it head-on!*

Kristian watched until the great doors blocked out the fading shadows of his brother, sister, and Grandpa, sealing him in; and his family out. He winced as they slammed completely closed and briefly wondered if he would ever see them again. His heart ached, but he quickly pushed those feelings down. He couldn't afford to be weak at this point, not now that he had his chance to be the warrior of his dreams! He had much to learn, much to do, and much too much to prepare for versus worry about such things.

He was brought out of his reverie as the crowd sauntered away from the doors and back toward the city. Heramon was standing twenty paces away, watching him. He finally motioned for Kristian to catch up. The boy ran at a slight jog, lurching a bit as he ran, not fully comfortable with the new sword slapping at his thigh. He slowed to a walk when he was within a few paces of Heramon and matched his mentor's stride as they made their way back down the path from where they had just come.

Heramon leaned over. "We need to teach you how to use that sword, if not to simply run with it." He jabbed an elbow at the boy and nodded his head in the direction of Kristian's hip where his sword was sheathed.

Looking up at Heramon with a look of pain etched on his face, Kristian sighed. "I can manage well enough!" he retorted as he puffed up his chest.

Heramon looked down at the boy with a smile and winked.

Kristian burst out in laughter.

Heramon straightened back up and pulled a hand through his hair. "I hear you are quite good with a sling though," he continued. "You can use that to your advantage over long distances . . . However, we need to give you the fighter's edge with the blade . . . if you come into close quarters with your opponent . . . ," he added as Kristian studied his mentor again with a reflective stare.

"Yes, but I'm sure an opponent can't do this . . . !" Kristian squinted his face and said "yangin," and a small flame burst in his palm and flittered for a few moments before he shot it into the sand, leaving a visible scorch mark.

A few of the gnomes that were walking in front of them hurriedly turned around, chattering in their local dialect.

Heramon noted the worried little men and nodded at Kristian with a maniacal grin. "Impressive, but can you do it under pressure and with enough power to overpower your foe?"

Kristian shrugged. "Of course," he guessed. They both lapsed into silence for a few moments as they walked.

"Heramon?"

The older man looked over at Kristian.

"Will we ever see them again?"

"Hmm . . ." Heramon reached over and patted the young man on the back. "Aye, you will, that you will. As long as you're trained up right. I have a feeling you will do just fine." He smiled down at the would-be soldier.

Kristian thought quickly about it and convinced himself that he would see his family. *BeeSting, we have training to do!* he announced.

The red drake perched easily on his shoulder, turned his head, and mouthed a toothy grin in understanding. The little drake was not very talkative most of the time. It was a trait that Kristian was very happy about. Lola was always blathering about something, and it drove him nuts.

But one dream resonated between the boy and his drake. They dreamed of becoming accomplished warriors. Of course, none of it would be possible without the help of Ethan, Kristian thought. His younger brother taught them to talk and to listen to each other. Kristian hadn't realized the importance of this at first. But with time, he noted that all of the other drake holders around him had immeasurable difficulty commanding their drakes without a lot of verbal strain. In fact, most of the boys at the school had never even dreamed of talking with their drakes through their minds. A sly smile curled on Kristian's lips. He nodded and promised himself that he would be sure to thank Ethan the next time they met.

The rest of the journey back to the city passed quickly. When they arrived at their quarters, Heramon and Muschle were immediately summoned to the war room. This left Kristian free to do whatever he wanted with his time.

He wasn't sure if he wanted to venture back into the palace after what had happened last time. He also hated doing things alone. He'd always had Ethan or one of his friends he could scam into doing it for him. But he could use more training, and it would keep his mind off his family. At least for a time.

Mesa was busily cleaning the house. She gave Kristian curious looks now and then, but was silent, other than the swishing of her broom.

"I'm going to train . . . ," Kristian suddenly announced, pointing awkwardly at the door with his thumb.

Mesa was in the process of lifting a glass flower pot off one of the shelves to dust underneath of it. She glanced up at the sudden interruption.

Kristian cleared his throat. "Um . . . in the palace. I'm going to train at the palace." He again clumsily pointed in the direction of where he thought the palace might be. "I'll be back in time for supper," he finished half-heartedly.

Mesa gave the boy a quizzical glance at his odd behavior then half-nodded and silently returned to her dusting.

He resolved to follow through, spun on his heel, and walked out the front doors. Two guards were posted at the bottom of the stairwell. They both looked very tense as they took up their positions next to him as he walked, but Kristian barely noticed. His mind immediately turned to

Ethan, Lola, and Grandpa as he made his way through the city streets. He admittedly missed them already.

He pushed the feelings aside and thought instead of the great victories he and BeeSting would lead in the charges for the people of Qara. He savored and rolled it over in his mind a few times, tasting the victory, the glory of the great battles of valor he had imagined to himself many, many times before. He always came out on top, of course, standing atop a sandy knoll, his hand and *new* sword raised in triumph, and a crowd of warriors cheering him on.

Kristian looked up at the tower in front of him and blinked in surprise. He had walked the distance to the palace without noticing his surroundings. His mind had been so engrossed in his own thoughts. He nodded at the lions on either side of the great palace doors. They nodded in return and relieved his present escort as he was led through a smaller set of doors and into the purplish interior he'd remembered from before. He had to admit that this inner world was breath taking, even after already seeing it once. He was quite sure that it would continue to amaze him on the third time and every time thereafter. It was, unnaturally, beautiful.

He shrugged the last thought off and retraced his steps to the training hut. As he strolled through the inner palace city, his mind again drifted. He hoped that Grandpa, Ethan, and Lola were faring well in their trip. He suddenly had a brilliant idea. *BeeSting, can you reach Seon or Deseret?* It was a good idea, but only an idea nonetheless.

BeeSting gave Kristian an expressionless look and didn't respond. The drake remained quiet, as at most times.

The boy sulked onward and quickly reached the sparring hut's door, set into the gigantic intertwining tree roots, forming the same small opening with a neat wooden door nestled in their embrace. He pulled on the latch and pushed open the door. With a sharp intake, he entered to train.

The same great hall met his gaze, and he wondered again how such a large room could appear out of such a small hut—only this time he didn't have Ethan to trip over. He was tempted to poke his head back outside and measure the structure, but decided otherwise. He shrugged at the thought and briefly considered that it must be a powerful magic, like the one that gave the purple tint to the palace skies.

The room was full of the sound of swords, spears, all clanking against one another—shouts from little men and roars from lions as they openly sparred. He glimpsed medics running from ring to ring, using their magic to heal accidental injuries incurred from the matches.

The Drake Epics - Journey to Qara

Kristian stopped to rethink if he should even spar with anyone or just practice on one of the dummies set up in one of the corners and almost turned back once or twice to leave the hut. His ambition got the better of him though, and he noticed a particularly interesting match in play. *Couldn't hurt to watch a little match*, he figured with BeeSting. Hey, he might even learn some techniques he could later use against the little men, if he had to.

Two gnomes were fighting an unusually large lion, and they weren't faring well. The cat easily evaded an otherwise-lethal blow from one of the gnome's spears. The attacking gnome was wearing a green tunic and gripped a small shield in his hand without the spear. The lion snarled in contempt and swiped its paw at the little man. The gnome reacted just in time, bringing the shield up to absorb the blow, but it sent him sprawling to the ground nonetheless. The gnome muttered something under his breath and gingerly got to his feet, careful to keep his spear raised in the direction of the larger animal.

The other gnome, this one in full armor, had only a one-handed mace that he swung menacingly about his head. He wore a mixture of anger and determination on his face. He grimaced and took advantage of the situation, lunging at the lion, expecting to catch the feline off guard. The larger opponent gracefully swiveled his body and, in one fluid motion, brought one of his paws up, pinning the gnome to the ground with a clang before the little man could react. His mace spun away on the floor and out of his helpless hands.

The gnome furiously pounded at the lion's paw, yelling something unintelligible, but to no avail. Kristian assumed the words coming from the little gnome couldn't be all that pleasant.

The lion immediately glanced sideways at the other gnome, who had positioned himself behind the big cat, hoping for a surprise attack; but he had waited a few moments too long. The sand lion scraped the armored gnome across the ground, still under his massive paw. As it turned, there was the sound of armor grating against stone that left huge gouges in the floor as the gnome was dragged along, as well as the fact that the gnome was still kicking and screaming. Kristian thought it must be mostly out of embarrassment rather than out of pain.

The spectator had to momentarily plug his ears as the hair stood straight up on his neck. Even BeeSting winced at the noise.

The stalking gnome suddenly bolted for the lion, shouting his battle charge. As soon as he entered the lion's reach, the feline lifted the paw from off the screaming gnome and took a swipe at the charging opponent. The gnome sacrificed his shield, throwing it into the air and ducking, where the lion's paw made contact, gracefully sliding on his side under the attacking lion's leg, coming up by his companion. The gnome that had been pinned unsheathed a small dagger from somewhere on his body, and both were now on their knees, weapons drawn ready for another assault.

Kristian whistled softly to himself—their moves were gutsy, he gave them that. He could see one of them moving his lips and assumed he was voicing a quiet countdown for the next charge at the big cat. However, before they could react, the lion let out an unearthly roar leaping sideways and over the two gnomes, landing just behind them. Before either could respond, the lion had pinned them both from behind, each under one of his enormous padded paws.

The match was over. The lion let out a victory roar as his final challenge.

Kristian clapped his hands together and grinned sideways at BeeSting. *I wonder how we would fare, think we could take him?* he asked with a crooked smile.

*We could!* the boy felt the encouraging reply.

"Yes, you could!"

Kristian spun around, and to his surprise, the queen stood towering over them.

Her eyes were filled with courage, and a reassuring smile spread across her lips. She summoned the lion with a quick nod of her head. "Shall we see how well you fare then?" she asked.

The boy felt a lump form at the base of his throat. He didn't answer, pointing at himself with a questioning look.

"Yes, you!" The queen confirmed. She lifted one of the ropes to admit the boy and his drake into the ring. "Let us remove the rules of this combat and see what you can both do." the queen injected. "No Rules!" she declared.

Kristian gulped and slipped into the ring. He watched the lion advance toward them. The beast appeared much larger and formidable than just a few moments ago, he realized.

The lion walked with grace as powerful muscles rippled with each step the cat took. A long gash extended from one of its ears to just below its eye. A shaggy mane that Kristian could now see much better sprouted from around the crest of its head and lay clumsily on the beast's neck.

BeeSting hissed at their adversary as he tasted the air with his forked tongue.

Kristian found momentary pleasure in his companion's determination as he stroked the crest of the little drake's head.

After only a few moments, the lion had reached them and crouched as if to pounce, studying the boy and his drake. It wasn't the sheer size of the lion, Kristian realized, that gave him pause for concern. No, it was those oversized eyes that were the most disconcerting part of all—enormous yellow pupils that studied him—just waiting for the boy to make his first move. Kristian could have sworn that he saw his own reflection drowning in the beast's eyes and felt as if he were going to suddenly throw up.

The feline appeared to menacingly smile at the boy's discomfort.

Kristian shook his head. Cats don't smile, he thought. It was most likely a silent snarl.

The lion shifted its giant shoulders up and down and barred its colossal fangs at the boy. Kristian unsheathed his sword and braced for an attack that was imminently coming. Instead, the beast rose to its feet, growled, and turned its back, making its way toward the center of the ring.

"Go on! It's your chance to prove you are truly a warrior, Young Sheikh," the queen urged.

He couldn't tell if she were mocking him or not. All he knew is that this isn't exactly what he had intended when he came here. A straw dummy or even a wooden pole would have suited him just fine. Something to strike at and practice his swings and blows. He had never thought to match up with a live foe, let alone with a massive lion and in a test without rules. He swallowed hard again then scanned the area as he had been taught to always size up his surroundings. *Awareness and diligence is what keeps the solider alive!* he silently recited to himself.

The ring was all fenced in by rope with big wooden posts every few paces that ran along its perimeter, something he hadn't really observed before now. It spanned forty or fifty paces wide and the same length with small obstacles and hazards that littered the interior of the ring for partial defense or hindrance, whichever way you preferred to look at it. He himself preferred to think of them as potential defense points that he could use to his advantage as he mentally strategized on a few paths he could charge from or retreat through.

The two gnomes that had just completed their sparring with the lion now passed him on their way out of the ring. One helped the other through the ropes as he was still slightly limping from a sprain. The other paused, putting his hand on Kristian's arm, and said, "Good luck, my boy! You're going to need it!" before quickly ducking out of the ring. Both gnomes took up spots on either side of the queen, intent to watch this particular challenge.

This did little to make Kristian feel the least bit better. In fact, it had quite the opposite effect on him, and he suddenly questioned why he wanted to be a soldier in the first place. Perhaps, the soundest counsel was that he should have abandoned the honor and glory he dreamed of in battle. Perhaps, he should have gone with his family instead.

"I have faith in you," the queen uttered and motioned for the boy to engage.

Kristian turned his head back toward the lion, who was patiently waiting on him. It continued to intently study the boy.

*Strategy, strategy—what's my strategy?* he asked himself, more out of desperation rather than to calm himself down.

BeeSting must have sensed this too because Kristian immediately felt a surge of power flow through his body.

He looked at the little drake and smiled in gratitude. *Let's do this!* he growled as a sudden burst of adrenaline flowed through his veins. He sheathed the sword and drew out his sling. fumbling around in his pouch, he found a smooth stone that he nimbly placed into the sling's leather interior. He slowly walked toward the massive animal, counting his steps and memorizing the distance between the little blockades he passed through. After what felt to him as a long while, he figured the lion was within twenty paces, and he halted to study the vicinity. The sling only needed twelve or so paces to strike a precise blow. The attack would be utterly useless beyond fifteen or sixteen paces.

Kristian slowly inched his way forward until he was within range as he started to swing the sling above his head. He then started to sidestep in a circle around the animal in order to get a better vantage point, keeping a close eye on the lion. All the while, he swung the sling around at a steady pace.

The lion snarled, possibly trying to startle Kristian, but he hardly noticed. His attention was on where he would strike. He continued to circle around, watching and being watched. If only he could get into the animal's blind spot before he launched the missile. It would catch the lion off guard. Just a little more.

But much to the boy's dismay, the lion grew uneasy at his planned out movements and paced back and forth, seemingly to keep his opponent in sight. Suddenly, the lion let out a roar and leapt off the floor and directly at Kristian with amazing agility.

Kristian didn't have time to think. He squared up the lion's head, spun the sling extra hard to ready the strike, and let the stone fly. It struck the cat just above one of its luminous eyes, and the feline dropped to the ground with another roar of fury. The beast rubbed at its eye with the side of its paw and angrily eyed Kristian.

A crowd had started to gather around the ring, and some of the gnomes were cheering the boy on.

However, Kristian kept his focus, he saw the anger in the big cat's eyes—those voluminous eyes. *That can't be good . . .* , he thought. He heard BeeSting laugh in his thoughts, but didn't linger on why. He quickly slipped another pebble into the sling's pouch and started the spin.

The lion was back on its feet now, pacing back and forth. This time, a little more wary, but more angry as well. It shook its head from time to time, probably to help with the throbbing.

Kristian continued to circle the lion, complaining to himself that he was much too close to the lion at this point. But just as he was starting to inch away from the cat to a safer distance, the lion charged for a second time.

It lunged forward at Kristian with another roar, zigzagging back and forth in an attempt to avoid another missile from the boy.

Kristian whirled the sling overhead for another strike and let the second stone fly. This time it harmlessly pelted off the side of the cat's torso. The boy instinctively reached for his sword and got it halfway out of its sheath when the cat struck him with one of its paws. He saw a red blur streak away from his shoulder, followed by an intense pain that shot through his body, as he was hurtled to one side and struck the ground. His mind went numb, and his vision was blurry. He half-heartedly pushed himself off the floor with one hand, but felt dizzy. He grabbed at his sword, which had made its way out of the sheath, but the blade had already spun away from him, clattering on the ground as it went.

BeeSting was squawking in alarm as he darted at the lion's eyes. The cat was swinging its paws at the small drake, which BeeSting easily avoided at the much larger and therefore slower animal's attempts.

That's all he needed. Kristian scrambled to his knees to make a lunge for his sword, but a sudden rush of new pain shot through his head is if it were split wide open from the inside out. He groaned then drove himself to ignore it as best he could. He lowered his shoulders, intent on reaching the sword, and lunged for it a second time. Wrapping his hand around the sword's hilt, he rolled to a kneeling position and readied his assault.

The lion continued to roar and swat at BeeSting, and Kristian had a sudden idea. "BeeSting!" he yelled to get the drake's attention. *BeeSting, keep it busy!* he thought.

The drake hovered for a moment, just out of the lion's reach, then dove.

The aggravated lion swiped at the air without reason trying desperately to connect with the little nuisance.

BeeSting easily avoided the blows, except for one that caught the little drake by the wing and sent him into a spiral before slamming hard into the ground.

Kristian instantly felt the pain from his little companion. His face countered in a mixture of shock and concern. *BeeSting, can you hear me? BeeSting?* No answer. *BeeSting, can you hear me?* he shouted in his mind.

The lion roared in triumph.

The little drake gave a feeble answer, *That hurt.*

Kristian could sense the pain, and he entirely forgot about the match. All he could think of was that his closest friend was on the ground, the victim of the lion standing above the small drake and roaring its head off. A new feeling rose within him, it drowned out everything else. It was a seething anger.

The lion turned to face off with Kristian and started its prowl of the wounded boy. Kristian hardly noticed; his rage continued to fuel him as he stared helplessly at BeeSting. He felt a power well within him he'd known only a portion of a few times before, but this time was different. It surged, it bubbled and boiled over.

*Let it grow, Kristian, let the power grow within you.*

The boy gave himself over to the queen's prodding within his head, subconsciously following the counsel.

*You are a mighty warrior, Great Sheikh!* her silent voice now reverberated throughout his awareness.

The lion continued its prowling advance.

Kristian stood motionless as his power grew in strength.

*Feel the power, stoke it . . . wait, wait . . . ,* the queen urged.

The lion gave up its prowl, roared, and launched itself at Kristian again. n*ow, Kristian, use your strength now!* the queen demanded.

The boy clenched his teeth in fury and uttered a single word, "Yangin!"

The lion drew up short and stared at the boy in abject horror. The ring's ropes all burst into flame, forming a great blazing square around the three of them.

BeeSting was on his feet now, and Kristian could feel his anger as well. The drake launched himself into the air and circled the cringing lion.

Kristian stood poised, ready to strike. A tower of flame erupted from his hand; he was ready to strike. His breathing was slow and deliberate. Sweat streamed steadily off his face. He was ready to strike. He reached back to heave the flame.

The lion had now become the prey and looked into the boy's eyes, horror plainly visible in its own luminous yellow eyes.

Kristian stared back intently, but without feeling. His anger had turned brutally cold. He studied his reflection in the cat's eyes, the flame enveloping his hand and arm. The lion continued to cower with a look of pleading fear plainly visible in its face.

Kristian reached back to let the inferno go, ready to strike his foe down, smiting its remains upon the ground.

"No . . . !" a man's voice broke Kristian's concentration. He half-turned his head and vaguely saw a man standing within the circle of flames. He didn't recognize him, not at first.

"Kristian, no . . . ! Stop . . . ! What are you doing?" the man continued yelling. It was annoying, he malevolently thought. This was followed by a bout of confusion. The man was eerily familiar.

Kristian looked back at the lion then back at the man again in bewilderment. Who was he? The man's face was drawn out with a mixture of anger and fear. The queen was nowhere in sight.

Then it dawned on him, it was Heramon. Kristian shook his head to clear his senses. Where was he?

Time slowed to a halt as Kristian looked at the lion again in slow motion. It was now on its belly, both paws were wrapped over its head as it trembled in terror. He couldn't quite figure out why it was so scared; then he looked down at his arm in wonder at the flame roaring from *him*. He looked up to see the square of fire all around them.

*Did this come from me?* he asked himself, suddenly realizing it had.

*Yes!* came two replies in his head at once. One reply was from BeeSting. He could feel BeeSting's wonder as well, his anger now gone. But who was the other? Then he realized the obvious: the queen!

He reached out to her *Where are you?*

Silence.

*Answer me!* he demanded. *What did you do to me?* He listened intently, waiting.

*I am here*, came the reply after a few moments.

Kristian spun around. The queen was behind him, only it wasn't the queen. At least, not by sight. In her place stood a magnificent beast. A beast of folklore—something Kristian would never have expected to see in his wildest dreams. Confusion crowded out all anger. *What is happening to me?* He shook his head and looked again.

Two massive paws lay stretched out toward him, with dagger like claws extending from each toe, followed by a massive body covered in golden brown scales that shimmered in the half-light. Two leathery wings extended outward, as if for balance; and a long, slender neck arose from the body. A large head with a ridge of pointed scales climbed up her back and onto the ridge of her head. Her tongue flicked in and out of her mouth.

Kristian shook his head again and squeezed his eyes shut as hard as he could. He took a deep breath, chancing another look. It was like looking at a massive version of BeeSting—a very massive version of BeeSting, *no*, a dragon. His mind knew something was wrong. *Where was BeeSting . . . ?* he began to think. But the enormity of the situation completely overwhelmed him, and the thought drowned everything out with a sudden wave of confusion and bewilderment at what he was now witnessing.

The enormous body shifted, flexing its wings before they snapped back, folding neatly onto her back. She gave a great yawn, then lowered her head, such that her snout was inches away from the boy's astonished face.

He could feel hot—*sweet?*—breath wafting over him as the dragon breathed. Kristian looked beyond the snout and into two enormous blue eyes—those eyes, they were endless, penetrating orbs. He felt for an instant that he could easily sink into them and his deepest, most secret thoughts would be easily revealed. He shook himself free. *Focus, Kristian, focus!* he thought angrily to himself. *A true solider is stronger than this!* Kristian fixated on this for a brief moment, but it was pointless. His eyes wandered back to the orbs. He was drawn to them as if in a trance. The eyes looked familiar. He had seen them before; and then it registered—that voice, those eyes, they were the queen's eyes, it was the queen's voice he'd heard. Shock registered on his face as his mouth hung open, *The queen?*

*I did nothing, this was all you,* she answered his former question. *Your brother handled this knowledge much better than you, but I suppose that he had seen a dragon before; whereas, you have not.* the queen amended.

*But . . . ?* Kristian fumbled for words, any words. He wasn't quite sure of what was happening to him. It was all too foreign, but then again, a lot had happened to the three children throughout their travels. He sucked up his courage to speak again, *I . . . I don't . . . understand . . . how . . . ?* His mind raced ahead of his words.

*You see me as I am!* She paused for emphasis. *As you must see me . . . if we are to be victorious.*

He still didn't understand. It was too much for his mind to grasp. He realized that he felt unusually warm, but he couldn't tell if it were from the hot breath rushing over his face or his own discomfort that caused his head to throb and burn. His perplexity continued to wash over him, and he suddenly felt completely alone inside as if the answers were slower in coming than usual. He hadn't had this feeling, not since before . . .

He spun around again to target BeeSting. *BeeSting, BeeSting!* he screamed. The drake was nowhere to be found. As he strained to find his companion's thoughts, he realized that he was lost in a haze of colors, all blurred together, as if in a dream. The lion, Heramon, and BeeSting were all gone. He was no longer in the sparring ring!

*You are quite safe here, Young Sheikh . . . Your little drake and Heramon are quite safe as well*, the queen spoke up again. Her voice was melodic and soothing.

Kristian turned back to her. *What did you do to them?* he haltingly questioned this time.

*I have done nothing. You are now here with me, you will return to them shortly.* She paused, as if to reassure him, before continuing, *You have a great talent, Young Sheikh. A power, if you will. I sense this is the first time you have discovered it.*

Kristian shook his head. *What power? What are you talking about . . . ?* He now paused to think it through as the memory of his burning arm and the burning ropes all flooded back into his mind. He raised his arm quickly and felt it for an answer—an ethereal flame rose from it.

*I did this? I mean, I know I can create fire, but I've never done anything so wild!* he said in amazement as the realization dawned on him. *I mean . . . I've never . . . I don't have the . . . how could . . . ?*

*You found your core!* the queen finished for him. *Yes, you can do these things, but you must control them. This power is to your credit, but it could be used against you. If you are not careful!*

Kristian's head was spinning faster than ever. He felt a dizzying intoxication, yet also at the same time, queasy. He cupped a hand to his mouth, just in case. He had never experienced anything like this with Ethan before. Not in all of his training or practice. This was new to him, entirely new.

*No, you haven't felt this way before, Young Sheikh. This is something that only a master can teach you. Alas, I only have time to expose you to your power. There is not enough time to train you how to control it completely. You must learn this on your own.*" The queen paused again, but Kristian had already felt the guilt in her voice.

*Not enough time? Why?* Kristian barked out before he could properly compose his thoughts. It felt as if a great discovery was within his reach, then suddenly yanked from his grasp.

*Great Sheikh!* the dragon soothed. Her voice was patient, but yet strangely filled with sorrow and perhaps a twinge of fear. *The day is upon us, the forces that would destroy Qara, Ethan . . . your family. They are without our walls. They've only just arrived.*

Kristian wasn't quite sure what this last statement meant. He would stand and fight. His family should be far away—that is, if they hadn't been intercepted already.

*No, they are beyond immediate danger, but they yet have a long journey ahead of them . . . I have already revealed myself to your brother . . . but I must yet visit your sister,* she said.

"Lola? Where is she? Is she all right?" a torrent of questions followed, but he was silenced by a stern look from the queen.

*They are exactly where they need to be, young one . . . For now, you must stand by Qara's side—that is your oath as a sworn solider of Qara.* Again, she paused. *You will yet be a great soldier, my Sheikh!* she concluded.

Too many questions flooded Kristian's mind, his head felt like bursting. *This is how Dingus must feel.* He mocked, thinking of his younger brother's penchant for day dreaming and asking too many questions.

Well, if BeeSting couldn't tell him now, at least he had a glimmer of hope from the queen, but it wasn't enough. How could she withhold this from him? Anger started to rise in his chest for the queen, replacing the confusion and anxiety he felt before.

*You will have answers in time. For now, learn to control your power—feel it within you, nurture it. Strong emotions will bring it to the front. If you are not careful, those emotions could be used to your ruin. Let it flow through you—nurture the power, but do not let it engulf you. In time it will provide you with a path through the questions you seek your answers to.*

The queen lifted her enormous head and stretched her neck back into its original position when the boy had first seen her.

*Wait!* Kristian barked again. *What do you mean? That doesn't make any sense!* He groped in desperation.

The queen's form flickered slightly, and she seemed to become even more transparent than before. He couldn't tell if his eyes were playing tricks on him as he focused on her, but the harder he strained, the more out of focus she became.

Her form smeared into a colored haze that started to fall away as if to dissolve entirely—more slowly at first, then with increasing speed.

*Wait! Don't go . . . ! You still haven't told me how to control it!* he pleaded.

*Let it run through you,* she repeated. This time, he could barely hear her voice.

He closed his eyes to concentrate. *Wait!* he begged again, pleading for more time. He opened his eyes; the queen was gone.

He looked around. He was standing alone as before the dream. He immediately felt BeeSting's presence enter his mind. The drake was worried; Kristian could tell that the drake also sensed a change in the boy. The lion was still cowering, just a few paces in front of him. He half-glanced over at Heramon, who still wore the same look of anger and surprise on his face.

The Drake Epics - Journey to Qara

Suddenly, Kristian was aware of the power burning within him. As he noticed this, he could hear the crackling of the fire all around him. He glanced back down at his arm and saw the inferno harmlessly rising from off him. In a moment of clarity, he realized that no time had passed. The discourse with the queen had taken no time at all! *Was it all a dream?* he wondered.

His senses came back to him, interrupting his train of thought. He had to douse the fire.

Kristian closed his eyes and concentrated on the source. He dug deep into his core until he could feel its raw energy, near his grasp. In his excitement, he reached out to grab hold, and immediately felt a searing pain shoot through his body. He yanked his senses back, reeling in astonishment. *It hurt!* A penetrating fear enveloped him. The power—he wasn't controlling it, it was controlling him!

His mind raced wildly—the vision, the queen—what had she said? He had to let it run through him, course through him. He had to control the power. He knew that he had to get it back under his control. He knew what he had to do. He reached out the second time and thrust himself into the power's core. He immediately felt the pain, almost unbearable at first. It pulsated, as if with each expansion, it would blow him apart. He willed himself to control it; the pulsing subsided. He took courage and thought harder, *You are mine!* He cast all doubts aside and willed himself to harness it. To his surprise, the pain continued to wane. He was controlling it!

*You are under my control!* he repeated. He pushed harder until all the pain left him, and he only felt the power itself. It felt thrilling! All of his senses seemed to be heightened, and the world around him slowed. He could hear the lion shivering; he could feel Heramon's anger and feel BeeSting's awe.

*You need to put the fire out!* BeeSting's thoughts came into his mind.

Kristian nodded. He snuffed it out as he closed his hand, and all was quiet. He opened his eyes and looked around him. The fire that had enveloped the ring, the posts, and the ropes was gone; and they appeared as they had before. He glanced at his arm; the fire was gone.

A broad smile spread across his lips. He had controlled it!

His attention now turned back to the present. He had a lot of explaining to do with Heramon. He wasn't sure of what frightened him more, what he had just experienced or Heramon's stern rebuke.

Kristian gulped, looked at Heramon, and started to sluggishly walk toward his mentor.

# Chapter 23

## Blood, Fire, and Wind

*Fuel it! Mold it! Control it!*

E than blinked in the rising morning sunlight. He rubbed at his eyes to clear his vision. It had been a little over four days since they had abandoned Qara and left Kristian and Heramon behind. The nights were bitterly cold, and the days were intensely hot. Right now, he didn't know which of them was more unfortunate—Kristian waging his war or his own forced march through the Nejd. *Besides, Grandpa is already used to this*, he thought miserably.

*The Drake Epics - Journey to Qara*

He let his mind wander a little about the last few days. It had seemed like an eternity, an eternity of discomfort and uneventful boredom. His thoughts drifted back to their departure from the fair land of Qara. After making their way up the main tunnel corridor, they had traversed the outskirts of the Forbidden City, mostly hugging to the cliff's walls and careful to stay as far into the shadow as possible. Must have worked as they escaped any discovery that he was aware of, or at the very least they had avoided the wolves altogether this time. That, and there had been no sign of the camping armies that he had seen within the Kur-ne.

The small company had marched in this manner until they were almost halfway across the valley floor before reaching a set of rudely covered tunnels, camouflaged behind brush and rock.

Once inside, the tunnels rose sharply from the valley floor, weaving their way into the cliff face, with frequent gaping shafts that permitted brief views of the valley below. The tunnels would then dive back into the earth, as if their builders couldn't quite make up their minds whether to stay near the light or go deeper into darkness. Again, fortunately for them, they hadn't seen any opposing army crowding the sunken valley, even when they crested the outer ridge of the plateau.

Still, Ethan had a gnawing feeling that they were there. *Perhaps in hiding?* he'd asked Seon.

To which the drake simply shrugged, not having a better answer.

He shook off the thought and continued through his morning mental backlog. From the plateau, they had proceeded in an eastwardly direction across the barren, sandy plains.

Of course, everyone was on high alert for the initial part of their march. Grandpa had insisted that Ethan relay his dream to the group in vivid detail to ensure that they avoided any potential confrontation. Not that it would do the small party any good—after all, Ethan and Seon had flown through this space and most of what he saw was only a blur of the landscape below.

Ethan found himself expectantly scanning the horizon with almost every step of the journey, anticipating the army that he had seen in his vision; but up until now, he saw no army, no auditor, only the sandy expanse of a bleak desert. He had begun to doubt whether he had seen the future in the Kur-ne at all.

The first night they had posted camp without fire, eating a quick and silent evening meal. Grandpa had said this was to avoid detection by others, and that any sort of flame in the Nejd would cast light for miles in the darkness. So they huddled together and ate without fire. Besides, they had their noble lion guardians with them for protection. *It wasn't the most pleasant experience*, Ethan grumbled. He didn't particularly enjoy eating raw meat. It left a tangy aftertaste, and the aroma of blood lingered on his taste buds for far too long. Although the lions literally wolfed down the meal as fast as they could, preferring it raw. Lola refused to eat any meat at all, folding her arms in protest. The only saving grace was the bits of bread, a few dollops of sweet honey, and the dried dates they were rationed. Breakfast was the same story.

The next few days had been just as tedious. For Ethan, it was morning study followed by a forced training through the blistering heat. Because of the extreme conditions, Grandpa had required both Ethan and Lola to be wrapped tightly in black cloaks with loose turbans (or Jamadani, as it was called) to shield the children from the scorching sun. It was a pain keeping all of those long strips of blackened cloth in order, and he had to admit that he wasn't very good at winding it anew each morning.

Lola fared a bit worse and had fallen into constant whining about the clothing and heat. Grandpa reprimanded her a number of times when she unwrapped her black shawl from around her head and face. "This is to protect you from the sun's heat, Lola!"

"But I can't breathe in here!" she complained. "It's suffocating me, and Deseret agrees," she said with a humph and folded her arms in protest.

Ethan sensed a touch of frustration growing in the older man's voice. But Grandpa always finished in a tender rebuke, "It is for your own good, little one."

Of course, this had made Lola even angrier.

The sound of footfalls and breathing interrupted the boy's reverie and made his heart jump. He looked sidewise just in time to see one of the massive lions, *Helam, is it?* the boy thought to himself, passing close to where he lay as the beast skirted their camp on its nightly rounds. Ethan had felt safe enough with the sand lions constantly standing guard, but not as safe as one would expect. He still didn't fully trust them yet. Besides, they were not social creatures and rarely talked about anything. In fact, he couldn't remember them having said anything more than a few words for the duration of their journey, which made them all the more mysterious in his eyes. He made a mental note and promised himself to take the next opportunity he had to talk with one of them.

As he watched the lion saunter beyond him, the giant feline waved its head from side to side with purposeful study before vanishing again behind a rock formation.

With Helam out of sight, the boy again fell into another reverie as he surveyed the countryside around him with increased interest. He recalled from last night that they had entered a strange rocky terrain with large

The Drake Epics - Journey to Qara

boulders that peppered the landscape, haphazardly jutting out of the sand. Their edges were sharp and jagged, as if a terrible earthquake had pressured them into ruthless spears, puncturing the soft ground beneath them in some epic battle. It gave him sudden chills, he concluded, shaking his head. Their jagged edges twisted and scratched against their shadows cast by the rising morning sun. Ethan admitted he wouldn't be overly surprised if the rock formations hid something evil, watching them, waiting for the right moment to attack the little group.

Even the large lions seemed on edge, he thought. They constantly paced around the camp perimeter, in and out of the rocky outcrops they went. He didn't particularly enjoy the feeling and had sent Seon up to canvass the countryside. *Besides, it's good for you to get some exercise,* he thought with amusement. Seon wasn't tickled about it.

*All clear!* Seon had reported as he weaved in and out of the boulders, which helped relieve some of Ethan's anxiety, but not entirely.

Another thing worried him even more so, he hadn't remembered this landscape from his vision. This gave him pause for concern that he might be leading the group in the wrong direction.

But Seon was sure they were on track.

Besides, when Ethan had mentioned this to Grandpa last night, the wise old man patted him on the back and said they were at least on course for the next waypoint and could get better bearings when they reached it. Although Grandpa wasn't forthcoming about what that waypoint might be.

Yet, the boy trusted his patriarch implicitly. He convinced himself that he must have been focusing on something else during the dream and missed this detail due to the speed at which they had flown overhead.

Seon agreed this must be the case.

At least Ethan could now see the Caucasus mountain range much more clearly in the distance, which gave him a shimmer of hope that Seon and Grandpa were both right after all.

Other than Ethan's anxiety, their journey had been completely uneventful, boring, compared to the excitement they'd had over the weeks leading up to the discovery of Qara. Boring, all except for Lola's constant whining. Ethan paused, his mind was taking him in circles, he realized.

His thoughts quickly returned to his frustration with his little sister on the previous day. She was really getting on his nerves. *She's getting worse . . .* He shook his head, thinking of her last episode. Whenever she didn't get her way, she would melt down into screaming uncontrollably at Ethan until Grandpa had to step in.

*It's not my fault she's cranky!* Ethan thought angrily about his grandpa's disapproving looks. He hadn't even done anything wrong—well, not really. All he did was disagree with her—once or twice—and perhaps stick his tongue out as well or poke her in the ribs. He smiled to himself, in spite of the fact he knew he was being a tad immature to liven things up. "Just a tad," he said softly with a grin on his face.

He turned over in his bedroll to shift his weight to the other side and realized that he had been lying on his hand, as sharp pricks exploded across his fingers. Ethan tried to shake the sleep from the hand and smacked it on the ground a few times before he felt the warm sensation of blood returning through his veins. He then propped himself up on one elbow and now studied their small encampment, stifling a silent yawn.

Lola was asleep next to him. *Thank goodness.* Of course, Deseret was curled up at her side. The little drake's blue scales glinted in the rising sun.

They were quite mesmerizing, he realized. He had never really studied the drake in any detail before and now couldn't think of why he hadn't. Her scales were slightly larger than Seon's, and her snout was narrower, eyes bigger and teeth longer. However, what he found most intriguing were her ears. Unlike Seon's ears, Deseret had furry tassels that rose from each, giving her the appearance of a small miniature feline. Ethan wasn't sure why he hadn't noticed it before and shrugged it off.

The fire had burned out sometime the night before, something that Grandpa had finally allowed last night, much to the delight of the children. He suddenly grinned with delight, his teeth showing in an accidental snarl, as he realized that last night's meal was the best he'd had since they left Qara. *Cooked rabbit sure beats uncooked rabbit, hands down!* he thought cheerily as he picked at his teeth to remove leftover scraps. Raw meat never appealed much to him, even when it was sweetened with Grandpa's desert herbs. Still, the lions insisted their meat not be cooked.

Ethan glanced up and noted Grandpa squatting just outside of the small camp. The old man was examining the landscape while twisting the hair in his beard. The boy briefly smiled to himself again. Grandpa had a strange habit of twirling strands of hair on his beard with his pointer finger when he was in deep, deep thought. Every other time, he would just tug at the beard, itself. He and Kristian had often mocked the old man that he would lose all of his hair if he continued this.

Grandpa always responded, "So be it!" and then went right along with the twirling.

On either side of the old man, both lions now stood at attention, their morning patrol of the perimeter complete.

Again, his attention was drawn to them and Ethan marveled if they ever slept. He secretly confessed that he had tried to stay awake to catch them falling asleep last night, but he passed out far short of his goal. He thought he had glimpsed Grandpa doing the same and knew that the older, wiser man didn't fully trust them yet either. But Lola couldn't stop talking to the brute beasts as they were captive attention for her.

A profound grimace etched across Ethan's face. *Uggh, I'm doing it again.* His mind again made the full circle and returned to his previous thoughts about his sister. If he had been paying more attention, he would have been more annoyed that his mind seemed to gravitate to his frustration with the little imp. The boy sat up and rubbed the scruff of his neck, this time yawning more loudly in spite of himself. He sheepishly glanced around, but realized that no one had taken note.

He lamented about his treatment of Lola and his immature behavior. He should be grown-up enough not to fight with his little sister, but it was kind of fun to annoy her to break up the monotony of their trek, and he realized he was lapsing back into old habits—before Seon and Deseret had come along.

*Oh . . . Seon.* He looked sheepishly in the white drake's direction, who lay peacefully asleep, nestled in a white ball a few paces away. The drake wasn't overly amused at his behavior with Lola either and had sternly rebuked Ethan for his immaturity. *Just because Seon never fights with Deseret doesn't mean he knows everything about being a good brother!* Ethan grimaced. His frown turned into a look of playful guilt as he watched his sleeping companion. *Ah, he's probably right anyways*, the boy thought to himself as he rubbed his head again. *I'll apologize when they all wake up*, he settled.

*At least I'm learning something*, he thought sarcastically. Ethan was starting to understand just how much Grandpa knew of drakes and Kesem.

The old man didn't have any practical knowledge with Kesem of course. But he seemed to know a lot of the textbook techniques.

*Textbook is right*, he mused. Grandpa had him memorizing every free moment he had—it was worse than back in Julfa when he was learning from Limnah and Ezera. *At least back then, I got the chance to practice as well as read*, he thought. The last few days' study took every spare moment he had. Not just in the morning and evening, but constant quizzing while they walked. Probably another reason he was picking on Lola so much, out of his own sheer irritation. He could tell that Seon was getting tired of the ban on practicing their Kesem together too.

Grandpa was pushing him to fill his mind with every technique possible, every tidbit of information about drakes. *Repetition, repetition, repetition . . .* , he thought tiredly as he rubbed his temples. Every time Grandpa reached into his pouch, Ethan feared yet another scroll was coming out for him to read, and if not a new scroll, then one of the same scrolls he'd already read. *I've read one of those scrolls at least one hundred times . . . of drakes, Kesem, and wonders.* He silently imitated his grandpa's voice. It was almost more than he could bare. When would he get to practice the techniques?

But every time he even thought about complaining, Grandpa would give him a stern look that would immediately silence the boy. Besides, the studies left him stir-crazy and frustrated. *I bet Kristian isn't having to put up with this!* he mumbled.

"Ethan? You're awake. Good. Come over here and sit with me a moment," Grandpa suddenly interrupted.

Both lions momentarily turned their big heads to look in the boy's direction, then swiveled back and continued passively scouting the country side.

Ethan winced then sluggishly pushed himself into a standing position and started for Grandpa. Glancing down at Seon, the boy realized the drake was also awake. He found a seat next to the old man and tried to compose himself with the relaxation technique he lately found to be an invaluable exercise, if only to relieve him of his thoughts about squashing his younger sister.

Seon apparently sensed the boy was calmer and flew to his usual perch on Ethan's shoulder, while starting his ritual morning preening.

Rubbing the drake's chin, Ethan welcomed his little companion, momentarily forgetting all about his anger. *Rest well?* He queried.

*Indeed.* came the reply. *And on a full stomach.*

A mental image of the little drake fat from his feast and laying on his side burst in on the boy's thoughts, and he refrained from laughing.

Grandpa looked tenderly at the boy. "I know this hasn't been easy for you," he started then cleared his throat. "It is difficult to understand why you must learn these scrolls by heart. You must understand that preparation is the key to survival." The old man paused and now focused his eyes gently on Ethan, who was still a bit grumpy, but softening a little. "Remember how you practiced building the hives . . . ?" he started again.

"Grandpa, is this going to turn into another lecture about beehives?" Ethan slapped his mouth shut as soon as he realized he had said it aloud.

The old man ignored the comment altogether. "In this is wisdom, learning is about knowledge and application. You can't apply something that you have not fully studied out in your mind first. It simply doesn't work that way." Grandpa paused again while scratching at his beard. At least he wasn't twisting his hair this time.

Ethan's face brightened at the mention of applying knowledge. For a brief moment, he hoped Grandpa would give him some real practice time. He was sorely disappointed.

"That is why it is time for you to read this scroll!" Grandpa pulled out a worn, leathery scroll from within his pouch.

*Can't he just lose that darn pouch?* Ethan grumbled to himself as he shook his head. He quickly stopped and awkwardly looked away when Grandpa glanced over at him. Embarrassed, he grabbed for the scroll, but missed it altogether.

Grandpa nimbly held it out of his reach. "Do not treat this lightly, my son. This scroll is of great import to you for your journey . . ."

Ethan finally burst out, "Grandpa, why is it always riddles and pieces of a story. Why can I never get the full truth out of anyone? I always hear of prophecies, of emperors, of the journey, or things about me that can't be true? I'm sick of all of it. I wish none of this had ever happened."

Seon gave a tiny indignant squawk.

Ethan knew he had said the wrong thing. *I didn't mean you, Seon, never you!*

*Watch what comes out of your mouth, you need to think before you speak, Ethan!* Seon retorted then went back to preening himself under his other wing.

*You're starting to sound like Grandpa!* Ethan spat.

*Ah, I knew he was smart.* Seon smirked.

Ethan smiled in spite of himself then glanced up at Grandpa. He was not as amused. *Uh-oh,* he thought and braced himself for a stern reprimand.

"Feel better?" Grandpa gave Ethan a wry look. "Ethan, you're not meant to know everything just now. You have to find it out for yourself . . ."

"See, that's just what I mean, first Limnah, then the queen, and now you! You all tell me the same thing—you'll find out when you're ready. You're not ready yet. Be patient! Well, I say that I'm ready now! I've done more than my fair share. Isn't it time for someone to trust me, instead of the other way around?" Ethan folded his arms and stared angrily at nothing in particular. He stomped his feet in the sand, kicking up a small dust cloud.

Grandpa slowed as if selecting his next words carefully. "Ethan, what I wish for is my youth, again—oh, what a time it was. I had my whole life laid out in front of me—every bit of it an adventure just waiting for me to discover it . . ."

Ethan wasn't quite sure where this was going, and he certainly couldn't tell how this related to anything they had been discussing. But at least in this case, he decided to be prudent for once and keep his mouth shut.

"But I wanted to grow up too fast," the old man continued. "All of my actions were to prove myself to . . . well . . . myself." Grandpa looked down at Ethan and reached out to pat the young boy's shoulder. "Do you see, Ethan? I wanted all of the answers given to me. I didn't want to work for it on my own. The foibles of my youth, and it cost me . . . greatly!" his voice wavered for a moment.

Ethan perked up. After a few moments of silence, he thought Grandpa might lapse into another tangent and tried to keep the subject alive. "How, Grandpa?"

The old man gave him a quizzical look and then shook his head. "I had answers given to me, they led me down a hard path and they forced me—no, I forced myself to follow them . . . blindly . . ." He paused again, shaking his head. "If I had sought the answers on my own, studied them, my path would have been simpler." Grandpa lapsed into silence again.

Determined, Ethan decided to push the subject. "Grandpa?"

The old man looked back at him. "Yes?"

"I'm not sure what you're talking about, what paths? What answers? What choices did you make?" He knew that he'd asked too many questions and risked the old man waking from his stroll down memory lane. But he was intoxicated with the possibility of Grandpa opening up a window into the older man's much younger life.

Ethan had only heard tiny slivers of his grandfather's life before. The old man kept them very close to him and, on occasion, would let out pieces of the puzzle. But not enough to ever build a complete picture from, let alone a fragment of one. He was always dodgy on the specifics and only talked of his past as if it were another time and place altogether.

Seon had stopped his preening and was now intently listening as well.

Ethan softly chuckled to himself.

Grandpa gave the boy another wry smile. "Let's just say that I learned my lessons the hard way. It is up to you to find your path. But . . . ," he said in a warning tone, "I won't be part of that path by giving you free answers, answers always come with a price."

*Ughh,* Ethan thought. He wasn't going to get *any* answers.

Seon must have realized this as well as he immediately went back to preening.

The old man chuckled, breaking the momentary tension. He lowered the scroll back into Ethan's grasp. "Think of your questions as you read this scroll. Perhaps you will find some of the answers inside. Most likely more questions, but perhaps some answers as well." The old man smiled and placed the scroll in Ethan's hands. "I will attend to the camp while you read."

Ethan looked blankly at the cylinder resting in his hands.

Seon paused and looked eagerly at it as well.

Standing slowly, Grandpa flashed the boy another smile and turned back toward the camp. He glanced back once more, "Read, Ethan!" he urged in a gentle, yet commanding voice.

Ethan untied the scroll, rolled it out on his lap in front of him, and began to read.

### ~ Blood, Fire, and Wind ~

*I, Corian, emperor of all that I purvey, write this by mine own hand and stand with the three guardians at the head of my armies, Shimlah, Osirach, and Tumar-si. We four stand in defense against the black dragon and have placed him in purgatory by excellence of our strength, nobility, and with aid from the white drake.*

. . .

*Black dragon?* Ethan gasped. *Seon, there is a black dragon . . . I'm not crazy . . . it . . .*

*Seon!* he interrupted his own conversation. *Another white drake!*

*Could it be?* the drake asked, forgetting all about his morning preening ritual.

Ethan rushed on with his reading, hoping to find more.

. . .

*But it is all for naught. He will escape, with time he will bring destruction and folly. After all, he is only the servant of one greater than he. He will find a way.*

. . .

*What does that mean? I mean, c'mon. How is this supposed to help me?* He glanced sidewise at the small drake. *Help us?* he amended apologetically.

*Read on!* Seon urged, now looking over the boy's shoulder and peering down at the scroll in anticipation for what would come next.

. . .

*But there is hope in us. We establish a prophecy to be had by all generations to come. The chaos dragon, Tiamat, will be overthrown, even as the sand shifts. Three, who are strangers among us, will defeat him. The prophecy of the three shall vanquish the dragon for eternity if but to speak blood, fire, and wind. It is in three that all are saved—one in purpose, unified under the great God. The white emperor will lead, the other to serve and return hope for doubt. The other will fall.*

. . .

*More riddles. Ugghhh. Any ideas, Seon?* Ethan asked, again looking at the small drake expectantly. If anyone could interpret it, Seon could.

*None. It's the prophecy we've heard of. But it doesn't tell us how*, came the obvious answer, and much to Ethan's disappointment. *Unless . . .*

Ethan raised an eyebrow.

The drake's eyes blinked momentarily with a thin transparent membrane shielding his eyes from a sudden gust of wind. *Yes, unless . . . for the three to defeat him . . . Could that be you, Kristian, and Lola? Perhaps it is about your dream of the tree?*

Ethan shot him a credulous look.

*Stay with me*, the little drake pleaded.

*But how does that answer anything?* Ethan grumbled. *What does it mean to speak three words . . . Ughh, I hate riddles. I've never been good at them.*

*We know the dragon's name—Tiamat!* Seon continued. *So . . . maybe it's a puzzle that we need to pull together from your dreams!* the drake concluded, looking quizzically back at Ethan.

*OK . . . and that leads us where?* the boy retorted.

*Don't know, but it feels right*, Seon thought reassuringly. *You had the dream of the black dragon, the One God, and the mounting sand. You were all at the tree*, the drake thought, reflecting on the dreams. He then suddenly turned his interest back to the scroll. *Is there more?*

Ethan nodded. *What?* he asked, not expecting the shift in the discussion. *Oh . . . yeah, one last sentence . . .*

. . .

*Only then must the chosen one continue on and will move beyond our abilities. He will remove the master from his place. He must seek out the One God, sit down at the feast, draw power to fortify, and vanquish the foe.*

. . .

Ethan scratched his head in frustration.

*OK . . . so we need to take the building blocks from your dreams and construct them. The dreams may be the key to unlock this . . . we just need to think through them all*, Seon plodded through. *We just need some time.*

*Well, we have plenty of time to talk about it now*, Ethan countered. *Besides, I still don't understand what this means. I mean, moving beyond abilities to remove the master from his place, sitting down to a feast to draw power and fortify? Fortify what? Arghhh, these riddles only give more questions than answers!* Ethan barked.

Seon looked consolingly at the boy.

The Drake Epics - Journey to Qara

Before either could discuss this further, Grandpa called for the camp to be broken down and the day's march to begin.

They had been so tied up in their discovery that Ethan had completely lost track of the time. He noticed that Lola was sidled up next to Grandpa, working on her morning memorizations with the old man. He felt a moment of envy. She was not a good reader, so she got quality study time with Grandpa instead of reading.

*But . . .*, he protested, pulling his mind back to what he and Seon had been studying.

"We need to move on!" One of the lions suddenly announced.

Ethan jerked around. He hadn't noticed the cat behind him and was amazed at how stealthily the creatures could move when they wanted to.

"If I'm right, we should be nearing Hosap Kalesi by midday," Grandpa stated. "We'll make camp there. The journey beyond that is the hottest area I know of, and we'll need to cross it extremely early in the morning in order to avoid the . . . dangers that lurk there." Grandpa paused, and Ethan sensed the old man's hesitation. But it was only for a moment.

"That and the direct sun upon us," Grandpa amended.

—  —  —

After hiking for half the morning, the group broke through the eerie rocky outcroppings and began to descend into a great valley that seemingly formed out of nowhere. The sands changed from a light tan hue to a rusty brown color that gave it an unearthly appearance. The valley was flanked by the great Caucasus Mountains looming in the distance at the other end of it, now visibly bluish brown against the sky. They were surprisingly closer than Ethan had thought they were earlier in the day, at least what he caught glimpses of between the large jagged rocky terrain they had to navigate through.

Far ahead of him in the center of the valley, Ethan could just see a gigantic rocky outcrop jutting up from the valley floor. He strained to look harder at the valley protrusion. There lay the ruins of a brownish clay brick castle gracefully set atop it, almost entirely camouflaged into the cliff itself.

Grandpa paused, throwing his arm out in front of him for the small company to see. "There lies castle Hosap Kalesi," he said proudly as if he himself had built the structure.

The children were too tired to even cheer. The sun was taking its toll on them already. After too brief of a rest, they were off again, hiking toward the castle.

403

Lola stumbled on a stone and Ethan reached out to help, but she yanked her arm away from her older brother in protest. "I don't need any help!" She snarled.

"Fine!" he countered, but Ethan could tell that the hike was having the biggest impact on her—she was more tired than he had ever seen her before. *Most likely why she is so quiet,* he thought to himself.

*Yes, she is so tired,* Seon joined in.

*Seon,* Ethan started. *We shouldn't have brought her. She can't keep up with this for much longer,* he mused.

*But where would she have stayed? Surely not with Kristian. It was too dangerous for her and Deseret, you know that!* countered the drake.

Ethan knew it was true. But it didn't make him feel any more confident. He turned his attention back to the decaying fortress as they neared it.

He could now distinguish the upper battlements from the lower courtyard. The castle was set high on the outcrop. The upper portion was shrouded in cliff, making it impossible for most anyone to climb its steep sides, let alone the towering wall rising vertically from the cliff face. The outcrop sloped downward and toward the courtyard at a steep angle until finally reaching the only entrance to the castle from a winding dirt road leading up to it.

"Grandpa?" Ethan suddenly asked.

The old man halted, turning to look at the boy. He looked relieved for another brief rest.

"Does anyone live in that castle?"

"Hmm? Oh, no, no," the old man remarked. "Although I have had to chase out some . . . well, unwanted creatures when I've stayed here in the past. But usually they keep their distance from me, and I from them." He scratched at his beard in thought for a moment, picking out small pebbles from the tangle of hair.

"It was once a proud sanctuary, you know, for any who risked the crossing, and there were but few who made that crossing. As legend goes, a great Sheikh lived here, but she sinned and a great evil befell the castle and it fell into ruin."

Lola spoke up for the first time that day, "What happened, Grandpa?"

He gingerly looked down at his granddaughter and stared hard at the castle as if that would provide the answer. "Well . . . the legend speaks of a great tempest, that by the way is also a curse to befall any who venture into its halls, although I have yet to experience it." Grandpa wandered off course before reclaiming his senses. "Although the caravan storytellers who tell this story tell it as a nightmare of sorts and the bravest claim

## The Drake Epics - Journey to Qara

they have weathered the storm itself. In any event, the castle is surrounded by a dark and dreary wasteland. Darkness is the main source of terror in the stories, the heat and glare of the day are second . . . ," Grandpa started to wander again.

Ethan quickly pulled him back on course, not wanting to lose the story. "What about the darkness?"

Grandpa paused. "Hmm? Oh, yes. Where was I? Ah . . . well, the culminating horror is the mist of darkness, a depressing mixture of dust and clammy fog, which adds to the night and completes the confusion of any who wander in the waste."

"But that doesn't explain the storm," Ethan added.

"No, it doesn't, but I'm not quite through yet," the old man said in a rebuking tone. "Do you see that slight crevice leading down and to the castle itself? Just there?" Grandpa pointed just beyond the castle where a depressed crevice in the landscape could be faintly seen.

Ethan and Lola strained to see it and then nodded in unison.

"Well, that is a true desert river. It used to be a clear stream a few paces wide with its underground source but a hundred paces away that gave life to the palace. The great dark mist raged around the castle, and the stream turned into a raging muddy wash, a *sayl* of filthy water that overwhelmed the castle, even from its height, and swept all people away to their destruction." Grandpa finished and looked up at the sun. "But that is enough talk. It is time to get moving," he announced and, turning, started walking again. "We need to get into the shade before you all fade away."

The children weren't yet through with the story though.

"And then?" they both chimed in unison as they trotted to keep up with the old man.

"What then what?" Grandpa asked. "That's it. The Sheikh and her household were never heard of again. That and caravan storytellers like to embellish on the curse for any who venture near the premises. I doubt any of them even believe that this place still exists. I'm the only one who ever ventures out this far."

The children lapsed back into silence as they conjured up the mist of darkness in their minds along with the people being swept away by the great waters. Although Ethan noticed that Lola was walking a little closer to him on the remainder of their descent into the valley.

The little group continued to briefly pause as Grandpa pointed a number of times to mention bits and pieces of facts about the castle as they walked. "Look at that, it's complete with an old granary, a water cistern full of long-weathered holes, and a dungeon, now a deep hole filled with rubble." As they neared the old ruins, the old man pointed out a series of arrow slits along the walls. Each arrow slit was long and thin, with a short horizontal opening extending to the left and another extending to the right, several finger widths higher.

"Do you know why the slits are arranged so?" Grandpa asked, more to amuse himself rather than anyone else. He didn't wait for confirmation. "Well, the theory behind this split-level slit design was that if you had a single horizontal slit cutting straight across the vertical slit, an archer from the ground below would have an easier target. But by splitting the horizontal slit into two slits at different heights, it makes a more difficult target for there is no single converging point on which an opposing archer could concentrate."

After Grandpa's latest boring fact, the group lapsed into silence until they reached the castle. The lions indicated that the others should wait while they scouted out the ruins for any lurking danger. Both lions reappeared a short time later and approved the party to move into the castle proper.

They entered through the great stone doors, one of which was completely off its rusted hinges and the other leaning dangerously across the entrance. The small group passed a once-great feasting hall, now in shambles, with a few side hallways and multiple other chambers. Most of the roof had long since decayed or fallen in, leaving much of the grounds exposed to the elements.

They made their way through the covered areas, which the children welcomed as the shade provided momentary relief from the blazing sun.

Ethan imagined to himself how grand it must have been as he walked along. He had to pick his way through the rubble, feeling slightly uneasy within the grounds.

Grandpa presently halted in a covered alcove and stated that this was camp for the night.

The lions immediately went to work setting up a perimeter.

The group would retire early, Grandpa announced. On the morrow, they would set out on the most dangerous part of the journey—they would cross the valley of heat.

However, first he wanted to show the children a few of the castle's sights and mysteries.

# Chapter 24

## Dust Demons

*There must be opposition in all things.*

Lola walked along silently behind the others. But she soon grew weary of the conversation. *Who cares how they used to lock up prisoners?* she thought in protest as Grandpa launched into another dissertation about the castle.

Deseret gave her a consoling look as she felt entirely bored as well.

The girl tiredly peered behind her. The lion they had left behind, Helam, seemed to be preoccupied watching the immediate vicinity of their little encampment. The other lion, Koran, was intent on leading them to wherever it was they were going.

"I'm tired!" Lola abruptly announced.

Both Grandpa and Ethan stopped the conversation and turned with questioning looks.

"I'm going back to take a nap," she said in as weary of a voice that she could muster.

They both looked beyond her to size up Helam who continued to scout around their camp area. Grandpa slowly nodded without another word. They waited for her to turn and walk back to camp.

She got halfway there and glanced back over her shoulder.

The two had already turned and were engrossed in some discussion, most likely just as boring as about the prison tour. As always, Koran was already scouting ahead of them.

Lola sighed in disgust. But as she turned to walk back, something caught her eye. Something she had not intended to see here.

She glanced back at Helam and realized he had not yet noticed her. *Did you see that?* she thought to Deseret.

*Yes, what is it? It was small and quick!*

The little girl felt the excitement from her companion—Deseret loved to chase small animals! She turned to face the crevasse in the wall where she had seen the movement. It was just large enough for her to squeeze through. She looked in both directions at the camp and then at the others. Upon finding it was all clear, she stepped briskly to the wall, peered into it for a brief moment, and slipped into the darkness.

*I don't feel good about this . . . ,* Deseret warned.

Lola ignored her. She had a funny feeling she had seen this creature before. It was only a ghost, a phantom in her mind. She urged her thoughts to organize around it to reveal what it was, but it continued to stay just out of reach from her thoughts. Tantalizingly out of reach.

The crevasse opened into another hallway. This one more intact than the others. At the end of the hall, she saw another movement in her periphery, but it disappeared around the corner before her eyes could focus on it.

She galloped after it, rounded the corner, and peered into another long hall. To her amazement, she saw a small white animal sniffing at the corner of a wall a few dozen paces from where she stood. The animal raised its head and looked in her direction. Lola immediately froze as did Deseret.

*Food!* craved the small drake. Deseret lowered herself, the same as any predatory cat would do before pouncing on its prey.

*No!* Lola thought back in a desperate attempt to keep the peace. *This has meaning. I'm not sure how, but you are not to eat this creature!*

Dessert cast a withering look at the girl. *But I'm hungry . . . I haven't had a good meal—I mean a very good meal today. I was not meant to live on honey and wafers and that rancid meat your grandpa feeds us.* The blue drake stuck its tongue out in disgust.

*Well, Seon seems to like it. But I know what you mean.* The little girl remembered declining any taste of that horrid food, if you could call *that* food.

*Then let me have my juicy meal—fresh meat!* the drake thought ravenously.

Lola didn't seem to notice. *Don't you feel that we're connected to it somehow?* She paused again, trying in vain to seize hold of the thoughts evading her consciousness.

*More like connected to my stomach . . . ,* the drake returned sarcastically.

Now it was Lola's turn to cast a withering look at her companion.

Deseret fell silent for a moment before suddenly changing tone. *No, wait! I feel it now too—that's strange indeed. Why didn't I feel this from you before? As if . . . as if you two have met before . . .*

Lola looked away from the little white creature and at Dessert. She refrained from scolding the drake as she recognized her little companion was deep in thought trying to unlock the mystery of her thoughts that she herself had failed to gain access to. A sly smile spread across her lips.

Just then, the white animal bolted.

*Quick!* she thought. *We can't let it escape.*

*Easily done!* Deseret launched from her shoulder and toward the fleeing animal, what Lola now recognized as a little white bunny.

"No!" she yelled.

This seemed to spook the bunny even more. It changed direction back toward the approaching drake, in a quick succession of erratic turns, trying to evade what it thought was certain death.

Deseret was upon her prey in moments. She held it firm to the ground as it squirmed under her talons.

Lola felt that Deseret meant no harm and relaxed a little as she chased after them. *Thank you for not harming it*, she thought gratefully to her champion. She felt Deseret return the warmth of a welcome, along with a slight pang of hunger.

The girl neared them and stood still with her hands on her hips, staring down at the little bunny. It was still struggling, but didn't seem as concerned as might be expected, if it were just about to be eaten. Perhaps it felt it wouldn't be. She still couldn't figure out how they were connected. It all seemed totally impossible in her mind, but her heart told her otherwise.

The bunny had now stopped struggling altogether and cocked its head around to look at Lola. "I've been awaiting you," it said in an unusually low voice for such a small creature. Well, besides the bunny talking at all, that is.

Lola took an involuntary step backward, putting her hands to her mouth. "You talked!" she exclaimed. She took a moment to recompose her thoughts and then quickly recovered, much to hers and Deseret's surprise. "We're not going to hurt you," she said consolingly.

Then she nodded to Deseret. *Let it go.* The drake shot her a concerned look and then reluctantly glided back a short distance, pacing back and forth and ready to pounce again upon the slightest provocation.

The bunny pushed itself back up. It no longer appeared to be frightened in any way. It proceeded to lick itself clean from the dust that had collected on its fur when it was so rudely thrown to the ground. "Oh, but you will try. But that won't matter when I'm through with you." It snickered in a tone bereft of any emotion.

"Now what is that supposed to mean?" Lola questioned. "We can rescue you from this place, if you like." She looked around and raised her arms at the musty surroundings. Then, she paused, changing tactic, focusing her attention back on the creature. "Have we met before?" she asked in a soft voice.

The bunny giggled. Not the kind of frolic giggle you would expect from a creature of fun and mischief. More like a dark and foreboding giggle. "Ah, yes, we have, and you've said that before."

"Before?" Excitement leapt in Lola's chest. She knew they were connected. She just knew it!

"Yes. But you don't remember me, do you?" It presently looked deeper into Lola's eyes.

Lola felt an icy cold reach into her soul, and she withdrew her eyes for a brief moment in stunned alarm. It almost felt like what Ethan had described to her about the auditor.

Deseret had grown uncomfortable with the dialogue and was ready for action as she now started to circle her would-be prey. *Should I dispatch it?* she asked wistfully.

*Be calm Deseret. Not yet,* Lola thought back. *Not until we know what is going on. I have a bad feeling about all of this now too,* she added on a cautionary note.

*Please do hurry,* the drake concluded, and Lola thought she actually heard the little drake's stomach growl.

Shaking her head, Lola looked back at the bunny after a moment. "Should I?" she asked.

"Oh, but it was I who led you here. It was I who led your brothers and grandpa here. You have me to thank for everything. You should be groveling at my feet and thanking me for everything." The bunny boldly plodded on. "But you are in the wrong place at the wrong time, my dear. You mustn't dawdle here any longer. You must return to your brother . . . or I fear the worst." The bunny stopped licking its paw and looked mournfully back up at Lola.

"Ethan?" Lola looked around and readied to race back.

"No, not Ethan, you fool!" the bunny scolded in a stern tone. "Kristian," it declared sarcasticly, once again going back to licking its paw.

Lola stopped midstride and turned back to the creature. "Kristian?" her eyes narrowed at the mention of her eldest brother. "How do you know about Kristian or even about Ethan for that matter?" She paused then slammed her foot down with her hands again on her hips. "Who are you really? Tell me now!"

"Your brother!" the creature snarled in disgust. "He will be facing my master shortly," the creature said in a nonchalant tone. "He won't survive, not without your help anyways." A fiendish smile spread across its face. "And that will never be!" It manically chuckled.

Lola stared harder at the creature, as if this would clarify for her just what the little bunny was saying. Things were not as they appeared, she finally realized.

The little bunny suddenly stopped cold, and for a moment, Lola thought she saw its eyes turn a deep red. It crouched ready to pounce in Lola's direction. "Once again, you are in the wrong place and at the wrong time!"

Before Lola could react at the sudden change in behavior, the little creature launched itself at her throat. It would have been too late, but with a deafening roar sounding in her head from Deseret, the small drake took the bunny mid-flight with her talons.

The creature let out an unearthly shriek of rage at its displeasure with the missed attempt.

Lola covered her ears and winced at the horrible sound.

The drake landed a few paces away and looked regretfully back up at Lola. *I'm sorry, it couldn't be helped*, she declared. *But . . . at least I eat well on this day.* She bent her snout toward the creature, taking it in her jaws. She finished the job with a smooth slice of her razor-sharp teeth, and it was all over.

The bunny uttered one final word just before it died. Neither Lola nor Deseret understood its meaning, and then the creature went limp in Deseret's jaws. "Kalesi."

A sudden harsh wind stirred from nowhere, even though the hallway was almost completely enclosed and there were no visible windows. Lola strained to look for the source, but had to shield her eyes as dust kicked up in all directions.

As she squinted to see through the windy onslaught, the dust collected itself around the limp creature, and it began to change form. It's little white paws lost their fur, turning bony black as they grew. Curled black talons emerged from somewhere within. Its arms and legs followed and then the body. Finally its ears retracted, and its head changed into a black leathery maw. It appeared quite like Deseret, like a drake, only much blacker than anything Lola had ever seen before. It was eerily beautiful.

The body presently began to quickly grow in size.

Deseret held tight to the creature, not wanting to give up her hard-earned meal. But in the end, the growing mass proved too much of a challenge and she was compelled to let it go.

Lola took another faltering step backward as the form now reached high above her. She shot a terrified look at Deseret.

*We've got to get out of here!* she frantically thought, but found that she couldn't move a muscle in her body. She was transfixed. She desperately tried to find the control to shield or protect herself. But it felt as if all her strength had been sapped. She was perfectly helpless.

Deseret sensed her distress and, having lost her kill, was now extremely agitated. She growled and sliced at the large creature with her jaws and talons. When this approach appeared to do no harm, she set to flight, repeatedly striking at the growing monster's head; but she passed through the specter with every lunge.

A throaty laugh gurgled from the creature's mouth, apparently amused at the pointless attacks by the small drake. The laughter stopped as the monster focused its attention on the young girl, bringing its massive head around, as it glared down at her. It paused for a brief moment, and then all at once, it reached to strike at her.

Deseret took one final lunge at the monster in a desperate attempt to protect her companion, but in dismay, passed through vapor yet again.

The monster struck, one of its talons protruding from its once-white paw as it sliced at Lola.

Lola squeezed her eyes shut and curled back away from the monster, ready for the blow—nothing happened. Suddenly, she felt a familiar warmth. She realized it was the warmth she had felt in Qara—it was the queen.

*I am with you, young one,* she heard the queen whisper. *Be at peace.*

She opened one eye in surprise. She was sure she would see the queen. At least she should have felt the attack. But there was no queen. The monster was still there, but with a look of confusion spread across its face as its eyes darted back and forth.

The black monster recoiled its paw and looked at it with disdain. It paused for only a moment more, then it lunged again. But its claw passed through Lola once more without any injury to the girl, not even a scratch. But Lola felt an icy cold breeze pass through her entire body, and she shivered uncontrollably for a few moments afterward. She was quickly realizing that this was a specter of some sort, and she began to take courage that she would come to no harm.

The creature laughed, but Lola could sense its discomfort and shock at the failed attempts. It hovered in the air for a moment, directly in front of her. Lola could see the hatred and loathing for her in its eyes. What had she done to make such an enemy? If she had known this creature before, and she still couldn't remember any such encounter, why was it so angry at her? After all, she was only a little girl.

The creature gave one throatier laugh and then hissed at her in contempt. It began to again shrink until it was the size of Deseret.

This was all the opening the blue drake needed, and she launched herself at the creature in a last attempt to eat.

The black specter looked malevolently at the pouncing drake, then folded inward on itself and spun into a swirling black stream of smoke that streaked upward, disappearing into the rocky ceiling above.

Deseret reached it too late and burst through the smoke. Upon finding that she had missed her meal for a second time, she grunted and returned to the girl, quite bitter about the whole experience. But her concern for Lola overwhelmed her anger. She peered into the girl's eyes. *Are you all right?* she asked.

Lola paused for a moment, still shivering and still frozen in thought about what had just happened. She slowly shook her head. *I . . . I couldn't use my Kesem. It happened too fast,* she whimpered.

Deseret looked lovingly at the girl and nuzzled her head against Lola's cheek, as if this would comfort her and help her to forget.

*I felt the queen by my side. But she can't be here!*

*Oh, but I am, my child,* came the reply to Lola's surprise.

Lola turned to see a ghostly image of a golden dragon before her. *Who are you?* she asked. *You have the queen's voice, but you are not the queen!* she exclaimed.

*Look harder, little one*, the queen answered.

Lola squinted hard and realized that the dragon had the queen's eyes—it was the queen. *But how?* she asked. *I don't understand.*

*You will, little one, you will. For now, you must warn the others. Your brother is in great peril.* The vision started to blur and became harder to see. A light appeared overhead, and the dragon queen began to ascend into the ceiling.

*Wait!* Lola exclaimed. *What was that thing? Where are you going? Is Kristian safe?* she asked all at once.

*You will meet the monster again. Warn the others . . . ,* the voice trailed off as the image began to disappear from view, followed by the light that drew itself upward and also vanished. *Warn the others . . . ,* the voice echoed for the third and last time.

*What are you seeing?* Deseret's thoughts abruptly came into Lola's mind. *Where did you go just now?*

Suddenly Lola straightened up, with a new look of resolve. *We have to tell Grandpa and Ethan!*

*But . . . ,* Deseret thought back.

*No time, Kristian is in trouble! I'll tell you on the way.* Lola turned with Deseret perched uneasily on her shoulder and bolted back to the others.

# Chapter 25

# Royal Mastery

*Self-control is at the root of all understanding.*

The last week had been hectic. Kristian couldn't remember if he'd gotten any sleep or not. Anxiety buzzed in the air as the city of gnomes and lions readied for battle. Armaments had been cast up and otherwise reinforced both in the city proper as well as in the surrounding Qara deserts including the forest island groves.

For the most part, the battlements were ingenious traps of spiked shafts placed at strategic choke points and buried so they wouldn't be noticed by advancing troops. Long, deep trenches had been dug out at the

# Royal Mastery

tunnel gates, casting mountainous hills of sand behind them, upon which spiked fortifications were set to provide troops an advantage of height over incoming assaults.

Kristian thought they might not hold against the giant wolves he had seen earlier, but all of this mobilization paled in comparison to the layers of Kesem that were being woven across the landscape. The city walls crackled with blue sparks. Magical gnomes that Kristian had seen only once before when the children had been challenged were now everywhere, placing powerful rune spells on gates, doorways, and at random points on the earthen floors in order to deter marauders from the least bit of mischief. The young man could not fathom how the gnomes kept all of this straight in their minds. When he had to walk through the city, he had an escort wherever he went for fear of tripping one of these magical defenses.

One particular gnome he had watched, had cast a wrapping spell rune on a doorway. The only way he knew the spell had been cast was that the gnome accidentally tripped it after absentmindedly walking through that same doorway. The spell threw the little man to the ground, and seismic waves of air held him tight, such that he couldn't move any part of his body, before the spell had knocked him unconscious. As a trepid soldier, Kristian attempted to free him, but had himself barely escaped the same fate, thanks to another gnome who had stepped in, disarming the trap in order to rescue them both in time, much to the boy's relief.

BeeSting had lit off the boy's shoulder, having predicted the event, and hovered over the boy, helpless to give aid.

Kristian often conjured up scenes of how well the battlements would hold, or how valiantly he would stand against the invasion. He tried to conjure up realistic visions of attacks and counterattacks in his mind, trying to capture every scenario available to him. Still, he'd had no experience at any of this, and all he had to pull from where his previous tactical strategic studies at Julfa or from analyzing the tactics that gnomes and lions used when they sparred.

Aside from helping throw up more bastions of defense, the boy took great pride in practice with his newfound weapons. He thought that this gave him a considerable advantage over any opponent. After all, he had his magical sickle sword—truly a kingly gift. Although the sword halberd continued to annoyingly smack against his thigh whenever he walked around with it strapped on.

But he had also discovered a much more effective weapon. The day after his family had left, Queen Ashteroth had gifted him a copper blade socket axe. It was an impressive weapon for piercing armor, and it gave him much better mobility than what the sword provided. The axe handle was elegantly designed with copper at its base, midsection, and at the head, next to the axe insert. The remainder of the body was decorated with a mahogany wrap, wound tightly to enable a better grip, and he could elongate the shaft to a longer pole that stood as high as his chest. But what was most intriguing about the weapon was the ability to replace the axe heads with various shapes and sizes, one of which was a particularly wicked blade exposing a narrow point at one end for piercing, and a razor-sharp spine on the other for slicing with. He had used this against makeshift wooden opponents in the ring and had hacked off more than a dozen wooden limbs. But by far, his most favorite insert was a magical copper trident head that he could set flame to. The trident scorched anything it came into contact within mere moments.

Still, it occurred to him that these were not enough to win in battle, considering how new he was at this sort of thing, and Heramon helped him see this more clearly.

"All of your training with a sling, a sword, or an axe," he recalled Heramon pointing at the boy bristling with his precious weapons, "if you don't harness that power I saw in the ring! That is where your true advantage lies."

And so, Kristian carved out time to mediate on his magical qualities and to harness his core power the queen had exposed him to. Of course, she had again shared this counsel when he received the sickle axe—after all, the axe was merely an extension of his own powers, she'd said. Nonetheless, he wore all three weapons wherever he went, just in case the occasion arose to randomly spar with someone, or in the case of something far more sinister that he felt brewing just outside of Qara's gates.

Reports had steadily poured in about movements within the Forbidden City. From what little Kristian could pick up from conversations he overheard, the destitute landscape was now completely overrun by roving wolves and camps of armored troops. The front guard of Qara, only hundreds strong, lined the only entrance into the land, with the bulk of the force encamped just beyond, extending into the Forbidden City.

He had not seen the fortifications there, as yet, but was under strict orders to remain within Qara by Heramon as well as by Muschle, even if his curiosity got the better of him to go and see. After the incident in the ring, he didn't want to upset his mentor any more than he had already done. So he was content to practice and help out where he could.

He assumed the reports were why he had seen less and less of Heramon in the ensuing days, attending long strategy councils with the king and queen and their generals at a secret location somewhere within the palace proper. In fact, Heramon had only returned late at night, looking more tired than usual and speaking little at meals before politely retiring to his bed. The boy couldn't blame him. Still, he would have liked to see more of his mentor, at least to receive additional training and sage advice from the seasoned warrior instead of the handful of comments he made to the boy here and there.

Notwithstanding Heramon's absence, Kristian had already improved threefold since he had started to spar. A gnome and a lion, in particular, had taken a special liking to the boy and took him under their wings as sparring partners. Remarkably, their friendship blossomed in a matter of days until they all felt they had known one another since birth.

The gnome, named Shalamar after his father and his father before him, looked a little like Muschle. He differed only in that he had a neat trimmed goatee, still a light brown due to his youth. Shalamar had a funny comment about everything that went on. In fact, he easily countered every witty comment or comeback Kristian could come up with, and Kristian thought his sides would burst a few times from laughing so hard at the little gnome's jokes.

The lion's name was Bortex, and he was slightly bigger than many of the other cats Kristian had previously seen, bigger even than the lion the queen had him face off against. Bortex was quiet, only ever speaking a word or two in conversation; but he laughed at all of Shalamar's jokes along with Kristian, even when they weren't all that funny. He made up for his quietness by his sheer strength and warm personality.

Together, they made quite a team and often fell into mischief when they sparred. But their playful banter was all in preparation to defend Qara. Since Heramon was so busy, Kristian found that he was spending most of his time with his newfound companions. Much to his liking, they did everything together, whether it was the hard manual labor on Qara's defenses or taking every opportunity they could to spar with one another.

The boy had also found out much more about the gnomes and the lions than he and Ethan ever could have. At first he'd thought that gnomes and lions could change their forms at will. But the two openly laughed at him when he broached the topic. He learned that each individual was born as a gnome or a lion, but at the age of *al-ghezihm*, or accountability similar to what boys underwent at Julfa, the gnome or lion had the choice of remaining what they had grown up as or to go through the transformation, as they called it, into the other form. He was shocked to hear this and couldn't imagine why any of them would want to ever choose to be a gnome. The lions were magnificent and far stronger than any of the gnomes or any other animal for that matter, he thought. But every individual had the choice. This was celebrated at their sixteenth birthday and was one of the most important events of their lives.

Bortex was sixteen years old and had just gone through his transformation. He had been born a cat and stayed a cat. Shalamar was fifteen years old and hadn't reached the age of choice, although he adamantly professed that he would remain a gnome.

"I'm telling you, lions are better!" Bortex had said.

Shalamar pinched his nose while waving with the other hand. "And stink like one too." He countered as he scrunched up his face into a comical ball of wrinkles.

Bortext laughed sarcastically. "Very funny!" he said in a mock whining voice and then proceeded to pounce on the youth.

"C'mon, guys, it was just a question," Kristian apologized. "Let's get back to sparring. It's not like I get the chance to turn into a lion or anything," he finished grumpily.

The other stopped midwrestle, giving the picture an awkward appearance.

"Yeah, humans are even worse than a gnome!" Bortex chuckled.

Before Kristian knew what was happening, the lion reached out with one paw and swiped Kristian's legs out from under him, dragging him into the tussle.

BeeSting wanted no part in the upcoming wrestle and launched off Kristian's shoulder. He flew a few paces from the three and settled on the ground, content to watch in peace from the sidelines and preen himself.

Kristian glanced back up at the small drake in between flailing arms and legs and motioned for the drakes help. When it appeared he'd get none, he spat, "Ah . . . don' need your help to get out of this anyways!" He dug deep within and found his core, then uttered the word *yangin*. A familiar flame cropped out of his hand, and he held it under the lion until the cat gave a soft yelp at the heat and pulled his weight off the boy. Kristian took the opportunity and lodged one foot under Bortex's underside for leverage and launched himself around and up onto the cat's massive shoulders. He let out a shout of triumph at his accomplishment and pounded harmlessly on the cat's muscled back.

Bortex, on the other hand, was too busy trying to wrap Shalamar into an unnaturally small gnomish ball.

The gnome grunted and wheezed, not overly pleased with his situation. He presently reached out with a swipe of his hand, missing the first time, but landing the grab on the second try and pulled hard on Bortex's hair tuft under the cat's right leg—a very sensitive area for sand lions.

Bortex let out a howl and reared back.

Kristian whooped and hollered as he kicked into the cat's sides, much like someone riding a giant hairy horse that had risen up on its hind legs.

This gave Shalamar just enough time to roll out from under the cat's massive paws. The nimble gnome whipped off his rope from around his waist (he always had it tied around his waist) and skillfully swung it around the cat's hind legs, tying it into a quick makeshift noose. He gave it a quick tug, satisfied it would hold, and pulled on it harder, grimacing at the strain. The noose tightened around Bortex' legs, burrowing into the cat's fur. Pulling on the lion's hair tuft again, he waited for the lion to shift his wait, then drove his shoulder hard into the lion and pushed the massive animal over and onto his side.

"Who's the boss? Who's the boss?" the gnome taunted and did a little jig.

Kristian, still ecstatic at his own feat, flailed his arms around in victory. He didn't notice the lion start to tumble and therefore didn't jump off in time as Bortex fell. He hit the ground with a thud, stretching out his arms to soften the blow, but pinned his right leg under the cat's side in the process. Fortunately for him, the lion's padded fur cushioned the blow from the fall, but Kristian was now completely trapped and couldn't pull his leg out no matter how hard he yanked on it.

Shalamar took a quick step back and admired his handiwork, then giggled with glee, and flung himself over the cat's body and directly onto Kristian, putting the younger boy in a rough headlock.

"OK, OK!" Kristian yelped. "You got me," he resigned.

"Not until you beg!" Shalamar barked with a gigantic smile on his face.

The boy was just about to give in when Bortex roared and swiveled around, his hind legs still tied. The lion pinned Shalimar under one of his giant paws, much to the gnome's surprise.

Shalimar shrieked as he thrashed his arms and legs around to somehow free himself. But it was no use, and he stopped, taking in a lung full of air. "You win. You win." He sighed.

Free from Bortex, Kristian took advantage of the opportunity and lunged a counterattack on Shalamar to repay the smaller gnome in kind with his own version of a headlock.

Bortex was too quick and caught Kristian in his thigh, knocking the boy down and pinning him with a quick stroke of his other paw.

Kristian struggled to free himself as much as the gnome had tried just moments before.

"It's no use, Kristian," the gnome said in an unexpected pleasant tone.

The boy momentarily stopped thrashing and glanced sideways at the gnome.

Shalamar lay perfectly still with both arms behind his head, looking exasperatedly up at the cat. "Yes, Bortex, we both know how strong you are!" With that, he rolled his eyes in an exaggerated expression so that both could see him.

The other two broke into laughter in response, as the lion presently rolled over, pulling both paws off his companions, such that all three were now lying on their backs, looking up at the ceiling.

Seeing that the wrestling competition was at an end, BeeSting flew back over to his companion. He landed on the boy's chest and curled up in a ball as Kristian stroked at the drake's neck. Apparently, the boy had forgotten all about the drake's unwillingness to help out just moments before.

"Good thing I didn't have my axe, or you would both be crying right now," Kristian bragged as he continued to stroke the red drake.

Shalamar took the opportunity to roll his eyes again. "Yeah—that would have been something else. If only you could use it as well as you talk about it." He retorted sarcastically.

Bortex stifled a silent chuckle. But both Shalamar and Kristian could hear the deep rumble in his throat.

Kristian smiled in spite of himself. "You have to admit that we're getting better."

"Better? No, not nearly. We still can't take them on." Shalamar nodded over toward another ring where two gnomes and a lion were sparring.

"They're older than we are, and more experienced," Bortex answered. "Not fair to compare us."

Shalamar's tone turned unusually serious. "Doesn't matter. When we get out there . . . you know . . . in battle, no one is gonna give us a break, just 'cause we're younger," he remarked with a faraway look in his eyes. "Besides, my dagger will do all the talking for me."

Kristian knew this was all talk—just like him, neither Shalamar nor Bortex had ever been in battle before. In fact, both were very interested when Kristian told the story of how the children had fought off the wolves in the Forbidden City. They'd already asked him to repeat it a hundred times in the few short days since they'd met. Kristian was growing tired of retelling it.

"We'll do all right, as long as we watch each another's backs," Kristian confided.

"Yeah, well, we're sure to do that," Shalamar answered. "And with BeeSting scouting above, we should be right good at it," he concluded.

Bortex grunted in answer.

Shalamar suddenly changed topic. "Why did your grandfather leave you behind again?" he blurted out.

It was now time for Kristian to roll his eyes. "Seriously. I told you already. He said I was man enough to stand on my own," he snapped. "Besides, I have BeeSting, like you said," he concluded. But deep down, he felt a sudden pang that he missed his family and the fact that he couldn't protect his younger siblings anymore.

Again, another nagging feeling tugged at him that he belonged somewhere else. Vague memories flooded his mind as he removed his hand from BeeSting to stroke his white necklace. He couldn't remember where he had gotten the necklace from, he had always worn it and assumed it was a great treasure bestowed on him by his parents.

The drake raised his head and peered around at Kristian, then lay back down and closed his eyes.

"But it doesn't make sense," Shalamar persisted. "I mean, I thought that you three were supposed to . . . you know . . . stick together. Why leave you behind when they are off trying to fix everything?"

Kristian sighed and resumed stroking BeeSting. "Cause I can help here," he said in his usual annoyed tone. "Let's talk about something else, OK?" He searched his mind to find something he could latch onto. He didn't have to think for long before he was interrupted.

"Kristian! Kristian! There you are . . ."

Kristian jerked up and looked around. It was Heramon. "Heramon, what are you doing here? I thought . . . ?"

"No time, we need to go now!" Heramon interrupted again. "Get your stuff and let's go. I'll explain along the way."

Kristian looked at his companions. Both were watching him with excited, inquisitive looks etched in their faces. Then it occurred to him.

"Heramon, can Shalamar and Bortex come along?"

"Who?" Heramon asked distractedly as he looked over his shoulder at something else.

Kristian took a deep breath and then took the plunge. "Shalamar and Bortex," he repeated more clearly. "They are assigned to me. You know, to fight?" he lied and let the last comment fall from his lips, not knowing what to expect from the other two. He winked at Shalamar, who in turn gave Bortex a jab with his elbow, and Kristian knew that both were all right with it.

"Assigned?" Heramon asked, again absentmindedly. "I didn't know you had assignments. I haven't heard of anything like that. Who assigned you?" he asked. "Never mind, fine. They can both come along, but they have to be quiet. The first peep I hear from either of them, and that's it," he said, pointing a finger at both.

The gnome and the lion nodded in excited understanding.

"Now, let's go," Heramon concluded quickly as he briefly sized them up.

The boy nodded and motioned for the others to collect their things and to follow.

Heramon didn't explain much of anything as they walked along. He seemed completely preoccupied by something else entirely.

So Kristian lapsed into quiet discussion with his friends, who were both beyond eager of what would happen next. As they walked along, Kristian soon discovered that they were heading in the direction of the palace war room. The anticipation grew, and he suddenly felt a little queasy. He had only been allowed there once before when he had first volunteered. Afterward, he hadn't been invited back. He wasn't sure what this meant.

Kristian leaned closer into Bortex, who was lumbering next to him, and motioned for Shalamar to do the same. "We're going to the war room!" he whispered hoarsely.

Shalamar shot him a quick, nervous look. "The . . . the war room?" he asked back in a whisper, slightly stuttering.

The boy nodded quickly and decided to prod Heramon for further information. "Stay behind me," he whispered and quickened his pace to catch his mentor up, clearing his throat. "Heramon," he ventured.

Heramon turned to look at him in apparent surprise, as if he didn't expect Kristian to be there in the first place.

"Heramon. What's going on? Why are we going to the war room? Why are you so . . . ," he paused to find the right word, "so distracted?"

The older man shook his head, more to clear his own thoughts than anything else. "Sorry, Kristian. I've not been overly helpful the last few days. It's been . . . extremely hectic. But you have stayed safe," he let his voice wander off.

After a few moments of quiet, Kristian grew annoyed. "OK . . . ," he started. "And?"

Heramon looked back at him apologetically. "I should have sent you with your grandfather and the others. It's too dangerous for you here." He shook his head again. "Not now, more later when we get to the war room. I need to think right now."

Kristian let his pace slacken, and he fell back in line with the others. He wasn't used to speaking with BeeSting, and when Ethan and Lola had left, he had quit it altogether. Besides, he still felt the emotional connection, but this situation felt unnatural to both of them. In fact, he sensed the same uneasy feelings from BeeSting, so he pressed his companion. *I don't like this. Something doesn't feel right*, he said in his mind.

The drake responded with an increased feeling of uneasiness, preferring that to thoughts or words.

That was all Kristian needed. He nodded.

Shalamar interrupted his thoughts. "Well?" he said expectantly.

Kristian shrugged, not knowing how to explain it to him.

"Shalamar and Heramon are both right. You should have gone with your family," Bortex suddenly chimed in.

Both Kristian and Shalamar shot the cat questioning looks at such a comment.

"We lions have an amazing gift of hearing," Bortex concluded. "I heard what Heramon said!" he added at the utterly confused looks on the others' faces.

They continued in silence and presently made their way up a path that led to a large tree that housed the war room. Two large lions stood at attention on either side of a large wooden door set into the tree.

Heramon nodded at the guards as they opened the door and admitted the little group.

Kristian took the chance to size up the lions' sizes versus Bortex and found that Bortex was bigger than both by a hand or two. He felt a little more confident, having such a massive friend on his side.

As they filed in through the door, Kristian recognized the giant wooden table arranged in the center of the room. The room itself was large with huge swirling wooden patterns forming the deep brown walls. Other than this, the room was devoid of any chairs, with a small group of gnomes and lions at the other end of the table.

He let his eyes quickly pass over the room's occupants and immediately recognized the king, who stood hunched over the table, peering deeply at a map spread out in front of him.

The queen stood at his side, also looking at the map. Kristian swore he saw a worried look of concern visible on her face. That bode ill for them all, he gathered.

Heramon interrupted his thoughts, as the warrior coughed into his hand.

The queen looked up and warmly greeted them from across the room. All traces of worry were momentarily erased from her visage. "Heramon, Kristian, come in, come in." She cast her eyes on the other two visitors, a quick look of surprise registering before it was again gone. "Bortex, Shalamar, good for you to join us as Kristian's aides," she finished.

*The Drake Epics - Journey to Qara*

Both the gnome and cat froze as the remainder of the crowd all looked up from the table. Neither knew how to react to this last statement.

"I guess you are really assigned to me now?" Kristian said under his breath so that only the lion and gnome could hear him. Still, he was a bit shocked himself looking back at the king and queen and smiled just as awkwardly as he made a brief bow. The others followed suit.

The boy took a quick inventory of the remaining gnomes and lions, most of which he recognized as generals and advisors. From what little he knew or remembered from his last visit to the war room, Qara consisted of a seven corps army, including raw lion power, chariots, a phalanx, spearmen, archers, light troops and axe caters. Three seasoned generals led the charge, and Kristian found that Qara had fought many more battles than he was fully aware of, although the last was one hundred years ago, meaning many of the soldiers were in need of the constant sparring and training that took place in the training pit—but not all. To his surprise, he'd found that many of the citizens in Qara were hundreds of years old, even if they didn't show it.

He presently let his eyes fall on one of the lions, named Roteck after his warrior grandfather. Roteck was the general of the forward mobile division, including the light guard and chariot garrisons. It was their strategy to find out enemy weak points and exploit them by opening them up, such that the heavier divisions could move in and disrupt their lines. Roteck was flanked by his two advisors, also lions. Kristian couldn't recall either of their names off hand.

Roteck was smaller than most lions Kristian knew of. In fact, he was probably only three-quarters the size of Bortex, but still huge by any comparison to a man. He likely made up for his smaller stature, in lion terms, with his incredible intelligence and strategic insight.

Kristian had witnessed both of the mobile garrisons up close as he watched them scrimmage over the last few days. The light guard consisted entirely of lions and were absent any weapons, except for their fangs and claws that could deliver death at every stroke, at least, if not more effective than any sword or spear. The chariots were all pulled by lions and driven by gnomes (the only gnomes under Roteck's command). The gnomes were either expert spearmen or short-range archers and could deliver volleys of missiles with deadly precision. The combination of the chariots and light guard were extremely fast and could work havoc in quick procession.

Next to the lions stood two gnomes. The lead gnome closest to the table, Shemnon, was the general of the heavy phalanx and archery garrisons. This was the same gnome the children first saw talking to the king and who had marched his garrison out of the palace. Their strategy was simple: cover the other divisions with a barrage of long-range missiles and strike at the heavy-armored sections in opposing forces with the phalanx.

In the latter regard, the heavy phalanx was amazingly deadly. Following the quick precision strikes from the forward mobile division, they simply pushed their way into the opposing enemy ranks by sheer weight and discipline of their locked shields in a steady advance. The spearmen delivered death at every stroke and avoided all counterattacks due to the heavy shielding. The result was catastrophic for the resulting disorganized enemy forces, leaving them completely open to the chariots and light infantry, who finished them off. He'd also seen some of their scrimmages and was impressed at how effective they were.

Kristian's eyes were now drawn to Shemnon's single advisor standing by his side. He also couldn't remember his name offhand. However, he was leaning on a magnificent composite bow that Kristian remembered all too well and was similar to Heramon's bow.

He wished he knew how to make use of one of these magnificent weapons. He was only equipped with a sling, and which only ever worked against unarmored targets. He was quite expert at its use, but Shalamar had jokingly mocked him for carrying around a child's toy. That, and it would be of little use to him in battle. So he hid the sling from view under his belt, not wishing to be made fun of.

As he inspected the bow more closely, examining it longingly, he found it was made of a fine wood that he couldn't identify. From what he knew of composite bows, they were formed from a combination of wood, animal horns, animal tendons, and sinews. These were glued and bound together, and before the bowstring was attached, the bow's shaft was constructed such that the two arms bent away from the body of the bow. This created the proper amount of tension. In some cases, beeswax was applied to the bowstring, as Grandpa had mentioned, to give the string a better twang and therefore more distance. The effective range of such a bow was 250-300 paces; whereas, his sling was 15 paces on a good day. This made for a formidable long-range attack providing cover for the forward mobile division and for the phalanx garrison.

The last gnome in the room was unfamiliar to Kristian. But he looked the part of the last general, Shiz, who led the axe men division. Kristian had overheard his name from Heramon and Muschle. Shiz was unusually large for a gnome, almost the full height of Kristian's mentor, Heramon, in fact. He wore a patch over one eye and had a long flowing mane and beard, both of which were pulled tight into ponytails. He had a rabid snarl painted on his face, and Kristian feigned not looking at him any longer, for fear of accidentally insulting him.

The Drake Epics - Journey to Qara

He pulled his eyes away and looked back across the others in the room, suddenly realizing that they were all intently studying him. He felt a twinge of embarrassment, and his cheeks flushed bright red. He did not like being the center of attention, at least not in this way. He almost threw his hands out, as if to say, "What? What is everyone looking at?" but thought better of it and decided to stay quiet for once.

The king cleared his throat, breaking the tension in the room. "Good, you're back, Heramon. Just in time. Roteck has proposed a strategy to flank the enemy by surprise."

"Your Highness . . ." Shemnon coughed into his hand. "It's too risky. It leaves us exposed here and here." The gnome pointed at the map. "We need to find another way . . ."

"Spare the forward and send in my axe men. We will cut them to the ground and run them out of the valley," Shiz chimed in. His voice was low and gruff.

"No!" Shemnon countered. "We can't spare the axe men. They will be needed if we find their armaments are stronger than anticipated. We also don't have the information on the contents of their wagons as yet."

"Enough!" The king slapped his hand down on the table. "We've been debating this for too long. We will post half of the archery garrison in the surrounding cliff tunnels." The king pointed to a line on the map. "We will send a squad of axe men with the archery units to defend and cut off any enemy scouts." He looked around the room, making eye contact with all of the generals. "The remainder of the force will make three lines here." He again pointed at the map, poking at it three times to signify where they would line up.

"The phalanx will take up the front center with the remainder of the archery division to the rear." He paused and looked at Shemnon to get his confirmation.

Shemnon obediently nodded.

"The chariots will line up here." He pointed to the map farther away from where he had previously pointed. "And will route the enemy from the left. The light infantry will line up here." He pointed to another section of the map. "And will route the enemy from the right." He looked up at Roteck, who grunted.

"The axe men will hold the tunnel retreat," he said firmly. "Upon a call of retreat, the archer and axe men units will retreat back into the main body of the corpses. The main body will hold until they have joined them. We then have Qara itself as the secondary defense point."

The king looked around the group of generals. They nodded, but grumbled at the compromise.

Shiz spat on the ground and wiped his mouth with the edge of his sleeve.

"To the matter of Kristian . . . ," the king announced as the room fell silent. "We will have him present in the negotiations tent. But that is as far as it goes."

"Excuse me," Kristian piped in.

The king looked up at him.

Kristian gulped but continued on. "What do I have to do with any of this?" he asked.

The king now looked in Heramon's direction. "He's not been told?" he queried.

"No. I still am not comfortable having him present. There's too much at risk—the entire prophecy is riding on it . . . his grandfather would not approve of it."

"That can't be helped now," the king said brusquely then paused to regain his composure. "We will provide adequate protection for him. He will be well guarded. Even if he is challenged, another can volunteer in his place." The king looked consolingly at Heramon. "I am loathe to do this, but it will buy us much-needed time. He is our champion," he spoke in a measured tone, imploring for understanding.

"But at what cost?" Heramon retorted. "Up until now, he would have been hidden—they wouldn't have known who he was. Exposing him like this is folly. We can't risk it, we at least owe him some amount of secrecy. That and you know full well of what that monster is capable of. Once he finishes with"—Heramon looked at Kristian before continuing in a more forceful tone—"finishes with us, he will certainly go back on his word. He is not to be trusted!"

Kristian was now completely annoyed, and he forgot his place entirely. "Look, I'm right here. Stop talking about me as if I weren't here. What is this about a prophecy? What do I have to do with it? Why do I even have to be at the negotiation or whatever it is?" He drew himself up and stood as erect as he could, trying to give a sense of his own majesty, even if totally self-imagined.

Shiz chuckled in response and spat on the ground again. The other generals and advisors looked at Kristian in shock at his outburst.

"Kristian, I know this is all a little hard to understand," the queen suddenly remarked. "You are needed now. This does not mean you need to fight him. You only need be at the negotiation, and we fill find a proxy to fight for you."

"Now I'm a coward? I still don't understand. I want to fight, that is why I am here! I'm protecting my family . . . This is what I'm meant to

The Drake Epics - Journey to Qara

do!" the last part came haltingly. He admitted to himself that he was a little scared. But just a little. He had to stand up for what he believed in.

He looked around the room and tried to read the tribunal's faces.

No one responded. They all simply looked at him expectantly. Even the king appeared to be waiting for something more.

He turned his head to look at his companions. Shalamar and Bortex stood behind him. The gnome had his arms folded, trying to show his support. Bortex had a snarl on his face as he looked at the others. BeeSting perched on his shoulder with his wings spread, as if we were ready to launch into the air.

Kristian took courage from the show of support and turned back to the war tribunal. A new question dawned on him, "Who is this man or beast? Tell me now!" The question came out more harshly, and he instantly regretted it.

"Beg your pardon?" the king asked, raising up to his full stature. He was clearly not amused by the tone of the question. Except for the queen, the tribunal wore looks of contempt and outrage.

"I'm . . . I'm sorry it came out that way, Your Majesties." He bowed quickly. "What am I up against? Who is asking for me?"

The king's face softened slightly, but he still looked displeased.

Kristian awaited an answer from the king, but it was the queen who responded, "We're not sure, Kristian. He is the apparent commander of the opposing forces . . . ," she paused for a moment, as if she didn't want to relay the rest of the message. "He has threatened to raze Julfa and Qara to the ground if you don't show," she finished but Kristian felt she knew something more—she knew who the commander was. Why wasn't she honest about it?

"You see!" Heramon blurted out. "This is exactly why Kristian shouldn't be there! We can't risk it, it's too dangerous. It's a trap. I will not allow it!"

The king shook his head. "Heramon, please see reason. Kristian can draw him out, but he doesn't have to fight him. We can use this to our advantage. You must see this. Without the boy, we have no chance to deflect bloodshed. No chance at all," he implored.

"I will do it!" Kristian volunteered.

The room went perfectly silent as the crowd gazed at Kristian with an intensity he didn't appreciate.

"Are you sure?" Heramon now looked intently at Kristian, searching his eyes. "This may have repercussions that you don't understand."

Kristian studied Heramon for a moment then drew himself up into as noble of a stance as he could muster and vigorously nodded his head.

429

"If we can save them"—he nodded at the tribunal—"and everyone in Qara."

"And what if he challenges you directly?" Heramon asked. "What will you do then? You are not ready for this, Kristian."

The would-be champion hadn't expected that question. He hadn't quite thought beyond appointing someone else, a more seasoned warrior to fight as the champion. Still, he was not above volunteering to do this on his own. After all, it was his right.

"If the commander will accept none but you, are you willing to die?" Heramon's next question burned into the boy—was he ready? Was he ready to die?

Kristian had never thought about dying before. When he went to war in his own mind, he was always victorious. True, he tried to study every scenario and detail, but his thoughts always ended in victory. There was no place for defeat. Death wasn't an option. But now it faced him head-on, there was no escape. This was reality, and when it all boiled down to this, he realized he *could* die!

He scanned the room. Everyone hung on his next words. What would he say? How would he say it? He knew the answer already—it sat there before him, nodding with approval. It gave him all the resolve he needed. "Then I will face him!" he concluded.

There was a brief pause. Then, the tribunal pounded their fists on the table in support of his response.

Heramon looked at him, shocked and helpless. It appeared that all of the blood had drained from his face—he looked paler than Kristian had ever seen him before. Kristian knew that his wise mentor struggled inward and that he both approved of the matter, yet rejected its outcome. But finally, he gave in.

"So be it," he whispered only loud enough for Kristian and the others directly behind him to hear it. He then announced "And I will defend Kristian to the death!" loudly enough so that all could hear him.

The tribunal pounded their fists even louder.

Suddenly, Bortex, who had remained silent as a statue, spoke out. The pounding stopped as all strained to hear the large cat speak.

"I exercise my right to stand as the champion." The lion looked around the room. "I will fight in Kristian's place. I will fight this . . . man!" He spat on the ground, and Kristian could hear a distinct deep rumble in the great lion's chest.

Kristian spun around. "No . . . Bortex, you can't . . ." He turned to face the council. "You can't let him do this!" he implored. He looked around at Shalamar with pleading eyes to talk the cat out of it, but Shalamar

The Drake Epics - Journey to Qara

wouldn't meet his gaze. He looked back at Bortex, desperate to dissuade him from this course of action.

The lion wore a hurt look on his face. "Kristian," Bortex said in a hushed tone, "you offend my honor, I will defend you. I have been raised on the prophecy, it is my whole honor to do this."

Kristian shook his head in disbelief. "I don't even know what the stupid prophecy is about." He almost sobbed back. He did not intend to send his new friend to his death. They were all supposed to fight together and win this together. This wasn't right. It wasn't supposed to turn out like this, not alone; and if alone, he should be the one to do so.

He looked back up at the king, now frightened of what his friend had sentenced himself to.

Heramon placed a consoling hand on Kristian's shoulder. But Kristian could tell that his mentor was relieved.

"Would you take his agency from him, Kristian? Did we not afford you with the choice just moments ago?" the king's words stung him to his core, but he knew the king was right.

Kristian bowed his head, squeezing his eyes shut, shaking his head again. Then he slowly nodded. "It is his right." He kept his head down, feeling much like he wanted to scream.

"Then we have our champion!" the king announced. A round of thunderous applause echoed through the tent. "Get him whatever he needs."

The sound of pounding fists echoed in Kristian's ears. But his hearing had grown dull, and the pounding fists seemed to slow in time. He wished within himself that such measures were not necessary. That this was all a dream.

He suddenly felt something touch his mind, a memory, as if it were a faint breeze that entered the tent. For a moment only, he felt that his fleeting dreams of another land were the reality and that what he now was living was in fact just a dream. Kristian's world ground to a halt, and he knew deep within himself that this was as true a thought as he had ever had. What was more, BeeSting agreed with him. Strange indeed.

# Chapter 26

## Dreams Again

*The future depends on will and effort, and sometimes you get hints along the way.*

A moment of serene calm emanated around the room they had just entered. Grandpa stood, looking up at the ceiling, studying its decor, while shuffling his feet, such that he turned in a full circle. He whistled to himself at the sight. "I've never been in this room before," he stated flatly.

Ethan glanced at the ceiling, but he didn't understand what all the excitement was about, other than all of the animals that were painted racing across it. Their color was dull, as if the painting had been drained of all life with a fissure that ran the length of the ceiling and branched out into tens of other smaller cracks. There was nothing remarkable about it! Then it dawned on him. *This must be what Grandpa is so excited about!* he exclaimed to himself. Grandpa always did have a keen interest in animals *of every kind!* Ethan admitted. That is, when he wasn't talking about bees.

Ethan looked away from the mural and noticed that their companion guard, Helam, was busy pacing around the room's perimeter, scanning for other entrances into the chamber. Once satisfied that there was no impending harm, the large cat took up his post at the only visible entrance.

The boy studied him for a short while before boring and proceeded to the far end of the room that had a slit in the wall, most likely only used as a window to allow a shaft of light to enter. He reached the wall and stepped up on his toes to peer out of the opening.

He could only see portions of the broken courtyard below as the slit provided a poor view. However, he could make out the rubble strewn everywhere. It was nearing dusk, and long shadows cast themselves across the courtyard below from the larger pieces of debris. It reminded him of the Forbidden City. They'd spent most of the afternoon exploring the once-proud castle, and the construction seemed very similar to that of the city, but Ethan fully admitted he was no expert on the subject.

He let his mind wander on their adventure for a while, and he realized that he missed his older brother much more than he'd expected. Not just fleetingly, but that he missed him immensely, although he would never admit that to himself, much less to anyone else.

Seon nuzzled his cheek, and Ethan could feel the sadness in the small drake as well.

He glanced around at his grandpa, who was still studying the ceiling, but had now picked up talking to himself and twirling his beard.

Ethan smiled to himself as the old man pointed with his finger to different animal caricatures, naming them and asking himself questions about them. It was a comical scene.

The boy suddenly felt tired and sat down below the window's opening. His attention turned to the blade of light casting its glow into the room, and Ethan concentrated on the specs of dust visibly floating within the beam. He reached his hand out and passed it through the light a few times, watching the dust swirl around it.

After a few moments, he grew tired of this and glanced back at his grandpa, still mesmerized by the ceiling mural, continuing his one-sided dialogue. Ethan smiled and shut his eyes to rest for a few moments. His head sagged and he slept.

—   —   —

Darkness crept in upon him. Ethan felt the gloom. He could no longer feel Seon's presence and he panicked. His dreams never lead him to a place of safety, and he longed for the sanctuary of his sleep without the dreams.

A rough whisper broke the silence, but from where? The boy spun around to see who it might be, casting his hands out as he blindly groped at the air in front of him. He neither felt nor saw anything. Another whisper sounded in his other ear. He whirled around again only to come up empty handed, this time barely keeping his balance at his sudden movement. A chorus of voices broke in on the whispers. Soon, it sounded as if a wave of rushing water were flowing all around him, *Just like back in Seon's cave,* as he liked to call it.

The noise intensified all around him, climaxing in high-pitched, shrieking sighs. Ethan laid down and curled up, clapping his hands over his ears as he tried to unsuccessfully shut out the maddening frenzy. He couldn't understand what they were saying, but the voices carried malice and hatred, and he somehow knew those voices wanted him to fail; they were trying so hard to thwart him. He felt the darkness begin to squeeze in upon him, much like a constrictor does with its prey. He had seen this many times before in the markets with snakes that the caravan merchants would bring with them. His breath momentarily left him as the darkness continued to bear down upon him. No longer worried about the whispering, he wrapped his hands around himself, rolling on the ground, trying to evade the pressure.

A ragged cry for help escaped his lips. But none came to aid him. Images of the dragon tore through his mind. The breath of fire hurtling at him. He was helpless again and instantly recognized the dream he'd dreamt so many times before. Yet, this dream seemed more real than the others. Of course he had thought this before, but, this one was . . . somehow . . . *different.*

He cried out for help again, the usual terror overtaking him even though deep down, he knew that no harm would befall him. But, no matter how he struggled against it, he could not avoid this feeling's horrific embrace. He reached out for a joyful memory; any memory: Seon, his family, the queen, his parents. These memories were all strangled in turn and ripped from his thoughts.

A fleeting memory of the queen's gift remained behind, but hung by a thread along with the thought to seek out his maker like what Grandpa always taught. The memory was enough and the boy clung to it, pleading for mercy, begging to be freed from the darkness that encircled him.

Immediately, he found himself free of the darkness, standing in the same room as before he dozed off. He was untied and unchained from the dark night.

The boy paused, taking in great gulps of renewing breath and he involuntarily shuddered, his close encounter still fresh in his mind. This dream of his was getting worse; yet his emotions were always the same, and he felt exhausted after every encounter. It was as if he were destined to face the same challenge over and over again in his mind—alone, with no one to help him. *Is there no end to this madness?* he moaned.

Ethan cast his eyes about him as he slowly got to his feet, and he realized that although the room was the same, it had somehow changed. It was beautiful!

Looking around, he quizzically noticed candlelight emanating from candlesticks resting comfortably in the walls around the room. They embraced him in their warmth and glowed more brilliant, he realized, owing to the shining marble flooring. He hadn't remembered marble there before, only a dusty cracked floor with bits of ceiling debris scattered throughout the chamber, none of which was visible now.

Turning himself about, the boy looked at the window slit and found that it was dark outside. Night must have fallen while he slept. Strange that he would have missed this—had he slept for that long?

Ethan suddenly thought of the mural and looked up. What he saw caught his breath. The animals were vivid and lifelike, not the faded figures he'd seen before. But what was more surprising—no, it couldn't be! He had to squint to make sure. Yes, it was! The animal pictures were moving across the ceiling in fluid motions, as if dancing.

Ethan rubbed his eyes and looked again.

Some of the moving creatures he'd never seen before and had no name to call after them. Others were terrible and imposing, and yet others were mysterious and beautiful in a way he couldn't describe. They danced, they pranced, and they frolicked across the painted countryside. There was no antagonism, they simply enjoyed the moment—it was hypnotic. He could lose himself in their whimsical little world, observing their every move. *It can't be all that hard,* he settled.

"Beautiful, aren't they?" a familiar soft voice asked just behind him.

Ethan whirled on the spot.

The queen appeared, dressed in a beautiful gown. She glowed. Ethan couldn't tell at present if she radiated from the candle's amber light or on her own.

He inspected her more closely, and to his surprise, she seemed much younger; and he now realized her beauty was tenfold that of how he had seen her a few days ago. He had never completely noticed this fact before, feeling an odd sensation of love and yearning for her to be at his side. He embarrassedly blushed at the thought when he remembered she could read his mind. He bowed quickly and threw his head down, squeezing his eyes shut in order to cast the thought from his conscience.

The queen smiled back at him. She had heard his thoughts! She strolled toward him with her hand extended. "Rise, Great Sheikh!" she commanded softly.

Ethan regained his composure and met her gaze. He put his hand in hers and obediently followed as she turned to walk from the room.

"How did I come to be here?" he ventured. "I mean, I don't understand, I was just resting over there . . ." It then dawned on him that he was still dreaming.

"You are both wise and quick to realize such things, Ethan. Yes, you are sleeping," she answered. "Your dream has brought you back in time when this castle . . . my castle . . . was a place of rest to those who journeyed through this land."

"So you were the Sheikh that my grandpa mentioned!" he realized.

"But . . . ," Ethan started, "I feel at peace now, what was the darkness I encountered?" He shivered. "It was . . . suffocating!"

The queen halted and turned to look at Ethan.

He could read the concern in her expression. Her eyes pierced his own, and he sensed the urgency of her thoughts. He turned his head away in an attempt to avoid her sudden intrusion into his privacy.

She gently reached out and turned his head. "Ethan?" she pleaded. "Ethan, look at me."

He reluctantly opened his eyes and met her gaze.

She smiled at his faith. "There is little time . . . ," she paused momentarily, selecting her next words carefully. "The dragon will engage our lands in battle. His armies have already moved on Qara!"

Ethan wasn't following. "Dragon?" he exclaimed.

"Yes, Ethan." She continued, "The black dragon of your dreams is he who attacks us, and as you have seen, the people of your village are now his minions, trapped within their own minds by his power . . ."

"But what can I do?" Ethan blurted out. "I mean . . . I . . . I need to finish the quest . . ." Then it hit him!

The Drake Epics - Journey to Qara

"Kristian!" He gasped. "Kristian is there! Is he safe?" Forgetting his previous embarrassment, he now looked intensely into the queen's eyes, desperately probing for the answer he sought. All of his shyness evaporated. But he already knew what the answer would be.

"We did not foresee this," she said softly, a single tear streaming down her cheek.

"No!" Ethan shrieked in pain. He jerked himself out of her grip, taking a step backward. "I know what you would say!" he screamed. "I will not let it happen, I must go back!" he swore the oath out loud.

"Ethan . . . ," the queen pleaded, reaching out to him with her trembling hand.

Ethan took another halting step backward, shaking his head in rejection.

"You cannot save him, Ethan." She stopped short of the boy and raised her hands, thought for a moment, then awkwardly dropped them to her sides. She bowed her head. "You must continue on your quest! It is the only way," she said in anguish. She raised her head to look into his eyes again.

He saw the resolve in her. But he had already made a resolve of his own. He would not abandon his brother! Nor his people! He would not allow for this to happen!

Ethan shook his head. "No!" he paused to emphasize what he would say next. "I will return to finish my quest another time . . . but not alone . . . I will do so with both Kristian and Lola!" he concluded. He mustered all of his strength and stood his ground before the queen, staring defiantly back into her eyes. His flash of temper softened with a sudden discovery. "But . . . that's what I was supposed to do all along," he said to himself as he searched deeper within.

Another tear formed on the queen's cheek.

"This was a test! A test to see what I would do." Ethan could tell she was holding back from sobbing out loud, and he wondered about her feelings for him. It was intoxicating. Her mind now seemed attached to his, and for the first time, he realized that her feelings for him ran somehow deeper. He couldn't quite tell how or why, but he realized that he knew her from before, yet how could this be? He was young and unacquainted with such feelings. They threw him into a brief world of chaos and confusion.

"You will understand these feelings in time. As you grow older, I grow younger until at last we meet, and . . ." The queen trembled, her hand partly extended toward him, and she nodded. One more wave of feeling raced across her face. Then, she closed the door to her emotions, regaining her royal composure without feeling or passion.

Yet he felt a sense of clarity now. His quest was never to be in his travels. His quest had always been back in Qara. He knew what he had to do.

"Then you must accept a gift," she agreed.

"Gift?" Ethan remarked, still puzzled, but now mingled with bewilderment about how quickly she gave in to his decision. Besides, he had already received her gift.

The queen drew an orb like his own from a pocket in her flowing gown.

Ethan's blood ran cold. He grabbed for his own, and reaching into his pocket, felt its cold smooth surface. A wave of relief washed over him as he drew out the orb and, studying the other, quickly realized that they were identical.

"You must join this orb with your own," she explained. "They are alike . . . only mine is from the past, and yours . . . ," she paused, "the future." She looked at him and sensed his disorientation. "You must take this, but I cannot tell you why, only that as I told you, I did not lose the orb . . . ," the queen halted again. "The dragon once sought for this precious gift, but I tricked him and kept it safe." She looked pained, then shook her head to clear her thoughts. "And . . . I now gave it to you freely!"

Ethan's mind was awash. He could not fathom what this meant for him. Why all the secrecy and riddles. Could no one explain this insanity to him?

"Take it and merge it with your own orb." She besought in a strange tone of grief. "It will teach you what you need to know in the exact moment that you need to know it. It will speak wisdom, peace, and knowledge to your soul." She reached her hand out to him.

Ethan paused and then reluctantly accepted the orb. As she placed it in his hand, he delicately closed his fingers around it. He looked at the two orbs in both hands, standing awkwardly, not sure of what to do next.

"Bring them together!" she urged him gently. "This will set you on the right course. But remember that you must hold true to your vow of the quest. This is our last hope." She made a sweeping motion with her hands, bringing them together into a clasp.

The boy slowly nodded and eased the two orbs together. A light emanated from within both orbs and intensified as he brought them closer together. Sudden sparks and waves of light ran between them. Ethan could feel them invisibly push against one another, as if they were magnetized, and he strained all the harder to drive them together. At last they touched,

# The Drake Epics - Journey to Qara

but to his surprise, the invisible force keeping them apart fled and they folded into each other with ease. A great light shone from them until they were completely merged into one.

"One in purpose," the queen uttered, followed by a few words in a tongue unknown to Ethan. The queen concluded, as if she were reciting a verse from some ancient text, and she sagged under some unseen burden.

Ethan reached out to her as if to hold her upright, but she shook her head. Her eyes now drained of some of her power.

He realized that he felt immediate strength enter him, a surge of knowledge and wisdom of spells he had not known of before. But now he knew them, as if he had studied and practiced them for years. He even knew how to use them and when to use them, similar to when he had joined with Seon. More so, his understanding expanded. He knew the prophecy—he understood it! It came to him as if it were a memory clear in his mind. But what was more, he also understood his part to play within the prophecy. It all made sense to him now!

Ethan's attention turned back to the combined orbs as he stared at their dazzling light. They continued to grow brighter, filling the room, overtaking, and vanquishing any shadows through their brilliance. He glanced up at the queen again, her face once again soft. Sensing her emotion for him, he watched her openly weep giving up all pretense. He wanted to reach out to her and comfort her. But the light soon swallowed her figure, and she was no longer visible, as was none of the room.

Warmth filled him, and he was at peace within his dream. His dream had become the sanctuary that he had so desperately yearned for previously. In fact, he now knew that his dreams would be nothing but sanctuary from this day onward. The real battle had moved beyond his thoughts and dreams into reality. The real battle was with a dragon. Not just any dragon, the chaos dragon known as Tiamat!

—  —  —

Ethan abruptly awoke as his little sister's high-pitched voice echoed throughout the chamber. The sound was shrill and made his skin crawl as it reverberated off the walls. As she reached the doorway, Helam snarled and growled at her sudden intrusion.

Grandpa, who was still staring at the ceiling, spun around and took quick strides in Lola's direction.

Ethan got to his feet and rushed to follow him. His head felt momentarily dizzy at the rush of blood as he stood and he had to balance himself. As he raised a hand to his head, he realized that he was back to the present and noticing the debris on the dusty ground, peered up at the ceiling, now dim and cracked with age.

"Grandpa!" Lola looked up at the old man and then at Ethan. "Ethan!" She paused to momentarily catch her breath. "Kristian . . . Kristian . . . ," she panted.

"I know!" Ethan said as he closed the gap between them. "I just had a dream about it. He faces the dragon! We don't have much time!"

Both Lola and Grandpa stared at him in disbelief.

"But how?" Lola blurted.

"How did I know?" the boy countered. "The queen appeared to me in my dream and told me. No time to talk right now! We need to hurry. If we don't make it in time . . ."

Ethan shrugged off a sudden impulse to burst into tears. He pushed his feelings down and resolved to be stronger. He looked back at his family. "I will explain to you along the way, but Kristian is in real danger! We have to go *now!*" he exclaimed.

# Chapter 27

## Duels and Dragon Sieges

*Vengeance destroys the soul.*

The march to the battlegrounds seemed like an eternity. Kristian never thought that the tunnel to Qara would ever end. He remembered it as being a much faster hike than this slow-moving procession he was stuck in. It began to wear on his nerves, and he felt like lashing out at someone.

He turned to look at Bortex and Shalamar. Neither had spoken one word to him, not since the war tribunal. They hadn't had time. Bortex had been whisked away to prepare for the challenge. Shalamar had accompanied him, while Heramon briefed Kristian to bring him up to speed.

Kristian still thought it all folly. He couldn't stand the thought of his friend dying on the battlefield and, even more so, dying for him! He quickly brushed the thought aside—of course he wouldn't die. The general of the other army was in for a surprising turn of events. Bortex was not only the largest of the lions, he was very fierce. Yet all the play that he and Shalamar did with the cat was just that—playing. Still, Bortex would never let his guard down. The general wouldn't even get close to him. He'd swipe his paw, and that would be the end of it.

The boy suddenly felt a little better. This wouldn't end so poorly after all. He turned and flashed a triumphant smile at Bortex.

The lion tried not to notice, to keep his regal appearance. But he winked back at Kristian. "You know this will soon all be over with!" He paused for a moment, considering his next words. "I have my two friends there to cover me!" he finished then looked back directly in front of him, as if the conversation had never happened.

Kristian smiled to himself again. "Hear that, BeeSting?" he asked out loud. "We're in for a real treat!" he cheerfully concluded. Yet a warning lingered in the back of his mind, and he knew that battle was nothing to be overly confident about.

The entourage now approached the entrance to the tunnel. *Finally!* Kristian thought in an annoyed whine.

BeeSting snorted.

As they passed into the light, Kristian could see concourses of lions and gnomes, all standing at attention. The troops formed a direct path out and toward the Forbidden City. This was on a scale that the boy had never witnessed before and would likely never encounter again. His breathing came in raspy waves. His adrenaline was pumping. He was ready for this!

First, they passed row after row of archers. He assumed the remainder of the regiment lay hidden in the surrounding cliff precipice. Next, he passed through the phalanx division, followed by rows of great, iron chariots, and lastly through the mobile infantry of lions. They all bowed before them. It was quite embarrassing, but Kristian figured he could get used to this—one way or the other.

BeeSting grinned in agreement.

Before they reached the end of the line, they banked hard right and toward a set of tents that he assumed were occupied by the king and queen and their generals and advisors. He strained to look over the heads of the soldiers to catch a glimpse of the opposing forces, but the valley floor dropped slightly from where they stood, such that he could

The Drake Epics - Journey to Qara

see nothing. Disappointed, he turned his attention back to the soldiers he now passed by.

They reached the tent, which Kristian now realized to be much taller than he had anticipated. Apparently, it was built on a platform of wood that provided for two levels. Perhaps, he would be allowed on the upper level to look out and across the battlefield to see what they were up against. He would be sure to ask.

The group paused, and Kristian took a moment to look back over the concourses of soldiers. It was much more impressive then when they first exited the tunnel. It appeared to be tens of thousands of soldiers. He marveled at the sheer size of the army.

Suddenly, a pair of trumpets sounded from somewhere within the ranks. The entire army started to applaud them and chant Bortex's and Kristian's names.

Kristian didn't know what to think of it and simply smiled and waved.

Shalamar stayed behind the lion, not wanting more exposure than he felt he deserved.

Bortex, on the other hand, drew himself up to his full stature and let out a deafening roar. This made the crowd applaud even louder.

Heramon tried to say something, but Kristian couldn't hear him over the applause. So the man cupped his hands around his lips and yelled at them, "Stupid foolery, get in here. Get in here!" He did not look the least bit amused, and they all quickly entered the tent.

The army continued to applaud and chant for a while before dying back down, and the divisional captains started barking orders to shore up loose lines.

To Kristian, it seemed an eternity of glory, just as he had dreamed of so many times before!

"Well, he knows we're all out here now! That's for sure!" Heramon scathed at no one in particular.

"It boosts the morale of the army," the queen said soothingly in her melodic voice.

Kristian noticed her approaching them in welcome.

Heramon grunted in contempt and sidled over to an edge of the tent, folding his arms, content to pout about it in silence.

The queen didn't seem to notice. "Come in . . . we've been awaiting this moment." She smiled as she took Kristian's hand in her own.

The same generals and their advisors all mingled within. Only, this time, there was no table to crowd around. They all looked a little awkward, just standing there, all decked out in their armor. But nonetheless, it gave Kristian a sense of security.

443

Shiz and the king were in midconversation, and Kristian caught the tail end of the king's comments. "We will be ready for any sign of a trap. On your word, you signal any mischief to be put down, is that understood . . . ?"

The king looked up and realized that the others had arrived, stopping midsentence. "Ah, Kristian, and our champion! Are you well? Are you ready?"

Both nodded.

Kristian thought to himself that the king always seemed so distant. It was almost as if he didn't really care about them at all, as if they were simply pawns in his personal game of war. Although, he knew as soon as he thought it that he was dead wrong. He'd seen the actions of the king, he did care about his people. He just seemed to be a distant magistrate, keeping himself aloof from what Kristian considered to be important for a king to do. Even the Grand Sheikh of Julfa knew better, he thought to himself. Still, Kristian had no prior experience being a king, and he must simply be wrong about what mattered most.

"Good, good." The king coughed slightly and changed course. "Bortex, are you sure you wish no armor? The opposing general is a man, but he could be . . ." The king stopped and appeared he was not going to continue. "He . . . could be something more," he finished the sentence awkwardly.

"No, Your Majesty! I will have Shalamar and Kristian by my side," the lion responded with a confident tone.

Both Kristian and Shalamar looked at each other and shrugged. They resolved to back him up, but neither knew what that really meant.

Bortex kept his eyes planted on the king. He always seemed to take these types of situations way too formally, Kristian thought to himself. Not that this situation wasn't serious, but he didn't have to keep at full attention all the time. Another thing that Kristian didn't really understand, he'd always had challenges with authority. It's what made him different. He liked to counter what adults said. It gave him a sense of purpose and proved how very smart he was indeed.

"Very well," the king finished. "Then let us to the top of the platform to scout out what lies before you."

Kristian's excitement welled up within him. *At last!* he mused to BeeSting. He felt his companion was excited too.

With that, the king motioned for them all to follow him up a slight stairwell near the other end of the tent that Kristian now just noticed. "Except for Shiz, the generals will remain below," he announced with the wave of his bony hand, and much to the dissatisfaction of the others. But no one argued the point.

The small regiment made their way to the top landing of the tent. As Kristian cleared the last step, the battleground came into view; and he paused, dumbstruck at the sight. Before him stood an array of tens of thousands. He could not number them and quickly turned off the counter running through his head.

Instead, he focused in on the types of soldiers he could see in the opposing forces. They were too distant and too numerous to tell much in detail, but he saw droves of wolves, like those the children had encountered before. A great many hooded figures stood with great staffs in their hands, and creatures of various shapes and sizes, but that he couldn't put a name to, as he had never encountered their like before.

As he let his eyes wander the crowd. What next he saw, he never expected. The flag of Julfa and what looked to be the people of his village stood left of the center. Kristian's heart sank. How could this be?

The king had been watching the boy and put a steady hand on his shoulder with an understanding sigh. "They are not in their right minds, son," he ventured. "They are . . . under the command of some other source . . . They do not know what they are doing . . . Their minds are confused."

Kristian looked at the king, questions flooding his mind, but he decided to keep them to himself. He felt numb, as if he had been struck by a great hammer. Even if they were "confused" as the king claimed, they could still die by the sword; and many of them would die, *perhaps even by my own hand*, he mourned.

The king turned to speak to all of them. "This is the army before us. They outnumber us seven to one, as far as our scouts can tell. Our defenses will hold for only so long, Kesem or not," he stated flatly, now turning to look at Bortex. "You will face their leader!" he added. "And we hope you will be victorious. It will mean avoiding much bloodshed," he said with finality.

On cue, a guttural shout sounded from thousands of soldiers in the opposing force, drawing everyone's attention to the other end of the valley.

Kristian could make out a large gap forming in the center of their ranks.

The shout continued for a while until a lone figure emerged from within and now strode into the open.

Kristian squinted to see him better.

The man was dressed all in black. A great cape billowed in some invisible wind, as the valley was deathly calm, and the shouting stopped. In fact a deathly still permeated the entire valley. As the man drew toward the center of the free zone, he halted and his voice rang clear throughout the valley, much louder than a natural voice of one man should carry over such a distance.

"I am here to recover the would-be emperor, his sister . . . and his feeble brother!" the figure called out then spat to the ground beside him. He stood erect, awaiting a reply.

The king uttered a few words in some dialect Kristian could not discern and replied with an equally clear and loud voice. "And what would you have of us? To release the three of them to you with the thousands you have brought to destroy our freedom, to reduce us to slaves, and to submit and bow to your demands?"

Kristian glanced at the king in awe, a newfound respect forming within him at the audacity of the king. The boy actually felt proud to be on the king's side.

The response was a loud, deep laugh from the man, as he threw his head back in amusement. "And you, O King, are man enough to match me? I think not . . . still, it would be a great challenge to face you. But no, no. You will hand over the three *children* . . . ," he emphasized the last word with contempt. "You will submit to me and be honored to serve in our kingdom. You can do nothing more than to accept this great honor. To so do otherwise would be . . . reckless!" the man snarled.

Kristian could see the veins bulge on the king's neck, as he refrained from shouting oaths at the other man. However, he regained his composure and spoke, "Then, I'm afraid that we are at an impasse! We will hold our ground, and either you or we will be victorious on this day!" he said with regal pride.

The man laughed again. "Very well, then. Send forth your champion. I shall meet him on my own to demonstrate my strength. At my hands, you will agree to your submission to my demands. But enough, send him forth, I shall meet him now. Send two, send three, or send hundreds. It matters not, for I shall defeat them all!" the man exclaimed.

"It is time," the king turned and spoke to Bortex, Shalamar, and Kristian.

They somberly nodded in acceptance and made their way down the crudely constructed staircase. As they reached the bottom, the commanders all bowed to the three in reverence. All except for Shiz, that is, who spat on the ground and mumbled that this was a despicable practice and no way for armies to meet in battle.

Kristian made his way with his friends through the tent, but ended up being much easier than what he was next to encounter. As the flaps of the tent were drawn back, there stood the thousands of soldiers of Qara. A loud cheer went up through their ranks again, and they all

*The Drake Epics - Journey to Qara*

parted as if they were one to allow the king's entourage to proceed to the front line.

The men's and lion's faces were all drawn out in hard expressions of war, some with fear. Kristian could tell that most were veterans of seasoned battle. Although he'd never found out the story behind who they had battled with so long ago. He himself had pushed away all fear, clenching his fists tightly together to force any anxiety out of his system. Defeat and death were not an option in his mind, and he had resolved that he was to return, no matter the outcome that lay ahead of him.

The king led the small group quietly onward; Shiz and another advisor walked on either side. Bortex followed directly behind the king, towering over them all. Kristian could see the proud manner in which his friend carried himself; but he knew the lion had doubts, even though the big cat would never admit it, let alone show it to anyone else. Shalamar was at his side, head also held high, determined to aid Bortex in whatever situation he got himself into. Kristian followed next, accompanied by Heramon, who strode alongside him. Heramon's features were cold and calculating, Kristian thought. No emotion registered on his face, except that of concentrated thought—*strategizing*, Kristian assumed.

The walk took longer than Kristian had expected. Finally, they emerged from the ranks and into the open field. The king raised his hand for them to halt. He turned and motioned to Bortex to approach him, motioning for the large lion to bow himself toward the king. The king placed his hand on Bortex's shoulder and wished him well by all the kings that went before and of the gods and the one true god. Bortex then stood erect, and the king bowed before him, as did the rest of the party. Finally, it was Kristian and Shalamar's turn.

"You stay out of harm, Bortex," Kristian plead.

The lion gave him a quizzical look, and Shalamar gave Kristian a quick jab in the ribs.

"I mean it!" Kristian said in a serious tone. "This general is nothing like us! Who knows what he has up his sleeve. Stay alert and be safe. I'd never forgive myself if anything happened . . . ," he paused to control his emotions.

Shalamar jumped in to save him from his discomfort. "Kristian is right. You can take this guy, just make sure to watch your flank." The gnome gave the lion a quick slap on his shoulder.

Bortex grunted and swatted playfully at them both. "Shalamar, I will finish this without your help." He smiled a toothy grin. "Kristian, I've only known you a short while. But I know that you are chosen, both Shalamar and I can feel it. I will serve you in this way to bring you glory."

This time both lion and gnome nodded in agreement. The three huddled for a few moments more in silence with unspoken words exchanged between them. Then, Bortex walked slowly ahead, a low rumble coming from deep in his throat. As he approached his opponent, the lion let out a yawning roar and leapt out into the open, running at full tilt toward the challenger.

Shalamar looked at Kristian and shrugged as if he couldn't help himself. Kristian knew he couldn't hold the gnome back. The little man joined Bortex, running behind at slightly less of a cadence to keep ample distance between them. Kristian made to join them, but Heramon put an arm on his shoulder and shook his head in silence.

"Let them do this," he said.

Kristian paused for a moment, then agreed and watched in earnest. He sent BeeSting up to scout and relay details of the battle back to him. At least it was better than watching from afar.

He could now make out more detail about the man. Bortex had reached him and came to an abrupt halt. The lion nodded out of respect. The general simply smiled. Bortex began his stalking, slowly circling the man, who appeared to be perfectly calm and uninterested in the lion's intentions. As a sign of contempt, the general brought his fingernails up to inspect. He breathed on them, then wiped them along his chest and inspected them again.

This infuriated the big cat, and Bortex threw all caution to the wind and lunged at the general from the side, attempting to catch him by surprise. The man casually stepped aside, letting the lion fly past him. In the same fluid motion, the general landed a stab of his fingers in the lion's side, extracting a painful hiss from the large feline.

Bortex landed easily, a bit dazed and bruised at the attack, limping on one of his legs. He snarled and spun around to face his opponent, who was still casually inspecting his fingernails, as if the lion's lunge hadn't happened at all.

Bortex continued to again slowly circle the man, more wary than before, but Kristian could tell the lion's anger was about to peak.

"Take your time, Bortex. C'mon, don't lose your cool," he muttered under his breath.

The large cat bode his time well until he had made the circle directly behind his prey.

The general continued to add insult to injury, as he began inspected his other hand, paying no attention to the prowling animal.

This was the opening Bortex had been waiting for. In a flash, the large cat charged silently from behind. He sized up his adversary moments before he struck, trying to anticipate a potential countermove. He tilted his head sidewise as he closed the gap and went for the man's neck, bearing down on him. At the last possible moment, the general sidestepped the lion's charge for a second time. But this time, Bortex was ready for his counter. He caught the man's hand by the tip of one of his claws, spraying blood into the sand, which quickly swallowed up the red liquid. The man yelled in surprised pain, clutching at this hand.

Bortex landed, pleased with his quick reaction, and a cheer sounded from Qara's armies.

Perhaps this man was not as tough as he thought himself to be, Kristian entertained to himself. *His pride will be his undoing*, he thought to BeeSting.

The little drake sneered as BeeSting continued circling the general from above.

Heramon, on the other hand, wore a look of worry on his face. Kristian hadn't expected that and tried to whisper to his mentor asking what was wrong.

Heramon put his fingers to his lips and simply said, "Watch."

The man glowered at the lion as Bortex moved backward a number of paces and again began to pace in a circle around his opponent.

This time, the general shifted around, watching the lion. He wouldn't make the same careless mistake twice. A light suddenly flared between his fingers that enveloped his injured hand, likely in an attempt to heal it.

"Kesem!" Kristian said in a worried tone. He looked back at Heramon. "Bortex can't stand against Kesem, he hasn't the skill. We need to help him!" he urged.

Heramon shook his head again. "If we were to do anything, we would breach the contract and the battle between our forces would commence. No, we must do nothing but watch. If . . . if Bortex is defeated, another may step in to avenge him, but no more. Besides, Shalamar is next in line."

"He wouldn't last either. I know these two—they have big hearts, but they don't stand a chance."

Heramon looked at Kristian with a mournful face as he leaned into the boy. "Kristian, there will be more to die today," he said as softly as he could.

Kristian shook his head. He couldn't let his friends die and stand around watching idly by. But he didn't have time to think on this longer. He readied himself.

A sudden voice echoed throughout the valley, "You will pay for that, young lion. I will teach your comrades what it means to anger me!" The man said something more in a foreign language that Kristian couldn't

*Duels and Dragon Sieges*

understand, and a spear sprouted outward from his hands. An angry smile spread across the general's lips as he gripped the spear with the hand that had been injured, apparently now completely healed. He joined the lion's prowl, each now circling the other.

"Just a little more time, Bortex," Kristian mumbled. "Don't push your position."

But Bortex was through stalking his prey. Avoiding any further pretense, the lion roared and lunged toward his foe in one giant leap.

The man smiled and ran at Bortex.

As they reached each other, Bortex thrust his massive paw, attempting to crush or impale the general's arm with his claws. At the same time, he swiped with the other to deflect the man's spear, and again went for the kill with his giant fangs.

The man yelled a battle cry, jumping into the air, while his body twisted and turned in an aerial display. He came about and out of Bortex's reach, thrusting the spear deep into Bortex's side.

The lion let out a painful whelp and fell to the sand with the spear set within his chest. He panted a few times and then exhaled and lay still.

The man landed in a crouched position with his head down. One fist plunged into the sand and the other held straight out as if he had just concluded an epic dance. He took a single breath and stood, turning to inspect his victim. He brushed his dark hair out of his eyes and triumphantly proclaimed the lion was dead with the same maniacal smile still on his lips.

A cheer erupted through the opposing ranks at the sudden victory.

Kristian's world crashed to a halt, not daring to believe what had just happened in mere moments. He let a ragged scream of rage escape his lips, and he leapt forward before Heramon could grab hold of him.

Muschle, who had up until now been silent, yelled and started after the boy as the small man sprang into action to halt Kristian's sudden flight, but the dark general raised a hand and shouted a single word. A surging blue shield erupted behind Kristian in a great dome, blocking anyone else from following him farther.

Muschle cried out in agony as the shield slammed into his leg, gouging deep into his flesh. He fell limply to the ground and passed out.

Kristian paid it no heed and sprinted toward his fallen friend.

Heramon shouted from behind the blockade, pounding his fists on its surface in brilliant flashes and sparks. "Nooo! Kristian! Come back!"

Shalamar was the first to Bortex's side, as he was the closest to him. He fell to his knees and screamed for the large cat to stand and finish the battle—nothing happened. He shouted again without any response, then

450

as his friend's death settled on him, he clutched at his mane and buried his head in the thick hair as he bitterly wept. "Bortex, you can't leave me." He sobbed.

Kristian struggled to close the gap to his friends as quickly as he could before Shalamar did anything rash.

But it was too late. The gnome threw his head back and yelled at the sky in anguish, "You can't leave me like this!" Then he turned to glare at the general, pure hatred evident on his face. He slowly got to his feet, shaking his head, then focused on the figure in front of him and shouted his battle cry, running as fast as his legs could carry him with his sword drawn.

"Ah, you have sent another to avenge the lion, I see!" the man cheered with glee. "This is always the better fight—one filled with hatred, malice, and anger!" he chuckled.

Kristian finally reached Bortex's side and rolled the large cat over with great strain. "Bortex!" he screamed again and felt for breathing or a pulse. There was none. "No, no, no . . ." Kristian whimpered at the loss of his friend. BeeSting landed on his shoulder and tried to console him, but nothing could bring Bortex back. *We need to try the healing technique Ethan and Lola taught us*, he thought frantically at the small drake.

BeeSting agreed and shared his power with Kristian.

The would-be healer focused on the core energy within himself and felt BeeSting's presence aiding him. He placed a hand against the lion, and with the other, he gripped the spear. He counted down from three and heaved the spear out of the lion's side. He threw it aside and placed his hands over the wound and uttered a short phrase, "Sefa vermak"; and to his utter joy and astonishment, the wound healed and closed in around itself.

Once he was self-assured that the healing was complete, Kristian cradled the cat's giant head in his lap and asked him to awake, uttering the word *Artim*. Nothing happened. Kristian checked the pulse and breathing, still no change. "Artim!" he said again. No change. "No, no, no. *Artim!*" he bellowed, but Bortex remained perfectly still, his eyes open in surprise. Kristian wept and closed the lion's eyes. It was done. Bortex was gone.

Through his tears, Kristian looked up to see the deadly battle that ensued as he was attempting to heal Bortex. He had paid no mind to it, his attention completely focused on the lion. But he could tell that Shalamar wasn't faring any better than Bortex had.

The gnome was more agile than Bortex and was quick to evade the sword that materialized in the general's hands. But he couldn't get close enough to the man to deal any lethal blows either.

Kristian wiped the tears from his eyes, placed the lion's head on the ground, and charged headlong toward the battle, asking for BeeSting to do the same. Just as he neared the fray, the general turned and looked at him with a giant smile spread across his face. "Just in time, Kristian! Your friend has been quite entertaining. He is nimble and angry." The man turned back to watch the little gnome as if he were a child playing in the sand, but of no greater consequence other than for the general's amusement. He turned back to the boy. "Alas, it is now time for us to duel!"

"You!" Kristian bawled, realizing who the general was. "The auditor is a traitor! I *will* end you!" he exclaimed.

The auditor laughed.

"Shalamar! Watch out!" Kristian bellowed, turning his attention to the little gnome who was readying for another lunge at his foe. "Let us take him together!" he urged.

Shalamar was beyond hearing. The bloodlust was too great in his eyes, and he only thought of avenging his fallen friend. He let out a deafening battle cry and rushed the auditor, throwing a series of darts that he pulled form his armor as he charged.

A blue light flashed, and the blades all fell helplessly to the sand. The auditor wore a wicked smile at Kristian, then turned toward Shalamar and in a quick succession of strokes, dispatched the small gnome, who fell lifeless to the ground, the same as Bortex.

"Nooo!" Kristian bellowed as he watched his second friend hewn down.

BeeSting was again in flight and started to harass the general.

Kristian added a shield around his companion to deflect attacks. Then he quickly focused on ridding himself of his enemy to clear a path to Shalamar. He dug deeper into his core than he ever had before and shouted the word *Yangin* at the auditor. The strength he used surprised him greatly. That he could tap into such power so quickly gave him more courage. Perhaps BeeSting's added strength was more than he anticipated; but for a moment, the word felt exhilarating and he felt freedom, the like he had only known once before in the ring with the queen.

He saw a glint of disbelief flash in the man's eyes before the general was enveloped in an inferno and flung a hundred paces away from the battle.

Kristian ran to Shalamar's side and attended to the same healing process he had done for Bortex, healing all of his fallen companion's wounds. In the end, the result was the same, and Kristian wept inconsolably.

Again, the mourning of his fallen friends was short-lived. Out of the fire, he heard an unearthly roar. He looked up to see a black form rise from the flames. He couldn't focus and had to wipe the tears from his eyes. At first, he couldn't see what it was clearly, then he stiffened as he realized the monster was a black dragon.

Kristian's blood ran cold. He'd remembered Ethan's talk about his dreams and about the black dragon, but he hadn't paid enough attention. Was it real? How could he defeat a dragon? "I can't defeat a dragon!" he exclaimed.

He looked helplessly behind him at Heramon, who stood just outside of the sparks of the blue shield. His mentor wore a look of utter helplessness. He was shouting words and pounding on the walls' surface as bright flashes of light erupted on contact. The king was doing much the same, only with magic, but without any noticeable results.

The boy turned to watch the giant dragon lumber toward him in slow motion. Fire billowed out of its nostrils, and it looked to be determined to finish him quickly.

"Where is the queen?" he roared. "You are a dragon! Do you send no help?" he continued.

*My Sheikh* . . . , came the reply. *I cannot breach the barrier. My powers are useless against Tiamat* . . . , her response broke off. *I . . . can . . . not . . . help* . . . She was gone.

It was up to Kristian. "Again!" he barked. Although how he would defeat the dragon, he did not know.

*You can do this!* BeeSting rallied in Kristian's mind.

*No, I have to do this!* the boy amended. He had to avenge Bortex and Shalamar. For a moment, his thoughts rested on Ethan and Lola, and he desperately yearned for them to be at his side now. But he let the rage take over and drive him to his true core. Kristian dug deep again, this time with the same ferocity he had used just moments before. He felt his blood boil and bubble.

BeeSting shared his intensity, returning to his perch on the boy's shoulder, he unintentionally dug his claws into Kristian's arms.

It hurt, Kristian thought, but it gave him a greater sense of clarity.

The dragon reared up and laughed. "You!" it spat. "You are an insect. I've foreseen this—you will not survive this day, how can you?" It laughed again.

Kristian didn't care. "This is for Bortex and Shalamar. They have *not* died in vain. This is for my family. They will *not* become your slaves!" He reached deeper within himself, and with his strength fully grasped, he thought through his arsenal of Kesem that Ethan had taught him.

Every muscle in his body tensed for the attack. This was it! Now to utter the words of death . . . With an ear-splitting battle cry, Kristian lunged himself at the monster.

# Chapter 28

# Howling Wind

*When all appears to be lost, self-conviction will find a way.*

The journey had already taken too long. Ethan could barely make out the trail, leading down to the edge of the giant sink hole in the distance, but he had to squint his eyes to see the chasm as waves of heat rose from the desert floor, interfering with his sight. *We're almost there!* he thought, overjoyed. "We made it!" he exclaimed with a smile to Lola. The boy quickly cast a refreshment spell on them, and they both started to run with unnatural speed.

"No!" Grandpa yelled after the children, but neither seemed to notice.

The Drake Epics - Journey to Qara

Helam was many paces behind Grandpa to ensure that the small company was not flanked from behind. Koran, the other lion, was off to the side scouting out another movement. Both lions lunged toward the children at Grandpa's sudden alert, but were too slow against Ethan's Kesem and newfound knowledge of quickening spells.

Adrenaline flowed freely through Ethan's veins. This second wind was surprising, considering they had been on a self-forced march taking little if any time to sleep. It had only taken the small company two days' journey to get back here. They were all intent on reaching the ledge and from there; *Kristian's rescue!*

*Ahh, Kristian's rescue.* Ethan suddenly realized that he hadn't thought about how he would liberate his older brother in the first place. He had been so consumed and preoccupied with reaching the older boy that he hadn't thought about what came next or how they would even escape.

Another sobering thought came to Ethan as they ran—*We have to be on time, we just have to be, or else* . . . He couldn't bring himself to think much more on that topic, but it was already too late. The vision of his brother and the dragon from his dreams flashed through his mind again. Kristian stood alone. There were none to stand by his side and protect him from the fiery onslaught. The dragon drew in its breath and unleashed the firestorm. Ethan winced, driving the vision away, and picked up his pace with renewed intensity.

Lola kept close by his side—she was always the little sportler.

The lions were quick on their heels.

Grandpa? Grandpa was a little winded and ran much more slowly.

After a moderate burst of speed, Ethan slowed to a jog to catch his breath. Lola slowed as well, thankful for the momentary reprieve. But that was not all that had slowed them down. Seon had noticed black shadows moving in the distance.

At first, Ethan couldn't make out what the movement was. He cupped a hand over his brow and squinted again to get a clearer view. Then all at once, the movement became clear—a group of black armored soldiers rose from seemingly nowhere in the sand and were slowly advancing on the approaching children. It was as if they had expected them!

Ethan dug in his heels and slid to a stop. At the same time, he reached a hand out to stop his sister and hauled Lola behind him.

She barely kept her balance and wrinkled up her nose at her brother, but realized something was wrong and didn't pursue her intended reprimand she had prepared.

*Seon, how many are there?* he asked.

*I'm not sure.* The drake tensed his muscles, pushing against Ethan's shoulder before spreading his wings, and launching himself into the air and toward the figures. He circled upward to get a better vantage point. *Twelve . . . maybe more,* the drake replied.

Ethan suddenly felt queasy. *How are we going to get by so many soldiers?*

Just then, both lions leapt overhead and landed, spraying a cloud of sand up in front of the children. They barred their wicked fangs and roared in warning at the advancing dark figures.

*Ethan . . . the lead man . . . he is waving a rag,* Seon suddenly announced. *At least . . . I think he wishes to talk . . . wait . . .*

*Talk?* spat Ethan in disgust, but he figured the lion's display had done the trick for the moment. *I don't have time to talk, we need to get down to Kristian, now!* He worried they were nearing the event, and if they didn't hurry, there was nothing to stop the black monster from incinerating his elder brother. He impatiently awaited Seon's next message. It took a few moments as Ethan grew more anxious.

*Wait, he's doing something with his hands . . . he's . . .*

*What, Seon? What is it? . . . Seon?* Ethan searched the skies for a little white spec, but it was no use; Seon had flown out of sight. Although he could still feel the little drake's presence, which gave him some small comfort. *Seon!* he repeated.

No answer.

Ethan bolted forward, inadvertently slamming against one of the cats' giant paws, which the lion had swiftly extended to hold him back. Helam turned his massive head toward the boy and shook it from side to side before turning back to the advancing line.

"This is taking too much time!" Lola blurted out.

Ethan grinned to himself at his little sister's insightful comment.

The boy pushed himself back from the lion's paw and paced back and forth a few times, trying to think of some way to expedite getting past the blockade.

Suddenly, Seon shot back in an alarmed tone. *Ethan, they're magi, I have a very bad feeling about this!* the drake finished with a feeling of dread.

A sudden jolt struck Ethan, and he momentarily forgot all about Kristian. This wouldn't bode well for them at all. He'd seen what the magi had done back at the palace and the many accounts he'd heard told in Julfa from the caravan storytellers—he knew what they were capable of.

*Seon, get back here now, we'll deal with this together,* Ethan demanded as a myriad of ideas, strategies, and resulting consequences shot through his mind all at once. The queen's gift had given him more knowledge than he could have achieved in a lifetime. He had to use that knowledge to get

The Drake Epics - Journey to Qara

himself and Lola through to their brother without harm, and he'd have to do it fast. He felt the little drake's acknowledgment and turned toward the lion closest to him.

Koran didn't seem to notice the boy was plotting and stood planted, glowering at the magi or whatever they were, with his fangs in full view.

Ethan settled on a plan, realizing it might just work. He readied himself to knock the lion aside with a forced blast, followed by a charge at the magi. They couldn't be more than a hundred paces from the children now, and interrupting their chants was the only way to stop whatever madness they were creating. He wished he were within reach to drive them off the cliff face, which was another few hundred paces beyond them. But, the boy couldn't risk telling his sister, as the lions had superb hearing. He nodded at her and reached out his hand while striking a pose as if he were ready to sprint ahead.

She nodded back at him and grabbed his hand as tightly as she could.

At the exact moment that Ethan readied to lunge forward, Grandpa flanked them and spun the boy around by the shoulder to face the older man.

The old man momentarily bowed over as he wheezed from his forced sprint and held his side with the other hand. "You can't, Ethan . . . ," he finally forced out in between ragged gasps of air as he wagged a finger. "Let the lions handle . . . and we'll try . . . to find another way . . . around." He bleated as his breathing slowly returned to normal. "You could have . . . been hurt!" he finished, taking his last large gulp of air. He straightened up and stared both youngsters down in a silent rebuke.

Neither of the children responded.

Ethan shook his head. This was the least of their worries right now. "Grandpa, they're magi!" he replied. A cold premonition shot down Ethan's spine, and all of the color suddenly drained from his face. He felt something. He felt Kesem, powerful Kesem. It—no, they weaved through his senses, intertwining with one another, building to create something, something sinister. He could feel it; it was palpable.

Apparently Lola had a similar expression, and when Grandpa heard about the magi and saw the children's shocked appearances, he wrinkled his brow in concern and slowly raised his head to look beyond them.

Ethan sensed what would happen next, as if he read the Kesem's intent. He looked up at Grandpa, then back over his shoulder at a rolling, tumbling mass of wind and sand. It was only a few moments before the sandstorm was on top of them.

"Children . . . stay together . . . stay . . . ," Grandpa's voice was drowned out by the storm as it reached them with a deafening roar.

The old man embraced the children; and they all dropped to their knees, cowering before the assault, wrapping their arms around their heads to protect their faces from the pellets of searing sand.

Ethan held tight to Lola's wrist, but the sand shards burrowed into his skin, and he momentarily released his grasp on her. It only took that moment, and Lola was gone. Ethan frantically thrust his hands out for his sister as the sand relentlessly scoured any surface it could strike at. When this failed, he tried to call out for her and drew in a mouthful of sharp daggers. Giving in, he tried to form a shield, but something held him back from using his Kesem.

*Ethan!* he faintly sensed from his drake. *I'm on the ground. Deseret is on the ground as well, and Lola is huddled next to her. Stay where you are, this will not last long. They . . . they don't have the power to keep this up for much longer.*

*I can't use my Kesem!* he bawled. The last word was jumbled, and Ethan soon lost all contact with his companion. He shivered, not from the onslaught of sand, but from the sensation of being solely alone. He couldn't feel Seon.

He reached out to the drake.

No answer.

He tried again and again and again.

No answer.

This was no dream and Ethan was perfectly alone. He drew his robe about him for at least some protection. It seemed an eternity before the storm passed and he'd forgotten all about Kristian at this point. All he could think of was his utter loneliness. It was foreign to him outside of his dreams, as if he'd never felt isolated before now. The darkness shrouded him, and the howling wind subsided. Soon, the shards of sand stopped the incessant prickling at his exposed skin. All was still, and all was perfectly dark.

Ethan tried to reach out to Seon again.

No answer.

He didn't feel or sense anything. He tried to yell and then scream.

Silence. The lack of sound was perfectly deafening.

The boy slowly stood and groped about in the gloom, hoping that he might stumble into someone. He wandered for a time without any mental or physical contact. The ground beneath him felt lumpy where he walked, sloping slightly away from him. Ethan had an eerie feeling of desperation that enveloped him. He'd been here before, but when or where? He couldn't remember, yet he had felt this moment would come. His dreams had foretold this. Had he dreamed of his future?

Ethan strained to recall what came next as he relived the dream that had so often invaded his sleep. His eyes played cruel tricks on him, and he thought for a moment that this nightmare would end momentarily, revealing the light. When it dragged on, he began to again feel discouraged, and he attempted to reach out to Seon once more.

Nothing.

Seon's consciousness was completely absent. Wait! Something else was out there.

He strained to make contact, but all he felt was Kesem weaving over and under itself in a fantastic tapestry of his surrounding environment. The Kesem lived and breathed, folding in upon itself in intricate patterns. It was intoxicating, but as Ethan greedily delved deeper, he realized the Kesem flowed with rancid decay.

"The magi!" he realized. His mind clung to his brother, or rather the memory of his brother, and he knew he had to put an end to the Kesem's destruction in order to reach Kristian in time. He had to somehow remove these magi and their foul kesem from the equation, but how?

Without hesitation, he drew upon the energy within him and raised his hands into the air. He forced himself into a calm state and concentrated to gather the Kesem. At first nothing happened, he felt nothing—the Kesem was absent. Then, as he continued to meditate, he slowly felt the power surge. This gave him more confidence and he strained to coax the flame. The Kesem surged again and rushed together all at once.

The ground beneath the boy began to swell, and Ethan experienced the sudden sensation of upward movement. He stood cradled within the safety of the earth supporting his feet and legs. Ethan took a deep, calming breath and thrust his hands forward toward the source of the weaving Kesem. He felt a slight breeze tug at his hair as he rushed forward through the darkness.

The earth ebbed and flowed beneath him, and a sudden alarm rose from somewhere in the back of his mind. The feeling was alien and became intolerable. He feigned turning back, but he knew that the conjurers were likely attempting to thwart him from his purpose. So he pushed onward. The cries reached a feverish pitch, and Ethan knew he was almost on top of them—one final screech in his mind, and then silence followed.

Ethan felt impressed to stop and wait for something more. His mind was now free of the cries, and he breathed with relief. He immediately retracted his hands, sweeping his palms out to calm the earth. It swayed underfoot for a few moments and began to subside until Ethan felt no more movement.

The darkness started to lighten ever so slightly. He cupped a hand to his brow and glanced upward as a steady curtain of sand fell all around him. The curtain thinned, and the sun broke through the darkness. Ethan found himself standing at the ledge, looking down upon a sunken valley that sprawled out before him.

The magi had all but vanished, buried beneath the earth. Ethan now knew what would come next as the scene played out before him. Concourses of people, in much the same formations as from his dreams, the opposing armies of Qara and those who belonged to the dragon, stretched out below. The dragon, to his horror, was already in motion, facing a small spec of a man. They seemed so small from here, much smaller than he'd remembered from his dreams—the man barely visible against the backdrop of the much larger lizard. Ethan immediately knew the man was his brother. He had felt it in his dreams, and when the orbs had been drawn together, it became clear that Kristian was the one to stand off with the monster.

Ethan ripped himself away from his reverie. He had to change the course of what would next happen. That must have been why he'd dreamed of it. He had the power to change what *would* have happened! With his renewed sense of purpose, he looked around, half-expecting his other companions to materialize. One by one, each reached his side, first Lola and Deseret, then Grandpa, then Seon, and finally the lions.

He didn't dwell on it. He had to act, and he had to act now!

*Seon! Good to have you back!* Ethan felt the warmth of his small companion's touch in his mind. He plodded on. *We need to create a shield for you and me and Lola and Deseret. Then we need to get down there!* He pointed at Kristian and the dragon. He knew that he only had a few precious moments before his brother would be consumed in a fiery grave.

Seon didn't argue or fight him in his request.

Both Ethan and Seon joined forces. As Lola came within reach, he grabbed hold of her and pulled her close to him. Now was the time to draw upon the power the queen had granted him. He didn't know if he could accomplish this feat, but he had to try. For Kristian's sake, he had to try!

Grandpa and the lions were stoic as statues, gazing down at the scene before them. They neither sensed nor realized what Ethan was about to do, completely drawn to the spectacle of the dragon.

The power coursed through Ethan's veins, and with a flick of his will, a sparkling blue shield materialized around them. He thought how amazingly easy this had become in such a short period of time—the queen's gift was complete. But now wasn't the time to boast. Ethan reached deeper and slowly levitated the sphere containing them off the ground. The drain wasn't as much has he had anticipated. Still, this was a new trick for him, and he wasn't completely sure of how well it would hold.

Grandpa took notice and frantically waved the children back. "No, Ethan! Lola! Come back, you can't do this alone!" But they were already over the ledge and beyond his grasp. After a few attempts to get Ethan and his sister to abandon their venture, he realized he could not detain them and let his hands drop helplessly to his sides. He knew there was nothing more he could do, but to get down the cliff face himself. He took a moment and looked longingly after his two grandchildren as he forced an ashen smile that looked to be a cross between a grimace and concern. Then he rallied the two lions, and all three sprinted for the entrance to the tunnels that led to the Forbidden City below.

The sphere hovered over the ledge for a moment. Ethan wasn't entirely fond of dangling so far above the earth, but he was fairly certain that this would work. "Yes, this will work," he said out loud

Lola, on the other hand, did not hear him. She was almost hysterical at the dizzying height. Her eyes grew big, and small whimpers escaped her lips. Deseret attempted to console her, without success.

"Cover your eyes, Lola. I'll get you to the bottom safely," Ethan reassured. "But you might feel a bit queasy, so best if you practice your calming Kesem," he encouraged.

The little girl looked at him in horror, then slowly nodded her head, sat down, and concentrated. A soft aura appeared around her, and she wrapped her arms about herself in a further attempt to put her mind at ease.

Ethan nodded in satisfaction, and taking another deep breath before the plunge, let go of the levitation enchantment. They fell for a moment, and he felt completely weightless, as if he were flying on his own. A sudden rush of blood flowed to his head—the experience was exhilarating!

Both Seon and Deseret had their wings completely outstretched to balance themselves.

The boy shook himself free of the sensation and directed the sphere's aim for the dragon as his marker as they plummeted diagonally downward toward the arena created by the encircling armies. He let gravity do its job as the sphere gained momentum and velocity. If anyone below happened to have looked up at that moment, they would have seen a streaming bluish star shooting across the sky. But none did. All were perfectly engrossed as the battle unraveled below.

Lola still had her eyes squeezed shut, but remained otherwise quiet. She hadn't appreciated the weightlessness she was experiencing, but the calming was helping.

The boy urged the sphere forward to hasten its descent. He didn't have much time left. But to his own horror, he detected another obstacle he hadn't noticed before. It appeared that some magical dome had been cast up that surrounded the entirety of the battlefield. He wasn't sure if he could punch through it at first, and it was fast approaching.

He had to test the crackling shield's strength and decided on a magical shard as the instrument to do so. He twisted a wrist and thought of the dagger of energy as it materialized just outside of their falling star. Another mental exertion, and he flung it toward the dome. Part of the shard made impact and exploded in a flash of sparks, the remaining piece glanced off the dome's surface. He shook his head in frustration. It needed more power. He doubled the next shard's strength, and this time it made its way through! But he figured he would need a hundred times that power in order for their sphere to break through, and he suddenly doubted if it were possible at all. Still, he didn't have an alternative, even if it meant draining most of his remaining energy. It would only be temporary, and he hoped he would have enough in reserve to land them safely.

Ethan squeezed his eyes shut to more fully concentrate on casting the Kesem while retaining their sphere's shield intact. Slowly, he drew upon his power and formed a tip at the edge of the sphere. Once he was satisfied, he elongated the ends to merge with the sphere itself, not unlike a giant wedge. Next, he added more power to the tip to strengthen it for impact; and with a last shout, he drove the last bit of his strength into the wedge and adjacent parts of the shield. It worked! The children punched a hole in the dragon's dome and continued their course.

Opening his eyes, Ethan smiled at the small victory as he chanced another look above him and could see the dome repairing the hole they had made. But the effort had sapped most of his remaining energy, and he needed a few moments to build it back up again before they made contact with the valley floor. He slowed his thoughts to concentrate in order to rejuvenate himself, but was prematurely pulled from his meditation.

In horror, he witnessed the scene from his dream unfold right beneath him. "I can't be too late," he said in shock. A torrent of flame erupted from the dragon's maw. Ethan saw Kristian brace for the impact before his brother was entirely consumed. The armies of Qara fell to the ground in abject horror as the inferno reached the domed shield, licking at its surface as it struck.

Ethan bore that no mind.

A glimmer of hope took root as he thought he saw an iridescent shield of flame materialize around his brother's form before the fire overtook him. A feat he'd never seen Kristian accomplish before. Could it be true? Ethan didn't dare to hope for it. He struggled to glimpse the shadow of a figure, *any figure* within the writhing flames, where his brother had stood just moments before.

*It's no use!* he cried within himself. *Nothing could survive that blast.* He balked if his own shield could have withstood such an impact.

*I can't reach BeeSting!* Seon thought in alarm.

Ethan shook his head, he couldn't have been too late! "No, no, no!" he ranted. He had to try something, and do it fast. It was mere moments before they reached the ground. Ethan measured where he thought to have seen his brother last standing, and with another push of Kesem, he drove the sphere to land directly in the line of fire.

As they slammed into the earth, the shock wave cast up a wall of sand high into the air and stopped the immediate flame from reaching them for a few stone throws on either side of the point of impact. The shield kept its consistency, protecting them from being flung about in the resulting crash. But unlike before, when they had punched through the dome, this time, the shield wobbled outward like a giant gelatinous bubble that saved them from burrowing into the sandy earth. The resulting thick dust cloud lingered in the air, and all of the remaining dragon fire was extinguished.

Ethan gasped with momentary relief, then fell on all fours, trying to concentrate to regain some of his precious energy. The shield remained intact for a brief moment and then winked out of existence.

*Ethan?* Seon asked. *Are you all right?*

He could hear the concern in his companion's voice, but only nodded in reply. He received enough strength to lift his head and turned to look behind him to where Kristian lay. A few moments of desperate scanning revealed a blackened form lying a few feet from him. "No!" he croaked, reaching a weak hand out in his brother's direction. "Kristian!" he bellowed again, then collapsed.

Lola, who still had her eyes shut, opened them and released her calming Kesem. She had felt only the slightest of impact from their landing and looked expectantly at Ethan. "Ethan?" she asked in confusion to see her brother kneeling on the ground panting in the sand.

"Kris-Kristian," he blubbered and reached a hand out to point in his brother's direction. "I'll be fine . . . Lola . . . Go see if he's all right." The last sentence was muddled. *You too, Seon,* he thought.

Lola shook her head, dropped to one knee, grabbing at Ethan's arm, and tried unsuccessfully to hoist him up.

"I need to rest, Lola," Ethan whispered hoarsely. "Just for a little while . . . Please, go help Kristian," he pleaded.

She looked at Ethan then slowly nodded. Rising to her feet, she saw Kristian's form and sharply inhaled as wisps of heat rose from his smoldering form. She whimpered in agony, looking back at Ethan in horror and started toward their eldest brother.

The drakes were already in flight and reached the boy first. Their feelings hit both children at once. Strange feelings—feelings neither Ethan nor Lola could interpret. Feelings of both joy and sorrow.

Ethan slowly climbed to his feet and stumbled in a half jog toward his brother, still in a weakened state, but fast recovering as he drew from the queen's Kesem.

Lola reached her brother's side and dropped to her knees cradling Kristian's head close to her. Tears streamed down her face as she looked up at her approaching brother. "He's alive!" she said. "He's not even burnt! Look at him!"

Ethan looked down and saw it now too. His brother was in perfect condition, although unconscious. Still, Kristian was breathing regularly, and he had not a single burn mark or a scratch upon him! He sluggishly dropped to his knees and grabbed for his older brother's hand, pulling it close to him. He too cried with joy.

Kristian lethargically opened one eye. He first saw Lola and smiled, then noticed Ethan to his side. Both siblings were still weeping over him. "Am I dead?" he asked to both of their surprise.

"No, dummy!" Lola squealed with glee.

He took his hand from Ethan and felt his chest to make sure then sighed in relief.

"Wait. Where did you both come from? You are supposed to be on the journey!" he exclaimed.

"Yeah, well, we knew you'd be in a heap of trouble here. Someone had to save your butt," Ethan said in between joyful sobs.

"Wow, what a rush! BeeSting, we did it! We escaped the flame! That stupid lizard never knew we could do it!" A gigantic smile spread across his face, but it was short-lived.

"BeeSting?" He sat up, almost bowling Lola over in the process. He looked at his siblings in terror. "I . . . I can't feel him. Help me find him!" He panicked.

Ethan felt a sudden wave of dread and pain hit his senses.

Kristian was on all fours, searching through the sand with his hands, as if he had lost a ring or precious jewel.

*Ethan* . . . Seon touched his mind. *Ethan, BeeSting is dead!*

The younger brother jerked his head around and toward his drake, just twelve paces away.

Kristian must have sensed the same as he drew himself up and charged the direction where both Seon and Deseret stood over the small figure of another drake.

"No!" Kristian howled as he slid to a halt near his fallen companion. Both of the other drakes leapt easily aside at the young man's approach. "Nooo!" he bellowed in agony. He cradled the limp form of the red drake in his hands. "Why? why? why?" he bawled.

Both Ethan and Lola reached him.

Ethan tried to place a calming hand on his brother's shoulder.

Kristian jerked his shoulder away. "Why did I push you to join my power? I knew it would hurt you. Why did you agree . . . to save me?" He whimpered. "Why?" he sobbed.

Ethan and Lola looked helplessly at each other. Neither knew what to do. They were both equally shocked at this turn of events. Grief overcame them all, and they all wept for their fallen friend.

Ethan glimpsed a brief vision of his brother going insane as he remembered stories of men losing their drakes to death. Were they true? Would Kristian lose his mind? He looked mournfully at his older brother, desperately hoping the stories weren't true.

Time seemed to stand still, crowded with grief and sorrow. The only audible sound was Kristian's heaving sobs as he nuzzled his lifeless companion. Then Kristian raised his head at a sudden premonition and stared at a pillar of light that formed around the little red drake. Much to the surprise of the children, the drake's limp body was taken up into the beam of light, levitating out of Kristian's hands.

"BeeSting?" Kristian said in a soft whisper. He shook his head, as if he didn't believe what was happening. "BeeSting . . . are you alive?"

The answer was not what any of them wanted to hear.

"No, he has gone to the other side. He has finished his sojourn in this realm and will continue his journey beyond." The voice was soft and soothing and quite familiar to all of the children now. It was the voice of the dragoness, the Queen of Qara.

"He can't be dead. He just can't be," Kristian's voice started loudly then ended in a whimpering plea.

There was another moment of silence.

"It is part of the plan of happiness," the queen continued. "All must learn and live up to their true potential. Then all must eventually die. For that is our purpose in this world. It is framed so that we may act for ourselves and learn, knowing good from evil," she concluded.

Kristian was shaking his head, not wanting to hear any more. But he knew it was true, even if he wanted to desperately push it away.

"But in this time of mourning, there is also hope and a blessing."

Kristian raised his head questioningly.

"BeeSting left this blessing in his last moments. He sent me a request. A request to have you clothed in his memory. Think of it as a precursor for your life to come where you will receive your true mantle."

"But . . . I don't understand." Kristian sobbed. He wiped at his eyes with the sleeve of his tunic. "None of this makes any sense! Your rhymes don't make sense! What do you mean clothed? What mantle?" His voice took on a stern tone.

"It is not meant for you to understand now. You must study it out in your minds, and with time, you will come to understand."

Ethan smiled in spite of himself in this dreadful situation. Up until witnessing the joining of his orbs, he loathed that phrase. But now? Now it made perfect sense to him. Although Kristian was not to that point yet, he grimaced.

The queen continued, "You are inherently good, Kristian, as are you, Ethan, and as are you, Lola. Your drakes are guides, albeit temporary ones, but guides nonetheless. Guides in your mortal sojourn here in this world."

Ethan couldn't figure out where she was going with this, but hoped she would get there fast. Kristian was not known for his patience.

"I now give you my blessing, Kristian. A blessing coupled with that of your drake."

BeeSting's form hovered in the air above them and began to spin. Slowly at first, then with more speed. Soon, the form whizzed around in a blur and slowly elongated, spreading out in a twirling cylinder. The spinning slowed to reveal a magnificent robe that pulsated in a prism of colored light. It was beautiful, like nothing the children had before seen. It glimmered with an intense brightness, even though no sun shone down upon them through the great dust cloud that the shield's sphere had launched into the sky.

The robe began to slowly descend toward Kristian.

He was overcome with its beauty. It filled him with a sense of joy, but also with bitter sorrow. For he knew of what this robe was made, and for a moment, he wished it to be gone entirely.

"It is only natural for you to feel this way in your grief, Kristian. You made a choice. You knew you needed to continue down a certain path. As your drake knew he must continue on his own—still, one different from that of yours. Let this be a symbol of joy unto you, not of sorrow, but also a reminder of the consequences of each and every action you make."

The robe hovered briefly in the air before lowering over his body. It rested upon his shoulders, and he felt alive in a way that immediately reminded him of BeeSting, his dear friend.

Kristian reveled in a brief exchange of companionship with BeeSting, and then the drake was gone. The robe continued to beam a few moments more, then began to fit itself around the boy before almost entirely disappearing from view. He felt that it had fit tightly around him and now shown as an aura.

"Yes, this aura will remain with you always. Only to be taken off and replaced with your mantle in the next life. But a blessing and a warning follows this. You must continue on your path for goodness. If you wander from this path, it will gradually weaken and eventually be taken from you, turning to your own condemnation."

The children all stood in awe. None of them knew what to think of what had just happened. But it was not meant for them to dwell on this now. Another danger lurked in the recesses of the dust cloud. Waiting for the moment to burst in upon them and threaten them with utter destruction.

As if on cue, their brief respite was interrupted, and they were all thrust back into the path of a real and present danger, its weight bearing down upon them. The brief moment of unity they shared vanished, replaced with a discernible deep-throated laughter. The laughter was twisted, even maniacal, and it came from behind them.

The children turned to see the head of the dragon emerge through the dust.

Tiamat was upon them once more.

# Chapter 29

# The Kur-ne Again

*"We end this, now . . ."*

Ethan felt a surge of strength flow through him, and he thrust out his hands to conjure a quick shield around the children. This time, he made an ingenious addition; a sphere within a sphere, such that he could spin the outer shield to move them around the battle field by the force of Kesem, but without the need of the children to walk or move. He also added an extra spell to the transparent armor, much as he had done when they arrived, hoping that it would hold long enough for them to defeat the monster or, at the very least, buy the children enough time for escape. He knew there was another outcome as a quick flash of BeeSting's recent departure burned within his mind, but he pushed it quickly away. He urged their sphere backward to buy them even more time from the slowly advancing monster, who launched short gusts of inferno at the children's fast moving sphere.

Briefly scanning the two armies as the dust vacated the battlefield, Ethan couldn't help but feel the familiarity of the scene from his dreams, with the dragon's contingent flanking the monster and the armies of Qara barring their path. Both forces stood in silent anticipation at what their champions would do next. Ethan momentarily imagined hopeful expressions worn on the faces of his troops. He looked toward the crags of the surrounding cliffs and thought he glimpsed his grandpa and the two lions charging through the open tunnels, or perhaps his mind had made it up? Either way, this gave him enough courage to silently construct his strategy.

*Seon?* he plead, thousands of tactics flooding his mind all at once. *I need you to scout for me. I need to know if we can back Tiamat into the cliff side.*

*Too far!* his companion rejoined. *There's no way we can get him there before he overpowers us.*

Ethan kicked at the sphere. That definitely lessened their odds of success.

"I know what we have to do!" he announced to his siblings, attempting to keep their morale high.

He chanced a look at Lola, who wore a look of rage, mixed with fear on her dirt-smeared face. The tear stains from BeeSting's murder were now a dark brown plunging down her cheeks.

"We need to hold our ground for long enough to defeat the dragon." He tore his eyes away from his sister and looked sidewise at Kristian, who stood angrily transfixed on their opponent.

But deep down, Ethan had no idea how they would succeed—which of the strategies would he choose? *My dreams never took me this far, Seon!* he admitted.

*Perhaps, they were only meant to point you in the right direction*, the drake volunteered.

Ethan turned and gave Seon a pitiful look. *And that helps me how?*

Seon shrugged. *Sometimes we only need to know just enough and the rest is up to us*, he wisely counseled.

The boy grumbled and went back to devising another strategy. *Think, think, think!* he implored of himself. *We don't have time for this.* He impatiently brooded as he tapped a finger against his thigh.

Then he had it! *Marduk!* he exclaimed.

*Marduk?* Seon asked.

*Yes, Marduk, the hero! He will save us, remember from the king's tour?*

The white drake gave him a blank expression. *I don't see how that is a viable strategy.*

*Just keep up. When the battle is at its . . . bleakest . . .* , Ethan paused, trying to recount what the king had said word for word, *Marduk will charge into the . . . fray, charge into the fray . . . and . . .* He shot the drake a quizzical look.

Seon lazily pruned at one of his wings, completely uninterested.

*And vanquish the dragon lord,* Ethan declared in triumph. Although he had to admit that relying on a mural relief of Tiamat's overthrow and the king's boring lecture felt like a stretch at the moment. Still, that had to be how they would get out of this situation!

*The strategy is to hold the shield for long enough for Marduk to get here.* Ethan kept the sphere moving, skirting the greater shield Tiamat had cast up. Once satisfied that he had enough momentum, the boy lowered himself to one knee and began to pray to the Great Spirit for the great warrior to appear.

Seon really didn't agree, but let the boy come to his own conclusions on this one.

Ethan stole a peek through one eye.

*Still not here,* Seon thought with a dry tone.

*Got to have a little faith, Seon.* Ethan urged as he stood back up. He immediately set to work building a plan to best conserve his energy in order to hold their shield until Marduk arrived.

Seon ignored him.

The dragon was still in close pursuit, keeping pace with their retreat. He glowered down at the three in contempt. "Enough!" the monster bellowed. He suddenly lunged forward with surprising speed, swiping at the shield with his talons.

To Ethan's relief, Tiamat's massive paw merely glanced off its surface, erupting in a shower of sparks. He could sense the monster's discomfort at seeing the three children all together. It was almost as if he hadn't expected this at all, and that the giant lizard feared their combined power. He brought their sphere quickly around the dragon and stood still.

The monster turned its hulking mass, while snaking his head around to meet the children, then paused as he came about. The dragon wore a quizzical look, as if Tiamat were listening in on the boy's thoughts and sudden change in tactic. He began to nervously pace back and forth, keeping his massive eyes locked on the children, looking like he were attempting to come up with his own strategy. Great curls of smoke rose from the dragon's nostrils as he dug a trail in the sand with his incessant pacing. His breathing was a little more erratic, and the smoke doubled in mass steadily puffing into the air.

Then he stopped pacing, and a thin, high laugh from the dragon broke the tension—very different from the deep-throated laughter they had all heard from him before. "You think that together you can now stand against me?" His breath again came in short, ragged gasps. "That you have the glimmer of a chance? But in this, you are sadly mistaken!" he rebuked with exaggerated remorse. "This is the end for you!" his voice quivered slightly, and both Kristian and Ethan took immediate note of it.

"I have waited for this moment of triumph," the dragon relished.

Ethan continued to agitatedly scan the surrounding armies for Marduk to appear. "Come on, Marduk, where are you?" he muttered under his breath. But no one came to their rescue. The monster's shield stayed intact, and all was still.

Kristian glared at the dragon with contempt, letting his fury slowly boil within him. He looked at where BeeSting used to sit on his shoulder and placed his hand there—a fresh wave of sorrow and anguish engulfed him as he dwelt on the memories of his little companion. He continued to stare at the spot, and for a brief moment he thought he saw the fiery red drake looking back at him. He instinctively reached out to stroke at his companion, but it was just a phantom of his friend, and the glowing red figure disappeared.

He shook his head in disgust, but something caught his eye, and Kristian realized, it was BeeSting! He was sure of it! He hesitated, not knowing how to react, but the comfort he felt was enough. He turned to look back at the dragon with renewed determination to finish this battle. "No! You're wrong, *monster*! We end this *now*, for BeeSting, for Bortex, for Shalamar," he bellowed. "Tiamat, you will die *here!*"

"No," Ethan said to his brother as quietly as he could. "Kristian, we must wait, just a little longer, we must wait," he pleaded.

Kristian grumbled, then he shook his head. "No, little brother. The waiting is over." Rejecting Ethan's counsel, the older boy clenched his fists and uttered the word of fire, *yangin*, bursting into flame, consuming his entire body. He was oblivious to his two younger siblings as the flames leapt skyward, glancing off the ceiling of Ethan's shield.

Ethan took a faltered step backward and raised an arm to shield his sister from the flame. Still, curiously, he didn't feel any heat from his burning brother.

Lola backed away, looking questioningly up at Ethan for an answer.

He shrugged at his little sister. He himself wasn't quite sure what was happening. He had never seen this intensity from his brother before.

"Kristian?" he asked out loud.

*He has found his true center*, Seon explained. *BeeSting is still with him, he will always be with him, deep within him*, the drake concluded.

Ethan momentarily paused, not understanding what his companion meant, then slowly nodded. He perceived a newness to his brother that he hadn't realized before as Seon shared the feeling with him. He didn't know how, but he felt that Kristian would be all right after all.

Lola apparently had a similar conversation with Deseret. Her eyes were trained on her brother, and her face was drawn out in a kind of relief mixed with determination. She turned toward the dragon and began to launch water missiles at him through Ethan's shield with all her strength. Each took a different shape. An arrow, a spear, an axe, a sword, and other weapons with increasing potency and size.

The dragon appeared wary of the attacks and took precaution by deflecting and dodging some of the more sinister-looking weapons that were flung his way. He busily swiped at the missiles, taking momentary pleasure in her failed attempts, as the shards of water glanced harmlessly off of his thick scaly hide.

Ethan desperately scanned Qara's troops for any sign of Marduk and realized with dread that the champion might not be coming to their rescue after all. He knew that his shield would only last for so long, and the worst had not even started yet.

*We must find another way*, Seon prompted reproachfully.

*I know, he isn't coming*, Ethan admitted in defeat. He thought hard of what their next step should be—without Marduk's help! *But what can we do, Seon?* he thought hard, trying to force himself into a successful strategy.

*Ethan, what about Kristian?* the drake suggested.

*What about him?* He momentarily considered his older brother, then it dawned on him too. *It can't be!* He shook his head to clear his thoughts, then studied his brother again. *Marduk is . . .*

*Kristian!* Seon finished the sentence for the boy.

*Kristian is Marduk!* Ethan plowed through his shock. *Marduk has been with us all along!* Ethan almost squealed in delight. With this realization, the strategy started to fall into place. He knew what had to be done.

*We may just make it out of this spot after all.* Seon beamed.

Ethan nodded with joy and looked warily back at the dragon, who had now stopped pacing and was fixated on Kristian, wearing a look of pure rage mixed with foreboding dread. *I can see the fear in his eyes.* Ethan nodded in Tiamat's direction.

The Drake Epics - Journey to Qara

Seon took a few puffs of air. *Yes, and I can smell his doubt,* the drake closed.

The dragon howled and spewed a torrent of fire at the children.

The double sphere pushed aside, narrowly avoiding the incendiary blaze, as Ethan pushed them back into a hasty retreat from the monster, zigzagging as he went to avoid the gusts of flame that catapulted at them.

*I just need to find some weakness we can exploit.* The boy deliberated as he studied Tiamat from head to toe.

*Wait!* Seon interjected. *There it is again. Do you see it?*

Ethan glanced at his companion and followed his eyes to the dragon, straining harder to see what he'd seen. *What?* he finally gave in. *What do you see?* The boy let his eyes drop to the monster's chest and, for the first time, noticed an old belly scar devoid of scales on Tiamat's hide. *That's it!* Ethan exclaimed. *If Kristian strikes at that gash, can he get through?* he asked Seon.

The white drake studied the wound and then surveyed the rest of the dragon. *Yes, there he's unprotected, vulnerable. See how he awkwardly shields the scar with his arm as he charges forward?*

Tiamat swung his arm back and forth and held it momentarily over the scar, as if the dragon didn't want anyone to notice.

*I have to tell my brother,* Ethan began. *If he and Lola can cause a distraction, the last piece may fall in place like a giant puzzle. I need you to keep the sphere moving away from that giant lizard while I'm . . . occupied.*

*Oh?* Seon prodded.

But Ethan had to be discrete about it. *I'm sorry for what I'm about to do,* he confided in Seon and, to his surprise, immediately felt the drake's understanding.

*Well, I guess the situation calls for it,* Seon rationalized.

The impish boy made a mental note to give the drake a good ribbing for his being a hypocrite later.

*Kristian!* Ethan reached out to probe his brother's mind. He felt a wave of sweltering heat from his brother's consciousness. It was ablaze, just as his brother was. There was a moment of burning at the violation. Ethan winced at its intensity, then redoubled his efforts and pushed onward. *Kristian, it's me, Ethan,* he announced, partly shrinking away from the searing heat as he waited. The scorching barrier suddenly softened to a pleasant warmth as Kristian acknowledged his younger brother's presence, but the older boy still didn't respond.

*You need to torch your trident and throw it into the dragon's gash. It's the only way!* Ethan paused, again studying the dragon's belly.

Kristian turned his blazing head in the monster's direction, then slowly looked back at Ethan and nodded. He slowly drew his axe from its sheath

473

and touched a finger to the trident tip as he repeated the incantation, "Yangin." The axe burst into immediate flame as the fire licked at the three fingers. The axe itself seemed to be otherwise fine, much as Kristian was, and Ethan marveled at the feat.

*Wait for it,* Ethan counseled. *Lola and I need to distract the dragon first.*

Kristian shot him a questioning look.

*See how he covers his scar with his forearm, we'll only get one shot at this and will have to time your throw perfectly,* he continued. *Throw it on my mark.*

Kristian complied. *Make it quick, little brother,* he thought back.

Ethan now turned to Lola and reached out to her with his mind the same as he'd done with Kristian. *Lola!* he projected and immediately felt her presence.

Her conscience was a frozen blizzard compared to her eldest brother's inferno, as the hostile cold burned him with the same intensity as the flames had. Only this time, Ethan shivered uncontrollably and winced at the searing ice.

Lola's conscience immediately shrank back from him, confused at the violation.

He pushed on, just as he'd done with Kristian, expecting the same outcome. However, this time, he felt a sudden jolt as Deseret's presence burst in on them. The drake's angry power pushed against him and almost drove him out before he could announce himself. The strained sensation was not pleasant.

He rallied more strength to keep the contact open, *Lola . . . Deseret . . . it's Ethan.* Each thought sapped his strength even more so, and he wasn't sure if he could keep this up, astonished by their combined power.

The blockade remained intact for a moment or two, then abruptly dropped, reluctantly permitting him to project his thoughts. He suddenly realized that Deseret's conscience was familiar to him, and he could feel the resemblance to that of Seon's. He also felt her resentment toward him for invading Lola's mind instead of working through her brother. Ethan also sensed Seon squirm a little as the drake's sister scolded his little white companion at the same time. He'd be careful not to do this again.

Still, he was relieved to get through, and he took a moment to regain some strength before continuing, *We need to help Kristian attack the dragon. I need you to create a windstorm around Tiamat.* He paused, *I'm going to probe the dragon's mind to confuse him enough for Kristian to strike. But I need time to do that. I need the windstorm. Can you do that?* he asked.

A moment of silence followed; then he felt a quick acknowledgment from his sister and her drake. He withdrew, resolving never to attempt that again. It had been necessary for Kristian without BeeSting, but not with Lola.

*No, Ethan, I'm not sure we can hold Tiamat back. He's too strong!* Seon burst into the discussion, having regained some composure after being thoroughly chewed out by Deseret.

*You have another way out of this?* he asked a bit impatiently. *Now is the time to call it out.*

A brief pause followed.

Ethan turned to look at his companion. *Well?*

*No, I don't. I . . . I feel that this is dangerous. You can't do it alone, we need to join our strength.*

Ethan thought about it for a moment. Would he risk Seon's fate the same way that Kristian had done with BeeSting? This could come at a great cost, and he looked at his brother in mournful sorrow. But Seon was right, he couldn't do this alone—whether he liked it or not, he needed Seon's help to overthrow the malevolent lizard. He slowly nodded.

Seon knew what he had been thinking and thanked the boy as he nuzzled against his cheek. *This is my choice, Ethan, besides, I have no intention of going anywhere without you,* he concluded.

Ethan looked at his sister and gave her the signal.

Lola closed her eyes, and a blue aura shrouded her form. It quickly grew around her, and Ethan was impressed at how far she had come in mastering herself. She now reached her hands outward, the strain plainly visible on her face.

For a moment, Ethan worried he'd asked too much of his little sister. He almost stepped in to stop her, but realized that would be more dangerous at this point. He watched her intently.

The aura suddenly shot outward in a rush of water. The water circled around them and rose above and through his shield. As it swirled, it transformed from a deep blue to a dusty brown, collecting dust as it spun. It continued to swirl, faster and faster. A sudden gust of wind joined the churning mass, and Ethan couldn't tell if this was caused by the elements coming in contact with the spell or if Lola had conjured it. The eddy reached a frenzied spin cycle and began to form into a giant howling storm. Flashes of lightening erupted from within as it grew outward. It hovered high over them for a moment, then Lola thrust her arms toward the dragon. The squall obeyed and consumed the black lizard in a barrage of howling wind, mud, and water, with sharp splashes of electricity. The monster howled in rage.

It was enough.

Ethan's turn had come. He drew power from the combined orbs and counted down from three in his mind; then he and Seon jointly reached out to the large monster.

He pushed too hard the first time and slammed into a wall. He reeled from the blow, then tried another wall, looking for any way in. The monster had obviously placed a permanent mental shield around itself. *I don't know how we will get in there, Seon*, he lamented. *I mean, we've been beating our heads against Tiamat's outer defenses, and there is no weaknesses.* Ethan paused to think their situation through. *What have we missed? How will we ever find a way into the black fiend's mind?* He'd have to think of something else.

*Wait! Look over there, Ethan.* Seon pointed his snout at the monster. *Do you see it?*

In the distance, Ethan discerned a tiny glimmer of light. *That's it!* he exclaimed. He quickly changed course and targeted the light with all of his energy. It grew slowly until it was large enough to breach.

Their combined consciences hovered just outside of the light for a few moments before taking the plunge. This time, instead of immediate ejection, they burst through into Tiamat's consciousness.

Ethan fell inward and pounded down into a spongy alternate reality. He was in some maze of seemingly endless hallways. So far, they had avoided discovery. Lola's wind storm had successfully distracted the monster enough to buy them valuable time. But he didn't know how much longer this would last. They had to work quickly.

The two companions scanned the corridors, looking for a place to anchor themselves. As they made their way through one passage, Ethan tried to remain in shadow as large specters patrolled the passageways. The apparitions were gruesome dragon heads, listlessly hovering in the air without discernible arms and legs. Red beams emanated from their eyes as they scanned their patrol routes. Ethan knew they needed to stay out of the paths of those beams.

Seon agreed.

The two intruders started to dig for a memory anchor in order to distract the monster, but at the same time careful not to alert Tiamat to their presence. At least not until they had found a safe place to launch their mental attacks from.

Ethan continued to scan the passages in the monster's subconscious. But there were too many, and still no memories. *Seon, we need to split up, we'll make better time this way*, he added at Seon's grimace. *You go that way*—he pointed down one of the corridors—*and I'll go this way.* He pointed a finger in the opposite direction.

*OK, but be careful, Ethan. We'll need to stay as close as we can and lock minds, if Tiamat discovers us?*

*Agreed*, the boy replied, not wanting to linger on thoughts of what would happen if they were caught off guard.

Watching Seon disappear around the corner, Ethan turned and walked in the other direction. Much to his delight, he found himself in a gallery of the monster's memories as he passed great screens of horrific scenes of the dragon's past. Ethan hoped to uncover something that would cause the most damage. He walked for a while before stumbling on something he did not expect. It was too easy in fact. He sensed a vague memory, but set in a semi sealed alcove with giant slits running from floor to ceiling, as if it were located in a cell of some kind.

*I found something*, he called out to Seon. *I think I've found what we've been looking for.* He peered through the gap for a better look and realized the memory took the shape of an orb, much like the one in his pocket. Yet this orb was dark and foreboding. It was shrouded in a small stream of smoke that orbited the sphere, creating the illusion of a moving web. This must be the memory he had been looking for. It appeared to be lingering on a pedestal, again like the Kur-ne when he first discovered it.

Seon arrived, and both boy and drake puzzled over the challenge of how to get in without being detected. The only apparent way in was to squeeze through a gap in the wall.

Ethan wasn't sure what would happen, but this appeared to be the perfect place to launch their attack from. Besides, the gap appeared to be too small for the massive ghoulish specters to fit through, at least, he hoped it was too small. He reached a hand out toward one of the bars.

*No, Ethan!* Seon warned. *What if you're detected? We need more time!*

*Seon, we don't have time. Can't you feel them closing in on us? No, time is something we don't have—they could detect us at any moment!*

The drake paused as if he knew not what to do. *Fine, but let us power up before you do.*

Ethan nodded and drew again from his combined orbs. He felt the power flow through him; then he pushed himself through the gap. Without another thought, he wedged himself into the gap; and after a few tries, he pulled himself through. Seon easily followed behind him.

Now within reach, they studied the memory. Ethan launched into a series of discovery techniques, but to no avail. Other than the black cloud that navigated around the little globe, there were no visible mental armaments either of them could detect.

*Is it a memory?* the drake asked.

*I think so*, Ethan answered. *At least I feel it is. But I don't know how to get past this black cloud*, he fussed. *I mean. If I touch it, will it set off an alarm and alert Tiamat to our presence?* he feared.

*I don't think it will*, the little drake said in an academic tone. *It appears to be a ward of some kind. It could be a trap . . . that will try to ensnare us?*

Ethan drew knowledge from his own orb and attempted a final time to discern this dark orb's meaning. But he found that it was beyond his understanding. He resolved to place his hand into the void and grasp the ball. *It's our best shot*, he said.

*Make it count then*, Seon sarcastically retorted.

Ethan smirked then reached out to grab hold of the memory. His hand passed easily enough through the black mist. He touched the orb and winced, expecting some defensive counterattack. When nothing happened, he peeked through one eye.

Before him lay an open wasteland, much like the one he and Lola had traveled through with Grandpa. He opened the other eye and slowly turned himself about in a full circle, inspecting the landscape.

Seon, he realized with relief, was next to him. The small drake adeptly leapt to perch on Ethan's shoulder. *We have been here before!* his little white friend claimed.

*I know, Seon*, Ethan said impatiently. *We were here with Lola and Grandpa . . .*

*No, that's not what I meant . . . this is different.* The drake furrowed his brow in determined concentration. *Yes, the scroll in Limnah's quarters, it must be!* the drake again paused as if in deep meditation. *But how?* the drake was now clearly talking to himself. *This is . . . this is not the memory, it is a defense meant to . . . to trap and ensnare the observer—ever seeking, but never finding . . .* , the drake's thoughts trailed off.

After a few moments, Ethan gave into his curiosity, *And?* he irritably demanded, realizing too that something was not quite right here.

Usually, he could perceive what his companion thought and felt, but his mind felt a void or an absence of presence from Seon. He could hear the drake in his mind. Still, the feeling was disconnected, as if Seon's mind were off-limits. "Perhaps this is part of the *defense*," he justified, as if it were causing a riff to occur between the two. When no answer was forthcoming from Seon, Ethan considered this for himself. If this image were from the scroll, then it had to be real; and if it were real, then he had foreseen his entry into Tiamat's mind. Somehow, this all tied together through his dreams and visions.

*Think, Ethan, think!* he mustered. The boy stewed for a few moments more before another thought came to mind—his dream of the sandy wasteland, the grove of trees. The answer had already been given to him! Others would have died here, but not him, and not Seon. It all made perfect sense.

*I know what it all means!* he blurted out.

Seon shot him a questioning look, and Ethan felt an odd sense as if Seon were attempting to probe his own thoughts, but without success.

*We must concentrate,* the boy urged as he looked into the dark blue eyes of his companion. *I know you have questions, but it is the only way, and I can't explain how I know right now!* This time it was Ethan's turn to be the knowledgeable one.

The boy lowered himself to his knees, squeezed his eyes shut, and called out to the Great Spirit in a quick plea. Then he focused his energy on the grove of trees with all his might and longing. He knew he could do it because he had done it before! He had done it in his dreams, but reality and dream seemed to mesh together now, and why not in this way? He blocked all else out and focused on the thought with all of his energy. For the moment, he felt that time itself no longer had its grip on him. Days and months passed, followed by years, centuries, and millennia. All time vanished from existence, opening his view to eternity. There he found the grove from his dreams, nestled in a cluster of stars. All around showed bleakness, except for the light from the grove. As he neared the place, a lone tree came into view, yielding precious fruit. He reached for the fruit, feeling eerily familiar in his grasp, as he tried to capture the dragon's memories.

Upon finding no harm, he caressed the memory with his fingers and began to probe, slowly at first; then with more vigor and with each moment, he grew bolder.

$-\quad-\quad-$

The memory was of a much younger dragon self, although Ethan couldn't tell how he knew this. The dragon didn't appear any differently, only in experience. The monster flew through a lush landscape, searching for something with every thought, although it was not completely clear for what. Ethan sensed bottled-up frustration in the memory as he watched the dragon float on its massive wings. He felt something more; he felt the monster's fear. It feared another being. It feared . . . its master!

Ethan paused in confusion. *Master?* Wasn't this the creature from his dreams? The great Tiamat whom all feared?

*I feel it too, Ethan.* Seon was still by his side.

The boy redoubled his efforts and pushed further inward to understand more about the master, but it wasn't the proper memory, and Ethan couldn't find any link that would shed more light on the feeling nor to the master's identity. A sudden pang of fear hit Ethan at the thought that Tiamat was only a puppet and that this war would not end with him.

*Focus, Ethan, focus on the here and now!* Seon encouraged.

Ethan shoved the thought aside.

The monster was now in a full-flight pattern, dropping with a sudden downdraft of wind and beating its wings to regain altitude. The dragon soared over fields of rolling hills, slowly at first, then with quick bursts of speed as it dove through air pockets, catching updrafts of air on the other side, sending the creature higher into the sky. The air whistled by him as the dragon flew onward.

Ominous cliffs appeared in a bluish haze in front of them, and the monster tilted its body sidewise, curling its tail upward as a rudder and beating its giant wings, throwing the dragon into another updraft, pushing them above and beyond the cliff face. Mountain after mountain stretched out in front of them—too many to count, some with the same strange white canopies.

Tiamat threw his body to the side and beat his wings to circumnavigate a large peak that rose into the sky and above the clouds. Beyond the mountain lay a great sea and a far off island. He beat his wings and ascended into the rolling white masses above and, for a time, flew through the white mist as great drops of water formed and clung to his scaly body. The wind was much calmer here, and the great dragon had to continuously flap his wings to maintain altitude and momentum.

Soon, he slowed yet again and dropped down through the clouds to expose a grassy stretch of savannah. In the distance stood a grove. Not just any grove, a grove of white trees, the trees from Ethan's dreams!

Above the grove towered a lone mountain peak, flanked on all sides by cliffs that plummeted to the grassland below. Tiamat circled away from the grove, avoiding it, and Ethan could feel the dragon's complete disdain for it. He landed on a cliff outcropping on the opposite side of the peak. It beat its massive wings a few times before folding them neatly to its sides. A blinding light ensued, and the horrific form transfigured into the figure of a man. The same man Ethan had recognized in the desert. The same man that struck fear into him. The inquisitor! The auditor! Tiamat!

The monster hated this form. Ethan could sense it. Still, it had its purpose and usefulness, the dragon thought.

The man scanned the surrounding landscape. It was beautiful. He let his eyes fall on the grove, and he grimaced again. He spat on the ground. "Qara!" he said in disgust and wiped his mouth with the sleeve of his arm.

"Qara?" Ethan said with surprise. "This must have been what the queen had meant about her loss, but how . . . ?"

Before he could grasp the importance of this, he lost track of the grove.

Tiamat whirled around so that the landscape was behind him. A small cave entrance opened before him, and he paused for a moment. However, Ethan sensed the frustration leave the man's feelings, replaced with a sense of foreboding and fear. He took a single step, then stopped with a shudder, and wrung his hands together. His face wrinkled, as if to forcibly jolt some courage throughout his body. He clenched his fists and looked back up at the cave.

He could just fly away. Ethan heard the thought. *No, the master would find me wherever I went. There is no escape!* He had to face the master. Tiamat, the man, shook his head and forced himself to walk into the cave.

At first, the cave was pitch-black. Tiamat paused to let his eyes grow accustomed to the darkness. After a few moments, his sight turned a faint red, and he could see through the blackness in a reddish tint. He threw his billowing cape to his back and proceeded forward through a series of tunnels. Presently, he approached a pair of massive doors. Two grotesque creatures stood at either side looking like horrific ants, standing only on two legs, with two more sets of arms folded across their abdomen and two more arms, grasping large cleavers in each, the weapons' butts planted firmly on the ground.

The ant-like creatures crossed the cleavers over the door as Tiamat neared.

The man looked at each in turn, tilting his head in a predatory manner, barred his teeth, and growled in a deep snarl that was more dragon than manlike.

The creatures withdrew their weapons and stood again at complete attention. The doors swung open, metal scratching on metal.

Tiamat paused and took a deep breath to gather his wits, then entered.

The room was barren, other than a few couches and a drawn set of curtains. From behind the curtains, the silhouette of a man stood. It appeared he had his arms folded, as if waiting on Tiamat's arrival.

"Well?" the man asked. His voice sounded eerily familiar to Ethan, but he couldn't place it.

Tiamat bowed. The figure behind the curtain nodded in acknowledgment.

# The Kur-ne Again

"Did you find her?" the man continued.

Tiamat kept his eyes lowered to the ground. "I have failed you," he gushed, "Master!" And he bowed again, ready to receive his due punishment.

"Arghhh," came the reply. "Not good enough, Tiamat. Not nearly good enough!" he said harshly. "Still, she will be helpless against you, although for centuries to come." The man began to pace out of frustration.

Tiamat raised his head with a questioning look. "By my hands?" he queried.

The man nodded his head. "Yes. But I need her brought to me now. I can diminish her impact. It may mean my ultimate victory. If we're not successful, I fear the worst."

"You fear? Master?" Tiamat uttered in shock.

"Yes, even I fear. Do not take that lightly, Tiamat."

Ethan thought he heard a distinct tone of loathing from the man at the mention of the monster's name.

"Arghh," the man interrupted himself. "We must find her!" he demanded at the air. He paused pacing and sat, striking a thinking pose with one arm across his torso and the other forming a fist upon which he rested his chin.

Tiamat stood motionless, obediently waiting on his master.

"Although . . . Yes!" the man stood holding a finger aloft and wagged it slowly. "We must scourge the land. It is the only way to discover her hiding place. We must turn all that is green and lush into sand and desert." The man was again pacing. "Only then can we flush her out. Yes, that's it! Only then will her quest fail. She will be disgraced, and we will draw the power from her!" the figure said in a malicious tone filled now with pleasure. He stood still and continued to wag his finger while muttering to himself.

"Tiamat!" the man commanded. "You will raze the landscape to the ground!"

"But!" Tiamat disagreed. "Destroy my kingdom?" His voice registered shock, then softly pleading, "Master? This is my kingdom, given me by He who cast me from paradise. This is my paradise to rule over as a god!" He said the last part more forcefully.

"Not your kingdom, only mine, and *yes*, you will do as I command. Or should I dispose of you and find another to take your place?" the man retorted in an icy tone.

Tiamat shook his head. "But it is I who created you. I gave you this life."

"Yes, and I rule over you now!" the man shouted back.

482

Rage filled Tiamat's eyes, but he softened and once again bowed. "As you command, Master!" The hatred in his voice was clearly audible. "I will raze the kingdom to the ground and create great gusts of sand to blow upon its face. I will find the Queen of Qara, and I will bring her to you!"

"Your response gives me great pleasure, Tiamat. Now go!" the man commanded, dismissing him with a wave of his arm.

"But, Master?" Tiamat tempted. "What of Qara's grove?"

"Why bother me with such trifles!" the man barked.

"Only that I lack the power to raze it, Master." Tiamat forcedly prostrated himself on the ground in expectation.

"Ah, yes." The veiled man's tone turned pleasant again. "You will hide it!" he simply said.

"Hide it?"

"Yes, yes, only you will require a pure crop in order to do so," he said with loathing.

"But how?"

"It matters not to me!" the man howled. "Find a way and see it done," he commanded in a steely tone.

"As you wish, Master!" Tiamat concluded now knowing what must be done to accomplish his task. He bowed again, whirled on the spot, and left the room. He walked along the corridors until he emerged from the cave, blinking in the bright sunlight. He winced at the sudden brightness and mumbled to himself as he strode to the same spot of ground upon which he had previously landed. A flash of light, and he was rendered back into his monstrous dragon form.

He beat his giant wings a few times to test them, sending great gusts of air into the nearby trees that bowed before the pressure. "I will destroy all, I will be avenged—cast out and forgotten. This is now my world. I will rule all!" he roared in agony, thinking about his rule over a soon-to-be bleak and lifeless land. Still, as long as there was pain and suffering, as he felt, that was something he would continue to fight for.

The dragon launched himself off the ledge and circled into the sky, gaining altitude. He scanned the landscape below him. Qara would have to wait. He would raze all the rest and come back to it. He dove earthbound, and with great gusts, he volleyed wave after wave of fire, incinerating all of the vegetation below him. In its place, mountains of sand piled up, and so it began. Tiamat turned the land from garden into wasteland.

─  ─  ─

Ethan was suddenly jerked away from the memory. Great waves of pain wracked his mind. Seon was nowhere to be seen, and Ethan tried desperately to reach him.

*We are discovered, Ethan! I've been driven from the dragon's mind!* came the reply.

The boy had no time to let the terror overtake him. Tiamat's onslaught kept him occupied, almost sending him into a tailspin as the waves broke over him in an endless torrent of grief and agony. However, the pain was minor compared to what followed. A series of direct attacks on his mind left him in an even weaker and more vulnerable state.

"Who are you?" a deep voice bellowed. "Why have you come? get out!"

He had not expected this. He'd hoped he could have found a more secure place.

"No, you will not escape me so easily. You have failed to attack me! I will now crush you!" the voice continued.

Ethan's own thoughts and memories began to crowd his mind, each attempting to take control, as they rushed in upon his consciousness. Apparitions of Grandpa, Kristian, Lola, Seon, the queen, Limnah, and even the bullies Hem and Yeb berated him all at once. Ethan hysterically screamed as the thoughts jumbled and packed into every recess of his mind. He felt as if his brain were ready to explode.

*Ethan! The shield is falling! Ethan!* Seon's thoughts magnified and burst through his confusion.

A moment of clarity burst in upon the boy with Seon's announcement, and he had enough sense about him to cast up a barrier protecting his mind and invoke a calming Kesem. It seemed to work for the moment, and Ethan found his sanity and relished in the brief respite from the attacks, even if his mind still ached from the previous assaults.

He knew that he couldn't hold out much longer. Ethan quickly scanned around him, seeking a better defense. He remembered what he was here to do. He couldn't fail now, not when he was so close to the finish line.

Upon finding no point of defense, he quickly inventoried his possible strategies and settled on withdrawal from the monster's mind. But as he tried to flee, the dragon held him tight and overpowered him, like a steel trap. It was unlike anything Ethan had encountered before. He could feel the power coursing through the dragon, as if redirecting itself all toward the boy. He felt almost as if he were battling twelve thousand soldiers all at once.

Somehow, he also sensed that his physical shield had lapsed, leaving the children's defenses completely vulnerable and that the monster had

The Drake Epics - Journey to Qara

broken through Lola's storm. In moments, it would all be over. They would all be destroyed or taken and absorbed as Tiamat's mindless slaves.

Ethan rallied his strength to push back against the dragon. He was deflected.

"Ah, it is *you!*" a voice suddenly boomed all around him. "I should have expected this," it said in a reflective tone. "Nevertheless, you will still bow to me! You are weak, I can feel it." There was a brief pause, as if the monster were inhaling the scent from a beautiful rose.

Then Ethan had it, he knew that he had to face the dragon on his own terms, if he could only draw him into his own conscience, it might just work. He slowly stood. "Then face me directly, you stinking lizard!" Ethan shouted back. "Or are you weaker than I am?" he finished.

For a moment, all was quiet.

"Ah, yes. You wish to prove yourself to me already, boy?" The monster laughed. "And ironically, once you have proven your metal, I will simply sap your strength and use it to reclaim my kingdom!" Tiamat materialized before Ethan in his human form, a maniacal grin spread across his face.

His robes billowed around him as he stared down at the boy. "But this will simply not do. No, no!" He snapped his fingers, and the environment immediately changed around him to expose an endless expanse with open skies. "We must have a proper battlefield," the monster said, obviously pleased with his selection.

Ethan drew once more from his power as he levitated himself to the same elevation as the dragon in auditor form. Even the brief discussion between he and Tiamat had given him valuable time to silently meditate and regain some of his energy that he would need for this battle. He could also sense that the monster was entirely consumed with this challenge and paid no attention to the physical one outside. At least for the time being.

The boy flexed his body and concentrated, raising his power level within him all the while. He felt Seon join him and welcomed the drake, even if his companion's conscience was not immediately with him.

"Are you ready?" The creature yawned.

Ethan nodded and launched himself through the air at the man. As he reached him, the man vaporized, and Ethan found himself hurdling through the space he had been moments before.

Tiamat materialized again behind the boy and struck him with a heel kick to the back, pounding Ethan to the ground and casting up a wave of dust.

Shaking his head, Ethan stood and turned to face his smiling opponent. This time he brought his hands together and watched his seismic wall of energy build, then lurched forward and thrust it at his

485

opponent. At the same time, the boy followed directly behind it, lunging to the side at the last moment to strike at Tiamat from his side.

The dragon prince responded with his own energy canon to deflect it, but was too slow to meet with Ethan's incoming assault.

Ethan slammed his fists into Tiamat's skull, landing a series of blurred punches and a final hammer kick that smashed down on top of the monster's head, sending him to the ground below. A great billow of dust plumed skyward at the impact. For a few moments, all was silent. *I did it!* he thought with delight. He hovered over the gaping hole he had created and watched for any sign of movement.

He knew his next move was to entrap the beast so that he could retreat into his own mind to give Kristian the signal. Slowly, Ethan formed the Kesem that he would cast, like a net over the dragon's conscience. He sensed where Tiamat lay and finished the incantation, launching it at the still form.

A screeching howl emanated from below as a black figure rocketed out of the gap, just missing entanglement. "You won't catch me that easy, *boy*!"

Ethan sensed the monster's renewed anger at its embarrassment. He brought his arms up in self-defense to block the assault, just as Tiamat reached him.

Tiamat threw a fist at the boy's face, which Ethan deflected with his left hand, followed by his own blow with his right hand. Tiamat blocked the attack and threw a kick, which Ethan blocked with his leg, launching a side kick. They exchanged a volley of blows, as the boy and the dragon took turns throwing punches and kicks at one another in an epic struggle.

The monster landed a palm punch to Ethan's chest that sent the boy flying backward through the air a few stone throws. Tiamat grinned and launched himself toward the boy.

Ethan recovered and charged the dragon. This time, however, his strategy was confusion. He projected a mental image of the dragon's master and his voice. "You will desist from this disobedience, Tiamat! Or I will find another to take your place!"

The mental attack seemed to momentarily work as Tiamat lost his focus.

This was all Ethan needed, and he cast another net around the monster, taking Tiamat in his trap.

The dragon struggled against it, fighting for his freedom and screaming in shock and confusion.

Ethan smiled in triumph and held the monster tight, sensing the confusion had drained his opponent's energy. He exercised all of his strength to keep Tiamat from escaping. Now all he needed was to keep the dragon bound. He added more energy to strengthen his binds, folding the Kesem over the top of itself to keep it taught. "This is your punishment for defying me, Tiamat. You will remain in this prison." Ethan continued in the master's voice.

The monster struggled for a few moments more and then whimpered in fear.

The boy continued to strengthen the cords and prepared the monster for transport back into his own conscience. He felt Tiamat's energy levels drop as fear replaced confidence.

"I have you now," he let slip. Ethan immediately realized his error and hoped the monster was too paralyzed to recognize Ethan's voice from that of the master's. But it was too late, he could feel Tiamat's strength spike.

"Enough!" a deep voice reverberated throughout the battlefield. Its power shook Tiamat free, easily breaking through Ethan's binding cords.

Ethan felt his own energy drain at an alarming rate, and he knew that Tiamat had regained his senses and was drawing energy from the boy. Then he felt a blow that wracked his mind with pain and found himself on the battlefield floor, reeling from the attack. He struggled against Tiamat's power, pinning him down and felt utterly helpless against it.

"How could something as pitiful as you have ever stood against me? Look at you cowering before me," the voice boomed.

Ethan felt another volley of attacks drive him back and outward. He realized that if the monster pushed him back out, Tiamat would follow him into his own mind and take control of him. He was helpless to stop it. With each attack, he neared the monster's outer consciousness. No matter how hard he and Seon rallied to gain ground, he lost more ground than he could take. It was no use, it was only a matter of time, and all would be lost. Was this how it was all supposed to end?

*Kristian! Throw the axe!* he desperately thought, no longer trying to mask his thoughts from intrusion. *Throw it!* he pleaded.

He sensed that time had ground to a halt and he didn't know if the message had gotten through. He despaired as he was continually pushed back, his heels dragging against the ground. He was nearing his own conscience. He volleyed with Seon in a last desperate attempt to free himself from Tiamat. It failed. The monster's control was complete.

"See, doesn't that feel better? Rest . . . Rest. It will all be over soon," Tiamat soothed.

Ethan gave in to despair. The dark oblivion was somehow welcoming. Why fight against it? Ethan's mind submerged in an ocean of intoxicating tranquility—no cares, no worries, no thoughts, simply blind obedience.

The Kur-ne Again

Suddenly, a flash of light erupted around Ethan. Confused and sluggish, he peered around himself. The light vibrated, and stars whirled and whizzed overhead. They vibrated and pulsed in a dizzying blur, and Ethan realized that the Kur-ne was adding to his strength.

Seon felt it too. Now, *Ethan! Strike at his memory* now! the drake shouted.

Ethan called upon his reserves, drawing from Seon, the queen, and the orbs all at once. He unleashed his attack on Tiamat. The dragon's defense held, but he could feel Tiamat's strain. Then he remembered all of his dreams about the dragon, the king and queen, the grove of trees, the crop from the monster's memory, and the white fruit from his dreams. It had all led to this! All he needed to do in his time of need was to have a righteous desire. He focused on his desire and strove for it. Instantly, the white fruit appeared in front to him, raised upon an altar. Ethan gratefully reached out for it.

Tiamat shrieked in fury and pain. "No! bow to me! I am your master!" His face contorted and twisted in rage.

Ethan wrapped his conscience around the fruit and consumed it. A fresh wave of energy broke over him, and he pushed on Tiamat's conscience. It held for mere moments, then shattered into thousands of grains of light. The boy felt all of his senses again, both in mind and in body. Realizing he was now in complete control of Tiamat's own strength, the raw power flowed over and through him. Instead of despair, he felt dominion!

Tiamat weakly beat against him, shrieking Ethan's name. "Bow . . . to . . . me."

"No," Ethan said matter-of-factly. "I will not bow to you. You will bow to me." He scoffed. Ethan bathed in the energy. This was all he needed. All other thoughts were distant. Nothing seemed to matter, he could use this power to control anything, bow anyone to his will. The King of Qara, Julfa's grand Sheikh, the village council, Hem! Ethan grinned to himself.

Tiamat cowered in fear. He continued to rant against Ethan, looking for any means of escape. It was no use.

Ethan easily wrapped the monster's mind into a small cage and placed it out of his way. All it was to him now was a source of power he could draw from.

He jerked his eyes open to look around him. Confident he could end the conflict. Confident that he could put down the remainder of the army with a single thought.

He looked upon Kristian with a cold stare. His brother was still ablaze. He had remarkable power, but it paled in comparison to what Ethan now wielded. It was insignificant. He looked at Lola with a sense of pity, still feebly trying to cobble together another weak water attack at an already enslaved dragon.

She looked up at him. Tears streaked down her cheeks.

Ethan felt a sudden flash of sorrow. Sorrow and guilt at the power he now possessed. It wracked his soul with torment he had never before known. He realized that he had something much more powerful than what was intended. He knew he loved his sister and his brother. He also realized that what had seemed like an eternity of seek-and-find in the monster's mind was in reality mere moments.

With renewed determination, he broke through his own power's barrier and yelled for Kristian to finish the monster off, "Now, Kristian, throw it into his heart!"

Kristian charged Tiamat with a battle cry. He pulled up just short of the monster and planted his feet firmly in the ground.

Tiamat didn't see him. The monster stood frozen, mentally writhing in Ethan's wake.

With another shout for strength, Kristian launched the fiery pitchfork into Tiamat's chest. He hit his mark as fire erupted from within the monster's belly. It poured out of him and enveloped Kristian in flame.

"No!" Ethan yelled as he looked wildly around. In his shock, he released Tiamat from his prison and withdrew from the monster's mind. He felt an immediate drain on his energy and fell to the ground, gasping.

The dragon, coming back to his senses, writhed in pain and agony, clutching at his chest. He tried unsuccessfully to draw the pitchfork out, but it had welded itself within his scaly hide. Great bursts of flame erupted out of the dragon's maw as he thrust his head around in the air. The flame continued to pour out and around Kristian, now completely submerged within the fiery inferno.

"Lola, put the fire out!" Ethan shrieked, turning on the girl.

She had tears in her eyes and fiercely shook her head. She was muttering, "Kristian, Kristian, Kristian."

Ethan grabbed her by the shoulders. "Lola . . . ," he said more gently, "you need to put the fire out around Kristian!"

She looked up at her brother for a moment then nodded, drawing up enough courage. She closed her eyes and concentrated. Her aura grew. She stretched her arms out in front of her and launched a flood of water at where her brother had been standing before the flames of lava had enveloped him.

Ethan drew from his power and thrust a shield in between Kristian and the dragon to prevent the flames from their continued course. *He's making a real habit out of this fire thing,* he muttered.

As Lola finished, a great cloud of steam floated skyward. Both Ethan and Lola ran to where Kristian had stood, but the heat was too intense, and they had to stop short and cover their faces with their arms to deflect it. They looked on, afraid of what they might discover.

Lola was openly weeping now, and both glanced back up at the dragon.

Tiamat continued to cry in agony and, with one last surge of flame, fell over backward, dead. His minions all cried out at once and fled the field. A number of them fell to the earth as if dead themselves. If Ethan had studied them more closely, he would have found that many of Julfa's villagers were among them. But his entire focus was on Kristian.

Suddenly, a desert wind rushed through the valley, and the steam began to fizzle.

Ethan cast a shield to protect them from the heat, and they both charged forward. They found Kristian lying on the ground in front of them. The shield around them consumed Kristian as Ethan knelt, putting his ear to his brother's chest.

Kristian was still breathing, and his heart was slightly beating. He appeared to be fine otherwise, but his arms were badly burned.

Ethan let out a yelp of joy. "Lola, he's OK. He's OK!" he stated numbly. "We need to get him out of here," he stated and grabbed hold of Kristian under his arms.

Lola grabbed one of Kristian's legs, not really helping, but with the intent to.

Ethan grunted and pulled Kristian slowly out of the steam.

As soon as the children had cleared the vapor, Grandpa and the armies of Qara maneuvered over to their location.

Ethan dropped the shield and set to work healing his older brother. He placed a hand each on his brother's arms and felt for his power to heal him. It appeared to work as Kristian's arms regained some of their color and looked much better. He put his head to his brother's chest and confirmed that Kristian's breathing was more regular. "Kristian?" he called out to him.

The older boy opened an eye. "I'm fine, Dingus," he said in hoarse whisper. "Is it done?" he asked, clearing his throat.

"It's done!" Ethan said with a smile as he started to tear up. He gruffly wiped away the tears and stood, reaching out his hand to help his brother to his feet.

The Drake Epics - Journey to Qara

Kristian accepted his brother's hand and stood. The older boy embraced his younger brother and started to laugh.

Soon, Lola joined them, she was already sobbing.

"Are you all right?" Grandpa suddenly announced, only just arriving from the tunnels.

Kristian quickly closed the gap to the old man and grasped him in a full bear hug, reaching out to pull Heramon into the same hug as the mentor came within reach.

Heramon willingly accepted the show of affection.

Ethan noticed that Kristian's necklace band had broken and the pendant lay half-submerged in the sand. He quickly retrieved it and rubbed the sand off it. "He'll need this!" he said to Lola before motioning for them both to meet their grandpa.

Heramon broke Kristian's grip and stood back to allow the family to embrace.

The king and queen appeared at the head of their armies and beamed smiles at their three saviors.

The children hardly noticed as they embraced their grandpa, all openly weeping for joy.

Deseret and Seon launched from the children's shoulders and merrily circled in the air above the happy family.

Grandpa hugged them close to him. "It is done! You are all right. It is done, it is done," he said in a soothingly tone. The children continued to uncontrollably sob in Grandpa's arms. "Let it all out, there, there. I'm so proud of you! I can't believe you did it," he said.

The army of Qara crowded around the three. Thousands of silent gnomes and lions looked upon the Sheikhs and worshiped them. The three heroes had destroyed the evil that had thrown their world into a continuous wasteland of chaos for thousands of years.

Kristian looked up and saw Bortex and Shalamar on the backs of other lions, racing toward the land of Qara.

*They are quite well, thanks to you.* The queen's thoughts pressed on the boy. *Even Muschle will make it through his ordeal, but his leg will never be the same again. Your magic is much stronger than you give it credit for. You healed them.*

The eldest wept even more so now that he knew his friends were safe.

A moment of silence was followed by immense cheering as the armies applauded the three children. The sound was deafening.

Kristian and Ethan looked around, a little embarrassed by all the attention. Lola continued to bury her face into Grandpa's chest.

# The Kur-ne Again

"It is done, my children. It is done. The people of Qara and Julfa are now safe!" Grandpa said proudly as he continued to hug them tightly to him for a few moments. Then, he pushed them slightly away at arm's length to look into their eyes, as if to tell them something more, but instead noticed Kristian's necklace in Ethan's hand. "I see that you have Kristian's pendant," the old man said as he looked down at Ethan with a tender smile.

Kristian felt around his neck at the sudden realization he'd lost it. He extended his hand in gratitude to Ethan for having found it.

"No, no, it must be brought together with the Kur-ne," Grandpa announced. Do you still have it, Ethan?

Ethan reached into his own pocket and drew out the orb, now glowing brilliantly.

*It is beautiful!* Seon purred.

The old man looked up at the queen, who nodded for him to continue. "But let me tell you three a secret," he said as he pulled them back into his embrace and bent his head to whisper into their ears. "Kristian and Ethan, lock arms with your sister just so." Grandpa pulled their arms together with one hand as he half-embraced them with the other. "There, there. Don't cry so. It will all be all right," he soothed Lola. "Now, Ethan, bring the two together, the pendant and the Kur-ne."

Ethan did as he was asked.

"Good, good." The old man applauded. "Now, repeat after me, *Biri dusecak iki artacaq, lakin butun Nejd ev qayıdacaqlar!*"

Ethan recited the line partly through, but interrupted himself with a bout of sudden joyful sobs. Grandpa had him repeat the line again, so he did. But something didn't feel quite right, he realized. He suddenly felt weak and groggy.

Once he was satisfied, Grandpa whispered clearly to three children, "Your prophecy is fulfilled, Ethan. But Kristian and Lola, yours has just begun," the old man cooed. "I love you all. You have done so well! Remember me and do not be sad. Where you are going, I cannot come. But, you had a chance to live a lifetime with me. A wonderful lifetime."

Ethan started to sag. He looked over at Kristian and Lola and noticed they were sagging too.

Seon's warm and happy conscience flowed lightly through Ethan's mind. *Remember me, Ethan. Remember me.* and then the little white Drake was gone.

"Seon!" he called out as he felt the drake's presence vanish. "What is happening? *Seon!*" he bawled. He sensed that Lola was calling out for Deseret as well. "Seon!"

The Drake Epics - Journey to Qara

Kristian suddenly passed out and fell over.

Ethan watched him fall, helpless to aid his brother. "Grandpa, what have you done?" he accused.

Lola now fell over onto the sand.

"What have you done? I don't understand." Ethan shook his head. With one last effort, he reached out to his companion. But it was no use, the drake was nowhere to be felt. The boy had a sudden flash of dread as he remembered what had happened to Kristian and to BeeSting. Had the same happened to him and to Lola? It couldn't be! Ethan struggled against the wall of fatigue that bore down upon him. He would *not* let this happen to them!

Suddenly, he felt the queen's mental embrace. "Be at peace, Great Sheikh, you have accomplished your quest, as has your drake and as has the Kur-ne. Do not struggle against this any longer, but be at peace."

Ethan realized that the Kur-ne was no longer in his grasp, but instead of fear and worry over the orb and about his white emperor drake, he only felt at harmony with the queen and momentarily forgot about his exertions. Her warmth flowed over him, and he willingly gave into her wishes.

Ethan toppled over and joined his siblings as they slept to the cheers of the people of Qara!

# Chapter 30

## Of Empires and Beehives

*Was it all a dream? And what is to come?*

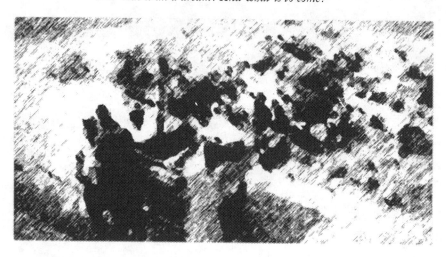

Ethan's senses slowly came back to him. The loud cheers he had fallen asleep to were still loud in his own ears. He forced himself out of the fogginess and haze of sleep. A faint alarm sounded in the back of his mind. He needed to wake up, but it was suddenly a very hard thing to do.

Finally, he managed to open one eye and realized that he was being dragged. Lola was being dragged directly behind him. A slight breeze blew across his face as he sputtered up some sand. Where was he? He

The Drake Epics - Journey to Qara

suddenly realized that he had neither the Kur-ne nor Kristian's necklace in his hands and wondered where they had gone. But, he was too groggy to search for them now.

The clapping continued, and he was finally laid down. A foggy face appeared in front of him, moving in and out of his blurred sight.

"Ethan! Ethan, can you hear me?" the man's voice was not immediately familiar. "Ethan, stay with me!" the voice continued. The applause started to lessen.

"Lola!" a woman's voice rang out clearly. It was not the voice of the queen, but it sounded familiar. "Lola, can you hear me?"

Who was it? Ethan couldn't remember.

"Are they OK?" she was now asking. "Travis, are our children OK?"

*Our children?* Ethan thought. *Are there other children here?* he asked as he strained to sit up.

"I think so," the man's voice replied to the woman. "Ethan keeps repeating the word Seon over and over again . . . wait, Ethan is sitting up . . . , and look . . . Lola is opening her eyes!"

Ethan felt strong hands helping him.

"You're OK, Ethan, just take it easy. We're here."

"Where am I?" Ethan tried to ask. His voice sounded raspy in his own ears, and his throat felt sore to speak. "What? What happened?" He knuckled at his eyes to clear the fogginess.

"You are here with us now. All is safe. You gave us quite the scare!" the man's voice said.

"I know! Is Tiamat dead?" the boy asked, still trying to get his eyesight back.

"You must have hit your head," the man answered. "Who is Tiamat? No one has died here."

"The . . . the . . . the dragon!" Ethan said out of frustration. He still couldn't see, and this line of questioning was completely disorienting. "The dragon over there!" He raised his hand in the direction he figured the hulking mass must be lying.

"There's nothing over there, son. There, there. Don't strain yourself. Just take it easy."

Ethan grimaced. How could the man not see that enormous lizard? That, and where had this man been through the most epic battle ever fought? Clearly, this man must be blind!

"Ethan?" Lola's voice rang out. "Ethan, are you there?"

"I'm here, Lola," he said. The boy could now hear the woman's voice crying.

"Ethan, Lola, we were so worried!" the woman now said.

495

"Grandpa. Where is Grandpa?" Ethan asked. "Lola, is Grandpa with you?"

"No. I don't know where he is . . . but . . . Mom and Dad are here!" Her words pounded into Ethan, and he knuckled at his eyes again so that he could see. A wash of memories poured over his mind. They flashed at him at a dizzying tempo. He remembered everything! He remembered their family was from Seattle. He remembered they were in Kurdistan for a burial dig. He remembered about the tank, about the well and its collapse. He remembered falling in and the children's rescue. "Mom? Dad?" he uttered.

"I'm here, Ethan," said his dad's voice. "I'm here."

Ethan's vision came back to him. All around him stood locals who were working on the dig. They had quieted down, but were all beaming at the children's rescue. Lola was sitting a few paces away from him. Mom had her in a bear hug. Dad was sitting next to the boy, his arm wrapped around Ethan in a half hug. The foreman stood over them with a look of relief on his face.

Ethan chanced a smile.

Lola stood with her mom's help, and they walked over to Ethan before kneeling in the sand.

Mom wrapped her arms around Ethan. "You had us so worried!" she said through her tears. "You all did!"

"Oh . . . OK, Mom." Ethan was beginning to feel smothered.

Mom released him and knelt back with one arm draped around Lola.

"Where is Kristian?" Ethan craned his head around for a glimpse of his brother, desperate to see him.

"I'm over here," Kristian said. He was lying in the sand a few paces away as he waved an arm. "I'm fine," he said to Ethan's relief.

"We pulled your brother out first," the dig's foreman replied. "But you have quite a gash on your head. Mr. Travis, sir, we should be getting young Ethan medical attention . . ."

Ethan waved off the comment, wanting some closure on what was happening.

Dad held his hand up and allowed him to speak a little further.

"What? What happened?" Ethan asked again, his mind confused at the abrupt change in the children's story.

"When we realized you weren't in the hut or anywhere at the dig"— Dad started and looked up at Mom and then at Lola before returning his gaze to Ethan—"your mother and I were desperate to find you three. We had search crews out all day and into the night looking for you. No one thought to look around the well, and we didn't have time to go for water due to the search . . ."

The Drake Epics - Journey to Qara

Kristian had now gotten to his feet and made his way over to the family, placing a loving hand on his dad's shoulder.

Dad smiled up at him and placed his own hand on his eldest son's hand then continued. "Early this morning, one of the men discovered the well's collapse. Fortunately for us all, he was clever enough to shine a light down inside and found you all partially buried under the sand. I don't know how he even saw you, that was quite a distance to fall." He cleared his throat, as if he were on the verge of tears, before continuing. "We're lucky you weren't more seriously injured. We thought we had lost you . . ." Tears filled his father's eyes, and he gruffly rubbed them off with the sleeve of his shirt as he let out a brief laugh of relief.

Ethan's mom started to openly cry again and pulled Lola closer to her.

Kristian dropped to one kneed and half-hugged his father from behind, placing his head on Dad's shoulder.

"But . . . but . . . ," Ethan stammered as his memories became more clear. "There was no tank shelling the village?"

"What tank?" Dad chuckled. "Really, you should take it easy, son." He looked at the foreman and nodded, who immediately moved off to get a stretcher for the boy.

But Ethan was determined. He looked over at where the well had collapsed. The battered, old wooden frame was mostly still intact, but the side of the well was completely caved in. There was no sign of a tank anywhere. "Right there!" He pointed. "And . . . Grandpa pulled us out at the bottom of the well . . ."

"Dingus!" Kristian said. "Let it go. We'll talk about it later."

Ethan looked at Lola and could see in her eyes that she knew exactly what he was talking about.

Mom and Dad, however, were exchanging nervous glances at each other. Exchanging sad glances.

"Grandpa isn't here, is he?" Ethan realized.

Dad shook his head. "No. We know how much you loved your grandpa, Ethan." He soothed. "He's been gone for some time."

"I know," Ethan admitted and looked up at his father, who looked lovingly back at the boy. "Dad?" he suddenly added. "I think you should give the bottom of that well another look. There's something down there," he offered more.

Dad smiled and nodded his head. "We'll look tomorrow," he replied. "OK, OK, I promise I'll look into it!" he added at Ethan's grimace. He ordered one of the digging foremen to secure the well for entry.

The foreman had the stretcher brought up and laid beside Ethan.

Of Empires and Beehives

"Well!" dad announced. "We need to get you all checked out. Ethan, we will move you over onto this stretcher so that we can get you back to the hut . . ."

"No, I can walk!" Ethan exclaimed.

Dad looked at Mom then nodded. "We can try." He waved off the stretcher.

"Can you walk?" Mom asked as she urged Lola to her feet.

Ethan grabbed hold of his dad and, with his help, stood slowly, feeling a bit dizzy.

Kristian was now already on his feet and stepped to the other side of Ethan to help the younger boy walk along. As the older boy draped Ethan's arm over his shoulder, Kristian whispered, "Ethan. Do you know what happened to my necklace?" as he felt around in his pocket with his other hand, searching for his most prized possession. "I remember you found it . . . you know where. But I can't find it now." He gave his brother a pitiful look.

Ethan shook his head. "I'm sorry Kristian," was all the younger boy could say.

The older boy gave him a sorrowful look and nodded in silent understanding as they made their way to the family home.

The next few hours were a blur. The children had little time to think about what had happened to them as the local doctor ran a barrage of tests on them to ensure they were healthy. The children were not happy about the check-ups. They took forever.

Kristian was particularly annoyed and therefore completely irate. "I'm fine!" he said as much as seven times to the doctor. He had a few severe lacerations on his arms that looked like burn marks from when he fell into the well and rubbed his arms raw against the sand.

Thirty minutes after the doctor had started his tests, the dig site erupted with excitement. The diggers had discovered a tunnel at the bottom of the well.

Dad had ordered a crew to investigate, but refused to go with them and stayed behind with his family. Mom was the most surprised by this, as dad usually threw himself entirely into his work. After all, this find was why the family had relocated here in the first place.

But before too long, the children had received the doctor's bill of health; and after he had reminded Kristian and Ethan to carefully watch after their wounds, they all crowded around the dig site in eager anticipation. Given the children's near-death experience, they were not allowed to go in and had to keep some safe distance. This was at their mother's request, who presently watched over the children like a hawk.

498

The Drake Epics - Journey to Qara

Once satisfied the children were healthy, Mom had allowed Dad to lead a small expedition farther into the tunnel. Within minutes, he found evidence of a submerged temple, although he calculated the temple proper was much, much deeper and would require more time to access. The entire camp was abuzz about the temple's discovery.

The children all wondered if it was the same temple they had been drug into. This was the topic of their conversation as they huddled together and quietly verified their stories with each other. They soon concluded that they were not crazy, but that they needed to keep their experiences completely secret.

"Or else, they will lock us up and throw away the key!" Kristian exclaimed.

Neither of the other children wanted this to happen, so they vowed not to talk to anyone about this again. That is, except for parts and pieces that wouldn't raise any alarms.

Because of the children's interest and vivid descriptions of the temple, dad had promised that tomorrow, they would get the chance to explore with him. This had taken another round of convincing of their mother, who said that she was coming along with them, much to all of their dismay.

That night, all three children sat outside of the hut, looking at the stars and watching the bright lights around the distant dig's new epicenter. Dad had excused himself and had crews removing blockages within the tunnel to get at the hoped-for temple's entrance.

"Was it all just a dream?" Ethan volunteered when he was sure that Mom had left and gone back into the hut to finish cooking dinner. He didn't want to alarm her again with talk of another life. Besides, surprising to all of the children, no time had elapsed from the moment they had all gone back in time and returned. The best that they could figure, it must have been something like a dream they had all lived. A very real dream. However, he still felt a void and a sadness that his little white companion, Seon, was missing entirely from the picture.

"How could it be?" Kristian asked at the air. "I mean . . . we all experienced it, didn't we?" he said. "Muschle!" the older boy suddenly interrupted himself. "That crafty devil is the one who gave me this!" He went for his pendant before realizing it was gone and sighed. "The pendant I lost . . . They all knew we were coming," he pronounced at the other's questioning looks. "They had this planned out from the start," he mused.

"But I miss Deseret," Lola said with sudden tears in her eyes. She had been unusually quiet the entire day. Mom was worried about her as she was usually so boisterous.

"I do too. But I'm sure they'll always be with us," Ethan said consolingly.

"Seon too," Lola added.

Ethan smiled at his younger sister.

The children lapsed into an awkward silence, looking at the lights. Each of them walked through their experiences in their own minds.

"And . . ." Ethan wasn't sure he could make it through the next part. "And Grandpa?"

"Don't start, Ethan!" Kristian ordered. "We all remember him. We practically lived our whole lives with him!" he exclaimed. Then he leaned back in his chair with a faraway look, and his face clouded over. "Of lost empires and beehives . . . with Grandpa always there to guide us . . . It's not a dream after all."

"What?" Ethan asked, not immediately following what Kristian was trying to say. Then he realized Kristian had a dazed look that he had seen before. The same look Lola had when she talked with her drake, and he instantly knew that Kristian was being fed a thought from somewhere else, or from someone else.

"Oh?" Kristian shook his head and leaned forward on his chair again.

"What's going on?" Lola interrupted.

"Oh, nothing. But I have a strange feeling that we will see him again!" Kristian winked, much to both Ethan's and Lola's surprise.

"Really? Wait! See who?" Ethan said with a mixture of excitement and confusion.

"Shhh!" Kristian rebuked the two. "Keep it down." The elder boy looked around and made sure that no one was looking.

The other two children moved in closer, not knowing what to expect next, but Ethan had a pretty good idea.

From the look on Kristian's face, this was serious stuff. The older boy stretched out his hand for them all to see it clearly. "I have a feeling that this story is not finished." He pointed to his hand. "Now watch closely." He paused a few moments more.

The excitement built as Ethan and Lola stared at their brother's hand.

"Yangin," Kristian finally stated.

A small flame started in the palm of his hand, much to all of the children's delight.

They all stared at the fire in a momentary trance as it danced there in Kristian's palm. It was eerily beautiful. It meant that this wasn't just a dream, the temple of Marduk was real, they had lived another life with Grandpa, and they had defeated the chaos dragon, Tiamat!

Ethan felt a sudden rush of exhilaration. If this wasn't a dream, then Seon might not be as far away as he had thought. There was hope of getting him back!

"Time to eat!" Mom suddenly announced, startling the children as she emerged from the hut with two plates of food.

Kristian quickly snuffed out the flame with his other hand and grinned at his two siblings. He put a finger to his lips.

"Your father just called over the radio, and he will be here shortly to eat with us," Mom said as she handed the two plates to the younger siblings. She placed both hands on her hips and looked at the children. "Now, what are you three up to?" she asked.

"Nothing," they all said in unison, but the guilty looks were evident on their faces.

She shook her head. "Fine, don't tell me. Just know that I love you all." She turned and went back into the hut for the rest of the food. Dad was now walking up to the little group as well, wearing a giant smile.

Kristian quickly sat forward on the edge of his chair for emphasis. "This story is definitely not over!" he said to his siblings before greeting their father.

Dad placed three large and well-worn books on the table. "Do you know what these are?" he asked the children in disbelief.

They all looked at each other and then shook their heads.

"What are they?" Lola asked.

"These are your grandfather's journals," came the revelation, "found just inside the temple's entrance." He opened the cover of one of them with Grandpa's name printed in the interior. "I cannot explain this." he said with tender emotion in his voice. "But the full search starts tomorrow, once we are all rested."

The children beamed excited smiles of understanding at each other.

"Read it to us?" Ethan implored.

"I will start at the beginning." Dad said resolutely as he sat down and began to read.

The family ate their evening meal together and listened to their grandpa's story about the great sand lions and the temple ruins of Marduk.

# QARA'S POSTLUDE

Two old and weathered men and a beautiful woman stood on a lonely desert dune. A tattered and ancient scroll lay on the ground before them, as they looked down upon it, watching three children revealed within.

"Do you think *my* children know that this is only the beginning?" One of the men asked.

"Perhaps," the woman answered. She placed a loving arm around the old man. "They love you," she whispered into his ear.

"The emperor will guide the other two, just as I have taught him to lead so many times before in the Temple of the Lion." the third mused as he looked up at the sky. "Tiamat's master is coming, we must go," he announced." The plans are in place . . . we must be vigilant."

A great and dark shadow appeared on the horizon, bearing down on the three figures. A ragged cry ripped through the early evening calm.

"Then, let us go and meet them," the woman nodded at the children in the scroll, as one of the men rolled it and picked it up. She raised her hand high into the air as the men huddled closer to her.

All three vanished in a blinding flash of light, just as the shadow reached them and shrieked with rage as it passed through where the figures had stood only moments before.

"Tiamat was nothing compared to me!" the shadow bellowed and vanished into the night air.